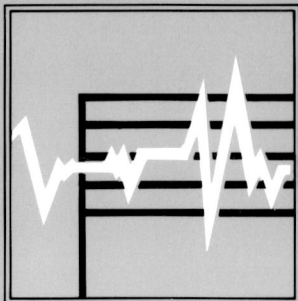

CONTEMPORARY MUSIC

REVIEW Editor in Chief **Nigel Osborne**

Music and the Cognitive Sciences

Stephen McAdams and Irène Deliège
Issue Editors

Volume 4

Proceedings from the 'Symposium on Music and the Cognitive Sciences'

14–18 March 1988

Centre National d'Art et de Culture 'Georges Pompidou'
Paris, France

ISSN 0749-4467
ISBN 3-7186-4953-5
CONREES 4, 1–467
Volume 4 (1989)

harwood academic publishers

chur ● london ● paris ● new york ● melbourne

CONTEMPORARY MUSIC REVIEW

Editor in Chief
Nigel Osborne (UK)

Regional Editors
Fred Lerdahl (USA)   Takemitsu Tōru (Japan)

Editorial Boards

UK	USA	JAPAN
Paul Driver	John Adams	Joaquim M Benitez, S.J.
Alexander Goehr	Jacob Druckman	Kondō Jō
Oliver Knussen	John Harbison	Shōno Susumu
Peter Nelson	Tod Machover	Tokumaru Yoshihiko
Bayan Northcott		
Anthony Payne		

Aims and scope: Contemporary Music Review is a contemporary musicians journal. It provides a forum where new tendencies in composition can be discussed in both breadth and depth. Each issue will focus on a specific topic. The main concern of the journal will be composition today in all its aspects – its techniques, aesthetics and technology and its relationship with other disciplines and currents of thought. The publication may also serve as a vehicle to communicate actual musical materials.

Notes for contributors can be found at the back of the journal.

Subscription rates. Each volume comprises   approximately 346 pages with an irregular number of issues scheduled. Issues are available individually as well as by subscription.

Subscription rates per volume: corporate, SF 322.00. Special reduced rates are available to university libraries and individuals; please write for details or see the journals checklist pertinent to your territory. Subscribers will be invoiced in the currency applicable to their geographical area at our current exchange rate.

Orders may be placed with your usual supplier or directly with Harwood Academic Publishers GmbH, c/o STBS Ltd., P.O. Box 197, London, WC2E 9PP, U.K. Claims for nonreceipt of issues should be made within three months of publication of the issue or they will not be honored without charge. Subscriptions are available for microform editions. Details will be furnished upon request.

License to photocopy. This publication is registered for copyright in the United States of America, and is protected under the Universal Copyright Convention and the Berne Convention. The Publisher is not a member of the Copyright Clearance Center, and has not entered into agreement with any other copyright payment centers in any part of the world. Accordingly, permission to photocopy beyond the 'fair use' provisions of the USA and most other copyright laws is available from the publisher by license only. Please note, however, that the license does not extend to other kinds of copying, such as copying for general distribution, for advertising or promotional purposes, for creating new collective works, or for resale. It is also expressly forbidden for any individual or company to copy any article as agent, either express or implied, of another individual or company. For licensing information, please write to P.O. Box 161, 1820 Montreux 2, Switzerland.

Reprints of individual articles. Copies of individual articles may be obtained from the Publisher's own document delivery service at the appropriate fees. Write to: Document Delivery Service, P.O. Box 786, Cooper Station, New York, NY 10276, USA or P.O. Box 197, London WC2E 9PX, U.K.

Distributed by STBS Ltd, P.O. Box 197, London WC2E 9PX, UK.

Printed in the United Kingdom by Bell and Bain Ltd.

November 1989

Music and the Cognitive Sciences

STEPHEN McADAMS and IRÈNE DELIÈGE,
Issue Editors

Proceedings from the 'Symposium on Music and the Cognitive Sciences'
14–18 March 1988,
Centre National d'Art et de Culture 'Georges Pompidou',
Paris, France

organized by

the Institut de Recherche et Coordination
Acoustique/Musique
(Centre National d'Art et de Culture 'Georges Pompidou', Paris, France)

the Unité de Recherche en Psychologie de la Musique
(Université de Liège, Centre de Recherches Musicales de Wallonie, Liège, Belgium)

and

the Institut de Pédagogie Musicale et Chorégraphique
(Etablissement Public du Parc de la Villette, Paris, France)

Volume published with the help of IRCAM and the
Cultural Affairs Directorate of the Ministry of the French Community of Belgium

781,1
5989 m

94 - 981

ACW-1190

Contents

Part III. Experimentation and Modeling

Part IV. Musical Performance

Foreword

This year marks the fourth centennial of the birth of Marin Mersenne (September 8, 1588), who is generally regarded as the dominant figure of the scientific revolution in its early stages. It is noteworthy that Mersenne's primary scientific interest lay in music, and indeed that many of the major scientists of his day, including Galileo, Descartes, Kepler, and Huygens, were trained musicians and wrote extensively concerning musical issues. Pitch perception, tuning systems, consonance and dissonance, musical aesthetics, and related topics were hotly debated by the leading thinkers of the time, and where possible subjected to experimental investigation. It is also noteworthy that during this enlightened period, scientists and technologists interacted frequently with composers, performers, and other practicing musicians, so that the pursuit of music was truly interdisciplinary in scope.

Given the central nature of Mersenne's involvement in this revolutionary movement (his cell at the Place Royale in Paris served as the international meeting ground for some of the most eminent thinkers of the time) it is particularly fitting that the present international Symposium was held in Paris on the fourth centennial of his birth. For once again there is emerging a strong spirit of interdisciplinary cooperation in the study of music. As evidenced in this volume, music theorists, composers, psychologists, computer scientists, neuroscientists, and others are interchanging ideas and working in collaboration, both to further the scientific understanding of music and also to develop new means of musical expression.

Thus in the firm belief that music is finally establishing itself as a unified field, I dedicate this Foreword to Marin Mersenne – music theorist, mathematician, scientist, technologist, and strong champion of interdisciplinary cooperation.

Diana Deutsch
University of California, San Diego
September 8, 1988

Preface

In August 1985, the fifth and last *Workshop on the Physical and Neuropsychological Foundations of Music,* organized by Juan Roederer, was held in Ossiach, Austria. This important gathering had for more than ten years served as an inter-disciplinary forum for various aspects of musical science. The news that the tradition would not be carried on was met with mixed feelings by many of us who had attended the workshop. This forum was an ideal setting to "knock heads" for a week over the burning issues that occupied us, but a certain resistance to many new trends, particularly with respect to cognition, made themselves apparent and privileged the more physical and psychoacoustic aspects of music. A sadness was thus accompanied by a certain feeling of liberation.

Compared with the early Ossiach meetings, attempts to account more for the complexities of *music* as opposed to elementary *tone* perception were beginning to appear. The necessity of following out the debates in this new direction and of finding another framework within which to meet was strongly expressed by Oscar Marin. He was the moving force behind the lengthy discussions with Eric Clarke, Carol Krumhansl, Fred Lerdahl and Bernard Vecchione – the other members of the organizing committee – on the form and content of a new kind of symposium that would deal more comprehensively with music cognition. We may hope that a new "tradition" has begun since a second symposium is already programmed for 1990 in Cambridge, England, at the initiative of Ian Cross.

The growing interest in the cognitive sciences that is manifest today is extending into the realm of the arts. Music composition, performance, and per-ception are among the primary concerns. The *Symposium on Music and the Cognitive Sciences,* held at IRCAM in March 1988, took stock of some of the most advanced directions in these domains. This collective volume is the fruit of that symposium, and relays the presentations of the specialists from several disciplines that met for the occasion – theorists, composers, computer scientists, musicologists, psychologists, mathematicians and neurologists. This event sought voluntarily, if perhaps somewhat dangerously, to address a *very* broad range of approaches to music cognition. Several of us felt all too keenly in many previous conferences the absence of composers at one end of the spectrum and of computer scientists at the other end. We can certainly claim this time to have achieved the goal of breadth.

This breadth bore witness to a diversity of basic assumptions, vocabularies, concepts, aims, methods, interpretations, and reasoning methods that often seemed at first view to be irreconcilable. Discussion, as one might imagine, was not always facile. The confrontation between art and science does not arouse only idealism and a will to understand, but also reveals reserve and criticism.

Five themes were debated by thirty researchers selected beforehand by the Organizing Committee. The difficult and ungrateful task of directing the discussions and of drawing things together was entrusted to session chairs specifically invited as a function of their reputation and of the session theme: David Osmond-Smith (the notion of musical language), Hugues Dufourt (form-bearing elements in music), Jay Dowling (experimental and theoretical approaches to listening and comprehension), André Riotte (modeling approaches to listening and comprehension), and Gerald Balzano (music performance). Their analyses of what was presented and discussed in their sessions are printed in this volume. In the interests of coherence, however, the five themes are rearranged here into four parts. Furthermore, to assure the level of quality of the volume, the symposium presentations were subsequently subjected to critical review and were revised for this publication.

Musical language and theory, the theme of the first section, presents approaches that are both theoretical (Eric Clarke; Eugene Narmour; Fred Lerdahl), and practical (Mario Baroni, Rossana Dalmonte & Carlo Jacoboni) from semiological, grammatical, generative and psychological perspectives. The question that has already been raised many times of the appropriateness of the concept of language for music and the implications that surround this conception was taken up by Eric Clarke. The impact exerted by the theoretical thought of Fred Lerdahl and Ray Jackendoff was notable at the Symposium. Their work, *A Generative Theory of Tonal Music,* some five years after its publication, remains a point of theoretical reference and is found at the heart of the development of several research programs. A generalization of the model to other idioms is also envisaged: Fred Lerdahl proposes an extension to pre-serial atonal music.

The analysis of *musical form,* a particularly sensitive subject for any musician today, is by far the one that attracted the greatest diversity of approach. In the second part of the volume, as one might have expected, chapters by composers and their close collaborators are collected (Jean-Baptiste Barrière; Marco Stroppa; Francois Bayle; Jean Petitot). They express their current preoccupations in terms of the architecture of the musical work. These concern the interaction between form and material: the evolution of language and the introduction of electronic instrument design open up as yet unheard perspectives. At the same time however, they perturb both the norms of compositional technique and the conception of musical form of the composer, and they require new listening habits of the audience. This provokes an occasion for fundamental reflection on the concept of form-bearing elements from historical (Marie-Elisabeth Duchez), psychological (Stephen McAdams; Irène Deliège) and theoretical (Célestin Deliège) points of view.

The last two parts of the volume, *experimentation and modeling* (III) and *musical performance* (IV), focus the concerns and state-of-the-art research in those areas of psychology where the marks of the cognitive current and artificial intelligence are preponderant. The experimental psychologist (Carol Krumhansl) questions, but also defends and justifies, the procedures and methods of investigating music in the laboratory, starting with experimental stimuli that are reductive objects, while being faced with recent tendencies that move towards music perception in more realistic circumstances. Neuropsychology (Oscar Marín; Robert Zatorre; Isabelle Peretz & José Morais) is at the very heart of the problem of cognition: based on experimental results and analyses of cerebral deficits, it reveals the role that may be played by specific regions of the cortex in the processing of musical information. The data from these two fields converge quite naturally on an advanced sector of current research: modeling. Several subjects give rise to attempts at the formalization and simulation of human behavior with computers: perceptual activity (Michael Baker; Jamshed Bharucha & Katherine Olney; Marc Leman), perceptual-motor activity (Henry Shaffer; Neil Todd; Rolf Carlson, Anders Friberg, Lars Frydén, Björn Granström & Johan Sundberg), learning (Richard Ashley; Alan Marsden), and the comprehension of visual information that is achieved by the reading of musical notation and the establishment of relations with its sound attributes (Kari Kurkela).

*   *   *   *   *   *

The Symposium on Music and the Cognitive Sciences would not have been possible without the generosity of several cultural, scientific, and educational institutions: the Institut de Recherche et Coordination Acoustique/Musique, the Unité de Recherche en Psychologie de la Musique of the University of Liège and of the Centre de Recherches Musicales de Wallonie, and the Institut de Pédagogie Musicale et Chorégraphique of the Etablissement Public du Parc de la Villette in Paris. For their support in the organization of the Symposium we are particularly indebted to Laurent Bayle, Artistic Director of IRCAM, Marc Richelle, Professor of the Faculty of Psychology and Education Sciences of the University of Liège, Michel Schoonbrood, Administrator of the Centre de Recherches Musicales de Wallonie, and Jean-Claude Wallach, General Secretary (at that time) of the Institut de Pédagogie Musicale et Chorégraphique. Special thanks are also due to Florence Quilliard for her organizational help and patience during the long months of preparation for the symposium and to Marie-Isabelle Collart and Cécile Marin for their help with the preparation of the index.

The publication of this volume in two languages simultaneously (the French version, *La Musique et les Sciences Cognitives* is published by Pierre Mardaga Editions, Brussels) received financial support from IRCAM and the Cultural Affairs Directorate of the Ministry of the French Community of Belgium, wherein the initiative taken by Etienne Grosjean (Director General of Culture), Philippe Dewonck (Principal Attaché for the Promotion of Music), and Robert Jeukens (Administrative Officer) were particularly valuable to us. We would like to express to these people our sincerest thanks and gratitude.

Stephen McAdams & Irène Deliège
Paris and Liège, 19 October 1988

Contemporary Music Review,
1989, Vol. 4, pp. 1–7
Photocopying permitted by license only

Introduction:
The many faces of human cognition
in musical research and practice

Stephen McAdams

Institut de Recherche et Coordination Acoustique/Musique (IRCAM),
31, rue Saint-Merri, F-75004 Paris, France

The presentations at the *Symposium on Music and the Cognitive Sciences* covered a vast array of approaches and aims from disciplines such as music composition, musicology, music theory, music analysis, experimental psychology, neuropsychology, mathematics, and computer science. These different approaches are briefly described. A plethora of fundamental concerns were raised across these disciplines. Those discussed in this chapter include the perception and representation of musical attributes, patterns, and forms, the mental organization of musical material and form, the development and learning of musical skills, and musical universals. A number of problems in the cross-disciplinary dialogue are also noted and discussed, with emphasis being placed on the problems that the basic assumptions of each discipline pose when considering what is relevant in other disciplines.

KEY WORDS: Mental organization, mental representation, multi-disciplinary dialogue, music cognition, music perception, musical development, musical universals.

In this introductory chapter, I would like to examine some of the promises and problems of the diversity of approaches that confront the field of music cognition, with the aim of evaluating how we might best proceed as a community in the near and more distant future. I am especially concerned with how we might establish and widen the channels of communication among disciplines, rather than re-entrenching ourselves in our various restricted domains. With this aim in mind, the near future is certain to continue the frustration felt by many, but a serious consideration of what is "relevant" in other domains of musical thought, aside from one's own, is bound to be important if we are to understand something of the diversity of musical experience and research.

The approaches and aims

At the base of all musical study is the product of the one who creates the music, be it noted, improvised, or passed on by oral tradition. Our culture being dominated by what Trevor Wishart (1985) calls the "class of scribes", participation by creators of music at the symposium was not so surprisingly limited to composers, though all of those present use electro-acoustic technology in their works and thus do not confine their activity to notation on the page. When they write, composers most often reflect on their own creative concerns and on how they organize their thought and work. Some explicitly examine the way issues in the cognitive sciences have influenced their composing, and what their compositional approaches have to offer to cognitive study itself. But ultimately, their aim is to make music rather than words. That they consciously reflect and write on what they do should be considered a boon to the scientists interested in musical activity, since scientific studies on the processes and concerns of composition are extremely rare.

Musicology, music theory and analysis try, as a group of disciplines, to describe what forms music takes, to explain what the constituents are, and how and why these evolved, and even to evaluate critically the end results. Their concerns are perhaps much broader today than they were in the past. Many, like Jean-Jacques Nattiez (1987, p. 15), consider the *musical work* to be more than a notated text or ensemble of structures (configurations as he would prefer to call them). It also includes the processes that gave birth to the music (the acts of composition) and that manifest it in the world (the acts of performance and perception). The analytic endeavor often draws from formalization practices in other fields, such as linguistics, semiotics, mathematics, historical and epistemological research, biology, sociology, cognitive psychology, and so on. But their primary concern is most often considering and explicating the specifically musical in terms of the constituent elements of music. The particular interest of the work of theorists for more psychologically oriented researchers, is to have some reasonable formulations of the structure of music as a starting point for theory and experiment that aims at an understanding of how humans actually conceive, perform, and experience music.

Experimental psychologists seek to establish tendencies, constraints, and possibilities of the mental mechanisms that underly musical activity and experience. They try to find a way of describing musical structure and process in a way that reflects as much as possible the mental structures and processes by which music is created, reproduced, and understood. To do this, experimental method obliges the scientist to measure some kind of behavior that then allows one to infer the mental states and processes that underly it and to relate these to the original stimulating acoustic structure. The aim can be to use music as a means of understanding more about the human mind in general, or of using knowledge of the mind to explicate observable aspects of musical experience. The interest of psychological theory and data for other domains is that they can offer an empirical test of compositional or music theoretic hypotheses, and that theory based on empirical results can extend the base of the composer's, theorist's or music teacher's craft by advancing their *conscious understanding* of musicians' intuitions. This work also provides models and constraints for research in neuropsychology and for work in computer simulation.

Neuropsychology tries to elaborate the brain structures and functions underlying human activity. The musical neuropsychologist through a knowledge of neuroanatomy, neurophysiology, and clinical neurology seeks to determine which parts of the brain are involved in various aspects of musical activity and to understand the contribution of general and music-specific neural mechanisms to musical perception, thought, and production. Musical neuropsychology mostly proceeds with the methods of experimental psychology, testing both normal people and patients with various kinds of brain damage, in order to show how certain kinds of damage affect certain aspects of musical mental function.

The last domain that is represented in this volume is one where researchers try to formalize understanding of a physical, music theoretic, psychological or neurological nature in mathematical formulae or computer programs using techniques developed in artificial intelligence or in other computational domains. The approach of some modelers is to achieve an output behavior similar to that of humans when exposed to music. This is a way of testing our understanding of the operation of mental and physiological mechanisms in musical activity. Some people try to go further in assuring that the way the program functions is also a simulation of the way the human information processing system works, even in the intermediate stages. The interest for other domains is the concrete nature of this research. One might claim that to be able to formalize one's knowledge is to truly understand the phenomenon in question, though this is surely open to debate.

Some fundamental questions

In spite of this diversity of approaches and issues, several fundamental concerns emerge in cognitive considerations of music, some of which are presented below. The selection cannot help but be subject to my own biases as an experimental psychologist that is in constant contact with composers of electroacoustic music.

Perception and Representation of Attributes, Patterns, and Forms

This area concerns the mental representation of sound attributes and relations, and of their ordering in systems of relations, and the representation of specific musical patterns and forms. What are we capable of learning and storing in memory, and of comparing across time? This is clearly one of the important questions concerning what is possible as musical form.

Another important question concerns the psychological reality of reductional representation, a hypothetical construct dear to all Schenkerian analysts and their descendants, not to mention many other schools of music theoretic thought. The notion of reduction of several events to a single abstract one at a higher level of representation has a certain intuitive appeal at some levels of musical elaboration. But the psychologist becomes a bit skeptical when claims are made to extend this to a whole piece. Of pressing interest is a program of research that puts this notion to the test in order to determine to what extent reductional representation is real, to what levels it extends, what its limits are and why.

The notion of associational structure, evoked in several papers, particularly with respect to the notion of "parallelism" of musical structure is badly in need of formalization, or at least clarification, in music theory, and of empirical testing in experimental psychology. It seems clear that such relations can strongly influence musical perception, particularly when striking or repeated events or patterns adopt the function of Signs (cf. Clarke, this volume). It also seems clear that hierarchical structure is not sufficient to explain the experience of musical form, but we do not have a clear agenda for how to proceed. Explorations in the degree of perceived relations among patterns or "indices" of musical segments, and their contribution to form cognition, is an appropriate and important first step (cf. I. Deliège, this volume).

The distinction between declarative and procedural knowledge raised by Krumhansl would seem to be an important one. As Dowling discusses, there are aspects of musical knowledge representations and processing that may be more pertinently considered as procedural, many of which have to this point been conceived in declarative terms. This implies that they are less available to conscious verbal interrogation and may require the development of new methods of measure and experimentation. The shift of perspective necessary to digest this point of view is non-trivial. A lot of clarification is necessary in our thinking about what representations are good for in our explications of musical activity.

It is of capital importance to extend the few studies to date (and most notably work by Francès starting in the 1950's, cf. 1972/1988) that have made serious attempts to investigate musical dimensions and systems outside of pitch and rhythm as confined to the Western tonal/metric system. The reason for studying within these confines are surely justified, i.e., most of the Westerners that psychologists study have far greater experience within this system than outside of it. But for research in music cognition to claim an important place in the interaction with composers and theorists, the horizons need to be opened. Directions have been indicated for pitch research in non-Western cultures, in atonal and serial idioms, and to some extent with micro-tonal systems. Much work remains to be done both in theory and experimentation on the bases and possible future evolution of 20th century harmony. Similar efforts could be directed to rhythm research. At the top of the agenda should be work on timbre, and here the door is open for vital interaction between composers, theorists, and psychologists to determine the limits and possibilities of timbre as an essential form-bearing dimension in music. This has importance for the development both of orchestration and sound synthesis techniques.

Mental Organization of Musical Material and Form

It is encouraging to see an increasing concern with mental *process* in musical activity, after so many years of concern primarily centered on mental *structure* and representation. This brings into play the essential dimension of time and temporal experience. Two of the key notions that have been advanced which distinguish structure and process and, at the same time, show the way to their relationship, are abstract knowledge structure and event structure (Bharucha, 1984; Deutsch, 1984; McAdams, this volume), the latter being a representation that is accumulated through time in the process of listening, or generated through time in the process of performing. They depend both on already acquired knowledge as well as on processes of perceptual or motor organization. A concerted effort to more clearly define their respective natures and interdependencies will be important for our understanding of real-time music cognition. This also concerns the ability to draw together perceived materials widely separated in time, and to plan detailed temporal relations over long time periods in score-based or improvised performance.

One of the more elusive aspects of real-time musical experience is the generation, modulation, and resolution of expectation. This would have its counterparts in the conception of implication in composition and improvisation, in its realization and reinforcement in expressive performance, and in its perception and resolution in listening. Work on this problem at the level of music theory is included in the chapter by Narmour. A crucial psychological question concerns the relation between these music theoretical constructs and the theory of anticipatory mental schemata, addressed in part here and elsewhere by Bharucha. This problem area is very closely related to that of the accumulation of event structures. One might imagine that partially accumulated event structures that match well-formed or familiar schemata would tend to create a sense of expectation, that is, to imply the eventual realization of the schema in question. Understanding the conditions and time course of the realization and its experience may be a direction that allows the experimental sciences to at last approach some of the more affective and aesthetic aspects of musical experience that, for many reasons, have been left to the side for the time being (cf. Clarke, Krumhansl, this volume, for other points of view on this last question).

Development and Learning of Musical Skills

Omnipresent in any discussion of development is the question of those aspects of mental structure and process which exist at birth (the "initial state", as some call it). The degree of innateness attributed to various perceptual and cognitive capacities often depends on the (tacit) philosophical stance of the researcher. A wide spectrum was seen in the few papers that addressed such issues at this symposium, but no experimental work was reported on neonate or infant perception and cognition that might indicate the nature of precursors to musical skills. In fact, such work is relatively rare and extremely difficult to do (but see Zenatti, 1975, 1981; Shuter-Dyson & Gabriel, 1981; Hargreaves, 1986; for reviews of issues in the development of musical abilities). The question is: what do we possess at birth that allows the development of musical skills and to what extent are they specific to music, if at all? Or do general mechanisms of learning exist that allow either the acquisition of domain-specific skills in music listening and production, or the acquisition of general cognitive skills that serve musical as well as other activities?

Developmental problems in general, which could do much to advance techniques of music education, have not been much treated. It would be fruitful to examine the process of development of musical skills, including possibilities and limits at different ages, for the activities of listening, performing, comprehending, analyzing, improvising, and composing. How do these various skills develop in conjunction with other perceptual and cognitive skills such as language, seeing, reading, reasoning, calculating, and imagining? Do they in some ways share common cognitive architectures?

Learning is also important at adult ages, as we are forever encountering new musical works, idioms, styles, and cultures. Learning concerns the storage and accommodation of information and knowledge with the purpose of modifying existing knowledge structures, perceptual strategies, and action strategies. The learnability (whether by conscious effort or by passive exposure) of various musical systems, patterns, and forms is of crucial importance for an understanding of contemporary musical experience where those listeners who are interested in the "art" music of their time are constantly struggling with novelty of sound and organization and, at times, with what Lerdahl (1988) has characterized as a divorce between compositional and listening grammars.

Musical Universals

Much debated at the symposium and extensively discussed in the chapter of

Dowling, is the question of universals in music. Some people seem to have a tendency to confuse questions of innateness with those of universals. But as Dowling points out, the *capacity to acquire* certain mental structures for music could be universal throughout the human species. What he raises is the question of the appropriate level of consideration when discussing universality of some perceptual or cognitive capacity. For example, it may be that octave equivalence is not an *a priori* universal property of human hearing, whereas humans universally have the *capacity to learn* this equivalence if exposed to an appropriate musical environment. It seems likely that consideration of universal capacities to represent, organize, and learn musical structures, may be a more fruitful approach to the question than trying to make claims for specific structures found in individual cultures.

This cursory overview certainly does not exhaust the many fundamental issues confronting students of music cognition. But I feel it includes some of the more urgent ones that should be considered from the many disciplines currently investigating music cognition.

The challenge of cross-disciplinary communication

When one comes from another discipline, it is sometimes difficult to achieve an understanding of what researchers in a certain domain are trying to accomplish and of what methodological limits are posed by their discipline. Clearly none of us can take everything into account in any given study, whether it be of a musicological, music theoretic, music analytic, psychological, neurological, or computational nature. It seems that disputes across disciplines are often based on misunderstandings of the vocabulary, methods, aims, and a certain vision of what is "relevant" for the other discipine. The problem of what is "relevant" seems varied and elusive. The many concerns and approaches are, I believe, fairly clearly stated in the chapters that compose this volume. I leave it to the reader to ferret out their basic assumptions and limits.

The challenge and the stakes are clear. If this symposium showed us one thing, it is that we have a long way to go to be able to communicate freely among the disciplines. As I stated at the beginning, for those with the desire to continue the dialogue, a certain amount of frustration is still in store, and patience is called for. The members of each discipline have a lot to learn about the others. We have several sets of vocabulary and explanatory concepts that are only partially overlapping. Adopting an autodidactic will is a first step to resolving the problem of inter-education. One hopes that the making and appreciation of music itself will benefit from the attempt. One hopes also that such coordinated effort will help establish the study of music as a viable, important, central domain of research in human cognition, rather than leave it in the margins as the larger scientific community has a tendency to do with anything associated with the arts and letters. I personally feel we have a critical mass of good will and genuine concern to carry on the ancient dialogue between music and science. The diversity of relevant approaches is a testament to the complexity of the problem. It is necessarily the affair of a multi-disciplinary community.

References

Bharucha, J.J. (1984) Event hierarchies, tonal hierarchies and assimilation: A reply to Deutsch and Dowling, *Journal of Experimental Psychology: General*, **113**, 421–425.

Deutsch, D. (1984) Two issues concerning tonal hierarchies: Comment on Castellano, Bharucha and Krumhansl, *Journal of Experimental Psychology: General*, **113**, 413–416.

Francès, R. (1972) *La perception de la musique*, 2nd ed., Paris: J. Vrin; trans. by W.J. Dowling *The Perception of Music* Hillsdale, N.J.: Lawrence Erlbaum Associates (1988).

Hargreaves, D. (1986) *The Developmental Psychology of Music*, Cambridge: Cambridge University Press.

Lerdahl, F. (1988) Cognitive constraints on compositional systems. In *Generative Processes in Music*, J. Sloboda (ed.), 231–259, Oxford: Oxford University Press.

Nattiez, J.J. (1987) *Musicologie générale et sémiologie*, Paris: Christian Bourgois Editeur.

Shuter-Dyson, R. & Gabriel, C. (1981) *The Psychology of Musical Ability*, 2nd ed., London: Methuen.

Wishart, T. (1985) *On Sonic Art*, York: Imagineering Press (83 Heslington Road, York YO1 5AX, U.K.).

Zenatti, A. (1975) Le développement génétique de la perception musicale, *Monographies Francaises de Psychologie*, no. 17, Paris: Centre National de Recherche Scientifique.

Zenatti, A. (1981) *L'enfant et son environnement musical*, Issy-les-Moulineaux: E.A.P.

Part I
Musical Language and Theory

Contemporary Music Review,
1989, Vol. 4, pp. 9–22
Photocopying permitted by license only

Issues in language and music

Eric F. Clarke

*Music Department, City University, 223–227 St John Street, London EC1V 0HB,
United Kingdom*

This paper examines the different motivations and aims which lie behind various attempts to investigate or make use of the relationship between language and music, some from music theory and some
from the psychology of music. While the theoretical developments of linguistics and psycholinguistics
have helped to develop aspects of music theory and the psychology of music, it is argued that certain
theoretical distinctions that may be useful in linguistics, such as the distinction between syntax and
semantics, maybe inappropriate for music. Instead, a more general framework based on semiotics and
communication theory may offer a more flexible and ultimately more powerful context within which
to assess both the general relations between language and music as well as some of the more specific
correspondences.

KEY WORDS: Language, music, generative theory, semiotics, communication, syntax, semantics,
signification, meaning.

Introduction

An increasingly prominent feature of work in musicology and the psychology of
music is the use of ideas related to or derived from linguistics, or reflections on
various aspects of the possible relationship between language and music.
Different kinds of linguistic theory have been employed in these speculations,
and the term "language" itself has been used at various levels and with varying
degrees of specificity and rigor. The result is that a degree of confusion now exists
as to the nature of music's relation to language, and, more seriously, what the aim
of establishing such links might be. For some the importance of establishing such
a relationship is to show the unity or common foundation of human modes of
communication, and hence the universality of certain fundamental cognitive
characteristics; for others the attraction has been primarily methodological: by
demonstrating the links between language and music certain powerful conceptual and procedural tools that have developed in connection with language
research may be legitimately transferable into the musical domain. These and
other motivations that lie behind the various attempts to explore the relationship
between language and music merit closer investigation if we are to obtain a clearer
idea of the function of this kind of inter-disciplinary link. The purpose of this
paper is to examine these basic motivations and the manner in which they are
implemented in a number of different approaches, and to explore other possibilities for tackling this relationship.

It should be recognized from the outset that different authors have used the
word language with varying degrees of specificity: in Deryck Cooke's *The
Language of Music* (1959), for example, the term is employed in no more specific a
manner than to indicate a system that communicates an emotional state between

the composer and the listeners, incorporating a kind of informal lexicon of musical expressive units (see below). Lerdahl & Jackendoff, on the other hand, in their book *A Generative Theory of Tonal Music* (1983) propose some quite precise links between one component of their approach to music and prosodic features of language, as well as deriving the entire foundation of their theory from a specific linguistic tradition – namely generative linguistics. This greater precision is in part a reflection of the fact that Jackendoff is himself a linguist, but it also seems to express a desire to move beyond the kind of informal reference to musical styles as "languages", and to consider rather more carefully whether natural language and music really do share significant features, and if so, what this implies.

Before moving to more detailed discussions, it is appropriate to consider in a general way the intended function of establishing such links. There seem to be at least four related motivations:

1. Methodological or procedural transfer: linguistics and psycholinguistics are disciplines which have acquired considerable prestige and have seen the development of some very powerful conceptual and methodological tools over the past thirty years. Given the rather obvious resemblances between language and music, at least at a superficial level, there is an interest in discovering whether those same tools can be employed in this area, for the purposes of either music analysis or models in the psychology of music. Artificial intelligence (another discipline with high prestige) has developed in close association with linguistic principles, partly as a result of their common use of tree structure representations, with the consequence that A.I. approaches to music also reflect these linguistic origins more or less strongly. Examples of this kind of orientation are Lerdahl & Jackendoff (1983) and Longuet-Higgins (1979).

2. Common cognitive origin: a second reason for wanting to examine links between language and music is to explore evidence for a common origin for both language and music, or a single cognitive capacity which supports both. This interest may in turn be a reflection of recent controversies about the modularity (or otherwise) of the human mind. Sloboda (1985) discusses a range of studies that tackle various aspects of this issue.

3. Integration with other symbolic systems: strong links between language and music may provide a basis for establishing a more unified theory of human symbolic skills within a general framework such as semiotics or communication theory (e.g. Eco, 1977; Campbell, 1984). A possible benefit of achieving a unification of this kind might be the discovery of fundamental explanatory principles not immediately evident in any of the symbolic systems individually. This involves not only a principle of "theoretical economy", but also the possibility of making real discoveries.

4. Verbal culture: we live in a tremendously logocentric culture, in which our capacity to express ourselves in language seems sometimes to be regarded as virtually synonymous with knowledge. In view of the tremendous amount of *writing* about music (and mind), it is not surprising that there should be considerable interest in discovering the nature of the relationship between language and music (just as there is in the relationship between language and mind, and music and mind).

As this short list illustrates, the movitivations for examining the question of language and music are a mixture of practical and theoretical concerns, and it is in part the failure to be sufficiently clear about this distinction that has led to some of the difficulties and misunderstandings that I will touch upon in this paper. Since musicology has tended to focus more on the practical and terminological possibilities arising out of the relation between language and music, while the theoretical interest has been picked up by more cognitive approaches, I shall divide accordingly the more detailed coverage of some of the ways in which language and music have been related.

Language and music in musicology

The first and most specifically analytical example that I want to consider is the use by Cooper & Meyer of a system of poetic feet in their book *The Rhythmic Structure of Music* (1960). The theory is an attempt to analyze musical rhythm using a limited repertoire of five rhythmic types that are described using the terminology of poetic feet, according to the distribution of groups of accented and unaccented elements. The five types are: trochee (strong weak), dactyl (strong weak weak), iamb (weak strong), anapest (weak weak strong), and amphibrach (weak strong weak). They are identified at hierarchic levels ranging from the most detailed features of the musical surface up to a single foot standing for a whole symphonic movement. I have no wish to add to the body of critical evaluations of Cooper & Meyer's book since many of the discussions of its strengths and weaknesses are already well-known (e.g. Yeston, 1976). However, an aspect of the theory which is very much the concern of this paper is the use of an originally linguistic model for their method, and the consequences of doing so.

As Yeston (1976) points out, the use of a system of poetic feet to describe the rhythmic structure of music has a history that goes back to the time of Aristoxenus, and can be traced through Renaisssance and 18th century theorists to the 19th century music theorist Riemann. Cooper & Meyer therefore do no more than pick up and explore a theoretical strand that already had a long musical tradition. Nonetheless it is a tradition that is rooted in an analogy with language, and hence inherits an outlook that is in certain respects fundamentally linguistic.

A problem that stems from this is the rather striking omission of any detailed treatment of the low-level durational properties of rhythm. The authors deal with duration primarily as it contributes to accentuation, and pay virtually no attention to the way in which patterns of durational relations at the note-to-note level contribute to musical rhythm. A symptom of this comparative disregard for the temporal properties of rhythm is the way they treat their own "principle of metric equivalance" (p. 22), which states that the accented and unaccented elements of a group should tend towards durational equality. This seems to be a recognition of the role of duration in determining rhythmic structures, but turns out to be a principle which Cooper & Meyer are happy to violate in a quite dramatic manner, some of their analyses showing a ratio of 6:1 between the durations of accented and unaccented elements. This seriously undermines the integrity of their repertoire of rhythmic types, since it seems to allow them to squeeze rhythmic groups of all kinds into their five-fold categorization, but emphasizes the arbitrariness of the repertoire itself.

These difficulties relate directly to the different way in which time is organized in speech and music. In the tonal and metrical music with which Cooper & Meyer are concerned, rhythm is organized around a framework of repeating iso-chronous units (the pulse) such that larger timespans are related to one another by small integer ratios. This provides a stable framework which, amongst other things, facilitates the coordination of separate players in ensembles. Language by contrast has no need of such a tight framework, since apart from certain rather unusual contexts, people do not talk together in ensembles,[1] and certainly not with the degree of coordinated complexity that is found in polyphonic music. The temporal organization of spoken language is still not very well understood, but it appears that although it is based around some sort of rough periodicity (or "near-miss periodicity" as Shaffer, 1982, calls it), and imposes strong constraints on certain aspects of timing, it does not employ the same kind of metric framework that is found in music. As a consequence, individual units may be locally stretched or squeezed in a way that would be unacceptable in music, and may explain why the *temporal* definition of the accented and unaccented units in Cooper & Meyer's rhythmic theory (with its linguistic inheritance) is so weak.

Similarly, since the accent may be produced by length as well as intensity and a whole range of other parametric changes, in speech – where no strict temporal framework need be adhered to – one can maintain a comparative indifference to the manner in which an accent may be achieved. In music, by contrast, there are strong constraints on the use of duration for purposes of accentuation, since there are metrical requirements to be adhered to in addition to the considerations of accent itself. The use of a linguistic model may therefore explain why Cooper & Meyer fail to deal with the separate but coordinated aspects of duration and accent in a satisfactory way.

A rather different example of the relationship between language and music within musicology is Deryck Cooke's *The Language of Music* (1959), which makes use of a repertoire of "types" in order to address issues that are primarily aesthetic and loosely speaking psychological. The main thrust of Cooke's book is an attempt to demonstrate that for Western tonal music of the period from about 1600 to 1900, an essentially stable correspondence exists between melodic configura-tions (and to a lesser extent rhythmic features) and affective content. Cooke claims that this correspondence is a direct outcome of properties of the harmonic series that are embedded in the nature of tonality, and that the affective content of a composition must be understood as a content that the composer has inscribed in a deliberate fashion in the music in order to communicate it to an audience. Once again my aim is not to embark on a full scale critique of Cooke's ideas, but to con-centrate on the way in which the notion of "language" has been used.

A considerable part of the book is taken up with what is virtually a lexicon of musical expression – a detailed listing of numerous examples from the repertoire of Western classical music that (Cooke claims) illustrate unambiguously the stable relationship between a particular melodic formula (e.g. "scalar descending fifth in minor mode") and the affective content intended by the composer. This latter aspect is made "objective" by Cooke through the choice of examples that are almost invariably associated with a text in some way (sacred vocal music, opera, Lieder, programme music, pieces with definite titles and historical associations such as the "Eroica" symphony etc.), the textual content of which is then taken to be essentially synonymous with the musical content. This is a dubious approach for a number of reasons: it appears to adopt a naive view of textual meaning, it offers no way to accommodate ironic, contradictory or other "non-identity" relations between text and music unless by reference to another text, it is based on a restricted repertoire, and it offers no way to tackle instrumental music other than by regarding it as parasitic upon vocal music.

Two other primary features of Cooke's theory are similarly hard to defend. He insists on a very crude kind of communication model in which the composer is the "sender," the listener is the "receiver" and the piece is the "channel," with the result that the emotional content of a piece is essentially determined by its composer. A listener who fails to pick up the content of the piece (as defined by Cooke) is simply unmusical. Likewise, the harmonic series is identified as an absolute force which directly shapes the music's affective content as a result of the consonance/dissonance and stability/instability relations that are asserted to exist between those members of the harmonic series which Cooke claims constitute the building blocks of tonality. It would be redundant to repeat the arguments against this intentionalist theory of musical meaning and the "natural" basis of tonality; my purpose instead is to identify those aspects of Cooke's ideas that are worth preserving, since there is a danger of turning Cooke into a scapegoat and of adopting a quite different but equally indefensible position.

The "lexicon" aspect of Cooke's theory seems to me to be the least useful. Like the much more restricted typology of Cooper & Meyer, the effect of this kind of nominalism is paradoxically to highlight the cases which do not fit the model, and to provide in the way of real explanation for those that do fit. However, the issues of communication and the role of the harmonic series deserve rather more careful consideration, since under the influence of a certain kind of structuralism there has been a strong tendency to regard music as an entirely arbitrary system with no communicative aspect – both of which are suspect assertions.

First it seems highly unlikely (and is contradicted by cross-cultural evidence) that human musical cultures should evolve with no reference whatsoever to the regularities of naturally occurring sound sources. The environment, and in particular the human speech environment, continually floods our auditory systems with the properties of the harmonic series (and has done for millennia), and it would be strange indeed if such a pervasive influence had not left its mark on our musical cultures – analogous to an architectural tradition that did not reflect the influence of gravity. What must be stressed, however, is that this influence lies in the historically very distant origins of our present musical cultures, and cannot be invoked in a simplistic fashion to account for current or historically recent phenomena, which are more directly the result of specific cultural forces with a history and momentum of their own. (One would not expect to reveal much about a building by Le Corbusier in terms of gravity alone).

In a similar fashion, we should not let the peculiar characteristics of music in contemporary Western culture blind us to the fact that in most other cultures, in other periods of our own classical culture, and in contemporary popular culture, music has been or still is closely bound to a variety of social functions, in which it plays a very significant communicative role. The mistake is to assume that the composer acts as sender in this arrangement (in many circumstances there is no identifiable composer), to disregard the communicative role of performers (what is performance expression if not a communicative act?), and to imply (as Cooke does) that there is some determinate message that must be picked up by listeners

in a veridical manner. What is needed is a more effective approach to musical communication which distinguishes between various levels and kinds of content,
ranging from musical structures to social meanings.

My final example of language and music within musicology comes from the
music theory of Lerdahl & Jackendoff. Their approach to this relationship is
handled in a far more informed and sophisticated manner than in either of the two
pieces of work examined so far, and covers many issues that I will not attempt to
tackle here. A strong point in their approach is the clear distinction drawn
between the adoption of a general theoretical framework that is strongly based in
generative linguistics, but which they develop in terms of specifically musical
categories with no comparisons between music and language. This is important
since there have been attempts (e.g. Bernstein, 1976) to establish the existence of
direct links between language and music at various levels and in various ways
which, while appearing superficially attractive, have been theoretically
unfounded and somewhat misleading. In addition, when discussing the
similarities between time-span structure in music and prosodic structure in
language (which is the substance of their remarks on specific parallelisms),
Lerdahl & Jackendoff avoid the rather arid exercise of simply equating properties
in one medium with properties in the other, and focus instead on the more
interesting possibility that the phenomena are different manifestations of some
more general and abstract cognitive capacity concerned with temporal segmentation and organization which are a feature of other activities as well – such as
dance. This gets beyond the simplistic notion that a feature in language can be
directly compared with one in music, and focuses instead on the possibility that
two similar features which have some kind of common cognitive origin have been
elaborated in their respective domains according to principles which are specific
to that domain. This is more powerful as an approach since it separates general
commonalties, which are interesting from the perspective of common origins,
innateness etc., but which are usually too unspecific to reveal anything very
interesting in a concrete instance, from the particular differentiations of such
common capacities, for which more specialized theories are needed if anything
interesting is to be revealed.

Turning now to the more general approach of the theory, certain problems
result from the linguistic outlook on which it is modeled. The most serious and
pervasive feature is the transfer of a syntax/semantics distinction from generative
linguistics into music. While the authors recognize that syntax and semantics as
used in a linguistic context cannot be translated completely unmodified into a
musical context, they nevertheless approach music with a clear separation
between the supposedly neutral and objective structural properties of their
material, and the signifcance (and in some sense function) of those same events.
As they themselves express it: "Music is not tied down to specific meanings and
functions. . . . In a sense, music is pure structure, to be "played with" within
certain bounds." (p.9). This undoubtedly makes the task of developing a set of
generative analytical rules easier, since it limits the amount of context sensitivity
that must be built into the system, and confines decision making within these
rules to questions relating directly to structural properties that are directly visible
in the notation.

It is interesting, however, that the problems of this apparently neutral and
"value-free" approach are made manifest in the authors' analytical treatment of

the most fundamental building-block of tonal structure – the cadence. Because their timespan reduction rules work on the principle that at any level of structure only the most hierarchically stable elements should remain, they are left with the absurd result that every cadence would be reduced to a single tonic element. This outcome fails to convey the oppositional nature of the cadence, makes perfect and imperfect cadences indistinguishable, and removes all trace of interrupted cadences. To overcome this obstacle, Lerdahl & Jackendoff appeal to the very property that they claimed earlier was not appropriate for musical structures – meaning and signification. Of the distinction between a perfect (full) and interrupted (deceptive) cadence they write: "The full cadence and the deceptive cadence possess two members, joined together as a unit; in both, neither member would have remotely the same meaning if the other did not function with it." (p.134). And in introducing the solution that they adopt, they write: "To avoid [absurd] results . . ., we must regard cadences as signs . . ." (p. 134).

The justification for restricting this semiotic approach to cadences seems to be that only cadences are sufficiently prominent as formulaic devices to warrant such special treatment. This is a questionable position, both in its own terms (since other aspects of musical structure, such as pedalpoints or the rhythmic/harmonic/melodic treatment of codas could be regarded as similarly conventional) and because it seems curious to restrict a fundamentally different way of thinking about musical structure to a class of events simply because the events are particularly easy to identify. The kind of approach that Lerdahl & Jackendoff are obliged to adopt in relation to the cadence is, I believe, one that should be adopted in a much more generalized fashion, since the semiotic nature of musical structures is by no means confined to broad stylistic categories such as the cadence, but can be seen at every level of musical organization, including the most local and ephemeral. Some signs are established within a single piece and operate only there, others are common to style groups of varying sizes and periods of influence, and others are more or less permanent features of a whole musical tradition. In some cases the signs can be understood almost exclusively in terms of the criteria of musical structure and its historical development, and in other cases musical criteria and wider cultural issues are inextricably bound together. But in every case it is the fact that these events are *signs*, and hence point beyond themselves, that determines how we should understand their properties and our response to them.

This undoubtedly raises some difficult practical problems concerning the way in which musical analysis should be carried out, since it involves a type of relativism which requires that musical events be understood as participating in a network of relationships that is both specific to the piece and which extends beyond the piece to include other pieces sharing the same stylistic features at various levels. The analytical method must therefore do more than just consider the "notes on the page," since it has to be sensitive to the assumed norms of the style and to the way in which these norms affect the nature and degree of significance attached to the events of the music. At the same time it must be sufficiently open-ended to be capable of picking up the function and significance of what happens in the music in terms that may be specific to that piece alone, and must be able to convey these functions (both local and style-based) in a framework that has as much to do with the experience of music as with its appearance on the page. Meyer's (1973) idea of "archetypal schemata" and Narmour's (1977) distinction between style structure and idiostructure are pointers in the same general direction, as are the ideas of Perlman & Greenblatt (1981) in relation to signification and function in jazz.

Language and music in the psychology of music

Many of the issues raised in connection with the influence of linguistics on musicology are encountered again within the psychology of music. Modern cognitive psychology as a whole has been powerfully shaped by generative linguistics and, more recently, by artificial intelligence. The consequences of this for the psychology of music are both positive and negative. On the positive side there has been a rapid development of the subject around a core of shared principles and experimental approaches which have a considerable background of development and elaboration within psychology and cognitive science. Much of this has been directly inspired by the immediate similarities between language and music, and the possibility of applying readily available techniques and theoretical frameworks to a new domain. On the negative side there are the problems, discussed in connection with musicology, of imposing linguistic models on musical material, together with additional difficulties associated with the application of A.I. techniques to music. Rather than going over ground similar to that treated in the previous section, I shall deal with just two issues here: the notion of grammaticality in music, and psychological approaches to emotion and meaning in music.

The idea that musical structures are governed by, or subject to, systems of constraints or rules is hardly novel: in Western music theory one need only go back to modal and contrapuntal theory to find a considerable tradition of treating music as a rule-based system, a characteristic that is also found in many other musical cultures (such as North Indian classical music). The phenomenon is not limited to musical styles with a written tradition, and oral musical cultures may demonstrate rules of construction that are no less complex or rigorous. Since these constraints operate on aspects of musical structure in a way that is extremely reminiscent of syntax in language (namely, sequential and hierarchical relationships under the influence of strong context sensitivity), it is not surprising that the idea of musical grammar has attracted a good deal of attention.

The empirical evidence that something like a grammar exists is also very strong: when listeners familiar with an idiom are required to identify errors in musical sequences, their performance depends on the extent to which the idiom is constrained (the more constrained it is, the easier it is to spot errors) and the extent to which an error "violates" the rules (the more implausible it is as a member of the system the easier it is to identify). Similarly, in a study in which pianists sight read unknown but highly conventional pieces in a familiar idiom into which deliberate notational errors had been introduced, Sloboda (1976) demonstrated that readers failed to notice and unconsciously re-corrected the errors, presumably on the basis of their tacit knowledge of the stylistic norms. Finally, in different studies in which subjects were required to recall sequences of various lengths (either by singing them or by writing them down), Deutsch (1982) and Sloboda (1985) showed that a person's ability to perform the task depended on the extent to which the sequence was rule-based, and that errors in reproduction were not random, but structured according to the rules picked up, or imposed, by the subject.

While it is clear from these and other empirical results that our ability to make sense of music under a variety of different conditions depends on the acquisition of the appropriate set of principles or rules, the question remains whether we are really talking about a grammar: after all, virtually every aspect of perception and cognition relies on making use of regularities of one sort or another, but we do not regard all of this behavior as "grammatical". It is no easy matter to define grammar such that it is sufficiently general to cover all those phenomena that *are* clearly grammatical while not engulfing everything that has any systematic properties at all. In order to clarify the issues, let us return to the classic formulation of the proponents of generative grammar: a grammar is a finite set of rules that will generate all, and only the sentences recognized as sentences in the language. There are two critical features here: first there should be a finite (and ideally small) set of rules which will account for a large (in principle infinite) number of diverse utterances; and second, there must be a clear distinction between utterances that are acceptable in the language, and utterances that are not.

This allows ordinary visual perception, for example, to be excluded from the category of grammatical behavior. Although it operates in a systematic and regular manner and is hence potentially describable in terms of rules, there seems to be no sensible way to distinguish between visual perceptions that are "acceptable" and those that are not – in other words there is no identifiable equivalent to the concept of a *language* as used in the definition above. By contrast, it is clear that Chomsky, the originator of this kind of definition of grammar, is quite sure of the truly grammatical nature of music. In the course of discussing the way in which the innate basis of natural language grammars acts as both a constraining and an enabling force, he writes as follows:

> The fact that there are many imaginable languages that we could not develop through the exercise of the language faculty is a consequence of the innate endowment that made it possible for us to attain our knowledge of the English or some other human language. Similarly, the fact that there are no doubt many systems of musical organization that we simply could not comprehend or enjoy should be a source of satisfaction, because it reflects the same innate endowment that enables us to appreciate Bach and Beethoven.
>
> (Chomsky in Gregory, ed., 1987, p. 420)

The only sensible way to understand what is implied by this quote is to regard different musical styles as being directly equivalent to different natural languages – an equivalence that as a whole may not be too controversial. However, a problem with this equivalence is that different musical styles are in many cases much less clearly demarcated from one another than are different languages, particularly styles that are historically rather than geographically separated. It is relatively easy to identify stylistic differences between, for example, Balinese gamelan music and the traditional music of Ireland, but it is a very different matter to give a reliable account of the differences between late Romanticism and early atonality. Certain features are fairly clear, such as the loosening of the restrictions that apply to tonal harmony, but many characteristics of the more recent style are continuous developments from its predecessor, and do not allow definite boundaries to be drawn. In theory, this is no different from historical change in language (modern English is obviously different from Shakespeare's) and the need adopt a primarily synchronic approach to language structure, but there is a very considerable difference in the *rate* of change in music as compared with language that makes a synchronic perspective difficult for music. Musical styles (particularly those of the European literate tradition) are characterized by continuous stylistic transformation, including periods of almost bewilderingly rapid change.

The specific problem that this raises for the orthodox generative grammar approach is that it becomes exceedingly difficult to establish a definite boundary between what is or is not permissable (or acceptable) within the style. Examples such as the chorale harmonization in Berg's violin concerto (which would certainly not have been "permissable" before 1900) show both how dramatically style can change over a comparatively brief period, and the kind of complex interrelations and references that may exist between styles. The history of hostile reactions to new pieces of music is evidence for the disparities between different people's conceptions of what is acceptable within a musical style. By comparison, the occasional resistances to the introduction of new words and constructions into a language are of nothing like the same scale nor intensity.

Hostile audience reaction is also evidence for a related phenomenon – the stylistic pluralism which is particularly evident in European and American music since the second world war. The problem of identifying diachronic style boundaries becomes compounded by the existence of a number of parallel and more or less independent musical styles which may operate according to entirely different criteria and use very different musical and technical resources. American minimalism, contemporary electroacoustic music, total serialism, and aleatoric music, for instance, as well as many other styles with less identifiable labels, have all coexisted at the same time – and these are only a selection of "art" music examples. When the various forms of jazz and popular music are also included, the true scale of this parallelism becomes clearer. The difference in outlook between these traditions can be so great that the adherents of two different traditions may not even agree whether the same sequence of events is or is not music. Once again the problem this poses for generative theory is stylistic demarcation, given that the idea of grammaticality depends on identifying the limits within which a grammar should be expected to operate.

Lerdahl & Jackendoff (1983) argue that the correct response to this problem of interdeterminacy is to concentrate less on the idea of grammaticality in music and to concentrate instead on ambiguity – something that Bernstein (1976) also emphasizes. The passage in which they propose this, however, has a curiously *non sequitur* character.

> In a linguistic grammar, perhaps the most important distinction is grammaticality: whether or not a given string of words is a sentence in the language in question. A subsidiary distinction is ambiguity: whether a given string is assigned two or more structures with different meanings. In music, on the other hand, grammaticality per se plays a far less important role, since almost any passage of music is potentially vastly ambiguous – it is much easier to construe music in a multiplicity of ways.
>
> (Lerdahl & Jackendoff, 1983, p. 9)

While accepting the potential for ambiguity within music, and the argument for its importance, I fail to see how the recognition of this fact helps with the problem of grammaticality. Lerdahl & Jackendoff use the argument above as a motivation for establishing two kinds of rule in their theory – a distinction that has been widely commented upon. Their "well-formedness" rules are essentially grammatical in nature, though of a generality that does not permit them to reveal much about any particular piece of of music, while their "preference" rules are designed to identify the different parsings of the same (grammatical) passage that are the source of its ambiguity. The widely expressed criticism of this scheme is that the preference rules have no teeth: they allow too many equally possible parsings, and do nothing to choose between them. Despite the principled basis from which the rules come, the real decisions seem to have been left to the "intuitions of the analyst." As an analytical procedure this is not necessarily too damaging, but it undermines the theory's claim to be an explicit theory of tonal music in the tradition of generative linguistics, as well as its claim to empirical falsifiability.

The source for the various problems raised here in connection with grammar is once again the rigid distinction between syntax and semantics, since this distinction requires that every aspect of musical structure be accounted for entirely in terms of a logic of structural relations. To attempt to do so is to ignore the communicative and rhetorical aims which motivate musical development and which thrive in the context of music's functionlessness. Natural language is essential to the cohesion and survival of human social organization, and hence must make use of structural constraints (grammar) which, by remaining relatively unchanging, ensure successful communication. By contrast, music in European art culture, although serving as an important cultural indicator, does not bear the same functional responsibility, and thus has less need for long-lasting structural constraints. Each piece can make use of a substantial number of principles that are specific only to that work, and which are consequently inexplicable (or at best explicable only at a very general level) in terms of a broad and general structural theory.

Furthermore, an account of the relationships within a work cannot proceed without an understanding of the relationships that extend beyond the work – in other words the network of *meanings* in which it participates. This approach obviously must include the network of connections within the work itself as a vital element, but views them as relationships of signification rather than as "neutral" structural links, and recognizes that there is in fact no clear boundary between their intensional and extensional properties. A particular structural device clearly has to work in its purely musical context, but it also has to be (or become) part of the mental life of the people who create, perform or hear it – a mental life which consists of much more than just musical principles.

This can be illustrated with the idea from Perlman & Greenblatt (1981) that part of the meaning of the thematic content in a bebop jazz solo is its "personal origin" – the individual who first "coined the phrase" or with whose style it is associated. A melodic fragment borrowed, say, from Charlie Parker, or the American national anthem has to make sense in the context of the harmonic, melodic and rhythmic structure of the solo as a whole, and in this sense its signification has an intensional aspect: it may, for instance, be the initiator of a modulating harmonic sequence. But at the same time its signification extends beyond the limits (and time) of the solo to a network of people, institutions, and ideologies that takes one rapidly outside purely musical issues. Furthermore, there is no real separation between these intensional and extensional aspects, since the musical context has the power to cast a different light on what we may label the extensional component, and the cultural significance with which a musical fragment is imbued may influence its musical usage. We thus arrive at the final aspect of this paper – a brief consideration of the psychology of musical meaning and emotion.

Empirical work on emotion and meaning in music has primarily been concerned with the mapping out of a kind of "semantic space" for musical events, and with trying to establish the stability or cross-cultural generality of these findings (e.g. Gabrielsson, 1973; Imberty, 1975; Gabriel, 1978; Clynes, 1982). While this work is interesting in other ways, it does not really touch upon the primary concern of this paper, since the "semantic" aspect of the findings can be accepted or dismissed whatever the relationship to language. A more relevant approach to the issue is found in Dowling & Harwood (1986) who make use of semiotic ideas taken from Charles Peirce. Peirce (1931–35) defined three kinds of sign – Index, Icon and Symbol – which differed with respect to the relationship between sign and concept embodied in each. For an *index* the relationship is either casual or directly associative (e.g. a tune and the occasion on which it is played), for an *icon* the relationship is one of formal similarity or mimicry, and for a *symbol* the relationship is governed only by the systematic network of connections that make up the relevant semiotic system. This framework allows Dowling & Harwood to explain clearly and persuasively how it is that musical meaning can consist of such a variety of elements, ranging from the instrumental and purely performance impact of music, through its ability to mimic non-musical events, to abstract meanings that are specifically and purely musical, since the indexical, iconic and symbolic components of musical meaning are neither mutually exclusive nor even conflicting. This semiotic framework provides, in other words precisely the kind of theory that can accommodate the complex mixture of intensional, extensional, rhetorical and pragmatic components discussed above.

Their approach to emotion in music is to use the principle of arousal as developed by Meyer (1956), Mandler (1984), Berlyne (1971), and others, coupled with Peirce's semiotic. In brief, they suggest that the emotion experienced during musical listening is the result of two components: a global state of arousal that is related to general features of the music, such as loudness or speed, as well as subtler features that depend on the kind of patterns of expectation and surprise (or implication and realization) that Meyer has discussed; and a mediating network of meanings. The semiotic relationships carry the more differentiated, culturally mediated and specific component of the emotional experience, while the state of arousal carries the "charge." While the theory is not yet sufficiently developed to give an entirely satisfactory account of the extraordinarily subtle, continually evolving emotional flux that characterizes concentrated musical listening, it nonetheless is an important principle to acknowledge the different contributions of socio-cultural, cognitive and psycho-physiological components as co-determinants of a response to music that is experienced as a unified affective state.

Concluding remarks

I have argued in this paper that the relationship between music and language is both attractive and potentially hazardous. Music theorists and psychologists of music have used the abundant superficial resemblances between the two as a pretext for a somewhat ill-considered extension of linguistic theory into the study of the structure, aesthetics, meaning, mental representation and affective content of music. In some of these domains, the result has been an increased level of activity and interest, and some valuable insights. But it is also true that in some respects these linguistic models have restricted our ability to tackle some of the more important questions relating to the nature and impact of music, questions which call into doubt the neat separation between syntax and semantics as it applies to music. It seems more fruitful to regard music as a network of relations embodying musical functions that are both structural and signifying, and which extend not only throughout the various levels of musical discourse, but also beyond to the mediating networks of human culture. Wilden (1972) distinguishes between signification and meaning by proposing that while signification is contained within a local and specific system of relations which are primarily digital (based on oppositions) meaning is characterized by analog relations (based on differences) which spread beyond the immediate systematic context. It is the fact that music is simultaneously subject to its own constructive principles and a part of this wider semiotic network, that gives it the ambivalence of a system that is highly self consistent, and yet suffused with meaning.

Acknowledgments

I am grateful to Eugene Narmour and Stephen McAdams for helpful comments on a previous version of this paper.

Notes

1. It is striking that when people do speak together in coordinated groups (e.g. in the context of ecclesiastical responses or street demonstrations), they adopt a metrical style that is rather similar to that employed in music and poetry, and which is quite different from the more flexible rhythmic style or ordinary speech.

References

Berlyne, D. (1971) *Aesthetics and Psychobiology*. New York: Appleton-Century-Crofts.
Bernstein, L. (1976) *The Unanswered Question*. Cambridge, Mass: Harvard University Press.
Campbell, J. (1984) *Grammatical Man*. Harmondsworth, Middlesex: Penguin.
Clynes, M. (1982) (ed.) *Music, Mind and Brain: The Neuropsychology of Music*. New York: Plenum.
Cooke, D. (1959) *The Language of Music*. London: Oxford University Press.
Cooper, G. & Meyer, L.B. (1960) *The Rhythmic Structure of Music*. University of Chicago Press.
Deutsch, D. (1982) The processing of pitch combinations. In D. Deutsch (Ed.): *The Psychology of Music*. New York: Academic Press.
Dowling, J. & Harwood, D. (1986) *Music Cognition*. New York: Academic Press.
Eco, U. (1977) *A Theory of Semiotics*. London: Macmillan.
Gabriel, C. (1978) An experimental study of Deryck Cooke's theory of music and meaning. *Psychology of Music*, **Vol. 6,** 13–20.
Gabrielsson, A. (1973) Adjective ratings and dimension analyses of auditory rhythm patterns. *Scandinavian Journal of Psychology*. **Vol.14,** 244–260.
Gregory, R.L. (1987) *The Oxford Companion to the Mind*. Oxford: Oxford University Press.
Imberty, M. (1975) Perspectives nouvelles de la sémantique musicale expérimentale. *Musique en Jeu*, **Vol. 17,** 87–109.
Lerdahl, F. & Jackendoff, R. (1983) *A Generative Theory of Tonal Music*. Cambridge, Mass: MIT Press.
Longuet-Higgins, H.C. (1979) The perception of music. *Proceedings of the Royal Society of London*, B205, 307–322.
Mandler, G.(1984) *Mind and Body*. New York: Norton.
Meyer, L.B. (1956) *Emotion and Meaning in Music*. Chicago: University of Chicago Press.
Meyer, L.B. (1973) *Explaining Music*. Berkeley: University of California Press.
Narmour, E. (1977) *Beyond Schenkerism: The Need for Alternatives in Music Analysis*. Chicago: University of Chicago Press.

Peirce, C.S. (1931–35) *Collected Papers,* (vols. 1–6) (C. Hartshorne & P. Weiss, Eds.). Cambridge, Mass: Harvard University Press.

Perlman, A.H. & Greenblatt, D. (1981) Miles Davis meets Noam Chomsky: some observations on jazz improvisation and language structure. In W. Steiner (Ed): *The Sign in Music and Literature.* Austin: University of Texas Press.

Shaffer, L.H. (1982) Rhythm and timing in skill. *Psychological Review,* (**83** 5), 109–122.

Sloboda, J.A. (1976) The effect of item position on the likelihood of identification by inference in prose reading and music reading. *Canadian Journal of Psychology,* **30,** 228–236.

Sloboda, J.A. (1985) *The Musical Mind.* Oxford: The Clarendon Press.

Wilden, A. (1972) *System and Structure: Essays in Communication and Exchange.* London: Tavistock Publications.

Yeston, M. (1976) *The Stratification of Musical Rhythm.* London: Yale University Press.

Contemporary Music Review,
1989, Vol. 4, pp. 23–44
Photocopying permitted by license only

Relationships between music and poetry in the arias of Giovanni Legrenzi

Mario Baroni[a], Rossana Dalmonte[b] and Carlo Jacoboni[c]

[a]*Università di Bologna, Dipartimento di Musica e Spettacolo, via Galliera 3, I-40121 Bologna, Italy*
[b]*Università di Trento, Facoltà di Lettere, via S. Croce 65, I-38100 Trento, Italy*
[c]*Università di Modena, Dipartimento di Fisica, via Campi 213A, I-41100 Modena, Italy*

This paper presents in detail part of a project set up to analyze the arias of Giovanni Legrenzi. Its aim is to study the relationship between poetry and music. By means of a metric-syntactic tree describing the structure of the poem, it is possible to formulate the rules which govern the form of the arias and their tonal organization. A computer program verifies the completeness and self-consistency of the twenty-eight generative rules used in the analysis. This project on Legrenzi's arias is part of a wider project developing a theory of European melody.

KEY WORDS: Computer-aided analysis, generative grammar, music-poetry relationships, musical form, tonality, Legrenzi.

Aims and method of the research

The present work is part of a wider piece of research on the theory of European melody in terms of both its main structures and its historical development. Having completed an initial study of the melody of Lutheran chorales (Baroni & Jacoboni, 1978; Baroni, 1983; Baroni & Jacoboni, 1983), we have now taken into consideration other repertories: a book of melodic French chansons of the 18th century (Baroni, Brunetti, Callegari & Jacoboni, 1984; Baroni & Callergari, 1984) and a collection of arias by Giovanni Legrenzi . Other more modern repertories (Schubert's Lieder, melodies by C. Debussy) have been studied using analogous procedures by researchers not belonging to our group (Camilleri, 1984; Wenk, 1987). The final aim of our research project is to carry out a comparative analysis on a sufficiently large set of examples in order (a) to test the reliability of the theory (b) to distinguish general laws, valid for the "melody" in itself, from particular laws characteristic of different repertories, and (c) to sketch an historical description of the developments of European melody. In this paper we shall limit ourselves to a description of Legrenzi's arias. Some of the results will not hold for other repertories. A general theory should take into account similarities and differences in the results obtained from the different repertories.

The method used in the analysis consists of a description of the repertory under consideration based on a hierarchical set of rules expressed in generative form. The description must be exhaustive and the rules must be neccessary and self-consistent. These requirements are checked by a computer program able to produce melodies in the style of the repertory. In previous articles we have discussed certain practical and theoretical problems that have arisen in the course of our research, with references to the current literature on the subject. Here we prefer to present a detailed "case study" in order to give a concrete example of the method used. As regards problems of musical cognition, our research does not pretend to examine empirically the mental mechanisms implied in making music, due also to the early stage of theoretical research in this field. However, the results of the research do implicitly show how musical form reflects and implies some of these mental devices.

In the first two repertories examined, the rules have been divided into two categories: macroformal and microformal rules. The first category refers to the composition as a whole. They describe the number and length of the phrases, the symmetrical or asymmetrical sequences of identical or similar phrases, the general organization of their direction and extension, their tonal and rhythmic properties, the relationships between their cadences – in short, the whole system of formal features that give continuity and coherence to the melodic course of the composition. The second category refers to the internal structure of the single phrase, starting from the "kernel" interval that defines its direction and extension, and adding to it a number of figures (repetitions, neighbor notes, appoggiaturas, skips) that, according to a strictly defined syntax, give it its melodic shape.

In the repertory of Legrenzi's arias, both macroformal and microformal rules are made much more complex because of the problems posed by the harmonic relationships between the vocal part and the part of the thorough-bass, and by the presence of a poetic text that deeply interferes with the musical structures and upsets their regularity. This latter is, indeed, the main characteristic of the Italian vocal baroque style of the 18th century.

In the present work we will describe a part of the macroformal structure. We will present the rules that describe the number and the length of the phrases, the repetitions of identical fragments, and the tonal structure of the arias. These aspects of Legrenzi's compositions are exhaustively described by 28 rules. They will be given and explained with examples. A computer program based on these rules is used to verify their pertinence, their completeness and their self-consistency. An example obtained using this computer program will be examined at the end of this paper. It can be seen that the present state of research is much more complete as regards the description of the general structures of the aria obtained by processing the poetic text. Research is still being undertaken on other musical aspects regarding melody and harmony.

The repertory analyzed

Our sample includes the arias of the *Cantatas*, op. 12 by G. Legrenzi (Bologna: Monti, 1676), excluding the *Canzonettas* of the same collection. From the various aria-like pieces of the *Cantatas*, we made a choice based on the following criteria:

1. the piece had to start and end in the same key;
2. the tempo had to be the same throughout the piece;
3. the verbal text had to consist of more than one line.

These criteria may not give a general definition of "aria." They have nevertheless been useful in our repertory in order to exclude from the sample all the "arioso" fragments which are so frequent in Legrenzi's *Cantatas* and so typical of the style of this epoch. Moreover, only Alto and Bass *Cantatas* have been consi-dered – Soprano and Tenor *Cantatas* will be used later in order to check the results obtained. Our sample consists of a total of 17 arias.

Segmentation

Dividing an aria into phrases is the first step of the analysis. The first task facing the analyst is thus to find valid criteria on the basis of which this segmentation can take place. Our definition of the "phrase" implies here an inseparable connection between the music and the verbal text. This enabled us to look for our criteria both in the music and in the poem.

As we conceived of our analysis in principle as concerning a formalization of listening competence, we started by trying to define, explicitly and through general rules, the divisions in the musical phrases which we perceived in the text.

We noted that melodic, harmonic and rhythmic features could not give us seg-mentation criteria which were generally valid and unambiguous. On the other hand, the line of the poem and the verbal phrase offer some help but cannot solve the problem of musical phrasing.

A much more convincing solution is given by the interaction of the two dimen-sions. As the analysis showed, there are coherent indications at the end of a line which come both from the poetry and the music. According to the principles of post-Monteverdian musical aesthetics, music is no less than a sort of emphatic "pronunciation" of the poem, and has the function of strengthening the rules of verbal intonation and above all to stress the pauses between its metric sub-divisions. When a line is particularly long, as in the case of hendecasyllables (11 syllables), Legrenzi's music stresses its subdivision into two half-lines. Thus for analytic purposes, the line and the half-line can be taken as a basis for the segmen-tation of the piece into musical phrases. We found the same coherent indications of music and text in cases such as the opening of aria no. 7:

Disciaglietevi	[melt,
disciaglietevi in due fiumi	melt into two rivers]

Here the first half line is repeated and is separated from the next complete line by a movement of cadence and by a rest.

The following rule summarizes what we have shown up to this point:

RULE 1: Each aria is divided into musical phrases which correspond to the lines of the poem, or to its half-lines in the case of hendecasyllables (11 syllables) or of repeated half-lines.

The relationships between music, metrics and syntax

Even after a cursory glance one can see that repetition plays a very important role in the form of Legrenzi's aria. The composer organizes his musical material mainly through the repetition of phrases or groups of phrases.

Legrenzi's verbal repetition respects metric organization and, in fact, always consists of lines or half lines. On the other hand, the syntactic organization of the poetry models itself on the subdivisions of the lines, following the rules of classical versification: there is only one case of "enjambement" in the repertory (aria no. 6).

Our task, then, is to discover the underlying rules which can permit the combination of the various requirements of music, metrics, and syntax in the particular form of the aria. In other words we have to understand what it is possible to repeat and when it is possible to do so without breaking the syntactic and metric demands. In any case, it is clear that we are facing a "rewriting" of the poem by the composer, who (more or less consciously) acts within the limits given by the text. Our task is to make explicit in a formal manner the possible alternatives facing the composer. To this end, we constructed a metric-syntactic tree describing the structure of the poems in our repertory.

A metric–syntactic tree

Analysis showed that repetition can involve greater or smaller sections of verbal text. Sometimes they correspond to groups of phrases or even to the whole poem; in other cases only very short sections of the text are repeated, even if these are never shorter than the half-line. In any case, long or short repetitions never break the half-line. For this reason the half-line appears to be the fundamental metric unit of the text. Since lines inferior to the septenary also behave in the same way, that is they cannot be broken in repetition, they too can be considered fundamental metric units like the half-line. Dividing the poem into half-lines or short lines is the first step to the construction of the metric-syntactic tree. In order to obtain trees able to describe the poems of the repertory in a non-contradictory manner, we followed a clearly-defined procedure consisting of eight prescriptions. These prescriptions are not to be considered as rules with the same status as the others presented in this paper. They have to be considered as no more than a formalization of our competence in the metric-syntactic analysis of the poem.

> Prescription 1: Each half-line forms a final branch of the tree and pairs with the other half-line of the line. The bottom of the tree is normally formed by pairs of half-lines.

Example (aria no. 6 – octosyllabic):

[Half-line]	*Ad un cenno*		[By a lift
"	*delle ciglia*		of her eyebrows,
"	*gira l'alma*		my heart turns
"	*a suo talento*		to her bidding]

> Prescription 2: When two lines are tied by enjambement, the final half-line of the first line pairs with the initial half-line of the second. This couple pairs with the initial half-line of the first line. The final half-line of the second line pairs with the previous group.

Example (aria no. 6):

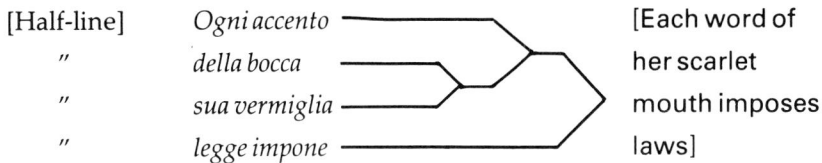

[Half-line]	*Ogni accento*	[Each word of
"	*della bocca*	her scarlet
"	*sua vermiglia*	mouth imposes
"	*legge impone*	laws]

Prescription 3: Lines shorter than a septenary are not divided into half-lines and pair with the adjacent line, if this is also shorter than a septenary. If not, the short line pairs with the couple of half-lines with which it is syntactically connected.

Example (aria no. 1):

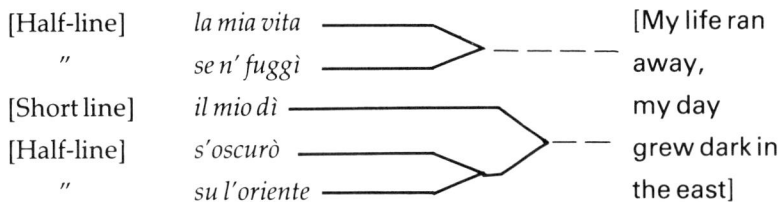

[Half-line]	*la mia vita*	[My life ran
"	*se n' fuggì*	away,
[Short line]	*il mio dì*	my day
[Half-line]	*s'oscurò*	grew dark in
"	*su l'oriente*	the east]

Prescriptions 1, 2 and 3 refer to the first level of pairing which concerns metric organization. The following prescriptions (4–7) concern syntactic levels.

Prescription 4: A line (or couple of short lines), not containing the predicate of its sentence, pairs with the adjacent line (or couple) if it contains this predicate. Two adjacent incomplete lines depending on the same predicate pair together before pairing with the line containing their common predicate.

Example (aria no. 9):

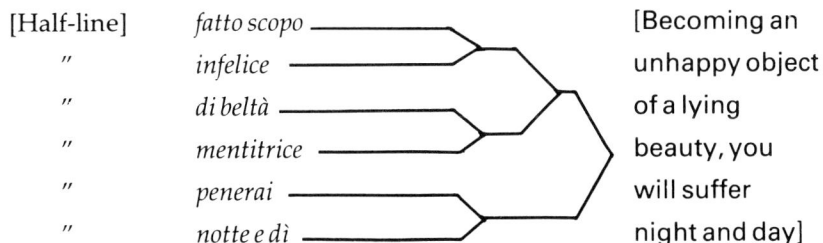

[Half-line]	*fatto scopo*	[Becoming an
"	*infelice*	unhappy object
"	*di beltà*	of a lying
"	*mentitrice*	beauty, you
"	*penerai*	will suffer
"	*notte e dì*	night and day]

Since the syntactic organization of the repertory is quite simple, only these two types of incomplete clauses are present.

Once the metric units are connected together to form syntactically complete clauses, the next step consists in pairing clauses into larger units on the basis of their function in the sentence (either as main or dependent clauses) and of their reciprocal relationship (coordination, subordination).

Prescription 5: Two adjacent coordinated clauses pair together in both main and dependent clauses.

Example (aria no. 6):

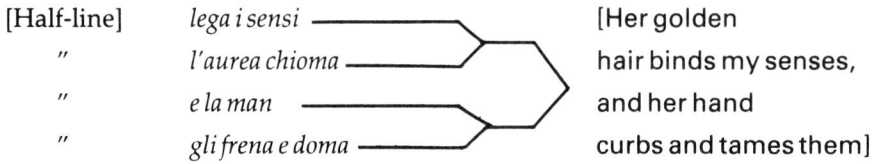

[Half-line]	*lega i sensi*	[Her golden
"	*l'aurea chioma*	hair binds my senses,
"	*e la man*	and her hand
"	*gli frena e doma*	curbs and tames them]

Prescription 6: Two adjacent clauses pair together when one is dependent on the other.

Example (aria no. 9):

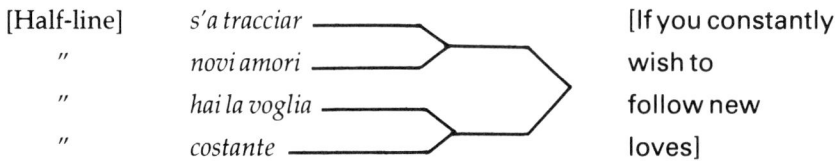

[Half-line]	*s'a tracciar*	[If you constantly
"	*novi amori*	wish to
"	*hai la voglia*	follow new
"	*costante*	loves]

Prescription 7: Once the clauses come to completion, if both the situations described in prescriptions 5 and 6 are present, they must be carried out in the order given in prescriptions 5 and 6.

Example (aria no. 2):

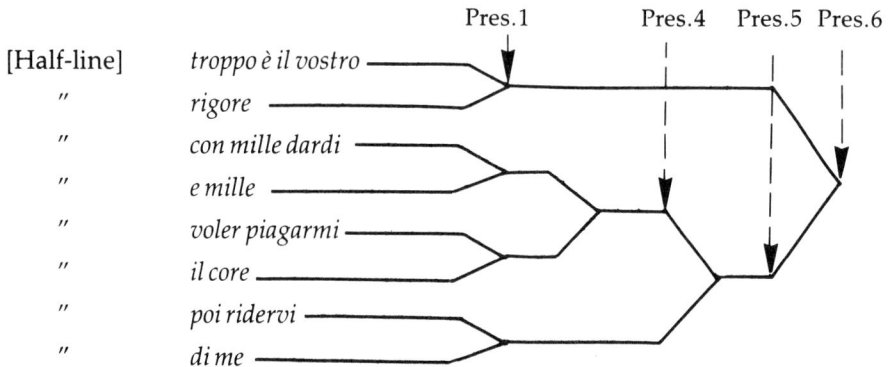

Pres.1   Pres.4   Pres.5   Pres.6

[Half-line]	*troppo è il vostro*
"	*rigore*
"	*con mille dardi*
"	*e mille*
"	*voler piagarmi*
"	*il core*
"	*poi ridervi*
"	*di me*

[You are too cruel when you wound my heart with thousands of arrows and then laugh at me]

In the example, the line is rebuilt by means of prescription 1, the clause is completed by connecting the complement with its predicate through prescription 4, two adjacent subordinate clauses are connected through prescription 5, and all the subordinate clauses are connected with the main clause through prescription 6.

> Prescription 8: Finally, independent clauses separated by a caesura are always connected. Through this operation more than two branches of the tree can be connected.

Example (aria no. 11):

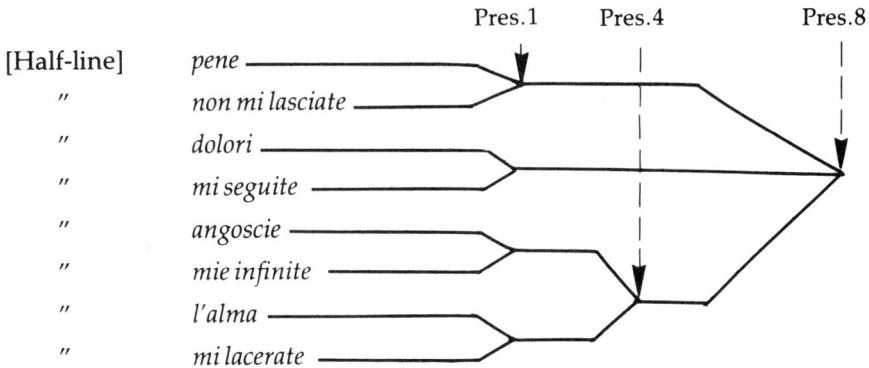

| | | Pres.1 | Pres.4 | Pres.8 |

[Half-line]   *pene*
"   *non mi lasciate*
"   *dolori*
"   *mi seguite*
"   *angoscie*
"   *mie infinite*
"   *l'alma*
"   *mi lacerate*

[Sorrows, you do not leave me; troubles, you follow me; my endless anguishes, you rend my soul]

In this example, that refers to the whole text of a poem, the tree can be completed by carrying out only three kinds of operation. Here the main branches of the tree connect clauses separated by a caesura, that is, complete and not coordinated clauses, but this condition is not always necessary.

Example (aria no. 15):

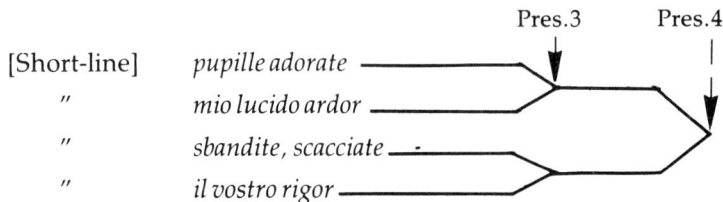

| | | Pres.3 | Pres.4 |

[Short-line]   *pupille adorate*
"   *mio lucido ardor*
"   *sbandite, scacciate*
"   *il vostro rigor*

[Beloved eyes, my shining ardor, banish, dismiss your cruelty]

Here too the whole text of the poem has been given, but the main branches of the tree describe the completion of the only clause forming the text (prescription 4). We can also notice that the coupling of half-lines is missing (prescription 1) because we are here dealing with short lines.

Musical form

The tree describes the interaction between metrics and syntax and divides the poem into two, three or four parts corresponding to the main branches. The structure of the tree does not only describe the subdivisions of the poem but also the musical form of the aria.

RULE 2:   The fundamental form of each aria is based on a division of the poem into two, three or four parts corresponding to the main branches of the tree.

The verbal text of an aria is never formed by the poem alone but is always enriched by repetitions.

There are two types of repetition, which we will define as major and minor repetitions.

Major repetitions increase the number of main branches of the tree and therefore modify the binary, ternary or quaternary structure of the poem. They repeat groups of lines, each group corresponding to a formal unit of music.

Minor repetitions increase the number of intermediate or final branches of the tree. They repeat the smallest metric units (lines or half-lines), each of them corresponding to a musical phrase.

RULE 3:   The verbal text of an aria is obtained by adding to the original poem either repeated sections of it or the smallest metric units (lines or half-lines). The repetition of a section of the poem involves the main branches of the tree; that of the smallest metric units involves intermediate or terminal branches.

Major Repetitions

The analysis of the whole sample shows that in Legrenzi two types of major repetitions are present, which we can define as adjacent and remote repetition.

Adjacent repetitions begin immediately after the conclusion of the part to be repeated. If we label with letters the main branches of the tree, we may have, for example:

ABB, ABAB, ABCBC, ABCABC

From the various possibilities, Legrenzi chooses only some of these schemes, which can be described using the following rules:

RULE 4:   Adjacent major repetitions only involve the last, or the two or three last main branches of the tree.

This rule allows, for example, the form ABB but not AAB; it allows ABCBC but not ABABC. As this rule counts the branches by starting with the last of them, it can include also the first. So for example, in the scheme of ABCABC, "A" is considered as the third to last branch of the tree.

Remote repetitions do not begin immediately after the conclusion of the part to be repeated, as for example, in the scheme ABC or ABCA. Only the first branch can produce a remote repetition, and only at the end of the aria.

Using traditional terminology we can call this repetition "reprise." A reprise, however, is not always possible. In Legrenzi's style, there are two conditions that have to be met before a reprise can become a possibility. There has to be a caesura at the end of the first branch, and one that rhymes with the last line of the poem (we may say that there is a caesura when the end of a sentence, even if this is made up of only one clause, is not connected with the following by means of a conjunction). In any case, no reprise can take place if there are more than two branches between the first one and its final repetition.

Example: ABBA but not ABCBCA

RULE 5: A reprise involves only the section corresponding to the first branch of the tree and it is possible only if this section is concluded by a caesura and rhymes with the last line of the poem. Between the first and the second occurrence of the section no more than two main branches of the tree can be present. Under these conditions, a reprise is always present.

Both adjacent and remote repetitions must observe the following rules:

RULE 6: No main branch of the tree can be repeated more than once.

RULE 7: Each aria is formed by no less than three and no more than six formal units.

The set of these rules, theoretically, permits the following formal schemes:

Tree	Formal units	Presence in the sample
binary: AB	ABB	7
	ABAB	3
	ABA	3
	ABBA	1
ternary: ABC	ABC	2
	ABCC	0
	ABCBC	0
	ABCABC	0
	ABCA	1
quaternary: ABCD	ABCD	0
	ABCDD	0
	ABCDCD	1

Not all the theoretical schemes are present in the sample. Some of them occur more frequently due to the fact that the binary tree is much more common than the others. But there is no reason to exclude a scheme such as ABCD since a larger form of it (ABCDCD) does exist. Thus the fact that some of the schemes are missing may be due to the low number of examples available in the sample.

Minor Repetitions

While major repetitions refer to formal units, minor repetitions concern the smallest metric units, that is, half-lines or short lines.

Minor repetitions are always adjacent and are situated at particular points in the poem. According to their place in the poem they are called: initial, central, semifinal, and final. Initial repetitions involve the first two metric units of the poem: a line or two short lines. For example (aria no. 1):

Resto un'ombra/ resto un niente	[I remain a shadow, I remain nothing]

or (aria no. 15):

Pupille adorate	Beloved eyes
mio lucido ardor	my shining fire]

Central repetitions involve the unit or the two metric units preceding a caesura (at the end of one of the main branches of the tree). Final repetitions involve the last or the last two metric units of the poem. Semifinal repetitions involve the unit or the two units preceding the final ones.

At this point it is necessary to add some further specifications to our former definitions if we are to avoid creating misunderstandings or falling into ambiguities. According to our definitions, the final lines of aria no. 6:

lega i sensi/ l'aurea chioma
e la man/ gli frena e doma

could be labelled in the following ways:

Final units:	Semifinal Units:
gli frena e doma	*e la man*
e la man gli frena e doma	*l'aurea chioma*
e la man gli frena e doma	*lega i sensi l'aurea chioma*

If the semifinal fragment includes two metric units, they cannot belong to two lines. For example, they cannot be:

. . . l'aurea chioma
e la man . . .

To sum up, we can say that the position of the semifinal repetition depends on the extension of the final one.

As can be seen, our definitions of central, semifinal, and final units are obtained by counting from the last unit. In very short poems, this can create some ambiguities, as, for example, aria no. 17 which includes only two lines:

Tornate poi da me/ che giusta l'alma
a chi vince di voi/ darà la palma

[(Love and virtue) come back to me so that my just soul will bestow victory upon the winner between you]

In this case, if the second half-line of the first line (also the penultimate) were repeated, the repetition could be classed as both initial and semifinal. However, such ambiguity is only terminological in nature and does not interfere with a correct application of the rules.

Finally, we should point out that there is an important relationship between major and minor repetitions. If major repetitions are present in an aria, a part of the poem occurs twice. In this case, if minor repetitions are also present, they behave differently in the first and in the second occurrence. Such differences will be explained in the following two sections.

Minor Repetitions in the First Occurrence

Our analysis has shown that initial repetitions act according to the following rule:

RULE 8: Initial metric units may or may not be repeated at the first occurrence. This is possible of the first or of the second unit, or of both together or separately.

For example, the first line of aria no. 1 *(Resto un'ombra, resto un niente)* could be expanded in the following four ways:

1. *Resto un'ombra, resto un'ombra, resto un niente*
2. *Resto un'ombra, resto un niente, resto un niente*
3. *Resto un'ombra, resto un niente, resto un'ombra, resto un niente*
4. *Resto un'ombra, resto un'ombra, resto un niente, resto un niente*

These four possibilities are all present in different degrees in the sample.

Central repetitions, depending on the existence of a caesura, are not frequent in the repertory, bearing in mind also that not all caesuras are followed by a central repetition. Their use is governed by the following rule:

RULE 9: In the first occurrence, central repetitions may be present or not. In the former case, the last or the last two metric units preceding the caesura can be repeated in the following ways: 1. Only the last unit preceding the caesura is repeated. 2. The last two units preceding the caesura are repeated. 3. The last or the penultimate unit is repeated, followed by their repetition together. If more than one caesura is present, central repetitions are possible only once.

Examples:
1. Aria no. 8, lines 1–2:
   Stelle ingrate/ rio destino   [Ungrateful stars,
   luci amate, e dove sete?   sad destiny, beloved
   e dove sete?   eyes, where are you?]

2. Aria no. 6, lines 1–2:
   Ad un cenno/ delle ciglia   [By a lift of her
   gira l'alma/ a suo talento   eyebrows, my heart turns
   gira l'alma/ a suo talento   to her bidding]

3. Aria no. 9, lines 1–2:
   Cessa/ d'essere amante   [Cease being a lover,
   mio cor/ basta così   my heart/enough!]
   basta così
   mio cor/ basta così

3b. Aria no. 14, lines 1–2:
   Nutro il serpe/ nel mio seno   [I nurture a snake in my
   alimento/ fiamme al core   bosom, I feed flames in
   alimento   my heart]
   alimento/ fiamme al core

Since the caesura is a sort of intermediate closure of the poem, central repetitions can assume the function of a temporary end, and this justifies the number of repetitions possible in this place.

Semifinal repetitions can be described in the following rule:

RULE 10:   In the first occurrence, semifinal units may be repeated or not. When repeated, repetition involves the last or the last two units preceding the final units. In the former case, two repetitions are possible.

The function of semifinal repetitions is to give some rhetorical support to the final ones. In some cases, they can improve their effect through a double repetition.

Final repetitions behave differently according to whether they are followed or not by a major repetition, as is described in the following rules:

RULE 11:   In first occurrences that are not followed by a major repetition, final repetitions may repeat the last or the last two metric units only once. In any case, however, their presence is necessary.

RULE 12:   In first occurrences followed by a major repetition, final metric units are never repeated if they are preceded by a semifinal repetition. If this is not the case, the last or the last two metric units may be repeated once.

As can be seen, Legrenzi does not abuse the rhetorical expansion that is given by minor repetitions at the end of a poem. This seems to be particularly typical of his style, at least when the first occurrence of the final repetition corresponds to the end of the aria. In these cases, Legrenzi, avoiding major repetitions and using minor repetitions only sparingly, sketches a model of an aria which is very simple and close to the poetic text.

Minor Repetitions in the Second Occurrence

In the second occurrence, the names we have given to the different kinds of repetition could be misleading in that they do not necessarily correspond to the place where the repetitions occur. For example, in the formal scheme ABA repetitions in A are always called initial repetitions, even if in the second occurrence they are situated at the end of the aria. In other words, the terms refer to the place in the poem and not to the place in the aria.

When studying minor repetitions in second occurrences, one cannot avoid taking into account the relationships between minor and major repetitions. Minor repetitions, in fact, behave differently according to the position of the formal unit to which they belong. For example in the formal scheme ABA, minor repetitions in the second A can behave differently from those in the first A, because their formal unit has assumed a final position. The relationships between major and minor repetitions can be summed up in the following rules:

RULE 13:   The second occurrence of every kind of minor repetition belonging to a formal unit not placed at the end of the aria but followed by another formal unit is identical to the first occurrence.

Examples of this rule can be found in formal schemes such as AB<u>B</u>A, AB<u>A</u>B, ABCD<u>C</u>D.

RULE 14: At the end of an aria, an adjacent repetition must be present. This can be a major or minor repetition or both. In the sample considered, the ending of an aria is always expanded by some kind of repetition.

For example:

- aria no. 3: formal scheme ABB: no minor repetitions in B
- aria no. 4: formal scheme ABC: final repetition in C
- aria no. 5: formal scheme ABB: final repetition in B

RULE 15: The second occurrence of every kind of minor repetition belonging to a formal unit placed at the end of the aria can add repetitions to those which may be present in the first occurrence, provided that the total number of actual repetitions respects the rules governing the first occurrence.

The following table shows the various possibilities that can be present according to this rule, using some examples from our sample:

I occurrence	II occurrence	Aria no.	Formal scheme
no rep.	=	3	ABB
no rep.	+	5	ABB
rep.	=	1	ABBA
rep.	+	2	ABA

It should be noted here that the second occurrence of a formal unit never takes place without any repetition that appeared in the first occurrence, and this is generally valid also for the situations described in rules 13, 14, and 15.

Observations

There are a few examples of repetition that are not, however, covered by the rules discussed above. The following points describe these examples:

1. In arias no. 2 and 17, there are repetitions of single words, shorter than half-lines:

| | *care, care pupille* | [dear, dear eyes] |
| and | *tornate, tornate poi da me* | [come back to me] |

In both examples the repeated words have an exclamatory emphasis. The same occurs in aria no. 11 where the exclamatory emphasis is not given by a repetition but by the insertion of the negative particle "no, no":

pene non mi lasciate, [Sorrows, do not leave me
no, no, non mi lasciate no, no, do not leave me]

2. In aria no. 2, the reprise of the initial line inverts the order of its two half-lines:

> *avete il torto affè/ care pupille*   [You are quite wrong my dear eyes]

becomes

> *care pupille/ avete il torto affè.*

3. In aria no. 17, the final repetition in the second occurrence reiterates four times the last short line, breaking the constraints of rules 15 and 11. This exceptional enrichment is probably due to the collocation of the aria at the end of the cantata. In this case, the expansion may be explained by the need for rhetorical closure in a cantata and not to those of a single aria. In aria no. 10, the final repetition in the second occurrence follows the rule of central repetition (Rule 9):

> *sol è pregno/ d'inganni*   [He is only full of deceits]
> *sol è pregno*
> *sol è pregno/ d'inganni*

The three cases discussed above are, however, isolated cases in a reduced repertory. The exceptions listed are perhaps important for a more complete definition of Legrenzi's style. However, their occurrence was too rare to allow the formulation of precise rules. As our aim is to describe regularities, we thus decided to disregard such cases, at least until such time as they can be considered in a wider historical context.

Tonality

In Legrenzi's cantatas, the tonal organization of an aria has no completely autonomous rules but is dependent on the form, which interferes with the duration of every key and with the point of its change. The following analysis attempts to point out the parallelism between formal and tonal organization and their different hierarchical levels.

Main Key

The majority of Legrenzi's arias, are written in a minor key: only three arias out of 17 are in a major key. This is due perhaps to the semantic content of the poems, which in all cases can be termed that of the lover's lament. However, a too strict correspondence between the pathos of the poem and the minor key cannot be assumed as the arias in major keys have the same pathetic character. Nevertheless, the distinction between minor and major keys is relevant as they correspond to different forms of tonal organization.

Simple Tonal Patterns

The particular tonal patterns correspond to the division of the aria into its formal units. As the concept of the main key identifies the hierarchically most important key of the piece and picks it out temporarily despite the complexity of the overall context, so it is necessary to do the same in order to identify the key which is hierarchically predominant in every formal unit.

For this reason it has been found useful to introduce the concept of the *extended key* in order to define a tonal space including relative major and minor keys. More precisely we can say that a minor key can be "extended" to its relative major and vice-versa. In other words, we found that in Legrenzi's arias the modulation from a key to its relative has to be interpreted differently from other modulating devices as it reflects aspects of the late modal tradition in its progression towards modern tonality. The concept of extended tonality has been used at the level of formal units because it permits a clearer and simpler initial definition of tonal patterns. At the subsequent level, this ambiguity will be resolved and a precise key will be assigned to every phrase.

We have already seen that Legrenzi's arias are made up of not less than three and not more than six formal units. Tonal patterns respect this organization and behave differently in each of the different cases.

A first distinction can be made between patterns in minor or in major main keys. We shall begin our description with the former.

RULE 16:   In minor keys, a three-unit tonal pattern remains in the same key or modulates to the dominant in the second unit. Both keys are to be understood as extended keys.

For example:

Formal scheme	Tonal pattern	Aria no.
ABA	I V I	2
ABC	I I I	6
ABB	I V I	7

RULE 17:   In minor keys, a four-unit tonal pattern can remain in the same key or it can assign the dominant key to the second and/or third formal unit. Both keys are to be understood as extended keys.

For example:

Formal scheme	Tonal pattern	Aria no.
ABBA	I V I I	1
ABCA	I V V I	11

Three and four-unit patterns are fairly frequent in the sample, but for larger patterns we have only the example of aria no. 14: ABCDCD. The existence of a six-unit pattern allows us to admit the possibility of a five-unit pattern whose rules can be derived from existing models. The following rule, therefore, must be considered only as hypothetical.

RULE 18:   In minor keys, five- and six-unit tonal patterns do not maintain the same key but assign the dominant key to the second and third formal units. Both keys are to be understood as extended keys.

The tonal patterns described by the three preceding rules are particularly simple. As such they are not only to be found in the repertory in these simplified forms (see examples to rules, 16, 17) but can also be found in one of the two following expanded forms:

1. A modulation to the fourth degree appears just before the last appearance of the main key in a few cases, probably due to modal memories.

2. The key of the first formal unit can extend to the first part of the second. In these cases, the modulation does not take place between two formal units, but rather between two phrases of the second one.

These conditions allow the existence of two extended keys in the same formal unit.

RULE 19:   In minor keys, a modulation to the fourth degree can be inserted immediately before the last appearance of the main key. In three- and four-unit tonal patterns, this insertion involves only a part of the formal unit. In larger tonal patterns, however, it involves a whole formal unit. The key of the fourth degree is never an extended one.

RULE 20:   In minor keys, the key of the first formal unit can extend to the first part of the second.

The following scheme shows the examples of rules 19 and 20 in the sample:

Formal scheme	Tonal pattern						Aria no.
ABB	I	I–V	I				3
ABA	I	V–IV	I				8
ABAB	I	I	I	IV–I			10
ABCDCD	I	I–V	V	IV	I	I	14
ABB	I	I–V	I				16

The three arias in major keys have three-unit tonal patterns. Two of them have the model I-V-I, the third (aria no. 5) is irregular, both because of the number and the kind of modulations, as its scheme shows:

A	B	C
I–V	V^v	V–I
(A–E)	(B)	(E–A)

It cannot be denied that this has the fundamental pattern I-V-I, but this kind of enrichment appears only once in our limited repertory and therefore it cannot be formalized with rules. Leaving aside this example, the use of tonality in major key patterns seems to be considerably more rigid than that of minor keys.

RULE 22: In any one formal unit, no more than two keys can be present.

Another primary requirement is to resolve the ambiguity implied in the concept of extended tonality. To begin with we can say that in our sample there do exist cases of keys whose use is not that of extended keys. This occurs for example, in formal schemes with reprise, where, in the first and last formal units, the first degree relates only to the main key and not to its relative.

RULE 23: In formal schemes with reprise, the keys of the first and last formal units are to be understood exclusively as main and not extended keys.

This is the only case in which identical formal units require identical tonal features. While in the majority of formal schemes major repetitions do not necessarily imply tonal parallelism (for example ABB/I-V-I), in the schemes which include reprise, it is necessary because the aria must begin and end with the main key. For example, in the case of ABA/I-V-I, it would not be possible to have a tonal sequence such as A minor–C major/E minor/A minor–C major. The following rule is based on similar considerations.

RULE 24: In external units, a modulation between the main key and its relative is possible, provided that the aria ends with the main key.

For example in the case of ABB/I-V-I, it would be possible to have a tonal sequence such as A minor–C major/E minor/C major–A minor. On the other hand, internal units are not governed by the restriction of initial and final main keys, and so the following rule is possible:

RULE 25: Internal units in minor tonal patterns can behave in three different ways: 1. They can remain in the real key of the tonic or of the dominant. 2. They can modulate between the real key and its relative and vice-versa. 3. They can use only the relative either of the tonic or of the dominant.

For example:

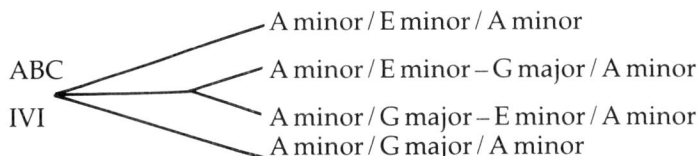

A minor / E minor / A minor
A minor / E minor – G major / A minor
A minor / G major – E minor / A minor
A minor / G major / A minor

In major tonal patterns, the choice between the real key and its relative is not possible in internal units, as stated in rule 21. The same rule implicitly allows a modulation between a main key and its relative in external units. However, since previous rules have exhaustively defined the tonal order also in major patterns, it is not necessary to add a specific rule here.

The difference in tonal organization in minor and major patterns can be explained on the basis of the different weight of the tonic–dominant relationships in the two cases. It is probable that this link is already perceived in a modern manner in major keys, whereas in minor keys, modal habits survive longer.

When in the "simple" form of tonal patterns described above (rules 16–21), two keys are present in a single unit, the modulation between the real key and its relative is not possible (see rule 22). However, we must have some criteria by which to choose one of the two keys – a choice necessitated by the concept of the extended key.

We must remember that in the first unit, the "simple" tonal pattern does not permit modulation and thus first units can be excluded from the present discussion. On the other hand in the last unit the "simple" tonal pattern permits modulation only between the fourth and the first degree. The former is never extended (see rule 19) and the latter, being at the end of the aria, must therefore be the main key.

The problem of the choice between real and relative keys only exists for internal units, whose examples in the corpus are the following four cases:

Aria no.	Formal scheme	Main key	Tonal pattern	Keys of internal units
3	ABB	A minor	I I–V I	A minor–E minor
8	ABA	G minor	I I–IV I	B flat major–C minor
14	ABCDCD	D minor	I I–V V IV I I	D minor–A minor
16	ABB	G minor	I I–V I	B flat major–D minor

The following rule can be deduced from the observations made above:

RULE 26: When, in internal units, one unit includes two keys, they can remain in the real tonality indicated by the pattern or one of them can be replaced by its relative.

The Key of Single Phrases

The complete tonal sequence of an aria has been defined by the preceding rules. Now it is necessary to formulate rules which are able to assign a key to each phrase. We may start with a general rule:

RULE 27: Modulation always takes place between two phrases, never inside a single phrase.

This rule points out that each phrase can be interpreted in only one key, even if the phrase may include, at the beginning, some tonally ambiguous fragment. Having made this preliminary statement, we can proceed to discuss two possibilities that may arise:

1. Only one key is present in a formal unit. In this case no problem arises as all the phrases of the unit are in the same key.

2. Two keys are present in one formal unit. No problem arises in this case either if the unit is formed by two phrases. The problem only arises when there are two keys and more than two phrases in the same unit. This is possible because, in accordance with rule 22, although more than two keys cannot be present, the

number of phrases, depending on the structure of the metric-syntactic tree, is not predictable.

The following rule can supply a solution to this problem:

RULE 28: When there are two keys and more than two phrases in one formal unit, modulation takes place at the beginning of any one of the minor repetitions (if they exist), and if they do not exist, it takes place at the division of the two highest branches of the tree present in that unit.

The following example is taken from the second formal unit of aria no. 8:

Dell'arciero vostro lume	phrase 1	B flat major
in qual parte i rai volgete?	phrase 2	B flat major
in qual parte i rai volgete?	phrase 3	C minor

[Eyes like archers, where you direct your beams?]

In this case, modulation takes place at the beginning of the minor repetition. Similar situations are to be found in arias no. 4, 5, 10, 13 and 14.

In the following example, the metric-syntactic tree of aria no. 3 has been partially reproduced:

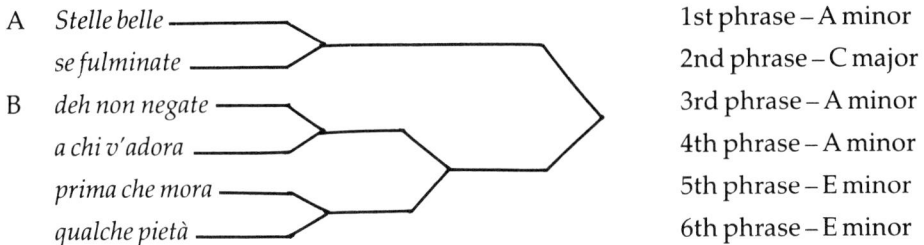

A	*Stelle belle*	1st phrase – A minor
	se fulminate	2nd phrase – C major
B	*deh non negate*	3rd phrase – A minor
	a chi v'adora	4th phrase – A minor
	prima che mora	5th phrase – E minor
	qualche pietà	6th phrase – E minor

etc.

[Beautiful stars, if you strike with lightning, oh do not deny the one who loves you some mercy before he dies]

In each of the two formal units, there are two keys. In formal unit A there are also two phrases, whereas in B there are four without any minor repetitions. Modulation takes place at the division of the two highest branches of the tree present in unit B. Similar situations can be found in arias no. 9 and 16.

If we remember that the particular tonal patterns correspond to the division of the aria into two formal units, units which coincide with the main branches of the tree, and that we have already observed the role of the tree in the assignment of keys inside a formal unit, we can affirm that the metric-syntactic structure of the poem not only dominates the musical form of the aria but also determines its tonal organization. More particularly we can say that the hierarchical structure of the tree is isomorphically reproduced in the hierarchical structure of the key-system.

The computer program

Our analysis has been expressed in generative form through rules, rules which are not, however, mere descriptions of our sample. They aim to describe a much wider hypothetical Legrenzian repertory to which the 17 arias considered belong. We have in fact even formulated rules which are not supported by concrete examples in the sample. In these cases we have assumed that the lack of an explicit example was due to a fortuitous absence in our limited sample rather than to any structural reasons.

As was stated in the introduction, a computer program, LEGRE.2, written in Basic for an Apple 2 computer, is being set up in order to obtain an automatic production of arias generated according to the rules formulated in the previous sections. The purpose of the program is to verify the capability of these rules to produce "correct" arias, "correct" that is, according to our competence. When "incorrect" arias are produced, the automatic production becomes a heuristic device which can uncover structural features which require deeper investigation.

The present state of the program reflects the state of the rules as we have formulated them. Thus it can produce the verbal text, expanded by all the different types of repetition, as well as the keys to be assigned to every phrase. Whenever the program has to choose amongst different possibilities permitted by the rules, a random choice is made according to a probability distribution obtained by an adaptation of the actual occurrences in the sample and of the results of automatic production. This adaptation is based on our own intuitive musical expertise.

The program contains as input data the verbal text of all the poems in their original forms (without repetitions). For each syllable, information is also given regarding its role: internal to the word, final of a word, final with the possibility of liaison with the next word, final of a half-line, final of a half-line with the possibility of liaison with the next word, final of a line, final of a line with caesura, final of a line with caesura and rhyme, final of poem. Finally, for each syllable its position in the metric-syntactic tree is given.

In the Appendix are given: 1) the original version of the poem no. 8 together with Legrenzi's expansion, tonal pattern and formal scheme, 2) two examples of output referred to the poem no. 8, and 3) Legrenzi's original score of the same aria.

Appendix

Aria no. 8

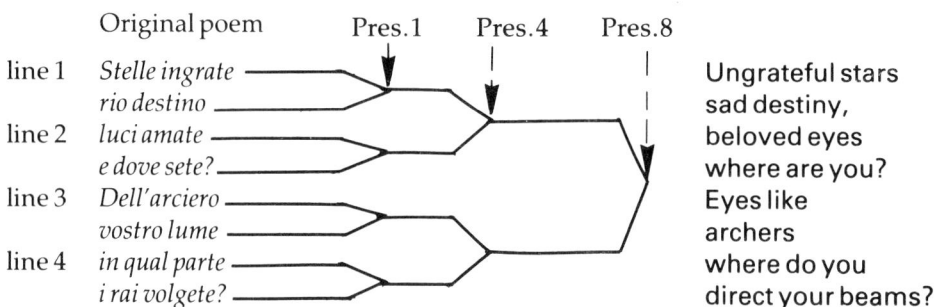

Tonal patterns	Expanded poem divided into musical phrases	Formal scheme
G min.	Stelle ingrate, rio destino, luci amate, e dove sete? **e dove sete?**	A
B-flat maj.	Dell'arciero vostro lume in qual parte i rai volgete?	B
C min.	**in qual parte i rai volgete?**	
G min.	Stelle imgrate, rio destino, luci amate, e dove sete? **e dove sete?**	A

Two examples of output

POESIA SCELTA N.8
Testo originale:

Stelle ingrate rio destino
luci amate e dove sete?
Dell'arciero vostro lume
in qual parte i rai volgete?

Numero di rami principali dell'albero = 2
Possibilità di ripresa: sì
Forma ABA

Ripetizioni iniziali:
Decide di non fare ripetizioni iniziali

Ripetizioni centrali:
Esistenza di cesura: sì
Ripete ultime due unità metriche centrali

Ripetizioni semifinali:
Decide di non fare ripetizioni semifinali

Ripetizionia finali:
Decide di non fare ripetizioni finali

Ripetizioni in seconda esposizione:
Decide di non fare ripetizioni semifinali
Decide di ripetere l'ultima unità metrica

Numero di frasi = 9
Tonalità: MAGGIORE

Tonalità estese:
I   V   I
Tonalità ristrette:
I   V   I
Numero di frasi nelle unità formali:
3   2   4

Frasi	Tonalità
Stelle ingrate rio destino	I
luci amate e dove sete?	I
luci amate e dove sete?	I
Dell'arciero vostro lume	V
in qual parte i rai volgete?	V
Stelle ingrate rio destino	I
luci amate e dove sete?	I
luci amate e dove sete?	I
e dove sete?	I

POESIA SCELTA N.8
Testo originale:

Stelle ingrate rio destino
luci amate e dove sete?
Dell'arciero vostro lume
in qual parte i rai volgete?

Numero di rami principali dell'albero = 2
Possibilità di ripresa: sì
Forma ABA

Ripetizioni iniziali:
Decide di ripetere la prima unità metrica

Ripetizioni centrali:
Esistenza di cesura: sì
Ripete ultima unità metrica centrale

Ripetizioni semifinali:
Decide di non fare ripetizioni semifinali

Ripetizioni finali:
Decide di non fare ripetizioni finali

Ripetizioni in seconda esposizione:
Decide di non fare ripetizioni semifinali
Decide di non ripetere l'ultima unità metrica

Numero di frasi = 10
Tonalità: MINORE

Tonalità estese:
i   i   i
Tonalità ristrette:
i   ir   i
Numero di frasi nelle unità formali:
4   2   4

Frasi	Tonalità
Stelle ingrate	i
Stelle ingrate rio destino	i
luci amate e dove sete?	i
e dove sete?	i
Dell'arciero vostro lume	ir
in qual parte i rai volgete?	ir
Stelle ingrate	i
Stelle ingrate rio destino	i
luci amate e dove sete?	i
e dove sete?	i

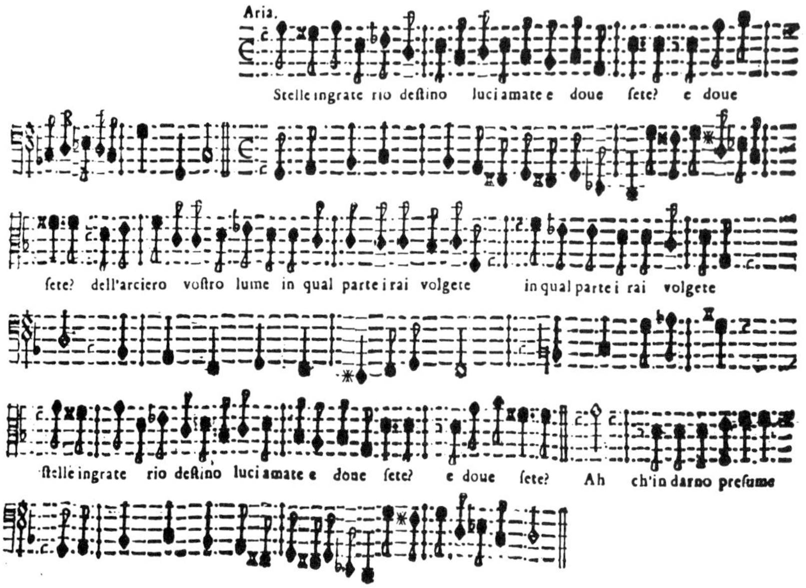

Figure 1   Original score of the aria no. 8.

References

Baroni, M. (1983) The concept of musical grammar, *Music Analysis*, **2** (2).

Baroni, M., Brunetti, R., Callegari, L. & Jacoboni, C. (1984) A grammar for melody: Relationships between melody and harmony. In *Musical Grammars and Computer Analysis*, M. Baroni & L.Callegari (eds), 201–218, Firenze: Olschki.

Baroni, M. & Callegari, L. (1984) Antiche canzoni francesi. Uno studio di metrica generativa. *Quaderni di informatica musicale* **5.**

Baroni, M. & Jacoboni, C. (1978) *Proposal for a Grammar of Melody. The Bach Chorales.* Montréal: Les Presses de l'Université de Montréal.

Baroni, M. & Jacoboni, C. (1983) Computer generation of melodies. Further proposals. *Computer and the Humanities,* 17(1).

Camilleri, L. (1984) A Grammar of the melodies of Schubert's Lieder. In *Musical Grammars and Computer Analysis.* M. Baroni & L. Callegari (eds.), 229–236, Firenze: Olschki.

Wenk, A.B. (1987) Parsing Debussy: Proposal for a grammar of his melodic practice. *In Theory Only,* **9/8.**

Contemporary Music Review,
1989, Vol. 4, pp. 45–63
Photocopying permitted by license only

The "genetic code" of melody: Cognitive structures generated by the implication-realization model

Eugene Narmour

Department of Music, University of Pennsylvania, 201 S. 34th Street, Philadelphia, PA 19104, USA

The general claim herein is that the analysis of melody rests on the perception of implications of continuation and reversal. Continuation is said to be governed hypothetically by the bottom-up Gestalt laws of similarity, proximity, and common direction (common fate); whereas reversal is hypothesized as a symmetrical construct. The hypotheses are context-free and scalable, producing several archetypal realizations (process, duplication, reversal, registral return). And they are recursive, generating hierarchical levels. Separately applying to the implicative aspects of interval, registral direction, and specific pitch, the twin hypotheses generate overall sixteen prospective and retrospective realizations. These types also appear in pair combinations (some 200 are possible), in chains of three or more structures strung together in an infinite variety, and in overlapping networks of different simultaneous structures. A melodic model of psychological encoding is offered, and top-down processing in the form of intraopus style is discussed.

KEY WORDS: Implication-realization, continuation, reversal, melodic encoding, melodic archetypes, melodic networks.

Introduction

A melody may be imagined as a single time line segmented into varying degrees of articulation (LaRue, 1970). Music theorists attribute such partitioning of melodic time to closure. Closure in this sense does not refer to the introspective and highly interpretive Gestaltist concepts of completeness, symmetry, or "good" definition but rather to the various ways musical parameters interact to create melodic "chunks," perceptual groupings whose beginning and ending nodes exhibit varying degrees of stability (Meyer, 1973; Narmour, 1977; Tenney & Polansky, 1980).[1]

Probably the most interactive parameters causing melodic grouping are duration, harmony and meter. For instance, incisive points of melodic closure creating pitch groupings take place when in the parameter of duration a short note moves to a long note (Woodrow, 1909, 1911, 1951; Mursell, 1937; Fraisse, 1956); we may mark such durationally cumulative places analytically with the symbol (d) over the closed melodic note, the "d" standing for durational interference in the continuation of the melodic line (see Figure 1). Points of melodic closure also occur when in the parameter of harmony a sufficiently dissonant note goes to a sufficiently consonant one; this we mark with the symbol (h) over the closed melodic note, the "h" standing for harmonic interruption in the melodic line (again see Figure 1). Lastly, the parameter of meter may also impose closure upon a melodic pattern. I mark this with the symbol (b) which signifies metric

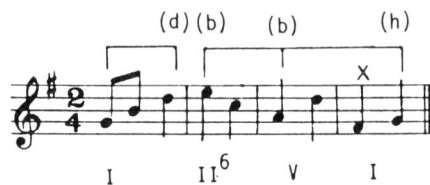

Figure 1

differentiation that is sufficiently emphatic by itself to segment a melodic line (see Figure 1; though "b" for "beat" is the mnemonic to help remember the symbol, it is important to understand that the symbol (b) does not actually stand for beat – or pulse, tactus, ictus, accent, or stress for that matter).[2]

I characterize the grouping influence of durational closure, harmonic closure, and metric differentiation on melody as interference, interposition, or incision because what is interrupted in a melodic line is realization of implication. Implication is simply the objective term in music theory for what psychologists call expectancy. That is, between the articulative and closural signposts of (h), (d), and (b) in Figure 1, melody frequently generates conscious and subconscious expectations in the listener as to what continuation seems most probable.

Implication of continuation

But what exactly is implied within the parameter of melody? The implication-realization model hypothesizes that intervallic continuation, registral direction, and specific pitch (when mode is known) are all *separately* subject to cognitive prediction and thus dependent on laws of implication and expectancy. Moreover, in order to qualify as a realization the model says also that both where a melodic realization is to occur (place) and how long it lasts (time) are essential to any understanding of implication (Jones, 1981). All other things being equal, the theory hypothesizes, for instance, that a pattern like that found in Figure 2 implies a continuing ascent (up to up), a continuation of intervallic similarity (M2 to M2), a continuation of duration (quarter to quarter), a realization on the level of the beat, and a specific pitch – in this case A, assuming mode is known.[3]

On what psychological foundation might such parametric hypotheses of constant expectancy be based? In the implication-realization model the separate registral and intervallic aspects of small intervals (like the major second) are said

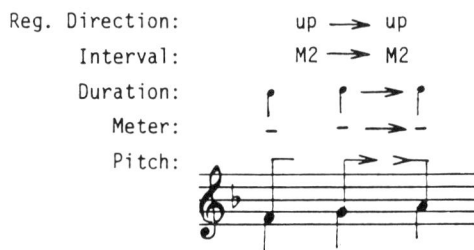

Figure 2

to be implicatively governed from the bottom up by the Gestalt laws of similarity, proximity, and common direction (sometimes called common fate). As regards Figure 2, for instance, the theory says that: the pitches F–G imply the closely proximate pitch of A (assuming mode is known); the major second of F–G implies another similar interval (in this mode, another major second); and the ascending F–G leads to directional expectations of a continuing upward register.

As perceptual–theoretical constants, what is important to notice about the invocation of such Gestalt laws is (1) that they have been shown to be highly resistant to learning and thus may be innate (Gleitman, 1981); (2) unlike the notoriously interpretive, holistically supersummative, top-down Gestalt laws of "good" continuation, "good„ figure, and "best" organization, which everyone rightly criticizes, the Gestalt laws of similarity, proximity, and common direction are measurable, formalizable, and thus open to empirical testing (Pomerantz, 1981); and (3) they are applied here from the *bottom-up* as nonclosural (implicative) *hypotheses*.

Definitions

To make the Gestalt laws operational in the bottom-up sense in the implication-realization model, I define pitch proximity (a+a) as any two tones the distance of a major second or smaller. And when registral direction is continued, I define intervallic similarity (A+A) as any two adjacent intervals that differ a minor third or less. Common direction obviously defines itself: up followed by up (C-D-E), down by down (E-D-C), and lateral by lateral (C-C-C).

Thus, the implication of the ascending F-G in Figure 2 could have been realized by an ascending A♭, A, E♭, B, or even C since any of these pitches would satisfy the intervallic definition of similarity and common direction, as defined here.[4] Of course, if the known mode were F major and A were construed as the specified pitch of implication, then a realization of A♭, B♭, B or C would be heard as a surprise – but mostly in light of the aspect of specific pitch: according to our definitions, the intervallic and registral "prophecy" of F-G – that similarity and direction will continue – comes to pass in either F-G-A♭, F-G-A, F-G-B♭, F-G-B, or F-G-C.

Process

I call such patterns where both intervallic similarity and registral continuation of ascent or descent are realized registral-intervallic processes (or simply *processes*) and symbolize such structures with the capital letter P between the initial and terminal tones bracketed by the closure that occurs in the parameters of duration (d), harmony (h), or meter (b).[5] A corollary to process is iteration or *duplication*, symbolized by the letter D within the bracket; unlike all other patterns, duplication always implies interval (a unison), registral direction (lateral), and specific pitch (e.g., C-C-C).[6] What lies behind both P and D of course, are the initiators, arrows, and tails seen in Figure 2.

Further, in the absence of any top-down stylistic interference or interference from other parameters, I hypothesize as a bottom-up constant that all intervals a perfect fourth or smaller (u, m2, M2, m3, M3, P4) imply a continuation of intervallic similarity and a continuation of registral direction in the mode of the initial pattern. Figure 3 illustrates a few patterns satisfying the intervallic and registral definitions of process (P) and duplication (D); note here the closural interaction of cumulative duration (d) in suppressing further implication and realization on the note-to-note level.[7]

Figure 3

Partial Denial (IP, ID, VP)

We saw with reference to the initial F-G of Figure 2 that if the known mode were F major, then realization of an Ab in an ascending pattern like F-G-A would be somewhat unexpected in terms of pitch implication even though in terms of inter-vallic similarity and continuation of registral direction the F-G-A pattern would not, overall, be perceived as a surprise. Since implication of specific pitch can be denied while implications of interval and register are realized, it follows that *both* implications of specified pitch and registral direction can be denied while only implication of interval is realized. The registrally zigzagging up-down patterns of Figure 4, for instance, realize only the implied intervallic similarity.[8] I call such partially realized patterns of similar intervals *intervallic processes* and symbolize them with the letters IP (note how the unison figures into this in the third example). Similarly, I call partially realized patterns where registrally zigzagging intervals are exactly the same *intervallic duplications* (ID).[9]

It also follows that implications of specified pitch and interval can be denied while implication of registral direction is realized. Partial realizations of this type – where initially implied registral direction is continued but intervallic differentia-tion (A+B) occurs instead of intervallic similarity (A+A) – I call *registral processes,* symbolized in Figure 4 as VP (mnemonic: V=vector=registral direction).

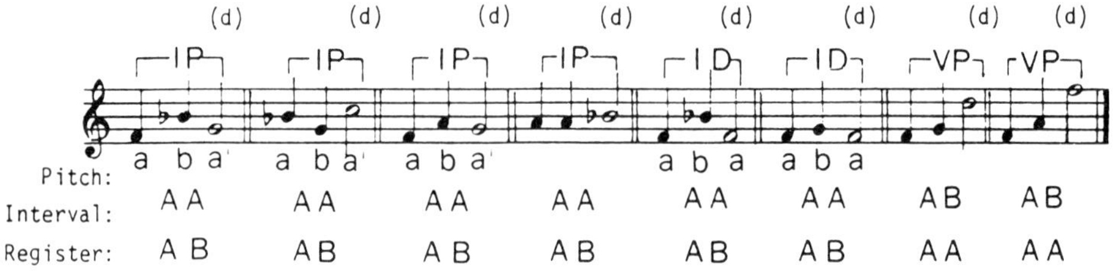

Figure 4

What I am hypothesizing, then, is that – all other parametric and stylistic things being equal (an important proviso) – listeners will hear melodic patterns like those shown in Figure 4 as partial surprises (registral surprise in the case of IP and ID; intervallic surprise in the case of VP). In contrast, the processes (P) of Figure 3 will, given a lack of mode, not in the main be heard as complete intervallic or registral surprises (though the specific pitch of a realization may not be the expected one).

Registral return (aba)

Realization of intervallic process (IP) or intervallic duplication (ID) draws our attention to another very important type of melodic structure, namely exact or near registral return (symbolized aba and aba^1, respectively, in Figure 4). Though not normally a melodically implicative phenomenon (unless the b-part is dissonant or unless return is indicated by a previously invoked style), registral return occurs when two discontiguous pitches lie within a major second of one another. Registral return thus obeys the bottom-up Gestalt law of proximity. Such return may be structural if underscored by duration (d), harmony (h), or meter (b). And because the perception of registral return is a cognitive operation independent of intervallic process and intervallic duplication, the simultaneous overlapping of IP and ID with aba or aba^1 frequently occurs (which can be seen in Figure 4). That overlapping structures on the *same* level can take place attests, of course, to the perceptual redundancies built into our cognitive systems, which the implication-realization model tries to account for (as we shall see in the discussion of Figure 9 below).

Implication of reversal

So much for how the bottom-up Gestalt laws of similarity, proximity, and common direction support hypotheses of implication and realization that generate P, D, IP, ID, VP, aba, and aba^1. Let us now, however, turn to the second major perceptual hypothesis in the implication-realization model, for not all melodic realizations remain implicative and ongoing until durational cumulation (d), resolution of dissonance (h), or occurrence of metric differentiation (b) takes place. Indeed, some patterns within the parameter of melody are capable of creating closure in and of themselves (though usually assisted by (d), (h), and (b)). One such type is intervallic-registral reversal or simply *reversal*, which I symbolize with the letter R between the brackets. The hypothesis concerning reversal says simply that when a listener hears a large interval (P5 or greater), he expects, all other things being equal, a change in registral direction (A+B) and a differentiation of interval (A+B; when register changes direction, intervallic differentiation is defined as a minor third or more).

A typical instance of such reversal is the NBC logo, shown in the first case of Figure 5. As can be seen, change of registral direction is defined either as up/down, up/lateral, down/up, or down/lateral (see the second case in Figure 5, and recall that what lies behind any R is an initiator, an implicative arrow, and a closural tail). Reversal, then, is the intervallic and registral opposite of process (and duplication) and moreover its functional opposite since realization of reversal creates closure (though that closure is not necessarily transformational to a higher level).

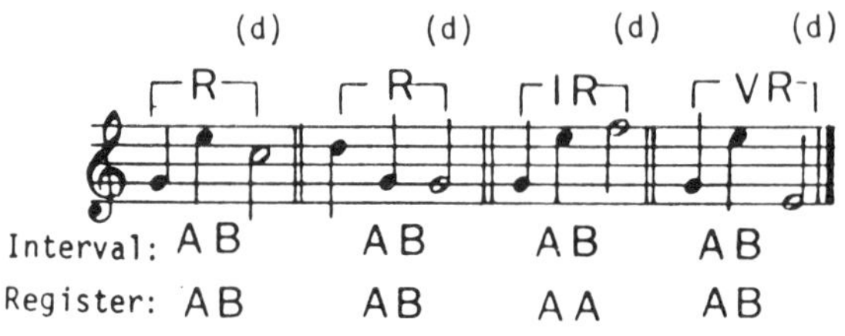

Figure 5

If process, in its various complete and partial realizations, is well founded on certain bottom-up Gestalt laws, then we may ask the question: on what perceptual-cognitive foundation is the hypothesis of reversal based? The answer is: none that I know of, because apparently no psychological evidence yet exists to support the concept of reversal as a hypothetical perceptual constant – reversal is not simply contrast since it involves a function of closure, and reversal is not simply the vertex of a registral "angle" since closure occurs after the change of direction[10] – it is thus treated in the implication-realization model as a *symmetrical construct*, that is, as a conceptual complement to the hypothesis of process. Symmetrical conception, of course, is a time-honored technique in the sciences for formulating hyotheses in the face of the unknown (other reasoning that comes to mind in this regard is Piaget's idea of the reversability of cognitive operations and Lévi-Strauss's notion of bipolar opposites).

Partial Denials of Reversal (IR, VR)

As with process, it is also the case that reversal implications can be realized in whole or in part. That is, the intervallic implication of reversal (that a small interval is to follow a large leap) can be realized, while registral implication (that direction is to reverse) can be denied. I call such partially realized patterns *intervallic reversals* and symbolize them as IR (see case 3 in Figure 5). Conversely, given a large initial leap, registral implication can be realized while intervallic implication is denied. This pattern I call *registral reversal* and symbolize it with the letters VR (see case 4 in Figure 5).

The closural aspect of intervallic reversal (IR) is the large interval moving to the small, differentiated one (A+B) since register continues direction; whereas the closural aspect of registral reversal (VR) is the change in registral direction (A+B) since interval moves differentiatedly from a large skip to an even larger one (A+B). Incidentally, now we can also see that both intervallic process (IP) and intervallic duplication (ID) possess an aspect of registral closure in that both reverse direction.

The hypothesized parametric scale

At this point two summaries are useful: first, we have eight basic melodic structures, not counting registral return (aba and aba[1]):[11]

```
        P                        D                         R
      /   \                    /                         /   \
    IP      VP              ID           –            IR       VR
```

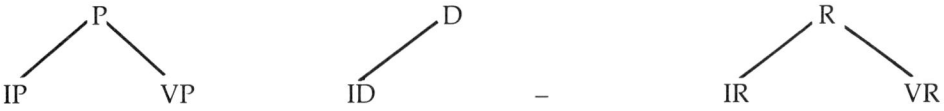

(P=process; IP=intervallic process; VP=registral process; D=duplication [iteration]; ID=intervallic duplication [intervallic iteration]; R=reversal; IR=intervallic reversal; VF=registral reversal)

And second, we may formalize on a *parametric scale* our bottom-up hypotheses of how small intervals imply process and large intervals imply reversal.

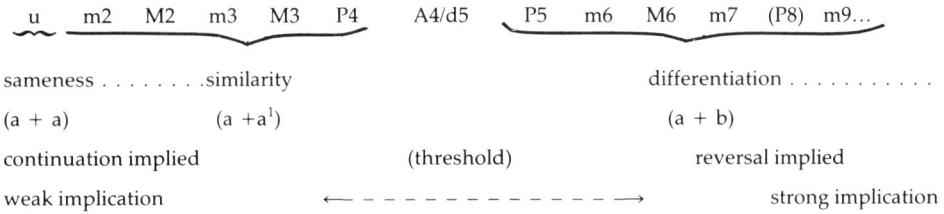

u	m2	M2	m3	M3	P4	A4/d5	P5	m6	M6	m7	(P8)	m9...

sameness . . . . .similarity   differentiation . . . .

(a + a)   (a +a^1)   (a + b)

continuation implied   (threshold)   reversal implied

weak implication   ← – – – – – – – – – – – – →   strong implication

The intervallic parametric scale is more than a convenient representation of the different implicative functions of small intervals and large intervals: it is itself a *perceptual hypothesis* in the implication-realization model against which degree of implication (in P, IP, ID, and VP), degree of closure (in R, IR, and VR), and degree of surprise are measured and evaluated. That is, the intervallic parametric scale is conceived not just to measure distances between pitches but rather to hypothesize an inborn mechanism embodying melodic syntax. In short, it is a cognitive matrix that both orders elementary patterns across a spectrum of similarity and differentiation, and fixes them in categorical "slots" of proximity concerning their inherent bottom-up implicative-realizational functions of closure and non-closure.[12]

Oriented from left to right, from small interval to large interval, the scale thus illustrates how implications of continuation gradually yields to the implication of reversal as the individual pitches making up the intervals become less proximate, more differentiated, an implicatively stronger.[13] The threshold – where change of implicative function is hypothesized to occur – takes place at the tritone (A4/d5), and whether that interval melodically implies continuation or reversal is reflected in the traditional nomenclature: augmented fourth=continuation (to P or IR); diminished fifth=reversal (to R or VR).[14]

There is, of course, every reason to believe that the very act of scaling, so prevalent in the sciences, reflects an inborn inherent ability in the physiological mechanism of the brain. Moreover, everything we have learned about perception in the past fifty years argues that scaling of stimuli is an inherent part of human cognition and memory. Of course, numerous scaling models (linear, circular, helical) have already been put to good use in the psychology of music.[15] In the implication-realization model, the important point to observe is that the intervallic parametric scale classifies the bottom-up implication of intervals both according to width (magnitude) and category.[16]

Retrospective realizations (complete denials)

To resume our discussion of the kinds of melodic structures there are, let us now consider realization from a retrospective point of view. Obviously, the very notions of implication and realization entail prospective perceptual evaluation, but it is also true that listeners retrodictively evaluate realizations, cognitively "looking backward" over what they have experienced. If this were not so, listeners could never correct their perceptual "mistakes", "rewrite" their short-term memories, or learn new implicative associations. For although perhaps not originally foreseen (in the absence of stylistic interference or closure from other parameters), it so happens that even if the pitch, interval, and registral direction implied by large intervals is denied, large intervals nevertheless can retrospectively come to be heard either as processes (P), intervallic processes (IP), or registral processes (VP). And it so happens that even if the aspects of pitch, interval, and registral direction implied by small intervals are denied, small intervals may still retrospectively come to be heard either as reversals (R), inter-vallic reversals (IR), or registral reversals (VR) even though none of these realiza-tions was originally implied. How this may come about may be seen in Figure 6, whose patterns should be compared to those in Figures 3, 4 and 5.

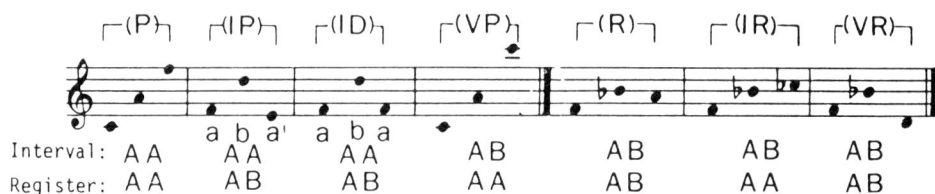

Figure 6

I symbolize retrospective realization by putting parentheses around the letters. As can be seen in Figure 6, the various retrospective patterns fulfill all the condi-tions of intervallic and registral similarity/differentiation that define the various complete and partial types of realizations. What I am hypothesizing, then, is that, although a listener tends to project continuation from, say, an initial ascending major third (all other things being equal), she would nevertheless have no trouble recognizing in retrospect that that interval could come functionally to mimic, say, an implication and realization of reversal (as in case 5 of Fig. 6).

To our original eight prospective structures, we may thus add eight retrospec-tive analogues (note again the parentheses denoting the retrospection):

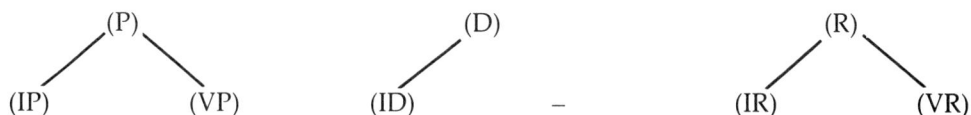

Some examples

How the theory works in analysis may be seen in the three melodies of Figure 7.

In the Mozart example the listener breaks measure 1 into two processes (P). Owing to dynamic change (from *forte* to *piano*), shift in interval (minor thirds to minor seconds), and the perception of an implied harmonic change from tonic to augmented sixth, a sense of metric emphasis (b) causes articulation on the F# on the third beat. Indeed, from the last beat of measure 1 to the downbeat of measure 2, the downward leap of the minor sixth (A♭–C) leads the listener to expect both a continuation in direction and a small interval: thus, the structure to emerge is IR.

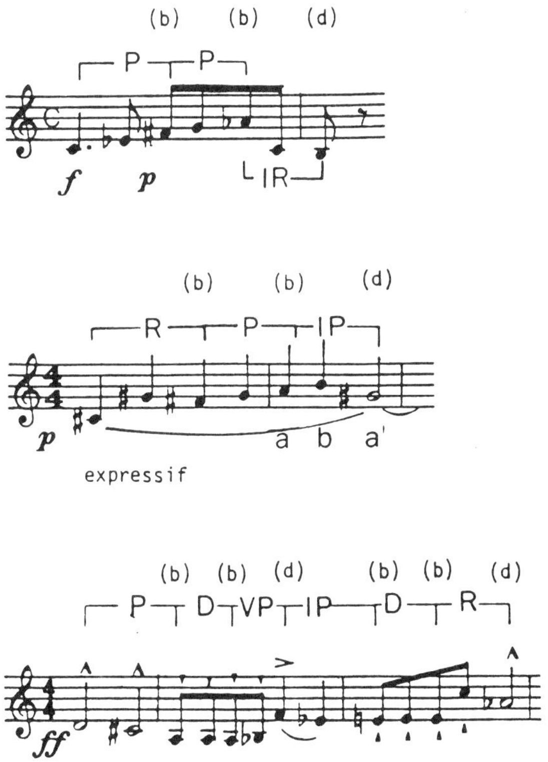

Figure 7 Mozart, *Fantasy in C minor,* K. 475 (Adagio); Debussy, *Pelléas et Mélisande,* Act 1, sc. 1, mm. 72–73; Schoenberg, *Fourth String Quartet,* I, mm. 1–3 (Allegro molto; energico) (Copyright held by G. Schirmer)

In the Debussy example, from the opening leap of the fifth (C–G#) the listener expects a reversal (R), which indeed is metrically realized on the F#. The ascending process (P) and change of chord every two beats establish metric articulations (b) which set off the intervallic process (IP) and the concurrrent near registral return (aba¹) that durationally cumulates in measure 2(d).

The interference of meter (b) and duration (d) in the Schoenberg example is much the same though what closes the duplicative structure (D) on the beat in measure 2 is the dynamic stress produced by the accented chords in the other parts. Note that although the metrically emphasized eighth-note A in measure 2 is the "wrong" length to follow the durational implication of the half-notes D and C#. The A nevertheless functions to end the process (P) because it occurs in the "right" place, on the beat. The cumulative F in measure 2 (d) is something of a surprise: the A–Bb preceding the leap indicates to the listener that a continuing ascent is to follow (A+A) but not in such an intervallically differentiated (A+B) way as the ascending leap to the F. This explains why the registral process (VP) is here such an effective aesthetic realization: it is partly unexpected. (Also note that the reversal implication is a surprise in terms of intraopus style since the earlier grouping of repeated notes is followed by a half step instead of a leap).

Combinations

The way in which duration (d) and meter (b) articulate the three stylistically different melodies of Figure 7 into structural "chunks" of P, IR, D, R, VP, and aba[1] is perceptually simple and cognitively economical. The question arises, however, as to what happens when two different kinds of unclosed structural contours occur without benefit of such closure in other parameters? The answer is that structural *combinations* – where the end of one pattern shares at least two tones with the beginning of another – are created. For instance, typical combinations of reversal incorporated with process (symbolized RP) can be found in certain examples of Meyer's (1973) gap-filling melody and in certain instances of Schenker's (1956) *Anstieg* followed by descending *Urlinie*.)

Figure 8 illustrates two combinational instances from the literature. On the first two beats of measure 2 an intervallic duplication of G#–F#–G# joins with a process of F#–G#–A–B to produce and IDP combination. And on beats 2 and 3 of measure 2 the B–A–G# to the cumulative A of measure 3 makes one PID grouping on the low level. That is, the B–A–G# process (P) connects to, and is reversed by, the A–G#–A intervallic duplication (ID).

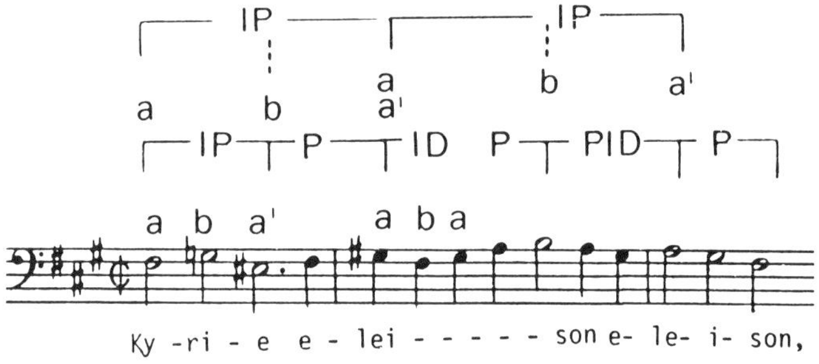

Figure 8 Bach, *Mass in B minor*, Kyrie Eleison II, mm. 1–3.

Observe also about Figure 8 that structures generated by realization of implication can occur on higher levels, for the theoretical rules outlined here are recursive: once the initial and terminal tones of each closed structure (the beginning and ending points of each bracket) become transformed onto a higher level (traceable through the dashed lines), new patterns of implication and realization (as well as registral return) occur, whether as single structures, combinations, or (as we shall see below) longer chains.

The sixteen basic types of single structures illustrated earlier in Figures 3, 4, 5, and 6 may, of course, combine in pairs *in any order*. I estimate that there are some 200 of these combinational pairs, and I have found musical examples of all the basic types (but not every prospective/retrospective possibility). Indeed, searching for examples from the literature has led to new discoveries about style. Certain combinational types, for instance, seem only to occur in twentieth-century music (e.g., IRIR, VPVP); other combinations appear to be favorites of particular composers or of particular periods.

Chains

In the absence of closure from other parameters, it is also possible for three or more of the sixteen basic prospective and retrospective types of structures to join into longer structural *chains*. Many typical ornaments are chains. An unarticulated trill with an ending, for instance, makes an ID . . . PID chain.

The number and variety of possible chains, of course, is theoretically infinite. The opening turn of Figure 9, for example, combines an ID (G#–A#–G#), a P (A#–G#–F#), another ID (G#–F#–G#), and a VP (F#–G#–E#), all of which also overlap exact registral return (aba). (Again, note how the rules of the theory are recursive on higher levels). The analysis hypothesizes that a competent listener hears the opening turn as an alternating sequence of partial and complete intervallic and registral realizations with little surprise, followed by a quite unexpected leap to the high E#. Here, the leap to E# is more of a surprise than the normal interpretation of a differentiated VP would indicate inasmuch as the IDPID realization and the overlapping aba's establish a top-down intraopus style that suddenly becomes violated.

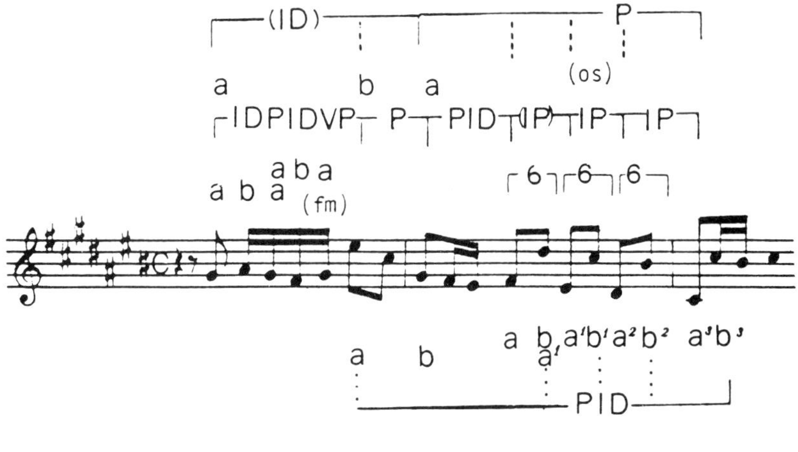

Figure 9 Bach, Fugue 3, *Well-Tempered Clavier*, I, mm. 1–2.

Chains are a form of melodic networking since the terminal and initial parts of different kinds of single structures dovetail. But near registral return (aba¹) in Figure 9 also creates complex structural networking, not only in measure 1 but also in measure 2 where the discontiguous tones overlapping the zigzagging IPs (shown by the dotted and dashed lines) cause two processes (P) to emerge.[17]

Incidentally, such overlapping is how the implication-realization model explains the psychological phenomenon of "fission" or "streaming" which we see in measure 2: the perception of near registral return (according to the bottom-up Gestalt law of proximity) splits the melody into upper and lower processes. Yet the listener is also acutely aware that intervallic similarity is being replicated in the zigzagging IPs (again according to bottom-up Gestalt laws).[18]

Top-Down Processing

Given that the invoked Gestalt laws governing continuation and registral return (in the various manifestations of P, D, IP, ID, VP, aba, aba¹) together with the symmetrical hypotheses of reversal (in the complete and partial realizations of R, IR, VR) operate perceptually and analytically from the bottom up, it is surprising how far the theory takes us in explaining how experienced listeners are able to comprehend melodies like those found in figures 7–9. Nevertheless, no percep-tual theory can claim psychological adequacy on the basis of bottom-up proces-sing alone, for the evidence is unequivocally conclusive that, in cognition and per-ception, top-down processing is simultaneously operative with bottom-up pro-cessing. As we saw in discussing the high E♯ of Figure 9, both bottom-up and top-down converge to make sense out of the incoming flow of stimuli entering the senses.[19]

Space does not permit me to show how the implication-realization role deals with that very large topic of top-down processing, which in music theory can be characterized as the influence of style or in psychology as the invocation of learned schemata.[20] But one place in Figure 9 may serve as a brief illustration: the E♯–C♯ leap of the sixth, which would ordinarily imply a reversal and thus would normally create a retrospective intervallic process (IP in parentheses), functions in measure 2 as a *prospective* intervallic process because it mimics the F♯–D♯ preceding it. I symbolize this top-down learning via schematic conformance – that upwards leap of sixths in additive durations in this fugue subject come prospec-tively to imply, and stylistically to realize, IPs instead of Rs – by the "os" above the E♯–C♯ leap and by the lack of parentheses around the letters IP. This shows that at this point intraopus style (os) interferes with the normal implications stipulated by the hypothetical rules of the theory and that E♯–C♯ implies a low D♯, mimicking the preceding F♯–D♯ (that went, as a retrospective IP to the low E♯).[21]

The "genetic code"

Top-down processing may be thought of as an "environment", as the "phenotyp-ical" influence of nurtured learning on the input. Bottom-up processing on the other hand may be imagined as "genotypical", as the operation of cognitive-per-ceptual constants mapped onto the incoming signal. There is no reason not to think that all melodies written and ever to be written conform to a "genetic code"

of perception, just as human evolution is partly controlled by DNA. From a par-
simonious set of principles (that also apply recursively to higher-level transformations), I have shown here how the nucleic concepts of P, D, and R, can be
extended prospectively to the various partial realizations of IP, ID, VP, IR, and
VR, and in turn have demonstrated how retrospective analogues can be extrapo-
lated from these eight types. I have also suggested how these sixteen prospective
and retrospective structures can be combined into two hundred pairs and ultimately how simple single structures are able theoretically to generate an infinite
number of possible chains.

The theory thus shows how great complexity can arise from extreme simplicity,
which accords well with what we know both about evolutionary physiological
systems like the brain and about human learning in general. It is not by accident,
for instance, that nursery rhyme tunes contain mostly simple melodic structures,
whereas sophisticated art music is full of complex combinations and chains,
which put much more "load" on short-term memory.

Since the bottom-up part of the theory is context-free, and applicable to all
learned styles of melody, the model should enable us to discover what kinds of
aesthetic strategies composers employ with respect to realization, denial, and
thus, by inference, degree of idiostructural surprise. And from the economical
symbology we should be able to learn (on all levels) what kinds of melodic strings
occur most commonly. The two melodies of Figure 10, for instance, exhibit
basically the same *syntactic* aesthetic effect (as opposed to temporal aesthetic
effect). Both are, for example, highly similar in their low level structural sequences
– the first three structures on level 2 being 6–D–IP, with (VR) and PIP or PID combinations nested underneath (note that differences between the two examples are
tracked on both levels as well).

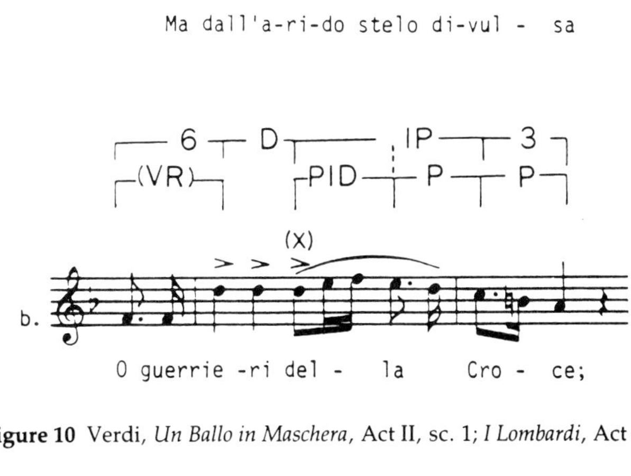

Figure 10 Verdi, *Un Ballo in Maschera*, Act II, sc. 1; *I Lombardi*, Act IV, sc. 2.

Encoding

Since the theory sees pitches, intervals and registral directions as syntactic functional relations of closure and nonclosure in formats of both similarity (a+a, A+A) and differentiation (a+b, A+B), we can, with a little imagination, thus conceive how the first melody of Figure 10 can be neuropsychologically encoded (italicized letters symbolize closure; small letters stand for pitches; capital letters for intervallic or registral patterns; letters read left to right and can be scanned up and down for transformational congruence):

LEVEL 1

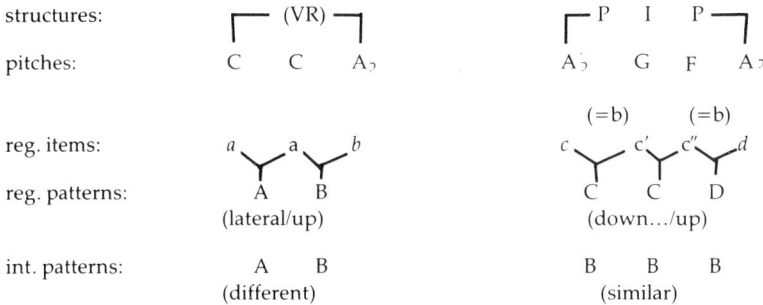

LEVEL 2

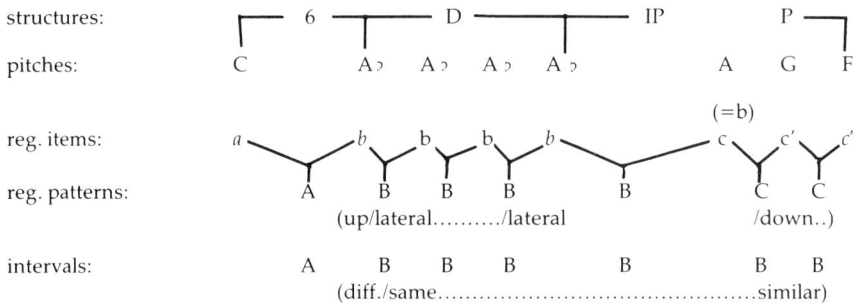

There are a number of things to be said about this encoding. To begin with, it is completely independent of style-structural schemata (as opposed to the style-shape learning of the elementary materials – pitches, intervals, durations, etc.) It would thus appear that a fairly wide-reaching musical expertise – or the construction of a reasonably competent "expert system" of melodic perception – could be based on a very few principles (A+A, A+B, parametric scale, continuation, reversal, registral return, definitions of similarity and difference). Indeed, it may be the case that, of all the arts, syntatical structure in music is the least dependent on learning. Assuming an inherent ability to scale parameters (to perceive up/down/lateral and to recognize large intervallic motions from small ones), and assuming an inborn capacity to recognize continuation and reversal in both register and interval, even a naive listener would have little trouble apprehending both the low-level structuring and the high-level structural tones of the encoded melody. We can imagine, for instance, such cognitive assimilation taking place through both "horizontal" processing (letters left to right) and "vertical" construction of hierarchical levels (italicized small letters from Level 1 to Level 2).

Conclusion

But much work remains to be done. Analytically, there is the matter of how low-level implication influences higher-level implication – and vice versa – and what effect this influence has on prospective and retrospective perception on all levels. Though suppression of implication via closure prevents realization on the same level of occurrence, it is nevertheless true in partially decomposable hierarchical systems (Simon, 1969) that suppressed implication becomes *embodied* in the closed note transformed to the higher level. Thus, inhibited implications continue to influence the listener's immediate expectations.[22]

Psychologically, we need to learn whether definitions of intervallic similarity and difference, including those asserted herein, are constant from listener to listener and style to style. Or do they vary according to degree of learning? Moreover, since in vision, parallels to process and duplication are recognized by everyone, can we find parallels to closural reversal in vision and speech?

Lastly, in the neuropsychological realm, one wants to know not only if parametric scaling in music bears a direct connection to the columnar modules of our cortex (Mountcastle, 1978), as Deutsch (1982) argues, but also whether such modules incorporate the more abstract closural and nonclosural encoding of melodic structure outlined here. Of course, neurophysiologically, it goes without saying that we also need to know how the neurotransmitters involved in learned "expectancy waves" (recorded electroencephalographically in numerous stimulus-response experiments concerning motor behavior; Walter, 1973) are different from those involved in the activation of the bottom-up Gestalt laws invoked here.

But one thing is clear: as Marín (1982, p. 454) put it, "one cannot study the neuropsychology of complex behavior without a prior understanding of the cognitive structures of the systems involved." I believe in this noble quest to understand the perception and cognition of melodic structures that the implication-realization model may prove useful.

Notes

1. Those familiar with Lerdahl & Jackendoff's (1983) grouping preference rules will notice in this article some similarities between their rules and mine. One difference, however, is that I believe grouping junctures take place more often *on* notes – at beginnings and ends of *structures* – rather than between segments. I. Deliège's evidence (1987) for the partial validity of some of Lerdahl and Jackendoff's rules to the contrary, I believe an experiment that asked subjects to locate precisely the initiation and termination of groupings (rather than just to parse segments) will yield results favorable to the model expostulated in this article – and contrary to some of Lerdahl & Jackendoff's rules.
2. Though meter has received considerable treatment in recent studies in music theory (Cooper & Meyer, 1960; Barry, 1976, 1985; Yeston, 1976; Lewin, 1981; Lerdahl & Jackendoff, 1983; Benjamin, 1984), how much metric differentiation (b) affects melodic structuring is in general less well understood than our knowledge of how durational (d) and harmonic (h) closure establish groupings. One obvious reason for this is that the listener's reliance on metric structuring rests partly on subjective cognitive limitations (for instance, it is not by accident that triple and quadruple meters on all levels are the most common ones since our short-term memories generally chunk three to four items more accurately and comfortably than five, seven, or nine; see Estes, 1972; Swain, 1986). Another

reason for our imperfect understanding of meter is that meter itself is the summarized result of interaction among all other parameters, which makes the study of it difficult. For instance, mere chord change, quite apart from properties of dissonance and consonance, brings about metric emphasis, as does durational cumulation, dynamic stress, repetition, or, for that matter, the patterning of melody itself – or any combination of these things. Space does not permit me to cover the topic of metric differentiation here; in what follows below the structuring effect of meter is explained on a case-by-case basis. Readers who wish to see a fuller discussion of the rules governing the operation of meter in the implication-realization model may consult Narmour (in press a, b).

3. The *locus classicus* for all studies concerning expectation of continuation is, of course, Meyer's *Emotion and Meaning* (1956).

4. That is, F–G–A♭ has an intervallic difference of a m2 (M2–m2); F–G–A, a unison (M2–M2); F–G–B♭, a m2 (M2–m3); F–G– B, a M2 (M2–M3); F–G–C, a m3 (M2–P4) – all within the definition of A+A).

5. In the parameter of melody, processes (P) are open and ongoing until terminated by closure in other parameters or by reversal (R, to be discussed).

6. Because duplication stays on the same registral plane, its pitches do not logarithmically "escalate" or "de-escalate" as those of processes do. For this reason, I separate D from P even though both are governed by the same Gestalt laws. For want of space, I cannot discuss the theoretical aspects of duplicative melodic structures in this article.

7. The theory has arithmetic rules stipulating what amount of closural cumulation inhibits what degree of melodic implication (see Narmour, 1989a, chap. 10).

8. The rules governing intervallic similarity when register changes direction are slightly different – a major second or less defines A+A, a minor third or more A+B – than when registral direction is maintained (recall that when register is maintained, A+A equals a minor third or less, whereas A+B is a major third or more). The reason for the slight difference in rule is that registral change itself adds a modicum of differentiation. Hence slightly less intervallic differeniation is necessary to create A+B when register changes direction.

9. Traditional nomenclature treats patterns like these entirely as harmonic phenomena; IP's, for example, are "escape tones", whereas ID's are "neighboring tones". Such names ignore the implicative melodic quality of these patterns. As we shall see below, both IP and ID are also partially closed because in retrospect they reverse registral direction.

10. Studies of visual perception which show that observers tend to fixate on corners – e.g., Attneave (1954); Baker & Loeb (1973); Watkins & Dyson (1985) – thus are not relevant to the concept of rehearsal.

11. "Registral duplication" – the missing symbol of VD – is not possible.

12. Readers of Krumhansl (1979, 1983) and Deutsch & Feroe (1981) will want to know what happens to the three-dimensional, hierarchical, conical concept of scale step in my hypothesis of a melodic parametric scale of intervallic implications. The answer is that scale step works *within* each intervallic class. For example, if we imagine the existence of goal notes (degrees 1, 3, 5), nongoal notes (2, 6), and mobile notes (4, 7), then a major third implication of continuation composed of degrees 1 to 3 (both goal notes) will be weaker than one composed of 5 to 7 (a goal note moving differentiatedly to a mobile note). This assumes, of course, all other parametric things are equal. If degrees 5–7 belonged to the same chord (e.g., a dominant), then differentiation would be considerably decreased. One cannot build an implicative melodic theory of how separate parameters interact solely on the basis of a fixed hierarchical space of scale step: there is no "melody of the spheres".

13. One problematic interval in an implicative melodic sense is the octave, which I do not have room to discuss here. Readers interested in seeing how the minutely differing implications and realizations of any intervallic sequence may be symbologically tracked my consult Narmour (1984).

14. Evidence of the confusability of the melodic tritone with either the perfect fourth or the perfect fifth – and thus by inference the tritone's potentially ambiguous function as the threshold interval in the intervallic scale hypothesized above – is discussed in Balzano & Leisch (1982). The authors show that melodically (as opposed to harmonically) the perfect fourth and perfect fifth are rarely confused – more evidence, perhaps, for the function of these intervals as having opposite implicative functions. A study showing the peculiarity of the tritone as a distance factor in melody is discussed in Divenyi & Hirsh (1978). For more on the strangeness of the tritone, see Deutsch, Kuyper, & Fisher (1987), and Deutsch (1988).

15. For a discussion of these, see, for example, Balzano & Liesch (1982); or Shepard (1982).

16. For arguments that intervals are top-down phenomena implicated in long-term memory – contrary to my and, for instance, Deutsch's (1975) bottom-up view – see Dowling (1982).

Nonmusical subjects seem to depend more on interval width than on category (Attneave & Olson, 1971); judgments of similarity also seem to be based on intervallic size (Kallman, 1982). Categorical perception on the other hand seems to result from "extensive utilization" (Marin, 1982) or, with well trained subjects, from a "high information load" (Burns & Ward, 1982),

17. In this theory, dashed lines show next-level transformation, while dotted lines represent low-level formation. The "6s" in the Figure refer to overlapping *dyads*, another kind of basic structure which cannot be discussed here. See Chap. 22 of Narmour (in press, a)

18. For other analytical applications of streaming in music theory, see Erickson (1975, 1982); on streaming from a psychological point of view, see Ortmann (1926); Bregman & Campbell (1971); Bregman & Dannenbring (1973); Dowling (1973); McNally & Handel (1977); Watkins & Dyson (1985) – to name but a few. The best summary of psychological research on streaming and its application to music is found in McAdams & Bregman (1979); for other good but less detailed summaries, see Davies (1978); Sloboda (1985); or Dowling & Harwood (1986).

19. On the necessity of convergence, see Rumelhart & Ortony (1977).

20. The parametric intervallic scale discussed above operates on primitive style materials and shapes (e.g., pitches and intervals) as opposed to complex style structures; see Narmour (in press, a).

21. Though not shown in this paper, the interference of extraopus style from "outside" the piece at hand – mimicry to a conformant melodic pattern from another piece or from a schema generally common to the style – is also treated in the implication-realization model (symbolized by "xs").

22. On why a concept of ebmodiment is necessary in true hierarchical systems, see Narmour (1983–84).

References:

Attneave, F. (1954) Some informational aspects of visual perception. *Psychological Review,* **61,** 183–193.

Baker, M.A. & Loeb, M. (1973) Implications of measurements of eye fixations for a psychophysics of form perception. *Perception and Psychophysics,* **13,** 185–192.

Balzano, G.J. & Liesch,B.W. (1982) The role of chroma and scalestep in the recognition of musical intervals in and out of context. *Psychomusicology,* **2** (2), 3–31.

Benjamin, W.E. (1984) A theory of music meter. *Music Perception,* **1** (4), 355–413.

Berry, W. (1976) *Structural Functions of Music.* Englewood Cliffs: Prentice-Hall.

Berry, W. (1985) Metric and rhythmic articulation in music. *Music Theory Spectrum,* **7,** 7–33.

Bregman, A.S. & Campbell, J. (1971) Primary auditory stream segregation and perception of order in rapid sequence of tones. *Journal of Experimental Psychology,* **89,** 244–249.

Bregman, A.S. & Dannenbring, G.L. (1973) The effect of continuity on auditory stream segregation. *Perception and Psychophysics,* **13,** 308–312.

Burns, E.M. & Ward, W.D. (1982) Intervals, scales and tuning. In *The Psychology of Music,* D. Deutsch (ed.) 241– 269, New York: Academic Press.

Cooper, G. & Meyer, L. (1960) *The Rhythmic Structure of Music.* Chicago: University of Chicago Press.

Davies, J.B. (1978) *The Psychology of Music.* Stanford: Stanford University Press.

Deliège, I. (1987) Grouping conditions in listening to music: An approach to Lerdahl & Jackendoff's grouping preference rules. *Music Perception,* **4,** 325–360.

Deutsch, D. (1975) The organization of short-term memory for a single acoustic attribute. In *Short-term Memory,* J.A. Deutsch & D. Deutsch (eds.) 107–151, New York: Academic Press.

Deutsch, D. (1982) the processing of pitch combinations. In *The Psychology of Music,* D. Deutsch (ed.), 271–316, New York: Academic Press.

Deutsch, D. & Feroe, J. (1981) The internal representation of pitch sequences in tonal music. *Psychological Review,* **88,** 503–522.

Deutsch, D., Kuyper, W., & Fisher, Y. (1987) The tritone paradox: Its presence and form of distribution in a general population. *Music Perception,* **5,** 79–92.

Divenyi, P.L. & Hirsh, I.J. (1978) Some figural properties of auditory patterns. *Journal of the Acoustical Society of America,* **64,** 1369–1385.

Dowling, W.J. (1973) The perception of interleaved melodies *Cognitive Psychology,* **5,** 322–337.

Dowling, W.J. (1982) Melodic information processing and its development. In *The Psychology of Music,* D. Deutsch (ed.) 314–429, New York: Academic Press.

Dowling, W.J. & Harwood, D.L. (1986) *Music Cognition.* Orlando: Academic Press.

Erickson, R. (1975) *Sound Structure in Music*. Berkeley. University of California Press.

Erickson, R. (1982) New music and psychology. In *The Psychology of Music*, D. Deutsch (ed.) 517–536. New York: Academic Press.

Estes, W.K. (1972) An associative basis for coding and organization in memory. In *Coding Processes in Human Memory*, A.W. Melton and E.Martin (eds.), 161–90, Washington, D.C.: Winston

Fraisse, P. (1956) *Les structures rhythmiques*. Louvain: Editions Universitaires.

Fraisse, P. (1982) Rhythm and tempo. In *The Psychology of Music, D. Deutsch (ed.)* 149–180, New York: Academic Press.

Gleitman, H. (1981) *Psychology*. New York: W.W. Norton.

Jones, M.R. (1981) Music as a stimulus for psychological motion: Part I. Some determinants of expectancies. *Psychomusicology*, **1**, 34–51.

Kallman, H.J. (1982) Octave equivalence as measured by similarity ratings. *Perception and Psychophysics*, **32**, 37–49.

Krumhansl, C.L. (1979) The psychological representation of musical pitch in a tonal context. *Cognitive Psychology*, **11**, 346–374

Krumhansl, C.L. (1983) Perceptual structures for tonal music. *Music Perception*, **1**, 28–62.

LaRue,J. (1970) *Guidelines for Style Analysis*. New York: Norton.

Lerdahl, F.& Jackendoff, R. (1983) *A Generative Theory of Tonal Music*. Cambridge: MIT Press

Lewin, D. (1981) Some investigations into foreground rhythmic and metric patterning. In *Music Theory: Special Topics*, R. Browne (ed.), 101–37, New York: Academic Press.

Marin, O.S.M. (1982) Neurological aspects of music perception and performance. In *The Psychology of Music*, D. Deutsch (ed.) 453–477, New York: Academic Press.

McAdams, S. & Bregman, A.S. (1979) Hearing musical streams. *Computer Music Journal*, **3** (4), 26–43.

McNally, K.A. & Handel, S. (1977) Effect of element composition on streaming and ordering of repeating sequences. *Journal of Experimental Psychology: Human Perception and Performance*, **3**, 451–460.

Meyer, L.B. (1956) *Emotion and Meaning in Music*. Chicago: University of Chicago Press.

Meyer, L.B. (1973) *Explaining Music*. Berkeley: University of California Press.

Mountcastle, V. (1978) An organizing principle for cerebral function: The unit module and the distributed system. In *The Mindful Brain*, G.M. Edelman & V.B. Mountcastle (eds.) 7–50, Cambridge, Mass.: MIT Press.

Mursell, (1937) *The Psychology of Music*. New York: Norton.

Narmour, E. (1977) *Beyond Schenkerism: The Need for Alternatives in Music Analysis*. Chicago: University of Chicago Press.

Narmour, E. (1983) Some major theoretical problems concerning the concept of hierarchy in the analysis of tonal music. *Music Perception*, **1** (2), 129–199.

Narmour, E. (1984) Toward an analytical symbology: The melodic, harmonic and durational functions of implication and realization. In *Musical Grammars and Computer Analysis*, M. Baroni & L. Callegari (eds.), 83–114, *Florence: Olschki*.

Narmour, E. (in press,a) The Analysis and Perception of Basic Melodic Structures: The Implication-Realization Model, Vol. 1, Chicago: University of Chicago Press.

Narmour, E. (in press, b) *The Analysis and Perception of Melodic Complexity: The Implication-Realization Model*, Vol. 2, Chigaco: University of Chicago Press.

Ortmann, O. (1926) On the melodic relativity of tones. *Psychological Monographs*, **25** (1), 1–45.

Pomerantz, J.R. (1981) Perceptual organization in information processing. In *Perceptual Organization*, M. Kubovy & J.R. Pomerantz (eds.) 141–80, Hillsdale, N.J.: Lawrence Erlbaum Associates.

Rumelhart, D.E. & Ortony,A. (1977) The representation of knowledge in memory. In *Schooling and the Acquisition of Knowledge*, R.C. Anderson, R.J. Spiro, & W.E. Montague (eds.) 99–135, Hillsdale, N.J.: Lawrence Erlbaum Associates.

Schenker, H. (1956) *Der Freie Satz*. Vienna: Universal.

Shepard, R.N. (1982) Structural representations of musical pitch. In *The Psychology of Music*, D. Deutsch (ed.) 343–390, New York: Academic Press.

Simon, H.A. (1969) *The Sciences of the Artificial*. Cambridge, Mass.: MIT Press.

Sloboda, J. (1985) *The Musical Mind*. Oxford: Clarendon Press.

Swain, J.P. (1986) The need for limits in hierarchical theories of music. *Music Perception*, **4** (1), 121–147.

Tenney, J. & Polansky, L. (1980) Temporal Gestalt perception in music. *Journal of Music Theory*, **24** (2), 205–241.

Walter, W.G. (1973) Human frontal lobe function in sensory-motor association. In *Psychophysiology of the Frontal Lobes*, K.H. Pribam, & A.R. Luria (eds.), pp. 109–22.

Watkins, A.J. & Dyson, M.C. (1985) On the perceptual organization of tone sequences and melodies. In *Musical Structure and Cognition*, P. Howell, I. Cross, and R. West (eds.) 71-119, Orlando: Academic Press.

Woodrow, H.A. (1909) A quantitative study of rhythm. *Archives of Psychology*, **14**, 1-66.

Woodrow, H.A. (1911) The role of pitch in rhythm. *Psychological Review*, **18**, 54-77.

Woodrow, H.A. (1951) Time perception. In *Handbook of Experimental Psychology*, S.S. Stevens (ed.) 1224-1236, New York: Wiley.

Yeston, M. (1976) *The Stratification of Musical Rhythm*. New Haven: Yale University Press.

Contemporary Music Review,
1989, Vol. 4, pp. 65–87
Photocopying permitted by license only

Atonal prolongational structure

Fred Lerdahl

School of Music, University of Michigan, Ann Arbor,
Michigan 48109–2085, U.S.A.

The early atonal music of Schoenberg and his school is emblematic of the difficulties in comprehending twentieth-century music. Music theorists have tried to analyze this music either through a modified Schenkerian approach or through pitch-set theory. After discussing limitations in these approaches, this paper develops at length a different theory for atonal music, one that adapts Jackendoff's and my *A Generative Theory of Tonal Music* in appropriate ways. Analyses of three Schoenberg pieces (from op. 11 and op. 19) illustrate the theory. The paper closes with an informal discussion of atonal pitch space.

KEY WORDS: Atonal, prolongation, pitch-set theory, Schenkerian theory, generative music theory, reduction, Schoenberg, pitch space.

Introduction

The Viennese atonal music of the early decades of this century continues to receive theoretical attention not only because of its aesthetic interest but because the problems it poses remain with us. As Schoenberg (1911/1978) confessed, harmonies in the first atonal works were composed more or less instinctively. The pitches had little explanation but sounded right. Here we have in pure form the theorists's nightmare: coherence in the face of no theory.

Just as Schoenberg was the first to enter this nightmare, so he was the first to seek an exit. But the twelve-tone system is a compositional rather than a listening grammar (Lerdahl, 1985; 1988a); it does not reveal in any direct way how the music composed by it is construed by the listener. The same holds for most of the other compositional systems that have been invented subsequently. Contemporary music analyses that concentrate on compositional method tend to give false security. Rarely do we know how to explain in any depth how a contemporary piece makes aural sense. The early atonal works thus represent a great difficulty. If only we could understand them, how much better we could understand ourselves.

In this article, in an extension of Jackendoff's and my tonal theory (Lerdahl & Jackendoff, 1983, *A Generative Theory of Tonal Music*, henceforth *GTTM*), I sketch a listener-based theory of atonal music. To put the issues in perspective, I begin with a review of other aproaches.

Problems of current approaches

There have been two broad ways of analyzing pitch structure in post-tonal music: pitch-set theory (Perle, 1962; Forte, 1973; Rahn, 1980); and adaptations of Schenkerian theory (Salzer,1952; Travis, 1970; Larson, 1987). Both approaches are valuable, but it suits my purpose to focus on their problematical aspects. We begin with pitch-set theory (Forte, 1973).

The first difficulty of pitch-set theory is that it provides no criteria for segmenting the musical surface into sets (Benjamin, 1974; Browne, 1974). The perceptual and formal issues are formidable, so it is understandable that theorists have avoided them. (Hasty, 1978, 1981, is an exception whose work dovetails with aspects of the discussion below.) Practitioners have in effect relied on two external criteria for set segmentation: its "musicality", and its capacity to provide what the theory denotes as significant set relationships. The first criterion is unexplicated, and the second is self-reinforcing.

A second problem concerns the absence of analytic connections among pitch classes within an assigned set. In a real context, some pitches are heard as more or less structural than other pitches. Adjacent pitches and chords form relationships that tug and pull at one another.

A third issue has to do with the criteria for equivalence and similarity among assigned sets. Are sets and their inversions really "equivalent"? What about Z-related sets? Such matters have spawned a technical subliterature, indicating uncertainty in how to decide the matter.

All these remarks point to a fourth and central problem. How does the theoretical description of pitch-class and interval-class content relate to the listener's organization of pitches at the musical surface? The relationship often seems remote. The very notions "pitch class" and "interval class" are abstractions from the pitch and interval content of a musical passage. And the various concepts invoked for set equivalence or similarity (inversional equivalence, normal form, interval vectors, Z-relatedness, the R relations, the inclusion relation, the K and Kh complexes) also create a distancing from the surface [1]. There is nothing wrong with this in principle: all theories generalize from phenomena. The question is whether these particular abstractions reflect and illuminate our hearing. The little experimental research that has been done on such matters (Francès, 1972/1988; Dowling, 1972; Deutsch, 1982; Bruner, 1984; Krumhansal, Sandell & Sergeant, 1987) has not been very encouraging. (In the last section I will suggest a way of thinking about pitch-set theory that weakens the charge that its abstractions are insufficiently related to musical surfaces.)

A fifth and related difficulty concerns the lack of hierarchical description in pitch-set theory. Basic to the *GTTM* theory is the distinction between hierarchical structure and associational structure (also see Meyer, 1973). Hierarchical structure is known to be central to learning and memory, both in the general case (Miller, Galanter & Pribram, 1960; Simon, 1962/82; Neisser, 1967) and for music in particular (Deutsch & Feroe, 1981; Deutsch, 1982; Krumhansl & Kessler, 1982). However, similarity among sets, like motivic structure, is associational in character: sets are perceived as closely or distantly related, not as subsumed by other sets. (This holds in part even for the "inclusion relation", as will be seen below.) Without a hierarchical framework, it is difficult to cognize sets.

A final problem concerns stylistic change. The conventional wisdom, at least in the United States, holds that Schenkerian theory explains diatonic tonal music and pitch-set theory explains atonal music (chromatic tonal music is a source of discomfort). This scenario is implausible from a psychological standpoint if only because it presupposes two entirely different listening mechanisms. We do not hear *Elektra* and *Erwartung* in completely different ways. There is a good deal of 20th-century music - Bartók or Messiaen, for instance - that moves smoothly between tonality (broadly speaking) and atonality. In short, the historical development from tonality to atonality (and back) is richly continuous. Theories of tonality and atonality should be comparably linked.

It does not suffice to apply pitch-set theory to underlying quasi-Schenkerian levels for atonal music, as Forte (1987) and J. Baker (1986) do for the transitional music of late Liszt and Scriabin, even though this technique may be illuminating in particular cases. Such a mixture is theoretically unsatisfying; it does not establish any real connection between the theories of the two idioms. What is needed is a theory that is general enough to underlie both idioms yet flexible enough to adapt to the ways in which the idioms differ and intermix.

Concerns such as these have led theorists, both before and after the advent of pitch-set theory, to propose neotonal analyses of atonal pieces. Sometimes these analyses change pitches at the musical surface in order to facilitate traditional harmonic analysis. This gambit is tempting because atonal pieces often share the gestural world of late tonal pieces. But which pitches are to be changed? No consistent criteria are imaginable. Whatever tonality and atonality have in common, it cannot be this literal.

Hindemith (1937/1942) attempts in an interesting way to generalize traditional fundamental-bass theory without resorting to the transformation of "non-harmonic" tones to fit the old triadic foundation. However, the psychoacoustical basis for his theory is shaky; and, what is worse, his analyses strike one as far-fetched. A modernized version of his theory may prove feasible, perhaps using Terhardt's (1974) "virtual pitch" theory. But such an extension would still shortchange the linear and formal aspects of post-tonal music.

Schenkerian adaptations to atonal music have proved controversial to both believers and nonbelievers in the Schenkerian faith. To believers these adaptations have diluted basic Schenkerian concepts to an unacceptable degree. To nonbelievers the resultant analyses have simply seemed unconvincing. On both sides the dissatisfaction provides small comfort, because the basic intuitions that Schenkerian theory addresses - the sense that musical material is elaborated, the recognition of local and global linar connections - also need to find a place in any theory of atonal music.

Straus (1987) discusses the difficulties in applying Schenkerian theory to atonal music. He explains "prolongation" in an orthodox manner and gives it four necessary conditions. First there must be a consistent distinction between consonance and dissonance. Second, there must be a scale of stability among consonant harmonies. (As he points out, this condition is a conceptual extension of the first.) Third, there must exist consistent ways that less structural pitches embellish more structural pitches. Fourth, there must be a clear relationship between harmony and voice-leading. He then shows that these conditions do not apply in atonal contexts, and concludes that a prolongational approach to atonal music is misbegotten.

Despite the clarity of Straus' argument, one cannot escape the impression that it is circular. He constrains the concept of prolongation to fit only classical tonal music and then demonstrates that other music does not fit it. True enough; but what about all those intuitions that made him want to think of atonal music in a prolongational way in the first place? It is not enough to settle, as he suggests, for a more modest atonal theory that just employs motivic associations in a set-theoretic manner. Straus regrets this posture, and has reason to.

I believe that an atonal prolongational theory can be developed in a way that sheds its Schenkerian origins. Such a theory can account for the important intuitions of elaboration and linear connection that atonal music evokes. Such a theory also can relate atonal to tonal prolongation at a more abstract level than Straus considers, thereby providing common theoretical ground between the two idioms.

A first attempt

Before outlining such a theory, I want to suggest an approach to pitch-set theory (derived from *GTTM*, pp. 299-300) that overcomes some of the difficulties mentioned above. This attempt will fall short for interesting reasons that will in turn set the stage for a genuine atonal prolongational theory.

The *GTTM* theory has a number of features relevant to pitch-set theory. Let me summarize the theory in the quickest possible way by sayng that *GTTM* proposes, and justifies on psychological grounds, a set of rules that together predict heard hierarchical structures from tonal surfaces. Figure 1 illustrates this schematically. For each component of the theory there are two main rule types: *well-formedness rules* (WFRS), which provide the conditions for hierarchical structures; and *preference rules* (PRs), which match possible structures with particular musical surfaces. Two aspects of the theory will concern us for the moment: *grouping structure*, which describes the listener's segmentation of the music into units of various sizes; and an underspecified *reduction*, which simply represents a pitch hierarchy.

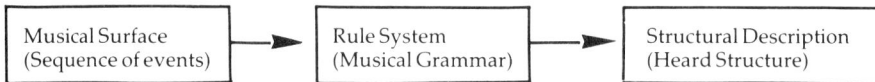

Figure 1

The *GTTM* theory can be made to apply to pitch-set theory in two steps. First, set segmentation can be viewed as a subspecies of musical grouping, so many of the grouping rules can be invoked for it. The grouping WFRs must be altered somewhat, pushing the atom of analysis down from the event (a pitch or chord) exclusively to the level of the pitch, and permitting horizontal, vertical, and diagonal segmentations. Overlaps can occur freely as long as contiguity of pitches within a set is not violated. Sets may contain smaller sets, producing a hierarchical analysis. In addition, the grouping PRs for proximity, similarity and parallelism find counterparts in set segmentation.

A formulation of segmentation in terms of WFRs and PRs could accomplish a degree of predictiveness that is currently lacking in pitch-set theory. It may be objected that such a rule system would not be as precise as the various formal operations on sets already given in pitch-set theory. Such precision, however, is misleading, since it begs the question of perceptual organization.

It is in any case beyond the scope of this paper to develop such a rule system (see Lerdahl, in preparation). Let us settle for a broad indication of how such a system might work. Level *b* of Figure 2 illustrates it with a segmentation of the opening phrase of Schoenberg's op. 11, no. 1. The sets marked *A* are established by their identical attack-points. The sets marked *B* are due to a combination of registral proximity and motivic parallelism. The set marked *C*, which includes the *B* sets, is assigned by linear similarity (it forms a "stream" in the sense of McAdams & Bregman, 1979); and likewise for the sets marked *D* and *E*. (This segmentation resembles that of Wittlich 1975; in contrast, Perle 1962 carves up the surface solely in terms of the [014] trichord.)[2]

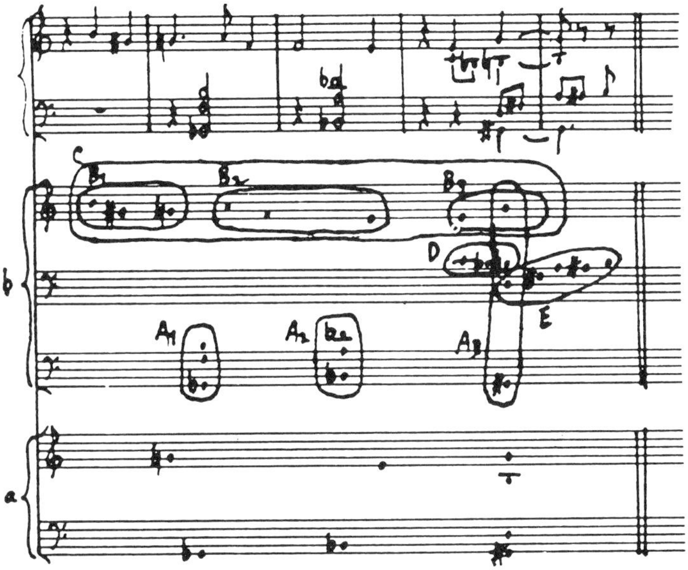

Figure 2

Set-theoretic analysis can now be applied to level *b* of Figure 2, revealing degrees of association among sets. The set types are given in Figure 3, cast in a format that roughly brings out degrees of similarity (the arrows mean "included within"). [03] is of course a subset of [014]. The "cadential" arrival at [0147] (m.4) contains [014] and [016], the two most prominent trichords in the piece. [012] is projected at the surface as a subset of [01258]. The largest set, [013457], includes all the smaller sets except [01258]. (To achieve an accurate overall projection of relative distance, we would have to invoke a multidimensional representation in which, for example, [03] and [014] would wrap around to be proximate to [01258], which includes them.)

A remark is in order regarding the hierarchical property of inclusion and its relation to cognition. It is one thing for sets to be included abstractly in a larger set, and another for them to be hierarchically related via the musical surface. For example, the *B* sets in Figure 2 appear within *C* at the surface, but A_1 and B_1 are separate from A_3 (even though [0147] includes [014] and [016]. Only the former case qualifies as inclusion in the sense of an "event hierarchy" (Bharucha, 1984; Deutsch, 1984; Lerdahl, 1988b). The latter is instead an instance of associational structure. (In the final section I return to this topic from another angle.)

The second step in applying the *GTTM* theory is to assign a hierarchy to individual pitches within a set, so that distinctions in structural importance can be

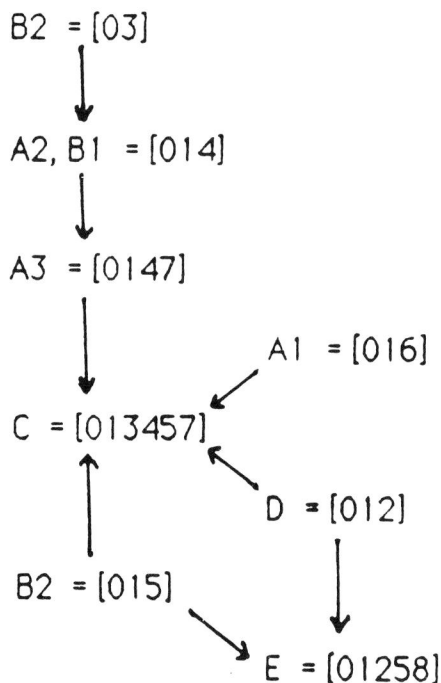

B2 = [03]

A2, B1 = [014]

A3 = [0147]

A1 = [016]

C = [013457]

D = [012]

B2 = [015]

E = [01258]

Figure 3

represented. This could be done with a tree notation, but it is simpler to delete less important pitches in a more or less standard reductional format. In Figure 2, level *a* gives the *head* (or dominating pitch) for each smallest set in level *b*. Generally, less salient pitches are removed so that only one pitch remains per set. In other words, the most important pitches are those in the outer voices, those that are relatively long or loud in their context, those that create motivic relations with other sets, and so forth. This steps creates a hierarchy not only among sets but among pitches within a set.

The motivation for equating salience with structural importance will be considered below. At this point, let us just assume some intuitive resonance with this procedure. But how do the pitches at level *a* connect to one another? How is the reduction to proceed to a further level? Even supposing an answer to the first question, there is no solution to the second. The notion of reduction depends on the establishment of hierarchically well-formed regions over which reduction is to take place. Except for the inclusion of the *B* sets within *C*, there are no such well-formed regions available in Figure 2. How, for example, are the vertical *A* sets to relate to the horizontal *B* and *C* sets? What about the overlapping sets in measure 3? How can the analysis be extended to the level of the whole phrase?

To perform a genuine reduction, in short, we must first develop hierarchical regions of analysis. Schenkerians (including Straus) tacitly assume this step. As we have just seen, pitch sets do not qualify for this role. Therefore an atonal reductional theory must discard pitch sets as the unit of analysis.

This conclusion may seem unappetizing, especially since the attractions of a reductional approach have yet to be demonstrated. Skeptics should keep in mind, however, that the psychological evidence points to the central role of hierarchies (reductions) in cognition. I propose now to develop a more thorough reductional approach to atonal music. From this vantage it will be possible to reconsider the role of pitch sets.

Tonal reduction

A good deal of *GTTM* is devoted to establishing intuitively relevant well-formed regions of analysis for its two reductional components. Here I outline this theoretical machinery so that it can be adapted to atonal music.

GTTM claims that listeners hear events within nested rhythmic units called time spans. At local levels time spans consist of the distances between beats; at global levels, of groups; at intermediate levels, of a combination of meter and grouping. Within these spans the listener compares events for their relative stability. Less stable events are recursively "reduced out" at each level, until one event remains for the entire piece. Such in brief is *time-span reduction*. Its essential function is to link rhythmic and pitch structure. This step is needed to develop a deeper stage of analysis, *prolongational reduction*, which requires rhythmic as well as pitch information in order to evaluate the prolongational importance of events.

The prolongational component is modeled on Schenkerian reduction to the extent that it describes the linear continuity, departure, and return of events in hierarchical fashion. However, the hierarchy is more restricted than Schenker's, insisting on direct elaboration of immediately superordinate events and permitting only three kinds of prolongational connection. These relationships are interpreted in terms of intuitions of tension and relaxation among events. And unlike Schenkerian theory's reliance on the *Ursatz*, prolongational connections do not require an *a priori* schema. Instead these connections derive from global to local levels of the associated time-span reduction. This top-down procedure is necessary because the prolongational function of an event is determined by its larger context. As each level of time-span reduction comes up for analysis, the events in question form a *prolongational region* (the prolongational analogue to a time span). These regions successively become embedded as the analysis progresses to more local levels. Events to be assigned within a prolongational region are evaluated in terms of their relative stability of connection at that point in the analysis. As in time-span reduction, this evaluation refers to a set of *stability conditions*.

Prolongational connections are represented by branchings in a tree diagram above the music, and, more or less equivalently, by slurs between noteheads in the musical notation. Right branches stand for a tensing motion (or departure), left branches for a relaxing motion (or return). The three kinds of connection are *strong prolongation*, in which an event repeats; *weak prolongation*, in which an event repeats in an altered form (such as triadic inversion); and *progression*, in which an event connects to completely different event. Figure 4 shows these relationships in schematic form (dashed slurs are reserved for strong prolongation).

Figure 5 gives the overall form of the theory. The grouping and metrical structures determine the time-span segmentation, over which time-span reduction takes place. The stability conditions provide input to both reductions. Prolongational reduction derives from the time-span analysis.

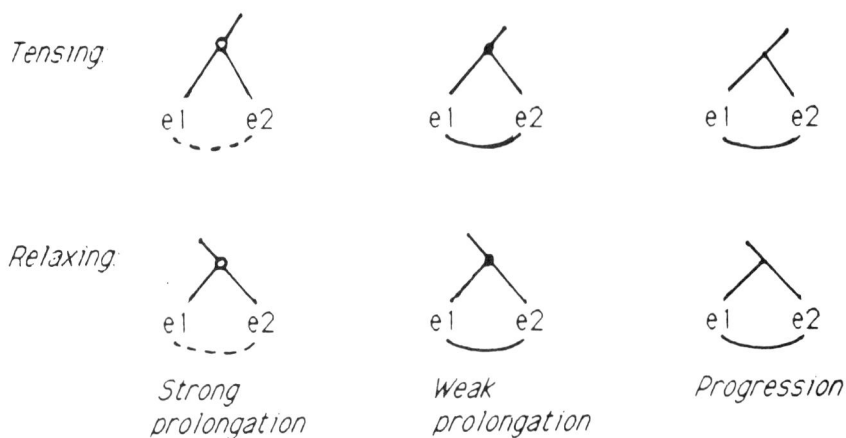

Figure 4

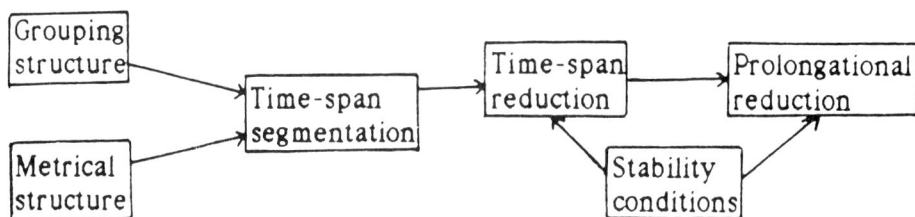

Figure 5

Since the writing of *GTTM*, I have proposed a number of revisions in the theory's reductional components (Lerdahl, 1988b, in preparation). Three of them must be mentioned here. First, time-span reduction has been demoted from a position of equality with prolongational reduction to a step in the derivation of the prolongational tree. This change allows the convenience of drawing only one graph per analysis. The prolongational tree appears over the music; under the music appears the metrical and grouping analyses and the time-span analysis in its "musical" notation; and beneath that appears the prolongational analysis in its "musical" notation (see the analyses below).

Second, in *GTTM* an event was assumed to have identical content as it proceeded up the tree to larger reductional levels. This was an idealization, not consonant with musical experience. In a global context one does not hear an event with the same degree of detail as in a local context. Therefore the content of an event must simplify as it proceeds from the musical surface to underlying levels. This new attitude was implicit in Figure 2, where less important events were deleted in moving from level *b* to level *a*. A sort of reduction thus occurs within as well as across events. Formally, however, deletion within an event is accomplished by a *transformational rule*. (Transformational rules are the third and least used kind of rule in the original *GTTM* theory.

The third change is that the stability conditions, which were stated impressionistically in *GTTM* have now been fleshed out in terms of a reductionally organized pitch space. In essence, if event *e1* is closer in the space to *e2* than to *e3*, then it forms a more stable connection with *e2*. The notion of pitch space will return below.

Modifications for atonal music

Let us now adapt the tonal theory to atonal music. The unit of atonal analysis becomes not the pitch or pitch set, but the *pitch event* – that is, any pitch or pitches that have the same attack point. An atonal surface is thus a sequence of events. This is natural enough, except that, as in *GTTM*, it idealizes away from the perception of polyphonic sequences (or streams). Such a simplification seems reasonable at this point.

We have seen that the establishment of prolongational regions depends on a time-span reduction, which in turn requires a time-span segmentation derived from grouping and meter. In short, all the structures of the *GTTM* theory are needed. Again, this seems intuitively right: atonal as well as tonal pieces have rhythmic structure that affects the understanding of pitch connections. This rhythmic structure is encoded in the time-span analysis. It would be surprising indeed if a coherent atonal reductional theory could be formulated in a temporal vacuum.

Now we come to the critical point. Atonal music almost by definition does not have stability conditions. Its pitch space is flat; sensory consonance and dissonance do not have any syntactic counterpart. How then is pitch reduction to be developed?

In this connection, I have found that the reductional PRs in the *GTTM* tonal theory fall into two classes, those that refer to stability conditions and those that refer to contextual salience. Given that two events connect, the more *stable* is the one that is more consonant or spatially closer to the (local) tonic; the more *salient* is the one that is in a strong metrical position, at a registral extreme, or more significant motivically. If one event turns out to be more stable and more salient, it unambiguously dominates the other. But if one event is more stable and the other is more salient, there is a conflict in the rules. In tonal music stability almost always overrides salience. One might say that the grammatical force of tonal pitch structures can be gauged by their ability to override surface salience.

Atonal music may not have stability conditions, but it does project the relative salience of events. The absence of stability conditions makes salience cognitively all the more important. I argue that listeners organize atonal surfaces by means of it. As a result, atonal music collapses the distinction between salience and structural importance.

In terms of Figure 5, the tonal stability conditions must be replaced by a set of *salience conditions* that interact to select the most salient event within each time-span of a piece or passage, with less salient events reduced out recursively from local to global levels. These conditions are needed only for time-span reduction; prolongational connections can then be read off global-to-local time-span levels, as discussed below. The salience conditions, which interact computationally with one another in a preference-rule fashion, may provisionally be stated as follows (the numbers in brackets are explained below):

Salience conditions: Of the possible choices for head of a time span, prefer an event that is

   (a) attacked within the region [3];
   (b) in a relatively strong metrical position [1];

(c) relatively loud [2];
(d) relatively prominent timbrally [2];
(e) in an extreme (high or low) registral position [3];
(f) relatively dense [2];
(g) relatively long in duration [2];
(h) relatively important motivically [2];
(i) next to a relatively large grouping boundary [2];
(j) parallel to a choice made elsewhere in the analysis [3]

At local levels the factors are right at the musical surface: attack, metrical position, loudness, timbre, registral position, density, and duration (conditions [a]-[g]). At global levels the rather more abstract factors are motivic importance, position in the grouping structure, and parallelism (conditions [h]-[j]). As in *GTTM* and all other music theories, the notion of what constitutes a parallel structure has yet to be explicated. Intuitively, an event qualifies if it is similar to another event that is in a parallel place in the grouping structure.

    After each condition there is a number suggesting its relative strength of application, where [3] = strong, [2] = intermediate, and [1] = weak. I add these numbers simply to avoid the impression that all conditions are equal. For example, registral position (e) will generally override durational length (g).However, this quantification is only a rough indication, since for any condition the salience of an event is relative to its immediate context. The salience of a relatively loud event (c), for instance, depends on *how much* louder it is than its surrounding events.

    Condition (f) calls for a brief comment. In tonal music density is syntactically marginal, but without stability conditions it becomes a real factor in assessing an event's importance. This is why postwar composers became obsessed with density.

    We turn now to the prolongational component. The meaning of prolongational connections must be modified for atonal use. Without stability conditions the sense of patterns of tension and relaxation among events is attenuated, so it is best to abandon these interpretations and just say that right branching means departure and left branching means return. *Strong prolongation* (repetition of an event) and *progression* (movement to a different event) can then be carried over intact from the tonal theory. *Weak prolongation*, however, has no obvious counterpart in atonal music without the abstracted triad as the referential sonority (the *Klang* of Riemann,1893), it is less easy to say what constitutes "the same event in an altered form". Obviously a vertical rearrangement of the same pitch classes qualifies, but I would also like to include situations where a significant number of pitch classes – say, about half – repeat from one event to the next. Though this move seems intuitively justified, it creates a fuzzy boundary between weak prolongation and progression. Such cases can be represented by placing parentheses arund the node for weak prolongation.

    Figure 6 illustrates these connections for simple cases. If *p1* ("pitch one") and *p2* are in the same region and repeat, the result is a strong prolongation (6a). If *p1* and *p2* invert (6b), or if one of them repeats and the other does not (6c), the result is weak prolongation. (Note in 6c the combination of solid and dashed slurs for weak prolongation; this is a useful variant on the *GTTM* notation). If both pitches change – if *p1* and *p2* become *p3* and *p4* – the result is a progression (6d). A fuzzy case might look like 6e, where more pitches change than repeat.

(a)   (b)   (c)   (d)   (e)

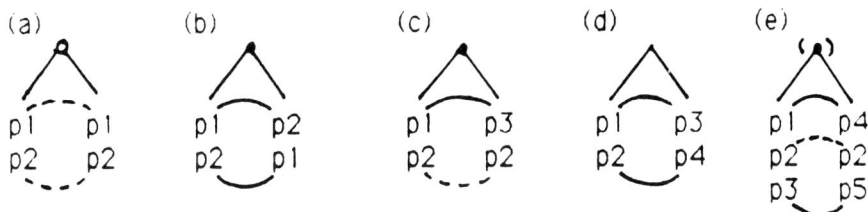

p1 p1	p1 p2	p1 p3	p1 p3	p1 p4
p2 p2	p2 p1	p2 p2	p2 p4	p2 p2
				p3 p5

Figure 6

This scheme for prolongational connections circumvents Straus' four conditions (enumerated above) for Schenkerian prolongation. His first two conditions address stability conditions, which, as discussed, are inoperative here. His third condition constrains linear embellishment along the lines of species counterpoint – neighboring tones, passing tones, and arpeggiations. No such voice-leading constraints are invoked here. Consequently there is no analogue to the concept of the *Zug* ("linear progression"), which is so central in Schenkerian theory. Right and left branching simply and only mean departure and return within a prolongational region. His fourth condition concerns the differentiation in tonal music between voice-leading and harmony, where, for example, the interval of a second is stable horizontally but dissonant vertically. No such distinction in the treatment of intervals applies here, with the result that in atonal music the horizontal and vertical dimensions tend to merge.

In short, it is the very generality of these connections – the same, the same in altered form, and different – that facilitates their adaptation at an abstract level from the tonal to the atonal idiom. Presumably they could be adapted to other idioms as well, and even to nonmusical phenomena such as narrative structure in literature.

We must now establish the principles for determining the most important event within a prolongational region and for making the most stable connection within the region. As we have seen, one event dominates another in the time-span structure by virtue of its time-span salience. These time-span events gradually become available for prolongational connection in a top-down fashion. This procedure may be stated as:

Preference Rule for Prolongational Importance:
    In choosing the prolongationally most important event e_k (event "k") within the prolongational region (e_i-e_j) prefer an event that appears in the two most important levels of the corresponding time-span reduction.

Events within (e_i-e_j) that are of more local time-span importance lack the rhythmic significance to be considered at that point in the prolongational analysis.

Next, how is e_k to be connected within the tree? There are two main factors in deciding whether e_k attaches to e_i or e_j:

Preference Rule for Prolongational Connection:
(a) *(Stability of Connection)* Choose a connection in the following order of preference:
    (1) e_k attaches to e_i as a strong right prolongation;
    (2) e_k attaches to e_j as a left progression;
    (3) e_k attaches to either e_i or e_j as a weak prolongation;
    (4) e_k attaches to e_i as a right progression;
    (5) e_k attaches to e_j as a strong left prolongation;
(b) *(Time-span segmentation).* If there is a time span that contains e_i and e_k but not e_j, choose the connection in which e_k is an elaboration of e_i; and similarly with the roles of e_i and e_j reversed.

The two factors within this second rule have counterparts in *GTTM*, and interact in the normal preference-rule fashion. Factor (a) encourages analyses in terms of superordinate events that are either extended (condition [1]) or returned to (condition [2]). Factor (b) favors a congruence between time-span segmentations and prolongational regions. This second factor appears to be stronger for atonal than for tonal music, probably because atonal pitch relations are less organized and therefore rhythmic structure plays a more dominant role.

The two overall prolongational rules also interact in a preference-rule manner. If the globally most important time-span event can connect as a strong right prolongation or a left progression, the rules are mutually supportive. But if these best connections are not available from the globally most important time-span level, the two rules are in conflict, and the most stable connections are sought from the next time-span level. If these connections are still not available, less stable connections are then assigned from the most global time-span level.

There is a final matter to consider. Along the lines of Figure 2, it is desirable to delete pitches at underlying reductional levels. At present I am uncertain whether this operation should take place in both reductions or only in the prolongational reduction. In any case, the salience conditions play the major role in retaining pitches at underlying levels – particularly registral prominence (condition [e]), supplemented by features such as relative loudness (c) and motivic importance (h).

However, as will be sensed in the analyses that follow, there is often a greater difference in deleting inner voices in atonal music than in tonal music. There are two reasons for this, one normative and the other psychoacoustic. In tonal music the vertical norm is always the triad, which consequently is understood even when the inner voices are not present. This understanding is reinforced by the greater tendency of verticalities to fuse (in the psychoacoustic sense of McAdams & Bregman, 1979) if they possess a high degree of sensory consonance. Atonal chords, by contrast, are distinctive and, due to their sensory dissonance, tend to be heard out in their details. Thus the deletion of less salient pitches at underlying levels is a less convincing operation for atonal than for tonal music.

Analyses

Now it is time to see how these theoretical considerations can yield illuminating analyses. Three passages from Schoenberg's atonal period will be examined.

Schoenberg: Op. 19, no. 6

This little piece, given in Figure 7 along with its analysis, is a good place to start because it clearly builds off reiterations of the opening sonority. I will take shortcuts in the derivation, the purpose being to convey the basic intuitions and representations for atonal prolongational structure. (Those interested in pitch-set theory may want to compare the analysis in Forte, 1973, plus briefer remarks in Lewin, 1987.)

No metrical analysis is given in Figure 7 because (despite the fascinating discussion in Lewin, 1981) the distances between attack-points at the musical surface do not facilitate the inference of a hierarchy of periodic beats. Beneath the music appears the grouping structure, which falls into four little phrases (measures 1–4, 4–6, 7–8, 9) by virtue of the intervening silences. At the next larger level, overall symmetry causes both the first and second phrases and the third and fourth phrases to group together. Phrases one and three subdivide. The time-span

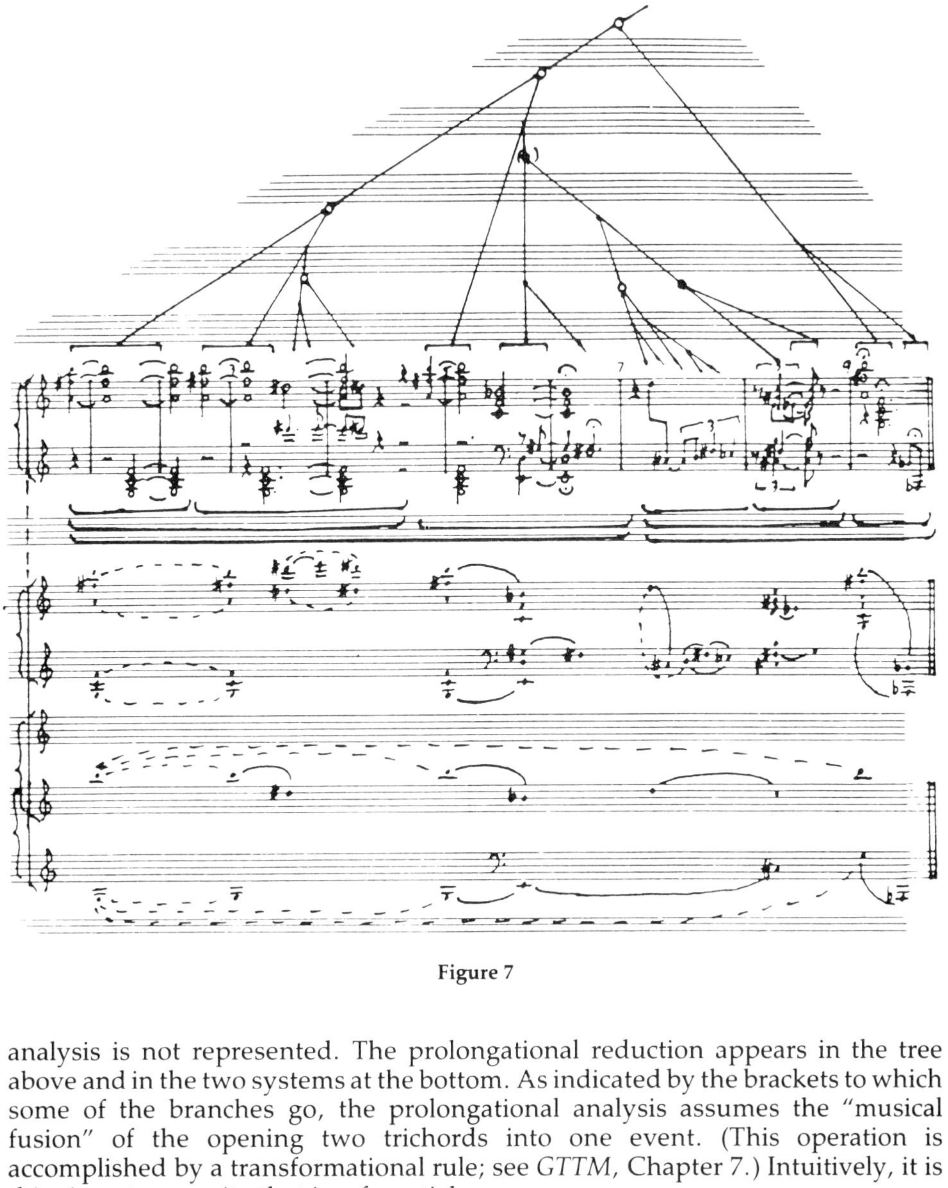

Figure 7

analysis is not represented. The prolongational reduction appears in the tree above and in the two systems at the bottom. As indicated by the brackets to which some of the branches go, the prolongational analysis assumes the "musical fusion" of the opening two trichords into one event. (This operation is accomplished by a transformational rule; see *GTTM*, Chapter 7.) Intuitively, it is this six-note sonority that is referential.

The tree shows that the opening sonority is strongly prolonged first to measure 3, then to measure 5, and finally to measure 9. After each of these prolongations there is a right-branching progression to a "melodic tag". Measures 7-8 develop this feature into the entire third phrase, shown as an elaboration off the second phrase. Measure 7 becomes an interpolation between the denser sonorities in measures 6 and 8. As suggested by the node in parentheses, these surrounding sonorities can be understood as weakly prolongational, due to the repetition of pitch classes C, D, E and G#.

The system at the bottom of Figure 7 shows an underlying reductional level with the inner voices deleted. This, together with the slur notation, helps project the voice-leading of the piece.

Figure 8 isolates the melodic tags to reveal a prolongational rhyme between phrases one and three and phrases two and four. The tag for the first phrase is a neighboring motion (D#-E-D#), represented by a progression within a strong prolongation. This motive inverts and transforms at the beginning of the third phase (D-C#-D), after which further elaboration takes place. Similarly, the descending whole step at the end of the second phrase (G#-F#), turns into the descending major ninth at the end of the fourth phrase (Bb-Ab). The arrows in the graph point out these correspondences.

Figure 8

Despite the attractiveness of this rhyme, the analysis on which it is based (Figure 7) fails to capture some underlying voice-leading features. So let us consider an alternative analysis. Two fundamental issues arise concerning fusion and register. First, should measure 7 be fused? That is, is measure 7 a melody or an arpeggiated chord? Of course it is a melody; but if regarded also as a chord, certain linear connections emerge more easily in the analysis. Figure 9a fuses both the tag in measure 6 and all of measure 7. Now the tenor F# in measure 6 can be analyzed as prolonging, via the same F# in measure 7, to measure 8; and the bass C# in measure 7, assigned a local neighboring function in Figure 8, now prolongs to measure 8 at an intermediate level. These connections are quite audible.

Second, what is the "real" bass line in measure 5-9? Is it just the lowest notes, as in Figure 7, or is it a combination of bass and tenor notes that make a good linear connection? Figure 9b shows the second possibility: the bass G in measure 5 moves to the tenor G#-F# in the same register; the F# prolongs for two measures, as discussed above, and then returns to an anticipatory G in measure 8; and this brings the music back to the strong prolongation of the opening, again with G in the bass. Finally, if the other voices are deleted and the remaining skeleton is registrally normalized, as in the bottom system of Figure 9b, the result is an inversional neighbor-note symmetry between the outer voices.

This last step employs three transformational rules – deletion, octave transfer, and fusion. In tonal as well as in atonal music, it is debatable how much to change

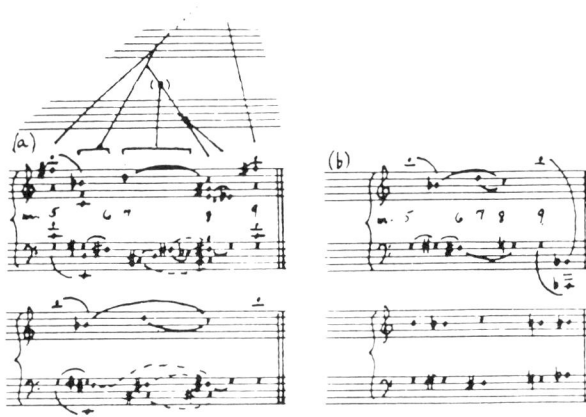

Figure 9

the surface in search of underlying regularities. Schenker (1935) relies a great deal on transformations; *GTTM*, in line with recent linguistic theory, mostly avoids them. Now I would advocate a moderate and constrained use of deletion and octave transfer for both the tonal and atonal idioms. Fusion seems to be needed more often for atonal than for tonal music, which as mentioned above, lacks the harmonic and voice-leading constraints of tonal music. In atonal music it is far easier to hear a succession of widely-spaced pitches as an arpeggiation. This is one reason why so much contemporary music sounds static.

Schoenberg, Op.19, no. 2

This piece, shown in Figure 10, also elaborates a pervasive sonority – in this case, the G-B dyad. But there is an ambiguity: is this dyad the main thing, or is it accompanimental to events in other registers? Which is figure and which is ground?

Figure 10 analyzes the G-B dyad as central. Again the metrical analysis is omitted; it rarely goes beyond the quarter-note level. The grouping structure is ambiguous (see the dashed grouping as an alternative for measures 5–7, based on the silences in these measures). The grouping interpretation taken here emphasizes the return of the opening dyad in measures 4 and 7, yielding three 3-bar phrases. The time-span reduction is included beneath the grouping slurs, starting at the quarter-note level *e* and progressing to level *a* . For each span at each level the most salient event is selected according to the criteria stated above. It may be helpful to play the piece and then successive levels of the time-span reduction in tempo.

The prolongational analysis again appears in the tree and in the musical notation at the bottom. For clarity the latter is given in two levels. The analysis derives from global-to-local levels of the time span reduction, in the manner discussed above: level *a* of the prolongational analysis builds off the events available at levels *a* and *b* of the time-span reduction, and so forth to more local

Figure 10

levels. The inner voices are deleted at underlying level *a*. The dense chord in
measure 6 can be understood as a displacement at the musical surface; so it is
transferred up two octaves at level *a* bringing out a connection with the high Ds
in measures 2 and 9.

The overall sense of the prolongational analysis in Figure 10 is as follows. Level
a strongly prolongs the G-B dyad from measure 1 to measure 4 and then to
measure 7, and within each such prolongation the music elaborates in parallel
ways. Level *b* shows more local elaborations. Of particular interest is the approximate retrograde between measures 2-3 and meaure 6: first the D-B dyad moves
through D#and A to C and A♭; this motion reverses in measure 6.

But there are weaknesses in this analysis. It does not explicitly represent the
prolongations between the high Ds at level *a* and it treats the final chord as an
afterthought rather than as a goal. Both shortcomings are due to the emphasis on
the prolongation of the G-B dyad. It is easy to shift one's listening focus instead

to the "densities" in measures 2-3, 5, 6, and 9, with the G-B dyads functioning as background. This second interpretation is given in Figure 11. For convenience the time-span notation appears below the prolongational musical notation, to which the tree is drawn directly. Events in measures 2-3, 5 and 9 are gradually fused at levels *e* to *c* in the time span analysis so that the proper prolongational connections can be made. (The most debatable fusion concerns measure 9: does the C-E dyad carry over conceptually into the final chord, or is it left hanging?)

Figure 11

In the tree the high Ds now connect as weak prolongations – "weak" because the events they are part of share some but not all pitch classes. The high F♭ in measure 5 becomes a quasi-neighbor between the Ds in measure 2 and 6. The final chord is now globally superordinate. Finally, the E♭-C dyad on the second beat of measure 4 (prefigured in the previous bar at an immediately underlying level) now becomes a weak prolongational anticipation of the density on the downbeat of measure 5, like the G-B dyads in measures 1 and 7 to the densities in measures 2-3 and 9. In all three cases, a dyad elaborates into a more complex sonority.

Travis (1966) offers a quasi-Schenkerian analysis of this piece in which the G pedal becomes a dominant, prolonged and resolved to the tonic low C in measure 9. The analyses presented here, in contrast, do not evoke traditional tonal analytical categories. Yet they are able to convey intuitions of elaboration and linear connection that are fundamental to any understanding of the piece.

Schoenberg, Op.11, no. 1

We return now to the musical passage with which we began. Figure 12 gives the opening section of the piece, minus the repeated material in measures 5-8. The metrical and grouping structures appear beneath the music (from the end of measure 4 to measure 9, the meter goes into 2/4). The only doubts in the time-span analysis concern the choice of melody notes in measures 3 and 11. In measure 3, the E is selected because it is next to a grouping boundary (stability condition (i) above) and because it forms a [0147] set, motivically close to measure 4 (condition (h)). The B♭ in measure 11 is selected because it too is next to a grouping boundary and because it is parallel to measure 3 (condition (j)). The prolongational analysis follows in a straightforward fashion except for the choice of head of the passage, which can be determined only on a more global view. The chord in measure 4 dominates over that in measure 2 because the former connects prolongationally with parallel events in measures 34 and 54, both of which begin large-scale groups.

A number of motivic relationships emerge from the prolongational analysis. At the surface, for example, the [026] trichord beginning the second phrase (measures 9-10) is a variant of the opening [014] trichord. Such an obvious relationship, which is not easily treated in pitch-set theory, depends on contour, position in the grouping structure, and other contextual factors. Though Figure 12 does not represent contour, it does show the two trichords in parallel groups and receiving parallel branching descriptions.

There are underlying motivic relationships as well. As shown at level *a* of Figure 12, the melodic E-G ending of the first phrase (measure 4) derives from the melodic heads of measures 1-3; that is, the ending of the phrase compresses and reverses the surface of the first three measures. One would expect an analogous pattern after the second phrase (B♭-C, since C and B♭ are the heads of measures 10-11). Instead comes the interruption of measures 12-14. When the slow tempo resumes in measure 15, there is a summarizing reference to the beginning of the first phrase and then a slightly altered version of the second phrase, after which the expected B♭-C in fact arrives in measures 19-20. The material in measures 19-20, parallel to that in measures 4-5, also repeats twice with small variations, but the third time (measures 23-24) it changes to B♭-G, an inversion of the original E-G (measure 4). These relationships are illustrated in Figure 13. Finally B♭ and G happen to be the melodic heads of the entire passage shown in Figure 12; thus the process of reversal and compression has continued down one more reductional level. This is the deeper reason why the B♭-G motion in measures 23-24 has such a closural effect.

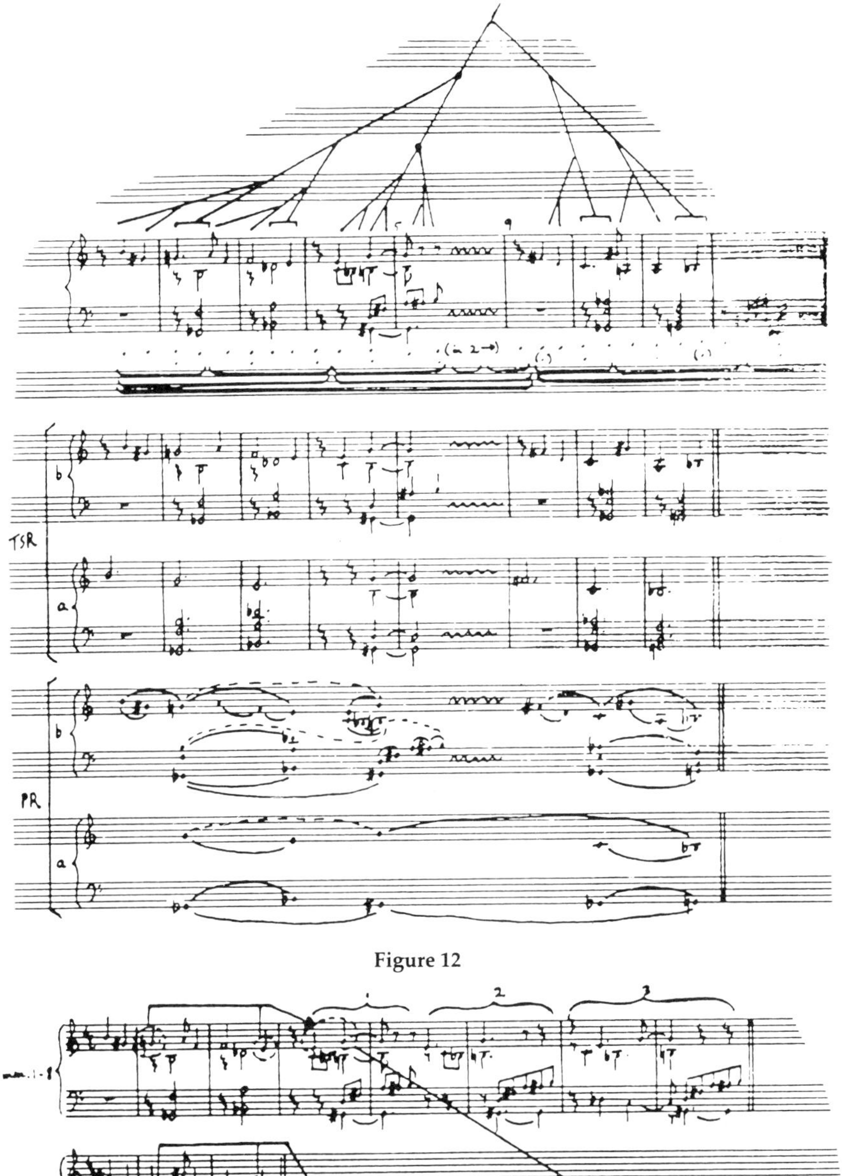

Figure 12

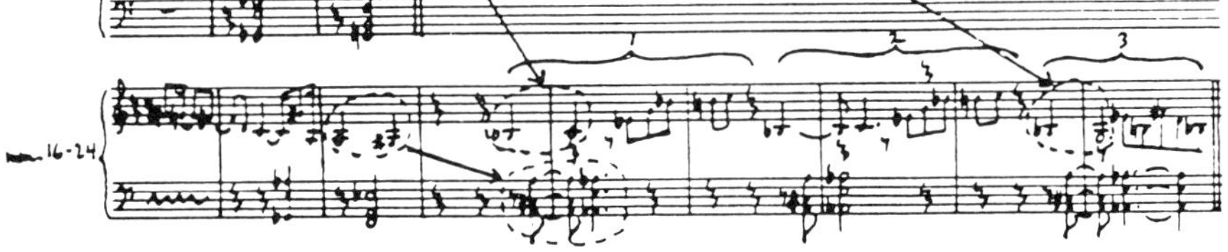

Figure 13

That these examples bring out non-obvious but satisfying motivic relationships is, I believe, an indication that theory is on the right track. I could continue in the same vein, but prefer to rest the case here, in the hope that the analyses developed so far have intuitive appeal and that their logic is clear. Let us now step back and consider some broader issues.

Discussion

The crux of the theory outlined above is the decision to regard contextual salience in atonal music as analogus to stability in tonal music. This step amounts to an acknowledgement that atonal music is not very grammatical. I think this is an accurate conclusion. Listeners to atonal music do not have at their disposal a consistent, psychologically relevant set of principles by which to organize pitches at the musical surface. As a result, they grab on to what they can: relative salience becomes structurally important, and within that framework the best linear connections are made. Schoenberg had reason to invent a new system.

How well does this theory apply to twelve-tone and other twentieth-century music? Though I have not yet explored this question in detail, my impression is that, at least as it stands, this approach is less illuminating for twelve-tone music. For example, the salient events in the first 20 or so measures of Schoenberg's *Violin Concerto* do not seem by themselves to combine into revealing patterns. From this one may conclude that, like tonal music, twelve-tone music has a listening grammar that diverges in interesting ways from surface salience. What is this listening grammar? Few theorists have addressed this important issue though, see Samet, 1985; Mead (in preparation). At a minimum, a listening theory of twelve-tone music would have to include both a quasi-grouping component that segments the aggregate appropriately and a prolongational component that establishes connections over these segments. Aspects of the above theory could be adapted to such a purpose. However, as discussed elsewhere (Lerdahl, 1988a), there are reasons for thinking that such a grammar is much harder to learn than is its tonal counterpart.

As for other twentieth-century music, I believe the theory will work rather well for music that combines tonal and atonal elements. Such music has various kinds of stability conditions that also must play a role in the analysis. For instance, Bartók's axis system (Lendvai, 1971) provides limited distinctions in relative pitch stability, and these mix with salience to produce his "centric" effects. I also think the theory has promise for coming to grips with some of the atonal music of the postwar avant-garde. In Boulez, for example, the twelve-tone organization (Koblyakov, 1977) is so hidden as to be irrelevant to the listener, and compensation is made by pedals and proliferations that are eminently prolongational in character.

The relationship of this theory to Schenker has already been discussed. But what is the relationship to pitch-set theory? The answer depends on how one thinks of pitch sets. On the one hand, they are concrete, be it a motive or a chord. In a piece such as Op.11, no. 1, a motive is a horizontal version of a chord, a chord a vertical version of a motive. On the other hand, pitch sets are abstract, a network of possible relationships that lie behind the atonal idiom and manifest themselves in specific ways in actual musical passages. An analytic study such as Schmalfeldt (1983) uses them in both senses.

The abstract view of pitch sets might be further considered as follows. For tonal music, psychologists (Bharucha, 1984; Deutsch, 1984) have distinguished between an *event hierarchy* and a *tonal hierarchy*. An event hierarchy is part of the structure that listeners infer from temporal music sequences. Schenker (1935/1979), *GTTM*, and others provide examples of this sort. A tonal hierarchy is a non-temporal mental schema that listeners utilize in assigning event hierarchies. Examples appear in Weber (1817), Riemann (1902), Schoenberg (1954/1969), Longuet-Higgins (1962/1987), Shepard (1982), and others. Lerdahl (1988b) points out that the tonal hierarchy and *GTTM's* stability conditions are in principle identical and formulates them in a hierarchal, multidimensional pitch space.

As Figure 3 roughly suggests, I prefer to think of pitch sets in terms of a multidimensional atonal pitch space in which similar sets are proximate and dissimilar ones are distant. This approach allows the atonal theory to look more like the tonal one. Both theories then map non-temporal pitch abstractions onto rhythmically realized pitch sequences; and in so doing, both utilize stability and salience factors, though in tonal music the former, and in atonal music the latter, is more significant. The difficulty with this approach is that atonal space is so much more unstructured than tonal space, which has precise levels of elaboration and distinct paths in moving from one structure to another. An atonal space would look more like a free-for-all "associational" space that plots similarity relations among motives. Thus we come back to pitch sets in their motivic aspect. Motive, harmony, and pitch space tend to merge into one another.

Nevertheless there is reason to keep a non-temporal atonal pitch space theoretically separate from the temporal, surface phenomena of motives and chords. In tonal music listeners organize pieces in part from their internalized knowledge of distances among pitch classes, chords and regions. Likewise, in atonal music listeners hear actual surfaces partly in terms of the relative similarity of the pitch and interval classes within pitch groupings. Accusations of the excessive abstraction of pitch-set theory should therefore be qualified. The real question is how these abstractions contribute to the organization of atonal event sequences.

There is a suggestive passage at the end of Wason (1985):

"When . . . Schoenberg (1911/1978) remarks that in (atonal) music 'one might reach conclusions concerning the constitution of chords through a procedure similar to figured bass . . .', we think of recent set-theoretic approaches to twentieth-century music. Earlier attempts to transfer Schenker's ideas to this repertory proved to be naive and premature. Indeed, with this music we are still in the figured bass era."

I take Wason to mean that pitch-set theory, like eighteenth-century figured bass theory, treats music in terms of intervals, and that no one has found a higher-level approach to actual atonal pieces, as Schenker did with tonal ones. In a sense the theory sketched here, along with the ruminations about pitch-space, is an exploratory response to Wason's remark.

Beyond its analytic promise, the present theory bears a potentially productive relationship to composition and to music psychology. How composers analyze music affects how they compose. It is not uncommon for composers to use set-theoretic concepts in their music in an incoherent or trivial way. It is easy to fall into such a trap precisely because pitch-set theory is so remote from musical surfaces. A virtue of the present approach is that it directly concerns musical surfaces and the relationships inferred from them. Perhaps on this account it can serve as a compositional aid. For the same reason it may prove useful in guiding experimental research in how listeners make sense of atonal music.

Notes

1. It is my purpose to explain the concepts of pitch-set theory. Briefly, *inversional equivalence* means that two pitch sets are in a sense identical if one can be made to invert into the other; for example, the major and minor triads are inversionally equivalent. *Normal form* is the compression of a pc (pitch-class) set or its inversional equivalent into the smallest space possible, in ascending order, and transposed by convention starting on pitch-class C, so that all versions (transpositions, inversions, registral spacings) of the set can be referred to as the same. The *interval vector* of a pc lists its total ic (interval-class) content ("interval class" equates an interval and its inverse, such as a major third and a minor sixth). Two sets are *Z-related* if they have the same interval vector but cannot be reduced to the same normal form. The *R relations* establish degrees of relatedness among sets of the same cardinality (of the same number of pcs), involving pc or ic similarity. The *inclusion relation* refers to sets of different cardinality, where one set is a subset of another. The *K complex* is a set of sets or of their complements (all the pcs not included in a set) associated by the inclusion relation; the *Kh complex* is a subcomplex of the K complex, whereby sets *and* their complements are associated by the inclusion relation.
2. In the integer notation, 0 = C, 1 =C# (or Db), 2 = D .... 11 = B. Pitch-set references are to normal form and hence include inversional equivalence (see footnote 1). For example, C-C#-D# and F#-G#-A are both [013]. It is often convenient to think of 0 as movable.

Acknowledgments

My principal debt is to John Covach, my research assistant at the University of Michigan while I was formulating the ideas in this paper. My colleagues Andrew Mead and William Rothstein also provided useful suggestions. Various versions of the paper were delivered during winter 1987 at the Michigan Music Theory Society, the University of Chicago, and the Université de Liège. Finally I would like to acknowledge similar and concurrent work by Mariko Hirosaki,a student of Tokumaru Yoshihiko at Ochanomizu University in Tokyo.

References

Baker, J. (1986) *The Music of Alexander Scriabin*. New Haven: Yale University Press.
Benjamin, W. (1974) Review of Forte's *The Structure of Atonal Music Perspectives of New Music*. **2**, 170-211.
Bharucha, J.J. (1984) Event hierarchies, tonal hierarchies, and assimilation: A reply to Deutsch and Dowling. *Journal of Experimental Psychology: General*, **113**, 421-46.
Browne, R. (1974) Review of *The Structure of Atonal Music* by A. Forte. *Journal of Music Theory*, **18**, 390-415.
Bruner, C. (1984) The perception of contemporary pitch structures. *Music Perception*, **2**, 25-40.
Deutsch, D. (1982) The processing of pitch combinations. *The Psychology of Music*, D. Deutsch, ed., New York, Academic.
Deutsch, D. (1984) Two issues concerning tonal hierarchies: Comment on Catellano, Bharucha and Krumhansl. *Journal of Experimental Psychology: General*, **113**, 413-416.
Deutsch, D. & Feroe,J. (1981) The internal representation of pitch sequences in tonal music. *Psychological Review* **88**, 503-522.
Dowling, W.J. (1972) Recognition of melodic transformations: inversion, retrograde, and retrograde-inversion. *Perception and Psychophysics*, **12**, 417-421.
Forte, A. (1973) *The Structure of Atonal Music*. New Haven, Yale University Press.
Forte, A. (1987) Liszt's experimental idiom and the music of the early twentieth century. *Nineteenth Century Music*, **10, 3**, 209-228.
Francès, R. (1972) *La Perception de la Musique* (2nd ed.). Paris: Vrin; Tr. W.J.Dowling, Hillsdale, NJ: Erlbaum (1988).
Hasty, C. (1978) *A Theory of Segmentation Developed from Late Works of Stefan Wolpe*. Doctoral Dissertation: Yale University.
Hasty, C. (1981) Segmentation and process in post-tonal music, *Music Theory Spectrum*, **3**, 54-73.
Hindemith, P. (1942) *The Craft of Musical Composition* (Vol 1). New York: Belwin-Mills. (Originally published 1937).
Koblyakov, L. (1977) P. Boulez 'Le Marteau sans Maître': Analysis of pitch structure. *Zeitschrift für Musiktheorie*, **8** (1) 24-39.

Krumhansl, C. & Kessler, E. (1982) tracing the dynamic changes in perceived tonal organization in a spatial representation of musical keys. *Psychological Review,* **89,** 334-368.

Krumhansl, C., Sandell, G. & Sergeant, D. (1987) The perception of tone hierarchies and mirror forms in twelve-tone serial music. *Music Perception,* **5,** 31-78.

Larson, S. (1987) A tonal model of an "atonal" piece. *Perspectives of New Music,* **25,** 418-433.

Lendvai, E. (1971) *Béla Bartók: an Analysis of His Music.* London: Kahn & Averill.

Lerdahl, F. (1985) Théorie générative de la musique et composition musicale. In *Quoi? Quand? Comment?: La Recherche Musicale,* T. Machover (ed.), pp. 101-120. Paris: C.Bourgois.

Lerdahl, F. (1988a) Cognitive constraints on compositional systems. *Generative Processes in Music,* J.Sloboda (ed.), 231-259. Oxford: Clarendon Press. 231-259.

Lerdahl, F. (1988b) Tonal pitch space. *Music Perception* **5,** 315-349.

Lerdahl, F. (in preparation) *Composition and Cognition.* Oxford University Press.

Lerdahl, F. & Jackendoff, R. (1983) *A Generative Theory of Tonal Music.* Cambridge: The MIT Press.

Lewin, D. (1981) Some investigations into foreground rhythmic and metric patterning. In *Music Theory, Special Topics,* R. Browne (ed.), New York: Academic.

Lewin, D. (1987) *Generalized Music Intervals and Transformations.* New Haven: Yale University Press.

Longuet-Higgins, H.C. (1962) Two letters to a musical friend. *The Music Review,* **23,** 244-248 and 271-280. (Reprinted in H.C.Longuet-Higgins, *Mental Processes: Studies in Cognitive Science.* Cambridge: The MIT Press 1987).

McAdams, S. & Bregman, A. (1979) Hearing musical streams. *Computer Music Journal,* **3** (4), 26-43 (Reprinted in C. Roads & J. Strawn, eds., *Foundations of Computer Music,* Cambridge, The MIT Press, 1985).

Mead, A. (in preparation) Twelve-tone listening strategies.

Meyer, L.B. (1973) *Explaining Music.* Berkeley: University of California Press.

Miller, G., Galanter, E. & Pribram, K. (1960) *Plans and the Structure of Behavior.* New York: Holt.

Neisser, U. (1967) *Cognitive Psychology.* Englewood Cliffs, N.J.: Prentice-Hall.

Perle, G. (1962) *Serial Composition and Atonality.* Berkeley: University of California Press.

Rahn, J. (1980) *Basic Atonal Theory.* New York: Longman.

Riemann, H. (1893) *Vereinfachte Harmonielehre, oder die lehre von den Tonalen Fünktionen der Akkorde.* London: Augener.

Riemann, H. (1902) *Grosse Kompositionslehre,* Vol 1, Berlin: W. Spemann.

Salzer, F. (1952) *Structural Hearing.* New York: Dover.

Samet, B. (1985) *Hearing Aggregates.* Dissertation: Princeton University.

Schenker, H. (1979) *Free Composition.* New York: Longman (Originally published 1935).

Schmalfeldt, J. (1983) *Berg's Wozzeck: Harmonic Language and Dramatic Design.* New Haven: Yale University Press.

Schoenberg, A. (1969) *Structural Functions of Harmony* (rev. ed.). New York: Norton, (originally published in 1954).

Schoenberg, A. (1978) *Theory of Harmony,* R. Carter, trans.. Berkeley University of California Press (originally published 1911).

Shepard, R. (1982) Structural representations of musical pitch. In *The Psychology of Music,* D. Deutsch, (ed.), New York: Academic.

Simon, H. (1962) The architecture of complexity. *Proceedings of the American Philosophical Society* **106,** 467-482. (Reprinted in H.A. Simon. *The Sciences of the Artificial,* 2nd ed., Cambridge: The MIT Press 1982).

Straus, J. (1987) The problem of prolongation in post-tonal music. *Journal of Music Theory,* **31,** 1-21.

Terhardt, E. (1974) Pitch, consonance, and harmony. *Journal of the Acoustical Society of America,* **55,** 1061-1069.

Travis, R. (1966) Directed motion in Schoenberg and Webern, *Perspectives of New Music,* **4,** 85-89.

Travis, R. (1970) Tonal coherence in the first movement of Bartok's Fourth String Quartet. In *The Music Forum* (Vol. 2) W. Mitchell and F. Salzer, (eds.), New York: Columbia University Press.

Wason, R. (1985) *Viennese Harmonic Theory from Albrechtsberger to Schenker and Schoenberg.* Ann Arbor: UMI Research Press.

Weber, G. (1817) *Versuch einer Geordeneten Theorie.* Mainz: B. Schotts Söhne.

Wittlich, G. (1975) Sets and ordering procedures in twentieth-century music, *Aspects of Twentieth-Century Music,* G. Wittlich, ed., Englewood Cliffs, N.J.: Prentice-Hall.

Contemporary Music Review,
1989, Vol. 4, pp. 89–100
Photocopying permitted by license only

Between music and language: A view from the bridge

David Osmond-Smith

*School of English and American Studies, University of Sussex, Falmer,
Brighton BN1 9QN, Great Britain*

This paper develops points arising from the papers presented by Peretz & Morais; Clarke; Lerdahl; C. Deliège; Baroni, Dalmonte & Jacoboni; and Nattiez, and the discussions that followed from them during the Symposium. These include the implications of a predisposition to hierarchic pitch structures; the relationship between a "discursive" period in the evolution of Western music and the analytical methods devised to comment on it; the complementarity of holistic and syntactic musical perception; the limitations of syntactic analysis; the lacunae of Nattiez's semiological framework as a cognitive model; and the possible relationship between holistic perception and the semantics of music.

KEY WORDS: Syntactic music perception, holistic music perception, musical semantics, modular pitch perception, semiology, cognition.

It must be clear from the group of papers discussed in this chapter that the conjunction of music and language has suggested a wide variety of experimental and analytical pursuits. The common ground between them is, however, relatively sparse. Rather than attempt a resumé, I shall therefore try to develop some of the points raised that open up problematic vistas for music researchers.

Of these, one of the most contentious was that set out by Isabelle Peretz and José Morais. Their summary of the evidence for modular processing in music perception underlined the possibility that there may be the possibility of innate dispositions that underlie the abstract and seemingly universal structure of musical scales, which become tuned to the specific scales of a culture, namely tonality in Western societies (Peretz & Morais, this volume). Indeed, they did not hesitate to assert that the tonal system seemed to mediate perception of musical pitch in an automatic way and without conscious awareness, so that we cannot override the musical tendency to interpret tones in terms of the diatonic scale. Apologists for the music of this century such as Célestin Deliège were quick to protest at the implied hegemony of tonal music, though Peretz responded that tonality was simply a powerful example of a more generalized predisposition. In subsequent discussion of the topic, Helga de la Motte questioned the ideological premises lurking behind the notion of "universal structure", and Jean-Jacques Nattiez reinforced her arguments with a trenchant list of ethnomusicological examples.

We are, however, confronted with a growing body of experimental evidence regarding tonality within our own culture. Musicologists might choose to dismiss it by asserting that our friends in the cognitive sciences have merely gone looking for what they wanted to find (for apart from Irène Deliège, few of them show much affection for post-tonal music). And it remains to be seen whether experimental evidence from a wider range of ethnomusicological sources will corroborate Peretz & Morais' assertions. But let us for the moment take these at face value, and explore some of their consequences.

In the first place, does our apparent predisposition to organize pitch structure hierarchically work only on a rather generic, global level, or does it imply that the more highly hierarchized, and strongly syntactic a system is, the more susceptible we are to it? If the latter is the case, perhaps we have means to explain (though by no means justify) the insidious invasion of popular cultures the world over by cheapjack tonal harmony. Perhaps indeed the highly developed refinements of nuance with regard to timbre, attack, intonation and rhythm that musicologists have demonstrated in so many non-Western cultures can only flourish in a society not overly fixated upon pitch syntax (or one that, like jazz, is shrewd enough to deploy "readymade" harmonic clichés merely as background). Euro-American "high" culture has cultivated its susceptibility to syntax in a relatively sophisticated fashion: once the addiction got out of hand it even began to develop antidotes. But the popular culture surrounding it has seized upon the detritus of that addiction to whet its own appetite. The alarming spread of the resultant confection – a sort of aural Coca Cola – has shown how innate predispositions may produce results that are desirable neither ethically, nor aesthetically.

Clearly, then, the findings that Peretz & Morais report cannot be taken to have normative implications. Yet a glance through the papers at this conference might tempt one to conclude that psychologists of perception consider post-tonal composers to be "throwing the sand against the wind" as Blake put it.[1] Culture perverts nature all the way from medicine to music. Tonality itself, in its most highly developed form, is an exquisite artefact that, through equal temperament, systematically perverts our responses to the "harmonic" nature of sound (to which Eric Clarke, in turn, proposes that we may have "natural" responses; cf. this volume). There is no obvious point at which it becomes expedient for a culture to stop challenging "innate" predispositions.

A little pitch syntax can be made to go a long way in the music of Dufay or Ockeghem. Yet three hundred and fifty years later, Mozart employs a pitch syntax of substantially greater power to produce a discourse of equal subtlety. Clearly there is a rich problem here for the historian of culture: why at a certain phase in its devleopment has Western music given such prominence to probabilistic rules? The answer must inevitably be complex, but some small part of it can perhaps be gaged from one of the ancillary consequences of this phase of our musical history.

Discourse feeds off discourse, as the unending shelves of literary criticism in any university library will attest. A non-verbal medium such as sculpture or painting generates discussion most easily in those areas that have the greatest affinity with language: iconographic studies show an elegance and penetration that discussion of abstract art can rarely match. And so it is with music. Only once the "para-linguistic" aspect of Western music had reached its apogee in the late 18th and 19th centuries did that form of discourse that we now label music analysis begin to proliferate and consolidate itself into a discipline. Naturally, in order to build up its confidence, it has concentrated upon saying the sayable. So to this day, analyses proliferate around the Viennese Classical Style, and the second Viennese School. but apart from some demonstrations of the ingenuities of Flemish counterpoint, the 15th and 16th centuries receive a good deal less attention, and 20th century pan-tonal harmony is only rarely discussed confidently and at length. This is not because such musics are any less aesthetically valuable; it is because the satisfactions of elegant discourse are less easily achieved when talking about them.

Those aspects of the psychology of perception that have derived their agenda from music analysis have of course adopted this bias. A frequent point of reference among the papers presented at this symposium has been the work of Lerdahl & Jackendoff (1983). Eric Clarke in particular commented extensively on their theories, and although I wouldn't wish to recapitulate his observations about the utility of "grammaticality" as a metaphor for music, (cf. this volume) I would venture one supplementary point. This is best illustrated by recalling one of the exchanges that followed Fred Lerdahl's own paper (cf. this volume) on the possibility of constructing prolongational trees for atonal music by adapting some of the procedures that he had previously elaborated with Ray Jackendoff for tonal music. Having asserted that without structure (which within a prolongational context essentially involves process) there was "no aesthetic response", he was asked whether such immediately perceived qualities as timbre, texture, and so forth did not therefore contribute to music's aesthetic impact. He replied that they clearly did, but only at a very low level. Now that is the response that I would expect from someone who views the world through syntactic spectacles. Perhaps it rings true if you are listening to Bach or Beethoven. But are there not many other musics where probabilistic rules governing the association of elements provide at best only a rather elementary scaffolding for other forms of perception?

Let us take atonal harmony, the subject of Lerdahl's own discussion. Its use presents composer and listener alike with a vast range of pitch agglomerates that may or may not be linked to each other by voice leading or pitch identities. Each chord, whether or not thus linked, is savoured for its own individual "color" – in which pitch content and spacing play practically equal roles. We can look at the score and analyze its structure in those terms. But is that how we *perceive* it? Surely our perception tends to be both global and imprecise, half way between our lucid aural mapping of an augmented sixth or a dominant ninth in tonal music, and the global synthesis that our ear automatically performs upon partials when distinguishing oboe from clarinet (an experience in no way modified by our knowledge of physics). We "go fishing" in an atonal chord, suspended among a variety of possible focuses, and are more or less able to separate out some of its internal relationships according to how it is laid out, and how long we have to listen. But such things are not confined to atonal music. Take the many instances in Mozart where we are suddenly brought up short by a passage which owes its impact as much to chord spacing and instrumentation as to surprises of harmonic syntax: bar 57 of the first movement of the Quartet K.499 for instance, or the c minor episode from the Larghetto of the Piano concerto K.491, or the second subject from the orchestral exposition in the first movement of the Concerto K.503…

I'm not even sure that such global, asyntactic factors are confined to simultaneities. Take any line from a motet by Ockeghem – surely one of the most inventive melodic thinkers. Voice leading or prolongation are only of modest help in guiding the ear through a formidable variety of melodic shapes: even when following that single line, we grasp at more global entities - a series of imbricated gestures, each with its own center of gravity (and often no exact sense of an outer boundary). And consider what happens when four or five of these marvellously intricate lines are all sounding at once (as, say, in the motet *Intermerata Dei mater*). The ear cannot possibly follow everything, so once again it floats suspended amongst the superabundance of melodic gesture, and is only guided into a momentary overview when the non-directional harmony engendered by this counterpoint focuses into a cadence. Perhaps that is why neither Schoenberg nor Ockeghem are all that popular with a public bred on discursive music by the Classical Music industry. In both cases the ear is at best only partially in control of what is happening to it. But as Rilke observed,

> . . . das Schöne ist nichts
> als des Schrecklichen Anfang, den wir noch grade ertragen,
> und wir bewundern es so, weil es gelassen verschmäht,
> uns zu zerstören.

> (. . . Beauty's nothing
> but beginning of Terror we're still just able to bear,
> and why we adore it so is because it serenely
> disdains to destroy us.)[2]

Might not that terror be the motive force behind the 17th-19th centuries' enthusiastic exploration of discursive music? We are offered a means of mitigating our impotence in the face of beauty. Beyond the concert-hall there are no such consolations: if you turn the corner and encounter a strikingly beautiful man or woman, what help are structure and syntax (save perhaps as a posthumous defence, in the manner of Gustave Aschenbach[3])? In music too we are made to turn corners: indeed, Mozart uses the most banal of syntax to lead us up to and propel us round them, only to leave us defenceless in the face of a magically spaced and orchestrated chord. But the syntax catches us up again, and our *amour propre* is saved.

This delicate balance between discursive control and holistic abandon is one that has become intensely valued in Western culture: in effect, Célestin Deliège's eloquent *plaidoyer* for the restoration of narrativity within post-syntactic music bears witness to the strength of the tradition (cf. this volume). So too, in a rather more paranoid way, does the vengeful systematicity of post-war discourses on music. It is this quality that leaves me admiring, but uneasy in the face of the paper by Baroni, Dalmonte & Jacoboni (cf. this volume). On one level their venture is calculatedly tautological. Their patient elaboration of a set of rules to describe what may and may not happen in a corpus of arias by Legrenzi models explicitly and logically a competence that we would already possess, but probably could not as coherently conceptualize after listening to those arias attentively and repeatedly. We have gained an increment in our sense of control, but almost by definition the resultant theoretical construct will be devoid of critical content: it cannot challenge our pre-formed responses because it sets out to reproduce them. And surely if we are going to talk about music rather than practice it, that challenge is the vital creative contribution that theory can make.

Yet the zeal and exactitude with which they extend their domination over this corpus of music might conceal a more hubristic ambition. If the tentacles of their tree diagrams could be extended far enough into the intimate detail of music, if the range of possibilities thus defined could be calibrated in terms of relative prob- abilities, and further sets of rules established to govern the balance between surprise and redundancy, then might they at last be able to fulfill the classicists's dream, and produce rules for generating beauty? It is perhaps a sign of their musicianship that they instictively veer away from such hubris, and content themselves with defining the well-made, for they have circumspectly chosen Legrenzi rather than Monteverdi or Berlioz to submit to the meticulous sacrilege of scholarship.

Jean-Jacques Nattiez shares with them a pleasure in systematic investigation. But rather than pursue a single methodology through to its ultimate consequ- ences, he collates and compares. It is an essential task, and one that by its very nature throws up a whole host of detailed technical questions. But this is not, perhaps, the most apt forum to debate details of analytical method. So I shall confine myself to considering the theoretical framework within which he conducts his comparisons. This, as is by now well known, is based on a model proposed by Molino (1975) which Nattiez considers to be constitutive of a semiol- ogy. It distinguishes the "poietic", concerned with the creation of a work of art, the "neutral", concerned with structural description, and the "aesthesic", concerned with perception. In this study Nattiez subdivides the first and last categories by distinguishing "inductive" hypotheses deriving from analysis of the music text from "external" evidence. These five levels are then collated in order to determine whether what the composer meant has been perceived and under- stood, in other words whether "communication has really taken place".

There seems to me to be a number of problems here. In the first place, this model might do well enough for poetry or painting, but it appears to dismiss as ancillary the activities of the musical performer. Yet s/he it is who is often respon- sible for determining to which structural features we "aesthesically" respond. In interpreting the work, the performer undertakes a further "poietic" process that fills out what the score cannot notate, but does so on the basis of an "aesthesic" response to what s/he reads in the score. This in turn underlines a further problem, for our response to a work read in score, and projected on to the inner ear, may differ from our aural experience, but is surely equally significant: do we only respond "properly" to a poem when it is read aloud to us? Thus the simple "aesthesic-neutral-poietic" triad might provide an adequate model for what goes on in Nattiez' own study as he delves into Debussy's score, save that he then proposes to verify his "aesthesic" propositions by testing the experience of listen- ers. (Significantly, when Michel Imberty (1985) conducts such a test for him, Nattiez is obliged to explain one of the resultant "anomalies" by noting how slowly Gieseking plays the piece).

However the very distinction between "aesthesic" and "poietic" seems to me to rest upon dubious ideological premises. Perhaps it confirms our more gloomy assumptions about an average concert-goer listening to a Beethoven symphony. But what of an 18 year-old at a rock concert (or indeed one given by the Ensemble Intercontemporain)? He has the option, if he doesn't like what he hears, of going away and trying to write something better. In other words, he listens *competitively*, with flashes of "poietic" activity constantly informing his "aesthesic" perception. And surely it is just that "parapoietic" experience that constitutes the positive face of syntactical analysis, enabling us to listen interrogatively, and with a sense of alternative paths not taken - a crucial adjustment of perspective if we are to continue repeating classical musical texts to ourselves over and over again, while placing a firm taboo upon composing in the style of Mozart or Mahler. Similarly, although all sorts of arcane strategies may enter into the "poietic" process, composition involves a good measure of sheer *listening*, and trying to find a notational equivalent for what you hear. When Nattiez tries to enrol Meyer, Narmour or Lerdahl & Jackendoff under the banner of "inductive aesthesic analysis", he therefore does them less than justice.

The "neutral" level, on the other hand, is all too conveniently accomodating. We are instructed to place on it anything that does not *a priori* declare itself to be of "aesthesic" or "poietic" pertinence. But where do those pertinences cease? Because Nattiez does not engage in the "aesthesics" of the inner ear, the listening activities that go into constructing and checking one of his "paradigmatic" analyses are relegated to the "neutral" level. (Presumably this would not be so if I played my students a melody and asked them to give an aural analysis?) The more one interrogates the confines of the "aesthesic" and the "poietic", the more the domain of the "neutral" recedes into metaphysics: a last resting place for Kant's "thing-in-itself".

"Neutrality" also appears to privilege repetition. It thus perpetuates a distortion of musical experience common to much "traditional" analysis. Nattiez' "paradigmatic analysis" offers us no criterion for determining how similar one structure must be to one another before they appear as paradigmatic variants, though it has the merit of offering up its intuitions for assessment in a clear, easily read fashion. But what of the significance of placing two dissimilar entities side by side? The relationship created between them is every bit as significant as that of recognizing repetition and variation. But it is not so easy to talk about. So music theory remains silent and Nattiez, disappointingly, colludes. (He does however illustrate my previous point by also assuring us that recurrences may be presumed to have "poietic" pertinence).

Finally, Nattiez' criterion for communication is that the listener should perceive and understand what the composer "meant". That style of communicative model will do for morse code, but I'm not persuaded that it adequately describes what goes on within an artistic medium. I am incompetent (or more accurately devoid of "competence") in a vast range of non-Western musics, and am therefore unable to follow what a composer/improviser "means". But that does not stop me from finding my own response. And I can take intense aesthetic pleasure in a stone or a cloud formation (but having resisted the blandishments of metaphysics, I must now do the same for theology, and so will not enquire from whom these "messages" come). The nature of the cognitive activity stimulated but such objects – man-made or otherwise – clearly is something other than that modelled by information theory, with its senders and receivers of messages. We return to great works time and again, because we find ourselves able to make "meanings" proliferate from them in all directions. We have no reason to suppose that all of those meanings were envisaged by the composer: his is often as much a process of astonished discovery as is ours.

It may seem ungrateful to dwell upon the deficiencies of Nattiez' model, for there is much to be learnt from the comparative analyses that he conducts within it. But those deficiencies do underline just how rich a range of problems await discussion if musical cognition is to be satisfactorily mapped. And the one to which I have just referred, that of musical "meaning", is potentially the richest of all. Like Eric Clarke, I find difficulty in assigning cognitive (or indeed semiological) significance to music on the grounds of intra-musical, or purely formal relationships alone. How, for instance, could we begin to answer Peretz & Morais' question about the survival value of music, and thus the reason for its existence, without going beyond such criteria? They judge the various answers so far advanced to be no more than "plausible", but there might be a way forward in a closer scrutiny of what lies beyond discursivity in music.

My discomfort in the face of the general drive towards syntactic models in musicology is not motivated by some semi-mystical appeal to intuition and spontaneity. It is simply that such models follow the line of least resistance when using language to illuminate music. And in so doing, they evade the challenge issued by Stephen McAdams, and reiterated by Peretz & Morais in their paper: that of trying to understand where music is wholly unlike anything else. Analysis is atomistic. It looks to identify discrete entities, and then to establish probabilistic rules governing their association. Musical perception can of course function in that way: we often train it to do so. But even within the highly syntactic music of the Western classical tradition an alternative form of perception is operating alongside, one that siezes upon global entities - harmonic/contrapuntal textures, the melodic gestures etched out by syntactic means etc. - each relished for its own sake, and at best simply "setting off" the next as it retires into the background of our perception. Within that holistic mode the entities englobed by a percept (entities that we would *analyze* as constituent parts) remain in a dynamic state of free play rather than being polarized by pre-established hierarchies. It is the sort of playful, exploratory cognition brought to the front of consciousness by Stravinsky with his permutational treatment of melodic material.

Now that form of cognition is fundamental to the way we explore our environment. It underpins a pre-causal mode of perception that sorts out the sense data in terms of similarity, and produces a world-picture that we as products of discursive and causal thought are pleased to label as "primitive". (It is no accident that our culture's most obsessive explorer of this sensibility, Claude Lévi-Strauss, has constant recourse to musical imagery in order to convey his ideas). This process implies an infinite semiotic regression (*a* is like *b*, which is like *c*, which is like *d* etc.), which can only be halted by the intervention of recognition and language (*c* looks like a *carrot*, *d* sounds like a *bird*). Thus abstract art, whether musical or visual, sets complex, but usually non-specific waves of activity running through those parts of the brain devoted to formal analogy. And a single oboe note, as yet quite innocent of syntax, or a single tonal chord, acquires instant musical "meaning" through this process. The more multi-valent a percept, the richer this process will be. Thus it is that we pick out from the eloquent syntax of a Mozart quartet certain moments of holistic sublimity that seem loaded with infinite (and infinitely unspecific) significance.

Now while a culture may seek in some small measure to codify such a process by specific conventions of emotional connotation, to try and construct a musical lexicon of the type discussed by Clarke *à propos* of the theories of Cooke is doomed from the start. However maddeningly it contradicts our linguistic habits, we cannot specify *what* music means, but we can investigage *how* it means. We can in other words attempt to gain a fuller understanding both of how a perceptual whole is more than the sum of its parts (indeed in some sense nullifies those parts), and of the cognitive mechanisms whereby various dimensions or aspects of that whole may trigger off a chain of similarity perceptions. The obsession with repetition and variation that characterizes both traditional analysis, and its resurrection in the semiological fancy dress of "paradigmatic" analysis would, within this perspective, be a rudimentary intra-musical mimesis of the cognitive processes that render music significant to us. If our world is our past, then music pulls the world together. Out of a faculty for detecting similarity that is fundamental to man's survival, we have abstracted a mechanism for flooding perception with significance so powerful, that many of us can't live without it.

Notes

1. In his poem *Mock on, Mock on Voltaire, Rousseau* from a manuscript of c.1803.
2. In the first of the *Duino Elegies*. The English translation is by J.B. Leishman and Stephen Spender (1963).
3. *Death in Venice* is, after all, a fine cautionary tale for musicologists.
4. I here recapitulate a proposition first touched on in Osmond-Smith (1972.)

References

Imberty, M. (1983) *La Cathédrale engloutie* de Claude Debussy: De la perception au sens. *Revue de Musique des Universités Canadiennes*, **5,** 90-160.
Lerdahl, F. & Jackendoff, R. (1983) *A Generative Theory of Tonal Music*. Cambridge Mass.: M.I.T. Press.
Mann, T. (1928) *Death in Venice*, tr. Lowe-Porter, H.T. London: Secker and Warburg.
Molino, J. (1975) Fait musical et sémiologie de la musique . *Musique en jeu*, **17,** 37–62.
Osmond-Smith, D. (1972) The iconic process in musical communication. *VS*, **3,** 31.42.
Rilke, R.M. (1964) *Duino Elegies*, tr. and ed. Leishman, J.B. and Spender, S. London: The Hogarth Press.

Rules of modules are not rules of art : Reply to Osmond-Smith

Isabelle Peretz and José Morais

In our paper (Peretz & Morais, this volume) we examine the possibility that some aspects of music perception are subserved by highly specialized computational systems, with reference to the contemporary notion of modularity. We argue on the grounds of the available facts, that the tonal organization of pitch may well correspond to a module. This proposition arises from the observation that encoding of pitch information in terms of tonal scales appears to be made in an automatic way and to be acquired very precociously without explicit tutoring. We also speculate (following Dowling, 1978, 1982; and Shepard, 1982) that particular structural properties exhibited by tonal scales, such as having an asymmetric internal structure that affords reference points and making use of a very small set of pitch categories, may correspond to natural propensities, or innate predispositions, of the human cognitive system. Note, however, that postulating innate dispositions for dealing with these abstract structural properties of musical scales does not entail, as David Osmond-Smith seems to fear, that we are endowed at birth with a device already tuned to one specific tonal system or even to the organization of tonal systems in general. It is obvious that a certain amount of exposure to pitch material is necesary. However, we are in no position today to predict whether some post-tonal musical pieces, for example, possess the sort of structural regularities to which the module can be tuned or is able to infer and reconstruct. Thus, we agree with David Osmond-Smith that there is at present no obvious point at which various musical forms can challenge innate predispositions.

Nevertheless, David Osmond-Smith jumps to the conclusion that our claim can explain the "alarming spread" of tonal clichés in popular music and shows "how innate predispositions may produce results that are desirable neither ethically, or aesthetically". This is an unfair charge. First, the existence of mental capacities does not explain, and certainly does not justify the direction of their exploitation. The nuclear bomb is not explained by the human capacity to understand matter; racist slogans are not explained by the human capacity to speak. Second, mental capacities do not dictate norms and more importantly have no prescriptive value with respect to art. Cognitive psychologists and neuropsychologists have accumulated quite strong evidence for the existence of special systems devoted to speech comprehension and to the recognition of visual objects such as human faces. However, not one of them has attempted to refute non-figurative paintings as art or has denied the possibility of using agrammatic speech for artitistic purposes. Nevertheless, not all agrammatic speech and not all non-figurative paintings are art. So is it for music. Art has its own set of criteria, and to ennunciate them is not our intention.

References

Dowling, W.J. (1978) Scale and contour : two components of a theory of memory for melodies. *Psychological Review* 85, 341-354.

Dowling, W.J. (1982) Musical scales and psychological scales : their psychological reality. In *Cross-cultural Perspectives on Music*, R. Falk & T. Rice (eds.) Toronto : University of Toronto Press, pp.20-28.

Shepard, R.N. (1982) Geometrical approximations to the structure of musical pitch. *Psychological Review*, **89**, 305-333.

Reply to Osmond-Smith

Jean-Jacques Nattiez

I decided not to publish my symposium paper devoted to a fragment of an analysis of *La Cathédrale engloutie* because the examination and analysis of the relationships between the three poles of the semiological model that I use (poietic, neutral, aesthesic) require such extensive development and diagrams that the normal "symposium proceedings" format - roughly twenty pages - doesn't provide enough space for my demonstration to be convincing.

This decision doesn't invalidate Osmond-Smith's remarks concerning my work, however, since with only two specific exceptions his comments relate to certain aspects of my general model. I should therefore like to counter with several quotations from my readily accessible books *Fondements d'une sémiologie de la musique* (1975) and *Musicologie générale et sémiologie* (published in March 1987). Readers can thus judge for themselves whether his criticism of the "deficencies" and "lacunae" in my model appears "ungrateful", or otherwise.

Osmond-Smith's criticisms challenge the poietic/aesthesic distinction on three points (not taken up in order here):

1. He attempts to challenge the legitimacy of the distinction by stressing that the poietic process entails a considerable measure of sheer listening. I have never

claimed the contrary since, in the conclusion to my 1975 book I wrote: "There is another cause for resistance concerning the trichotomy, and this involves the presence of poietic elements in the aesthesic and vice versa. For it is obvious that on the poietic side, the composer takes into account (in theory) the auditory effect of his music, first of all on himself. He is the first hearer of his own work. Phenomena of 'internal perception' cannot be disregarded in poietic description". (Nattiez, 1975,pp. 408-409). In a footnote,I added, "This is what Varèse fittingly called the 'internal ear'" (p.419).

It is moreover symptomatic of recent research in cognitive musicology that the theme of the poietic/aesthesic discrepancy is beginning to recur. The following was heard at the *Society for Music Theory's* "Music Cognition Group" in 1987: "Many of the leading psychological theorists seem to have adopted the stance that many composer-theorists have taken, which is the viewpoint of the composer (with score in head) or analyst (with score in hand), rather than the viewpoint of the listener. [. . .] We are learning [today] that it is erroneous to believe that listening is the mirror image of composition" (Butler, 1988, pp.24-25). And Meyer's brilliant statement at the same conference furnishes me with a final argument. After discussing contemporary music, he said: "It by no means follows that the constraints that guide the composer's choices are, despite the suggestions of some theoretical gurus, the same as those that are pertinent for – that facilitate and shape – the comprehension and experience of listeners. And, being heretical, I would suggest that this may also be true of some aspects of tonal music as well. Perhaps, for example, high-level key schemes in a Wagner opera or a Mahler symphony to which theorists and musicologists devote so much attention, should be interpreted as belonging to the realm of compositional rather than comprehensional constraints. The same is sometimes said to be the case, for instance with isorhythmus. If these observations have merit – and I grant that there is a continuum from idiosyncratic compositional constraints to ones belonging to a shared stylistic universe of discourse – then it is a mistake to assume that all musical relationships serve aesthetic ends such as enchancing unity, fostering closure etc. Some relationships exist because they facilitate composition rather than comprehension" (Meyer, 1988, p.5).

2. The passage in which Osmond-Smith refers to flashes of poietic activity constantly informing aesthesic perception seems to me to lack clarity. If he is trying to say that the listener can conceive that the work heard could have been written otherwise, I don't see how that undermines the poietic/aesthesic distinction. While admitting that rock music fans are often known to rush to put pen to music paper "in order to write something new" after having heard a dissatisfying concert, this simply means that the person in question moves from the role of listener to that of composer. Which is what all composers the world over do all the time.

If Osmond-Smith means that when we listen to music, we form hypotheses on the poietic strategies which generate what we hear, this is also a situation that I have explicitly acknowledged: "Theoretical knowledge plays its role in the perception of a work, and in particular in poietic elements such as, for example, the rules of counterpoint and the structural framework of the sonata form" (Nattiez, 1975, p.409).

3. Finally, Osmond-Smith charges me with not having included interpretation in my model: "In interpreting the work, the performer undertakes a further

'poietic' process that fills out what the score cannot notate, but does so on the basis of an "aesthesic" response to what s/he reads in the score." Yet in my 1975 book one can read: "if a work is conceived as an entity composed of relations laid down in the score . . . the aesthesic begins from the moment that the performer interprets the work . . . If, on the other hand, it is assumed that a work has not been completely produced until it has been played, then the poïetic extends up to the completion of the performance" (1975, p. 110). And I took this problem up again in my latest book (1987, p. 100). Must I conclude from that that Osmond-Smith doesn't know how to read?

But perhaps it would be better to raise the discussion to the level of musicological methodology. Several of Osmond-Smith's inaccuracies should first of all be corrected. He asserts that "neutrality" privileges repetition. But what analysts of the neutral level have privileged – by means of the paradigmatic technique, up to this point – are repetition *and* transformation. And this is just what distinguishes my approach from that of Lerdahl and Jackendoff, who don't deal with the "variation" dimension of the musical event: "When two passages are identical they certainly count as parallel, but how different can they be before they are judged as no long parallel? . . . It appears that a set of preference rules for parallelism must be developed, the most highly reinforced case of which is identity. But we are not prepared to go beyond this, and we feel that our failure to flesh out the notion of parallelism is a serious gap in our attempt to formulate a fully explicit theory of musical understanding. For the present we must rely on intuitive judgments to deal with this area of analysis in which the theory cannot make predictions" (1983, pp. 52-53). Osmond-Smith at least grants my approach "the merit of offering up its intuitions for assessment in a clear, easily read fashion" but he reproaches me for offering "no criterion for determining how similar one structure must be to another before they appear as paradigmatic variants."

It could hardly be otherwise, because what is the point - in this specific instance – of neutral level analysis? Precisely to catalog a set of *potential* relations whose aesthetic pertinence will be determined by the very techniques of perceptual analysis. Now, I'm convinced 1) that the problem of transformational distance cannot be resolved by what I call inductive aesthesic analysis (Nattiez 1987, p. 178), but rather through experimentation, which is why Lerdahl & Jackendoff could not propose rules *a priori* , and 2) that if experimentation intends to take into account what goes on in the works, it will have to be based on empirical cataloging of paradigmatic relationships. It is thus clear that my critic is absolutely wrong in claiming that the "checking of [my] 'paradigmatic' analyses are relegated to the 'neutral' level". To the contrary *verification* (and not construction) is transferred to the experimenter. I broached this issue back in 1975 when I expressly wrote that, "A *specifically* aesthesic experimental technique is needed in order to determine the degree of relationship between two musical units in each concrete case" (Nattiez,1975, p. 276).

Osmond-Smith also taxes paradigmatic analysis with perpetuating "traditional" analysis. Maybe, but doesn't it do so a shade more precisely and systematically? Osmond-Smith does, however, indirectly raise a real question: why is paradigmatic analysis so essential? Because it corresponds to what is probably a *universal* characteristic of all musics throughout the world – the dialectic of repetition and variation. All this does not mean, of course, that paradigmatic analysis is *sufficient*; it would certainly appear that it is not, and I will return to this point elsewhere. No method, for that matter, fully answers *all* questions. But the fact that it can offer, among other things, a way of describing techniques of development and variation is no mean thing, as will be appreciated if the global situation of musical analysis is considered with a modicum of attention.

Thus a rapid review of my work shows that the neutral level is not a vestige of metaphysics, but is rather a tool which, based on the *description* of a text, supplies elements and raises questions that only the poietic and aesthesic points of view can *explicate*.

Osmond-Smith's final remarks concerning my conception of communication are mind-boggling. For in the first chapter of *Musicologie générale et sémiologie*, I analyzed at length the standard communication theories (Jakobson and Eco) to show that they were incorrectly based on an identity between what happens in production and what happens in reception. And if I had more space I could even demonstrate that, historically, information theory was the model used by Jakobson and by Eco in elaborating the notion of the code! It is ironic, to say the least, that Osmond-Smith dishes this same argument up to me. What I've said is completely different: and that if there is communication, then it is only established *after* having rendered to the poietic and the aesthesic what is properly theirs. For me, the confirmation of communication remains a potential result of research, not its initial hypothesis. Osmond-Smith is perfectly correct to cite the example of the aesthesic perception of natural objects - Molino's triadic theory was partly based on his reading of Caillois' work on rocks. Caillois' fine analyses show, in fact, that meaning can be constructed by the receiver in the complete absence of intention since no sender exists. I am therefore grateful to Osmond-Smith for providing yet another argument in favor of the poietic/aesthesic discrepancy. But how could he not realize that in describing this process, he was no longer speaking of what he wanted to criticize in my work (the *communication* between a sender and a receiver), but indeed of *aesthesic* processes alone? Does Osmond-smith assume that in speaking of communication it is sufficient to focus on reception? And would he deny that, in writing *La Cathédral engloutie*, Debussy used compositional strategies, or that, on a semantic level, Debussy wanted to at least paint a picture, if not recount a story? Should he someday want to contest these points, I wish him luck. In so far as poietic (syntactic, morphological, semantic) strategies exist, it is perfectly legitimate to ask, whether or not there is communication. And I don't see how and why semiology, any more than cognitive research, should evade this question.

Translated from the French by Deke Dusinberre

References

Butler, D. (1988) (Non-) convergence of cognitive and speculative theories of music. *Music Cognition and Theories of Music* (Session of the 10th Annual Meeting of the Society for Music Theory, Rochester, November 6, 1987) H. Brown & P.McFall (eds.), Purdue University, mimeographed, pp. 23-25.

Lerdahl, F. & Jackendoff, R. (1983) *A Generative Theory of Tonal Music* Cambridge,Mass: MIT Press.

Meyer, L.B. (1988) Music cognition and theories of music. *Music Cognition and Theories of Music* (Session of the 10th Annual Meeting of the Society for Music Theory, Rochester, November 6 1987). H. Brown & P. McFall (eds), Purdue University, memeographed, pp. 4-6.

Nattiez, J.J. (1975) *Fondements d'une sémiologie de la musique*. Paris: Union générale d'éditions, 10/18.

Nattiez, J.J. (1987) *Musicologie générale et sémiologie*. Paris: Christian Bourgois.

Part II
Compositional and Psychological Aspects of Form

Contemporary Music Review,
1989, Vol. 4, pp. 101–115
Photocopying permitted by license only

On form as actually experienced

Célestin Deliège

Conservatoire Royal de Liège, 14, rue Forgeur, B-4000 Liège, Belgium

The following are considered, in turn: (1) *Form as assimilated experience.* Form is conditioned by a dialectic between internal and external determining factors related to detailed compositional writing while external determining factors are dominated by architectonic elements. Also, the form-content relationship is reconsidered here. (2) *Temporal transformation of the discursive process .* Debussy and Schoenberg, in particular, fostered a contraction of the discursive process that Webern, followed by Boulez and Stockhausen, finished and radicalized. Can perception adjust to the resurgence of the unpredictable? Husserl's *Vorlesungen zur Phänomenologie des inneren Zeitberuusstseins* helps to address this question on a conceptual level. (3) *Possibility of a new compositional approach.* This would postulate adherence to a grammar which, after the ravages of chance systems, could only be reconstituted by works providing descriptive principles comparable to those suggested by "weak" generative grammars. In addition to this requirement, the value accorded to "events" has to be enhanced.

KEY WORDS: Form, determining factors, content, 20th century, transformations, grammar, event.

> *To be beautiful, a living creature, and every whole made up of parts, must not only present a certain order in its arrangement of parts, but also must not leave its dimensions to chance.*
>
> Aristotle, *Poetics*

In 1950, the problems confronting music composition were problems of language. These were handled with varying success, depending on the imaginative skills of the protagonists and on the collective commitment made. Ultimate success, however, was thwarted by desertions, by unevenness in outlook, and by a certain complacency which went so far as to disregard the need for an aesthetic position. Today, questions relating to language are probably less removed from the broad range of considerations concerning *écriture* ("compositional writing")[1]: that somewhat vague, often-used term invoking a level of abstraction but at the same time linked to a notion of syntax and passage-connecting tactics – form and discourse.

Could it be that consideration of the burning questions facing musical composition at the end of the 1980s necessarily concerns the field of the cognitive sciences? The answer to this question depends on the limits assigned to the term cognition: it is perhaps preferable to leave the question open for the moment, confining ourselves to the hypothesis that the crucial area of debate concerning composition indisputably bears on the cognitive approaches adopted by those involved in creating music, and that secondarily a *critical musicology* must come to terms with this.

It is in this context, and in the hope that a critical musicology (up to now almost exclusively the prerogative of the more enlightened composers) will come into being, that I would like to offer the following comments and propositions. For that matter, such discussion does not at all stem from musicology itself, but rather emerges from issues recently raised by composers, in particular Giuseppe Sinopoli (private conversation with the author, March 1979) and Pascal Dusapin (1988).

Form as assimilated experience

It is always difficult to deal with questions relating to the concept of form without re-invoking concepts designed to explain the reasoning employed. Nevertheless, there is no intention here to proceed with a new examination of the concept of form from a phenomenological perspective, as the very title of this article might suggest[2]. The point of view defended here belongs to a strictly practical and critical perspective. First, however, it would be appropriate to go over several notions which vary according to period and ideology and which, as a result, can lead to ambiguity. It nevertheless remains possible to view musical form from a standpoint sufficiently general to encompass the historical situations which have shaped it.

Since its origins in popular culture, musical form has been determined by the poetic text on which it was based. The consequence of this for instrumental music was the perpetuation of the same type of configuration, as most clearly manifested in the classical period and beyond by four-bar phrase symmetry. Here it is a question of an external determining factor of form, one which probably found its fullest expression in the West in the thematic organization of sonata forms. Opposed to this external determining factor is an internal determining factor resulting from the grammatical system and from the specific compositional approach. The weight of an internal determining factor is, in every instance, the greater of the two, regardless of period and type of form. This preponderance is due to the inevitable collusion between grammar and style which can generate extreme diversity, while the external givens of the distribution of global organizational elements, much like an outline, can never exceed a small number. Combinatorial organization symbolized by the series A B C D, usually involving the repetition of certain of these symbols, is a limit that practically no form, except the rhapsody, has exceeded. It is no coincidence that Debussy, an opponent of abstraction, never sought to escape the schematic constraints of tradition; nor is it a coincidence that he usually worked with the simplest of these, thereby revealing the feebleness of their effect on the concrete form he sought.

Philosophical and religious reasons have also reinforced external and internal determining factors, depending on the context: it is striking that sonata forms flourished in the southern parts of Europe, that is to say in regions subjected to Catholic domination, while the fugue, a form much less externally determined, but fundamentally engendered by the movement and dynamics of its internal composition, rapidly escaped its southern origins, truly establishing itself under the aegis of northern Protestantism. It would be hard to maintain that the various forms of Viennese sonata are as diverse as those of Bach's fugues which, as has been justly pointed out, are all different in conception and design.

From the days of the baroque sonata, sonata forms were built according to an intuitive, linear-type logic where hierarchically structured units were linked according to an order of derivations governed by relations of complementarity or contrast. Although open to invention, this order was relatively predetermined, and always organized within a geometric framework. The fugue, on the other hand, resulted from a concept based on a largely deductive logic, which could then be worked out using combinatorial techniques. Pre-established factors were determining to only a small degree. The form of the fugue was progressively defined through its contrapuntal combinations and relatively free tonal progression, of which only the development of the classical sonata has retained any traces. Analysis of the fugal process invokes highly elaborate methods of formalization. From this standpoint, it is significant that no method of generative grammar has succeeded up to now in penetrating this technique.

It may appear a risky extrapolation to see the sonata as having philosophical features inherited from Descartes while the fugue would reflect traits inherited from Leibniz. Yet if their opposing epistemological positions are examined along the lines of Belaval's (1960) insightful critique, such an analysis would prove valid. And it would then be no riskier to link the fugue, with its search for constant renewal, to the free interpretation of the Scripture in conformance with Protestant theology, and to link sonata forms to the dogmatic imperatives of Catholicism. Of course, we know that classical musicians didn't load their forms with as many predetermined concepts as the teachings of Adolphe B. Marx and Czerny would suggest; the work of Charles Rosen (1971, 1980) has sufficiently dwelt on this point. The above comments are obviously addressed quite specifically to the organizational framework and norms of the two forms in question.

The subject of a work's external determining factors (its phrase and thematic structure) versus its internal determining factors (specific compositional technique and grammar) should also be dealt with from the angle of the form/ content relationship. But the concept of content in music still remains relatively evanescent: just when you think you've grasped it, it vanishes, and just when you've decided to turn your back on it, it sneakily reaffirms its existence. Even Hegel, who wanted to grant a major role to musical content, couldn't offer a definition of it, nor even a fair translation. He admitted that of all the arts, music possesses the best means to liberate itself from content; but he was living in an age where instrumental music, while winning autonomy, was still socially precarious – a point stressed by Carl Dahlhaus (1982, p. 26ff). Hegel, however, in his effort to distinguish between content and form – even in music – and driven by his determination to affirm the priority of content, couldn't content himself with the combination of sounds alone, with what would be purely musical. Music couldn't remain empty; it had to *signify*, in spite of its handicap vis-a-vis the other arts. Without being able to be more specific, Hegel invoked categories of the sensory capable of expressing the mental, and at the height of his argument he declared that music must make "the listener more clearly aware of the workings of his inner self." (Hegel, 1928/1965, p. 176).

On those occasions when, outside of strictly Marxist-inspired circles, musical content has been discussed with greater precision, efforts at understanding have been rather hesitant and attempts at definition have adopted a rather negative tone. Adorno, in his theory of aesthetics (1970/1974), when dealing with the form/ content relationship, managed finally only to extend his discourse on form (to which he assigned clear priority) without managing to convey the slightest concrete notion of what musical content might be. Now it is well known that musician-philosopher Adorno, although developing a general theory of aesthetics, referred constantly to music in his book. And when the art under discussion isn't specified, the reader has the feeling that Adorno's sole aim was to allude to music. In basically defending contemporary music practice rather than a theory of form and content, Adorno leaned totally in favor of form and concluded: "The campaign directed against formalism overlooks the fact that the form given to content is itself a sedimented content" (Adorno, 1974, p. 194). Poles apart from Hegelian Marxism, the structuralist position may seem more logical through its radicalism which no longer accepts the distinction between form and content, asserting that they are identical. It is significant that Boulez adopted Lévi-Strauss' argument basically defending the idea that *form and content are of identical nature and amenable to the same analysis* (Lévi-Strauss, 1960, p. 21–22). The anthropologist's position achieved enormous success in so far as it corresponded to the sensibility of the times, giving it an aura of truth. I myself greeted it as an advance, in the conclusion to an article written in 1962 on the form/content relationship in Debussy as revealed in *La mer* (C. Deliège, 1986, p. 136). Yet today I believe that the distinction between form and content is accepted or rejected depending on which aesthetic conception historically prevails in establishing the concept of art. It is hard to disagree with Jean Wahl when, using "matter" to refer to what several lines earlier he named *content*, he writes:

There is therefore no separation between matter and form, but the human mind constantly needs to make such a separation. The mind has a life of its own which involves making separations and subsequently making them disappear, making initially differentiated terms melt into one another. In this sense, ideas on the distinction between form and matter will always reappear, although in another sense, as we've seen, they're obliged to disappear.   (Wahl, 1957, p. 84).

Despite legitimate regret over the author's lack of precision in alternately using *matter* and *content* for the same concept (in the context from which this quotation is taken), the basic idea behind the argument is striking in that it draws its point of view from *the life of the mind itself*. This sanctions the option which now appears inescapable: accepting that it is the products of history – the works themselves and the ideology which inspires them – which confer legitimacy either on the form/content distinction or its rejection. The final arbiter of that decision can only be *actual life experience*. And if it is finally recognized that, depending on period and school, musical signification arises from the identity of, or distinction between, form and content, then Nattiez' recent definition of signification may well be adopted:

A given object assumes signification for an individual apprehending it when he places that object in relationship to other sectors of his life as actually experienced, that is to say the totality of other objects belonging to his experience of the world.   (Nattiez, 1987, p. 31).

Applying this general definition to music in the context of the foregoing comments means first considering the "other objects" as external contribution to both form and content, whether they arise from history, from expressiveness, or even from the sphere of overall organization. The apprehended object itself supplies its own contribution, its originality; one could even postulate that this originality is based on the object's material, its compositional articulation, and its grammar. Linking this musical application of Nattiez' general definition of signification to Wahl's shifting concept of the form/matter (content) relationship leads to the idea that a work's signification stems primarily from its form or its content depending on whether the internal or external determining factors of the apprehended object predominate. But given the constant complicity between form and content, fluctuating between mutual assimilation and relative independence, it is unlikely that just one of the two poles can ever be exclusively relied upon in experiencing the meaning of a work (except perhaps in the case of thoroughly explicit formalism).

I am tempted to illustrate this with an example comparing radically opposed aesthetic concepts: a highly formalist piece by Xenakis, for example, against one of Milhaud's more casual or folkloristic works. I am not proposing anything particularly subtle in saying that Xenakis' work makes an impression on my acquired experience primarily through internal factors, while Milhaud's work takes me back to a much more common type of experience, confronting me with factors mainly determined externally. In neither case, however, is the internal or external element completely pure; it's rather a question of weighting, of the predominance of a given type of factor coming from one pole or the other.

Any essentialist philosophy based strictly on the ontological properties of a work would challenge such reasoning, even though there is no pretense here of dealing with the way in which reality is organically constituted. Yet this reasoning has practical implications; it could thus be said that the more the composer invokes external factors, the more he or she tends to differentiate between form and content, and the more musical "events" must be incorporated into the form. Conversely, the more the composer relies on abstract factors of composition and grammar, the more the work moves toward the pole of material and structure. It could even be said, though at somewhat greater risk, that a latent opposition exists between the *formed* and the *forming*, depending on whether the composer is primarily oriented toward external, already existing, elements or toward internal elements expressed as combinatorial relationships of constituent parts.

Having established these preliminary points, we can now take a global look at how form's internal and external determining factors have been actually experienced during the 20th century, from the moment music ceased being tonal.

Temporal transformation of the discursive process in the 20th century

As a whole, 20th-century musical forms – highly elaborated ones, at least – have progressively reduced the influence of form's external determining factors. The major reason for this development should be understood in terms of composers' new-found obligation to establish individual yet coherent grammars. The resulting *mannerism* – or, if you prefer, *formalism*, or *structuralism* – which characterized the first decades of the second half of this century is no historical accident, but rather the logical outcome of the attention paid to language events.

As was just pointed out, already in Debussy the organization of sequences was much less important than their internal fashioning. It could even be safely asserted that overall structures were used by Debussy only to assure a certain level of conventionality. For the essence of his work is never found in the order of thematic contrasts and reprises, this order being simply a sort of mold into which the wealth of substance comprising all inventive and original elements could be poured. To cite just one simple and readily accessible example, Prelude no. 10

from the first collection, *La cathédrale engloutie*, which many musicologists have dealt with recently (at the symposium Nattiez cited no fewer than twelve analyses of the piece): the interest of the work most certainly does not lie in the general thematic outline A B A C B C A which, even if rare, is no less banal and offers only a very low degree of coherence. Nor could the underlying key of C major alone greatly influence the listener's judgment. The most original aspects of this piece are obviously related to the introduction of modes into the basic key, to the charm of their potential ambiguity, to the quality of the timbres largely resulting from the use made of the instrument's registers and resonance, to the true meter determined by holds and the measure's underlying time signature, and finally to the evolution of the form as underscored by shifting dynamics.

A similar observation could be made concerning Schoenberg, in spite of differences between the two composers. Boulez' harsh criticism of Schoenberg's determination to shore up his new material by using classic forms is well known. While this criticism is understandable coming from another composer – himself motivated by specific designs on the evolution of his own creativity – it should be acknowledged that in Schoenberg's case it is also the quality of the internal substance which gives life to form and not the opposite. Schoenberg only superficially resembles classical models, despite care taken to work from derived forms and basic shapes *(Grundgestalt)*. His phrasing is completely modified by the level of unpredictability arising from the intensity of variation. It would probably not be too difficult to select several minor works from Schoenberg's oeuvre to prove the opposite of what I wish to stress; minor works, whatever their origin, provide no insight regardless of the light in which they are examined. And apart from these contentious cases, Schoenberg's oeuvre leaves no room for doubt on the question under discussion. Take, for example, *Klavierstück op. 11, no. 3:* it is true that this is a piece which, in terms of its external organization, can be considered bi-partite and bi-thematic. But is this what really holds perceptual and analytical interest? Even the work of phrasing variations derived from basic shapes is only distantly related to classic derivation, which is nevertheless evoked through the presence of motivating form and the high degree of cohesiveness. What strikes the listener even more on initial contact, however, is the polyphonic writing unique in musical literature, where voices remain distinct, sometimes diverging, sometimes converging into chords. The voices move according to a system, one which includes the possibility of doubling. This counterpoint and state of variation, these movements within the phrasing, result in a perturbation of the external two-part, two-theme structure to the extent that it is difficult to assert that the second part is a re-exposition rather than a development. Powerful structural contrasts determine the actual site of perception so much so that the two-theme organization itself leaves the potential trace of a sonata form in the background. Through constantly varying equivalences, it is the paradigmatic characteristics which finally offer the listener recourse in the form of reference points to be noted (consciously or not), thus reinforcing listening and expectation.

Models such as those just mentioned are highly relevant in showing how form's external determining factors are minimized, but these works nevertheless retain a discursive and process-oriented nature to a large extent. The notion of structure and event, however, here finds an equilibrium which would not be so plainly assured during later stages in the evolution of forms during this century.

I would now like to propose two important and related postulates, namely:

(1) that as the discursive and process-oriented aspect of a work diminishes, and analysis by reduction and rewriting is no longer possible, and (2) that it is generally of little interest, in such cases, to conduct an investigative analysis of the entire trajectory of a piece. From the standpoint of the second postulate, it is significant that Stockhausen himself limited analysis of his own *Klavierstück I* to the type of information he felt it important to present (Stockhausen, 1963, p. 63–74). As to the first postulate, opponents of all reductive analysis will perhaps refuse to take the remark seriously; it is nevertheless true that, whatever virtues or vices are accorded analysis by rewriting, information contained in a message undergoes transformation depending on whether or not the analytical approach permits any given technique.

Proposing these postulates in no way represents an attempt to make value judgments. Rather, they are intended to represent nothing other than the swift change in the status of musical form from the moment that serialism was introduced. Although little disposed to a reductive analysis, classic Viennese serial works renew interest in an analytic reading all through their development, and it is their stylistic quality which plays the most important role in this renewal of interest. Webern's serial grammar apparently admits no reduction as a result of the absence of a true pitch hierarchy – it is generally understood that his main formal and syntactic structures are organized around the canon, the mirror-form and timbral relationships. Yet did this provide sufficient satisfaction concerning discursive development, even in the composer's eyes? In the first movement of the *Second Cantata, op. 31*, for instance, Webern's reintroduction of periodicity in the distribution of vertical clusters of six sounds, maintaining relationships of equivalence among them, would suggest that the composer himself felt the need to confer prerogatives on discursive form. This concern also extended to the treatment of variations, in so far as compatible with the system – one thinks especially of the second movement of the *Symphony op. 21* and the third movement of the *Variations for Piano op. 27*.

Separating the variables within the overall series led to the total equality of all components in the sound field. These variables, which up to then had been on "naturally" good terms given their relative independence (from a strictly morphological point of view), suddenly found themselves drawn into relationships of interdependence stemming from combinatorial procedures.

Completely integrating a whole set of components into the statement of each series contributed largely – if not predominantly – to the elimination of the discursive process in the post-Webern period. The absence of a vocal text continued to pose problems (already sensed by the Viennese) for the renewal of form. In a piece such as *Structure 1a,* Boulez resolved the problem through variations in density; in *Kontrapunkte,* Stockhausen built his formal project on the periodicity of tempi and the progresssive "farewell" of instruments, with the transference of density to the remaining instruments – yet this remains, in effect, an external project which substitutes itself for that level of information which the compositional articulation itself cannot sufficiently renew.

The tempo series found its extension in Stockhausen's acoustic practice in the years immediately following *Kontrapunkte,* and at any rate the conclusions he drew from this experience were decisive. By arriving at the conclusion that the postulated unity between pitch and duration could lead to what I will call the *well-tempered organization* of tempi (cf. his article "Wie die Zeit vergeht," Stockhausen,

1963, p. 99–139, and especially *Gruppen, Zeitmasse,* and *Klavierstücke V to X*), he transformed musical time to the point of no longer allowing for any predictability in listening, nor for the fully efficient use of memory. The choice of the distribution of striking events (*Gruppen, Carré, Kontakte*) obviously constitutes a corrective measure, but the concept of process, in the sense that it had been progressively developed since the instrumental pieces of Bach's Cöthen period, and as inherited by the 19th-century, was bankrupt.

This fundamental transformation of musical time led Stockhausen to the perfectly logical conclusion of *Momentform.* Moment-form should probably not be conceived of as an arbitrary association of moments; the dramatic power of a work such as *Momente* affirms the discernment underlying its composition. But it is nevertheless undeniable that the pole of interest in works stemming from or deriving from moment-form is basically that of material, for discourse can no longer emerge in the form of a linear process. A purely instrumental work such as Boulez' *Eclat,* related to moment-form through the monadic nature of its structures and their material diversity, mobilizes a form which reveals itself to the listener via the unexpected.

A great deal of congratulating went on in the early 1960s concerning recent accomplishments in transforming musical time, without the reasons for such rejoicing ever being questioned. It was at Darmstadt at about this time (1965) that a conference on form was held. On this occasion, Carl Dahlhaus adopted a certain distance from what was tending to become a new norm:

One would not include Stockhausen among those who despise form; yet the concepts "pointillist" and "statistical", though they were introduced as formal categories, do not refer to form but to compositional technique. They describe the structure of individual sections, not how they cohere. A complex of notes can be defined as "pointillist" or "statistical"; to say as much of a relationship between two sections would be meaningless. The concepts "pointillist" and "statistical" say little or nothing about form, the relation of parts to one another and to the whole.

Dahlhaus stressed the historical import of his comments by adding:

However, vocabularies that contain the word "form", although they may describe nothing more than compositional technique, are misleading with regard to the fact that *the problem of form, or of musical coherence, which they have seemingly solved, has not even been posed.*
(Dahlhaus, 1987, p. 252, emphasis added).

It might be felt that the distinction Dahlhaus makes between *form* and *compositional technique* is a little too sharp. What pertains to compositional technique can often be considered as pertaining to language; and history shows that transformations of language imply transformations of form. It is nevertheless true that circumstances fully justified Dahlhaus' argument in so far as "moment-form" never questioned its own motives, in other words the reasons for which the "discursive process" – only lately acquired by Western music after a long and difficult assault – had been eliminated.

Mental representations, to be sure, determined behavior then just as they did during the classical period. How could composers working with the microstructure of sound, for example, remain uninfluenced by microphysics? They discovered an image of the world which had been previously hidden from them, an image which enabled them to envisage (though this entailed a prevaricating interpretation) their work as a reflection of the universe of subatomic particles. All fields, moreover – artistic ones as well as scientific ones – were led by new techniques toward an epistemology drawing them closer together by subjecting all thought to the generic concept of "structure". Few answers were proposed as to the question of what was behind this convergence – typical of an entire civilization – which was merely affirmed rather than explained; it might be hypothesized that the development of operative techniques, particularly in physics and biology, and the enormous fascination they held for the collective imagination, had something to do with this.

Dahlhaus' comment seems to have made no impact at the time. That type of concern simply wasn't in the air. Luciano Berio was practically alone among those who composed without making concessions to the collective anamnesis, who didn't lose sight of concepts concerning hierarchy and discourse. The simple comparison of titles such as *Sequenza* and *Chemin* on the one hand, and *Gruppen, Momente* or *Structures, Eclat, Eclat-Multiples* on the other, reveals more than a play of metaphors – it places a whole program concerning continuity and temporal dimension into perspective.

A critical evaluation of the body of ideologies of creativity as formulated in the works and writings of Stockhausen and especially of Boulez nevertheless requires that an additional distinction be made. It has just been asserted that Stockhausen was never indifferent the way "moments" were to be linked; he soon sensed the danger of pointillism, to the extent that his retrospective analysis of *Klavierstück I* led him to consider it from the standpoint of "group technique" rather than "pointillist composition" which nevertheless seems to have been the principle behind the work (Stockhausen, 1963). As for Boulez, right from *Le marteau sans maître* and his article entitled *Recherche maintenant* (Boulez, 1966, p. 27–32), he euphemistically expressed his exit from pointillism and explicitly stated his concern with formal rhetoric. Yet it remains true that Boulez, like Stockhausen, was preoccupied by acoustic questions (though from a different standpoint) and was fundamentally oriented toward problems of constituting and structuring material. Therein, he felt, lay the source of a new poetics. Boulez was present at Darmstadt in 1965, where Dahlhaus spoke on form, but he offered an ironic monologue (much in the manner of Joyce's well-known character Leopold Bloom) on the subject which had given rise to a "conference". So – perhaps, because form was a problem in abeyance and was probably beyond the audience – he mused at the height of his presentation: "And is the virgin forest a form?" (Boulez, 1981, p. 97). The aptness of such a question should be acknowledged at a time when such confidence in disorder had authorized such allegiance to the virtues of chance! But the harshness of the reaction perhaps also indicated that a temporarily taboo subject had been raised.

Although resisting the confrontation of points of view, Boulez had nevertheless spoken out seriously on form two years earlier, in that same august – if slapdash – temple of contemporary music, presenting his comments as a sort of assessment. Contrasting conventional forms with new forms, he defined the former as those of predictability and the latter as those of *a posteriori* reconstitution:

Formerly, the perception of a form was based on immediate memory and on an *a priori* "listening angle." Now perception is based on para-memory, so to speak, and on an *a posteriori* "listening angle."
(Boulez, 1981, p. 88).

There's no reason to challenge this; yet hasn't the problem become more serious? And couldn't Dahlhaus' contribution be seen as premonitory? Young musicians who didn't harken at the time have now been imitated by an entirely new generation.

But what sinks into the para-memory? How much confidence can be placed in it? How efficient is recollection? Charles S. Peirce warned against the experience of recollection, however familiar it may appear:

> . . . it is plain enough that all that is immediately present to a man is what is in his mind in the present instant. His whole life is in the present. But when he asks what is the content of the present instant, his question always comes too late. The present has gone by, and what remains of it is greatly metamorphosed.   (Peirce, 1974: 1.310, p. 154).

This dovetails with Husserl's comments in the *The Phenomenology of Internal Time Consciousness*, lectures delivered at Göttingen between 1904 and 1910 (Husserl, 1928/1964). Husserl speaks in particular of the apprehension of given forms in an immanent duration. It would be useful to summarize Husserl's point of view here, in so far as the problem raised by Boulez relates to the receiver's state of consciousness.

Husserl distinguishes three stages in the *flux* of form: the *impression* received at the present moment, the *retention* experienced as a *shading off* of *what has just been*, and the *protention* which involves foresight. Retentional "shading off" is compared to an object in space whose dimensions appear smaller as the space between observer and object increases. There comes a moment in retention when what Husserl calls *primary remembrance* is no longer active or at least insufficiently active; it is then a *re-collection* which is *presentified* to consciousness in the form of an *external object*, because no longer present.

Husserl himself summed up his conception of the apprehension of form in a striking way:

> The form consists in this, that a now is constituted through an impression and that to the impression is joined a train of retentions and a horizon of protentions. This abiding form, however, supports the consciousness of a continuous change (this consciousness being a primal matter of fact, namely, the consciousness of the transformation of the impression into retention), while an impression is continuously present anew or, with reference to the quiddity of the impression, the consciousness of the change of this quiddity while the latter, which until just now we were still cognizant of as "now" is modified into the character of "just-having-been".   (Husserl, 1964, pp. 153–154).

Such is the perceptual description of form at the moment it takes place. But when the time of reconstitution arrives, and of the recollection which presentifies the object, this is then introduced into general consciousness as a "substrate" which loses its immanent temporality even though internal reflection confers consciousness of a duration on the substrate of this object in memory. In addition, perception at this "reconstitution" stage being an objectifying perception, the substrate of the object may be an "empty presentifying one" (1964, p. 178), associated with various affective contents which may mask reconstitution.

It is no coincidence that Husserl's model has been invoked here in an attempt to deal with the problem of reconstitution of form as raised by Boulez. The notion of immanent temporality in *The Phenomenology of Internal Time-Consciousness* often refers to the duration of a sound, to its constancy or change, as well as to the phases of melodic form.

Husserl could perhaps be paraphrased without doing his philosophy injustice by comparing two types of temporal structures: on the one hand, that of the apprehension of immanent duration, that is to say of form as exposed, and on the other, that of re-memoration ("secondary remembrance" in Husserl's terminology) or "para-memory" (according to Boulez), where the object emerges in its totality in the way recollection may assail memory at any given moment. It can be easily seen that in this latter case the structure of the reconstitution, regardless of the form involved, will always be much more precarious in nature than will the apprehension of the immanent form. It can be deduced that the form will be all the more difficult to reconstitute if apprehension encounters resistance at the moment it takes place. Furthermore, the apprehension of a form which only allows perception of "now" and a "train of retention" which "shades off" (a striking image which Husserl compares to a "comet's tail which is joined to actual perception," p. 57) *without* offering a real "protentional horizon", runs the risk of not proposing a sufficient extension to perception, thereby reducing the quality of its comprehension. It could be argued that such forms will be apprehended successfully through repeated listening; yet this remains a resource which is not always readily accessible (even less so to the extent that recorded music doesn't provide the standards of spatialization required by contemporary music). It is therefore legitimate that some composers take up this problem, wishing to test current conditions for a rediscovery of the discursive process. Boulez himself, for that matter, seems to have implicitly adopted a certain distance from his Darmstadt remarks of 1963: *Répons,* his major piece of the 1980s, though it renounces neither the strong polarity toward "material" nor the heavy marking of local processes, reveals broad unifying structures which perhaps suggest the re-introduction of linear compass. If I had to describe the form taken by the high points of *Répons* in a single phrase, I would speak of powerful arches rising above the tight harmonic columns supporting them. Whatever the case, one of the fundamental features of 20th-century aesthetics, mainly since Webern, will prove to be the negation of the concept of discursive process in the sense in which the two preceding centuries experienced it. It is by no means certain that the time has come to reclaim updated and newly-engaged discursive norms – that is up to the composer to decide and consider. Nor is the issue likely to produce new work immediately, the major danger being mimetic works of the "revival" type. Moreover, paths of research in this direction may be that much more cluttered in that an exploration of material itself remains as important as ever (cf. Barrière, this volume). But it is possible that the two lines of research can or even must meet up. Will critical musicology, in the event, have the courage to speak out? It should commit itself only with full awareness of its limitations, as well as full awareness of its responsibility. Music is not the sole property of those who create it, and among those who have claimed to contribute to its production there are many who have profited from the pickings for thirty years. Will they be pardoned by being dismissed as cranks rather than being suspected of having plundered the commonweal? It just may be – some signs point to it – that ethics has recently reacquired a certain substance and rectitude. Perhaps it is not vain, then, to hope for the founding of a new *communal spirit of musical development*?

Possibility of a new compositional approach to the discursive process

Berio defined music in a way which initially delighted me enormously: "Music is everything that one listens to with the intention of listening to music" (Berio, 1981, p. 7). Finally one was free to decide for oneself, without reference to anyone or anything whatsoever! And it is true enough that this constitutes an advance over the prattle about the *art of sounds . . .* Cage has always recommended this approach, never having placed, apparently, the least restriction on listening intention. No natural ordering, goes the theory, can be formless – as demonstrated by crystals (Cunningham, 1964, p. 7–80). Can it be left at that, or did Varèse have some justifiable reason for believing in sounds only if they are organized?

In any event, if we place cooled crystals side by side after their constituent elements have been heated, the resulting structure runs a high risk of resembling a meaningless sentence, even assuming the vocabulary belongs to an identifiable language. If we refuse to credit meaningless sentences in which it is impossible to even determine a threshold of correctness, that's because it is indispensible to take the notion of grammaticality into account. On that basis, though Berio's relativization is delightful in the freedom it proposes, a certain reordering is called for (. . . defining music certainly turns out to be difficult). I don't know how far Berio would go concerning listening intentions in terms of discovering a threshold of musicality, but his work as a whole would indicate that he places the bar of minimal requirements fairly high (for which even Cage himself might be grateful). I'm aware that referring to an alignment of crystals formed by chance and mean-ingless verbal sentences may appear annoyingly arbitrary in justifying the need for a musical grammar; if I took that path, it's precisely because Cage's argument led me there. And if I added the intervening example of a verbal sentence, it was simply to indicate that, if it's a *grammatical* sentence, then a sculptor trying to imitate it in crystal would give the alignment of those crystals a certain type of grammar, too. Such reasoning would probably be immediately convincing if it weren't a question of music; the difficulty here remains knowing how to attack the concept of meaning or signification. Cage's reasoning, via crystals, is seductive: for as long as there's only one crystal, the proposition holds true. But it becomes false as soon as one questions whether there can be the least connection between the natural fact of formation and the cultural level of formalization.

One would therefore like to retain Berio's quip-definition of music while adding a restriction on the level of intentionality: the necessity of pre-ordering. If this does not seem thoroughly convincing, one could perhaps in the last instance turn to human experience by inquiring of ethnomusicology if there are any known musical processes based on *happenings* in a given culture, where such an arbitrary combination of sounds is asserted to be music by the group which produces and perceives it.

The topic of this essay perhaps dictates a return to the elementary level of syntactic articulation, since it is a question of restoring the discursive process. Granted. More fundamentally, though, it should not be overlooked that a consid-eration of the development of this process must proceed via a revision of syntactic relationships conceived in terms of apprehension of long durations. Nor should it be forgotten that things come hard these days, and there's nothing to be gained in pretending to ignore the reasons for this. In addition, the question of grammar is problematic today in so far as no preliminary elements compel universal recognition. Even Viennese twelve-tone music didn't succeed in systematizing its theoretical project apart from several simple operations; and serialism, as commonly applied by several composers, proposed no overall definition apart from the very general one given by Stockhausen: work on a "limited number of different magnitudes" (Stockhausen, 1953, p. 128).

Broaching the question of musical grammar nevertheless requires extreme prudence. Recognizing that it is ultimately up to composers to decide, it will be postulated here that in the absence of a system from which generative rules describing that system can be extracted (which the tonal system seems to permit), understood in the sense of a *strong generative grammar*, then aesthetic conviction must insist that a work creates conditions allowing the rules of its generation to be determined in the *weak* sense as understood in the context of generative grammars. One rarely meets with this insistence, although it implies no common code (which in any case cannot, in current circumstances, be demanded). I will go further by pointing out that the requirement of a coherent grammar in the weak generative sense does not impose the concept of a code, which is probably much too rigid, but implies that the work offer a requisite degree of intelligibility. Such a general suggestion, in so far as it infringes on the composer's role, is intended to insure a level of clarity that the person to whom the work is addressed has a right to expect.

From this perspective, when considering the major forms which characterized the first half of this century, certain of Bartók's works offer an interesting model. The first movement of the *Fourth Quartet* reveals a construction of intervals which are deployed horizontally and vertically along the same symmetrical axes; their horizontal, contrapuntal deployment extends equivalents of harmonic entities over large time-spans. The potential unity of horizontal and vertical produced in Webern's pitch structures here finds another, certainly less generalized, type of application which projects local features across that range of the horizontal field. (For a detailed analysis of this phenomenon, see Antokoletz, 1984, pp. 109–125).

The grammatical perspective in its broadest sense, as I've tried to present it here, immediately implies compositional *writing*. This concept has often been raised in articles by young composers in recent years, which is far from surprising. The difficulty posed by this problematic is that sometimes what relates to compositional technique is posited without first raising questions of grammar. It would seem that this oversight has led to systems which were scarcely verified, or in any case hardly verifiable by those to whom the work is addressed. Such techniques on their own can lead to disaster, though when verified with the help of a legible grammar they can produce the very best. Berg can hardly be said to have written within the framework of a strict grammar, but the generative rules that he adopted enabled him to arrive at a very horizontalized compositional approach. In a serial work such as *Kammerkonzert*, the obvious discursive structure is backed by a highly economical elaboration allowing for a progressive unfolding of the series, which are often handled according to discrete areas. Was Berg led along this path by his penchant for symbols? The distinction between series and thematic elements was very clear in his work, more so than in Schoenberg's work; and since in the work in question the names of the Viennese trinity are key words, and since the three letters A, B, and E are shared by the three names and G is found in two of them, the allocation of "areas" suggested itself right from the outset. Moreover, the shared "A" initial of the three first names allowed for a valorization of the octave in a contrapuntal context at a time when that interval was considered highly suspect, to say the least. But perhaps what really enabled Berg to rescue process was the directionality of the compositional technique which he strongly sustained and which permitted broad deployment. Such features are truly those which condition form from the interior, and they can still function as models, whereas Berg's external determining features of form – including those in the *Kammerkonzert* – stem from a neoclassicism which has ceased to concern us.

Yet the event structure also retains its full weight when the evolution of the process is invoked. Bartók and Berg both had, in their major works, a sharp sense of it. In Bartók this manifested itself mainly through the play of contrasting structures with their own internal metric variations. In Berg, it can be seen in the relationship of oppositions between very audible and highly efficient structures, a sort of elaboration in close-up. However, the anecdotal events scattered throughout the work, to stress one of the inventive features of the *Kammerkonzert*, are not heard (such as the "midnight" of the low C# struck by the piano in the second movement, or the unexpected play by the violinist on the open strings of the instrument during the first movement in which the violin doesn't participate, or the waltzing forms of the second variation and the syncopated forms of the third). It should be recalled that, from the position argued here, external, allusive, anecdotal and other such factors appear to belong rather to the domain of content.

In conclusion, one might cavil at the relevance of raising the problem of form at this time. Yet justifications have been put forward: picking up on concerns previously formulated or simply hinted at; the desire to struggle against the crumbling of the musical commonweal; and finally the right to express one's faith in an attainment reached by recent tradition and perhaps too swiftly abandoned. The anesthetizing aggressivity of *avant-gardes,* so violently rejected by Adorno, has unsettled many, as well as facilitating the progress of mediocrity, but theories sometimes prematurely uttered before being durably confirmed by creative output have also played a role. Twenty years ago, Dahlhaus' warning went unheeded; today some symptoms must truly exist so that a comment which was once immediately forgotten now stands out as one of its author's major analytical insights.

Translated from the French by Deke Dusinberre

Notes

1. *Ecriture,* a term currently used extensively in French theoretical articles on music, carries numerous connotations: from the abstract process of representing musical ideas symbolically, to a composer's specific "writing" style to the concrete act of composing a score. Stephen McAdams' translation/ definition of *écriture* suggests that the term broadly conveys "the act and product of notating one's thoughts, as well as a kind of symbolic reasoning. . . ." Since it cannot be adequately translated by a single term in English, it is variously rendered here as "composition", "compositional articulation", "compositional writing" and "compositional technique". [*Translator's note*].
2. The original French title of this article – *De la forme comme expérience vécue* – embodies two slightly diverging meanings. *Vécu* is a fairly common expression referring to "actual experience", whereas *expérience vécue* is an allusion to the Husserlian phenomenological concept rendered in English by Calvin Schrag as "lived experience". In this passage, the author is adopting a certain distance from the phenomenological connotation. [*Translator's note*].

References

Adorno, T.W. (1974) *Théorie esthétique*. M. Jimenez (trans.) Paris: Kincksieck; English trans., C. Lerhardt, *Aesthetic Theory*, Routledge and Kegan Paul, London (1987); 2nd German ed., *Aesthetische Theorie* (1970) Frankfurt aM: Suhrkamp.

Antokoletz, E. (1984) *The Music of Bela Bartok, A Study in Tonality and Progression in Twentieth Century Music*. Berkeley, Los Angeles, London: University of California Press.

Belaval, Y. (1960) *Leibniz critique de Descartes*. Paris: NRF, Gallimard.

Berio, L. (1981) *Intervista sulla musica, a cura di Rossana Dalmonte*. Rome: Bari.

Boulez, P. (1963) *Penser la musique aujourd'hui*. Paris: Gonthier Médiation.

Boulez, P. (1966) *Relevés d'apprenti*. Paris: Seuil.

Boulez, P. (1981) *Points de repère*. Paris: Bourgois/Seuil.

Cunningham, M. (1964) L'art impermanent. *Tel quel*, **18**, 78–80, Paris: Seuil.

Dahlhaus, C. (1982) *Esthetics of Music*. W.W. Austin (trans.), Cambridge University Press.

Dahlhaus, C. (1987) *Schoenberg and the New Music*. D. Puffett & A. Clayton (trans.), Cambridge University Press.

Deliège, C. (1986) *Invention musicale et idéologies*. Paris: Bourgois.

Dusapin, P. (1988) Une filiation problématique. *Entretemps*, **6**, 71–76, Paris, Lattès.

Hegel, G.W.F. (1965) *Esthétique*, tome 8, Paris: Aubier-Montaigne; anonymous trans. from *Sämtliche Werke*, **14**: Aesthetik, W. Glockner (ed.), (1928) Stuttgart: F.R. Fromann.

Husserl, E. (1964) *The Phenomenology on Internal Time-Consciousness*. Bloomington, London: Indiana University Press; trans. by Calvin Schrag from *Vorlesungen zur Phänomenologie des inneren Zeitbewusstseins*, Niemeyer, 1928.

Lévi-Strauss, C. (1960) La structure et la forme, réflexion sur un ouvrage de Vladimir Propp. *Cahiers de science économique appliquée*, **99**, Series M No. 7, 5–36. Paris.

Nattiez, J.J. (1987) *Musicologie générale et sémiologie*. Paris: Bourgois.

Peirce, C.S. (1974) *Collected Papers*. Cambridge, Mass: Harvard University Press.

Rosen, C. (1971) *The Classical Style: Haydn, Mozart, Beethoven*. New York: Norton.

Stockhausen, K. (1953) Situation actuelle du métier de compositeur. *Domaine Musical*, **1**, 126–141, Paris: Grasset.

Stockhausen, K. (1963) *Texte zur elektronischen und instrumentalen Musik*, Band 1. Cologne: Du Mont Schauberg.

Wahl, J. (1957) *Traité de métaphysique*. Paris: Payot.

Contemporary Music Review,
1989, Vol. 4, pp. 117–130
Photocopying permitted by license only

Computer music as cognitive approach:
Simulation, timbre and formal processes

Jean-Baptiste Barrière

IRCAM, 31 rue Saint Merri, F-75004 Paris, France

In this article, I consider timbre to be the set of material/organization interactions leading to the ela-boration of a form. Given this framework, the goal is to formalize constraints through a process of unifying control over these interactions by exploiting the theory of formal systems: composition is con-sidered first as the action of composing symbols, combined into propositions which are mutually generated through the application of inference rules. In addition, the emergence of new structures is explored through materials produced via simulation methodology, in the evolving processes of modeling, hybridization, interpolation, extrapolation, and abstraction. There then arises the question of a theory of references which can describe centripetal and centrifugal elements, controlling and structuring them. The critical and selective process of arriving at discrete structures can be performed in a heuristic fashion as a function of causal determination based on the classic distinction between excitation and resonance modes. In this context, the representation with which (and on which) one can operate becomes a key issue. The ambition is to develop a grammar of formal processes, a morpho-genesis. The conceptual graphs and semantic networks thus developed can be considered as veritable generators of forms, offering control over the trajectories and paths along which musical material can be elaborated, diverted, transformed.

KEY WORDS: Timbre, synthesis, simulation, representation, modeling, hybridization, interpola-tion, hypermorphosis, computer-aided composition.

Introduction

Back in the late 1950s, early pioneers of computer music had the impression that the entire universe of sound was opening up for them: the computer was hence-forth able to synthesize all possible sounds. But strategies for conquering this new, unexplored territory remained to be defined, for without them newly designed maps might eventually be mistaken for the territory itself.

The early years of this long quest were devoted to resolving essentially technological problems such as increasing the speed with which travel took place within this new domain. Sound had to be computed ever quicker in an attempt to approach real time, largely in order to return to a live feed back situation between the production and perception of instrumental performance.

Research in this area produced interesting results as of the mid-1970s, but the battle is still far from over: the goal has constantly receded just when it seemed attainable. For another difficulty emerged at that time, one perhaps with deeper conceptual implications: while all sounds could be synthesized by the computer, they were not all potentially interesting. To the contrary, most resulted in fictive sound objects which remained functionless, outside any network of relationships or musically relevant constraints.

In order to make real progress, a theory was needed. A first step, related to the combinatorial concerns which held center stage in music of that period, involved employing all sorts of abstract mathematical models as formulae for generating sound. While it would be unfair to reject all of the research done at that time, it should nevertheless be acknowledged that most of these approaches tossed the baby out with the bath water: they ignored the fact that our ear is culturally shaped, and at the same time they forgot that creativity should spring from the need to make something meaningful. Overlooking those two factors reduced such approaches to a fruitless, empty game.

Like many other artistic endeavors, composition sometimes seeks pretexts for *getting started*. But when these pretexts take over completely, the quality of the music and of the work in general will suffer. Scientific knowledge, the dominant ideology and obligatory touchstone of our times – purportedly objective – has supplied musicians with a great many such pretexts, right from the beginning of Western musical history. These pretexts usually gravitated toward totalitarian templates, i.e., a form of musical reduction. Even a metaphor can be totalitarian.

At the same time that these primarily technological developments were taking place, a second approach emerged. This could be described as a cognitive approach, in both the classic and contemporary meanings of the term. It was based on an acknowledgement of the fact that musical sound is a complex cultural object which must obey precise and highly structured laws if its validity as musical discourse is to be recognized. Instrumental sounds, for example, are the product of several centuries – indeed, several millenia – of cultural maturation representing the (natural?) selection of certain details at the expense of others, rendering everything meaningful. The cultural ear is fashioned (fastened?) by those unstated constraints which underlie all artistic practice. While one may wish to reject this stratification – this sedimentation – of culture, it is impossible to ignore it totally, since any discourse of rejection situates itself as a reflection – even if in negative – of what it impugns. This leads us to appreciate the idea that every artistic procedure entails an unacknowledged cognitive undertaking: the search for an absent structure, a deep, hidden structure which the artist attempts to disinter, to display, via non-scientific means. Any approach to sound synthesis, then, must be built as an extension of our collective memory, in a dialectical movement between memory and creativity, tradition and invention.

Simulation

It is in this respect that the use of simulation as a methodology for understanding musical phenomena can be justified. As distinct from imitation pure and simple, simulation involves mimesis with the remarkable quality of providing the composer with a whole base of constantly evolving knowledge in the computer, knowledge often left implicit for want of proper tools to *formalize* it. The artist can in turn re-engage this knowledge – thanks to the computer as a powerful formalization tool – reassembling it and putting it back into play, thus trying to enrich it with new meaning, making a new creative contribution.

This approach also tends to reinstate hierarchies and orders of importance within the composition, which sometimes gets shuffled during the cultural process of sedimentation. The totally arbitrary thus gives way to a logic of continuity within the creative process. The artist can in fact, if he or she so wishes, control all stages of the creative process, becoming at once instrument maker, composer, and performer.

This total control over the creative process can, however, lead to a burdensome freedom if the composer isn't prepared for it. It's all too easy to fail to take various consequences into account, to get technologically sidetracked by a tool whose fascinating complexity can become a disastrous mirage, or to try to master an instrument for which one is neither suited nor capable of making truly necessary to a piece. Novelty is never in itself a significant criterion of artistic production, and should not be confused with progress which is a process of accumulation built up from foundations which are constantly reassessed and reconstructed. Making novelty a positive value in itself condemns musical discourse to mercantile sterility: swiftly produced – swiftly consumed.

Composers who, like other artists, turn to the computer, will only take from sound synthesis what they bring to it, finding answers only to those questions previously and correctly raised. There are, of course, special encounters (that is to say, true inspiration) which occur in front of – and only in front of – the instrument. But these are very rare, and generalizations shouldn't be drawn from them.

Sound synthesis is a particularly demanding experience which leaves little room for chance, unless one resorts to the use of prefabricated structures. Synthesis always proceeds from a form of preliminary analysis, including abstract analysis, of the target phenomenon. This might be performed in a heuristic, non-experimental and conceptual manner, or to the contrary in a literal, multi-dimensional and laborious way. What's at stake is the elaboration of models which offer a satisfactory representation of the phenomenon. Satisfactory here means that it is operative, enabling the musician to get a hold of the phenomenon and effectively handle the model.

A process of progressive abstraction can be performed on models thus established, through which the composer can elaborate his or her own discourse. The point of simulation is not the simulated object itself, but its representation, its model – the model as a generator of knowledge concerning the object *under question*. A model's ultimate role includes adaptation by a creative mind and evolution toward other models, a conjugation made possible through the emergence of a grammar which itself is encouraged by simulation methodology.

In the domain of sound synthesis, a fundamental point of reference was speech synthesis. Speech synthesis enjoyed rapid growth compared to other fields such as image or music synthesis, for various reasons: military and industrial requirements, prior systematization of knowledge in the fields of linguistics and phonology, its intimate, even reflexive nature, and finally the relatively reasonable cost of its technological implementation.

It was a useful point of reference on the methodological level particularly through the process of rule-based synthesis, i.e., the organization of knowledge according to rules describing a phenomenon primarily in a declarative way, as a set of relations or constraints.

Subsequent research, notably in acoustics, followed a similar approach in describing physical models of sound production for string instruments, for the piano, and more recently for wind instruments. Sound production is broken down into each of the physical stages which contribute to its perception as an organized entity: how hard the key is pressed, the striking of the hammer, the impact of felt on the string, the string's vibratory modes, the sympathetic resonance of other strings, filtering by the sounding box, the interdependence of all these stages, etc. . . .

Such research offers the composer excellent models, even if it weren't initially geared to problems of artistic creativity. For it defines a synthesis paradigm which obeys what might be called a *continuity hypothesis*. No longer confined to an opposition between tradition and transgression, this hypothesis seeks to maintain links with acquired culture as an ineluctable seedbed of creativity, representing the manifest potential, the transformation, and the extension of accumulated knowledge.

Science rarely encounters art with such fertile results, yet here the two approaches are complementary. Scientists find musicians' formalized (if not explicitly formulated) knowledge extremely useful, because much faster and more efficient than long and fastidious observation of instrument, composer, score or performer. Scientists also have the equivocal satisfaction of finding themselves confronted by a problematic undergoing constant change and evolution. Musicians, on the other hand, benefit from the explicit formulation of their own knowledge, making it accessible in a new, operative form which is both purified and enriched (and to which is added a whole new range of previously unfamiliar knowledge). This establishes a universe of possibilities to be carried out to their logical consequences. Musicians are also constantly challenged by scientific discourse which suggests numerous rich metaphors for artistic creativity.

What's being postulated here is that music can be made using scientific knowledge, and that this change is not as radical as it may appear – musicians have always worked this way, but the knowledge was for the most part implicit (manifested in a poetic, analogic or proscriptive way in treatises, or in a symbolic manner in notation and scores). Today this knowledge is explicit, becoming in a way both more objective and more manipulable.

Simulation is both a *maieutic* and *mimetic* process, meaning that it gives birth to and apprentices musical complexity to the benefit of both researcher and artist. Sound synthesis thus assumes its role as a veritable cognitive approach: research into our knowledge of sound phenomena as well as research into appropriate representations of those phenomena. Representations are considered appropriate in so far as they may eventually legislate relationships between the representations themselves and a potential internal formal language, thus making advances in our understanding of the cognitive system. Sound synthesis can then develop a logic going beyond the game-playing stage of random experimentation. Experimentation must proceed from theory in order to produce results: here again, one usually only finds what one is looking for. Simulation offers theory, methodology and proposed project all at once.

It doesn't offer simple recipes however. It should be pointed out moreover that this approach is still costly in terms of research time and computing power. But it encourages a *heuristic* strategy which structures the creative universe via the computer. In other words, it offers a particularly fertile paradigm for artistic creativity.

Nor should the reality shift which takes place be overlooked, for it implicitly raises the ubiquitous question, characteristic of the late 20th century, of the status of the interaction between the real and the artificial. Creating simulacra forces the question of the true identity of the artificial, which in turn raises questions about the identity of the real. Playing the sorcerer's apprentice certainly has its risks. The question of potential political (or simply criminal) uses of a face or voice which seems only too real can't be dealt with here. It is, however, important to raise strictly artistic questions about this new type of relationship between the real and the artificial.

It seems to me that simulation, as a methodology for formalizing knowledge and subsequently as a medium for artistic creativity, should enable us to get beyond the dilemma posed by the relationship between abstraction and figurative representation by offering a handle on the real which authorizes multiple levels of flight toward the artificial, from simple anamorphosis to total abstraction.

Timbral hybrids, transitions and interpolations

In this respect, one of the most interesting problematics in the field of sound synthesis would seem to involve hybrid models, where properties typical of two or more models are mixed in order to construct a single new entity. Thus what might be called acoustic chimera can be used in composition. The same idea can also be applied across time, in order to obtain timbral transitions or interpolations: the model of a given instrument can be transformed more or less slowly into another "real" (i.e., referential in this context), or completely abstract, model. An axis of timbral variation can thus be defined which begins with modeling and then proceeds through hybridization, interpolation, extrapolation, and finally abstraction.

It's not a question here of an aesthetics of anamorphosis, nor of meta-morphosis, whose special representational status art history has shown to be inevitably limited to a rationale of merely enhancing a given effect. Because simu-lation proceeds from a language describing phenomena and their causality as well as their perception, it permits the emergence of what I call an aesthetics of *hyper-morphosis* involving the search for something beyond form: the constant biologi-cal, metaphysical (in the etymological sense of the term), and metaphorical evolution of form. Its language-like aspect justifies the use of operative knowledge developed in simulation methodology as a medium of artistic creat-ivity, constituting its fundamental originality. Organic metaphors invoked to describe the type of generation and mutation at work stress the ambiguity and destabilizing force of sound thus produced, yet they should not mask the funda-mental difference between hypermorphosis and simple metamorphosis.

The most interesting thing about a genetic/generic mutation is neither its point of departure nor its ultimate destination (just as in simulation the interest lies not in the model as an imitation, but rather in its potential diversions.) Rather, it might be described as the path linking these two points, through various stations, each with its own identity. Thus both the continuous and the discrete underpin this concept; a language cannot be constructed in a pure continuum, for discrete units are required in order for language (and therefore articulation, form and dis-course) to emerge.

Computer music has made work on the material of sound possible, in turn leading to work on timbre, which revolutionizes composition. It is in fact possible today for composers to freely think out their material and shape it according to their musical requirements. These might be based, for example, on the varying needs of a series of compositional contexts, in the manner of renewable, flexible and adaptable instrumentation. But the composer may also want to establish a tighter relationship between sound material and its organization, for example setting up a dialectic between micro, macro and intermediate structures. This prospect is enhanced by the fact that controlling these structures goes hand in hand with working with computers, and is potentially amenable to the same descriptive structures.

The interdependent development of timbral structures and formal processes nevertheless poses complex cognitive problems. Given deadlines and production constraints, composers are often obliged to resort to heuristic strategies instead of an authentically scientific method. This doesn't necessarily compromise the musical results, however, since such results depend largely on a constantly shifting balance of intuition and calculation.

The advantage offered by simulation here is that it functions as a substratum, an approach guaranteeing an unusual degree of coherence. Let us look a little closer at the development of sound objects via progressive stages of extrapolation and abstraction from an instrumental model. The first problem the composer confronts is their constitution as autonomous sound entities, and not only as transformations of a basic model. In fact, while the model usefully supplies reference points guiding both the composer's formal operations and the listener's perception, it should also be noted that the reference model provokes a centripetal effect which tends to obliterate small differences between objects derived from a model by assimilating them to the model itself, or conversely by exaggerating major differences by placing them outside the sphere of the model. What's involved here would seem to relate to a "theory of reference", sadly lacking up to now and increasingly needed; such a theory might in the future become a key area of psychological research in audition.

This problem retreats or vanishes in the context of continuous timbral variation, which plays a primarily expressive rather than formal role (such as timbral ornamentation weaving an aura around a real instrument in mixed electroacoustic and instrumental music, for example). On the other hand, the use of timbre as a constituent medium for formal elaboration, particularly in the case of music for tape alone (that is to say in the absence of an "immediate" referent), almost inevitably requires the recognition of "well-formed" identities which are defined and delimited. This entails interaction between a hierarchy on the one hand, based on the segmentation of a continuum between two or more objects into perceptually significant units, and the work of memory on the other hand. In other words, formal elaboration must be based on a thorough knowledge and mastery of the *tensile-strength of materials* employed, to use an architectural analogy.

A "selective" discretization (almost in the sense of natural selection) of the timbral continuum, made possible thanks to computer synthesis, also helps avoid the impasse to which the composer is sometimes led in arbitrarily building such hybrids and transitions: the situation of operating on found (and at the same time unfindable) objects on which it is hard to get a handle, and which can therefore only be organized as a more or less elegant arrangement of pure juxtapositions, like a catalog.

The highly crucial discretization process can also be handled in a heuristic fashion, based on a causal factor taking into account, for example, the classic acoustic distinction between excitation and resonance modes. This allows the structure of relationships between production and perception to emerge at any given moment. This process is largely compatible, in fact, with mechanisms of perceptual categorization, and thus permits the organization of a virtual timbre space, a topology integrating the ideas of trajectory and directionality essential to formal elaboration.

Using IRCAM's Chant/Formes sound synthesis programming environment, Yves Potard, Pierre-François Baisnée, and myself developed an integral modeling technique based on the analysis of instrumental sounds – mainly of the percussive type – in order to establish a library of timbre models (Baisnée, Potard & Barrière, 1988). These models describe the spectral behavior of the instruments, and can be implemented in such a way as to produce timbral assemblies and/or trajectories: they can be combined or linked to form hybrids, arranged to form interpolations, transformed to produce extrapolations or progressive abstractions.

Such simple or compound models are designed to represent the resonance of an instrument, serving to control banks of filters. Filters can be triggered by an excitation source such as enveloped white noise or digitized concrete sound, or any abstract model given in algorithmic form, as for example physical models of sound production.

This coupling of excitation and resonance can be extended to the coupling of synthesis and processing. With this method, an instrument on stage can become the excitation source for a resonance model of another instrument stored in the computer, (as is done in my piece *Epigénèse*). In practice, any instrument can filter any other, and conversely any instrument can act as exciter for any other.

The original idea behind this approach came from research into simulating a special way of playing wind instruments in which the musician sings into the instrument at the same time as he or she plays it almost normally. An extremely rich hybrid is produced, comprising:

- the normal sound of the instrument
- plus the sound of the human hum filtered by the tubing (the instrument's resonances),
- further enriched by a phenomenon of amplitude modulation of the two corresponding spectra, which produces a third, highly heterogeneous spectrum (resulting from the sum and the difference of their respective partials).

For me, this way of playing functioned as a real metaphor for the idea of a timbral hybrid. With the technique we developed, it is now possible to imagine infinite variations on this model. I notably reversed the prototype situation and filtered the sound of a wind instrument through the resonances of vocal phonemes. The results produced are astonishing from a perceptual point of view, although most often recognizable only in so far as the causal mechanism is justified or introduced, i.e., more or less explained by a formal mechanism. For instance, if the sound of the wind instrument filtered by voice follows the playing of voice through wind instrument, the causal connection is obvious. Of course the opposite may be desired, that is to say surprise, in which case playing these two in reverse order would allow an *a posteriori* explanation of the connection to emerge from the creative participation of the listener's memory.

Timbral interpolations using this technique raise the discretization problems mentioned above. Here work on short-term memory is essential. The temporal proximity of the model to its derivatives is indispensible – through re-presentation effects, for instance – to enable the memory to regularly resituate the different variations stemming from the model(s) between which interpolation takes place. The temporal distance between the model and its derivatives can provoke perceptual non-recognition or assimilation to a poor image of the model, having a destructive effect from a formal standpoint. What the listener hears is a poor imitation and not progressive derivatives based on a reference model (nor is the vector leading from one model to another perceived). There is always the risk of creating a halo – a zone of uncertainty – around a model, or the risk that the interpolation trajectory between two models is nothing more than a desperate leap from one fuzzy image to another. Interpolation can thus no longer function as a formal device but remains a mere effect of "color".

In mixed electroacoustic-instrumental music, this risk can be avoided by repetition of the original and the model. More generally, there could be a play on repetition and difference between two models, or between the original and a progressive series of models matched element by element, alternately near and then far away. The difficulty, indeed the impossibility of considering here a polytimbral, not to mention polyphonic, interpolation should be noted: it is almost impossible to distinguish more than two timbral interpolations simultaneously, and it is all the more difficult to follow polyphony under similar conditions.

Extrapolation and abstraction raise similar problems concerning proximity or distance in relation to the reference model, as well as of course the competing parallel existence of various processes. These are less crucial, however, in so far as here the formal vector is less specifically directional (because it is a question of starting from a model in order to clearly distance oneself, potentially detaching oneself entirely, completely forgetting the reference model). Extrapolation and abstraction techniques are by definition infinite, since it is no longer necessary to stick with the reference object. Total freedom is possible, but once again it is perception which in the last analysis will arbitrate via complex coding/decoding of the structure by perceptual and cognitive processes.

I myself decided to transpose part of the simulation approach into this domain, too, rather than strictly apply abstract formulas. For example, I placed abstract algorithms on models which were not directly derived from a strict detailed analysis of the way an instrument functions, but rather were superficial and simplified representations of the concept behind such functioning. Thus I applied, for instance, a "cymbalization" algorithm to various instrumental and vocal models, retranscribing in an imaginary and inevitably reductive way the idea of what happens spectrally within a cymbal sound. The resulting "cymbalized" choir or tuba is not a hybrid since two models are not cross-bred, nor is the formula applied to the model designed to be recognized as an "instrument". It is rather a question of an extrapolation since what is perceived is the modulated model which is more or less recognizable according to the extent of application of the formula; the model is drawn, as it were, towards a mysterious, evanescent and fleeting otherness, an absence of specific identity.

Any acoustic phenomenon can thus be used as metaphor or trigger. By way of example, I've modulated various models through:

– amplitude modulation observed in the complex method of playing mentioned above,
– spectral enrichment formulas corresponding to a brassy effect,

- spectral envelope deformations corresponding to the observation of vocal phonemes,
- and even a formula found in the acoustic literature describing the behavior of square metal plate resonators.

Freedom is even greater in the field of abstractions. One idea, among others, involves using Ernst Terhardt's alorithm for detecting spectral pitch in a complex timbre to extract those pitches endowed with the most perceptual weight and therefore of most import (Terhardt, Stoll & Seewann, 1982), in order to literally abstract the most significant harmonic information from the model. The completely abstract model thus elaborated will subsequently assume a life of its own, undergoing the same specific transformations, totally detached from the original model, remaining linked only through memory and ongoing formal elaboration. Kaija Saariaho, for example, used this technique on double bass sounds in *Io*, a mixed electroacoustic-instrumental piece. Another abstraction process involves chain filtering different models, or even rendering them progessively inharmonic until their intitial constituent identities are completely lost.

Such timbral operations lead to preconstrained formal compositional techniques that are based mainly on patterns of opposition which some may find too simplistic and linear. I don't feel that this is the case, however, for it is entirely possible to build elaborate and complex forms with oppositional systems and with gradual progression between two extremes. After all, it is simply a question of restoring hierarchies, systems of tension/release based on new factors (Saariaho, 1987). Musical experience has already proven – and will continue to prove, as mastery over the phenomenon is gained – that constraints thus expressed do not fundamentally differ from those encountered in conventional orchestration and composition. Rather, they extend them, though we lack enough experience to completely rationalize them at present.

In comparison, it will be noted that conventional orchestration remains at the same time extremely empirical. I will advance the hypothesis that simulation, thanks to the new perspective it affords, will have a significant impact on the development of more rational and satisfactory attitudes to orchestration. A system of computer-aided composition, for instance, should include sophisticated orchestration functionalities which will only be truly efficient if they are implemented with tools derived from simulation rather than simply through sparse sampling of the orchestral ensemble. The difference here lies precisely in the cognitive nature of simulation, which doesn't merely provide composers with a pure and simple replica of the reference object, but rather offers them an evolving body of knowledge on that object.

From a heuristic standpoint, this is a highly powerful method because it can easily and intuitively generate families of complex and living sounds, which in the context of a mixed piece can fuse remarkably well with the instrumental sounds from which they spring, yet can also evolve independently thanks to a rich palette of transformational possibilities. In fact, it is easy to produce a complete palette of sound colors with this technique, from total heterogeneity to complete fusion of synthesized material and real instruments on stage.

It should be stressed that the reason which led to coherence within sound synthesis through simulation is the same one governing an external coherence between synthesis and instrumental composition. Generally, it would seem that this approach offers a new and constructive perspective on orchestration, based on a reinterpretation of the perception of resonance and its role in composition technique. Which is why it is of particular interest to composers specifically concerned with the relationship between timbre and harmony (cf. Saariaho, 1987; Dalbavie, in press).

Moreover, nothing prevents a multitude of bases of description/variation from becoming so many dimensions or relationships on which formal structure can be elaborated. This requires only that the stages stemming from the discretization process, in the case of timbral interpolations for example, be hierarchized among themselves and finally validated perceptually.

Material/organization interactions: Computer-aided composition

Through this approach, timbre progressively constitutes itself as the set of dynamic material/organization interactions which enable a form to be elaborated. With this in mind, I tried to formalize constraints through a process of unifying control over interactions between materials and ways of organizing them, by using the theory of formal systems. Composition is thus first considered as the action of composing symbols which group themselves into propositions, statements or phrases, which mutually generate one another through the application of rules of inference.

The main problem then becomes that of the representation with which (and on which) one can operate. I used the theory of conceptual graphs to model musical concepts and relationships with which I wanted to work. "Conceptual graphs form a knowledge representation language based on linguistics, psychology, and philosophy. In the graphs, concept nodes represent entities, attributes, states and events and relation nodes show how the concepts are interconnected" (Sowa, 1984, p. 69).

Based on these conceptual graphs, I developed semantic networks: "the collection of all the relationships that concepts have to other concepts, to percepts, to procedures . . ." (Sowa, 1984).

Form was then built up step by step as a type of bi-polarization, a search for opposites (and their potential resolution) through elaborating or borrowing elements from a library, creating perpetual movement between:

- the choice of one or several materials (i.e., simple or compound models, etc.)
- the definition of interactions (i.e., conceptual relationships, rules etc.)
- the definition of paths (i.e., directionalities, trajectories, such as interpolations, extrapolations, abstractions)
- the definition of contexts (i.e., "scenes" which constitute the different parts of the piece)
- instantiations of variables (at all levels, e.g., various parameters for form and synthesis).

My goal here, which I began to sketch out in *Chréode* (Barrière, 1984), is to produce a grammar of formal processes, a morphogenesis. The semantic networks thus generated can be considered true generators of form because they lead to the control of trajectories, the paths by which the musical material will be elaborated, shifted, transformed.

Obviously, I don't claim that this formalization process in any way guarantees or validates the musical quality of the resulting material. I nevertheless think this process can be extremely fertile in the field of computer-aided composition, especially in compositional contexts which integrate synthesized material requiring a great number of control parameters, although it could also be useful in a pure instrumental context.

I am progressively attempting to integrate all the various aspects of composition (representing distinct functionalities at the levels of practice and tradition) into a single, continuum-like system of conceptual control:

- conceptual tools used to elaborate musical ideas (literally the forms of the piece),
- analytical tools used to elaborate models based on simple or complex instrumental sounds,
- which then undergo operations performed by the various functions in the *Esquisse* composition environment at IRCAM by P.F. Baisnée and a group of composers (Baisnée, Barrière, Dalbavie, Lindberg & Saariaho, 1988), and
- to subsequently control synthesis and/or processing.

This desire to unify the entire compositional space (starting from conventional musical categories, the conceptual environment, including metaphorical work with its visual and psychological – indeed, dramatic, etc. – analogies, extending up to the parameters controlling every detail of synthesis) corresponds to both the practical necessity of managing such complexity, and the wish to implement a compositional logic which is all-embracing and synoptic.

Despite – or rather because of – this project of formalization, I think that an extremely pragmatic attitude should be adopted when it finally comes time to move from experimentation to musical production: just as the research and development stage requires a radical rigor which attempts to model the composition in every aspect, so the final composition stage demands a freedom of movement uninhibited by any formal constraint. I would therefore argue that a computer-aided composition system should retain the basic function of random access to free will, restoring the possibility of expressing that part of intuition which remains (provisionally?) non-formalized. A very simple way of fulfilling this need involves integrating a good text editor for musical representation into a compositional environment. In a more systematic way, a computer-aided composition set-up which includes grammatical mechanisms must be able to handle exceptions satisfactorily. Systems of compositional constraints should thus be harmonized on global and local levels, for example through re-write rule systems, provided that they're context-sensitive and can at all times be modified by a system of priorities.

At a later stage it is also important to be able to benefit from automatic learning systems which "track" this fundamental phase of composition and suggest models which themselves become available to abstract manipulation by the composer, making conscious certain intuitive operations and transferring them into the realms of computation.

The long term goal is to make all conceptual operations in the compositional process explicit and accessible in an efficient representational form, that is to say at once economical (just the information relevant to the processing of specific musical material), comprehensive, and operational.

More than just a sophisticated problem of notation, this issue seems to me to be the most important one currently facing computer music, along with the big wager riding on the encounter between music and the cognitive sciences, which could be described as an effort to further extend *compositional artifice ("artifice d'écriture en musique"*, Dufourt, 1981). The implications of research in this area specifically involve composition yet also concern performance, analysis, and perhaps even more so those fields of the cognitive sciences interested in the processing of mental representations.

The choice of a system of representation can never be innocent or neutral: musical thought must be able to take whatever shortcuts are necessary. This places both material and cognitive issues at stake: attempting to find representations appropriate to compositional operations also means uncovering clues to related processes.

Musical notation could be thought of as an instrument used to move from metaphor – from the symbolic – to control. This is especially true of computer music where, as opposed to the world of instrumental music and standard notation, the score can be both production code (i.e., for composition) and execution code (i.e., performance). During the early decades of computer music, compositional artifice moved progressively toward synthesis, via the computer, and consequently the notation of control of sound production. Synthetic and operational symbolic representations of these phenomena have yet to replace explicitly numeric and algorithmic representations. Today, however, and in the years to come, the major challenge would seem to be to extend this artifice to conceptual structures which underlie and guide compositional activity, as well as the search for representations ever more appropriate to formalization and manipulation.

For example, exploring the question of whether music is "special" in the sense that Fodor uses the term (cf. Peretz & Morais, this volume) – that is to say whether it benefits from a special neural processing module – would seem to be perfectly feasible given the fertile soil of experimental investigation undertaken in this direction. It is also perhaps one of the rare problematics where scientists' and composers' efforts can truly progress in parallel, because both work on exactly the same types of representation.

Conclusion

The hypothesis of a continuum subtends this entire approach: a continuum between everyday real-life experience and culturally sedimented experience, a continuum between musical intuition and mental representations, between systems of production and perception, a continuum of referents across different media, a continuum between sound synthesis, processing, instruments – in short a continuum between various categories which are constantly reassessed along an axis leading from the natural to the artificial.

The use of computers in musical composition, beyond mere sound synthesis, raises other acute cognitive problems, as has been pointed out. Though research into computer-aided composition historically preceded research into synthesis this former field of investigation is still relatively immature. The reason for this lag is due to the impoverishment of approaches attempted to date, linked to the lack of experts involved in this field, not to mention inadequate technological resources. The same bent which exists in computer sciences in general, from the computational toward the symbolic, exists in computer music: while synthesis basically involves problems of signal processing which are now being mastered, composition is more amenable to artificial intelligence techniques which remain poorly developed.

This computer-aided composition calls into play a whole sophisticated problematic, including the development and handling of multiple representations – notably graphic – of musical structures. Here again the issue of research first of all involves restoring the fundamental complexity and flexibility of the composer's conceptual environment – once again justifying a simulation approach – before being able to offer new possibilities. This issue represents another challenge for scientists who increasingly realize the extent to which the musical field is a fertile one for high-level research, especially in the areas of computer technology, artificial intelligence, psychoacoustics, and the sciences of the mind.

No doubt research in years to come will be devoted to these rich yet complex aspects related to the description of high-level music-organizational phenomena (rather than sound production which, as pointed out, has been largely mastered), as well as their perception/reception, the former being hierarchically superior to the latter, thus structuring and encompassing them.

Are we equipped today to correctly raise all the theoretical and practical questions on which this new aesthetic dimension will be built? How can the experience of some best profit others, that is to say how can we accumulate knowledge in a creative way, particularly in the context of interdisciplinary exchanges between scientists and musicians? How can we get beyond the frustrating stage of technological tinkering to finally arrive at a true, serious professionalism without however rejecting values of experimentation and speculation? How can we encourage veritable transdisciplinary exchanges which are more than battles between cliques over turf, struggles for power? How can we avoid ideology, positivism, irrationalism and make this new field a living laboratory for artistic and scientific ideas? All these questions deserve consideration.

It is unfortunately the case that people in many artistic fields employing computers continue to make the same perpetual mistakes. A lot could be said about the scientific-technocratic tendency which tries to deprive artists of their creative status to the benefit of an equivocal yet domineering technological discourse claiming to encompass and surpass artistic practice. The grandiloquent naiveté and incompetence of these cads are matched only by their pretentiousness and their power to block things. It wouldn't matter much except that on the one hand irresponsible scientists waste their time by spoiling important research and displaying a regal contempt for the naiveté of composers, and on the other hand technocrats try all too often to block artists' access to research and production facilities. Obviously, in the final analysis artists are responsible for their fate, and it is up to them to obtain, indeed to build, their own instruments. It might be regretted, though, that so few artists call for this loud and clear, just as their often timid and paradoxically conservative attitude could be regretted, along with their poor degree of involvement in, indeed motivation for, this type of research. Though it is true that the situation is hardly designed to encourage them.

Yet there are potential solutions to this political and sociological malaise. On the one hand the extraordinary development of personal computer systems will progressively enable artists to resolve their own problems through a new appropriation and progressive mastery of the production tool, without having to rely on institutions rendered sterile by technocrats on the lookout for a little spiritual uplift for their own benefit. On the other hand, it is probable that a new generation of composers will emerge with a real scientific background as well as scientists having real musical training, which allows us to envisage true interdisciplinary research once the sterilizing cleavage wrought by our overspecialized society has been healed.

But this new movement should not be allowed to mask and hinder what could be a renewed role for institutions confronted with such developments to centralize issues concerning research and creativity in order to decentralize solutions; to think through, elaborate and promote relay structures capable of taking over development and dissemination of knowledge now required of musical creativity undergoing transformation and renewal; and finally to create meeting places for scientists and artists which allow them to develop that notorious "shared language" to which Pierre Boulez referred when IRCAM was founded, and which remains the condition for the long hoped-for consummation of the encounter between art and science.

Translated from the French by Deke Dusinberre

References

Baisnée, P.F., Barrière, J.B., Dalbavie, M.A., Lindberg, M. & Saariaho, K. (1988) Esquisses: A compositional environment. *Proceedings of the International Computer Music Conference 1988, Cologne*, San Francisco: Computer Music Association.

Baisnée, P.F., Potard, Y. & Barrière, J.B. (in press) Modèles de résonance pour l'élaboration et le contrôle de structures de timbre. In *Le timbre: Métaphores pour la composition*, J.B. Barrière (ed), Paris: Editions Christian Bourgois.

Barrière, J.B. (1984) *Chréode I:* A pathway to new music with the computer. In "Musical Thought at IRCAM", Tod Machover (ed) *Contemporary Music Review*, **1(1)**, 181–201. London: Harwood Academic Publishers.

Barrière, J.B. (1987) Mutations du matériau, mutation de l'écriture. *InHarmoniques* 1, 118–124.

Dalbavie, M.A. (in press) Pour en finir avec la modernité. In *Le timbre: Métaphores pour la composition*, J.B. Barrière (ed.), Paris: Editions Christian Bourgois.

Dufourt, H. (1981) L'artifice d'écriture dans la musique occidentale. *Critique*, **408**, 465–478.

Saariaho, K. (1987) Timbre and harmony: Interpolations of timbral structures. In "Music and Psychology: A Mutual Regard," S. McAdams (ed), *Contemporary Music Review*, **2(1)**, 93–133. London: Harwood Academic Publishers.

Sowa, J.F. (1984) *Conceptual Structures: Information Processing in Mind and Machines.* Reading, Mass: Addison-Wesley.

Terhardt, E., Stoll, G. & Seewann, M. (1982) Algorithm for extraction of pitch and pitch salience from complex tonal signals. *Journal of the Acoustical Society of America*, **71**, 679–688.

Contemporary Music Review,
1989, Vol. 4, pp. 131–163
Photocopying permitted by license only

Musical information organisms:
An approach to composition

Marco Stroppa

IRCAM, 31, rue St. Merri, F-75004 Paris, France

This text is the beginning of a formalized reflection on some poetic aspects of my present compositional world. After a brief survey of our historical background, a general conceptual framework,
inspired by research in knowledge representation and categorization, is established. Using two complementary representational systems, I develop a microworld paradigm, the paradigm which first
sparks my imagination. Higher-level musical structures, considered as evolving societies in morphological spaces, are then examined, including the overall form of a piece. Excerpts from my own
work are analyzed in terms of the writing techniques which are adopted. Finally, a few extensions to
this compositional approach are succinctly discussed, together with some of the consequences that
challenge traditional perception, analysis, performance, and interpretation.

KEY WORDS: Concept, *écriture*, knowledge representation, language, metaphor, morphology,
poetics, similarity, society.

The context

We live in a musical age where common languages and common models no longer
exist. One of the most immediate consequences is that an analysis of a piece of
contemporary music requires the invention of a new model which describes some
aspects of that specific piece. In spite of its intellectual interest, this attitude is
often too passive from a composer's perspective. The model often has to be built
on the visible surface of a piece, does not necessarily correspond to the composer's creative process, and can rarely be reused.

However, an analysis might point to some abstract compositional principles
which could be adopted to generate a piece. It is not important then that these
principles correspond to the ones that the composer followed. Indeed, this will
not generally be the case. But they can be used – as a metaphor or as a technique
– to generate new music. Such an analysis yields a way of exploring a compositional world.

This text is the beginning of a formalized reflection on some characteristics of
my own musical world, in terms of the abstract writing techniques which have
given rise to a particular compositional system. It is not my aim to provide at
present an exhaustive picture of my current poetics: a more elaborate description
of it will be discussed in future works. The main conceptual effort had to be an
inductive one, since it was applied to a set of pieces which had already been completed. It was in the attempt to account for intuitive work of my imagination that
I suddenly saw more sharply into some of the inner principles that spurred the
growth of my musical thought.

The first clues of a different poetic direction can be traced in a short orchestral piece, *Metabolai*, written in 1982. Some of the writing techniques described in this article were already used there in an intuitive and somewhat simplistic way. In *Traiettoria* for piano and computer-generated sounds, a cycle of three works (*Traiettoria ...deviata, Dialoghi, Contrasti*) which followed *Metabolai*, the experiments became more accurate and their use more conscious: proof of an emerging compositional system[1]. *Contrasti* in fact, represents the first conscious use of such a system and therefore provides an ideal field from which to draw most of the examples analyzed here.

Defining a new compositional system entails establishing a general conceptual framework suited to the specific compositional process. Within this framework, one or more representational systems, together with some operative methodologies, can be specified. At this stage, the choice of appropriate representation(s) is critical, because of the consequences it will have on any further developments. I will employ two complementary representations to describe a compositional system used to analyze various musical examples. As a composer, I will mainly take a creative and poetic perspective and focus on the system's influence on musical composition.

A survey

The Historical Context

Let us imagine, for a moment, that we are listening to Beethoven's *Archduke Trio*, with its gentle, almost Schubertian initial melody, carefully arranged above a calm accompaniment and barely wrinkled by a final crescendo and two fleeting trills. If we wonder how to analyze what we are hearing and ask the same question of various people from different backgrounds, the range of answers we would get is enormous. If they tell us something about the way (rather, the ways) people perceive, represent, and think about music they will probably be either too vague or too analytical, that is, either not specific enough or too narrowly concentrated on isolated musical dimensions. A very important feature might still remain unaccounted for: if, for instance, the whole first theme is considered as a unique stimulus, how then can our perception relate to it? This stimulus must be seen from another perspective, as a complex element made of simpler parts whose interactions give it a certain, easily perceivable character or identity. Each part roughly corresponds to a classic dimension and does not have the same perceptual relevance with respect to the stimulus as a whole: some dimensions will be more important, other ones less so.

If we develop this perspective a little more formally, we suddenly realize that there are no tools in traditional music theory to help us cope with it: no ways to represent it adequately, no operators available to pursue it further. How to describe, for instance, the relationship between the whole first theme of a sonata-form and its development section? Is it possible to perceive which parts of it are developed? Does the theme's identity stay the same or is it transformed into something else? How are these transformations related to the global structure of the piece? If some kind of relationship is effectively grasped, this implies that long-term memory has been involved, because of the temporal distance separating the two episodes. Since information is stored in long-term memory mainly on a semantic base, some structural, or, to use a personal term, some identity-based encoding of the material must have occurred. How can a composer represent and control it directly?

A Poetic Standpoint

If a better description of the approach that has just been put forward could be imagined, then a compositional technique might be derived and exploited. The first step is to find an adequate framework, a framework with a positive, generative quality, which can be directly related to the act of composing, that is, to symbolic writing, and not only to the auditory surface. Which is the best paradigm to tackle this kind of musical behavior?

Summarizing its most hard-to-represent characteristics, we have to take into account the issue of *definition*: the parts a complex musical element is made of are difficult to specify, quantify, and enumerate, and may be irrelevant under certain conditions. Their importance also varies according to the current context. A tempting strategy would be to consider them as "musical chunks", thus establishing a direct reference to short-term memory needs as far as complexity, size, number, and encoding strategies are concerned.

Another issue is *abstraction*: the behavior of a musical element has an identity which cannot be totally explained by the mere presence of its actual components, since it may not be affected by the change of some of them.[2] The real perception of this identity varies along a continuum and is a complex function of personal, cultural, historical and contextual factors. Their mutual influence, probably the most thorny issue to understand for someone who has never composed, is usually dealt with intuitively by musicians, and is virtually impossible to quantify satisfactorily.

A final issue is *similarity* how to describe the fact that many different elements may be an instance of the same identity, and are therefore similar? Tversky's *contrast model* has shown that the notion of similary is asymmetric, directional and can be biased by the differential availability of examples (Tversky & Gati, 1978). What is the role of attention and of such visual cues as the analysis of a score on the perception of an identity? Can one envisage something like linguistic "hedges" in the auditory world? Will an expression like "loosely hearing" ever make sense?

An Appropriate Framework

When I started looking at music in this way, I groped after some conceptual help in classic music theory, but unsuccessfully. Context-dependent behavior, for instance, was at best tacitly accounted for, but never dealt with explicitly. It was only some scientific ideas that provided me with the correct terms and a satisfactory framework to think about it. A close correspondence will then be found between the questions raised by my own complex musical stimuli and some issues tackled both by knowledge representation in artificial intelligence and by research on categorization in cognitive psychology. Explicit references to these areas will be given throughout this text.

Musical Information Organisms: The microworld paradigm

The *basic level* (as defined in Rosch, Mervis, Gray, Johnson & Boys-Braem, 1976) of composition, the level which first sparks my imagination, is not the development of pre-compositional material, like pitch relations, or any kind of work on single dimensions, but the birth of a *Musical Information Organism* (or OIM, from the Italian - *Organismo di Informazione Musicale*).

The term "organism" is used in a technical and formal way to refer to a complex and dynamic entity whose evolution cannot be described or predicted by synthetic rules (such as analytical functions, stochastic processes, deterministic or combinatorial procedures[3]). An organism is something active and consists of several *components* and *properties*[4] of varying complexity, maintaining certain *relationships* and giving rise to a particular *form* . Its *identity* is a cognitive representation of such a form. An OIM has a well-defined *life-span:* it comes into existence, develops, and fades away after some time. Its *evolution* is usually guided by a plan and is goal-oriented: it starts at some point and reaches a goal following various trajectories. The perception of the form of the trajectory is at least as important as the perception of the form of a single organism. Two apparently similar organisms can still be discriminated if they belong to two different trajectories. This mobile network of cross-references produces a complex *microscopic society* within a single OIM. However, this internal activity is perceived or dealt with non-analytically, as a whole. An OIM's identity is undoubtedly related to this holistic aspect as well as to various other factors, such as a particular behavior, a prominent attribute, an emerging relationship, a special musical figure, or an outstanding instrumental gesture.

An OIM's attributes or relationships are not of equal importance. They have different time-variant *weights* which are connected to perceptual or structural relevance. Perception and composition, on the other hand, are not automatically related: a component can be given more weight because of its structural relief, even if it is hard to perceive. Since the weight is also a measure of a component's contribution to the OIM's overall identity, it affects the choice and the use of a particular writing technique. A first, general rule is that the lower the weight, the more dramatically a component can be modified without influencing the identity, whereas the higher the weight, the more exposed and sensitive to small changes a component becomes, demanding a much more refined technique (see the notion of "family resemblance score" in Rosch & Mervis, 1975). During analysis or composition, it seems pointless to use an extremely sensitive technique for low-weight attributes, unless this is motivated by other structural reasons. Modifications applied to high-weight components or properties tend to have a structural significance: they might weaken an OIM's identity, change its place within the existing context, be a sign of a major formal change, and so on. Modifications applied to low-weight components or properties are more often due to local conditions and do not usually affect the global context.

A Complementary Representation: Energy Fields and Morphological Spaces

The representation of an OIM as an active element is best suited to describe the micro-structural characteristics of single instances. This corresponds approximately to the level of musical material. However, when dealing with macroscopic, context-dependent properties – which play an important role at a higher formal level – as well as with the mutual interactions among several OIMs, this paradigm is insufficient. Another representation must then be used. Some means to pass from one to the other also need to be specified.

If the weight of a single property is seen as a measure of some *energy* radiating from it, and that we concentrate on this energetic aspect, then the overall strength of an OIM's identity will correspond to the total energy that results from the interactions of all its components' energies. From this perspective, the total energy generates a *field* around an OIM. Since each property's energy is varying and different from the others, the field will be stronger in the directions corresponding to heavy components, and weaker in the lighter ones. The field's main attributes are its *morphology* and its *identity*. The former is related to the concept of form defined earier, whereas the latter can be seen only from this viewpoint.

An energy-radiating OIM projects its action away from its core towards neighboring fields. The stage where all these fields interact, in other words, the musical context itself, is a *morphological space* with its own structure and constraints. As we will see, describing the evolution of such a space is one of the possible ways to deal with the issue of form in a piece.[5]

An Example: Static Identity

Let us now turn to a real OIM, the one starting the piano solo cadenza of *Contrasti*. It's final form is presented in Figure 8. A first, essential remark is that it is very pianistic and has a particularly strong sound identity attached to it. In fact, all the OIMs used in *Contrasti* are highly influenced by specific instrumental gestures.

If we emphasize only the most salient components (Fig. 1), the OIM can be divided into three parts:
a) *head*, made of a relatively long note (usually an accented chord), followed by two short repeated notes (usually less dense chords) in a different register of the instrument.
b) *middle part*, ascending pattern which uses a slightly extended version of the pianistic technique of alternate hands.
c) *joint*, composed of some flexible material that can be easily "bent" so as to fit whatever comes next. Because of its dependence on the context, it cannot be further specified at this stage.

By applying what has been worked out so far, it is fairly straightforward to analyze most properties of the present OIM and to recognize and learn the main aspects of its identity. However, it is only the *static identity* which is referred to here, that is, what can be inferred from just one instance of an OIM. Before being able to analyze its *dynamic identity* which derives from the behavioral properties of a class of OIMs, some writing techniques appropriate to this level need to be introduced.

Some Writing Techniques

The musical elements to which these techniques are applied are:
1) *Single items.* They span from traditional dimensions (such as a note, a duration,

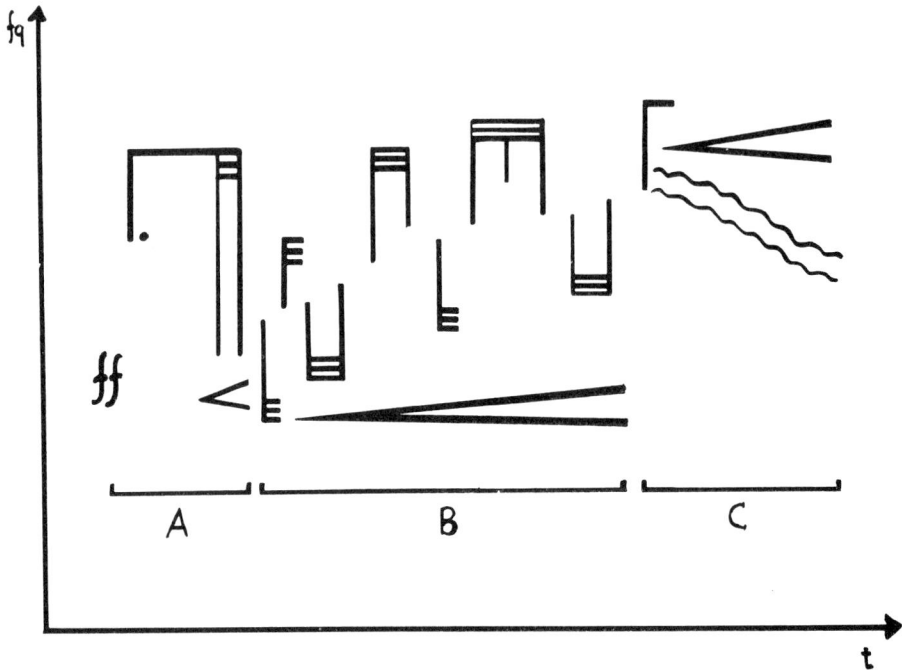

Figure 1 Synthetic view of *Contrasti*'s first OIM (A: head; B: middle part; C: joint).

an amplitude, an instrument's register, etc.), which have little or no identity, to single properties with their own micro-identity, and finally to single relations between dimensions and/or properties.

2) *Sets of items.* This is a collection of single items of any kind, size and order, which yields a unique pattern. Examples of sets are: a crescendo (a set of amplitudes), a musical figure, a chord, a special rhythm, and so on.

3) *Space.* This is the distance between two or more items or sets of items.

4) *Direction.* It refers to the evolution of a set of items and is represented as a vector with a certain magnitude.

5) *Energy.* This is a way to deal with the global force of a certain pattern, independently of how it is distributed and is computed by taking into account the weights of all the OIM's properties.

When one or several simultaneous techniques emphasize the same aspect of a given item, they are said to be *coherent* with respect to it. Otherwise, they are said to be *incoherent*. A coherent behavior has a particuarly strong perceptual relevance.

Defocusing

This technique consists in altering the sharpness of a given item, that is in putting it out of focus. One must distinguish the kind of item that is defocused from those that are used for defocusing. Figure 2 presents a few applications on an idealized note or chord. It is crucial to realize that the overall effect should be considered and played as a whole. It is still a single item which has gone out of focus,

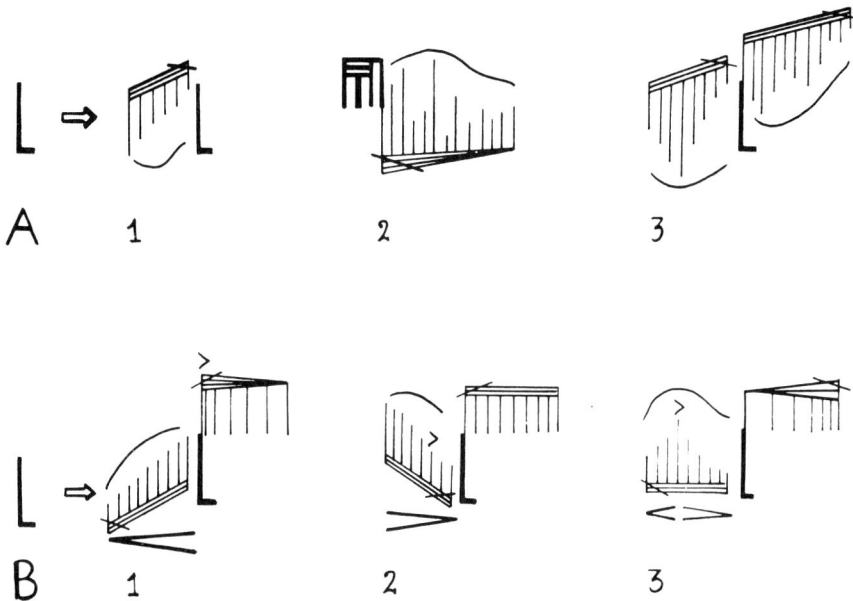

Figure 2 Defocusing Technique. A: simple cases. 1 = smooth up-beat arpeggio; 2 = smooth up-beat rhythmical anacrusis similar to remultiplication + rough down-beat melodic structure; 3 = smooth up-and down-beat melodic structure. The second structure repeats the pattern of the first one twice, with an upward melodic trajectory. B: example of coherent and incoherent use of a melodic structure (MS), a dynamic change (DC), an accent (ACC) and a rhythmical inflection (RI). 1 = all coherent; 2 = MS/DC coherent, ACC incoherent, RI neutral; 3 = MS/DC/ACC coherent, RI incoherent.

it is not a set of items!

To understand a simple use of coherence vs. incoherence, the case of Figure 2b should be studied in detail. A dynamic accent, a dynamic change, a fast melodic figure and a rhythmical inflection are used simultaneously. An accent is a source of energy coming from one point with a single value at any given time, while a dynamic change is a source of energy spread over a certain time and evolving within a certain range of intensities. The melodic figure has a smooth contour with a single highest point, where most of the energy is concentrated. Its evolution is always correlated with the dynamic change: higher pitches correspond to louder dynamics and so on. The energy of the final inflection is controlled by the speed of repetition of each element: accelerando (increase of energy), decelerando (decrease of energy) or no change (equally spread energy). Each component then, modulates energy by concentrating it in a certain temporal region, with different degrees of strength and sharpness. When acting on the amount of overlap of these regions, their energies can be made to converge or diverge at will.

A discretized variant of this technique is *remultiplication,* in which an item is blurred by modulated repetition. Among the various control parameters, the *duration, rate* and *regularity of the repetitions,* as well as the *arrangement* of the *anchor points* ought to be mentioned. A rough sketch of some cases of remultiplication of the second half of the head of our target OIM is shown in Figure 3.

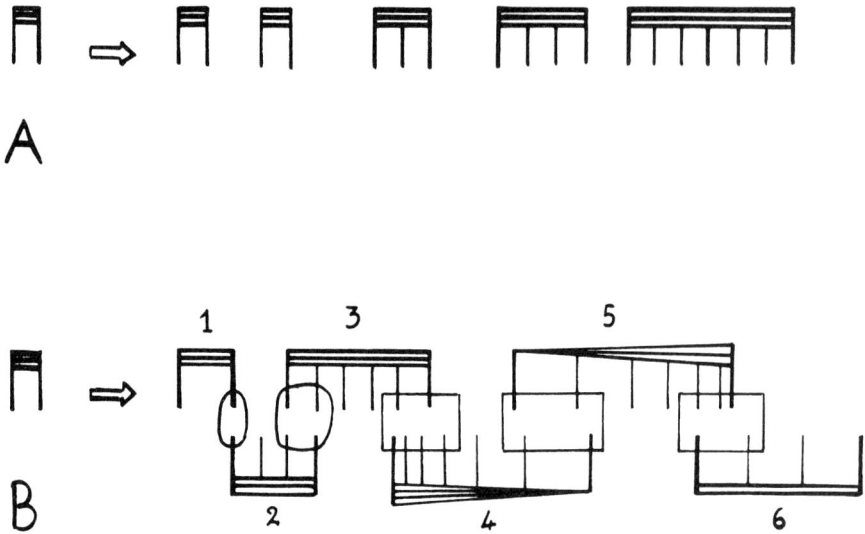

Figure 3 Remultiplication. A: separated remultiplication with five regular, fast repetitions. The distance between repetitions increases and decreases smoothly, the number of repeated notes increases smoothly at first and abruptly at the end. B: remultiplication with six overlapping repetitions and five variable anchor regions (circles = synchronous superpositions, rectangles = asynchronous superpositions). 1 to 3 are regular, fast repetitions with an increasing number of notes, 4 and 5 are smoothly accelerated and decelerated repetitions with the same number of notes, 6 is a short, regular and slow repetition.

Space filling and stretching
The space between items or sets of items can be filled in several different ways. As above, one has to distinguish between the nature of the items which delimit the space, the nature of the items which are employed to fill such space and the nature of the space itself. Some examples of a temporal space bounded by the two main components of the head of the OIM of Figure 2 and filled by various kinds of items are presented in Figure 8 (nos. 8, 11-14, 17). It is worth noting that the action of a certain technique can be considerably reinforced by profiting from the inherent limits of the instrument and/or the performer. For instance, a simple recombination of the order of presentation of the notes in a musical figure may transform it from a very natural one to play, to a nasty, awkward one. The smoothness of the final outcome will therefore be affected in ways which eventually depend on the performer.

The space can also be overfilled, so that no human being can play or perceive it without stretching the items which frame it. A *space filler* can be easily turned into a *space stretcher* by simply increasing the number of its components or the complexity of their behavior (see, for example, Fig. 8a, nos. 13-14).

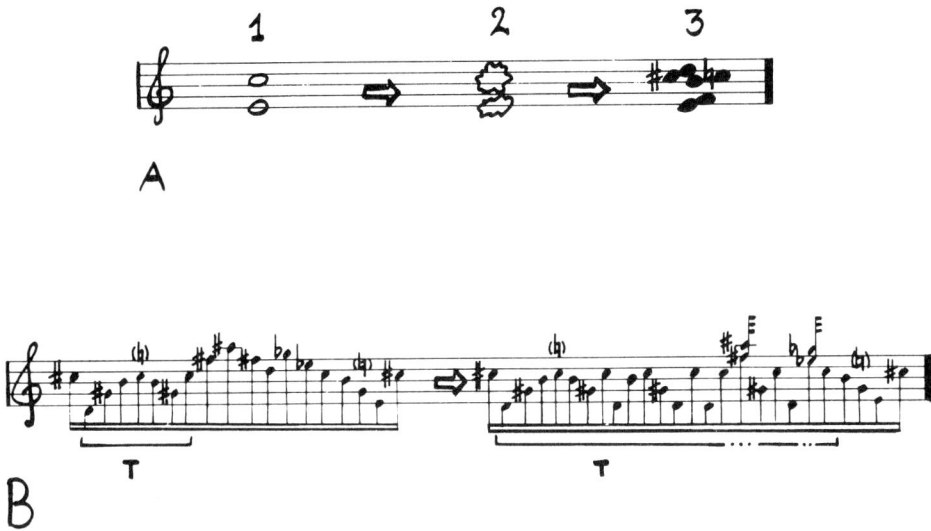

Figure 4 Tumoral Expansion. A: vertical tumor, which generates the first chord of Fig. 8, no. 1 (1 = reference pitches; 2 = ideal expansion; 3 = actual expansion). B: horizontal tumor (T), from *Contrasti*, part of the OIM labelled as XE2 in Fig. 13.

Vectors
A vector is characterized by a *direction* and a *magnitude* : musically speaking, the former is related to the direction of change within a certain domain, the latter refers to the width of such a change. For instance, in the frequency domain, an upward vector means higher frequencies; in the amplitude domain, it means louder sounds; in the complex domain of an energy field, it might mean increase of overall energy, or it might refer to the orientation of the field within the morphological space. In *Contrasti*, for instance, the head alone of the OIM of Figure 8 is developed by applying different vectors to it.

Energy modulation
This can only be applied to sets of items. In the frequency domain, for instance, the total energy of a given figure is approximately proportional to the quantity of notes of which it is made, provided they are played fast enough to be considered as a single unit. In the OIM under examination, the middle part ("b" in Fig. 8) maintains the same overall energy while gradually passing from an average density of two notes per hand (as in Fig. 8, no. 1) to an average density of one note per hand twice as fast (as in Fig. 8, no. 11).

Tumoral expansions
A tumoral expansion is a deviation from a "healthy" reference item, which proliferates abnormally via more or less modified repetitions. The exact order of such repetitions does not follow a precise rule, is not important, and may be completely chaotic. Usually "thicker" than the original item, a tumoral expansion can be

applied to every dimension and is an exclusively local phenomenon: its final details cannot be determined in advance and take shape only once the context has been defined. An example in the pitch domain is shown in Figure 4. When affecting a vertical structure (Fig. 4a) the tumor closely resembles a cluster. When affecting a horizontal structure (Fig. 4b), it looks more like an ostinato melodic elaboration.

Surface, density and contour

These techniques, together with those yet to come, are particularly varied and will only be outlined here. They deal with items' visible profiles, their phenotypes as opposed to their internal structure. When an item occupies some space along a given demension, this space can be schematically represented as a *surface*. The *density* corresponds then to the average number of components per unit of surface. An item is *smooth* if it is regularly distributed along that dimension: it does not change abruptly. Otherwise, it is *rough*. The transition between the two extreme cases is continuous.

For instance, the fast melodic segment used to defocus the item of Figure 2a is smooth along the pitch dimension in 1 and 3, whereas it is fairly rough in 2. The rhythmical dimension of the "B" part of the OIM of Figure 8 is perfectly smooth at the beginning, while during the evolution it gets at first progressively perturbed and then smooth again until it disappears in the last instance of the class. A final example (Fig. 5) shows a progressive increase in surface with an approximately constant density (nos. 1-10), followed by a decrease in density over a constant surface (nos. 11-16), along the domain of another of *Contrasti's* OIMs.

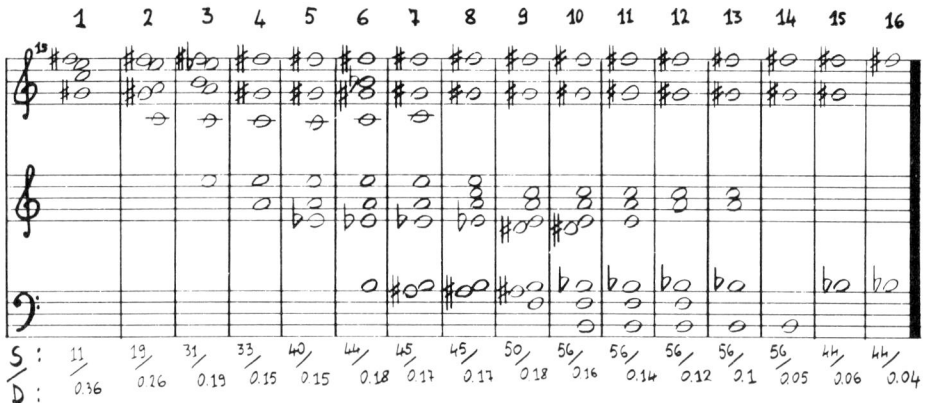

Figure 5 Modulation of Surface and Density along the pitch dimension of *Contrasti's* "B" OIM of Fig. 13 (S = surface, in semitones; D = density).

Control of acoustic behavior

"Acoustic behavior" refers to a special attitude towards both the surface and the deep sound structure per se of OIMs, rather than towards the ways they are put together. The musical potential of work on sound structures is unlimited. A natural ally is found in the computer, the only instrument with which sound can be radically explored and composed. Techniques to deal with the acoustic behavior may affect a single note, the most complex color "blob", a sophisticated sound texture, and so on. They are used to isolate parts of sounds, or to splice various pieces together, in both the frequency and time domains. Control of multiple acoustic behaviors is one of the main concerns of all my music.

Figure 6 presents three ways to modify the amplitude envelope of a sound with exclusively pianistic tools: a simple merging of two different touch qualities (staccato and tenuto, Fig. 6a), an attempt to artificially compose an amplitude envelope (dashed line of Fig. 6b), and various combinations of the defocusing technique creating a complex acoustic behavior (Fig. 6c). For the first two examples, both the actual pianistic implementation and the time domain representations are given.

Magnets
Magnets are a source of pure energy which exert an influence on an OIM's property and bend its field. They can seldom be seen in a piece, but their action is easily felt. A straightforward application of a magnetic bias is the driving principle of the last section of *Metabolai* . A magnet sweeps across the amplitude and duration fields of three reference pitch structures (Fig. 7a), from low to high register, at different speeds, deforming the fields' original shape (Fig. 7b-c). In the actual piece, the magnetized structures are interleaved so as to produce three overlapping trajectories.

An example: Dynamic identity

All the writing techniques described so far can freely interact with one another and be mixed with more traditional techniques. So, the items employed for space filling may resort to vectors to accomplish their task, remultiplication with variable anchors can be increasingly blurred by defocusing some of its components with rough patterns, which, in turn, may be derived from tumoral expansions, and so on. A prodigious variety can be achieved starting from relatively few basic tools. What is more important is that, even at this stage, the reality is deeply hierarchical and cannot be explained with a linear approach. The highest levels correspond to the most synthetic expressions of OIMs and are more explicitly related to their perceptual outline. The lowest levels constitute the structural substrate on which OIMs are built, but much harder to perceive.

Combining various techniques, one can modify an OIM's behavior and make it evolve according to certain trajectories. It is the abstraction and understanding of some principles of the way they evolve that yields the dynamic identity of a class of OIMs. Figure 8 shows the 19 instances which form the evolution of our target OIM. Its main principle consists of a progressive reduction of the differences between the identities of the OIM's three parts, until they turn into a kind of minimal inchoate matter. This is a good example of an "organic evolution" in that the sense of direction is clear, but its fine structure contains many local exceptions. The reference pitch contour is detailed in Figure 9.

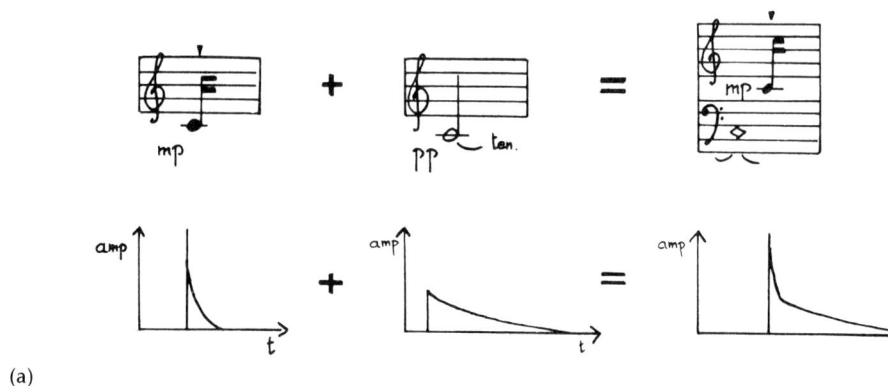

(a)

Figure 6 Control of the Acoustic Behavior: Modification of an Amplitude Envelope. (a) (From *Traiettoria . . . deviata*): the note has the character of a *mp*, dry staccato attack followed by a *pp* resonance (1 = time domain representation; 2 = actual pianistic implementation).

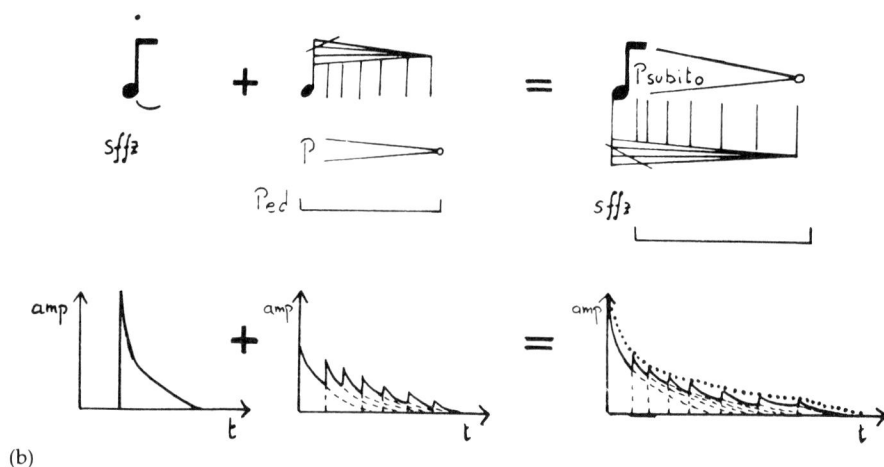

(b)

Figure 6 *Cont'd* (b) (From *Traiettoria . . . deviata*): artificial amplitude envelope (1 = time domain representation; 2 = actual pianistic implementation), built by combining a hard attack with a sequence of soft, rapid repetitions of the same note. The result is the effect of a single note, longer than the first one, with a perceivable amplitude tremolo added to it.

143

Figure 6 *Cont'd* (c) (From *Dialoghi*): complex acoustic behavior obtained with combinations of the defocusing technique.

(c)

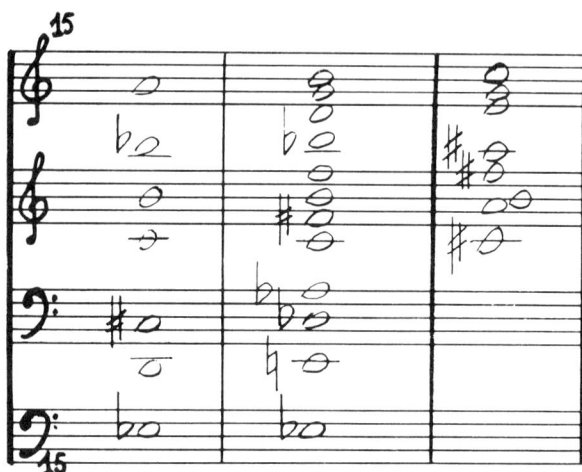

(a)

Figure 7 Magnet affecting the amplitude and duration fields of the last section of *Metabolai*. (a) Reference pitch structures.

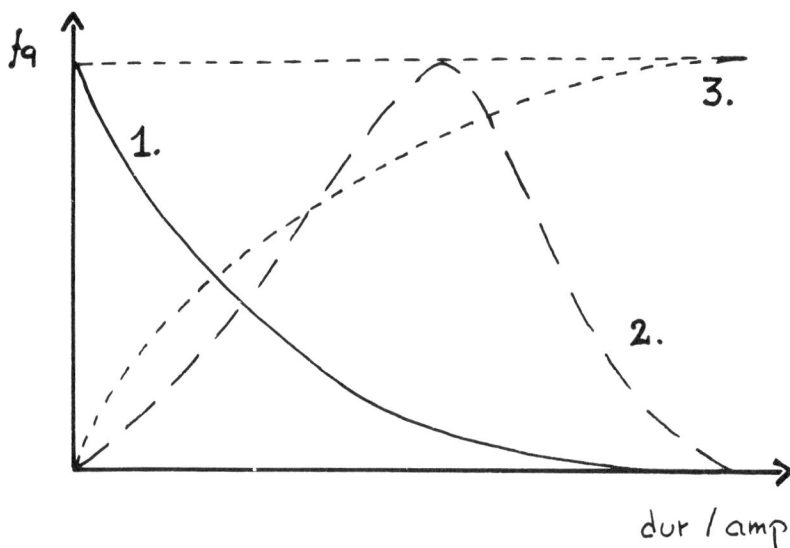

(b)

Figure 7 *Cont'd* (b) Magnetic field (1 = initial position, 2 = mid-way position, 3 = final position).

145

Figure 7 *Cont'd* (c) Actual writing of the first structure corresponding to the three positions described above. The total durations are all normalized to four quarter-notes.

Figure 8 Complete evolution of an OIM from *Contrasti* (RM = remultiplication, DF = defocusing, SF = space filling, SS = space stretching, CAB =control of the acoustic behavior).

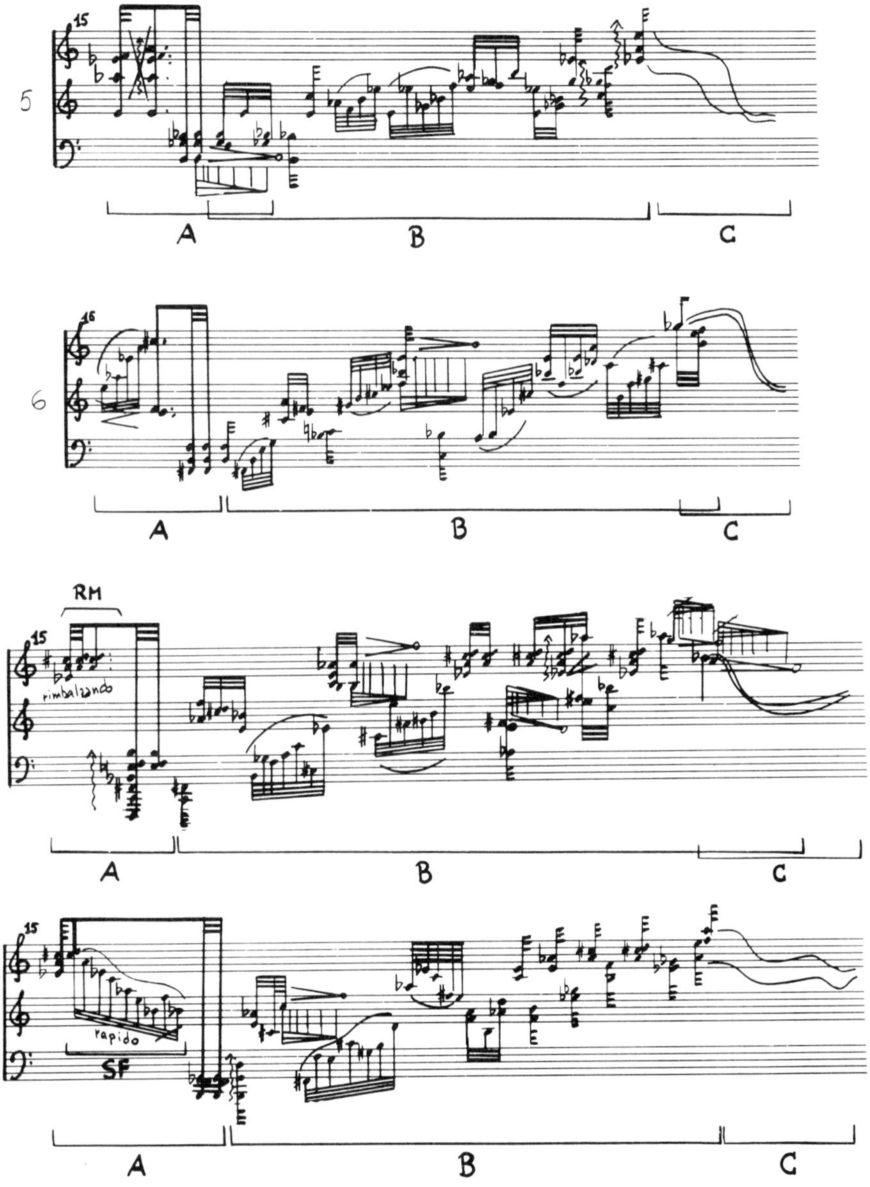

Figure 8 *Cont'd*

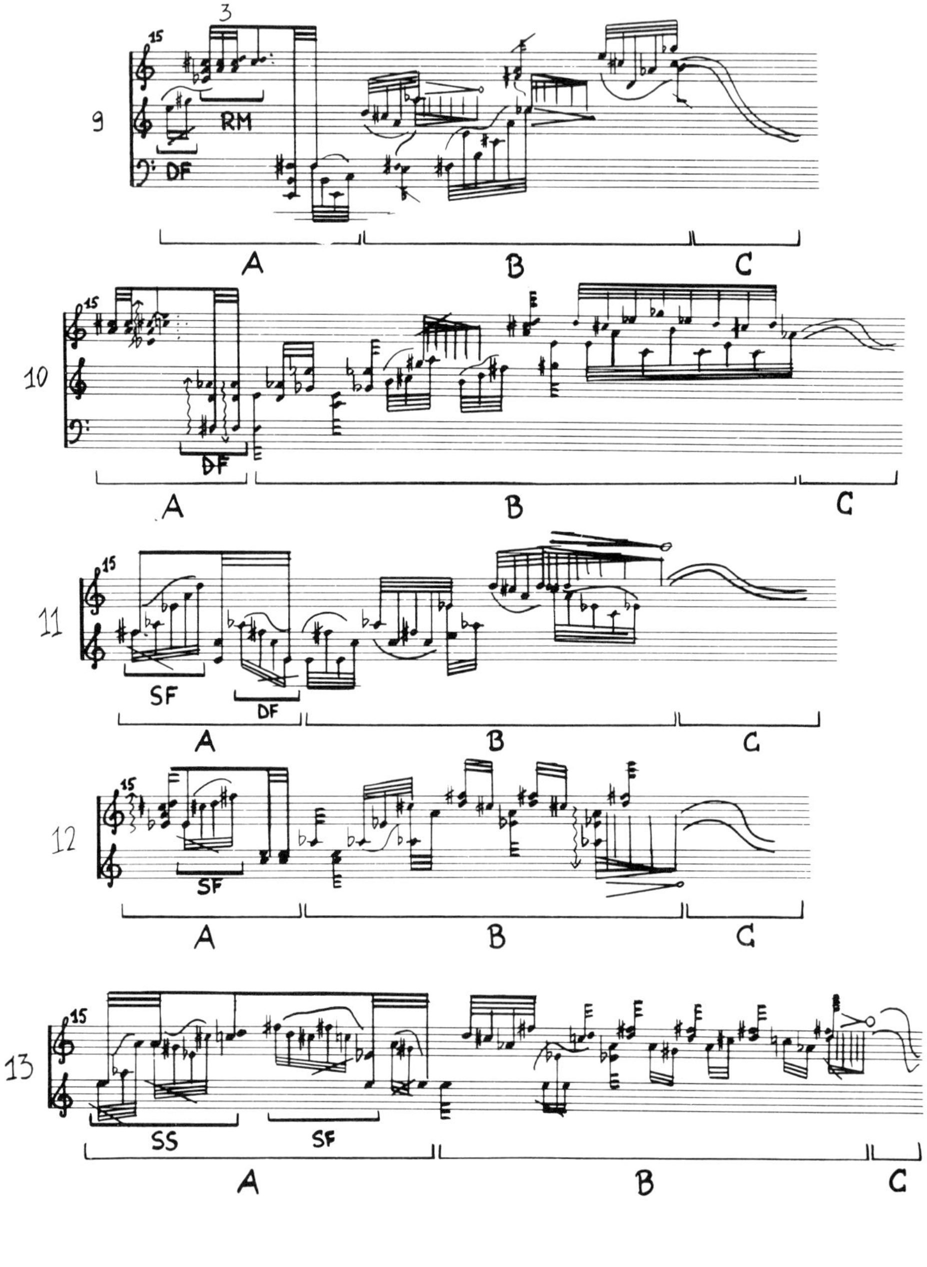

Figure 8 *Cont'd*

Figure 8 *Cont'd*

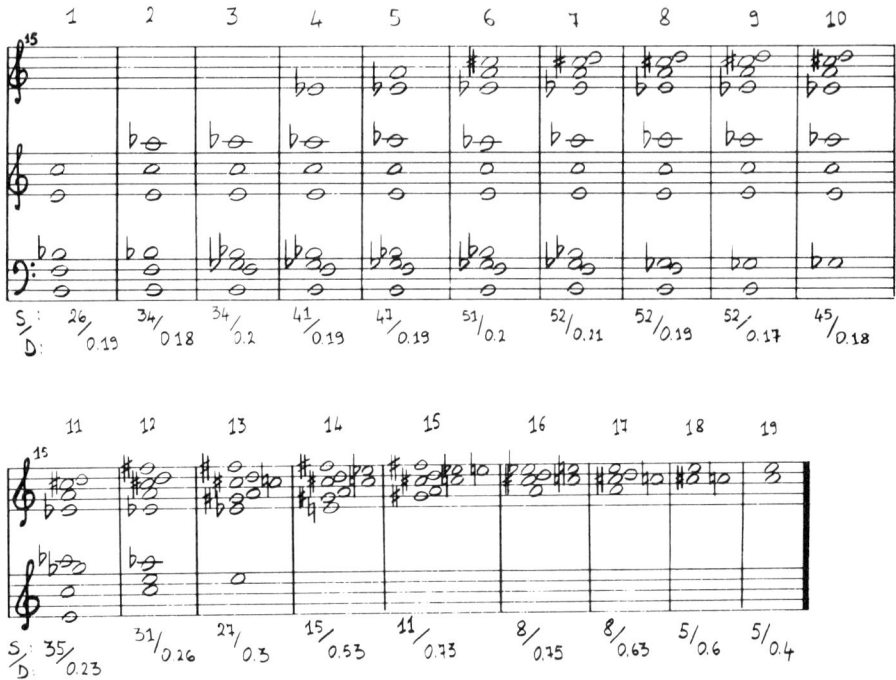

Figure 9 Structural pitch contour for the evolution of Fig. 8 (S = surface, in semitones; D = density).

The Society of OIMs

Social Constraints

A whole piece, or a large section, can be thought of as a *society*, where a group of OIMs interact and evolve according to certain *common laws* which affect their macroscopic characteristics and some microworld features. Although there are no limits on the definition, it is convenient to make a distinction between *arbitrary* laws, under the composer's complete poetic responsibility, and *compulsory* laws which are inevitable and used as a protection against those instrumentally impractical solutions which may arise when some OIMs are combined. It is only at this level that joints and other context-dependent elements, as well as an OIM's *life-span* (the interval between its first and last appearance in the structure), *speed*, and *regularity* of evolution will be defined. The form of a piece is therefore related to its *sociology* , i.e. to the study of the changes that affect a *community* of OIMs. The place where such a community evolves is the morphological space.

At this macroscopic level, an OIM's inner details are no longer important. It is only the interactions between different active OIMs sharing the same space which are to be taken into account. New problems arise; adequate writing techniques must be invented. I will distinguish between *local* and *global* techniques. The former deal with a very limited number of OIMs; the latter are chiefly concerned with larger musical segments and are directly responsible for major structural changes.

Some Local Writing Techniques

Unbiased coexistence
This is the only neutral technique and the easiest and least disruptive way to link OIMs together. OIMs which are simultaneously active maintain their own independent life and place and simply ignore each other.

Adapted coexistence
This term succinctly summarizes various techniques which modify an OIM so as to fit it into the context. Adaptation may either be the result of an arbitrary compositional choice, or be forced by undesired or "illegal" results.

Among the procedures which are involved I will include:
- *spatial* or *temporal shifting*, like horizontal/vertical juxtaposition, fragmentation, stretching, shortening, etc.
- *local changes* of varying importance
- *register relocation* from a single pitch to a whole OIM.

During adapted coexistence, the OIMs usually maintain their own identity, in spite of a few modifications, even though their simultaneous presence tends to favor the establishment of local perceptual *bonds* between some of them. The balance of identities will be affected and new illusory ones will arise as a consequence. In addition, an OIM may be subject to transformations so drastic that it looses its identity completely, while others will tend to predominate and to attract weak OIMs within their own field. New hybrid structures emerge as a result.

In such cases, the following are among the most frequently employed techniques:
- *deletion:* a weak OIM is purely and simply scratched away. It is a quick, if not very elegant, solution to the problem.
- *parasitical reduction:* a weak OIM is turned into a *parasite* of a dominating one. Parasites are full-grown OIMs which cannot live on their own and are bound to stay attached to other OIMs in order to survive. Because of the necessity to adapt themselves to a preexisting context, they are often made of flexible materials similar to those used in joints. With respect, to their *target*, parasites can be *selective* (live only on certain OIMs and neglect the others) or *unselective* (able to plug themselves into whichever OIM is available at a given moment). Their *use* is exclusively under the composer's control who can literally *infest* a piece with a parasitical *epidemic!* With respect to their *effect*, they can be *benign* (do not substantially modify the OIM they live on) or *malignant* (modify it in an irreversible manner). *Viruses* are a good example of deadly parasites.[6] With respect to their *range of activity* parasitical reductions can be *local* or *global*. Figure 10 presents a benign, unselective, local reduction which could not have been avoided, since the dominating OIM calls for the pianist to use both hands. The head of the reduced OIM manages to keep its own identity, but the second half is completely splintered.
- *satellite reduction:* when a weak OIM becomes a satellite, it looses both its autonomy and its identity and is degraded to the role of a component of the

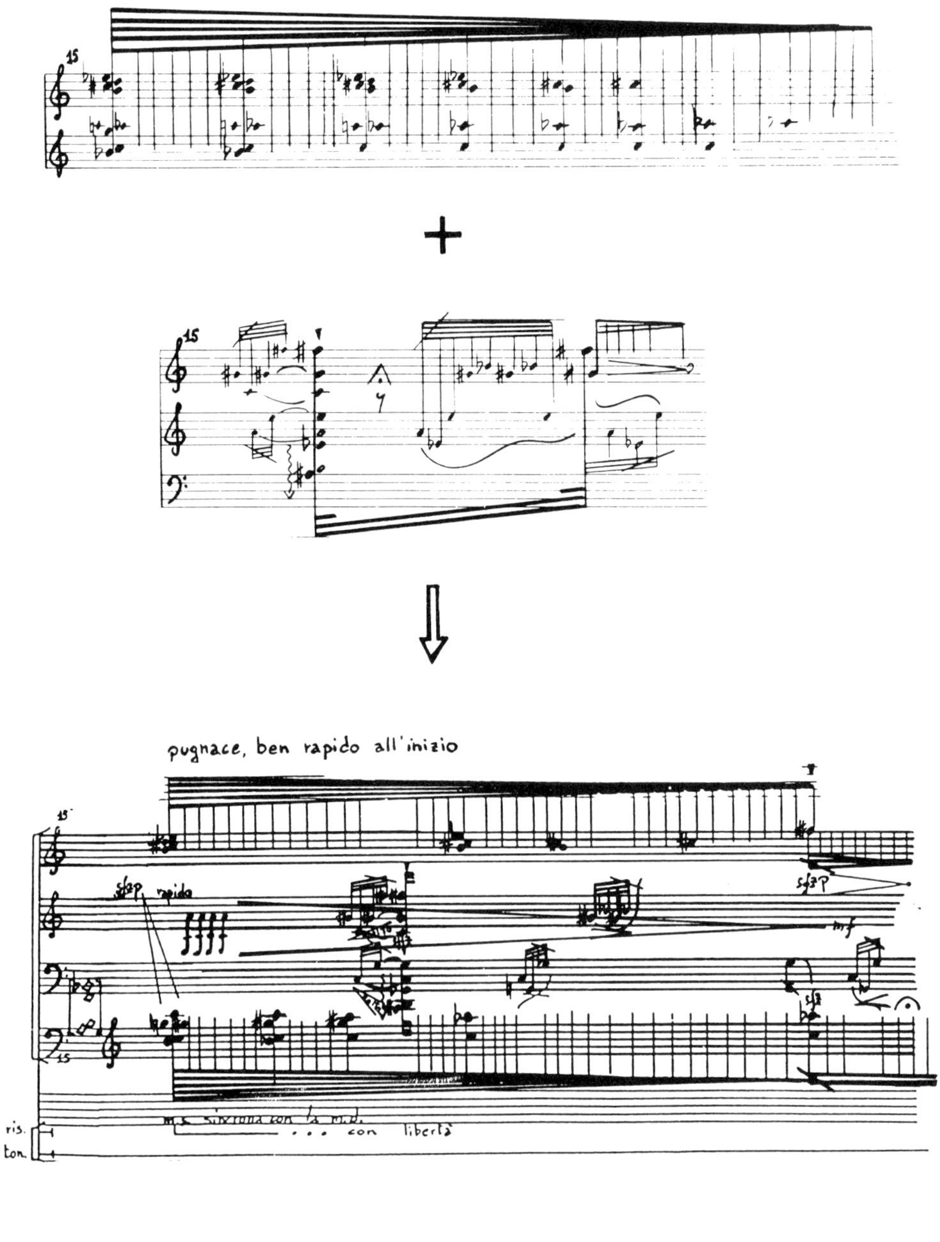

Figure 10 Adapted Coexistence (from *Contrasti*,© G. Ricordi and Co., Milan; reproduced with permission): parasitical reduction of OIMs C4 and B7 of Fig. 13.

Figure 11 Adapted Coexistence (from *Contrasti*,© G. Ricordi and Co., Milan; reproduced with permission): satellite reduction of OIMs C13 and B14 of Fig. 13.

predominating OIM. This case is shown in Figure 11. Since satellite reductions entail the degeneration of an OIM, there is a qualitive leap from one level to another, whereas parasitical reductions maintain all the OIMs' identities, even if one is actually living on the other.

Some Global Writing Techniques

Magnets

Magnets are the only processes that can be found at any point within a musical structure. Depending on their intrinsic power, they operate on either simple musical dimensions, or on more elaborated structures, such as OIMs' properties or OIMs themselves. An example of their use is found during the first five minutes of *Dialoghi*. The magnet exerts a centripetal force in the pitch domain towards the absolute pitches C and E. At the beginning its energy is weak and therefore not very effective: the registers are variable and one of the notes is sometimes missing. It then becomes increasingly stronger, until the whole musical context has been obliged to comply with it and to take the form of a fast tremolo pianissimo.

Enzymes

A musical enzyme is a concrete entity with its own life-span – and not just a pure source of energy – which catalyzes some formal changes. Its structure is extremely varied: it can be derived from ongoing material or be completely new; it may change over time and even be endowed with a built-in regulatory mechanism which will automatically monitor its action and stop it when it is completed. Enzymes may remain *inert* for a long time and then suddenly wake up in response to some signal.

Figure 12 presents the pitch contents of the nine instances of the only enzyme of *Traiettoria*. It is a predominantly melodic structure which spirals around middle C at increasing speed and sweeps all the registers of the instrument. It catalyzes the transition between the two parts which form the starting section of *Dialoghi* by occupying the space used by the musical structures which had settled in from the beginning of the piece [7] (see also Fig. 14c-d).

Distribution functions

A distribution function is a two-dimensional graph whose x-coordinate is time and whose y-coordinate is the repetition rate of a class of OIMs: the higher the y-value, the shorter the interval between two adjacent instances of an OIM. This is the simplest technique which is actively concerned with the creation of large formal sections; when many functions are simultaneously active, the overall form emerges from their dialectical relationships. In spite of their straightforward definition, distribution functions can generate a virtually infinite amount of different forms, depending on their profile, envelope, life-span and maximum value.

The piano cadenza in *Contrasti* is entirely governed by eight distribution functions whose round shape mostly recalls the effect of a filter (Fig.13). When it exists, the peak region of each function lies at different places and corresponds to a moment of maximum density of a certain OIM, which will therefore tend to predominate over its neighbors. This specific choice produces a kind of overtly round form, with extremely bevelled angles.

Figure 12 Musical Enzyme from *Dialoghi*: pitch structure.

Structural molds

Structural molds generate new forms in ways which are more refined than distribution functions, in that the structure of the materials making up a given piece is also taken into consideration. Quite often, it is the rhythmico-temporal structure which is processed and mapped onto the formal space: each component of the rhythm becomes an articulation point of the form. The mapping process may end up being completely incorporated into the existing context or artificially imposed on it. The formal articulation points may be used to control the inner temporal structure of an OIM, to trigger a new OIM, or even to give the starting signal to an entire sequence.

The whole form of *Dialoghi* is regulated by a single structural mold derived from some elementary cells which are found in the two rectangular frames at the end of *Traiettoria ... deviata* (Fig. 14a). The superposition of seven different rhythmic layers generates the reference mold of Figure 14b which is used from the time 1:40. Figure 14 c-d, on the other hand, is an example of the close interaction between the mold and the various musical structures which are present at that time. Later on in the piece the mold is slowed down by a factor of two or four and is used less strictly to trigger progressively longer compositional structures.

Advanced issues

The purpose of this final section is to skim over some plausible extensions and

156

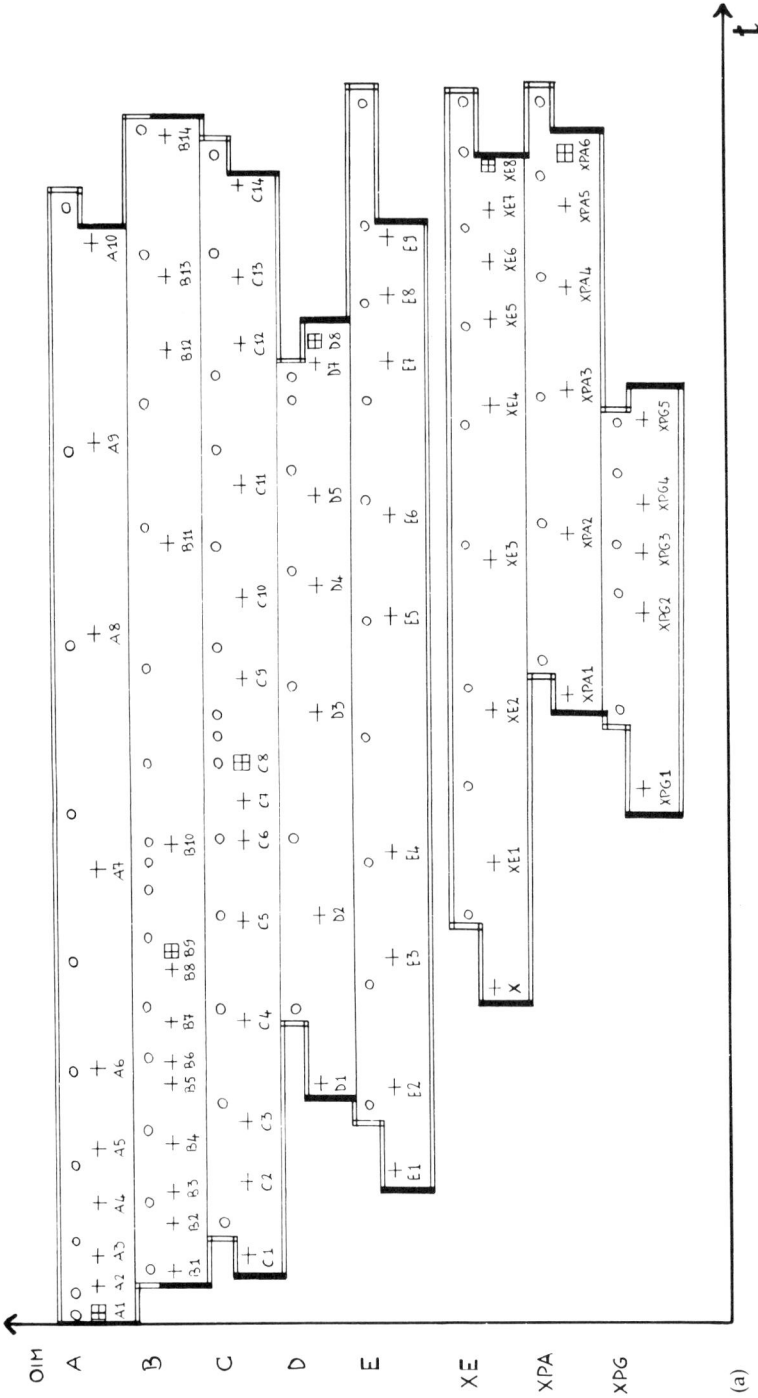

Figure 13 Simplified Morphological Time-Space, reduced to just one dimension representing the start time of each OIM, for the piano cadenza of *Contrasti*. (a) x-axis = time, y-axis = OIMs, o = ideal sequence issued from the distribution functions, + = actual sequence after the needed formal adaptations, + in squares = highest-density point, A-B-C-D-E-XE-XPA-XPG = classes of OIMs.

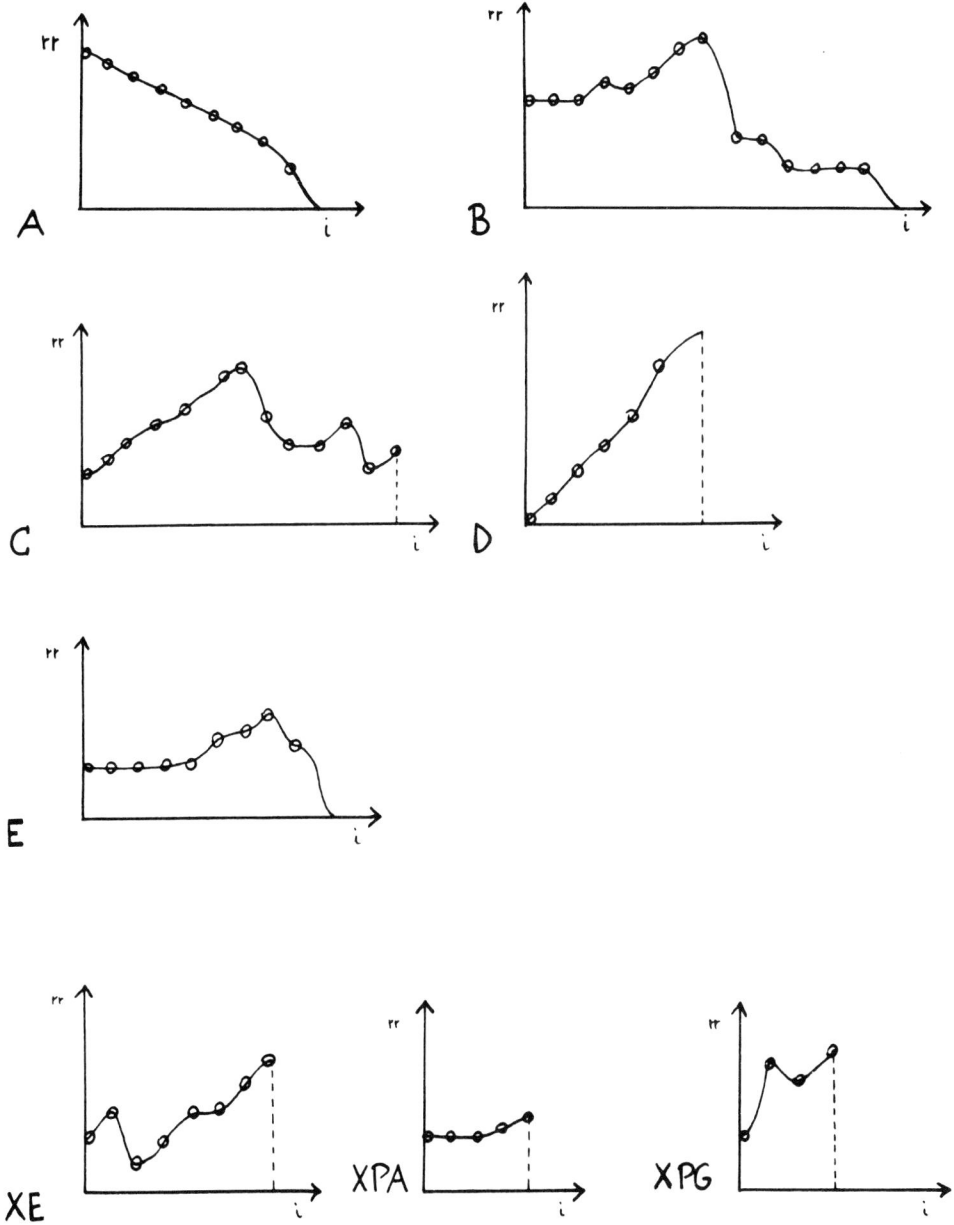

(b)

Figure 13 *Cont'd* (b) Distribution functions for each OIM, i = time interval between two consecutive instances, rr = repetition rate)

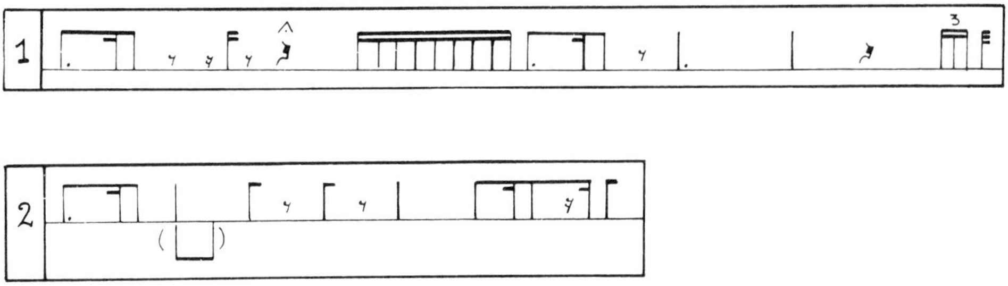

(a)

Figure 14 Structural Mold for *Dialoghi*. (a) Reference rhythmic patterns from *Traiettoria . . . deviata.*

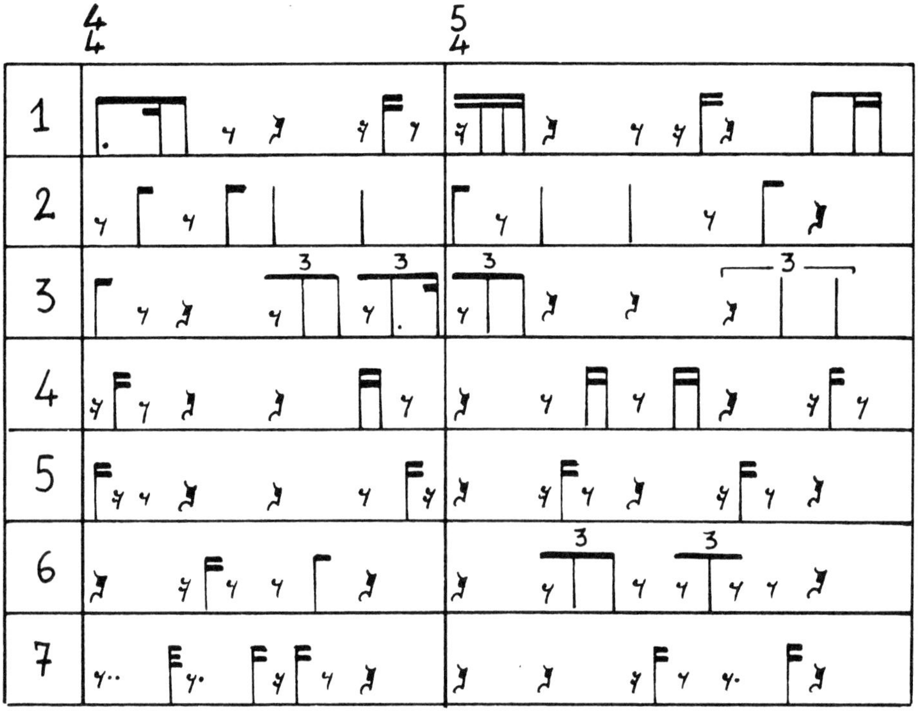

(b)

Figure 14 *Cont'd* (b) Structural mold from time 1:40 of *Dialoghi.*

(c)

Figure 14 *Cont'd* (c) Interaction between the mold and various simultaneous musical structures, before the control of acoustic behavior (1 - 7 = low-register rhythmic pedals, A - C = first three instances of the enzyme of Fig. 12, WS = waving structure.

some immediate consequences of an advanced use of the compositional approach I have just put forward. One such extension is to apply it to a hierarchy of OIMs, so as to create the state of *meta-OIM*, a higher-level structure made in turn of lower-level OIMs. Aside from its conceptual interest, such an extension opens up new ways of thinking about form, since a meta-OIM whether it evolves or not, already represents the form of a piece. Microworld writing techniques might then be applied to such a global shape with the same rights as social techniques. An entire piece will result from the behavior of a single meta-OIM. Another extension

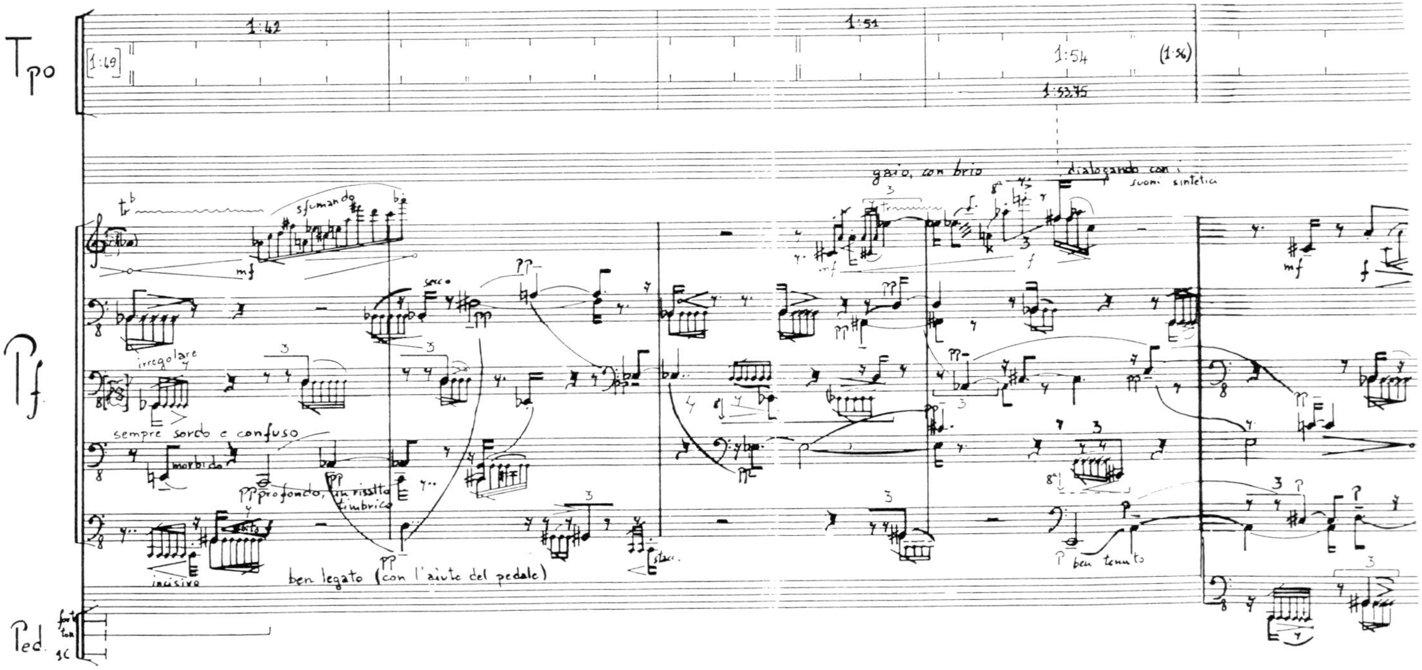

160

Figure 14 *Cont'd* (d) Final score, © G. Ricordi and Co., Milan, reproduced with permission.

(d)

is to use this approach to control single musical dimensions, so as to think of them as rudimentary OIMs. A chord, a sequence of durations, even an absolute pitch do have identities, a timbre – not just traditional timbres, but mainly those fascinating computer-generated sounds which are hard to describe and use – is already a multidimensional OIM.

Perception, analysis and interpretation

Further research in cognitive psychology is needed before one can tell what is really perceivable by ear or by score analysis without clues given by the composer, even though some implicit knowledge about the OIM paradigm might already exist. I am convinced that the metaphor is audible – whether or not this is under the same conditions as those imagined by a composer is not important at this stage – and can therefore be used to parse a complex musical flow. In fact, from this perspective, it is a refinement of McAdams' (1984) auditory images.

The metaphor can also be used as a model to account for some features of other pieces, even if they use different compositional systems. I will demonstrate this in a later text.

Finally, even though it is not always essential that a performer be aware of the compositional structure of a piece in order to interpret it correctly, in the case of OIMs a certain familiarity can hardly be avoided. A different playing and listening attitude, including a performer's very physical movements, has to be found so as to respect an OIM's correct structure and interactions. A good performance can do wonders for perception, and although the remark is true for any real intepretation, it is especially valid in this case, because the performer is directly involved with all the levels of the system. From my personal experience, I was able to appreciate how important it was that the performers' attention be focused on the salient compositional principles before they were able to find the most appropriate instrumental gestures and play correctly.

I hope that a new species of "organic performers" will be educated and sensitized to the infinite facets of this compositional world!

Acknowledgments

I wish to express my deep gratitude to Deke Dusinberre, Andrew Gerzso, Stephen McAdams and Alvise Vidolin for their valuable remarks and suggestions. Before taking their final form, many of the ideas around OIMs were discussed within the IRCAM "Groupe d'Ecriture", composed of Pierre Boulez, Marc-André Dalbavie, Thierry Lancino and Philippe Manoury, whom I sincerely thank.

Notes

1. A *compositional system* may be considered as a collection of writing techniques operating on certain musical material.
    Musical material is what exists or is dealt with by a composer as such, independently of its use in a given piece. It is extremely varied: simple or complex, concrete or abstract, structured or unstructured, etc. Its definition may or may not need a preexisting compositional system and, with the

exception of the simplest material, is normally bound to the system and the historical context in which it originated and/or which used it. Within the tonal system for instance, the following are examples of possible material: an absolute pitch, an instrument, an interval, a chord, a melodic fragment, a long rhythmic pattern. Any kind of material requires an appropriate representation in order to be operated upon efficiently.

A *writing technique* is a set of useful directions, from vague principles to strict rules, that can be used to give a shape to *(mettre en forme)* the material available within the context of a piece. The generality and the power of extrapolation of a certain technique is inversely proportional to the complexity of both the material per se and the chosen representation. As an example, one might note that a technique as sophisticated as "tonal fugue writing" can only be applied to relatively neutral sound material and would not work if the very sounds were too complex.

The *function* of a compositional system is twofold: it can be used as a knowledge base to *analyze* a piece of music as well as an overall framework to *generate* new music, even though it can only describe standard cases and will never account for the "short circuits" which are probably the most interesting aspect of a composer's activity.

A compositional system is therefore concerned with the poetic side of musical creation, and should not be mistaken for a *compositional model*, a specific embodiment of a certain *theory of composition*, which can, in turn, be used to understand and test compositional systems. So, theories and models of composition are usually built on and account for already existing musical examples, while compositional systems are to be used in a conscious or tacit manner, independently of any theories.

2. There are at least three level of identity: the identity of the component itself (for instance, the identity of a figure such as a trill), the identity of the component as a part of the element (for instance, its place or function in it), and finally the identity of the element itself. One can imagine that any kind of modification would affect all these levels more or less dramatically.

3. It is very important to understand the purely formal meaning attached to the word "organism". It would be wrong and misleading to oppose organic matter to inorganic matter, or to hint at possible affective feelings towards living entities. I am simply trying to convey specific behavior with this word; possible alternatives to "organism" (such as objects, elements, processes, concepts, frames, crystals, etc.) all seemed too static, mechanic or artificial.

   OIMs have nothing to do with Stockhausen's use of "formulas", a mystical attempt to merge the characteristics of classic themes and of integral rows. Formulas contain all the musical parameters, control the development of a whole piece, if not a whole cycle of pieces, do not evolve and are mostly processed with traditional combinatorial techniques. As we will see, none of the ideas supporting formulas can be used when dealing with OIMs.

4. I will use Garner's (1978) distinction between components and properties and their further subdivisions. The main keywords of my compositional system are italicized the first time they appear.

5. This double perspective may seem puzzling at first: why not using a single, comprehensive representation? In fact, I purposefully forced a separation between the two levels of material and form so as to exploit their dialectical potentialities. This separation is also called for by my using multidimensional materials and complex forms.

6. A "malignant viral epidemic" is the principal cause of change between the first and the last section of *Metabolai*. Both sections are made of the same rhythmical and pitch structures, but the last one is "sick": it proceeds much more slowly and is continuously shaken by the parasite whose main symptoms are the tremolos, the use of mutes, the bow on the bridge and the presence of the magnet which was analyzed in the previous section (Fig. 7).

   An evident case of a "benign epidemic", on the other hand, can be observed in *Contrasti*. Here, the parasite is a trill, a continuous source of motion. At first, it infests the pianistic introduction unselectively; during the piano cadenza it becomes selective and attacks only one family of OIMs (those whose label starts with X in Fig. 13); finally it again infests all but one OIM and is eventually fought off by a new percussive OIM in the lower register of the computer sounds.

7. Since the most important structure is a rhythmic pedal in the low register, the enzyme starts from it so as to be more effective. In order of appearance, the other complex structures are: soft notes in the middle-high register using double-escapement, four prominent accents on C-sharp, A, C and A-flat, and the waving pattern shared by piano and computer in the medium and high registers. The fact that the enzyme always converges towards middle C is a sign of the magnet which has previously been described (see also Figs. 12 and 14).

References

Garner, W.R. (1978)Aspects of a stimulus: Features, dimensions and configurations. In *Cognition and Categorization* , E. Rosch & B.B. Lloyd (eds), pp. 99-133. Hillsdale, N.J.: L. Erlbaum Associates.
McAdams, S. (1984) The auditory image: A metaphor for musical and psychological research on auditory organization. In *Cognitive Processes in the Perception of Art*, W.R. Crozier & A.J. Chapman (eds), pp. 289-323, Amsterdam: North Holland.
Rosch, E. & Mervis, C.B. (1975) Family resemblances: Studies in the internal structure of categories. *Cognitive Psychology*, **7**, 573-605.
Rosch, E., Mervis, C.B., Gray, W.D., Johnson, D.M., & Boyes-Braem, P. (1976) Basic objects in natural categories. *Cognitive Psychology*, **8**, 382-439.
Stroppa, M. (1982a) *Metabolai*. Ricordi Ed. n° 133531, Milan.
Stroppa, M. (1982b) *Traiettoria ... deviata*. Ricordi Ed. n° 133770, Milan.
Stroppa, M. (1983) *Dialoghi*. Ricordi Ed., n° 134 014, Milan.
Stroppa, M. (9184) *Contrasti*. Ricordi Ed. n° 134261, Milan.
Tversky, A & Gati, I (1978) Studies of similarity. In *Cognition and Categorization*, E. Rosch & B.B. Lloyd (eds), pp 81-98. Hillsdale, N.J.: L. Erlbaum Associates.

Contemporary Music Review,
1989, Vol. 4, pp. 165–170
Photocopying permitted by license only

Image-of-sound, or i-sound: Metaphor/metaform[1]

François Bayle

INA-GRM, Maison de la Radio,
116 avenue du Président Kennedy, F-75016 Paris, France

Taking the case presented by the acousmatic situation (radio, records, and especially works of organized sound designed for concerts), the central question discussed is that of conditions or criteria of the listenability of organized sounds projected into a listening space by electroacoustic means. Based on their morphological "appearance" – raw material, transformation stages, composed sequences – effects of salience and pregnance, as well as distinguishing features of reference and coherence, will be assessed. A recognition model for perceptual forms in the musical dimension is drawn from compositional experience for the acousmatic stage. A function-flowchart is proposed as a "bridge" between the physical and the symbolic, between hearing sound and comprehending its meaning, between listening and understanding.

KEY WORDS: Acousmatic, coherence, listenability, musical form, sound image, metaphor, experimental music, musical operations.

> *I paint what I can't photograph and photograph what I can't paint.*   Man Ray
>
> *Music is pure non-sense.*   Beethoven, to Goethe

Yet the representation, the image, the staging of this non-sense involves recourse to a profound meaning at the very root of all complexity, of morphology. The body of acousmatic[2] music would thus appear to constitute a valid element in the investigation into music and the cognitive sciences. Investigation understood here as raising the question of whether correspondences usually affected by sounds in music – accents, influences, relationships, correlations, polyphony, polychromy, polyrhythms, etc. – are related to the emergence of "meaning". Or even to a "meaning of meanings", a meta-meaning produced by the play of symbols, metaphors, metaforms (forms of forms[3]) – all correctly tuned. Correctly tuned not only among themselves (acoustically) but also in tune with experience in general, with the sense of life. . . . If this can be assumed, then perhaps the way in which the audible is segmented should be taken into consideration. Correctly segmenting means correctly *depicting*. That is to say making an accurate image of the contours of the audible and its perceived coherence on several planes (planes in immediate and constant juxtaposition):

– the first plane of motor-sensory appearance (hearing),
– the second plane of attention focussed on relevant details (listening),
– the third plane of corrrespondence (understanding).

> "I *heard* you without *listening,* neither *comprehending* nor *understanding.*"   Pierre Schaeffer

This trichotomy of the audible accomplishes its role of "rendering understandable" through its very circularity, a constant back and forth play (Peirce, 1978).

For the audible *in general*, understanding means first of all taking the environment into account based on the phonic trace of things, events in the objective world. Which means intelligently identifying the sound residue of acts and objects, whose conflicts and frictions are manifested as phenomenological "appearance" which signals, informs, anticipates and explains other planes of consciousness, notably tactile, gestural and visual appearance. While understanding what is *musically* audible (both more specific and much more broad than the audible in general) means taking the subject and the subject's body into account, in this projected world. Reverting, then, to this body of sensory pleasure, of ideas, where new, "utopian" (in short, *symbolic*) connections arise. Which also means re-situating and constantly recycling a library of referential musics, invoking a realm of objects (simple notes or clusters . . .) and a treasure of timeless values (the classics . . .).

A major technological feat then intervenes: the possibility of fixing or creating sound, then listening to the trace it has left. This new capability (roughly contemporary with the arrival of photography and cinema) serves our argument in so far as the notion of *image* constitutes a scale model of appearance. As well as constituting a new object – or *i-sound* – an intermediate object which in a certain way includes appearance, where it can be followed and seen to work. A misunderstanding should perhaps be quickly cleared up here. At once banal and highly original, acousmatic production was born of recordings (on cylinders, records, tape) designed to facilitate, to "relay", the musical act, bringing it nearer in time and space. Listening without seeing, via radio and recordings henceforth constitutes a common practice where the *relay* pretends to – without ever achieving – transparency. From this context emerges the truly original situation of the creation of a domain *specific* to acousmatic music. This *sui generis* acousmatic situation now stands in opposition to the initial context. Every skill of art and sound technique is invoked to substitute image for object, to generate fictional objects, forging a new compositional writing, a rhetoric, a poetics.[4] Thus montage, insertion, extraction, stretching and filtering become method and content, medium and message, as do the shattering of time and place, the shifting of contours, their superimposition and mixing, and even the introduction of speed and spatiality. And all the cognitive skills needed to mark out and identify these new objects are also called into play. Certain "dotted lines" have already been traced in order to distinguish the planes of hearing, listening, comprehending.[5] Considering a scaled-down version of the acousmatic domain reveals at least three points of significant interest:

- This field proposes "texts" of direct sound, arranged according to the limits (yielding reference points) of the authors' know-how and hear-how, with no reinforcement from any additional element or ally (performer). This means that during listening, the absence of reinforcement provided by visible clues obliges the author to express the meaning *inscribed in the text* (other reference points).

- The acousmatic field is relatively recent. Compared to the scope of traditional music, it constitutes a relatively pure micro-field where certain clear behavioral features emerge, free of cultural overdetermination. These features constitute the "primitives" of cognitive auditory practice. For example: more or less predictable assemblage of percussion/resonance, translation/resistance, apparition/growth ... by inversion, interversion, stimulation.

– But the most original point concerns above all the question of content. The acousmatic field, to a greater extent than any other, is predisposed (most probably in my own musical composition, but also more generally in the "musique concrète" style) to the experience of morphological singularity, whether this be the constitution of sound material reacting to constraints, or an auditory vigilance open to de-realized, idealized potentialities.

Cognition thus constitutes one of the evaluating procedures which compare and distribute direct or induced psychic energy. The trichotomy mentioned above can be taken up again in reference to levels of faculties engaged in attentive listening:

– First: our ear becomes interested in perceiving the circumstances, typo-morphological details, and interactions between sound materials. This *auditory faculty* works as a detector limited only by *physiological thresholds.* Detecting salience, attack, contour, bursts of sound. . . .[6]

– Second: Our being becomes interested in perceiving origins and evolutions, coherences (fusion) and distinctions (identification). The natures of these entities (things, complexes) surpass the field of the audible, which they traverse not only in the "before-after" direction, but also along paths of inertia, velocities, temperatures, coloring, densities . . . that is to say qualities of "during". The corresponding *cognitive faculty* works as a modeler according to *psychoacoustic schemas.* Detecting forms (prey), space (landscapes), actors (characters).[7]

– Third: Our mind, "stuck in its body" (Merleau-Ponty, 1964), constructs a misadaptation, a body undergoing growth. The *symbolic faculty* works as opening, current, exchange, incompletion. Detecting pregnance. . . ."[8]

This proposition suggests that the cognitive function, truly ungraspable "in itself", is apprised from "above" and "below". The symbolic function exercises remote control from above, rearranging the real according to a "projected" world. And it is conditioned from below by the qualitative structuring of the morphological world which "serves as input to our perceptual apparatus",to use Jean Petitot's expression. He reminds us that the

world that we apprehend is a phenomenalized objective world. The conditions of perceptual possibility are already given in this world, through matter's faculty of organizing itself, even organizing itself qualitatively. Physical, physio-chemical and thermodynamic processes possess what could be called catastrophic infrastructures, essentially related to those processes' singularities. Singularities which constitute the morphological component of phenomena. And of their qualities. It could be argued that it is these catastrophic infrastructures which are subsequently processed by our perceptual apparatus. (1985)

Thus we come, a third time, to the trichotomy of the audible:

– hearing and presentification (activating audition),
– listening and identification (activating cognition).
– comprehending and interpretation (which activate musicalization).

Following C.S. Peirce, this trichotomy could then be related to three degrees of intentionality concerning images-of-sound.[9]

- the isomorphic image (iconic, referential) or *im-sound*
- the diagram, a selection of simplified contours (indexical), or *di-sound*
- the metaphor/metaform, associated with a general concept (sign of) or *me-sound*.

We would thus have a conceptual framework providing a useful tool for the execution of both reception (understanding) and production (listenability) of a musical text composed of "organized" (Varèse's term)[10] im-sounds, di-sounds, and me-sounds. The function-flowchart (Figure 1) is an attempt at a schematic representation of this. But any attempt to describe the functioning of an "active" symbolic faculty can never do more than offer a space for tablatures, as a heuristic tool.

We will always have to "rise" to the level of music, higher and greater than ourselves.

> Music . . . is too far beyond the world and the designatable to depict anything but certain outlines of Being – its ebb and flow, its growth, its upheavals, its turbulence.

M. Merleau-Ponty – *Eye and Mind*

Translated from the French by Deke Dusinberre

Notes

1. N.B. This article complements the point of view expressed elsewhere in this volume by Jean Petitot, "Cognition, Perception and Morphological Objectivity", applying it to the domain of the musical.
2. *Acousmatic:* A pure listening situation, where attention cannot be drawn to or reinforced by a visible (or predictable) instrumental causality. Music conceived only in the form of images-of-sounds (i-sounds) and only perceived at the moment of their projection into space (potentially staged or performed cinematically).
3. *Metaform:* Every act of vigilance – including music listening, especially listening in the acousmatic mode – is necessarily established according to criteria of "emergence", made possible by a hierarchy of archetypal references constituting a dictionary of "forms of forms". These might be considered generalized words, or "ideograms", for the psychic apparatus. For example:
   - on the first, or "presentification" level, everything connected with sudden irruption: summoning, disappearing, clashing, extracting, scraping, bursting . . .
   - on the second, or "identification" level, everything indicating gesture and constraints concerning sound material: colliding, compressing, twisting, stretching, fragmenting . . .
   - on the third, or "interpretation" level, everything relating to a "world" or "ulterior world" of poetic, abstract relationships: echo or rebound, values, colors, brilliance, aura . . .
4. *Metaphor:* In the generation and proliferation of sound forms produced and perceived in an acousmatic situation, images-of-sound (i-sounds) enter into "projective relationships" with target-figures in the semantic field (dynamic verbs) such as: press, crush, draw together, penetrate, invade, envelope, engulf, and many others. Moreover, both production and listening situations involving i-sounds engage two forms – one external, entailing pure energy, the other internal, entailing pure perception. These are married under the auspices of an "imaginary thing", a fictional and metaphorical "as if", much more real and true than any veritable, indistinct cause. In relation to metaform (source-form), metaphor functions as target-form.
5. *Experience:* Experience first of all establishes consciousness of the coherence of a unique thing from the diversity of its various aspects. This capacity for synthesis uses stabilizing experience to reduce the world of appearance to a more restricted, more coherent, world of things. Experience then assumes the inverse aspiration from the success of this exercise: to successfully divide, to lose in order to rediscover. By implementing various operations and manipulations, experience locates and produces new coherences, peoples a new space with new "things" (experimental music).
6. *Technique – Operation – Manipulation:* Operation refers to the techniques used to "bring into being" new objects via physical constraints and transformations. Manipulation concerns a transformation

		Dertectors		Comparors	
		by state	by action	slow	fast
Image level **I-sound**	salience indication				
	complex contour appreciation				
	speed and flow of bursts				
	faces, landscapes				
Diagram level **D-sound**	stability / motion				
	homogeneous / heterogeneous				
	form / edge				
	coherence / cloud				
Metaphor level **M-sound**	known / unknown				
	unreal / simulated				
	new / comprehensible				
	saturated / incoherent				

World-behind-the-scenes

World

Map of "there is"

operation

Map of "I can"

manipulation

spaces of memory and games

Image

metaphor

Metaform

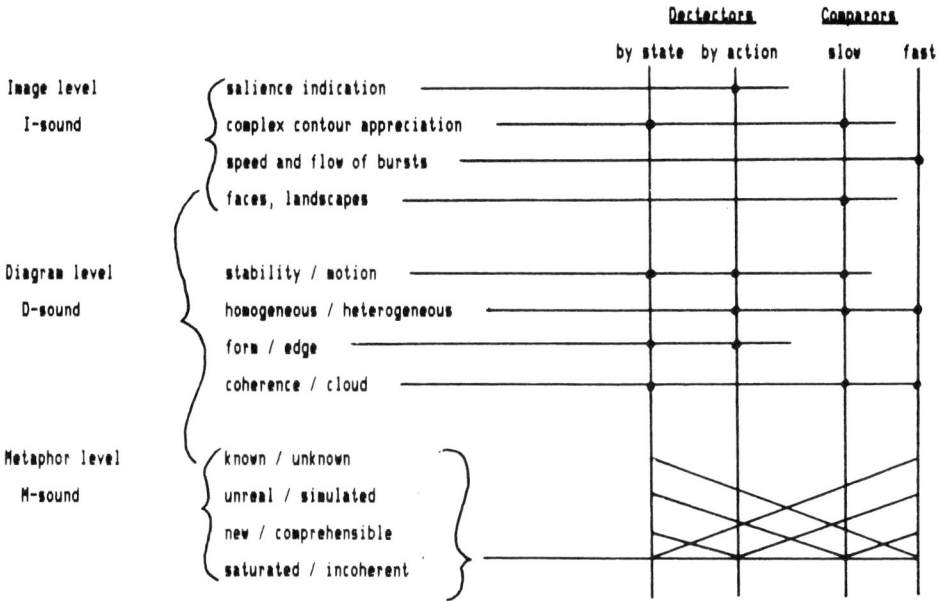

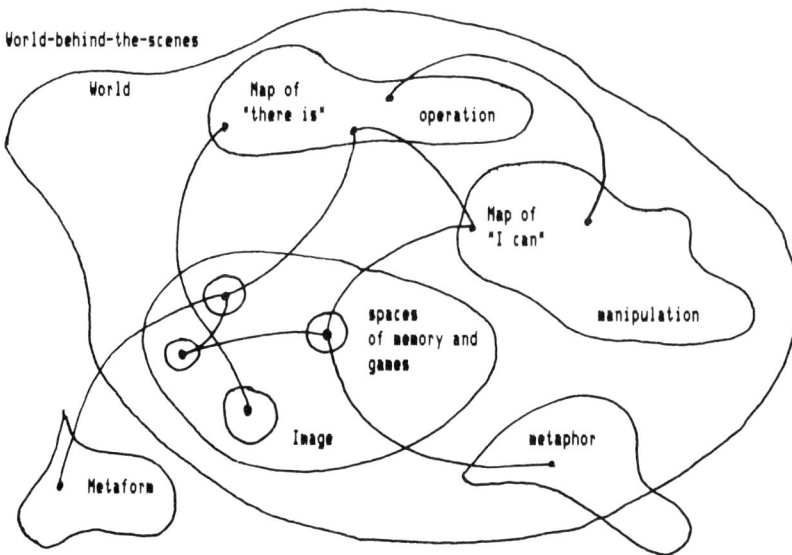

Figure 1 Function-flowchart.

of effects geared to targeted perceptual results. From operative "bringing into being" acting on morphological infrastructures arises a "bringing into appearance", full of surprises and anomalies in terms of categories (illusions – anamorphosis – syntheses – hybrids), contributing to eventual *savoir-faire* (a craft and its tools).

7. *Landscape – World and World-Behind-the-Scenes:* ". . . The apple . . . forms itself from itself and comes into the visible as if it had come from a prespatial world-behind-the-scenes". (Merleau-Ponty, 1964). The stream of sound projection peoples acousmatic listening according to a scenario of forms, a panorama carpeted with characters, hillocks, varyingly "stimulated" states within the sound continuum – a morphogenetic landscape. It is made by hand, but with the help of technology, that is to say that the handiwork is invisible though everywhere felt.

8. *Character:* In this landscape, the listening subject works – "symbolically replays" – the music. One "pilots" one's listening like a vehicle, an apparatus simulating spaces and forms . . . A tense relationship with appearances is established, full of risk, desire, antipathy, hope. This reproduces the same sensation of strangeness as when a tale is recounted.

9. *Image and I-Sound:* "I do not look at [a painting] as I do a thing . . . My gaze wanders around in it. . . . It is more accurate to say that I see according to it, or with it, than that I see it" (Merleau-Ponty, 1964).

"A photo is always invisible. It's not the photo itself which is seen . . . photos: signs which don't "take" too well. . . ." (Barthes, 1980).

The gaze defines images based on the trace they leave on a medium sensitive to the luminous energy emitted by an object. I-sounds are defined by audition in the same way, in an isomorphic appearance at the sound source (that is to say transmitted in the same way through the air to the auditory system). But, like images, i-sounds are differentiated from the source-sound by a double disjunction: the first physical, coming from a substitution of causal space, and the second psychological, coming from a displacement in the region of effects (awareness of a simulacrum, an interpretation, a sign).

10. *Coherence – Listenability:* A system of related qualities which emanate from a "thing", positing this thing as appearance, and constituting its degree of coherence. Its pregnance – its transmission of a clutch of qualities – lends credence to imagined, non-causal, free associations. For example, the coherence of "lemon" enables us to hazard the observation that "sourness is yellow" (Ponge).

". . . Without the notion of (coherent) thing, we are confronted with the sound object (i-sound) like a film viewer who doesn't know how to recognize a coherent character in the various close-ups and long-shots of different movements and still poses by the same actor, and who therefore soon becomes exhausted trying to itemize these movements second by second". (Chion, 1988).

In "natural" music, all "external" factors of coherence – for instance, instrumental identification ("clarinetness"), visible gestures (the participatory involvement of the gaze), etc., must be well "observed" so that in the staging of listening in an acousmatic situation they can be "relayed" by i-sounds/coherence markers and elements of rhetoric. Attention is thus held, during acousmatic production, by the maintenance of coherences, insuring the listenability of "i-sounding" compositions when played. New coherences are thereby created, coherences neither realistic nor causal, but truly phenomenal.

References

Barthes, R. (1980) La chambre claire. *Cahier du cinéma,* 18–136. Paris: Gallimard.

Bayle, F. (1984) La musique acousmatique, ou l'art des son projetés. *Enjeux,* 211–218, Paris: Encyclopedia Universalis.

Bayle, F. (1986) Ecouter et comprendre – In "La recherche musicale au GRM", *La Revue Musicale,* 394/397, 109–119.

Chion, M. (1988) Du son à la chose. *Analyse Musicale,* **11,** 52–58.

McAdams, S. (1984) The auditory image: A metaphor for musical and psychological research on auditory organization. In *Cognitive Processes in the Perception of Art,* W.R. Crozier & A.J. Chapman (eds.), 289–323, Amsterdam: North Holland.

Merleau–Ponty, M. (1964) Eye and Mind. In *The Primacy of Perception,* James Edie (trans), Evanston, Ill: Northwestern University Press.

Petitot–Cocorda, J. (1985) *Morphogenèse du sens,* 23–26, Paris: Presses Universitaires de France.

Peirce, C.S. (1978) *Ecrits sur le signe,* 230–239, Paris: Seuil.

Thom. R. (1983) *Paraboles et catastrophes,* 154–157, Paris: Flammarion.

Contemporary Music Review,
1989, Vol. 4, pp. 171–180
Photocopying permitted by license only

Perception, cognition and morphological objectivity

Jean Petitot

Centre d'Analyse et de Mathématique Sociales,
Ecole des Hautes Etudes en Sciences Sociales, 54 boulevard Raspail, F-75006 Paris, France

The study of "form-bearing elements" presupposes the possibility of developing a specifically morphological analysis of sound forms. For that, a physico-mathematical theory of morphogenesis is required. Its role is to suggest morphodynamic models of natural morphologies. In order to comprehend sound forms (and, more generally, perceptual forms) it is not enough to consider them as the "projection" of the results of cognitive processing of physical information onto the external world. For – as opposed to the "methodological solipsism" dominating the classic cognitive sciences, and in agreement with more "ecological" points of view such as David Marr's – recent morphodynamic theories (catastrophe theory, dissipative structures, synergetics, etc.) show that the morphological structuring of the external world is largely the result of physical processes of (auto)organization. These fundamental scientific findings should be incorporated into cognitive analyses.

KEY WORDS: Morphodynamic models, phenomenology of perception, phenophysics, principle of double organization, conceptual structure, projected world, catastrophe theory.

Foreword

This short article covers only one very specific theoretical point, and is a complement to Francois Bayle's chapter (this volume). It is the work of a mathematician (not a musician) who has applied morphodynamic mathematical models to certain basic cognitive problems such as categorical perception in phonetics (and, more generally, problems concerning prototypicality and categorization), relationships between language and perception, as well as, for example, David Marr's 2½ D sketch of visual perception.

   In the following pages, *morphological* refers to everything concerning the (spatio-temporal) qualitative organization and structuring of natural and perceptible forms. *Morphodynamic* refers to models of morphologies and morphogenetic processes based on mathematical theories of singularities and their universal unfoldings as well as of the bifurcations of non-linear dynamic systems.

Introduction

One of the most striking things about acousmatic music such as that of François Bayle – apart from its specifically aesthetic and artistic qualities – is its wealth of morphological components. The morphological, indeed morphodynamic, lexicon used by the composer in the *phenomenological description* of sound images, sound structures and sound organizations is very diverse; it includes forms, figurative salience, clear and fuzzy contours, attacks and fronts, not to mention deformation, stretching, mixing, stability and instability, rupture, discontinuity, harmonic clouds, crumbling and deviation of figures and so on. Should this vocabulary be considered as a vague, poetic approximation or, to the contrary, as the demonstration of an authentic morphological component on which higher semiotic levels of musical composition can be built? This second option is adopted here. The hypothesis is that a specifically morphological component of perceptual sound organization really exists, a component on which most *form-bearing elements* can be founded (cf. McAdams, this volume).

What then, is the *cognitive* status of such structures? The problem is a general one extending beyond music cognition. *It is central to the entire field of the phenomenology of perception.* In phonetics, for instance, the phenomena of categorical perception (which discretizes the audio-acoustic continuum and thereby effects the passage from the audio-acoustic level to the phonological level) are eminently morphological phenomena. They basically arise from the fact that phonetic perception of spectral morphologies is *qualitative*. Within the space of acoustic cues which function as control parameters for phonetic percepts, there are areas of *stability* bounded by areas of *instability*. As Kenneth Stevens pointed out in his "quantum" theory of speech, it is this mixing of stability/instability of spectral morphologies relative to control variations that produces the fundamental perceptual effects of *invariance* and *discretization* without which the audio-acoustic *continuum* could not function as substrate for the phonological *code* (cf. Petitot, 1983a, 1985b; Schwartz, 1987). Here it can be clearly seen how the morphological level serves as the basis for the higher – symbolic – cognitive levels of perceptual "languages", conceptual "grammars" and formal "syntaxes" currently undergoing intensive scrutiny by the cognitive sciences. The problem is that, for *intrinsic* reasons, this morphological level is one of the most difficult to theorize. It supports form-bearing elements, but is scientifically manageable only if a *physico-mathematical theory of form and morphogenesis* is made available. Yet following some not very convincing efforts by Gestalt theory, nothing was developed along these lines for a long time. It wasn't until the amazing developments of the early 1970s, such as the theories of morphodynamic catastrophe models, of dissipative structures, and of synergetics, that the situation was completely reversed. There *now* exists a physico-mathematical theory of morphology as such, *a theory to be integrated into the cognitive sciences.* The brief comments which follow will be devoted to this topic, stemming as it does from the epistemology of cognition.

Conceptual structure and projected world

In order to understand what it means to introduce a morphodynamic component into the cognitivist paradigm, it is appropriate to begin with a particularly relevant conception of cognitivism, the one developed by Ray Jackendoff. In *Semantics and Cognition*, Jackendoff introduced the hypothesis of Conceptual Structure (CS), in order to understand the semantic structure which enables us to speak of what we see: "There is a *single* level of mental representation, *conceptual structure*, at which linguistic, sensory, and motor information are compatible" (Jackendoff, 1983, p. 17). This hypothesis fits into the framework of computational mentalism (classic symbolic paradigm). Its role is to allow for a better understanding of the structural constraints imposed on a theory of cognition, and of the relationship between universal grammar, cognitive capabilities in general, and the structure of thought. It posits the idea that language "reflects" thought and the world, and that, there-fore, there exist *semantic* constraints which determine syntax (these constraints being themselves constrained by perceptual structures).

The CS transforms the real world (RW) of physical objectivity into a *projected world* (PW), namely the *sensory* world as *qualitatively* structured and *phenomenolog-ically* organized, the world of actual experience, the world of phenomenal events. Let us take the classic example, given by Jackendoff, of *color*. In the RW there are electromagnetic waves. The sensory quality of /color/, however, belongs to the PW. It is derived from the processing of physical information by a conceptual con-stituent, [COLOR], belonging to the CS. [COLOR] is the structure of /color/ as formally expressed in the internal structure of the related mental computation, the relationship between [COLOR] and /color/ raising the classic "mind-body problem" (Jackendoff, 1983, pp. 31-34) (see Figure 1).

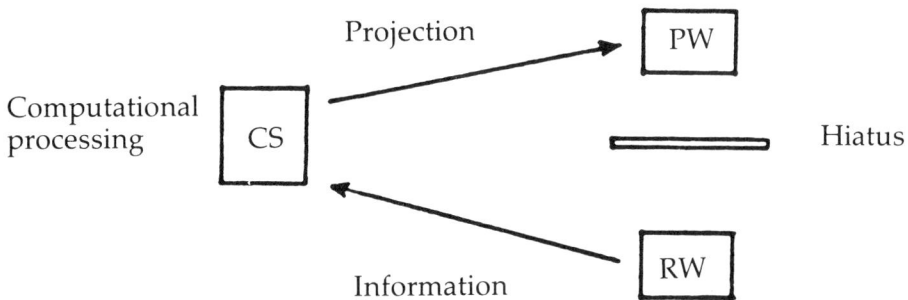

Figure 1

The projected world thus described is not, by definition, the real world. But it is not merely the perceived world, either. It is the world "for us" in the *phenomenological* meaning of the term. This phenomenological world is not subjec-tive-relative. It is not an imaginary world of appearances. It is obviously a *cognitive construction* but one which obeys genetic constraints and is therefore universal to the human species.

Jackendoff thus takes up all the central themes of the phenomenological tradition following on the guiding concept that phenomenological consciousness is the correlate of the PW. This means that consciousness is not the same as mental computation. Mental representation is derived from processing, from calcula-tions done by the constituent elements of the CS. But the major part of the internal structure of these constituents (such as [COLOR]) *is not projectable* (which moreover places intrinsic limits on introspection). Internal structure *is not manifest* in phenomenological experience. Which is to say that "projectability" is a basic *property* of the process of constituting the PW. This point of view is further developed in Jackendoff's latest book, *Consciousness and the Computational Mind*. The reconquest of a phenomenological point of view allows for the reintroduction of a *realist* conception of language and perception. Language and perception truly possess an *ontological* content, but it is a question of the ontology of the PW and not of the physical RW. Starting from these premises, Jackendoff undertakes a cognitive analysis of the CS in its projective relationship to the PW. This leads him to identify *ontological categories* of the PW.

It should be stressed that the CS standpoint represents a phenomenologico-computational mentalist standpoint in contrast to Russell's logic and Wittgenstein's pragmatism. Jackendoff's semantic approach reactivates numerous *Gestalt* and phenomenological problems and therefore inevitably leads to a critique of the various schools of formal semantics. It holds that the level of the CS constitutes the *same* level as that of semantic structure.

The problem of pheno-physics

Jackendoff's analyses and conclusions are fully endorsed here, with the exception of one major reservation. The phenomenological conception stemming from the CS hypothesis is, as just pointed out, purely *projective*. The PW appears there as a purely cognitive construction and is separated from the physical RW by an unbridgeable ontological hiatus (cf. Figure 1). The hypothesis that there may exist a *natural – non-cognitive – process of phenomenalization of the objective RW* is never raised. Nor is the possibility ever considered that the *qualitative structuring* of the world of things, forms, states of affairs, places, paths, states, events, processes, etc. may *partly emerge* from a spontaneous *morphological* organization of material substrates. In other words, Jackendoff's analysis is limited to a classic objectivist physicalist conception of physics and it is the *subject* (consciousness, the mind) who is responsible for the phenomenalization of the RW into PW.

A prejudice concerning the meaning of physics always legitimates this type of perspective, the prejudice that "it is well known" that physics "cannot explain" the qualitative organization of the world. Now – and this is the point – such "evidence" inherited from the history of modern physics *can no longer be accepted as such*. The past twenty years has seen considerable progress in physics and mathematics in terms of understanding (auto)organizational phenomena of material substrates. This entails:

(i) in mathematics: the theory of singularities and their universal unfoldings; theories of structural stability; the qualitative theory of non-linear dynamic systems and of their bifurcations; theories of turbulence and of the paths leading to chaos, etc.

(ii) in physics and non-linear thermodynamics: theories of critical phenomena in general; the theory of phase transitions and, more broadly, the study of phenomena of spontaneous breakings of symmetry within organized media; the analysis of catastrophes of diffraction and of dislocations of wavefronts in wave optics (caustics, asymptotic solutions to wave equations, approximation of geometric optics, oscillating integrals and methods of stationary phase, etc); numerous applications of the many theories mentioned above in various fields, such as shock waves, dissipating structures in kinetic chemistry and in non-equilibrium thermodynamics, defects in ordered media and in particular in mesomorphic phases (liquid crystals), etc.

All this converging research, the work of some of the most eminent contemporary scientists and engaging an enormous physico-mathematical problematic, has profoundly – radically, it could even be said – modified the image of physics. Three guiding concepts have been developed:

(i) In general, natural systems – such as thermodynamic systems – possess (at least) two levels of objective reality: a "micro" level, "intricate" and complex, corresponding to the system's fundamental physics, and a "macro" level, coarser and usually finitely describable, more of a morphological than of a physical nature. The "macro" level *emerges* from the underlying "micro" level and this process of transition can be mathematically checked, using models. It basically results from the coordinated and cooperative collective behavior of local "micro" entities (cf. statistical mechanics in thermodynamics, aggregation theory in economics, or connectionism in cognitive science).

(ii) The "macro" level is essentially organized around singularities (caustics, phase transitions, shock waves, defects, breaks in symmetry, etc.) of underlying physical processes. These singularities carry information and are phenomenologically dominant ("salient" to use Thom's term). The qualitative structuring – the morphological organization – of phenomena is thus effected through them. Spectacular examples of this include the explanation of caustics in terms of oscillating integrals and the explanation of phase transitions in terms of renormalization groups (cf. Petitot, 1986b).

(iii) There are abstract (formal, "platonist"), mathematically formulatable constraints imposed on critical phenomena in general. Analysis reveals strong properties of *universality* on critical behavior, that is to say a notable *independence* of organization at the morphological "macro" level (according to morpho-structural rules).

One can therefore properly speak of an emergent and autonomous *morphological level* as well as of *catastrophic infrastructures* of phenomena. Following a suggestion made by Per Aage Brandt, the neologism *pheno-physics* will be used to refer to this morphological level: basic physics can be understood as a sort of "genophysics" which is "pheno-physically" *expressed* through a morphological level possessing a relative autonomy and its own structural laws of organization. Pheno-physics deals with a morphodynamic approach to what is now currently called "qualitative physics."

The physicalist and objectivist prejudice mentioned above can then easily be formulated as follows: *no pheno-physical level exists.* This implies the corresponding projectivist cognitive thesis. But since the physicalist argument is no longer tenable, the projectivist thesis should be revised: *the phenomenological world – the natural sensory world (NW) – is both projected and pheno-physical.* There is therefore no ontological hiatus between PW and RW. The diagram presented above should be revised as in Figure 2.

Based on René Thom's work, a certain number of my articles have already offered detailed analyses of the status of pheno-physics (Petitot 1982a,b, 1983a,b, 1986a,b, in press-a), involving epistemological investigations of its physico-mathematical contents. Through these works, I dealt with – in my own way – most of the topics raised by Jackendoff long before I became aware of *Semantics and Cognition.* For example:

(i) The Gestaltist reconstruction of a form from its apparent contours. Here it is a

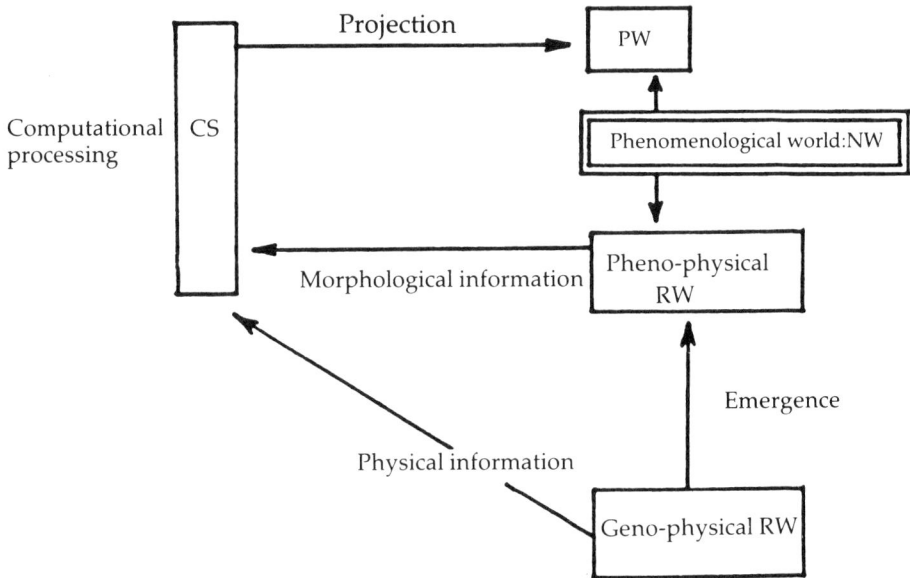

Figure 2

question of confrontation between Husserl's phenomenology and contemporary cognitivism, especially as developed by David Marr in *Vision,* where the inter-mediate level of the 2½-D sketch corresponds quite closely to Husserl's concept of perceptual adumbrations.

(ii) Problems of categorization and typicality. This involves interpreting the type-token dialectic in the context of the theory of structural stability, as well as the way a space can be categorized so as to become a paradigm (in the structuralist sense). As already pointed out, this is especially important for phonological paradigms and categorical perception (Petitot 1983a, 1985a, 1986c).

(iii) The localist hypothesis in structural syntax and perception–language relations (Petitot, 1988).

(iv) An explanation of the intentional orientation of consciousness.

This convergence reinforces the idea that an authentic phenomenology of the organization of the worldly substance should be not only projective, but also morphological (realist), thereby linking cognitivism to a philosophy of nature in the context of a search for a "physics of meaning" or, as Thom likes to say, a "semio-physics".

The principle of double organization

In order to integrate a specifically morphological component into a cognitivist phenomenology like Jackendoff's, the standard symbolic and functionalist (compu-tational-representational) paradigm must be significantly transformed. For this paradigm, symbolic mental representations are expressions of an internal formal language referring to the outside world by processing external physical information (understood in the geno-physicalist sense of the term). It is posited that "contact with the world enables the cognitive system to supply meaning to its internal symbols" (Andler, 1987, p. 7). In other words, it is posited that "the structural properties of the world are expressible, using a fairly rich formal language, in the form of facts and rules" (Andler, 1987, p. 8).

This perspective immediately gives rise to a weighty problem which Zenon Pylyshyn, in *Computation and Cognition*, calls the problem of the "bridge from Physical to Symbolic". From an objectivist physicalist standpoint, external physical information being *a priori* non-symbolic – and therefore without prior computational signification – it should be recognized that the interface between the cognitive system and external reality is reduced to the operation of peripheral modules – transducers – which convert this information into computationally significant information. This is obviously necessary since, in order for symbolic representations to represent (i.e., to possess semantics), they must be truly correlated with external physical events. Pylyshyn himself opts for a strict dualism as opposed to the monist naturalism sketched out here. For Pylyshyn, there is an *irresolvable* break between the cognitive (symbolic) and the physical. There is no physicalist description of inputs which are usable by a cognitive system (Pylyshyn, 1984, p. 166). The functional cognitive lexicon is without physical content. And given this "general failure", (p. 167), the transducers converting physical inputs into system-usable inputs must therefore deplete the "objective" ontological content of cognition, the remaining ontological content being projectively defined according to PW ontology.

Two enigmas remain, within this dualist paradigm.

(i) The object enigma – already mentioned – of *forms*. That is to say the enigma of the specifically morphological dimension of the natural sensory world.

(ii) The subject enigma of *meaning*. "How does meaning become affixed to the symbol?" (Andler, 1987, p. 18). As many authors have pointed out (Searle, Putnam, Dreyfus, etc.), the symbolic paradigm does not provide a good theory of the *interpretation* of mental representations nor of the *intentional* orientation of subjects toward objects (cf. Proust, 1987).

I think that a *double* theory of emergence is needed in order to shed light on these two enigmas. The object enigma requires the development of a phenophysics based on morphodynamic models of critical and (auto)organizational phenomena. Whereas the subject enigma urges elaboration of Thom's and Zeeman's seminal idea that a "macro" content can be assimilated to the topology of an attractor of an underlying "micro" dynamic, and that logico-combinatorial structures of competence must therefore be interpreted as stable and emergent regularities in the context of the theory of bifurcations of non-linear dynamic systems (yielding a principled analogy with thermodynamic models of phase transitions). This idea has been recently rediscovered and refined by *neo-connectionist* models of performance in the context of the so-called sub-symbolic paradigm. From a connectionist standpoint, entities possessing a semantic content are, at the micro level, complex and global patterns of activation of elementary local units which are interconnected and function in parallel. Semantics is therefore an emergent holistic property. Discrete and serial symbolic structures on the "macro" computational level (symbols, rules, inferences, etc.) are then interpreted as qualitative, stable, invariant structures emerging from the sub-symbolic level through a *cooperative* process of aggregation. Which leads back to the principled analogy with phase transitions. If, as Paul Smolensky suggests, a *harmony function* is introduced here (as the cognitive analog of thermodynamic *energy*, just as information is the analog of entropy) whose optimization defines *coherent and consistent* global patterns (Smolensky, 1986), then one arrives at the conclusion that sub-symbolic cognitive systems behave so as to optimize this potential function. Which naturally brings us back to models of the "catastrophe theory" type.

The natural world of phenomenological manifestation thus becomes the product of *three* interdependent processes:

(i) The emergence of a symbolic conceptual structure from an underlying sub-symbolic dynamic level;

(ii) The projection of this CS ("computational mind") onto the Consciousness – Projected World correlation;

(iii) The emergence of a pheno-physical morphological level from the geno-physical level.

This leads to the formulation of the following principle, challenging Pylyshyn and Fodor's projective and dualist notions: *Several* levels of reality exist whose ontological content is *objective*; the basic physical level (in the physicalist sense), of course: light waves, sound waves, etc.; but also the intermediate morphological level as well as the higher level of movements of objects in three-dimensional space. *Autonomous* (non-computational) mathematical and physico-mathematical theories of these objective levels are already available. Then from the subjective standpoint, several levels of *information explicitness* also exist. *And some of these levels possess objective levels of reality as objective correlates.* Consider the *visual form of objects*, for example, where the three basic levels of David Marr's perceptual theory all possess mathematically describable objective correlates:

(i) optics (geometric and wave) for the peripheral 2D primal sketch: propagation of wavefront singularities representing the apparent contour of objects, and their detection by zero-crossing criteria;

(ii) theory of singularities (Thom and Arnold's catastrophe theory) for the inter-mediate 2½-D sketch: apparent contours and reconstruction of a form based on the family of its apparent contours, etc.;

(iii) classic geometry and mechanics (Lie groups, movement of solids, etc.) for the central 3D level.

These objective theories are not computational. But they define *types* of infor-mation. The principle of double organization, as opposed to Fodor's (1980) "methodological solipsism", *finalizes* computational theories through objective theories: *when a level of explicitness (of representation) of information possesses an objective correlate it is the objective theory of this correlated reality which should determine the computational theory of information explicitness.* In other words, it is the *objective* determination of the *type* of information which must determine the theory of information processing.

This principle of finalization, when applied to the foregoing, is formulated in the following way. Information serving as input to the cognitive system is not only physical but also morphological. It is *pre-organized* in a way which is already system-significant on an *objective* basis. But this significance probably does not directly concern the symbolic level. A natural hypothesis is that it concerns instead the *sub-symbolic* level. Since the sub-symbolic and pheno-physical levels are governed *by morphodynamic formalizations of the same type*, it is easier to understand how one can *simulate* the other. Once represented at the sub-symbolic level, morphological information moves back toward the conceptual structure and, through projection onto the phenomenological level, transforms the natural world into a projected world. This is known as the *principle of double emergence and double organization* of the natural world (see Figure 3).

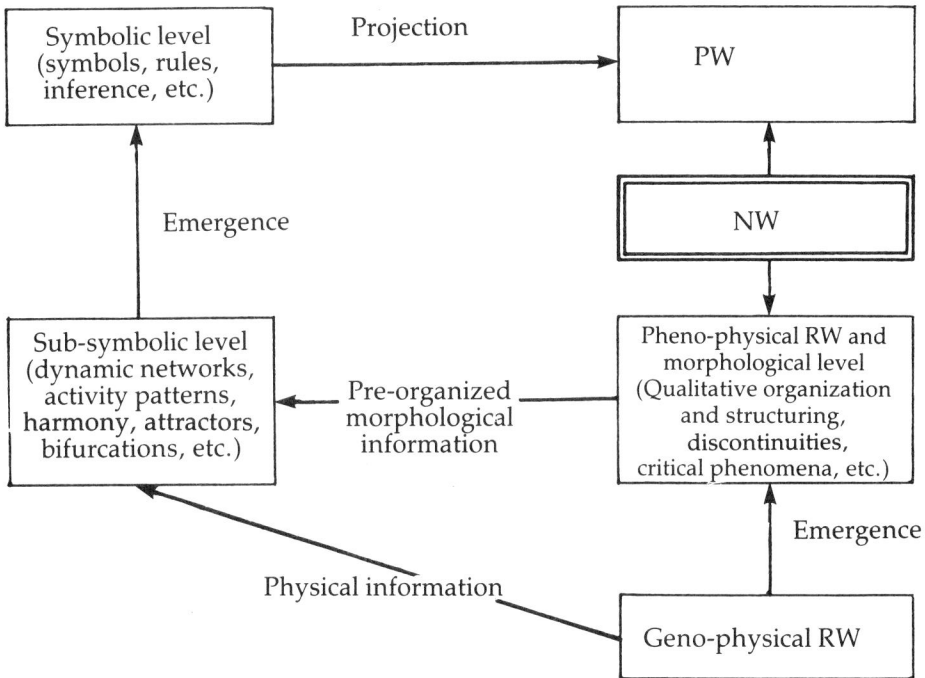

Figure 3

Conclusion

Theories of signal analysis, digital signal processing technologies, and the focus on symbolic representation – all of which are typical of computational mentalism – could be notably enhanced by taking into account the morphological information which is encoded through singularities. For the basic role of detectors of significant features is to reconstruct the geometry of these singularities. This is beginning to be appreciated, as indicated here, by theorists of visual and phonetic perception. Will it perhaps soon be appreciated by those concerned with musical perception?

Translated from the French by Deke Dusinberre

References

Andler, D. (1987) Progrès en situation d'incertitude. *Le Débat,* **47,** 5–25.

Fodor, J.A. (1980) Methodological solipsism considered as a research strategy in cognitive psychology. *The Behavioral and Brain Sciences,* **3,** 63–73.

Jackendoff, R. (1983) *Semantics and Cognition.* Cambridge, Mass: MIT Press.

Jackendoff, R. (1987) *Consciousness and the Computational Mind.* Cambridge, Mass: MIT Press.

Koenderink, J.J. & Van Doorn, A.J. (1986) Dynamic shape. *Biological Cybernetics,* **53** (6), 383–396.

Marr, D. (1982) *Vision.* San Francisco: Freeman.

Ouellet, P. (1987) Une physique du sens. *Critique,* **481/482,** 577–597.

Petitot, J. (1982a) A propos de la querelle du déterminisme. *Traverses,* **24,** 134–151.

Petitot, J. (1982b) Structuralisme et phénoménologie: la théorie des catastrophes et la part maudite de la raison. Printed in Petitot, J. (in press-b)

Petitot, J. (1983a) Paradigme catastrophique et perception catégorielle. *Recherches Sémiotiques* (RS/SI), **3** (3), 207–245.

Petitot, J. (1983b) La lacune du contour. *Anàlise,* **1** (1), 101–140.

Petitot, J. (1985a) *Morphogenèse du Sens,* Paris: Presses Universitaires de France.

Petitot, J. (1985b) *Les Catastrophes de la Parole. De Roman Jakobson à René Thom.* Paris: Maloine.

Petitot, J. (1986a) *Le "morphological turn" de la Phénoménologie,* CAMS Document. Paris: Ecole des Hautes Etudes en Sciences Sociales.

Petitot, J. (1986b) *Epistémologie des Phénomènes Critiques.* CAMS Document. Paris: Ecole des Hautes Etudes en Sciences Sociales.

Petitot, J. (1986c) Structure. *Encyclopedic Dictionary of Semiotics,* New York: Walter de Gruyter.

Petitot, J. (1988) Approche morphodynamique de la formule canonique du mythe. *L'Homme,* xxvii (2–3), 24–50.

Petitot, J. (in press-a) *Phénoménologie et Sémiotiquedu Monde Naturel.* Lisbon: Lisbon University Press.

Petitot, J. (ed.) (in press–b) *Logos et Théorie des Catastrophes.* Geneva: Patiño.

Proust, J. (1987) L'intelligence artificielle comme philosophie. *Le Débat,* **47,** 88–102.

Pylyshyn, Z. (1986) *Computation and Cognition.* Cambridge, Mass: MIT Press.

Rumelhart, D.E. & McClelland, J.L. (eds.) (1986) *Parallel Distributed Processing,* Vol. I, Cambridge, Mass: MIT Press.

Schwartz, J.L. (1987) *Représentations Auditives de Spectres Vocaliques* (Dissertation). Grenoble: Institut de la Communication Parlée.

Smolensky, P. (1986) Information processing in dynamical systems: Foundations of harmony theory. In *Parallel Distributed Processing,* Rumelhart & McClelland (eds.) vol. I, 194–281, Cambridge, Mass: MIT Press.

Smolensky, P. (1988),On the proper treatment of connectionnism. *The Behavioral and Brain Sciences,* **11,** 1–22.

Thom, R. (1972) *Stabilité Structurelle et Morphogenèse.* New York: Benjamin / Paris: Ediscience.

Thom, R. (1980) *Modèles Mathématiques de la Morphogenèse.* Paris: Christian Bourgois.

Contemporary Music Review,
1989, Vol. 4, pp. 181–198
Photocopying permitted by license only

Psychological constraints on form-bearing dimensions in music

Stephen McAdams

IRCAM, 31 rue Saint-Merri, F-75004 Paris, France

In raising the question of form-bearing dimensions in music, we are trying to understand the possibilities and limits of the apprehension of musical form in terms of the psychological mechanisms that operate on a received acoustic structure. To approach this understanding theoretically and experimentally, we need to define the notion of form-bearing dimension and to develop some ideas of the interactions that take place between perceptual processes and memory structures as form is accumulated in the mind of a listener. Three areas of psychological concern are discussed: perceptual grouping processes, abstract musical knowledge structures and event structure processing. For each area, the constraints on different musical dimensions such as pitch, duration, dynamics and timbre are examined in light of their potential to carry musical form.

KEY WORDS: Auditory grouping, event structures, form-bearing dimensions, knowledge structures, mental representation, musical form, perceptual invariance, psychological constraints.

Introduction

From the perceiver's perspective, the existence of artistic form is often intangible, fleeting, fugitive – evolving with new perceptions, new understanding. Form as experienced depends partly on the mind of the listener and partly on the structure presented to that mind. How, then, do we proceed to investigate the *psychological reality* of a musical form? What of a musical structure is *experienced* as musical form?

One approach to these questions would be to investigate the form-bearing *capacity* of the perceptual dimensions that are used in music. A dimension can bear form if configurations of values along it can be encoded, organized, recognized and compared with other such configurations. We can arrange a sequence of pitches, for example, that is easily recognized when it is heard again. We are also quite adept at noticing variations on such a sequence – the appreciation of melodic variation requires this psychological ability.

The *utility* of a dimension as a form-bearer, however, depends on some additional factors. A dimension that affords a greater number of perceivable configurations is more valuable to a composer than a dimension along which only a small number are possible. This restriction may be due, for example, to limits in the discrimination among the values available. Many pitches are easily perceived and discriminated, as are a vast quantity of their combinations. It is unlikely, though, that a large number of separate vibrato rates would be easily discriminated and, as such, only a very small number of configurations would be possible.

Limits on the encoding of complex patterns along the dimensions would in turn limit their potential for transformation and development of configurations. Our encoding of relative durations is fairly acute and highly structured, which allows for a rich variation and elaboration of rhythmic patterns. To the contrary, encoding of spatial location in audition is relatively poor, and one would imagine that the development of sequences of spatial positions of notes would not be easily apprehended by a listener.

Another factor is the capacity to encode patterns along a given dimension in the presence of changes along other dimensions. Duration may well be the strongest dimension from this perspective since many composers repeat rhythmic motifs across rather large variations in pitch and timbre pattern, and listeners have no trouble in recognizing the similarity. According to the above mentioned conditions we might predict that duration and pitch would be strong dimensions, that several of the timbre dimensions would be of medium power, but that vibrato rate and spatial location, for example, would be very weak.

We cannot, therefore, arbitrarily structure an available physical dimension such as spatial location and still expect it to be comprehended. The limits for a given individual may be tied to internalizations of relations in the physical world that would have proven useful to the human species through its evolution (Shepard, 1984). They might also be related to the degree to which the various dimensions are used in the music of a given culture. It may be that form-bearing capacities represent biological and psychological constraints on structure processing. We need to study the way in which such structures can be apprehended by a listener.

A form extended in time directly poses the problem of how to do research on the mental representation of its temporal structure. The experience of form is highly dependent on several cognitive processes involved in the mental representation of musical constituents and musical knowledge, and in the organization and comprehension of musical structures. These include perceptual grouping, abstract knowledge structures and event structure processing.

Auditory grouping processes serve to organize the acoustic surface into musical events (simultaneous grouping), to connect events into musical streams (sequential grouping), and to "chunk" event streams into musical units (segmentational grouping). These three basic grouping processes are important precursors to the organization of musical form in that they pre-organize the continuous "acoustic surface" into discrete entities and groups of entities. This organization is, in effect, the forming of mental descriptions of what is happening in the world, a mapping of acoustic sources and events into auditory descriptions that can be used in developing expectations and comprehension, in effect a kind of "auditory scene analysis" (Bregman, 1977, 1981, in press). To some extent these grouping processes precede the extraction (or "computation") of the perceptual qualities of events and the relations among these event qualities (pitch, timbre, density, rhythm, interval, consonance, etc.; cf. McAdams, 1987; Wright & Bregman, 1987). Musical form is built upon relations among perceptual qualities. To the extent that grouping processes affect the emergent qualities, they can affect the perception of form. Some perceptual dimensions are strongly correlated with the sensory dimensions along which grouping decisions are made, such as pitch and timbre being strongly correlated with the spectral changes that affect sequential and segmentational grouping (Bregman, 1978; McAdams & Bregman, 1979; McAdams,

1984; I. Deliège, 1987). Such dimensions will be important contributors to musical form. Thus, an important criterion for a form-bearing dimension is that changes along it should be able to induce distinctive transitions or contrasts at the musical surface.

The perceived qualities of musical events are anchored to a learned system of relations (scale, meter, harmonic field, etc.) that is more or less strongly evoked by the relations among events in the musical context. This system of relations may be considered as *abstract knowledge* about the structure of the music of a given culture that one has acquired through extensive experience. This knowledge is abstract in the sense that it embodies relations that apply across a large repertoire of pieces and serves to establish the relative stability or salience relations among the values along a given dimension. This domain is perhaps the most important for the consideration of form-bearing capacity because it is clear that if a system of habitual relations among values along a dimension cannot be learned, the power of that dimension as a structuring force would be severely compromised.

The incoming acoustic information is parsed and interpreted according to acquired musical knowledge structures which affect the subsequent encoding and organizing of the musical material in an accumulated *event structure* upon which the experience of form is based. This event structure is specific to a given listening to a piece of music. This area involves many psychological processes to which a dimension must be susceptible if it is to contribute to musical form, such as the encoding of values and relations on musical dimensions, the perception of the similarity, invariance, and difference of musical material occuring at different times, the combination of hierarchical and associative structures, the appreciation of the trajectory of development and the generation of expectations based on structural implications.

The remainder of this article will examine more closely the aspects of abstract knowledge structure and event structure processing that are important for evaluating the contribution of various perceptual dimensions to musical form.

Abstract knowledge structures

A lot of perceptions, decisions, and understandings are based on generalizations that we have learned from specific experience. In music cognition these abstractions seem to be of two types that are general to at least a whole repertoire of music or to a musical culture (though some may also apply across cultures): systems of relations among musical categories (such as pitch categories, scale structure, and tonal and metric hierarchies), and a lexicon of abstract patterns that are frequently encountered (such as gallop rhythm, gap-fill melody, sonata form or *rag* form). The former tend to be knowledge structures that are atemporal while the latter have a sequential aspect. Below, I will discuss the role of categories, ordered relations among categories, and a lexicon of patterns in the cognition of musical form. The discussion will focus primarily on pitch with brief mention of limits and possibilities for dimensions.

Categories

In the majority of the musics of the world, structure is based on dimensions that are divided into categories: classes of pitch, duration, dynamics and timbral identity. In many (though not all) cultures, this categorization is evidenced by the fact that the categories are coded in symbols either in notation systems or in language (e.g. solfège for pitch in Western and Indian music, and a kind of timbre solfège for tabla strokes in Indian music). Category systems serve "to provide maximum information with the least cognitive effort" (Rosch, 1978, p. 28). This is achieved when one perceives values along a dimension as equivalent to values of the same category and also as different from values in other categories. The interval class of a minor third is perceived as such within the Western 12-tone pitch system regardless of its precise tuning. It would however, be distinguished from a major second.

One of the aspects of this categorization is the discreteness of many of the musical dimensions. It is crucial that categories be easily discriminated from one another. If a listener cannot tell them apart then the use of one category rather than its neighbor cannot create a perceptible difference in structure. The semitone in the Western 12-tone pitch system, for example, is at least six times larger than the smallest interval most listeners are able to discriminate (Green, 1976, chap. 10). Even quarter-tones are still a reasonable interval size with respect to dis-criminability, at least in the middle and upper registers. Jordan (1987) has shown that listeners discriminate tonal function at the quarter-tone level but not at the eighth-tone level. A microtonal pitch system such as Partch's (1974) 43-tone per octave *Chromelodeon* approaches very closely the limits of discriminability which could present difficulties for perceiving the different pitch structures produced in the system.

The importance of discretization is that we remember discrete entities easier than continuous or unclearly demarcated ones, at least for the memory of struc-tures. This does not mean that continuous variation is not important in the appreciation of musical form. It is certainly vital for expressive variation of musical gesture. I am inclined, though, to remain close to Clarke's (1987) distinction between structure and expression, where discrete elements carry structure and continuous variation carries expression. But if a piece of music were to glide con-tinuously through its several dimensions, I fear that a listener would not acquire much of a sense of form. Expressive, interpretive gesture is certainly continuous in nature, but most often around a stable point of reference or between a couple of points of reference, which serve the role of category prototypes (Rosch, 1978). A specific category is still often evoked in such cases.

It is also important that there be a relatively small number of categories. How small this number is depends primarily on short-term memory limitations (our ability to encode and compare values over a relatively short time period). There is certainly an important interaction between these short-term processing limita-tions and the storage of an abstract system of relations among values. It is easier to encode values that can be anchored to an over-learned system of relations than those that are completely new for a listener, as would often be the case in one's initial contacts with new scale or rhythmic systems, or with new sound categories such as are found in electroacoustic music. Most pitch systems of the world are limited to 5-12 tones per octave, a limit largely superceded by Partch's *Chromelo-deon*. For musical qualities like timbre that have several perceptual "dimensions" such as brightness, tone color, roughness, attack character, etc., it would probably be necessary in building musical form with them to use only a few values along each dimension. These values should be widely separated so that the distinctive relations among them could be easily perceived and learned. Such is the case with distinctive features in speech sounds, where only two or three values are employed along any given speech dimension (Fant, 1973). This allows them to be meaningfully contrasted with one another.

It may be desirable, also for reasons related to memory limits, to have well-defined, perhaps fixed, categories or relations ("intervals") among categories. This fixity would certainly enhance the contribution of long-term memory to the encoding and organization of incoming information, primarily since the categories and relations could be generalized across a large number of musical situations. Dimensions like pitch and musical instrument timbre are, in many cases, more or less fixed in the fabrication of the instruments or are defined by cultural convention (though, again, there are important exceptions throughout the world). Duration and dynamics tend, however, to be much more flexibly chosen and thus the greater perceptual importance is attached to maintaining and contrasting relations among values in performance (Gabrielsson, 1979).

Relations are thus quite important components of musical material. Much psychological research on musical recognition memory has shown the importance of relations as building blocks of patterns. These relations would include pitch levels, timbre vectors and duration proportions. Our ability to recognize transposed or accelerated musical patterns testifies to the psychological reality of relational encoding. But in some cases it appears that these relations become strongly fixed in long-term memory. Shepard & Jordan (1984) presented listeners with a stretched C major scale such that the octave ended on C# 'instead of C'. They then presented probe tones belonging to C major, C# major or the stretched scale, and asked listeners to judge how well they fit with the previously heard scale. Listeners tended to judge tones from the C# major scale as better fitting, indicating that as the tones of the stretched scale deviated from the learned pattern, this pattern was "shifted" to accommodate the deviations. At the end it was thus "positioned" on C# and influenced the subsequent judgments accordingly.

The origins of the discretization of dimensions into categories are varied, depending on the dimension in question, and may be considered as either natural or artificial (cf. Rosch, 1973, 1978, for visual and semantic categories). Instrumental timbres would appear to be separated on the basis of their mode of production (attack quality and spectral evolution are related strongly to instrument family – such as brass, bowed string, single or double reed, and so on). This also appears to be the case with speech phonemes and implies the existence of possibly innate perceptual mechanisms that are tuned to the physical behavior of sound-producing objects (Neisser, 1976, chap. 9). The categorization of other dimensions (such as pitch, duration, dynamics and many synthesized timbres) results from a learned, artificial division of psychophysical continua of perceptual qualities (Dowling & Harwood, 1986, chap. 4). It is important to note that in the case of natural categories, it is difficult to achieve a continuous perception of some dimensions. The tendency to categorization and identification of the source is very strong. In the case of artificial categories, the continuity of the dimension is already there and a clear, reproducible system of discretization is necessary. The strong timbral identities of instrumental sound sources may to some extent be overcome by compositional artifice in orchestration where their blending into composite qualities gives one more flexibility in continuous variation between "composed" timbres (cf. Boulez, 1987).

Ordered Relations

It is necessary that the classification of stimulus categories and the ordering of their relations reflect psychological possibilities, in other words that there be a strong degree of correspondence between the stimulus structure and its mental representation. Otherwise the resultant structures will not be decodable by the listener, and they won't be able to contribute to the appreciation of musical form. The way of ordering the perceptual categories places more or less rigorous constraints on the apprehension of musical forms.

To begin this investigation, let us consider several properties that appear to contribute to the organization of pitch systems, (e.g., scale structures - Cross, Howell & West, 1985; and tonal hierarchies - Krumhansl, 1983) that we may postulate to be more or less easily processed by a listener. A recognition of these properties in a sequence of musical events helps to evoke and establish the system framework in the listener's mind.

Some researchers feel that the category values and intervals should be selected with respect to sensory considerations, such as sensory consonance (Helmholtz, 1877/1885; Krumhansl, 1987; Lerdahl, 1988; though this is contested by Brown, 1988). The organization of relations according to such sensory properties provides a solid psychoacoustic foundation for their function in musical patterns. Mathews, Pierce & Roberts (1987) propose this kind of constraint as a crucial consideration for the development of new musical dimensions. They call it the *acoustic nucleus hypothesis:* "With new materials, it is necessary to have an acoustic nucleus on which to grow powerful musical connotations via long-term learning. The acoustic nucleus consists of sound qualities that are perceivable at a low peripheral level, such as . . . relative dissonance . . ." (p. 83). However, we should realize that this constraint has been loosened somewhat in the establishment of the equal-tempered pitch system in order to gain other organizational possibilities such as being able to transpose a pitch pattern to any other pitch without seriously distorting the interval relations. Lerdahl (1987) has made some preliminary attempts at applying a generalized notion of sensory dissonance to the development of a system of timbral relations.

A property that seems to be special to pitch is the existence of a strong perceptual equivalence at the octave which allows the dimension to be organized cyclically with a given pattern of values being repeated regularly in each octave. This property is found in most of the musical scales of the world, though there are some notable exceptions (cf. discussion in Burns & Ward, 1982). As such one might hypothesize, as do Burns & Ward, that octave generalization in pitch is a learned concept which has its roots in sensory consonance. The innate vs. acquired nature of octave equivalence, however, is far from resolved in the debate between universalists and cultural relativists.

The psychological value of a cyclic dimension is that it allows a certain economy of mental representation and learning of the stimulus dimension: a large number and range of values can be used without overloading memory since a scale pattern with a small number of elements is repeated regularly. Once well-learned, these patterns tend to become very strong as components of structural interpretation, that is, as components of mental schemata that are used to organize and understand the incoming musical structure (Khumhansl, 1983; Shepard & Jordan, 1984).

One wonders whether the mere existence of a cyclic organization is in itself sufficient to enrich the dimension's form-bearing capacities independently of the actual repetition interval used. The very special status of the octave is due to its high degree of consonance. Aside from experiments by Mathews & Pierce (1980), little experimental evidence exists for scale systems organized on intervals other than the octave. They developed a "stretched" diatonic scale which had an "octave" ratio of 2.4:1 instead of 2:1. The tones that were played also had stretched frequency ratios, making them inharmonic. Subjects were asked to judge whether a short harmonic progression was in the same key as a longer passage. Both ended in a stretched equivalent of a cadence. Subjects were also asked to judge the finality of the cadence compared with unstretched tones and scales. The results suggest that subjects can match the "keys" of chord sequences in the stretched system, though the cadences lack a sense of finality.

In a great deal of contemporary Western music since the 1950's there has been a kind of obsessive avoidance of pitch pattern repetition in other octaves. Part of the reason for this was to avoid invoking the schemata of classical tonal music. Another was based on an æsthetic principal of continual renewal of material with as little repetition as possible (cf. Schoenberg, 1941/1975, 1948/1975). The resulting irregularities (often applied to rhythm as well) force listeners to adopt completely different modes of listening and remembering.

There is no evidence of true circularity in form-bearing dimensions other than pitch. One attempt at imposing circularity on timbre has been proposed by Slawson (1985). He takes a bounded two-dimensional representation of vowel-space (the dimensions corresponding to the center frequencies of two formants or filters) as a starting point for a theory of "sound color". From this he tries to develop a series of rules of organization of the space and of operations on the elements in the space based on serial procedures. He suggests that if an operation, such as transposition, forces one to leave the bounded space to the right, one should treat the right-hand border as coextensive with the left-hand border and simply wrap the pattern around. This has the effect of completely changing the interval and contour relations of the pattern. I would claim that this is the perceptual equivalent of using a two and a half octave instrument (C2 to F4) and treating the C2 as equivalent to F4. Transposing the pattern F3–D4–B♭3– A3–C#4 up a fourth and wrapping the notes above F4 around to C2 would give B♭–D2–E♭4–D4–C#2 which is clearly different from the original in both interval pattern and contour. The author recognizes that this is an unfounded premise that violates what one perceives. He proceeds nonetheless to base a large portion of his theory of sound color and many of his compositional efforts on this falsely imposed property of the space. It becomes clear through this intellectual exercise that one cannot "invent" a perceptual equivalence that has no psychoacoustic foundation. It also becomes clear that the lack of this property places some rather severe constraints on the possible range of operations along a dimension.

Balzano (1980), Dowling & Harwood (1986) and Krumhansl (1987) have delineated a number of other properties of the pitch dimension that are helpful in establishing a tonal pitch hierarchy. These criteria are examined in detail with respect to several existing and proposed pitch scale systems in Krumhansl (1987). *Focal values* are those that occur frequently, that have longer durations, and that tend to occupy strong positions in musical phrases. Frequency of occurrence and duration may, in particular, help to establish the system framework when a listener is faced with an unfamiliar musical style. Western listeners appear able to do this with Indian *rāgs* though certain subtleties of the Indian system escape them (Castellano, Bharucha & Krumhansl, 1984; see also Kessler, Hansen & Shepard, 1984, for Western and Balinese listeners). The effect of phrase position would depend a great deal on the listener already having acquired some under-standing of phrase structure, perhaps from cues such as slowing down and pauses at the end of phrases (cf. Carlson, Friberg, Frydén, Granström & Sundberg, this volume).

It is desirable for listeners to be able to rapidly discern their "position" within the system of pitch relations (Browne, 1981). This position finding may be due to both the *asymmetric structure of intervals* among the categories in a scale (e.g. in the major diatonic scale there are series of two and three major seconds separated by minor seconds), and to the existence of rare or *distinctive intervals* in the set (e.g. in the major diatonic scale there exists only one augmented fourth, two minor seconds, and a greater number of other intervals; cf. Butler & Brown, 1984). This property also *maximizes the variety of interval sizes* in a given scale. This property would distinguish the Western diatonic scales and many Indian *thats* from equal-tempered pentatonic scales found on Indonesian gamelan and Ugandan harp or from certain equal-tempered heptatonic scales found on Ugandan and Thai xylophones (cf. discussion in Burns & Ward, 1982, pp. 257–258).

The last criterion of ordering is the *predisposition to certain sequential relations* among dimension values (Butler & Brown, 1984; Brown, 1988). This criterion is enhanced by the existence of distinctive intervals. It tries to capture aspects of functional relations that are not merely related to the frequency of occurrence of individual values, but to the frequency of occurrence of pairs or sets of values in a given sequential order, that is, to statistical sequential asymmetries found in a body of music. For example, within the Western tonal hierarchy, the unstable leading-tone tends to resolve to a succeeding tonic. The statistical occurrence of this ordering of the pitches is much greater than the reverse. The learning of these tendencies through extended exposure to a given style of music is partially responsible for the sense of directed motion: a given value implies by anticipation its succession by another, giving rise to patterns of tension and release, or implica-tion and realization (cf. Narmour, this volume). This functional, sequential aspect of pitch relations has been stressed by Butler & Brown (1984) as a crucial cue in evoking a tonal center and a sense of key. What I would like to point out here is that many of these relations of stability and instability which occur frequently, can also become part of the abstract knowledge of the structure of a musical dimension such as pitch. This is the problem of the interaction between abstract knowledge structures and real-time event structure processing that is discussed by Deutsch (1984) and Bharucha (1984b) in terms of tonal and event hierarchies, respectively.

Much psychology research has demonstrated that information is more easily encoded, organized, perceived and remembered when it is hierarchically ordered (Restle, 1970; Deutsch & Feroe, 1981). One might postulate that this is, then, a desirable property of a stimulus system. There are two types of hierarchy that are often referred to here. One is a hierarchy of dominance or stability relations (what Simon, 1962/1982, refers to as a "formal hierarchy") in which some elements dominate other elements and are thus given greater structural prominence. The other type is one where combinations of elements at lower levels give rise to emergent properties at higher levels that are not easily derived from the properties of the individual constituents. Pitch relations in a scale are primarily of the first type, while the relations between pitch, chord and key are of the second type. There is a third type which is often used in connection with event hierarchies (see next section) which has a notion of parts within parts. This latter is the main type referred to in Lerdahl & Jackendoff (1983) in their well-formedness rules and structural trees. Hierarchization depends to a large extent on some of the criteria listed previously, such as the existence of reference points or focal values.

The derivation of harmonic function from the tonal organization of pitch is an example of the richness of hierarchization possible in a musical dimension (cf. Krumhansl, 1987; Lerdahl, 1988), though one wonders to what extent this richness might be limited to pitch and duration. The derivation of harmony from scale structure illustrates the fact that certain properties emerge at certain levels in a hierarchical system. A number of criteria for harmonic relations that mirror to some extent those of pitch relations listed above have been proposed by Krumhansl (1987). I won't examine these here, but will summarize her reflections by saying that the relations among the "emergent values" (chord types) at this higher level of the hierarchy are organized in strikingly similar ways to the simpler values (pitches) at the lower levels. This coherence between levels of the hierarchy distinguishes the Western tonal pitch system and is one of the properties that gives it such a high structuring potential.

The abandonment or weakening by many contemporary composers of the tonal pitch hierarchy, with its incumbent structural economy, and the resistance of some to using any other kind of hierarchy to replace it, might place a greater cognitive burden on the listener. To date little experimentation or psychologically oriented theory has been directed at trying to understand what listeners actually hear and understand in this kind of music, or to understand the extent to which one can learn to process these new combinatorial structures (though see Lerdahl, this volume). The work that has been done suggests that most listeners are more sensitive to contour than to precise interval structure in atonal and serial music (Francès, 1972/1988, chaps. 3,4; Dowling & Harwood, 1986, chap. 5). Krumhansl, Sandell & Sergeant (1987) produced evidence that both inexperienced listeners and those highly trained in contemporary musical idioms, when confronted with fragments of 12-tone serial music (Schoenberg's *Wind Quintet, op. 26*, 1924, and *String Quartet, no. 4, op. 37*, 1936) tend to interpret the pitches according to tonal implications in the fragments. The judgments of trained listeners tended to be negatively correlated with these implications. The authors interpreted these results as indicating that trained musicians hear the tonal implication and then give low ratings to tones that fit with it since such relations are not supposed to be present in this music: a kind of post hoc decision rather than an immediate perceptual experience. At any rate, it should be emphasized that relatively little work has been done on music outside the Western tonal idiom. Nor do we yet have a large population of people who have been as exposed to new musical organizations as they are to tonal/metric music. Some of the strong pronouncements about the psychological invalidity of contemporary musical idioms are certainly premature, though perhaps composers should also take a stronger interest in the speculations of music psychologists (cf. McAdams, 1988).

I have confined myself primarily to pitch in this section, but it is worthwhile briefly considering other dimensions. Another crucial form-bearing dimension is duration, upon which very elaborate metric and rhythmic systems have been developed. A relatively small number of well-defined relative durations are used. A system of strong and weak beats is often organized hierarchically (and re-presented mentally as abstract knowledge) to which duration patterns are anchored (cf. Gabrielsson, 1979; Lerdahl & Jackendoff, 1983, chap. 4; Longuet-Higgins & Lee, 1984; Povel & Essens, 1985; Dowling & Harwood, 1986, chap. 7). Some of the reflections on the relations between tonal and event hierarchies suggest that the temporal dimension is crucial for the establishment of relations that are encoded as abstract knowledge on other dimensions.

To my knowledge no systematic experimental or musical research has yet been done on the possibilities of "scale" systems of timbre, or how these might interact with pitch and duration systems. It has been demonstrated that musical instrument timbres can be easily discriminated. Timbre relations have been shown to have similar mental representations across several listeners and can be predicted more or less on the basis of acoustic properties (Grey, 1977; Risset & Wessel, 1982). Listeners can also make consistent judgments of analogous timbral *vectors* (intervals through more than one dimension, possessing both distance and direction components). This demonstrates that the notion of vector is relevant and that transposed vectors are perceived as being equivalent when distance and direction relations are held constant between the two timbres (Wessel, 1979). The existence of the vector is already an important step toward developing patterns and scales in timbre space. Some preliminary attempts at making hierarchically organized sequences of timbres are encouraging (Lerdahl, 1987). What is not yet known is the extent to which variation along the dimensions of timbre can maintain perceptual invariance in the face of changes along the pitch and duration dimensions, or the extent to which listeners can acquire stable abstract representations of an ordered system of timbre relations.

It will also be necessary to try to generalize the use of emergent properties of a hierarchical system (such as the relationship between pitch and harmony) to the timbre dimension. A combination of values must possess an emergent property that derives from the group configuration rather than being a new value along the dimension. In the case of pitch, a chord can have the quality of being major or minor, for example, and one can still hear out the individual pitches. The pitches do not fuse into a *new pitch* which replaces them (in spite of the fact that we are often limited by masking processes in hearing out inner voices). It is frequently the case, as a lot of 20th century music testifies, that multiple timbres fuse into a composite timbre, the individual identities being replaced by the newly emerged one. The non-fusion criterion may, in many cases, limit the possibilities of a superordinate system of timbral combinations. But then it may be pushing the rational urge too far to expect all form-bearing dimensions to behave in the same way or to have similar structural properties at all levels of combination.

A Lexicon of Patterns

Another type of knowledge we might expect experienced listeners to possess, and which would influence the ability of a perceptual dimension to bear form is that of classes of patterns and forms. There are, in any given culture, certain patterns of pitch, duration and perhaps timbre relations that occur frequently and in many different specific circumstances. Some music theorists propose a relatively restricted lexicon of pitch patterns that are the "genetic code" from which melodies are built (Narmour, this volume; in press), or that are a kind of archetypal substructure from which melodies are elaborated (Meyer's "melodic process", 1973).

Given that these patterns are sequential objects, it seems that the notion of "event schema" as the representation of a category may be appropriate. These abstract event schemata of stereotypic patterns and forms would correspond to some extent to the notion of "scripts" as developed by Schank & Abelson (1977). These researchers propose that we have abstract scripts for various kinds of macro-events, such as going to a concert or taking a bath. The script involves the main kinds of actions that are necessary such as leaving home, going to the concert hall, buying the ticket, sitting down, listening attentively, and going home. This is evidently very abstract and allows for all kinds of variation in its real-life manifestation. The same would hold for the notion of a melodic process. A "changing note process" for example, starts at an important pitch (such as a tonic), descends a step below this pitch on the scale, skips up to the pitch above and then comes down to the main pitch again. In its specific manifestation, each of these elements may be elaborated into several bars of music. What Meyer's theory proposes however, is that we recognize these processes as basic categories of melodic structure of which there are a very small number. This idea has been given some credence in analyses and experimental studies by Rosner & Meyer (1982, 1986).

This has several implications for form-bearing dimensions. Such patterns, if used extensively in the music of a culture, must be abstracted and generalized through experience by listeners. This means that for a lexicon of stereotypic event schemata to be established in long-term memory, the process of encoding and abstraction must be possible for that dimension. This is an area that certainly deserves more serious consideration as well as experimentation on several musical dimensions.

Event structure processing

Musical events, after passing through elementary grouping processes, are then processed in such a way as to recover aspects of their larger-scale structure. This more time-bound part of structure processing, specific to the information being received, may be contrasted with the abstract knowledge discussed in the previous section. This contrast mirrors that proposed by Bharucha (1984b) and Deutsch (1984) between tonal and event hierarchies. I prefer to use the term "event structure" here, since there are aspects of musical form, represented through event structures, that are not purely hierarchical, such as the relatively little understood associative relations established by similar patterns in different

parts of a piece. The area of event structures concerns the processes that underlie
1) the perceptual encoding of musical events and patterns within the context of
evoked systems of relations, 2) the perception of invariance and transformation of
musical patterns, and 3) the establishment of associative and hierarchical relations
across time in the building of a mental representation of a musical form. I will
discuss here the problems of pattern encoding and the perception of invariance
and transformation.

Encoding Values and Relations

The kinds of relations and patterns that are encoded include pitch intervals, pitch
contours, chord qualities, rhythmic intervals between event onsets, rhythmic
contours of sequences of long and short events, and vectors between points in
timbre space. The process of encoding the patterns of values and relations among
them as they occur in time is not neutral. Perceived relations are constrained by
grouping processes, and by expectations about events that are likely to occur.
These expectations result from anticipatory schemata representing abstract
knowledge acquired through previous experience and which are activated by the
incoming events. Such schemata have been shown to facilitate the perception of
certain tones over others in the cases both of tonal pitch relations (Bharucha &
Stoeckig, 1986) and of rhythmic sequences (Bharucha & Pryor, 1986). This
evoking or activation, of mental representations of tonality and meter may have
the effect of orienting perception toward a set of context-constrained alternatives
(Bartlett & Dowling, 1988). "Events are thus expected, implied, erroneously
judged to have occurred and rendered more consonant, to the extent that their
mental representations have been activated in anticipation of their occurrence"
(Bharucha, 1987, p. 3). Following this, one might conjecture that perceptual
dimensions for which listeners are capable of acquiring abstract structural knowledge, and which can subsequently be used to elicit more or less strong expectations in listening, would be good candidates for form-bearing dimensions.

An important property of the activation of a structural schema is the "assignment" of relative stability, dominance, or salience relations among the perceived
events. The fixing of events within an interpretive framework gives them musical
significance and to some extent forms the dynamic musical flow by the anchoring
or assimilation of less stable or salient elements to more stable and salient
elements. But the temporal order of tones can also strongly influence which ones
are interpreted as more stable (and, by implication, what the activated framework
is). For example, in the tonally ambiguous sequence B3–C4–D#4–E4–F#4–G4,
Bharucha (1984a) found that listeners preferred C major as an accompanying
chord over B major, though the pitches of both chords are present in the
sequence. To the contrary, when the sequence is played in reverse, listeners
preferred B major. Bharucha concludes that two constraints are in operation in the
anchoring of an unstable tone to a more stable one: the stable tone normally
follows the unstable one, and the tones must be either diatonic or chromatic
neighbors. Thus, the skips between C–D# and E–F# cause the sequence to be
interpreted as three sequential pairs and the stability relations to be established
within each pair. This is a point where grouping processes and knowledge structures strongly interact (Deutsch, 1978; Krumhansl, 1979; Bharucha, 1984a,b).
One wonders what responses listeners would give if the range of possible

accompaniments presented to them was greater or if the listener had had extensive experience listening to Arabic music where such a scale pattern is quite common.

Additional constraints on sequence order have been reported by Butler & Brown (1984) where the sequential position of the tritone in a melodic pattern was important in the degree of activation of a tonal center. This indicates that distinctive intervals in a scale structure are not sufficient in and of themselves to activate the representation of a whole system of relations. The import of the process of anchoring or assimilation is that the possibility of establishing such sequential tendencies is a strong factor contributing to the form-bearing capacity of a dimension.

Memory limits also need to be considered in the encoding of musical material. In order to be easily encoded and then to contribute to the perception of connectedness between groups of musical events separated in time, a musical pattern must satisfy a number of constraints. It should be small enough to fit within the perceptual present (about 2–5 seconds; Fraisse, 1978). It should be unified enough to be grouped into a chunk in short-term memory. (A limit on short-term storage is classically set at about 5–9 chunks in Miller, 1956, though this depends on the nature of the pattern). Patterns that are organized according to easily discernible rules of construction, such as hierarchical patterns, are generally remembered more easily and can have more elements in short-term memory than patterns organized in other ways (Restle, 1970; Deutsch & Feroe, 1981; 1981 Deutsch, 1982). Memorability may also be greater for patterns that have some kind of inherent stability or well-formedness or for those that are more easily assimilated to an existing knowledge structure. This latter hypothesis is suggested by work on recognition memory of tonal and atonal sequences (see Francès, 1972/1988; Dowling & Harwood, 1986). The question of "good formation" has not been considered much of late. What "well-formedness" means may well be quite varied for different dimensions and it is not clear to what extent it would be independent of cultural convention, and thus of acquired knowledge structures.

Invariance and Transformation

Pattern similarity perception may be considered an important basis for musical development, which involves the abstraction of invariances across transformations of musical patterns. The transformation of musical patterns figures among the quasi-universal characteristics of the world's music systems. A strong form-bearing dimension should allow a richness of pattern transformations that are perceived as related to the original material to a greater or lesser degree (Slawson, 1985). This raises the question of what remains the same and what varies when a musical pattern is transformed. Within the dimension of pitch, for example, transposition maintains exact interval pattern and contour, but can change key. Harmonic modulation maintains contour and interval class pattern (allowing for equivalence of major and minor intervals, etc. across keys). Inversion maintains interval size while inverting direction (and thus contour). In *Music for Strings, Percussion and Celeste* (1936), Bartók used expansive and compressive transforms that enlarged or reduced all intervals (constrained by some desired pitch set) which maintained pitch contour. Theme and variations treatment often uses hierarchical elaboration wherein notes of the original melody are ornamented or developed with melodic figures. It is hierarchical in the sense that a "reduction" of the elaborated melody would yield the original.

Perceptual invariance means that certain relations between categories along a stimulus dimension must remain constant after transformation. An interval of a perfect fifth (or a whole melody) maintains a relatively constant quality regardless of the register in which it is played (within the range of musical pitch). This means that transposition is an operation that is easily afforded by the pitch dimension. If patterns composed along a dimension are not predisposed to being varied and still being perceived as similar, then the dimension cannot make a strong contribution to musical form (White 1960). In cases of inversion and expansion transformations, we would intuit that the degree of similarity would be less than in the case of transposition where both contour and interval content were maintained. A simple retrograde transformation, on the other hand, reverses absolute pitch sequence, interval sequence and contour; though the pitch set remains constant, its order is completely changed and people tend not to perceive it as being very similar to the original sequence (Francès, 1972/1988, Exp. 6). From these cases, we might hypothesize that limits on the perceived relatedness of a pattern to its transformed version indicate the limits of viable musical transformations. Krumhansl, Sandell & Sergeant (1987) have shown that listeners are capable of classifying mirror forms related to distinctive original pitch patterns when there are only two sets of them. However, no estimate was made of how similar these forms were perceived as being with respect to their originals.

There would appear to be two basic classes of transformation: linear operations along a given dimension or set of dimensions (such as translation, expansion, rotation, etc.), and structural modifications of the pattern (such as changing a single element, splitting an internal beat in two, hierarchically elaborating a melodic process by developing musical figures around its main notes, or adapting a pattern to a different meter). In the case of linear dimensional operations, the comparison between original and transformed versions would remain at the structural level. For operations like hierarchical elaboration, the similarity judgment would necessarily be made at appropriate levels of the patterns depending on the degree of elaboration (Deutsch & Feroe, 1981; Rosner & Meyer, 1986).

It is not only desirable that listeners be able to recognize transformed material as being similar or related, but that they appreciate the nature of the transformation as well. This can contribute to a sense of direction in the musical development. The recognition and comparison of a more or less similar pattern after some kind of transformation at a later point in a piece, implies the existence of a mental representation of the original pattern that maintains certain structural properties during transformation. These properties may be perceptible as such: a contour for example. The existence of such representations suggests limits on the structuring of transformed musical materials. The majority of research in this area has been done in experiments on recognition memory for pitch patterns. Not much work has been done on other stimulus dimensions or on the contribution of perceived similarity to associative structuring. A more extended exploration may eventually open a rich domain of functional replacements for the classical variation process and propose new kinds of musical development (see, for example, Reynolds, 1987). It may well turn out, however, that certain kinds of transformation are limited to specific dimensions.

Conclusion

I have tried to set out in this article a number of ideas about constraints of a psychological nature on perceptual dimensions that are either well-known bearers of form, such as pitch and duration, or those that are serious candidates, such as timbre. These constraints fall into three areas as are summarized below.

A potential form-bearing dimension should be closely correlated with the sensory dimensions that effect perceptual grouping, whether it be of a simultaneous, sequential or segmentational nature. Current research indicates that the dimensions of timbral brightness, pitch, duration, dynamics and spatial location have this capacity. Future work should examine interactions and competitions among the dimensions with respect to perceptual grouping potential. Another important avenue of research would be the interaction between knowledge structures and grouping processes in order to understand the extent to which these latter, primarily bottom-up processes can be affected by previous knowledge and ongoing expectations.

A form-bearing dimension should be susceptible to being organized into perceptual categories and relations among these categories should be easily encoded. A system of salience or stability relations should be learnable through mere exposure and should affect the perception of patterns along this dimension. Certain recurrent sequential patterns of values should be easily learned as a kind of lexicon of forms. In other words, relations along the dimension must be susceptible to being acquired as abstract knowledge. Experimental research has focussed almost exclusively on pitch in this area though duration is beginning to receive more attention. In pitch, the vast majority of work is confined to Western tonal music, with some notable side trips to India and Indonesia. Future work should look at existing pitch systems of other non-Western cultures and at some of the new approaches to the compositional organization of pitch found in the work of our living composer colleagues. The same could be said of rhythm and meter. To my mind the next most important candidate for exploration and experimentation is timbre. Along which of its dimensions can we perceive, organize and remember musical relations? To what extent can they compete with structures of pitch and duration? It may be that the different dimensions have different general characteristics and that their relative contributions to grouping processes and knowledge structures will be varied.

Finally, there is much work of both theoretical and experimental natures to be done on the contribution of form-bearing dimensions to the building of hierarchical and associative event structures. A serious effort is needed to clarify theoretically the notion of associative structure and to develop experimental methodologies to verify its psychological reality. Other problems would include some of the following. To what extent can different form-bearing dimensions contribute to associative and hierarchical structures? What is the relative contribution of the different dimensions in these structures to the direction of attentional processes and to the development of expectation? How do the different dimensions interact in the accumulation of a musical form when the implications of their individual structures converge on structural coherence or diverge toward structural ambiguity? Perhaps with some clearer ideas of the mental representation and processing of musical structure and their result in an experience of musical form, we can approach some of the more fundamental questions of individual musical experience that have to this point eluded experimental and theoretical efforts.

Acknowledgments

This article has benefitted enormously from insightful discussions with Carol Krumhansl. I would also like to thank Eric Clarke, Fred Lerdahl, Eugene Narmour and an anonymous reviewer for helpful critiques of an earlier version of the manuscript.

References

Balzano, G.J. (1980) The group-theoretic description of twelve-fold and microtonal pitch systems, *Computer Music Journal*, **4(4)** 66–84.

Bartlett, J.C. & Dowling, W.J. (1988) Scale structure and similarity of melodies. *Music Perception*, **5**, 285–314.

Bartók, B. (1936) *Music for Strings, Percussion, and Celeste*, Vienna, Universal Editions/Philharmonia.

Bharucha, J.J. (1984a) Anchoring effects in music: The resolution of dissonance. *Cognitive Psychology*, **16**, 485–518.

Bharucha, J.J. (1984b) Event hierarchies, tonal hierarchies and assimilation: A reply to Deutsch and Dowling, *Journal of Experimental Psychology: General*, **113**, 421–425.

Bharucha, J.J. (1987) Music cognition and perceptual facilitation: A connectionist framework, *Music Perception*, **5**, 1–30.

Bharucha, J.J. & Pryor, J.H. (1986) Disrupting the isochrony underlying rhythm: An asymmetry in discrimination, *Perception & Psychophysics*, **40**, 137–141.

Bharucha, J.J. & Stoeckig, K. (1986) Reaction time and musical expectancy: Priming of chords, *Journal of Experimental Psychology: Human Perception & Performance*, **12**, 1–8.

Boulez, P. (1987) Timbre and composition – timbre and language. In "Music and Psychology: A Mutual Regard", S. McAdams (ed.), *Contemporary Music Review*, **2(1)**, 161–172.

Bregman, A.S. (1977) Perception and behavior as compositions of ideals, *Cognitive Psychology*, **9**, 250–292.

Bregman, A.S. (1978) The formation of auditory streams. In *Attention and Performance VII*, J. Requin (ed.), Hillsdale, N.J.: Lawrence Eribaum Associates.

Bregman, A.S. (1981) Asking the "what for" question in auditory perception. In *Perceptual Organization*, M. Kubovy & J.R. Pomerantz (eds.), pp. 99–118, Hillsdale, N.J.: Lawrence Erlbaum Associates.

Bregman, A.S. (in press) *Auditory Scene Analysis*, Cambridge, Mass.: Bradford Books, MIT Press.

Brown, H. (1988) The interplay of set content and temporal context in a functional theory of tonality perception, *Music Perception*, **5**, 219–249.

Browne, R. (1981) Tonal implications of the diatonic set, *In Theory Only*, 5(6–7), 3–21.

Burns, E.D. & Ward, W.D. (1982) Intervals, scales, and tuning. In *The Psychology of Music*, D. Deutsch (ed.), pp. 241–269, New York: Academic Press.

Butler, D. & Brown, H. (1984) Tonal structure versus function: Studies of the recognition of harmonic motion, *Music Perception*, **2**, 6–24.

Castellano, A.A., Bharucha, J.J. & Krumhansl, C.L. (1984) Tonal hierarchies in the music of North India, *Journal of Experimental Psychology: General*, **113**, 394–412.

Clarke, E.F. (1987) Levels of structure in musical time. In "Music and Psychology: A Mutual Regard", S. McAdams (ed.), *Contemporary Music Review*, **2(1)**, 211–238.

Cross, I., Howell, P. & West, R. (1985) Structural relationships in the perception of musical pitch. In *Musical Structure and Cognition*, P. Howell, I. Cross & R. West (eds.), pp. 121–142, London: Academic Press.

Deliège, I. (1987) Grouping conditions in listening to music: An approach to Lerdahl and Jackendoff's grouping preference rules, *Music Perception*, **4**, 325–360.

Deutsch, D. (1978) Delayed pitch comparisons and the principle of proximity, *Perception & Psychophysics*, **23**, 227–230.

Deutsch, D. (1982) The processing of pitch combinations. In *The Psychology of Music*, D. Deutsch (ed.), pp. 271–316, New York: Academic Press.

Deutsch, D. (1984) Two issues concerning tonal hierarchies: Comment on Castellano, Bharucha and Krumhansl, *Journal of Experimental Psychology: General*, **113**, 413–416.

Deutsch, D. & Feroe, J. (1981) The internal representation of pitch sequences in tonal music, *Psychological Review*, **88**, 503–522.

Dowling, W.J. & Harwood, D.L. (1986) *Music Cognition*, New York: Academic Press.

Fant, G. (1973) *Speech Sounds and Features*, Cambridge, Mass.: MIT Press.

Fraisse, P. (1963) *Psychology of Time*, New York: Harper; trans. from *Psychologie du temps*, Paris: Presses Universitaires de France, 1957.

Francès, R. (1988) *The Perception of Music*, Hillsdale, N.J.: Lawrence Erlbaum Associates; trans. by W.J. Dowling from *La perception de la musique*, 2nd ed., Paris: Vrin, 1972.

Gabrielsson, A. (1979) Experimental research on rhythm, *The Humanities Association Review* 30(1/2), 69–92.

Green, D.M. (1976) *An Introduction to Hearing*, Hillsdale, N.J.: Lawrence Erlbaum Associates.

Grey, J.M. (1977) Multidimensional perceptual scaling of musical timbres, *Journal of the Acoustical Society of America*, **61**, 1270–1277.

Helmholtz, H. von (1885) *On the Sensations of Tone*, republ. 1954, New York: Dover; trans. by A.J. Ellis from *Die Lehre von den Tonempfindungen*, 4th ed., 1877.

Jordan, D.S. (1987) Influence of the diatonic tonal hierarchy at microtonal intervals, *Perception & Psychophysics*, **41**, 482–488.

Kessler, E.J., Hansen, C. & Shepard, R.N. (1984), Tonal schemata in the perception of music in Bali and in the West, *Music Perception*, **2**, 131–165.

Krumhansl, C.L. (1979) The psychological representation of musical pitch in a tonal context, *Cognitive Psychology*, **11**, 346–374.

Krumhansl, C.L. (1983) Perceptual structures for tonal music, *Music Perception*, **1**, 28–62.

Krumhansl, C.L. (1987) General properties of musical pitch systems: Some psychological considera- tion. In *Harmony and Tonality*, J. Sundberg (ed.), pp. 33–52, Stockholm: Royal Swedish Academy of Music, publ. no. 54.

Krumhansl, C.L., Sandell, G.J. & Sergeant, D.C. (1987) The perception of tone hierarchies and mirror forms in twelve-tone serial music, *Music Perception*, **5**, 31–78.

Lerdahl, F. (1987) Timbral hierarchies. In "Music and Psychology: A Mutual Regard," S. McAdams (ed.), *Contemporary Music Review*, **2** (1), 135–160.

Lerdahl, F. (1988) Cognitive constraints on compositional systems. In *Generative Processes in Music*, J. Sloboda (ed.), pp. 231–259, Oxford: Oxford University Press.

Lerdahl, F. & Jackendoff, R. (1983) *A Generative Theory of Tonal Music*, Cambridge, Mass.: MIT Press.

Longuet-Higgins, H.C. & Lee, C.S. (1984) The rhythmic interpretation of monophonic music, *Music Perception*, **1**, 424–441.

Mathews, M.V. & Pierce, J.R. (1980) Harmony and non-harmonic partials, *Journal of the Acoustical Society of America*, **68**, 1252–1257.

Mathews, M.V., Pierce, J.R. & Roberts, L.A. (1987) Harmony and new scales. In *Harmony and Tonality*, J. Sundberg (ed.), 59–84, Stockholm: Royal Swedish Academy of Music, publ. no. 54.

McAdams, S. (1984) The auditory image: A metaphor for musical and psychological research on auditory organization. In *Cognitive Processes in the Perception of Art*, W.R. Crozier & A.J. Chapman (eds.), 289–323, Amsterdam: North Holland.

McAdams, S. (1987) Music: A science of the mind? In "Music and Psychology: A Mutual Regard", S. McAdams (ed.), *Contemporary Music Review*, **2**(1), 1–61.

McAdams, S. (1988) Perception et intuition: Calculs tacites [Perception and intuition: Tacit computa- tions], *InHarmoniques*, **3**, 86–103.

McAdams, S. & Bregman, A.S. (1979) Hearing musical streams, *Computer Music Journal*, **3**(4), 26–43.

Meyer, L.B. (1973) *Explaining Music*, Berkeley: University of California Press.

Miller, G.A. (1956) The magical number seven, plus or minus two: Some limits on our capacity for pro- cessing information, *Psychological Review*, **63**, 81–97.

Narmour, E. (in press) **vol. 1** – *The Analysis and Perception of Basic Melodic Structures: The Implication- Realization Model*: **vol. 2** – *The Analysis and Perception of Melodic Complexity: The Implication-Realization Model*.

Neisser, U. (1976) *Cognition and Reality*, San Francisco: W.H. Freeman.

Partch, H. (1974) *Genesis of a Music*, 2nd ed., New York: Da Capo Press.

Povel, D.J. & Essens, P. (1985) The perception of temporal patterns, *Music Perception*, **2**, 411–440.

Restle, F. (1970) Theories of serial pattern learning: Structural trees, *Psychological Review*, **77**, 481–495.

Reynolds, R. (1987) A perspective on form and experience. In "Music and Psychology: A Mutual Regard", S. McAdams (ed.), *Contemporary Music Review*, **2**(1), 277–308.

Risset, J.C. & Wessel, D.L. (1982) Exploration of timbre by analysis and synthesis. In *The Psychology of Music*, D. Deutsch, (ed), pp. 26–58, New York: Academic Press.

Rosch, E. (1973) Natural categories, *Cognitive Psychology* 4, 328–350

Rosch, E. (1978) Principles of categorization. In *Cognition and Categorization*, E. Rosch & B.B. Lloyd (eds.), pp. 28-71, Hillsdale, N.J.: Lawrence Erlbaum Associates.

Rosner, B.S. & Meyer, L.B. (1982) Melodic processes and the perception of music. In *The Psychology of Music*, D. Deutsch (ed.), pp. 317–341, New York: Academic Press.

Rosner, B.S. & Meyer, L.B. (1986) The perceptual roles of melodic process, contour, and form, *Music Perception*, **4**, 1–40.

Schank, R. & Abelson, R.P. (1977) *Scripts, Plans, Goals and Understandings: An Inquiry into Human Knowledge Structures*, Hillsdale, N.J.: Lawrence Erlbaum Associates.

Schoenberg, A. (1924) *Wind Quintet*, op.26. Vienna: Universal Editions/Philharmonia.

Schoenberg, A. (1936) *String Quartet, no. 4*, **op. 37,** New York: Schirmer.

Schoenberg, A. (1975) Composition with twelve tones:(1) & (2). In *Style and Idea*, L. Stein (ed.), pp. 214–249, New York: Saint Martin's Press; trans. by L. Black, (1) c. 1941 (2) c. 1948.

Shephard, R.N. (1984) Ecological constraints on internal representation: Resonant kinematics of perceiving, imagining, thinking and dreaming, *Psychological Review*, **91**, 417–447.

Shepard, R.N. & Jordan, S. (1984) Auditory illusions demonstrating that tones are assimilated to an internalized musical scale, *Science*, **226**, 1333–1334.

Simon, H.A. (1962) The architecture of complexity, *Proceedings of the American Philosophical Society* **106**, 467–482, republ. in *The Sciences of the Artificial*, 2nd ed., Cambridge, Mass: MIT Press, 1982.

Slawson, W. (1985) *Sound Color*, Berkeley: University of California Press.

Wessel, D.L. (1979) Timbre space as a musical control structure, *Computer Music Journal*, **3**(2), 45–52.

White, B.W. (1960) Recognition of distorted melodies, *American Journal of Psychology*, **73**, 100–107.

Wright, J.K. & Bregman, A.S. (1987) Auditory stream segregation and the control of dissonance in polyphonic music. In "Music and Psychology: A Mutual Regard", S. McAdams (ed.), *Contemporary Music Review*, **2**(1) 63–92.

Contemporary Music Review,
1989, Vol. 4, pp. 199–212
Photocopying permitted by license only

An historical and epistemological approach to the musical notion of "form-bearing" element

Marie-Elisabeth Duchez

CNRS, 43 rue d'Assas, F-75006 Paris, France

The perceptual emergence of a form-bearing – or "morphophoric" – musical element deriving from concrete conditions of musical production, and the articulation of this concept as derived from the cultural conditions in which it operates, are directly linked to the epistemological requirements of perceptual and conceptual knowledge as well as to the historical development of music and culture. The rational morphorphoric notion of pitch (perceptual salience and awareness, representative spatialization, conceptualization and measurement, symbolization) based on its treble-bass musical character, for instance, was the structural basis of Western music for a millenium, and a short historical and epistemological analysis of pitch reveals these links and interdependent relationships, as well as the epistemo-musical role of this notion.

KEY WORDS: Conceptual articulation, morphorphoric element, pitch, spatialization, monochordal measure, Tone, epistemo-musical value.

The historical and epistemological nature of musical morphophorism

The notion herein referred to as morphophoric – or form-bearing – element, has always and unfailingly guided musical action, that is to say strategies of production (inspiration, invention, representation, execution) and reception (listening, memorization). But this essential guidance is first of all only a more or less conscious, empirical practice based on immediate perception. Its efficiency, therefore, though direct and reliable, is limited, and it corresponds to what are generally called "primitive", orally-transmitted musics. As with all musical notions, the perceptual foundations of which cannot be ignored, the conscious notion arose with the development of discursive thought on/about music proper to certain musical civilizations, and in particular to Western music. This discursive and conceptual thought results from the fact that musical creativity, once it outstrips improvisational immediacy and ritual repetition, is not limited to the emotive act which relies on sensitivity and intuition to drive decisions, nor to the artistic act which invokes taste to guide choices; it demands an intellectual act concerning choices to be made and decisions to be taken. The idea of morphophorism is at the root of all discursive musical thought and of all music theoretic constructs.

Whether intuited or the object of rational knowledge, the form-bearing element belongs to the twin fields of action and perception characterizing the double movement of creativity, and is the intermediary between the mental anticipation of form and its practical determination. The passage from intuitive perceptual distinction to rational cognitive notion was achieved thanks to the elaboration of a perceptual, and necessarily objective, language needed to discursively guide an act which produces musical form, whether that act is creative or simply reproduces a pre-existing form. This passage initially required a constructive abstraction which, as an extension of an already abstracted perception, constituted discursive procedures for producing forms based on regular intuitive practices involving constant objects (practices and objects supplied by musical experience). It therefore remains closely tied to concrete conditions of musical production and to the structural and logical laws of language. Thus the actual morphophoric element of the relative pitch of a sound is determined and expressed differently by two different musical cultures – ancient Greek instrumental music, for example, and liturgical plainsong of the late Middle Ages – each corresponding to a different type of awareness. Pitch was altered on the Greek lyre by changing the length of the strings or more commonly by altering their *tension* (τάσιν), *stretching* them (τείνω) by adjusting the crossbar of the yoke according to the *tone system* (τόνοι) or *"Pitch Tropes"*. The length of the strings functioned as a measurable reference point for the system. The entire Greek vocabulary for treble-bass modification of sound entailed a vocabulary of tension, remaining linked in ancient musical consciousness to this simple, ordinary operation. Whereas in Gregorian chant of the first ten centuries of our era, auditory perception and vocal emission of treble-bass variations were done without concrete reference, according to cenesthetic sensations and their kinesthetic equivalents. Yet the efficient learning and performance of chant required the elaboration of an abstract notion, the notion of pitch height, at that time an absolutely new, rational, quantifiable notion whose impact on the future of music would be considerable. The difficult elaboration of this rational notion, which determined the principle – and formerly empirical – element in plainsong, could only be done, as will be seen, by taking quantitative concepts and methods of measurement handed down by Greek musical theory and applying them to Gregorian chant. Which meant that this element henceforth corresponded to a measurable dimension, the length of a vibrating string (monochord).[1] The language of pitch height slowly replaced the vocabulary of tension inherited from ancient Greek music (*intensio, tenor,* etc.), although the tension-relationed term *tone (tonus)*, nevertheless survived with full polysemic load.

This example, to which I will return in more detail, demonstrates the historical nature of morphophorism not only in terms of its musical content which shapes the musical reality of the times (perception, invention and material, performance), but also in terms of the specific awareness and constructive expression of the concept, which depend on objective knowledge of that musical reality and on the scientific and cultural context in which both music and knowledge have evolved. The general notion of morphophorism has been variously defined and labeled at different times, the form-bearing element being considered either as a differentiating qualitative property and a practical criterion imposed on perception, or as an essential dimension of the musical stimulus and a quantifiable physical parameter, still retaining its pertinent, structural aspect. But whatever term is used to describe it, the form bearing element is broadly, a variable distinguishing feature of the perceived musical material which, though transformable and constrainable, remains permanent and identifiable. This distinguishing feature can be represented, manipulated and organized materially and intellectu-ally. It implies operative potential, physical constraints (the objective structural limits of the stimulus), and cognitive constraints (the perceptual and conceptual limits of knowledge) which, like music and its material (and the knowledge and technological consequences with which these are associated), are historically determined. And the notion by which it is represented in consciousness possesses – as does all rational and developed, discursive knowledge – a scientific value, an epistemic value[2] related to the way in which constraints have been mastered, thus leading to the realization of potential.

Psychological analysis of the perceptual basis behind musical hierarchies, as well as their cognitive recognition and organization (the fundamental, obligatory point of departure for understanding the notion) takes into account neither the historico-musical circumstances nor the cultural legacy which intervene in these processes in a sometimes decisive fashion; nor does it appreciate their epistemic value. It therefore needs to be backed up by an historical and epistemological analysis[3] which takes into account not only the criteria and demands of psychological constraints on perception and knowledge, but also the concrete conditions of the production of music and the extrinsic knowledge and cultural context which historically determine the perceptual isolation and conceptual elaboration of the morphophoric element involved (for history has shown the inadequacy of perceptual knowledge alone in effecting this isolation and elaboration). An epistemological analysis of the process of elaboration of a form-bearing element – touching on its theoretical and practical value, its teleological scope, the historical evolution of the conceptual and perceptual knowledge behind it, as well as its mental and material representation – tells us about the past (and perhaps future) functioning of this element. It helps specify certain cognitive problems concerning the production and reception of music, and can thereby open up new space for analysis and new lines of reasoning. The constant interchange between historical investigation and epistemological analysis of the awareness and conceptual articulation of a morphophoric element provides dynamic understanding leading to an examination of the formal structures of music. I propose to examine here the specific example briefly cited above, concerning the perceptual and conceptual determination of the morphophoric element of *pitch* in the 9th–10th centuries. This determination implied the breakdown of the vocal continuum into *discrete sounds* and the formation of the *notion of musical scale.* It resulted from the search for concrete solutions to the difficulties presented by everyday musical tasks: *problems of the oral handing down of liturgical plainsong and the demands of memorization* (teaching and performance) and, in the 9th century, *the problem of stabilizing an emerging polyphony.* The theoretical solution which had to resolve all these problems, the notion of pitch, is not a direct perceptual given, but rather a later, rational construct privileging and conceptually elaborating perception of the preferential treble-bass quality of music. A geometrically discrete and mathematically simple value offering a manageable principle of differentiation and representation which could be assessed, organized, systemized, and hierarchized was developed for vocal music out of necessity. This morphophoric element, rationalized and conceptually articulated as "pitch height", rapidly became the overriding principle for the formal organization of instrumental as well as vocal music, and remained so for nearly a millenium.

History of musical morphophorism in the elaboration of the notion of pitch

The Perception and Expression of Variations in Form-bearing Treble-bass Quality According to Musical and Cultural Differences

The idea that one element of music is largely responsible for musical form was suggested in Greek music philosophy by the rather vague notion of *dunamis* (δύναμις). Whereas Pythagorean theory imputes all formal qualities of music to Number and numerical relationships (notably to variations in perceived, fundamentally differentiating *treble-bass.* (βαρύς-ὀξύς) qualities), instrumental practice – mainly that of stringed lyres and citharas, but also applicable in a different way to the bores of flutes – stressed the potentially formal psychophysical notion of *dunamis;* in the absence of a measurable absolute pitch (unknown at that time), the principle of *dunamis* skillfully enabled the relative but fixed tuning of instruments. The term *dunamis* (its general sense meaning the power or principle of change[4]) defined the musical property by which a change in the tension of voice, breath or strings gives the real relative pitch of the sound and its functional place in the System of sounds: it represents the *determining functional musical value,* the agent of treble-bass variation. Thus, given the usual fixed tuning (*thesis,* θέσις) of a seven string lyre in the middle register (*mesoides,* μεσοιδής) a new tuning could be created for the instrument without physically modifying the tension, by changing Tone, that is to say in mentally shifting the entire playing system on the lyre, thus changing the place of tones and semi-tones and the place of the system's functions (which then assume different degrees of highness and lowness).[5] This indirect intellectual operation replaced numerous direct material operations (which were limited and difficult) and required merely the immediate change in tension of several strings according to a simple interval. Thanks to the numerous possibilities of interval combinations it offered and its ease of use, everything could thus be played on the instrument. On a theoretical level, this represented for the Greeks a change in the *dunamis* of the sound.

It is not easy for those of us used to thinking in terms of absolute pitch to understand the Greeks' explanations of what was for them the relative degree of highness or lowness of a sound independent of any idea of pitch, and there have been numerous historical misunderstandings over the role of *dunamis* and Tones. There are no direct accounts prior to the 4th century B.C., the first being that of Aristoxenus (Macran, ed., 1902). Several Hellenistic reports exist, however[6], all agreeing with Aristoxenus. The most detailed of these is Ptolemy's 2nd century A.D. account (Düring, 1930), transmitted to the latin Middle Ages by Boethius, a philosopher of the waning Western Empire (Friedlein, ed., 1867). Medieval scribes, ignorant of Greek music and having a highly limited knowledge of instrumental music (little developed at that time), translated the Greek system of Tones and instrumental tuning into vocal modes, relying on it to develop their theory of modality in the 9th and 10th centuries (Duchez, in press,b).

In the early Middle Ages, when music was almost exclusively vocal in the form of ecclesiastical plainsong, the problematic of sound remained identical, in the abstract, to that of the Greeks. It entailed ensuring the simple euphonic manipulation of the greatest possible number of relational types and combinations of variations in the treble-bass morphophoric quality presented by instrument or voice, organized into a more or less hierarchized system. But in the vocal and verbal universe of liturgical plainsong in the early centuries of our era, variations of a treble-bass nature were not perceived and conceptually articulated as easily as in the instrumental and numeric universe of ancient Greece (where they were perceived both qualitatively and quantitatively through physical variations in the stimulus, appraised and measured according to instrument dimensions and tension). The treble-bass variations of the vocal stimulus being at that time difficult to evaluate and measure, musical problems concerning the mnemo-technical representation required by performance and teaching were therefore different. These involved a mental, then visual, representation which required of vocal music a more advanced abstraction and more sophisticated (precisely because less obvious) operative concepts. Cultural conditions, too, were different, as was the attitude of musicians (producers and receivers) and the way in which they analyzed and organized what they heard according to the learning at their disposal: the heritage of Greek musicography, then limited to several very abstract notions far removed from Gregorian reality and regularly reinvoked only as cosmic fact. It remained thus musically inefficient and inoperative on both practical and theoretical levels[7], up to the Carolingian Renaissance (late 8th – early 10th centuries).

From a practical standpoint, early medieval thought, describing music perceived as the movement of the voice *(motus vocum)*, still occasionally referred to a concept of potentiality *(potestas)* similar to that of the Greek *dunamis*.[8] Change in sound was attributed to a special active element *(proprietas)*[9] that could be varied at will and which was responsible for the degree of bass or treble. Following the Greeks, this form-bearing principle would be called the *Tone*. But in liturgical plainsong it was no longer a question of the instrumental pitch range as in the Greek system, but rather of *vocal intonation* of melodic formulas, phrases or chanted pieces, an intonation to be described melodically and fixed mnemoni-cally. The Tone, as a pliable expressive principle for language (in particular the sacred text to be enhanced by chant) accommodated the same goal and the same means – increasing the tension of the voice – to become at the same time the pliable expressive principle of the corresponding melody, inseparable from the text. Thus an identity was established between linguistic accent, musical tone, and melodic tenor; the three terms *accentus, tonus* and *tenor* were used inter-changeably (Duchez, 1985). The notions of morphophorism and of the mor-phophoric element itself, so essential in practice, still remained very vague in musical consciousness.

The notion of morphophorism and form-bearing element became clearer in the 9th century when the ancient texts were examined more closely in order to develop the teaching of the Liberal Arts (which included the *Scientia Musica*, the fourth of the mathematical subjects comprising the *Quadrivium*). It was at this point that the notion of *informitas* appeared, meaning non-existence due to absence of form, a defect which could be repaired by the action of a formative element. Thus an anonymous text which circulated widely in Northern France from the middle of the 9th century, commenting on a sentence in a late Western Empire text concerning the Apollonian lyre, asserts that sound is created out of *informitas* by the tension of the strings, and that a very slack string will form no sound, or only a very low, ugly sound, while a tightly stretched string gives the sound a form corresponding to a *higher, Greek Tone (or Trope) – the Hypodorian*. But this was simply a literary analysis with an allusion to antiquity which, like so many others, was without real import (Duchez, in press, b).

In reality, *Tone* seems to have signified at that time any variable and manipulable element which enables the movement of the voice and form of the chant to be created or modified at will. It corresponds to our notion of form-bearing element. Another text from the same period and region which may reasonably be attributed to John Scottus Eriugena, the first major medieval philosopher, distinguished pitch tones *(toni harmonici)* from time tones *(toni temporum)* and intensity of breath tones *(toni spiritum)*. Well in advance of his contemporaries, Eriugena thus distinguished the three parameters of sound which, for centuries to come, would determine musical form to a more or less structural degree (Duchez, in press, b). And it was in the second half of the 9th century and the beginning of the 10th century that the pressure of practical musical requirements (the description and memorization of vocal behavior) produced the transformation of the abstract and modulated perceptual criterion of treble-bass variation into a notion of pitch, becoming a conceptually articulated and measurable operative value which could be systemized and notated. This construct required substantial epistemic activity, as I described in detail in a presentation made at IRCAM in 1977 (Duchez, 1979).

Successive cognitive operations in the elaboration of the notion of pitch in the Middle Ages

Conscious Perceptual Emergence

A long period of melodic experience was required before treble-bass quality consciously emerged as having primary musical morphophoric value. This emerging consciousness was hampered by the difficulty in objectifying musical sound as an autonomous phenomenon, due to the phenomenal link and structural dependence tying music to the sacred language it was designed to convey. Simple perceptual isolation of treble-bass character was difficult, given the minor pitch difference in liturgical chant, where melody was not very marked *(modicus flexus, cantus planus)* and where plainsong merely represented a more expressive *pronunciation* (Duchez, 1981). Accounts written prior to the middle of the 9th century reveal the ambiguity of expressible conscious perception: there is a confusion in terminology between pitch and the intensity of sound (linked to the change in the nature of verbal accent in the transition from ancient Latin to medieval Latin), a rather late distinction between the role of pitch and that of beat and rhythm in musical expression, and difficulty in separating pitch quality from vocal timbre (Duchez, 1979, 1981).

Certain conditions were nevertheless favorable to a privileged perception of treble-bass quality and the conscious discernment of its relevance. Sacred melody unfolded in a mid-range tessitura, a zone where pitch is best perceived and handled, whereas other sound qualities accompanying pitch in Gregorian chant bore little salience; for ecclesiastical councils, imperial instructions, liturgical books, etc, all insisted that church music be sober, reserved, and moderate. This precluded, therefore, wide variations in intensity and rhythm; chant remained linked to the internalized and solemn flow of the religious text. Nor were there modifications in timbre (the very nature of plainsong demanding timbral homogeneity and stability); uniformity of timbre was interrupted only by the alternation of choir and soloist in antiphonal chants. Conscious vocal behavior was therefore limited to the modulation of treble-bass relationships, on which all objective attention and efforts at mastery were focused, with the main goal of fulfilling the requirement of memorization. But without instrumental reinforcement to concretize and quantify it, treble-bass quality didn't offer much of a handle to memory,[10] and in the 9th century cognitive efforts were redoubled to meet this need, a need which had grown as a result of the development of the liturgical repertoire and the spread of chant calling for several voices (diaphony becoming polyphony).

Representative Spatialization

The most significant and most original stage in this cognitive project was probably the *phase of representative spatialization of the treble-bass morphophoric character*, which had a decisive impact on the conception, manipulation and notation of musical sound. This spatialization involved the geometric and visual representation (psychologically, then graphically) of spatially heterogeneous relationships apprehended aurally, within the spatial conditions of human biological and intellectual existence. This was done by projection (mental, then material) of a high–low image onto the perception of treble-bass variations. This "musical space" is specific (at once psychological and imaginary, abstract and conceptual) and completely different from the empirical, physical and mathematical spaces which also belong to the sphere of the intelligible. But, symbolically appropriating their geometric properties (location, direction, orientation, system of references) it shares with them the status of being a space of operational representation in which objects can be distinguished (here, sounds) while maintaining their coherence, and in which a set of relations (here, in fact, qualitative) can function and be geometrically represented.

Impressions of sound spatiality had already appeared in texts on the behavior of the voice prior to the mid 9th century. Cenesthetic metaphors expressed an anthropomorphic vertical spatialization of vocal movements, and kinesthestic metaphors were drawn from chironomy.[11] But these fleeting spatial images were due to the naive geometry of language, so that expressions for ascending and descending corresponded to augmentation or diminution in general, and were applied to variations in relative degree of high or low pitch as well as to changes in dynamics and sometimes even in durations. More realistic and constructive were the descriptions of the voice's movements which relied on grammatical analogies, based on traditional comparisons between music and language and the phenomenal and structural correspondences uniting them in sacred plainsong. The cultural borrowing of concepts and analyses employed in Grammar made two very important contributions to the spatialization of the treble-bass morphophoric element. Firstly, by analogy with the letters of a language, *the notion of a graphically representable discrete sound*, as the primary irreducible element of vocal emission, would break down the sound continuum of plainsong formulas into units which could be described by a pitch. Secondly, assimilating musical tone with verbal accent in plainsong intonation lead to the description of vocal movements as accents. Such description had remained highly ambiguous when pertaining to Latin verbal accents which had become stressed accents but were still described using the terminology for Greek accents (a pitch accent with no spatial image). But this description became much more fertile once it dealt with a written sign representing the accent, a sign whose positions and geometric forms on the page were objective; writing thus spatialized the accent unambiguously, and introduced the clear notion of pitch into analogous descriptions of melodic movements (Duchez, 1981, 1983).

Rational Conceptual Articulation

This description of the treble-bass morphophoric element in gestural and verbographic space was nevertheless too vague to analytically differentiate, segregate and seriate sounds in order to firmly establish modal rationality. That is to say, to replace the ordinal scaling of liturgical tones proper to empirical, formulaic modality with a cardinal scaling of medieval modes characterized by the way they deployed intervals. It didn't lend itself to an accurate, organized superimposition of voices and therefore couldn't lead to the development of polyphony. It could only offer the elementary and imprecise graphic representation of *neumes*. These indicated only vocal movements and melodic contours, as a reminder of a chant already learned, and were incapable of initially providing a full grasp.[12] The search for greater efficiency in handling the treble-bass form-bearing element required a fuller abstraction of this operative notion as well as a more rigorous rationalization of its operational space. And the three practical problems faced at that time (Modality, Polyphony, Notation) could then be resolved through a single theoretical solution: the principle of the *distribution of successive or simultaneous musical sensations, different in their treble-bass morphophoric characteristics, in a vertical space according to mathematical relationships, which would be given the geometric term of Height*. This term (*altitudo* in medieval Latin) later lost its geometric connotation in the English word *Pitch*. The term *altitudo* was used from the middle of the 9th century by Aurelian of Réôme and by the commentators on Martianus Capella (Duchez, in press, b). It became current at the beginning of the 11th century with Guido d'Arezzo's synopses on scale and notation, although the geometric term "Height" ("Hauteur" in French) only really won out in the 17th century, after much debate (Duchez, 1979). *The concept of "height" (or pitch) nevertheless opera*-tated in musical consciousness well before having received its definitive name or even its rational formulation. This formulation developed from the elaboration of the quantitative notion of interval, the conscious perception of which preceded that of discrete sound, and led to the construction of the musical scale. The precise conceptual articulation of the morphophoric element of pitch, then, was definitely established through its quantification.

Precise Quantification

Notions of interval, discrete sound (characterized by its pitch), scale, and their quantitative measurement could only enter medieval musical consciousness thanks to the cultural reliance on the classic Pythagorean-Platonic tradition, which was conveyed to the Middle Ages by the arithmetico-musical cosmology of neoplatonism. Greek musical theory, with its elementary but scientifically exact acoustics, could not provide the notion of pitch (which it didn't possess), but it did introduce concepts of number and measurement into the musical analyses of clerics and into the musical experience of cantors, giving a theoretical and practical reality to this notion which up to that point had been vague and without empirical content. Contributory knowledge originating in the classic cultural tradition can be rapidly listed: *The Pythagorean theory of consonant intervals*, the first use of mathematics to describe the physical world; the diatonic scale as conveyed by Plato's *Timaeus*, and the double-octave on the Greek tetrachordal system revealing the structural importance of the cyclical octave; the interval distribution of *Pitch Tones or Tropes*, described above; *The Pythagorean-Platonic doctrine of the Harmony of the Spheres* which, in spreading a dominant cosmo-musical image throughout the medieval world (that of the celestial gamut as divine model of earthly musical scales), would make medieval thinkers familiar with the idea of a distribution of intervals according to relationships of consonance and of a serial distribution of discrete sounds according to their pitch (Duchez, in press, b); finally, *the method of monochordal measurement*, a precise and practical application of Pythagorean relationships of consonance to the measurement of relative pitch, by making perception of a sound correspond to the number measuring the length of the string capable of producing it.

The introduction of measurement, a critical moment in Western musical thought, definitively conferred objectivity on sound and on its treble-bass form-bearing nature, making number the intrinsic property of the measured object. This linked the qualitative apprehension of perception to the power associated with knowledge and its quantitative conditions, henceforth obvious and easily handled both conceptually and practically. This granted enormous theoretical efficiency and extraordinary operative fertility to the notion of pitch. The relative measurement of pitch made the establishment of structural hierarchies possible, whose accurate quantitative reference points were more rational than those of qualitative groupings and ordinal classifying of the previous era (aural grouping of Gregorian formulas and subsequent classification of *Liturgical Tones* into *Tonaries* and corresponding pieces,[13] *neumes* as memory prompts). These structural hierarchies became highly operational as soon as they were established, as evidenced by the theoretical stabilization of medieval *Modes*, the composition of *Tropes* and *Sequences*, and the rapid development of polyphony. And the measurement of pitch resolved the problem of memorization by establishing proportional relations[14] between the treble-bass form-bearing element and graphic vertical space, yielding the principle behind *diastematic notation*[15] which would adequately symbolize music for a long time. The conceptual articulation and measurement of the treble-bass morphophoric element transformed the verbal qualitative appreciation of vocal movement in the liturgical *pronuntiatio* into a numeric quantitative evaluation of musical sounds and intervals which could be notated, opening new paths to the apprehension of music.

Teleological Implications

It is not possible here to deal with all the consequences of the conceptual articulation of this morphophoric characteristic which, thanks to ease of representation and wealth of combinations, served as the foundation for Western musical structures for so long. Nor can we deal with the evolution of measurement (relative up to the 17th century, and then absolute) which became clearer with the development of science from Monochord to Electronics, transforming the very notion of pitch. For centuries, the discrete sound – theoretically considered an abstract and unchanging medium for generating variable relationships – would be ontologically characterized by its pitch, to which other parameters would be added (duration in the 12th–13th centuries, dynamic intensity in the 16th–17th centuries, timbre in the 18th–19th centuries). These additions modified the quality of sound without changing its theoretical nature, as far as musicians were concerned. During the classical period, the association established by scientific consciousness between the notion of pitch – a rationally spatialized and measured perception – and the *frequency* of the stimulus behind this perception reinforced (despite the paradox of the perceptual proximity of octaves and consonances between widely-separated frequencies) the notion of pitch in musical consciousness. And the primacy of polyphony (Counterpoint, Harmony) confirmed its unchallenged supremacy as form-bearing element: Rameau, who was nevertheless one of the first to mention the role of Timbre, asserted that "In Harmony, sound is distinguished only by treble and bass without paying attention to its force or duration" (Rameau, 1722).

The various cognitive operations superimposed on the primitive perception of the morphophoric element have transformed it into quantitative conceptual perception, concretized by the very notation for which it was elaborated and standardized through training and habit. So when the 20th century rejected the restriction of musical sounds to periodic sounds, and the restriction of the sensation of pitch to its fundamental frequency alone, the pitch-frequency link was weakened. The hegemony of the conceptual articulation of this perception was also weakened; it was reproached for having sacrificed musical values at one time less salient and hard to quantify and notate, but today scientifically controllable as form-bearing factors. It was also accused of having thus limited musical thought by forcing it into a pre-existing notional and graphic framework. The scientific development of knowledge (physical, psychological, psychoacoustic, psychomusical, technological) and the use of sound resources favoring other form-bearing elements led to a certain ebb in the role of the treble-bass morphophoric element and the shattering of the millenium-old concept of pitch height.

Epistemological conclusions

The historical analysis of the emerging consciousness and quantitative conceptual articulation of a musical morphophoric element could have been performed on any other form-bearing element (for instance, in the difficult theorization of the musical role of duration from the 12th to 17th centuries, or in the analysis of the emerging consciousness and cognitive and technological development of the morphophoric potential of timbre in the 20th century[16]). In considering these cases (cf. articles published or in progress, Duchez, in press, a, b) – all of which describe the historical transition from intuitive perceptual distinction to rational cognitive notion – different conditions of musical production and different levels of knowledge are encountered, not to mention widely varying levels of awareness and theoretical elaboration, yet the epistemological conclusions remain palpably identical.

The above historical analysis shows how a fundamental morphophoric characteristic was rationally constituted, and describes the development of that constitution. It fully agrees with results of research in music psychology. Moreover, it offers epistemological information on the intellectual processes through which "musical thought" (perception, memorization, imagination, invention) resolved certain cognitive problems in an operative fashion, based on an inescapable perceptual framework whose openness and potential is thereby confirmed.

Agreement of Historical Analysis with Data from Music Psychology

Modern music psychology has conducted research into the conditions of the apprehension of form in auditory perception which informs listening and guides musical creativity: perceptual constraints concerning both subject (biological and mental organization) and object (maintaining identity across various transformations), as well as cognitive constraints (coherence of the representational space, formation of a mental image). It has determined the perceptual and cognitive conditions for the functioning of form-bearing elements, that is to say those likely to play a role in musical structure, including fundamental salience requirements (categories, hierarchies, circularity, organization, memorization) and operative notional factors (differentiating into discrete units, relational functionality, complex combinatory ability – both relational and basic – not to mention the ability to be classified, ordered, systematized, and symbolized). These requirements and features insure the structural potential and musical richness of the form-bearing element.[17]

The history of the progressive elaboration of the rational and quantitative notion of the morphophoric element of pitch and the epistemological nature of this concept in its triple aspect (psychological, physico-mathematical and logico-ontological), corresponding to the rational and imaginative mental operations involved in this elaboration (perception, representation, measurement, and symbolization) address problems raised by music psychology. Historical epistemology supports and extends cognitive psychology. But psychology's fundamental, indispensable explanations overlook historico-musical circumstances, and the cultural context, which play an essential role in the resolution of these problems, even on the level of perception. Perception is already a partly historical and cultural operation since its chosen object depends on the mode of production of music and is influenced by structuring concepts (thus the reduced role of pitch weakens the spatial perception of music, and the technological separation of timbre leads to its perception as a more obvious form-bearing element) – there is a constant play between psychological "patterns" and cultural "models". Historical analysis throws into relief these facts of an epistemological nature.

Specific Epistemological Contribution of Historical Analysis

Historical examination has opened doors to an epistemological approach to musical knowledge (involving perceptual cognition as well as rational knowledge). Filling the void between what is perceived and what is thought, revealing the connection from perceptual preeminence to conceptual preeminence, and from there to structural preeminence, the epistemology of musical knowledge can accurately describe cognitive problems which are the perceptual and conceptual basis of the eminently structural morphophoric nature of pitch. It can reveal the historical appearance of the "why" (basic exigencies) and the development of the "how" (operative features). Demonstrating that the morphophoric notion is not elaborated by musical experience alone ("the naked ear" is necessary but not sufficient), epistemological analysis of the historical development of its elaboration revealed the role played by logical and mathematical cognitive mechanisms of a level higher than perception. And, as seen above, it stressed both the importance of the historical conditions to the general conditions of music production in the determination and conceptual articulation of the form-bearing element, and the founding role of cultural knowledge.

The mental processes involved in musical knowledge add specific musical conditions to the general conditions of psychogenesis. Cognitive mechanisms are the same, but function differently. This historical and epistemological analysis of the morphophoric notion of pitch has thus underscored the role of abstraction in transforming simple operational relations into a substantive relation starting not from the object to be abstracted (sound and its treble-bass quality) but the actions that the musician performs on that object (tension of voice or instrument).[18] It demonstrated that the conceptual articulation of the treble-bass form-bearing feature, which entailed making a conceptual structure into a psychomusical structure, fundamentally involves (spatial) imagination for its symbolizing construct. It has proved that the unavoidable role played by learning is ambivalent: there is a direct relationship between a high degree of knowledge and the complexity of musical organization and its morphophoric elements, yet on the other hand the extension of knowledge challenges the self-evident status of a form-bearing element and can favor the emergence of others by discovering new potential (as has happened to pitch and timbre in the 20th century).

But above all, this historical and epistemological analysis has led to an understanding of the need for a *symbolizable conceptual representation* for form-bearing features, the basis of hierarchical structures. This intermediate representation, which unites in a single notion the idea of morphophoric function and the concept representing the musical form-bearing element itself, is heterogeneous to auditory perception and imagination (the concept of pitch as "height" is not an aural concept but a geometric one). It functions like mental material which, in a constant back-and-forth creative mental flow between two perceptions (real or imagined), matches an external auditory *expressive form* to an internal auditory impression. The operative efficiency and musical richness of the morphophoric element depends on the epistemic value – or rather on the *epistemo-musical value*[19] of this intermediate representation, that is to say the appropriateness of its cognitive potential vis-a-vis physical and psychological musical reality.

Translated from the French by Deke Dusinberre

Notes

1. From Pythagoras to the 18th century, from the discovery of the numeric relationship of consonance to the measurement of frequency, the *monochord*, or single string stretched across a sounding box with graduated ruler, was the only instrument for the measurement and theorization of musical sounds.
2. I use the term *epistemic* to connote discursive knowledge and rational thought (dealt with by epistemology), as opposed to *cognitive*, which connotes all types of knowledge (sensory, scientific, imaginative, etc.)
3. An *epistemological* analysis examines the processes of elaboration, the bases, principles, the teleological implications, and the operative value of knowledge.
4. The Aristotelian theoretician Aristoxenus and his successors used the term *dunamis* in the sense of ability and power, corresponding to Aristotle's *power-form* duality.
5. Note that the theoretical scale (σύστημα) in the Greek musical *system of Tones or Tropes* is transposed

in pitch in its entirety, without modification; yet in practice, on the instrument, the value of real intervals is modifiable and the function of sounds changed.

6. As in the *Harmonics* by Cleonides, Gaudentius, and Bacchius (Jan, 1895).
7. Allusions to the Greek Tone-Trope system, quoted by Cassiodorus (6th century) and mentioned by Isidore of Seville (7th century) and Aurelian of Réôme (9th century), had no impact until they were assimilated to Boethius' theory of pitch tones in the 9th century. Note that this assimilation was based on a major (though fertile) misunderstanding: transposition being impossible for the voice without a concrete point of reference, the medieval *liturgical Tones*, initially designed to adapt the chant of the Anthems to that of the Psalms (for euphony they had to be in the same *Tone*) are theoretically different scales with differing intervals, unlike the Greek Tone-Tropes (Duchez, in press, b).
8. The term *potestas*, in the sense of pitch, is found in the first anonymous musical treatises dating from the end of the 9th century: the *Musica Enchiriadis* and so-called *Prague Anonymous* text (Duchez, in press, b).
9. Used in the 9th century in the texts cited above, the term *proprietas* sometimes still referred to pitch, the main property of sound, up to the 11th century.
10. Here it is a question of *long-term memory*, involving the storage of formulas, melodic phrases and Gregorian pieces, for their oral transmission. *Short-term memory* concerns the perceptual formation of psalmodic formulas linked to the chanted text (Duchez, in press, b); this role of segmentation and formal grouping, corresponding to short-term memory, is elucidated by research in cognitive psychology (Deutsch, 1975).
11. *Hand gestures*, with which the choirmaster led the chant, were vertically oriented and were seen and felt as lower/higher movements.
12. *Neumes,* written signs in forms which differed from region to region and whose origin (late 8th – early 9th century) remains obscure, sketched melodic phrasing above the text to be sung. Their vertical spacing, initially highly approximate, tended to become more accurate during the 9th century, at the same time that the notion of pitch was emerging (Duchez, 1983). Cognitive psychology offers information similar to that provided by history in terms of the perceptual grasp of melodic contour offered by neumes (Dowling, 1978, 1982; Dowling & Bartlett, 1981; Sloboda, 1978).
13. To make long-term memory storage easier, *Tonaries* classified types of formulas *(apechematic formulas)* perceived as being similar under the same *Tone* (see note 7, above), along with the textual *incipits* of the Gregorian pieces they governed (Huglo, 1971).
14. Spatial proportionality, the principle behind notating pitch, was later extended to duration *(ortho-chronic notation,* 16th century; Read, 1960), though only partly expressing it, other graphic modifications being necessary (Sloboda, 1981).
15. Notation based on the interval *(diastema)* first appeared in the 9th century in the vertical structuring of neumes *(diastematic neumes, line neumes)* and was definitely established in the 11th century by the *staff,* attributed to Guido d'Arezzo (Duchez, 1983).
16. *Beat* in Gregorian chant being determined by the verbal flow of the sacred text, problems of musical time were dealt with after those of pitch, that is to say when made necessary by polyphony (Duchez, in press, b). On the evolution of knowledge concerning *timbre,* see Duchez (in press, a).
17. Regarding this research, conducted over the last ten years, I rely mainly on the work of Stephen McAdams as well as the authors on which that work is based, as cited elsewhere in this volume.
18. Cognitive abstraction is here defined in the sense employed in Piaget's *genetic psychology (reflective abstraction)* and elsewhere (Piaget, 1961).
19. *Epistemo-musical value* is the value of knowledge which is not necessarily musical (it could be mathematical, physical, physiological, psychological, linguistic, etc), in relation to music (musical production, representation, and reception).

References

Deutsch, D. (1975) The organization of short-term memory for a single acoustic attribute. In *Short-Term Memory,* J.A. Deutsch & D. Deutsch (eds.), 107–151. New York: Academic Press.

Dowling, W.J. (1978) Scale and contour: Two components of a theory of memory for melodies. *Psychological Review,* **85,** 341–354

Dowling, W.J. (1982) Melodic information processing and its development. In *The Psychology of Music,* D. Deutsch (ed.), pp. 413–428. New York: Academic Press.

Dowling, W.J. & Bartlett, J.C. (1981) The importance of interval information in long-term memory for melodies. *Psychomusicology*, **1**, 30–49.

Duchez, M.E. (1979) La représentation spatio-verticale du caractère musical grave-aigu et l'élaboration de la notion de hauteur de son dans la conscience musicale occidentale. *Acta Musicologica*, **1**, 54–73.

Duchez, M.E. (1981) Description grammaticale et description arithmétique des phénomènes musicaux: le tournant du IXe siècle. In *Miscellanea Mediaevalia*, A. Zimmemann (ed.), Band **13** (2). Berlin: De Gruyter.

Duchez, M.E. (1983) Des neumes à la portée. Elaboration et organisation rationnelle de la discontinuité musicale et de sa représentation graphique, de la formule mélodique à l'échelle monocordale. *Canadian University Music Review / Revue de Musique des Universités Canadiennes*, **4**, 22–64.

Duchez, M.E. (1985) L'émergence acoustico-musicale du terme *sonus* dans les commentaires carolingiens de Martianus Capella. *Documents pour l'Histoire du Vocabulaire Scientifique*, **7**, 76–149. Paris: Editions du Centre National de la Recherche Scientifique.

Duchez, M.E. (in press, a) L'évolution scientifique de la notion de matériau musical. In *Le timbre: Métaphores pour la composition*, J.B. Barrière (ed.). Paris: Christian Bourgois.

Duchez, M.E. (in press, b) *Imago mundi. La Naissance de la Théorie musicale occidentale dans les Commentaires carolingiens de Martianus Capella et sa structuration par le "De institutione musica" de Boèce.*

Düring, I. (1930) *Die Harmonielehre des Klaudios Ptolemaios*, 49–62, Göteborg: Wetteren & Kerbers Förlag.

Friedlin, G. (ed.) (1867) *Boetti De institutione musica*, Leipzig: Teubner. Reprinted 1966, Frankfurt: Minerva.

Huglo, M. (1971) *Les Tonaires*, Paris: Heugel.

Jan, C. (ed.) (1895) *Musical Scriptores Greci*, Leipzig: Teubner. Reprinted 1962, Hildesheim: Olms.

Macran, H.S. (ed.) (1902) *The Harmonics of Aristoxenus*. Oxford: Oxford University Press. Reprinted 1974, Hildesheim: Olms.

Piaget, J. (1961) *Epistémologie mathématique et psychologie*. Paris: Presses Universitaires de France.

Rameau, J.P. (1722) *Traité de l'Harmonie / réduite à ses principes naturels*. p. 2. Paris: Ballard.

Read, G. (1969) *Music Notation*. Boston: Allyn & Bacon (2nd edition).

Sloboda, J.A. (1978) Perception of contour in music reading. *Perception*, **7**, 323–331.

Sloboda, J.A. (1981) The use of space in music notation. *Visible Language*, **25**, 86–110.

Contemporary Music Review,
1989, Vol. 4, pp. 213–230
Photocopying permitted by license only

A perceptual approach to contemporary musical forms

Irène Deliège

Unité de Recherche en Psychologie de la Musique, Université de Liège,
Faculté de Psychologie et des Sciences de l'Education,
Laboratoire de Psychologie Expérimentale, B.32, Sart Tilman, B-4000 Liège, Belgium .

This paper presents the following subject matter: First, a brief explanation is given of how *"perceptual approach to musical form"* is to be understood. Then hypotheses relating to the psychological mechanisms involved are proposed, along with predicted results and experimental methods employed (choice of works, subjects, and procedures). The results of three experiments, accompanied by a brief description of the musical passages as compared to these results, lead finally to a discussion of the hypotheses put forward. Musical works used in the experiment were: *Sequenza VI* (for solo viola) by Luciano Berio, performed by Walter Trampler (RCA SB 6846, 1971) and *Eclat* by Pierre Boulez, performed by the Ensemble Intercontemporain conducted by the composer (*Le Temps Musical 1*, a Radio France/IRCAM cassette).

KEY WORDS: Auditory grouping, groups, imprints, cues, invariants.

We all know that there are different ways of hearing music, from casually overheard background music to attentive listening which attempts to uncover the composer's aims. In between, there exists a range of fanciful attitudes which escape the work itself, projecting the listener's own, external content onto the music.

This research addresses attentive listening – *analytic listening* – which seeks an encounter with the work's structure. Here it should be pointed out, however, that this type of perceptual analysis does not involve a reconstitution of the score. For once a certain level of complexity is reached, perception can no longer handle all the information received in real time (this pertains to the auditory as well as to the other sensory modalities, cf. Moore, 1982, p. 202). The perceptual approach to form is here understood as the progressive elaboration of a simplified schema of the objective content of the piece. This initial stage of investigation concerns the listener's potential ability to constitute groupings of groups as a function of their perceived structural relevance, as well as the aptitude to detect links between structures and to situate them within the schema which emerged from the grouping operation. The interest behind this process does not, however, lie in a simple charting of boundaries between groups, but rather in the way this method reveals the content internal to these groupings and, consequently, the reasons that associations exist between grouped structures.

It has already been observed that rhythmic groups are demarcated by changes in register, dynamic, attack, timbre, etc. or by changes in the rate of durations (I. Deliège, 1987b). Musical audition thus invokes Gestalt principles of similarity and proximity as set out by Lerdahl & Jackendoff (1983) in their grouping preference

213

theory. Our focus here is on a subsequent stage of processing, that is to say access to hierarchically superior levels, or groupings of groups. An initial concern is to define the mechanisms on which such access is based.

Noizet (1974–75) states that perceiving "supposes an organism able to differen-tiate . . . ultimately concluding with an identification of objects or events." Between these initial and final stages, the perceptual act traverses intermediate stages comparing the current, newly delimited percept with previously known and memorized percepts. An appreciation emerges which is an evaluation in terms of degrees of similarity or contrast in relation to points of reference acquired in the more or less distant past.

Concerning musical perception, it has been postulated (I. Deliège, 1987a) that a mechanism for extracting *pertinent cues* (or *indices*) presented by the properties of the musical surface is intrinsically linked to the formation of rhythmic groups. At this basic stage of differentiation, auditory perception detects successive sounds and combines them in a series of groups whose size is limited to the psychological present or short-term memory capacity (Fraisse, 1974, p. 79). Cues thus extracted become abbreviations used to lighten the load on memory storage.

The concept of cue, or index, as used here is similar to the one suggested by Charles S. Peirce as a type of sign. Referring to indices, he wrote: "An *index* is a sign which refers to the Object that it denotes by virtue of being really affected by that Object" (Peirce, 1974: 2.248, p. 140). Elsewhere, he added that it points to the very thing or event evoked "because it is in dynamical (including spatial) connec-tion both with the individual object, on the one hand, and with the senses or memory of the person for whom it serves as a sign, on the other hand" (2.305, p. 170).

A cue should therefore facilitate the formation of groupings of groups at various hierarchical levels and enable the totality of the work to be circumscribed. These cues are nothing other than input tags. Most of them are temporary and fleeting, and not all are retained in memory. For a "natural selection" occurs in which only the strongest cues survive. These then act as signals, able to signpost the temporal progress of the work through their recurrent appearance.

Cues play an essential role in the perception of the fundamental articulations of a musical work. Once extracted, they acquire value as reference points for strategies of comparison; they enable structures to be identified and filed. Cues contain the *invariants within the discourse,* according to which a continual process of evaluating new input can be organized: a grouping of groups undergoing formation can be extended to encompass new candidates if the same type of invariant is recognized. A degree of variation is tolerated (Smyth, Morris, Levy & Ellis, 1987, p. 48), but when a contrasting structure is noted or predicted (depend-ing on whether the piece being listened to is familiar or not), the process is blocked and the boundary of the grouping under formation is set. This boundary can potentially become the leading cue for a new combination of units. It follows from the above that the process of extracting cues, from within the work or during suc-cessive listening sessions, progressively elaborates a memory imprint resulting from the accumulation of more or less varied reiterations. This constitutes a sort of summary (I. Deliège, 1987a) comprised of the major coordinates of a set of *percepts,* the specific details of each example "merging" into a single standard model.[1]

Two organizational principles, therefore, structure analytical listening to musical form: the principle of SAMENESS cements together structures which constitute groupings, while the principle of DIFFERENCE demarcates them. These principles illustrate a psychological tendency stressed in particular by Fraisse (1967, p. 126) relating to the perception of durations: following a law of assimilation, all variations closely related to an invariant kernal (or minor differences) will be minimized; in contrast, larger differences will be overestimated and established as boundaries, due to the law of contrasts.

Experiments

The processes just discussed were tested in three experiments. The formation of groupings of groups in listening to authentic pieces of music was studied in the first two, while the third reversed the approach and involved localizing extracts within groupings established by the first experiment. This first experiment is published elsewhere (I. Deliège & El Ahmadi, in press), but the results will be summarized here to lend coherence to this article.

This study extends prior observations made concerning Lerdahl & Jackendoff's grouping theory (I. Deliège, 1987b), here using a broader level of grouping. That research had shown that subjects' musical training had only a weak effect on their aptitude to perceive rhythmic groups. Consequently, the anticipated results of this study should logically reflect this already noted tendency. The formation of groupings is a question of preference: strictly speaking, there is no "right" or "wrong" answer. The organization of groupings on the basis of index extraction, as hypothesized here, should nevertheless reveal a stronger segmentation tendency when contrasting structures are introduced, that is to say at the moment that an invariant-bearing index ceases to be maintained. Finally, the test involving localizing extracts in their original grouping should provide a check on the efficiency of the index extraction process. For it is at this stage that the development of the imprint phenomenon resulting from their reiteration should take place.

Methodology

Stimuli

The choice of musical materials for the experiments posed a tricky methodological problem as regards observing the degree to which musical training influences grouping aptitude. It therefore seemed desirable to use pieces of contemporary music in order to resolve certain difficulties. Without pretending that it is easy to gather data free of possible influence, such material focused on the hypothesis by comparing the performance of professional musicians with that of non-musicians (for whom this represented their first contact with the music.)

Selection criteria from among the extensive repertoire available had to fulfill two other requirements. The first involved employing two works of the same duration so that subjects would undergo experimental sessions of equal length and effort, while the second deliberately aimed at testing the hypothesis of index extraction itself. This is why two experiments were conducted using works clearly differentiated in terms of compositional approach. In one, Berio's *Sequenza VI*, the invariant plays an important role, which should tend to favor the grouping of groups as a function of the similarity of cues encountered. In the other piece, Boulez' *Eclat,* it is a question of a framework in which relatively independent sound states are linked together. At first sight, the invariant is not a dominating compositional feature of *Eclat:* cue extraction should therefore logically be limited to a more local operation and be less effective in constituting large groupings. This twin perspective provided results which could be compared, thus offering a better assessment of the validity of the hypothesis.

In an effort to simplify the subjects' task of segmentation and to obtain cleaner data, it was also decided to use works which did not involve the superimposition or shifting of different rhythmic groups characteristic of complex counterpoint.[2]

For the third experiment, a set of forty-seven excerpts or groups of varying length (five to ten seconds) were marked out in Berio's work following Lerdahl & Jackendoff's Proximity, Slur-Rest and Intensification rules (1983, pp. 45 & 49). Clean breaks were produced using a tape recording.

Subjects

All three experiments involved two categories of subjects from 18 to 35 years of age: professional musicians fluent in contemporary music on the one hand, and non-musicians (college or drama students) on the other.

The first experiment (Berio's *Sequenza*) was run on 18 musicians and 18 non-musicians. In addition, as a point of reference, auditory analyses were performed by two young composers.

The second experiment (Boulez' *Eclat*) was run on 16 subjects from each category,the non-musicians not having participated in the first experiment.

For the third experiment (Berio, localizing extracts), 12 musicians and 12 non-musicians (*all* having participated in the first experiment) were involved.

Procedure

Hypotheses were tested through two distinct procedures:

a) To study the formation of groupings of groups on cue extraction (the first two experiments), instructions were given to subjects to segment the work as a function of perceived structures, that is to say to group together elements yielding convenient associations which would justify their being connected together. The segmentation exercise was open-ended, with no restraints imposed. As an analogy – and above all to make the task clear to non-musicians – two comparisons were suggested. The first involved demarcating architectural structures such as volumes and basic dimensions, the second involved picking out the major organizational structures of a written text, such as indentations, ends of paragraphs, and chapters.

Subjects heard the whole piece. Throughout every listening session, subjects could refer to the time elapsed as displayed on a screen. They listened once to familiarize themselves with the piece and to take notes relating to the instructions, particularly noting the time elapsed at the spots where they wanted to establish segmentation. This was followed by two other listenings, during which the requested tasks were to be performed; the second of these was designed to measure the degree of stability in segmentation judgments. Data was collected on a *Macintosh Plus* microcomputer. The tape was synchronized with the startup of the *Performer* (Mark of the Unicorn) program, which displayed elapsed time and recorded responses (entered by hitting designated keys on the keyboard).

For the first experiment (Berio), the two listening sessions were conducted in the same way: pressing a single key marked the boundary at the end of a grouping. For the second experiment (Boulez), however, the compositional approach involved groups highly demarcated by changes in pitch and instrumental timbre as well as long silences, so that a number of very similar segments could be expected to emerge, regardless of where they occurred. To be able to take this into consideration when analyzing results and to observe whether cue extraction supplants the formation of more local groups, the second listening session required an additional task which involved establishing a hierarchy of segment relevance, that is to say giving each a *weight* relating to its perceived importance. Weight levels were fixed at 1, 2 or 3, and were indicated by pressing the corresponding number of keys on the keyboard. Another special key was also designated as an "erase" key so that a segmentation judgment could be cancelled if a mistake was made.

b) During the test to localize extracts, subjects were informed of the results of the first experiment and the piece's subdivision into six main groupings – hereafter called "sections" (see below). They then listened to the whole piece twice, section boundaries being indicated by sound signals placed at the precise points. The experiment itself required that subjects listen to the forty-seven excerpts one by one, in random order, and determine the section to which each belonged. An additional measure of the effect of musical training on cue extraction was incorporated into this trial: subjects were to specify their level of certainty for each response, on a scale of 1 to 3, as well as how typical an extract was of the grouping to which it belonged, on a scale of 1 to 5.

Results and observations

Experiments 1 and 2

Figures 1 (Berio) and 2 (Boulez) show the groupings obtained. Elapsed time is indicated in regular increments along the X-axis so that places of segmentation can be cross-referenced to the score. The number of subjects having selected each segment appears along the Y-axis. For both experiments, segmentation pertaining to the two listening sessions can be read independently, as can the confirmations of segment selection (that is to say the fact that a given subject indicated segmentation at the same place in the work during both listening sessions).

Analysis of results was done using both score and performance. No segment was eliminated, but regrouping was done when the markers in the computer designated the same place in the score. In *Eclat*, for example (to avoid any ambiguity on this point), markers placed between 1'10" and 1'15" obviously indicated the perception of the same segment (number 3 on the score[3]), and so on for similar cases.

For Berio's *Sequenza VI*(Figure 1), subjects' results are compared with a reference perceptual trial conducted on two composers. Their breakdown into six major sections was probably suggested, according to their comments, by the

218

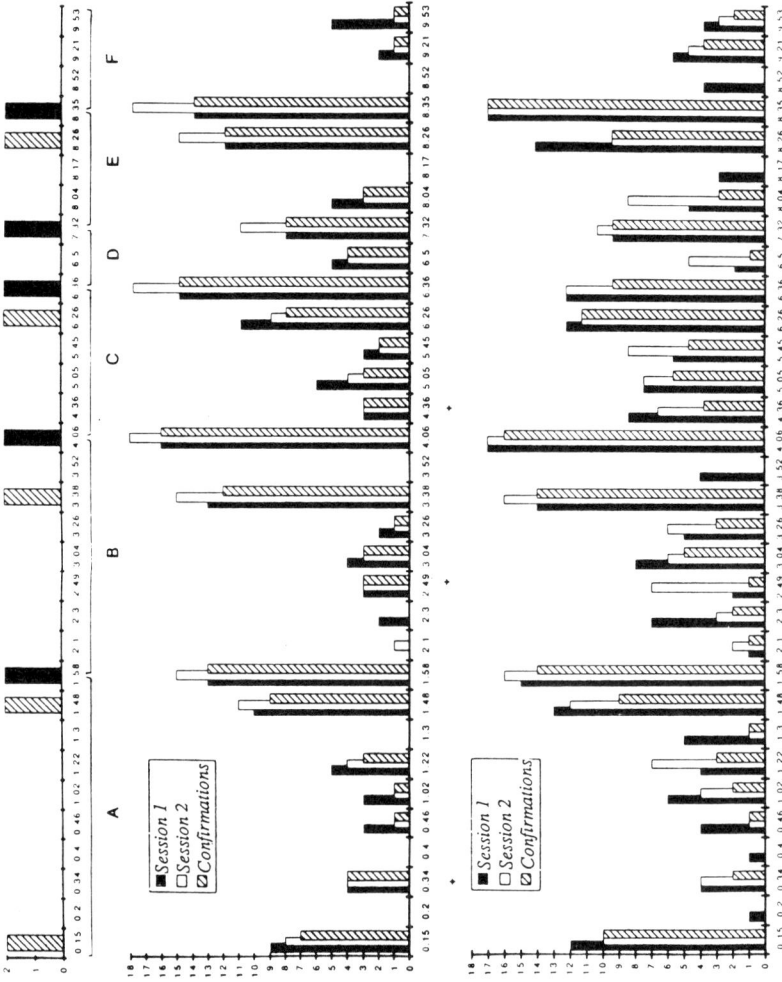

Figure 1 Segmentation of Berio's *Sequenza VI* (the entire piece) by two composers, 18 musicians, and 18 non-musicians.
(+) = Total stability in judgments of certain musicians at secondary points in the discourse.
(*) = Internal contrasts within sections perceived by non-musicians.

maintenance of characteristic figures and the statistical occurrence of sound events. Thus it followed the evolution of overall sound density. The composers moreover defined passages from one section to another as zones which "paved the way", by which they meant that a caesura (hatched lines) and a certain contrast in structures led to a temporary feeling of change in system when it was only a partial change anticipating the true segmentation at the end of a section (solid lines).

Subjects behaved in a highly uniform way. The few differences observed are negligeable (Table 1). All subjects indicated preferences along the same lines as the segmentations indicated by the composers. Musicians and non-musicians agreed extensively on how segmentation was to be carried out. At only five places (indicated by * in Figure 1) were non-musicians especially sensitive to contrasts within sections, as for instance the introduction of an up-and-down arpeggio-type sequence at 4'36" (Example 1) and the glissandi chords at 8'04" (Example 2), a structure particular to this spot in the work. For non-musicians, the stability of segmentation in the two successive auditions is highly correlated with the statistical relevance of the various points of segmentation (r = .815). On the other hand, several musicians manifested total stability for points of segmentation statistically less relevant (indicated by + in Figure 1) which resulted in a lowering of the level of correlation (r = .471).

Table 1 Significant comparisons (Fisher's Exact Test) between the proportions of responses by musicians and non-musicians for Berio's *Sequenta VI*.

Time	Session 1	Session 2	Confirmations
1'30"	.0227	—	—
3'26"	—	—	—
3'52"	.0519	—	—
4'36"	.0375	—	—
5'45"	—	.0137	—
6'36"	—	.0227	—
8'04"	—	.0375	—
8'35"	.0519	—	.0519
8'52"	.0519	—	—

It was demonstrated that the end of each section was marked by the introduction of contrasting structures. In addition, invariant cues were noted within the specific compositional approach characterizing each section. Section A uses a great deal of very sonorous tremolo-vibrato, with production of chords preceded by isolated sounds in a more or less arpeggiated configuration (Example 3) in the context of a chromatic tension moving toward the upper register. Section B inaugurates a descending system, but group cues share similarities with the cues of sections A, B and E in the use of tremolo-vibrato chords. Section C develops a more static and quieter compositional approach for two minutes and then produces a major

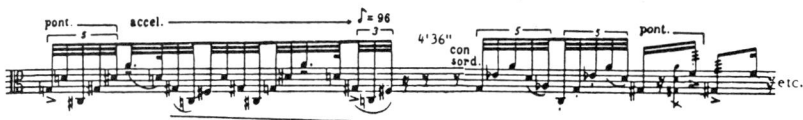

Example 1

Example 2

Example 3

Example 4

Example 5

Example 6 (Examples 1–6 from *Sequenza VI* by Luciano Berio, © 1970 by Universal Edition London, Ltd, with the kind permission of Universal Edition AG Vienna.)

contrast at the very center of the work (Example 4). *Pizzicato, arco,* and *col legno* chords are cues typical of Section D (Example 5) whereas section E re-adopts a system similar to Sections A and B. The final section stresses a high F and double string playing which produces intervals of diminished fifths (Example 6).

It is interesting that results produced for Boulez' *Eclat,* which is stylistically very different from *Sequenza VI* are analogous to those of the first experiment. Figures 2 and 3 clearly demonstrate similar grouping behavior on the part of all subjects. A reduced number of significant differences was noted (Table 2). Nor, moreover, was there any significant difference from one listening session to the next, nor in the way the hierarchic importance of segments was perceived during listening (Table 3), as is shown in Figure 3. The Y axis shows the sum of the weights (1, 2

Table 2 Significant comparisons (Fisher's Exact Test) between the proportions of responses by musicians and non-musicians for Boulez' *Eclat.*

Time	Session 1	Session 2	Confirmations	Hierarchization
3'25"	—	—	—	.0328
3'30"	.0506	—	—	—
3'35"	—	—	—	.0233
4'50"	—	—	—	.0253
5'15"	.0034	—	—	—
5'25"	—	—	—	.0556
7'45"	.0506	—	.0269	.0384
9'12"	—	—	—	.0439
9'40"	.0506	—	—	—

221

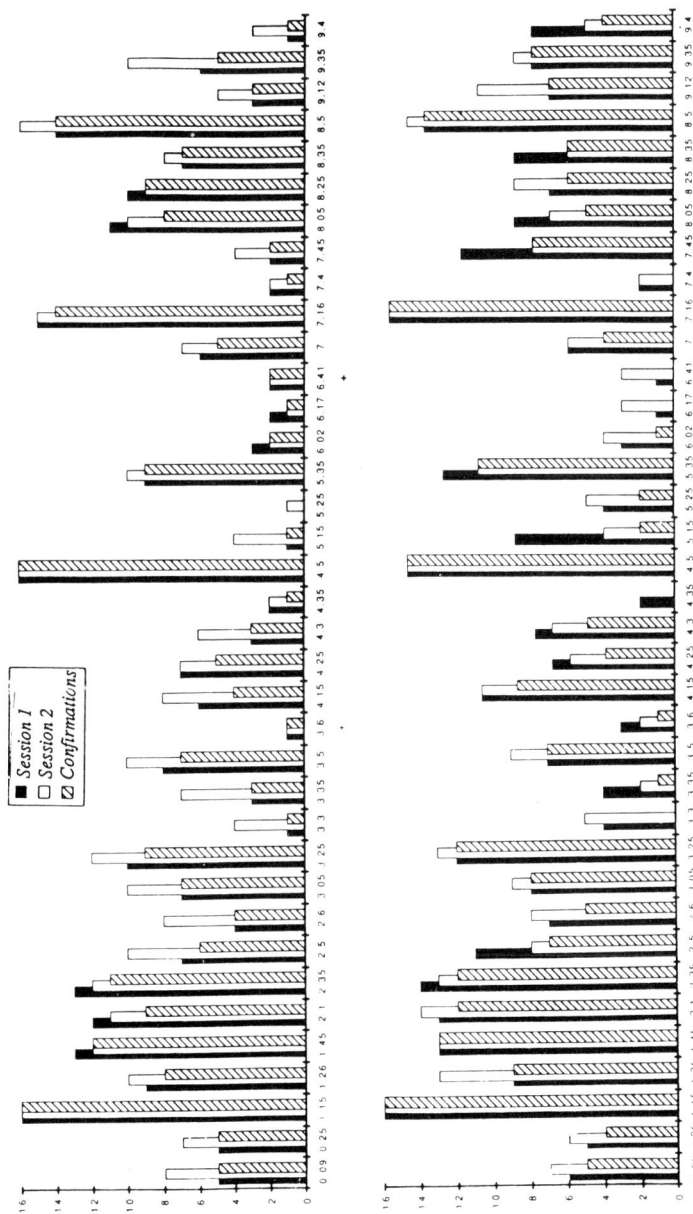

Figure 2 Segmentation of Boulez' *Eclat* (the entire piece) by 16 musicians and 16 non-musicians.
(+) = Total stability in judgments of certain musicians at secondary points in the discourse.

222

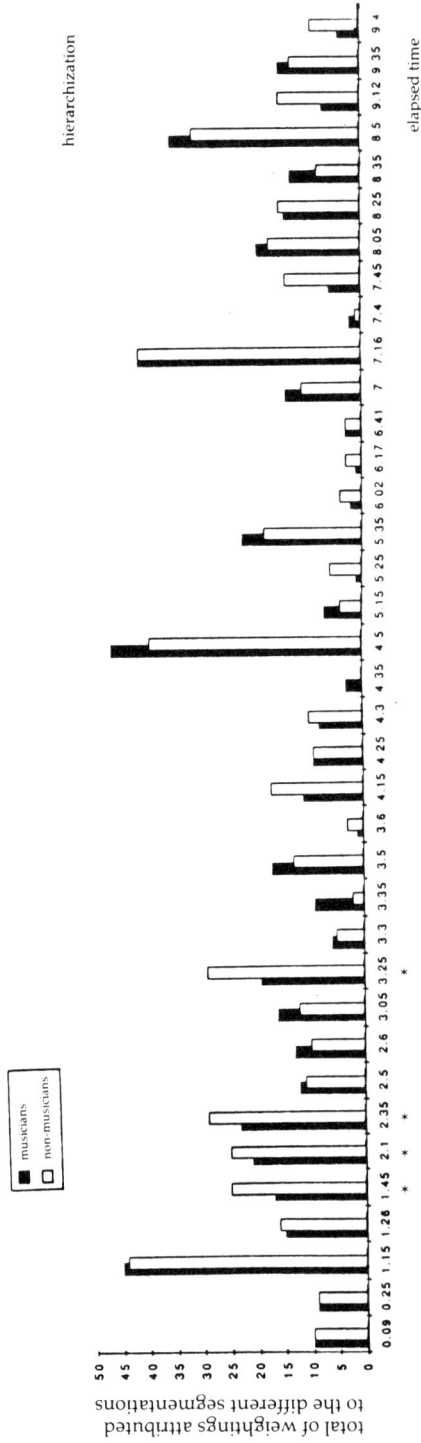

Figure 3 The sum of the weights attributed (1, 2 or 3) to each of the segments indicated in *Eclat* by 16 musicians and 16 non-musicians during the second experimental listening session.

(*) = Contrasts strongly perceived by non-musicians.

Table 3 Analysis of variance with repeated measures for two listening sessions of Boulez' *Eclat* by musicians and non-musicians.

Source of variation	d.f.	F	p
– effect related to category of subjects (musicians/non-musicians)	1,30	.92	.35 n.s.
– effect related to listening session (first/second)	1,30	1.43	.24 n.s.
– interaction	1,30	3.25	.15 n.s.
– effect related to perception of hierarchical importance of all segmentations	1,30	.04	.84 n.s.
– effect related to perception of hierarchical importance of four main segmentations	1,30	.42	.52 n.s.

or 3; cf. *Procedure*, above) attributed to the individual sequences (along the X-axis) by 16 subjects in each category.

Four major segments define the main groupings. A look at the score reveals the appearance of more marked contrasts at these points. At the beginning of the piece, after a long solo piano cadenza, the movement toward a structure including vibraphone, mandolin, and celeste (at roughly 1'15") is conveyed by the harp in regular steps (cf. rehearsal number 3 of the score). The composer then exploits the diversity of timbre within the instrumental ensemble through the predominance accorded to cells of rapid passages, moving toward long resonances (bells, glockenspiel, vibraphone) or to long-held trills. Boulez has spoken of this in terms of a double development of temporal flow: one active, the other contemplative – "elastic time" to be "played like an accordian" (*Le Temps Musical 1*, Radio France/IRCAM cassette). This atmosphere continues up to 4'50", giving way to several sharp, specific sound events, like unexpected flashes (rehearsal number 14) where the introduction of a resonant structure creates a counter-weight – a "cushion", to use Boulez' expression. A return to the piano solo at 5'35" (rehearsal number 16) then serves as "backdrop" (starting from rehearsal number 17) for other slow and occasional structures with resonant sounds. This system metamorphoses (rehearsal number 20) after a halt at roughly 7'16". The last major perceived segmentation is finally introduced after a long trill at 8'50" (rehearsal number 25) by a violent contrast in temporal flow.

In addition to this overview, it is worth taking a closer look at the few additional segments in *Eclat* (indicated by * in Figure 3) which yielded a marked perceptual salience (greater than 50%). These four instances, once again noted by non-musicians only, are found in the first third of the piece where a rapid run gives way to a trill and a long resonance (or the reverse – at rehearsal numbers 5, 6 and 7 in the score) or where the piano enters (at rehearsal number 9). It is therefore mainly a question of pitch and timbre contrasts in both cases. As in the previous experiment, these additional segments do not contradict the proposed hypothesis.

Another point in common between the results of the two experiments is the existence of a high degree of correlation between the statistically perceived salience of the different points of segmentation (Figure 4) and the stability of the non-musicians' behavior across the two experimental listening sessions (r = .805). Similarly, this second experiment once again shows a high degree of segmentation stability for musicians concerning secondary points in the musical discourse (indicated by + in Figure 2) which lowers the statistical correlation among all musicians (r = .571). Professional musicians would thereby demonstrate less spontaneity in fulfilling the requested tasks: they seem to control and anticipate their analyses more than do novice listeners, which is hardly surprising. If, on the other hand, only those points of segmentation defining the major groupings are considered, then the correlation between these points and segmentation stability is high for musicians (r = .88) as well as for non-musicians (r = .92).

Experiment 3

In Berio's *Sequenza,* subjects hearing 47 short excerpts one by one were instructed to determine to which section (from among the six that emerged from the first experiment) the excerpt belonged. The percentage of correct answers is conclusive, though somewhat lower for non-musicians (Table 4). A higher variation coefficient (standard deviation divided by the mean) was noted in performance averages for non-musicians (.19) than for musicians (.11). Table 5 provides important details concerning the results of the experiment. Essentially, it should be observed that on the whole there was a significant difference in the accuracy with which excerpts were localized as a function of the excerpt concerned. This difference is as marked for musicians as for non-musicians. These observations are corroborated on two levels. On the one hand, the degree of certainty with which subjects designated the section to which an excerpt belonged, as well as the extent to which that excerpt was felt to be typical of its section, differed from one excerpt to another. On the other hand, these assessments are not influenced by the subjects' level of musical training.

Table 4 Overall percentages of correctly localized excerpts, by section.

Musicians

	A	B	C	D	E	F
A	58.4	22.0	0.0	6.0	13.6	0.0
B	23.0	40.7	15.6	2.0	17.7	1.0
C	0.6	5.4	73.2	9.0	4.7	7.1
D	8.3	10.0	3.3	63.4	13.3	1.7
E	15.5	19.0	1.2	1.2	63.1	0.0
F	0.0	8.3	16.7	0.0	0.0	75.0

Non-musicians

	A	B	C	D	E	F
A	52.0	19.8	8.4	6.3	13.6	0.0
B	14.6	36.5	18.8	8.3	21.8	0.0
C	3.0	12.5	41.7	10.1	13.1	19.6
D	8.3	6.7	13.3	45.0	25.0	1.7
E	14.3	22.6	6.0	6.0	47.6	3.5
F	3.3	3.3	18.4	8.3	3.3	63.4

Table 5 Analysis of variance with repeated measures for results by musicians and non-musicians. a) Localizing the 47 excerpts from Berio's *Sequenza VI.* b) Assessment of the degree of certainty in their responses. c) Assessment of the extent to which the excerpt is typical of the section to which it belongs.

	Source of variation	d.f.	F	p	
a)	– effect related to excerpt concerned	46,1012	4.54	.0001	
	– effect related to excerpt concerned as a function of category of subjects (musicians/non-musicians)	46,1012	1.11	.29	n.s.
	– effect related to section as a function of category of subjects				
	for section A	1,22	.59	.45	n.s.
	for section B	1,22	.96	.34	n.s.
	for section C	1,22	25.03	.0001	
	for section D	1,22	4.98	.04	
	for section E	1,22	2.10	.16	n.s.
	for section F	1,22	.86	.36	n.s.
b)	– effect related to degree of certainty of subjects (musicians and non-musicians) according to excerpt	46,1012	5.60	.0001	
	– interaction as a function of category of subjects	46,1012	1.10	.31	n.s.
c)	– effect related to degree of typicality of excerpt in relation to section it belongs to, assessed by musicians and non-musicians	46,1012	4.85	.0001	
	– interaction as a function of category of subjects	46,1012	1.27	.11	n.s.

It is also important to point out that performances varied according to the section to which the excerpt belonged. Section B gave the poorest results, for both musicians and non-musicians, which was predictable given the decreased specificity of this section's cues (which, as described above, presented certain similarities with those of the preceding section as well as Section E). On the other hand, there was no difference between musicians and non-musicians concerning Sections A, B, E, and F, although the contrary was the case for Sections C and D.

It should be added that excerpts from three sections – A, B, and E – showed greater instability in terms of being correctly localized. This observation, the data for which is shown in Table 6, is especially clear when it is a question of localizing excerpts from section B. The percentage of correct answers is placed alongside the sum of the percentages of answers migrating to the other two sections: the comparison does not attain a truly significant difference.

On the whole, subjects performed this task in a fairly uniform way. The scores of non-musicians are however better for the opening and closing sections of the work, as opposed to the central sections, which might indicate the existence of primacy and recency effects as observed in the serial position curves for the recall of lists of words (Murdock, 1962). This effect perhaps diminishes as a result of learning and practice, since it did not occur among professional musicians.

226

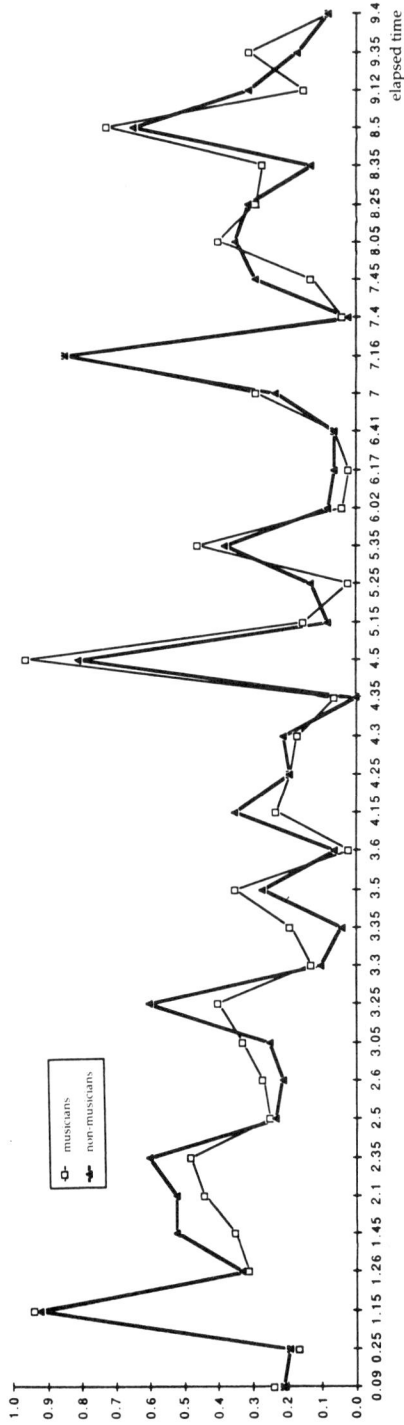

Figure 4 Plot of the pertinence quotients (proportion of subjects segmenting at a given moment) for musicians and non-musicians, pertaining to *Eclat*.

Table 6 Percentage of mistaken localizations of indices across Sections A, B and E in relation to the percentage of correctly localized excerpts.

	Section of origin	Percentage of correctly localized excerpts	Percentage of confusions	Level of significance
Musicians	A	58.4	B + E = 35.6	χ^2 2 d.f. =
	B	40.7	A + E = 40.7	4.109, p > .10
	E	63.1	A + B = 34.5	
Non-musicians	A	52.	B + E = 33.4	χ^2 2 d.f. =
	B	36.5	A + E = 36.4	1.825, p > .30
	E	47.6	A + B = 36.9	

Conclusion

Three points were raised at the outset of these experiments: the potential influence of musical training in grouping processes and the hypotheses of a cue extraction mechanism in perceptual analysis, in turn leading to the formation of imprints as a function of their reiteration. Do answers emerge from the overall results presented here?

Influence of Musical Training

The similarity of perceptual analyses is striking for both works examined, independently of the level of training of the subjects. Highly similar groupings were observed, as were evalutions of the degree of salience of the various grouping boundaries. The answer to the question concerning the influence of musical training therefore seems quite clear: it does not appear to affect in an obvious way the aptitude for auditory grouping regardless of the level of grouping structures considered. This corroborates prior observations concerning the perception of elementary rhythmic groups. At this point, it would be interesting to check the age at which this aptitude is acquired; an influence of language acquisition or level of schooling might emerge.

Cue Extraction Facilitating Grouping

The convergence of segmentation markings at certain specific places in the two works defined the major groupings of groups. Were these determined by the presence of any given invariant cue, however? Looking at the scores, one possibility immediately leaps to mind regarding the existence of a caesura (of greater or lesser importance) at these boundaries, and nothing more. Neither the role, nor the perception of these caesuras can be in doubt: any formation of a group is moreover accompanied by the perception of a caesura – even if subjective – at the boundary of a grouping. Yet this is not sufficient, and an analysis which recorded only the boundaries of groupings would of necessity be lacking and incomplete (cf. *Introduction*, above). Many caesuras do exist in these pieces, but only some of them produced an almost unanimous grouping preference among subjects tested. The reasons for this should be sought and the analysis pushed beyond mere grouping boundaries. Observation of surrounding structures showed clear contrasts at these precise spots. What is heard before and after the caesura is clearly different and signals specific belongingness in terms of groupings to be formed: one cue ceases, another begins. Their presence enables belongingness (Prieto, 1975, p. 15) to be determined for a given group and to indicate the boundaries – which a caesura alone cannot define, its main role of "pause" offering no other information.

If the two works selected are compared on the level of musical structure, cue extraction on the basis on invariants was far more predictable in Berio's *Sequenza* than in Boulez' *Eclat*. The obvious should be admitted, however: the effect of sound colors renewed by relatively individualized structures in *Eclat* progressively disappeared after the first three minutes of listening. A sort of assimilation was produced on the basis of pitch and timbre effects, perceived here largely as cues, leaving the role of demarcating groupings (and designating belongingness to those groupings) once again to highly contrasting structures alone. Cues can therefore be of several kinds – there is no pre-established rule on this point. It is the specific instance which is the determining factor, though the role of cues should be recognized as a basic mechanism in a perceptual approach to musical form.

Formation of Imprints

Results obtained in the procedure for localizing excerpts from Berio's piece reveal a majority of correctly localized excerpts. The cue extracted leads to a precise retrieval of the information and its specific localization. It should however be noted that when subjects had to localize an excerpt such as, in particular, the glissandi chords heard toward the end of the piece (see Example 2, above) – a passage containing cues rarely reiterated elsewhere – the number of correct responses increases. A greater number of errors was recorded, on the other hand, when localizing excerpts containing cues employed more frequently. This observation may seem paradoxical at first sight. How can the drop in performance be understood as normal when the effect of repetition should have aided memory? Here it should be stressed that the cues which reappear in the composition are usually not repeated in identical form. A varying degree of variation usually accompanies such reiterations. What results is the "imprint" form of memorization in which only dominant traits extracted across all reiterations remain. Identification strategies thus become less precise and more vague, the exact encoding of particular characteristics less certain, leading to the probable cause of the confusion observed between Sections A, B, and E where invariants of the same type occur.

It should also be noted that the poorer results of non-musicians in the third experiment and the greater possibility of interference between extracted cues could indicate that the number of cues they managed to take in was smaller, leading to the more rudimentary imprint formation and more marked inaccuracy in the identification process. But it could be supposed that the lack of musical fluency requires non-musicians to undergo a greater number of listening sessions before a sufficiently rich and efficient imprint can be developed. One effect of musical training would be demonstrated here, then, in the poorer aptitude of non-practitioners to memorize musical events.

To sum up, the psychological mechanism involved in analytical listening invoked both comparative strategies based on cues and imprints in the identification process, but it appears that the extraction of cues precedes the formation of imprints, which confirms the importance of this mechanism in the process of analytical listening to music. Yet once the stage of imprint formation has been reached, nothing allows us to postulate, concerning what has been suggested, that the two types of strategy leading to the identification of structures are necessarily present and operative at all times in the processing of information.

Translated from the French by Deke Dusinberre

Acknowledgments

Parts of this article were previously developed in presentations at the "Composition at Perception Musicales" conference at the University of Geneva in March 1987, when this research had just begun, as well as at the "Science and Music" conference at The City University in London in September 1987. I would like to thank Stephen McAdams, Carol Krumhansl, Fred Lerdahl, André Ducamp, John Sloboda, Claire Gérard and the anonymous reviewers for their encouragement and considered re-reading of the first draft of the article. I am grateful to Abdessadek El Ahmadi, Jean-Marc Sullon, Stéphane Lejoly, and Marie-Isabelle Collart for their help with technical aspects and overall coordination, as well as to all the subjects who agreed to see the experiments through.

Notes

1. An analogy can be drawn between the notion of imprint used here and a theory originally put forth by Posner, Goldsmith & Welton (1967) and subsequently developed by others (notably Franks & Bransford, 1971; Bransford & Franks, 1971; Solso & Raynis, 1982; Welker, 1982), which demonstrated the existence of a process of identification based on a memorized prototype. However, the concept of prototype may not really be appropriate here. For the concept of prototype, in everyday usage, refers to the primary exemplar, or model, of a whole series embodying all of its fundamental features. Subsequent reproductions are (nearly) perfect copies rather than variations in so far as the invariant dominates almost exclusively. The prototype is therefore a unique example representing a whole set, a sort of "zero model" which precedes all the other members of the series. Abdi (1986, p. 148) has pointed out that, in work done on the notion of prototype, the "various members" of a series can share a certain "representativity gradient" in their relationship to the series. The concept appears to have thus shifted toward a meaning which is almost the opposite of its original definition. It is possible that this shift is due to interference between the concept of prototype strictly speaking and the concept of category. For the notion of *typicality* as proposed by Rosch (1973, 1975) is behind the concept of category, suggesting that a class can be evoked by different representatives which all have the role of designating that class, the role of what Abdi calls the "psychological tide-mark". The specificity of the term prototype has thus undergone a certain transformation. At a time when these notions are being invoked to operate at the level of the perception of musical form, prudence dictates that ambiguity be avoided by eliminating terms that could lead to confusion. For the moment, then, it is a question here neither of prototype nor of category, of *imprint*, that is to say, for the sake of repetition, a standard model established by memory to sum up a set of information which shares invariants that are reiterated with a certain emphasis.
2. It should be pointed out once again that this research aims only to shed light on individual perceptual behavior, and makes no claim to aesthetic judgment concerning the works involved (much less normative recommendations of a compositional or pedagogical nature).
3. Given limited space, the examples raised concerning *Eclat* are not reproduced here. They can be easily located in the score, to which the reader is referred (Universal Edition UE 14283).

References

Abdi, H. (1986) La mémoire sémantique. Une fille de l'intelligence artificielle et de la psychologie: quelques éléments biographiques . . . *Psychologie, Intelligence artificielle et automatique*, Bonnet/Hoc/Tiberghien (eds.) Brussels: Mardaga.

Bransford, J.D. & Franks, J.J. (1971) The abstraction of linguistic ideas. *Cognitive Psychology,* **2,** 331–350.

Deliège, I. (1987a) Le parallélisme, support d'une analyse auditive de la musique: vers un modèle des parcours cognitifs de l'information musicale. Application au *Syrinx* de Debussy. *Analyse Musicale,* **6,** 73–39.

Deliège, I. (1987b) Grouping conditions in listening to music: An approach to Lerdahl & Jackendoff's grouping preference rules. *Music Perception,* **4,** 325–360.

Deliège, I. & El Ahmadi, A. (1989) Mécanismes d'extraction d'indices dans le groupement. Etude de perception sur la *Sequenza VI* pour alto solo de Luciano Berio. Actes du Symposium Composition et Perception musicales, 1987, University of Geneva, *Contrechamps,* **10,** 85–104. Traduction anglaise, Mechanisms of cue extraction in musical groupings, to appear, *Psychology of Music.*

Fraisse, P. (1967) *La psychologie du temps.* Paris: Presses Universitaires de France.

Fraisse, P. (1974) *La psychologie du rythme.* Paris: Presses Universitaires de France.

Franks, J.J. & Bransford, J.D. (1971) Abstraction of visual patterns. *Journal of Experimental Psychology,* **90,** 65–74.

Lerdahl, F. & Jackendoff R. (1983) *A Generative Theory of Tonal Music.* Cambridge, Mass: MIT Press.

Moore, B.C.J. (1982) *An Introduction to the Psychology of Hearing,* London, New York: Academic Press.

Murdock, B. Jr. (1962) The serial position effect in free recall, *Journal of Experimental Psychology,* **64,** 482–488.

Noizet, G.(1974–75) Les perceptions. *Bulletin de Psychologie,* **314, XXVIII,** 1–6, 167–205.

Peirce, C.S. (1974) *Collected Works,* Cambridge, Mass: Harvard University Press.

Posner, M.I., Goldsmith, R. & Welton, K.E. Jr. (1967) Perceived distance and the classification of distorted patterns. *Journal of Experimental Psychology,* **73,** 28–38.

Prieto, L.J. (1975) *Pertinence et pratique.* Paris: Minuit.

Rosch, E. (1973) Natural categories. *Cognitive Psychology,* **4,** 328–350.

Rosch, E.(1975) Cognitive reference points. *Journal of Experimental Psychology: General.* **104,** 192–233.

Smyth, M., Morris, P.E., Levy, P. & Ellis, A.W. (1987) *Cognition in Action,* Hillsdale, New Jersey: L. Erlbaum Associates.

Solso, R.L. & Raynis, S.A. (1982) Transfer of prototypes based on visual, tactual and kinesthetic exemplars. *American Journal of Psychology,* **95,** 13–29.

Welker,R. (1982) Abstraction of themes from melodic variations. *Journal of Experimental Psychology,* **8 (3),** 435–447

Contemporary Music Review,
1989, Vol. 4, pp. 231–236
Photocopying permitted by license only

Music and cognitive psychology: Form-bearing elements

Hugues Dufourt

Centre d'Information et de Documentation "Recherche Musicale",
CIDM IRCAM-CNRS, Centre Georges Pompidou, F-75191 Paris Cédex 04, France

Contemporary music offers cognitive psychology models that establish relevant and computable features for a theoretical field which had remained unspecified up to now. Cognitive psychology outlines a theory of the relations between memory and perception for which music functions as a test of effectiveness and coherence. The relationship of cognitive psychology to contemporary music is that of a theory to its models. Music composition offers new ways of thinking which extend the range of hypothetical constructions and offer proof of the fecundity of analogy. Cognitive psychology produces original theories which lend new insight into perceptual mechanisms and challenge the very foundations on which music is based.

KEY WORDS: Categorization, imprints, pitch, memory, timbre, source, texture.

This session of the symposium was devoted to potential form-bearing elements. This concept refers to the set of objective conditions which an acoustic signal – or indeed, developed musical material – must meet in order to be pertinently handled by the auditory system. The work in music psychology done by A. Bregman, S. Pinker, and S. McAdams initially dealt with the way in which the ear organizes sound (Bregman & Pinker, 1978; McAdams & Bregman, 1979). Psychology has described a hierarchy of perceptual and cognitive constraints which pertain to mental activity when it focuses on music. Stephen McAdams' work on the fusion and segregation of sound streams, for instance, is representative of this type of problem. The idea behind today's presentation is to reverse the perspective and ask what conditions sound must meet in order to be amenable to discriminating and assimilating operations performed by the human ear. The biological and psychological constraints characterizing what is called musical material have their own order, differing notably from the order of complexity of an acoustic signal. Following the psychologist J.J. Gibson, Jean-Claude Risset noted that psychoacoustics has stuck too closely to physics in analyzing perceptual operations according to parameters of pitch, duration, intensity and timbre (Risset, 1988, p. 14, 115, 20, 21). Psychoacoustics has neglected specific auditory work which "handles a very rich context, passing unconsciously from one level to another, performing an analysis or, to the contrary, a synthesis of perceptible data" (Ibid., p. 24). McAdams has proposed experimental procedures giving these questions an affirmative status, notably examining the conditions under which the auditory system detects a sound source. In order for a source to be perceived as such, it must have a common spatial origin, a coherent amplitude behavior, harmonicity across components and a regular system of resonance structures (McAdams, 1987, p. 41–42). This provides a set of determinations defining a new scientific object, halfway between psychophysic's methods of quantification and cognitive psychology's research into listening.

One of cognitive psychology's main contributions has been to reveal the role played by mental representations in perception. The exclusive consideration of automatic responses governing causal relations between stimuli and reactions is today given a back seat by the psycho-biological sciences in order to highlight more subtle conditioning (systems of correlation obeying criteria or optimization, suitability and self-regulation). Cognitive music psychology has therefore had to assimilate recent developments in acoustics, the brain sciences, and artificial intelligence as well as psycholinguistics and ethnomusicology.It has reintroduced concepts of image representation, of expectation, of attention, of anticipation, of learning, and of recognition. It stresses the role of memory in perceptual processes and shows that it involves a higher, complex form of elaboration. Jacques Paillard (1987, p. 9) comments that respective advances in the fields of cognitive psychology, neuropsychology and cognitive neuroscience must all be taken into account. One of the ultimate goals of these new fields is to understand the relation between perception and action, and to reveal mechanisms of behavioral conduct.

Cognitive psychology reconsiders afresh old philosophical questions which, in their original state, remained rudimentary and enigmatic. It is permissible to assume that perception notes those traits of a physical signal which are most useful to the survival of the organism. Acoustic causality – the identification of the sound source – is basic to hearing, which is a defensive sense. The ear can evaluate source direction and distance, and assess its initial energy, just as it is able to detect minor changes in signal emission, indeed distinguish several simultaneous sources. The phylogenesis of the human ear corroborates, thus informing us that the original function of the ear was to supply information concerning the direction and position of solids in an atmospheric medium. The ears possess remarkable sensitivity to the least disturbance, for which it localizes the origins and symbolizes the distance through additional cues such as intensity, spectrum (more or less truncated in the treble range), and the level of reverberation in relation to direct sound (Risset, 1988, p. 16). It is highly possible that this source identification function is indispensible to musical listening which, were it to be deprived of it (as is the case in electroacoustic music), would display a sort of fundamental dissatisfation with this artificial mutilation of its capacities (Cadoz, 1988). This is a crucial issue, for it calls into question the structure of auditory perception which seems above all centered on causality, conditioned by inference mechanisms and completely constructed on the process of grouping acoustic elements into source events. This pinpointing, this ordering of elements into an auditory image, precedes any appreciation of the quality of the source by the ear (McAdams, 1987, p. 43).

The validity of qualitative criteria, or the veracity of our senses and their aptitude for informing us about reality, all bear examination today. Everything leads us to trust what nature conveys to us by way of our senses, because sensory information takes into account the physical invariants on which it is modeled. In its very constitution, the human perceptual system retains that element of coherence and stability which derives from the physical models informing it. Because senses are congruent to their milieu (Shepard, 1984), an organism's overall grasp of its environment is assured and reliable. It is precisely these conditions of objectivity and consistency of sensory information that this session sought to bring to the fore through what are called "form-bearing elements". To fully understand the sense and extent of our adaptation to the physical environment, computer technology had to be able to dislocate natural data, to contradict the normal functioning of perception, to provoke disequilibrium, to perturb regulating and integrating mechanisms by offering perception paradoxical or discordant information. The computer can provide experimental conditions which take us beyond the normal, attaining through technological artifice what remains unavailable to our senses, thus provoking that which, precisely, never occurs in nature.

According to McAdams (this volume), perception is engaged in an objectivizing process which establishes the spatial and temporal coherence of perceived sound events via segmentation, simultaneous grouping or sequential organization. Perception only operates on distinct values, on well-defined attributes which enable it to classify and organize phenomena. Thus when physics provides us with continuous acoustic messages, the ear and brain strive to separate and discriminate. At the same time, it is the task of the auditory system to comprehend and unify, to convert – in the words of Maurice Pradines (1943) – "a quantitative multiplicity of identical impressions into a qualitative variation in differing impressions" (p. 521). McAdams uses the word "categorization" to refer to this task of discrimination proper to perception. Its values exclude any breakdown into parts, constituting such values into individualized, uniform entities suited to operations of organization, comparison and recognition; the coherence of a sound object depends on structural boundaries. Apprehending form in music depends on the aptitude of the sound medium to offer perceivable articulations to the listener, to engage the mechanisms of arranging and ordering. It requires clearly differentiated elements which can enter into functional relationships. It also requires the maintenance of certain invariants within the transformations the system undergoes.

Following Piaget, cognitive psychology has shown that mental structures active in perception are above all dynamic and integrating processes which unceasingly compose and transform data. The work of assimilation performed by brain and senses are not limited to pure categorical oppositions. Perceptual activity's substantiations are constantly reassessed as a function of perception's grasp on the acoustic object. The more complex the stream of information, the richer and more active is the auditory system's comprehension. In this regard, contemporary music holds great interest for cognitive psychology because it offers an indeterminate experimental field of composite and hybrid structures, of mutations of perceptual organization, of operations involving incessant fusion and articulation.

Kaija Saariaho's music raises an original problem for psychology since her work is located on the boundary between harmony and timbre. It uses sound endowed with a high level of inharmonicity and develops forms completely based on shifting relations of texture and timbre (see, for example, Saariaho, 1987). The global process prevails over any potential analytical-type pinpointing. The transformational act is no longer subordinated to a form of ordering. The works of György Ligeti, Roger Reynolds, Tristan Murail and Gérard Grisey also present processes in which perceptual categories remain unstable, where evolution is neither cyclical nor repetitive yet does not thereby become formless or incomprehensible.

Cognitive psychology must be able to account for the ceaseless readjustment effected by mental images, expressed as an experiential mutation, a qualitative transformation of perceptual organization oscillating between the homogeneous and the heterogeneous, between difference and variation. Cognitive psychology demonstrates that all mental activity is engaged in an incessant process of formation and specification. It stresses the work of coordination undertaken within perceptual organization, indicating the variety and mobility of forms such organization assumes, far from any fundamental invariance. It is therefore no coincidence that cognitive psychology and musical production today converge on this point. For both involve, in any event, an understanding of the rapport between order and transformation.

Marie-Elisabeth Duchez (this volume) provides an historical and critical analysis of the elaboration of the notion of pitch height in Western music. She reminds us that music psychology's interpretive framework supplies a set of conditions which are necessary but not sufficient for grasping a phenomenon which also issues from the cultural and scientific history of measurement. Her article retraces the stages through which successive generations managed to quantify and gain access to the realm of discursive relations, beyond intuitive modes of knowledge (whether these be on the order of the sensible, the geometric, or the causal). The concept of Pitch Height really only appeared with the institution of active comprehension in conjunction with operative formulae and explicit definitions. Understanding the history of music demands an elucidation of the genesis of rational forms which would extend, in fact, beyond the concerns of cognitive psychology.

Irène Deliège (this volume) presents a reverse viewpoint, so to speak, by showing that cognitive psychology can contribute to a better understanding of a cultural event through well conducted experimentation. She examines the performance of memory and identification strategies exhibited by attentive listeners who attempt to recognize a complex musical form. Musical education probably plays a role in a subject's aptitude to perform grouping operations and perceive structural hierarchies. Deliège hypothesizes that imprints become established through the reiteration of cues, during which memory performs the task of condensation and articulation. The brain seeks to grasp both the interdependence of various factors and the particularities of each specific arrangement. Memory's power of identification and construction through a discriminatory operation is used to coordinate and simplify elements, distinguishing them from the whole. Mental activity thus consists of an analytic, discriminating act and an organizing act which is indissociable from the former. Memory thereby performs the simultaneous task of articulation and composition within this order, demonstrating its power of schematization (in the philosophical sense of term).

Marco Stroppa (this volume) also deals with the problematic of memory by introducing the concept of "musical information organisms". A musical work can be conceived as the history of the reception, accumulation and assimilation of such organisms.

The contribution of David Wessel and David Bristow was devoted to timbre. Is timbre able to undergo differentiation similar to that practiced on pitch? The question is whether the idea of a timbral continuum with its hybrids and interpolations is perceptually pertinent, leading to hearable and decodable coherent structures. Does timbral music offer anything other than a continual shifting which disconcerts ear and mind, denying the listener any possibility of a categorical approach? Wessel and Bristow feel that acoustic properties which have perceptual value can be controlled with the aid of a computer, bypassing musical instruments and with no reference to relationships stemming from physical systems. It is simply a question of operations involving the distribution of spectral energy and on its variation across time. A multidimensional representation correlates physical parameters with perceptual attributes. Within this model, frequency modulation synthesis techniques create a timbral continuum allowing for the transposition of sequences. One might ask, as do psychoacousticians, what factors are involved in establishing timbral identity, enabling it to resist both distortions and variations in reverberation.

Jean-Baptiste Barrière (this volume) denies the notion of timbre its traditional status as those stable sound qualities which remain recognizable across changes in register, dynamics and articulation. He assigns timbre an entirely new meaning. Instead of being the residual remnants of everything in sound quality that escapes human analysis, timbre becomes an analytic environment encompassing a dialectic of categories. A category, for Barrière, is a way of comprehending and perceiving as well as a characteristic of what is perceived and comprehended. The form-bearing element is an ordering structure which includes both material and organization, the axiomatic and the descriptive. The substitution of one arrangement for another, interversion, transition, and permutation don't therefore generate confusion. Timbral composition is no longer situated on the plane of the immediate, on the plane of conventional practice in which the implicit still plays a large part. It shifts completely over to the plane of objectivity, that level where technological and symbolic structures meet, where formal analysis and material verification reinforce one another. Formalizing a language of timbre provides it with increased explicitness and clarity. It coordinates a plurality of expressions with distinct dimensional scales and different degrees of complexity. Composing means operating simultaneously on an order of operative constraints and on their symbolic formulation. And it also means insuring the cognitive relevance of these processes. The problem facing composers is radically new: cognitive sciences, psychoacoustics and specialized fields researching perception and memory are invoked to replace what history had accomplished through trial and error, making imperceptible progress within the impetuous continuity of tradition.

Formalization gains in rigor what it loses in intuitive proof, in practical utility. The development of operative capacities proper to formal systems must find a counterpart in the enhanced precision and salience of objects offered to listening. Barrière feels that a certain register of relations can be extracted from excitation and resonance modes, which will subsequently lead to the application of computational rules. The compositional algorithm is thus ordered according to a system of primitive articulations and simulation models. It enhances these models and performs predictable transformations. The idea of a hierarchy of sound parameters loses its traditional foundation. Timbre is capable of sustaining an organization equal to that of pitch. The elaboration of constructive procedures goes hand in hand with a reinterpretation and a complication of perceptible cues, which therefore entails a different conception of music.

This session's presentations were thus marked by the originality of the problems musical production raises today for cognitive psychology. Music offers psychology examples of auditory paradoxes of types of representation which would have been unthinkable prior to the advent of computer-aided composition. Conversely, the influence of science and technology on procedures of musical composition has become determining; the "natural" language of traditional music is progressively being replaced by artificial languages which reveal implicit categories of perception and higher mental processes and raise, in return, the question of the status of signifying forms.

References

Bregman, A.S. & Pinker, S. (1978) Auditory streaming and the building of timbre, *Canadian Journal of Psychology/Revue Canadienne de Psychologie*, **32**, 19–31.

Cadoz, C. (1988) Timbre et causalité. *Informatique, Musique Image animée*, Grenoble: ACROE-INGP; also to appear in *Le Timbre: Métaphores pour la Composition*, J.B. Barrière (ed.), Paris: Christian Bourgois Editions.

McAdams, S. (1987) Music: A science of the mind? In "Music and Psychology: a Mutual Regard", S.McAdams (ed.), *Contemporary Music Review*, **2**(1), 1–61, London: Harwood Academic Publishers.

McAdams, S & Bregman, A.S. (1979) Hearing musical streams. *Computer Music Journal* **3**(4), 26–43.

Paillard, J. (1987) De la perception à l'action. *Le courrier du CNRS*, 69/70, 9.

Pradines, M. (1943) *Traité de psychologie générale*, T.I., Les fonctions universelles, Collection Logos, Paris : Presses Universitaires de France.

Risset, J.C. (1988) Perception, environnement, musiques. *InHarmoniques*, **3**, 10–43.

Saariaho, K. (1987) Timbre and harmony: Interpolations of timbral structures. In "Music and Psychology: A Mutual Regard," S. McAdams (ed.) *Contemporary Music Review* **2** (1), 93–133 London: Harwood Academic Publishers.

Shepard, R.N. (1984) Ecological constraints on internal representation: Resonant kinematics of perceiving, imagining, thinking, and dreaming. *Psychological Review*, **91**, 417–447.

Part III
Experimentation and Modeling

Contemporary Music Review,
1989, Vol. 4, pp. 237–245
Photocopying permitted by license only

Issues in theoretical and experimental approaches to research on listening and comprehension

Carol L. Krumhansl

Department of Psychology, Uris Hall, Cornell University, Ithaca, NY 14853, USA

Music has been studied recently from the perspective of a number of disciplines, including experimental psychology, artificial intelligence and neuroscience. These disciplines compliment more traditional approaches to understanding music, such as music theory, music analysis, and musicology. Despite their common interest in music, the various disciplines have distinctive theoretical commitments and methodologies. This paper attempts to characterize those of experimental psychology. In particular it considers why it is that certain kinds of problems appear to be more amenable to experimental analysis than others. It discusses basic problems in experimental design, including the selection of stimulus materials, participants and experimental tasks. In addition, it treats briefly the application of analytical techniques to experimental data to uncover underlying regularities and reach theoretical generalizations. The paper closes by considering the problems and potential advantages of interdisciplinary research on music, particularly within the context of the developing cognitive sciences.

KEY WORDS: Music cognition, experimental methods, cognitive science.

It is now commonplace to say that there has been a great deal of activity in music research during the last decade. The number of articles and books concerned with the psychology of music has expanded rapidly over this period of time (see, for example, Clynes, 1982; Deutsch, 1982, Howell, Cross & West, 1985; Sloboda, 1985, Dowling & Harwood, 1986; articles in *Music Perception* and numerous other journals). The bulk of this research takes a cognitive orientation – focusing on the mental processing and internal representation of musical structures. Concurrently there has been an interest among music theorists (stimulated in part by Lerdahl & Jackendoff, 1983) in grounding their observations to psychological notions about perception and cognition. Despite this recent activity, it is important to remember that music psychology has in fact enjoyed a long history and has been influenced by various traditions within psychology, especially psychophysics (with the investigations following from Helmholtz, 1877/1954) and Gestalt psychology (notably, Meyer, 1956). Each of these psychological traditions bring with it certain theoretical commitments. These determine, in part, the kinds of problems chosen for study, the methodologies employed, and the way in which the empirical observations are summarized and interpreted.

What I will do here is to offer some observations about the place of music within the developing cognitive sciences. The term "cognitive sciences" refers to a rather loose affiliation among a number of established disciplines including cognitive psychology, philosophy of mind, linguistics, artificial intelligence and the neurosciences. Of these disciplines, cognitive psychology has probably had the greatest influence on music research recently, although definite influences of linguistics, artificial intelligence and, to some extent, the neurosciences, can also be identified. Because cognitive psychology has had the largest influence most of my comments will be directed toward the work carried out in that general tradition.

Cognitive psychology is the subarea of experimental psychology directed at describing complex mental activities. Stimulated in part by developments in theoretical linguistics and computer science, the approach is nonetheless experimental in nature. This is to say that the work proceeds from observations made in controlled (usually laboratory) situations; these observations generally take a quantitative form and are treated by a variety of analytic and statistical techniques leading to generalizations and theoretical descriptions. A varied collection of mental activities has been studied in this way, including how speech and visual patterns are encoded and interpreted, how perceptual and linguistic information is learned and remembered, how speech and motor behaviors are planned and executed, and how we solve problems and make decisions. Investigations in each of these areas have led to the view that the activity requires complex mental structures and processes. In other words, the observed behaviors can only be understood if one presupposes a mental system that encodes, transforms and combines information in particular ways.

The laboratory studies carried out yield a conception of a mental system with the following general characteristics. The results of early sensory processing are recoded according to various principles of perceptual organization giving rise to a short-term representation of the external event. Short-term sensory memory has a relatively large capacity for perceptual features or properties, but this memory decays rapidly. Over time, the information is recoded into a more schematic format. It is categorized and interpreted in terms of preexisting knowledge built up from prior experience. These interpreted representations are stored in a long-term memory whose capacity is extremely large. However, only a small portion of this memory is active at any time. Long-term memory is sometimes divided into what is called episodic memory (containing memories for experienced events) and semantic memory (containing knowledge of the meanings of words and symbols). One also finds the distinction between declarative knowledge (knowledge about "what") and procedural knowledge (knowledge about "how").

Within the cognitive system, specialized modules are presumed to exist which function autonomously. Modules have been proposed for processing speech sounds, carrying out syntactic analyses, and possibly other perceptual and cognitive functions. In addition, the literature describes a variety of strategies and heuristics for reasoning and decision making which, in certain cases, differ markedly from normative procedures. At present, there are certainly cognitive activities that are not well understood and important theoretical issues that remain unresolved. However, the field has achieved a notable degree of precision in formulating questions and devising laboratory techniques for their investigation. Conventions for summarizing and communicating the findings have been adopted, and theoretical frameworks for understanding the results have become accepted.

Music is a complex human activity, and so is a natural topic for cognitive psychology. Immediately, however, various theoretical and methodological questions arise, and it is to these that I would like to turn now. The first question, and the most general one, is why do laboratory research on music at all? In the final analysis it is, of course, a matter of one's intellectual predispositions. Certain individuals naturally adopt a scientific attitude and find an experimental approach to understanding music (in which one moves from specific observations to generalizations according to established procedures) congenial and fruitful. Others may judge such studies to be superfluous, arguing that they add nothing to their understanding of music derived from their experiences of listening, performing and composing. To draw an analogy, modern syntactic and semantic theories are based largely on linguists' own intuitions about language. Similarly, musical intuitions have produced sophisticated and powerful theoretical constructs. However, intuitions may be less useful for explicating the nature of internal processes and representations; these cannot be observed directly and may not be available to introspection. Thus, other techniques of a less direct nature may be required to examine the mental systems themselves. Psycholinguistics developed, in part, to fill this gap, and music psychology may play a similar role.

Additional impetus for laboratory studies comes from a desire to understand the way in which mental processes and representations involved in music perception and production are like those involved in other domains such as visual perception and language comprehension and production. Possible commonalities and differences can be identified if similar methodologies are applied. A final reason to examine musical behaviors in the laboratory is that the observations yield descriptions in a form different from those that derive from other approaches to studying music. In particular, for various reasons to be described later, experimental observations tend to take a quantitative form, and these have the advantage that they permit the application of certain analytic techniques. I will return to this point later, but for the present, I would argue simply that alternative modes of description may serve to sharpen our understanding of the musical phenomena of interest.

The next question that arises is: What can be studied using the methods of cognitive psychology? The answer to this is certainly not everything, and in particular not some of the things that appear to be of special interest to musicians: the affective or emotional response to music and the process of creation. At present, psychology unfortunately lacks a fully adequate theory of emotions. Physiological measures of emotional states are complex, variable, and inconsistently related to one another. Moreover, emotional states appear to be a combination of physiological and cognitive or interpretive factors whose interdependencies are a matter of continuing debate. Two additional problems arise in the context of music in particular. First, there is a rather indirect mapping between structural aspects of music (which can be identified objectively and manipulated experimentally) and the emotional response to music. Secondly, individuals differ markedly in the affective terms they will associate to particular selections of music. These considerations suggest a general theory of emotional responses to music may be elusive. As concerns creative processes, the psychological literature has even less of a definitive sort to offer, and so this topic might also be best set aside for the time being.

These remarks are not intended to diminish the importance of these questions for music psychology, only to note that theoretical and methodological advances may be prerequisite to progress in these areas. In contrast, cognitive psychology has developed a fairly complete theoretical framework and supporting methodologies for characterizing how structural properties of external objects and events influence how information about them is encoded, organized and remembered. Progress has also been made on the question of how external behaviors are planned and executed. So, in very general terms, these are the topics that tend to be addressed by experimental studies.

I would like to turn now to some more specific methodological considerations. The first has to do with the choice of musical materials to be employed. One finds two general approaches in the literature. The first approach is to identify some structural property of interest, and then build a special set of materials based on that property. To take a simple example, if the study is directed at examining the effects of diatonic structure on memory for melodies, then some of the melodies will be constructed so they conform to interval patterns found in the diatonic scale, others will not. It is necessary to control other factors so that they do not covary with the property of interest. In this example, it would be important to insure that the melodies of the two types have the same average interval size and contour complexity, because these factors are known to affect melodic processing. If these other factors are allowed to covary with the degree of diatonic structure, then a difference obtained in memory accuracy could not be attributed to the property of interest, but might instead depend on another factor that covaries with it.

Implicit in this approach to stimulus material construction is a reference to the law of statistical sampling. It says that the results can be generalized only to that population from which the materials are randomly sampled. More concretely, if the actual sequences used in this example can be said to be drawn randomly from the population of melodies that are diatonic and the population of melodies that are not diatonic, and a memory difference is found in the experiment, then one can generalize the result to all such melodies. In actual practice, this procedure is not followed exactly. Instead, the materials are constrained in various ways and the generality of the results is restricted accordingly. Typically, the constraints are chosen so that they should not strongly affect the results, but this is a matter of intuition and not a problem treated directly by the law of statistical sampling.

One final point in connection with this first approach to choosing stimulus materials concerns the variables to be manipulated experimentally. This choice is made with an eye toward extending the results to a fairly large class of music. Experimentalists naturally tend to focus on structural properties exhibited quite generally within broad stylistic traditions for the reason that the results obtained should have some quite general application. Incidentally, I think this is the real reason experimentalists have tended to focus on Western tonal music, and not a commitment to the notion that diatonic harmony has special psychological status. Notice, however, there is a rather large gap between the kinds of schematic or prototypical materials used in such experiments and actual pieces of music. The functioning in more complex musical contexts of the isolated variables needs to be demonstrated explicitly. This leads us to the second approach to selecting musical materials for experimental analysis.

This second approach selects materials from actual pieces of music. These materials may be short segments, extended passages, or even entire movements or pieces, depending on the questions of interest. The law of statistical sampling says that, in this case, the results obtained cannot be generalized beyond the actual stimulus materials used because they are not selected randomly from a larger population. Nonetheless, one naturally wishes to draw more general conclusions and so the piece or pieces of music are selected with certain considerations in mind. Firstly, they should be of inherent musical interest, possibly because they are representative or illustrative of a musical style or tradition. Secondly, they should pose questions of a psychological nature by exhibiting structural properties expected to have consequences for perception, memory or performance. Thirdly, these structural properties should be embodied in such a way that the results can be compared with results of experiments using more simplified schematic materials. This is important for guarding against inadvertent over generalizations that otherwise might be drawn from an intensive analysis of materials from one or a few pieces of music. In the end, the selection of materials depends to a great extent on one's interests and intuitions about the most fruitful questions to be investigated.

Having considered the problem of choosing stimulus materials, I would like to turn now to the question of what behaviors or responses are to be measured in the experiment. The first point to remember is that the cognitive psychologist is interested in describing an internal system that cannot be observed directly. The nature of internal processes and representations needs to be inferred from external behaviors that can be observed. For this to be informative, the response measured must be matched in some way to the musical experience itself. Playing and singing are natural behaviors, and thus a strong argument can be made for measuring such attributes as timing, amplitude and intonation in performances. These measurements would be expected to reveal something about how performers interpret the music, and plan and execute the performance to convey this interpretation.

However, performance measures may be less informative for understanding how music is perceived and remembered. A wide variety of different techniques have been developed for investigating these topics, including similarity ratings, direct judgments of structural attributes and recognition memory paradigms. There is little need to review these methods here. However, I would like to emphasize the desirability of using the strategy of convergent measures. Any particular experimental task may impose its own special characteristics on the data obtained. If, however, the same pattern of results is found using two or more measures, one can be more confident that the pattern depends on the internal system in which one is really interested and not the particular methodology employed. In this connection, I would suggest that a powerful argument can be made for basic psychological principles operating in music if performance and perception measures converge on the same conclusions.

The second, and final general point concerning experimental observations is the need for quantification. Cognitive psychology is patterned after the physical sciences in which advances have come largely through successful measurement of physical attributes and the discovery of laws relating these measures to one another. There are special problems involved in psychological measurement, however. The most notable is the complexity of human behaviors; any given situation is likely to evoke a multiplicity of responses. Consequently, it is necessary to constrain the mode of responding and record aspects that can be coded precisely. The numerical structures of mathematics are natural for this, but care must be taken not to make unsupportable assumptions about the nature of the quanitified response; this is a topic of considerable analysis and debate.

Additional problems come from the variability of observed responses. Under seemingly identical circumstances, different individuals may respond differently, and the same individual may produce different repsonses on different occasions. Various statistical techniques are routinely employed to test whether regularities underlie the observed responses. These techniques, based on the theory of statistical inference, provide a way of reaching generalizations from variable data; these generalizations still need to be interpreted in light of relevant musical and psychological issues. Moreover, numerical measurements, however precise, cannot substitute for an intuitive understanding of the phenomena of interest. Thus, qualitative observations and theoretical constructs play an important role in interpreting more quantitative measures.

This brings me to the final methodological question which is what kind of individuals participate as subjects in the experiments. Traditionally, cognitive psychology has been directed toward describing mental capabilities exhibited in the population quite generally, and so has not focused on individuals with special talents or deficits. Even restricting the subject population in this way, an important issue arises. That problem is to understand the relative contribution of fixed or innate psychological processes (which are assumed to be largely invariant across individuals) and the effects of prior learning and experience (which may vary considerably from individual to individual). The musical experience of even the "average" person is likely to be a product of general perceptual and cognitive capacities interacting with the individual's musical training and experience. Various strategies are employed to study this interaction.

One strategy is to take a developmental approach, using subjects of different ages. Another strategy is to take various summary measures of the subjects' musical backgrounds and determine whether these correlate with different patterns of responding. A third is to construct the experiment so that it provides considerable experience with particular musical materials and trace the effects of learning during the course of the experiment. Although these are the approaches that have been taken most frequently, important insights about musical behaviors can also come from studies of individuals who exhibit musical deficits, most often resulting from neurological damage. Such studies reveal dissociations between various musical functions and serve to localize these functions within the brain. At the other end of the continum are individuals with special talent or ability. The nature of these special abilities is a topic of inherent interest, but they are not well-understood at present. One promising approach to this question may be through studying skills present in musical performance; various notions from expert systems in artificial intelligence may be useful in this connection.

Having discussed the kinds of choices required by experimental studies and some of the considerations involved, I turn to some concerns I have about current directions. One motivation for experimental studies in music is to expand our knowledge of human intellectual functions. The vast majority of studies within cognitive psychology has focused on the internal processing and representation of visual and verbal information. This literature has given rise to the view that there are two primary formats for representing information: visual and verbal. Research in music reveals a system with rather different characteristics from either of these. Music requires the integration of information extended over time; as a consequence contextual influences and dynamically changing expectations become central to the experience. In addition, although music within stylistic traditions exhibits regularities, the notion of grammaticality (with clear differences between well-formed and ill-formed sequences) does not seem to have direct applicability. Finally, it is difficult to develop a precise notion of musical semantics, because the meaning of a musical event resides largely in its relation to other musical events, not to nonmusical objects or events. Yet, the domination of the other two areas in psychological theorizing, and the tendency to pattern experiments in much research after those in other domains, tend to obscure the differences. A thorough theoretical treatment of these differences is needed, but may still be premature.

At the same time, music psychology seems to be developing as a somewhat insular subdiscipline of cognitive psychology. This may be in part because researchers sometimes orient their work toward musical issues at the expense of psychological issues. The tension created by the pull of the two disciplines is inevitable, but it seems important not to lose the connection with the psychological tradition or traditions from which the individual research study extends. On a somewhat more positive note, music theory and analysis provide a wealth of information about musical structures which can guide the selection of musical materials and aid in interpreting the empirical findings. I will return momentarily to the potential of cross-disciplinary approaches, but would first like to mention one other strength I see in recent music psychology research. That strength is the diversity and ingenuity of experimental methods. Granted, some of these methods have been imported from other domains of psychological investigation, but their application has generally been well suited to the problem of interest. In addition, novel techniques have been devised for particular cases, and so far the field seems to have avoided narrow methodological disputes.

My comments to this point have been directed at music as it has been studied from the perspective of cognitive psychology. I close with some observations about music from a more broadly construed cognitive science perspective. One discipline that is central to an interdisciplinary approach to music is music theory. In addition to providing generalizations and interpretive constructs useful to experimentalists, music theory contains certain insights about the nature of perceptual and cognitive processes. This is rarely the primary focus, however, and to the extent that psychological considerations enter into the theory they are rarely anchored to specific empirical results. There are reasons to believe, however, that as music theory and music psychology develop, richer interconnections will be formed. Music theory can guide experimentalists to more subtle and musically interesting problems, while experimentalists can test and clarify psychologcial factors referred to in music theoretical treatments.

In this exchange certain inherent differences between the disciplines need to be kept in mind, however. The first is a difference in the level of generality of music and psychological theory. Psychological theories are based on specific empirical results, often concerning a limited range of variables, whereas music theory is direct at explicating structural properties of complex musical materials. This is not to say that empirical studies cannot deal with contextual factors or interactions among musical parameters; in fact, progress has been made on these problems. But, it does not seem likely that empirical studies will, or even should, attempt to provide comprehensive tests of any given body of music theory.

The second difference has to do with what are considered necessary features of a theory. Psychology, for the most part, adopts the standard scientific criteria:

that a theory should be stated precisely, that it should be consistent with a well-defined body of empirical data, and that it should make testable predictions. Ideally, two opposing theories can be identified, and critical experiments designed and conducted. It is not clear that these criteria are fully applicable to, or even desirable in music theory. Intuitive concepts, arising from the analysis of music, may be useful even though they may not be presented in terms of precise formalisms. Particular musical examples may serve to support a conclusion, rather than a demonstration that the conclusion is a valid generalization from a large domain of music. Finally, different orientations within music theory may coexist in as much as they are intended to explicate different aspects of music.

The final difference is in the use of various representational devices. Each discipline has developed certain descriptive systems and vocabularies. Borrowings across disciplines can be useful for identifying points of contact between the approaches, but these should not obscure the fact that these arise from rather different methodological and theoretical orientations. Nonetheless, the appearance of common descriptive formats, such as trees and hierarchies, invites further study. The cooccurrence suggests that the form that the empirical data takes gives rise naturally to structural descriptions similar to those that also come from the analysis of music.

The cognitive science of music is also likely to be strongly influenced by two other disciplines: linguistics and artificial intelligence. Apart from the fact that these disciplines occupy central positions within the cognitive sciences, they have special connections to music in particular. As these are treated explicitly in other papers, my comments here will be brief. Analogies between music and language are inevitable. They share a common sensory mechanism, and similar principles of perceptual recoding may operate in the two domains. Structural properties, such as stress and phrasing appear in both, they both have written notations, and they both involve vocal production. As has been noted elsewhere, however, uncritical application of linguistic theory may obscure musical phenomena of interest.

Artificial intelligence and computer science more generally make contact with music in a number of important ways. Computers have provided tools for composition and the means of sound synthesis. Automatic music analysis can serve as a way of testing and clarifying theoretical systems, and artificial intelligence models are useful for exploring the implications and limitations of empirical observations. The models developed in artificial intelligence can suggest ways in which information may be encoded, stored, and transformed internally. In this connection, it is important to keep in mind that linguistics has had a dominant influence on artificial intelligence modeling, and it is therefore necessary to evaluate the musical applicability of any particular type of model. It may turn out that special notions of representation and computation are needed for music.

Let me close by saying that I believe the apparent wealth of approaches to music we currently enjoy is not deceptive. We have at our disposal a great variety of theoretical constructs, methodological techniques, and descriptive systems. We share a common interest in the extraordinarily rich and varied phenomena which is music. Each of the relevant disciplines brings with it certain strengths and weaknesses, certain biases and commitments. Undoubtedly, we will experience difficulties in finding a common ground in identifying the most useful questions for study, and in respecting diverse intellectual traditions. These are problems, though, that will need to be addressed by the developing cognitive sciences more generally.

References

Clynes, M. (ed.) *Music, Mind and Brain: The Neuropsychology of Music*, New York: Plenum Press.

Deutsch, D. (ed.) (1982) *The Psychology of Music*, New York: Academic Press.

Dowling, W.J. & Harwood, D.L. (1986) *Music Cognition*, New York: Academic Press.

Helmholtz, H.L.F. von (1877/1954) *On the Sensations of Tone*, (A.J. Ellis, trans.), New York: Dover.

Howell, P., Cross, I. & West, R. (eds) (1985) *Musical Structure and Cognition*, New York: Academic Press.

Lerdahl, F. & Jackendoff, R. (1983) *A Generative Theory of Tonal Music*, Cambridge, Mass.: MIT Press.

Meyer, L.B. (1956) *Emotion and Meaning in Music*, Chicago: University of Chicago Press.

Sloboda, J.A. (1985) *The Musical Mind. The Cognitive Psychology of Music*, Oxford: Clarendon Press.

Contemporary Music Review,
1989, Vol. 4, pp. 247–253
Photocopying permitted by license only

Simplicity and complexity in music and cognition

W. Jay Dowling

Program in Human Development & Communication Sciences,
University of Texas at Dallas, Richardson, TX 75080, USA

There are three areas that have been touched upon in this conference about which I will comment. First, there is the issue of what I have come to call the "skimpiness" of stimuli in many experimental studies of music cognition. Second, there is the issue of whether there are cognitive universals constraining musical understanding and structure, and if there are, what we should make of them. Third, I take up the nature of mental representations involved in music cognition, suggesting that a considerable amount of the knowledge that guides listening and provides an interpretation of what we hear is implicit and procedural, rather than explicit and declarative.

KEY WORDS: Cognitive universals, stimulus complexity, procedural knowledge, explicit vs. implicit cognition, pitch perception, mental representations.

The three areas that I touch upon in this paper – the representativeness of stimuli in psychological experiments, the nature of the mental representation of musical structure, and the possibility of universals of cognition impinging on musical structure and cognition – are all interrelated. I shall return at the end to a discussion of some of those interrelationships.

The representative nature of stimuli

It has often been noted, here and elsewhere, that the stimuli used in psychological experiments purporting to investigate perception and memory for music are typically "skimpy" in comparison with "real" music. That is, they are usually brief, monophonic, and of uniform rhythm, loudness, and timbre, while real music is extended in time, usually involves more than one voice, and varies considerably, continuously, and subtly along numerous perceptual dimensions. When this observation is tied to a criticism of psychological research on music cognition the argument continues with the claim that since the stimuli are so different from music, experiments cannot tell us anything about *music perception,* but merely about some aspects of human information processing. To learn about music cognition, this argument goes, we must use as a stimulus actual music in all its complexity.

The counter-argument runs along the lines presented by Krumhansl (this volume). The skimpiness of stimuli in experiments stems from the desire to isolate important variables that affect cognition – to separate those variables from other variables present in complex music that may, within the style with which we are working, be correlated with them. For example, there are temporal cues that indicate the completion of a phrase, and pitch cues. In actual practice those two variables seldom vary independently of each other. Therefore, to separate the effects due to each we must contrive "unnatural" sets of stimuli. Further, once the variables are isolated we seek results that will generalize to a wide range of actual music. This leads us to represent critical variables in rather stark form in our stimuli, unaffected by the context in which they find themselves, and lacking the subtle alterations that context would impose.

This approach of using skimpy stimuli will work as long as the cognitive processes they evoke actually *are* components of the whole process involved in listening to and understanding music. What is important is the *representativeness* of the stimuli as well as that of the processes involved in interpreting them. For our claim to be investigating *music* to hold, the contrasts defined in the stimulus set must reflect contrasts relevant to musical structure, and the cognitive processes by which the stimuli are interpreted must reflect ones that figure in music listening. Whether we are successful in capturing essential properties of music is an empirical question. That is, as we make our stimuli more and more complex, taking them in the direction of actual music, the effects we had discovered with simpler stimuli should not disappear, but rather become qualified with contextual conditions of applicability. Simplified stimuli are successful to the extent that they represent relevant real world features accurately.

It is important to remember in this connection that we need not rely on just one set of stimulus representations to get a given musical feature. In general, we require a set of converging operations (Garner, Hake & Eriksen, 1956) to focus on an hypothesized internal process such as pitch encoding or temporal pacing. The use of converging operations to delineate complex internal processes has become a standard strategy of cognitive psychology. Its use here means that we don't have to settle for just one level of skimpiness – just one type of abstraction – in our stimulus representations of the features of music. Converging studies provide the opportunity for a variety of representations of one and the same musical phenomenon, each representation capturing it from a slightly different angle, with different nuances of emphasis. In that way varying contexts are sampled piece by piece, rather than all at once.

Thus, one direction the empirical program of applying cognitive psychology to music could take is to begin with the skimpy in an attempt to identify essential features, and then expand our stimulus patterns by including more and more complexity, continually monitoring the effects. The empirical program could equally well proceed in the opposite direction, starting with rich musical stimuli and gradually abstracting simpler features. Dowling & Bartlett (1981) did that, for example, in their investigation of memory for melodic contour versus exact intervals in long-term memory for melodies. They started with passages excerpted from Beethoven String Quartets and found the surprising result that listeners remembered intervals quite accurately. Then to specify the conditions on which that result depended more precisely, they proceeded to repeat the experiment with abstracted, simplified stimuli under more tightly controlled contextual conditions.

In this process of adding complexity the computer is invaluable. Computers provide detailed control over stimulus parameters and facilitate the exploration of increasingly elaborate structures. And given the technological capability to journey between the skimpy and the elaborate, we rely on theory to chart our course, pointing out features that are likely to be important and contextual aspects that should not be ignored. The relationship of theory and experiment is a two-way street. Experiments provide tests of theories, and theories show experiments how to define phenomena. In this venture, theories such as those of Narmour and Lerdahl are indispensable.

Universals in music cognition

The question of whether there are universals of music cognition, and in what sense they might constrain musical composition and practice, inevitably arises in discussions such as this. I myself am responsible for listing some of the universal features that appear in an overwhelming number of musical cultures around the world, including octave equivalence, seven or so discrete scale steps per octave, and hierarchical rhythmic organization (Dowling & Harwood, 1986, ch. 9). I have no doubt that these common features of the world's music have common origins in the structure of the human nervous system, as developed in its encounters with the world. To take the example of octave equivalence, it doesn't matter whether the octave is abstracted from complex sounds by the ear or whether it is innate; by adulthood virtually everyone treats the octave as a special relationship. And knowing that listeners are highly likely to judge octaves in a particular way is useful to composers and instrument designers.

Some of the proposed universals are more flexible, more malleable by experience than others. Thus the octave seems to be quite fixed, and the same size octave appears to be used the world over. Constraints on musical scale structure, in contrast, seem more general and to admit of a great many possible instantiations. The way the octave is filled in varies considerably from culture to culture. I think we can attribute this to the octave's being closely tied to the physical stimulus and to the innate structure of the auditory system, while the choice of scale intervals depends on more general constraints on human information processing that are not specific to music nor even to audition. The latter type of more flexible universal affords more possibilities for "bending" through perceptual learning. Thus for example, Schoenberg's dodecaphonic system increases the number of intervals that are used within the octave, but leaves the octave itself intact. Lerdahl's paper (this volume) outlines the way some of the more general structural constraints applicable to tonal music may be operating as well in atonal music.

Having said all that in defense of universals, I think we need to take seriously de la Motte's caution concerning them, which she voiced at the symposium. While remaining aware of universals as an empirical indication of highly likely states of our listeners, we still need to retain freedom of choice concerning their application. It would be sad indeed if composers were to be constrained by some list of what the general public is used to, in the way designers of utilitarian objects such as automobile seats are constrained by human factors, considerations such as the average length of the human torso. The composer is more like the designer of household furniture, who is free to decide that people might try a "chair" in which the knees provide much of the support, or to invent body-support devices for fanciful extra-terrestrial creatures. As Harry Partch (1974) commented, it would be unfortunate if composers had to be constrained in the choice of pitch intervals by the abilities of the least discriminating in the general population. The way to extend the range of human capacities is to explore new tonal relationships and let perceptual learning catch up.

In considering cross-cultural universals we should remember that there are large individual differences among people for the various cognitive and sensory capacities, and that a given person's strategy for processing a stimulus varies with its contextural setting and the person's goals in listening. To take one example, the quarter-steps that fall between the semitones in the standard Western diatonic scale are unusual and the listener's usual modes of cognitive processing. When such quarter-steps are presented as target pitches in a very rapid melodic sequence in which attention is narrowly focused and auditory processing is forced to operate quickly, the quarter steps that occur are heard as assimilated to neighboring scale pitches. However, if the stimulus is slowed and the auditory system is given more time, then quarter-steps are processed quite accurately (Dowling, Lung & Herrbold, 1987). Here context has a pronounced impact on how nonstandard elements are heard.

An additional issue that bears on this discussion, as well as on the previous discussion of experimental skimpiness, is that psychologists like myself often assume that cognitive processing (whether consciously explicit or not) proceeds in an analytic mode – that like Schumann's "ideal listener" the brain reconstructs the score as it goes along. This assumption feeds a theoretic position built on the experimental analysis of the brain's feature analysis. Much can be learned this way, but we should not forget that the brain and mind is not always so precise and analytic, and that cognitive processing can operate effectively on a more global level. Thus sound images (in Bayle and Petitot's sense; cf. their chapters, this volume) can be heard and remembered episodically (so that we can recall their occurrence and recognize them when they recur) without their having to be analyzed at a micro level. Just because the use of a particular microtonal interval makes such a sound image distinctive, doesn't mean that the brain has a systematic way of encoding such intervals. The types of universals listed as cognitive constraints refer generally to constraints on *analytic* processing, and not on ways of producing interesting or beautiful sound images. Such images *may* lend themselves to auditory analysis, but they also may not. But inaccessibility to auditory analysis does not necessarily rob an image of its cognitive effectiveness.

Because of human flexibility in perceptual learning and processing strategy we should, as de la Motte suggests, be very cautious about imposing rigid extramusical constraints on musical structure.

The nature of mental representations

Turning to a discussion of mental representations of musical structure, I will begin by introducing the distinction mentioned by Krumhansl between declarative and procedural knowledge. Declarative knowledge is explicitly accessible to consciousness – we can say what it is we know; for example, that Josef Haydn and George Washington were both born in 1732. In contrast, procedural knowledge is embodied in how the nervous system does things; for example riding a bicycle. Procedural knowledge is stored in sensorimotor schemes for the analysis of sensory input and the generation of organized behavior. Though for some abilities we develop parallel and largely consistent bodies of declarative and procedural knowledge, many abilities are represented only in one or the other form and the accessibility of one representation in the other system is severely limited. Piaget (1974/1976) provides a dramatic example of this limited access: though everyone knows how to crawl, few can tell you the order of placing the hands and feet when crawling. Further, even when a given domain of knowledge appears in both systems there is no guarantee that identical information is stored in both guises. Leonard Bernstein recounts amusing differences of conceptualisation by different members of the Vienna Philharmonic concerning the playing of waltzes, for which we can suppose agreement in practice. One said, "We stress the second beat;" while another said "The first beat is stressed and the third beat is held" (Knoelke, 1971).

Over the past few years I have gradually come to see pitch encoding less as involving declarative knowledge and more as procedural achievement, much like the nonverbal cognitive processes as described by Marin (this volume). That is, rather than thinking of the tonal pitch system as a separate knowledge structure used to interpret sense data after it has been encoded, I have come to see the tonal pitch system as embodied in the very way pitches are initially encoded. That is, the procedures for pitch encoding embody the schematic representation of tonal pitch. I am led to this conclusion by general considerations concerning the rapidity with which pitch encoding is accomplished, the typical conscious experience of pitches as already encoded in the tonal system (we hear a *do* or a *re* or a *mi* – we don't hear an undefined pitch that we later succeed in interpreting as a scale pitch), and the *gradual* efficacy of perceptual learning in improving pitch encoding. Long term familiarity with a musical style leads to the development of procedures for the perceptual organization of sounds, paralleling the organization encountered in the music (as Zenatti has suggested).

One piece of evidence that pushed me in the direction of thinking of pitch encoding as mainly procedural came from an experiment in which listeners were given the task of recognizing brief melodies. The melodies were framed by a chordal context that defined the tonal scale values of the notes, so that changing the context could change *do–re–mi* into *sol–la–ti*, or vice versa. Musically untrained listeners recognized the test melodies equally well whether or not the context had been changed and so appear to have remembered the melodies simply in terms of relative pitch values (and not tonal scale values). In contrast, listeners with about 5 years of musical training appeared to remember pitches in terms of tonal scale values; that is, when the context shifted their, performance declined to chance (Dowling, 1986). But though the latter listeners encoded the pitches in terms of tonal scale values, they could not have labeled the pitches with those values at all. Listeners with moderate training had developed a procedural scheme for tonal pitch encoding, without developing the parallel declarative system typical of professional musicians.

The notion of procedures for pitch encoding is quite consonant with the notions of brain modularity developed by Zatorre (this volume) and by Peretz & Morais (this volume). If pitch encoding is a declarative matter, involving a sort of dictionary for looking up the interpretations of sense data, then it can be handled in the nervous system like any general-purpose look-up device such as is used for the retrieval of memorized information. If, however, tonal pitch values are encoded procedurally in the auditory system, then the module that processes them can *only* be a special-purpose pitch module, and not a general-purpose device.

I believe that both musicians and psychologists have been slow to arrive at the idea of procedural knowledge as representing musical structure because, to use Eric Clarke's (this volume) term, we live in a "logocentric" culture. We tend to think of what we "really" know as what we can talk about, and to disparage knowledge that we can't verbalize. When we possess two representations of a musical structure, one declarative and the other procedural, we tend to prefer the declarative one because of its accessibility to theorizing and formal manipulation. We must come to realize that most of our brain representations of musical structure are first developed through years of perceptual learning in listening to and performing music, and that the corresponding declarative representations are typically in the form of rationalizations at the conscious level of subtler and richer implicit representations at the subconscious level. At the conscious level we inevitably discard information in the interests of clarity of formalization – information that the brain "knows" procedurally to be important and does not forget.

Interrelationships

The procedural nature of mental representations puts more severe limits on the malleability of cognitive universals than would be the case if the representations were largely declarative. With declarative knowledge representations, any formal symbolic system could be represented. But music is primarily to be heard, rather than reasoned with, and one consequence of that is that music is primarily interpreted via an essentially auditory procedural scheme. Universals inherent in the structure of auditory cognition constrain what perceptual learning can accomplish, while perceptual learning can stretch the capacities of the procedural schemes (though such stretching is less than what declarative learning could accomplish with declarative schemes.)

The issue between procedural and declarative schemes also has implications for the skimpiness-of-stimuli issue. Procedural schemes are typically quite literal minded – they come to expect *exactly* the same stimulus configuration again and again. Thus abstracting essential features from musical patterns incurs the possibility that they will be missed by the procedural representation, making the strategy of abstraction a risky one, though all the more impressive when it succeeds.

Finally, the abstractness of stimuli in many experiments leads us to a caution concerning the empirical basis for claims concerning cognitive universals in music. We need to be sure that a purported universal operates in musical contexts, and not only when isolated from context in the laboratory. For example, the evidence that octaves of the same size arise in musical instrument tunings around the world is a valuable addition to evidence concerning precision of octave tunings of pure tones out of context. (Dowling & Harwood, 1986). It is only through such explorations that we can discover how universal such "universals" might be.

References

Dowling, W.J. (1986) Context effects on melody recognition: Scale-step versus interval representations. *Music Perception*, **3**, 281–296.

Dowling, W.J. & Bartlett, J.C. (1981) The importance of interval information in long-term memory for melodies. *Psychomusicology*, **1**, 30–49.

Dowling, W.J. & Harwood, D.L. (1986) *Music Cognition*, Orlando: Academic Press.

Dowling, W.J., Lung, K.M.T. & Herrbold, S. (1987) Aiming attention in pitch and time in the perception of interleaved melodies. *Perception & Psychophysics*, **41**, 642–656.

Garner, W.R., Hake, H.W. & Eriksen, C.W. (1956) Operationism and the concept of perception. *Psychological Review*, **63**, 149–159.

Knoelke, B. (1971) "Der Rosenkavalier" and how it came about. Notes to R. Strauss, *Der Rosenkavalier*, Columbia album M3K–425564.

Partch, H. (1974) *Genesis of a Music*, New York: Da Capo Press.

Piaget, J. (1974) *La Prise de conscience*. Paris: Presses Universitaires de France. (English translation: *The Grasp of Consciousness*. Cambridge, MA: Harvard University Press, 1976).

Contemporary Music Review,
1989, Vol. 4, pp. 255–263
Photocopying permitted by license only

Neuropsychology, mental cognitive models and music processing

Oscar S.M. Marin

Laboratory of Cognitive Neuropsychology, Department of Neurology, Good Samaritan Hospital, 1015 N.W. 22nd Ave. Portland, Oregon, 97210 USA

Two separate and distinct problems are discussed in this article: 1) the relations between clinical cases of amusias and their lesional topography, and 2) the problem of defining more closely the nature of music, its cognitive structure and the possible ways by which the human brain (the mind) is capable of hearing and making sense of it. (1) Despite the lesional predominance of the right cerebral hemisphere, there are frequent exceptions and, within right-sided lateralization, there are very few topographical elements that allow a precise clinico-topographical predictability. Contrast with clinico-anatomical aspects of aphasias is noted. I propose that in the case of music the low degree of constancy in the functional topography is greatly due to the fact that music does not depend solely on its acoustic auditory sensory nature, but is primarily dependent on its internal organizational principles. This contrasts with language and speech which have more constant codes (letters, phonemes, lexico-semantic relations). (2) The importance of cognitive processing models is suggested and music is again contrasted with speech and language. Music hearing and understanding are here considered to be primarily non-verbal, non-semantic expertise, not radically different from expert behaviors in other perceptual or motor realms such as painting, chess playing, poetry, etc. Music is contrasted with speech and language with respect to the previous mental experience of individuals: for language, the mental process is considered primarily an arousal of already present verbal organizational representations, while in music no such previous experience seems to be indispensable. In music, the hearer must gradually develop and discover the musical perceptual organizational principles.

KEY WORDS: Music neuropsychology, amusias, cerebral localization, cognitive processing models, cognitive skills, perceptual organization.

Some neuropsychological aspects of amusias

Music perception seems to be somewhat lateralized to the right cerebral hemisphere, however, there is good evidence that we are dealing here with a preferential, but by no means absolute, hemispherical lateralization (Marin, 1982). In this sense, music is not the symmetrical counterpart of speech or language function which, in the right-handed individual, so strictly depends on the intactness of the left hemisphere cerebral cortex. Although some of the previous strict notions of lateralization for speech functions have also been reviewed and modified, there remains little doubt that for some aspects of language processing there is, in general, a well-defined, well-lateralized, hemispherical brain localization. This is particularly true for verbal phonetic encoding and perhaps also for syntactic processing. Such a similar situation has not been encountered for music, where clinical experimental evidence indicates a mere preponderance in the efficiency of one hemisphere rather than a strict lateralization.

From a more clinical perspective, one is confronted with a similar rather vague situation. Despite the valid criticisms of strict brain localization in aphasia, it still remains true that there is a certain degree of predictability with regards to the functional language deficits that one could expect in the right-handed individual according to the lesional topography. Thus, it is true, that predominantly anteriorly placed lesions in the inferolatoral frontal areas tend to originate disorders of speech and language that are predominantly expressive, while more posteriorly placed lesions, in the temporal regions, tend to originate predominantly receptive speech disorders (Marin, Schwartz & Saffran, 1979). But no strict localization may be expected for agrammatisms, although the lesions are usually more anteriorly than in patients affected with more typical perceptive disorders of the Wernicke type or repetition deficits as observed in conduction aphasias. Lexical disorders and anomias are the less predictable and most poorly circumscribed localized lesions. The difficulties in finding a precise brain localization for agrammatism may be due to the still unsettled question of whether agrammatism could be considered a truly autonomous nosological aphasic entity. Syntax, on the other hand, deals primarily with relations between words, word order in sentences, or phonological elements whose semantic meaning is not entirely transparent. Functions, such as grammatical syntactic rules, so dependent on language relations and so devoid of well-defined fixed codes, by the functional nature of the syntactic functions themselves, may be processed only with difficulty by a fixed, anatomically localized neuronal substratum and may depend on the functional efficiency of larger areas of the brain. We shall argue that with music we may be dealing with a similar situation.

From the clinical standpoint, despite the ongoing discussion as to the value of nosological classifications of aphasias, terms such as Broca's aphasias, Wernicke's symptom complex, anomia, conduction aphasias, at this time define rather well what is to be expected in the verbal behavior of those affected individuals. While one agrees that this nosological classification fails to define with precision the deficits or to predict accurately the lesional topography or the neurolinguistic details of the verbal behavior, at least, in general terms, they serve to delimit the main aspects of the verbal behavior that is affected. Thus, the classical nomenclature of verbal disorders will remain useful at least until psycholinguistic analysis provides a more precise set of functional parameters in terms of phonological, lexical, or syntactical operations. We shall only then be prepared to exchange the classical clinical labels for functional neurolinguistic nosological labels that will define the clinical and the neurolinguistic parameters that are compromised.

Though classical notions of localization and clinical nosology still remain as valid general indicators, in the case of aphasias, the situation in the case of musical perceptual disorders is quite different. The lesional localization of amusias is poorly lateralized and within the right hemisphere itself the localization remains rather inexact and the clinical deficit unpredictable. The classical characteristics of the various types of amusias, as described in the literature, are ill-defined and the overriding characteristics of their clinical manifestation depend strongly on the individual pre-morbid musical skills of the affected patients. A great deal of progress has been made in the study of the auditory cortices (Fitzpatrick & Imig, 1982; Imig, Reale & Brugge, 1982; Brugge & Reale, 1985; Whitfield, 1985). For obvious reasons this progress has been more restricted in the case of the human brain for which one must not only depend on the results of direct studies, but must also be able to interpret the direction and main evolutive trends observed in other vertebrates, mammals and primates. Similarly to what occurs in other sensory modalities, the primary receiving sensory cortices are not simple but multiple. The multiplicity has been studied and confirmed for both the sensory inputs as well as for the motor outputs. Instead of conceptualizing the incoming information proceeding from one single channel in each sensory modality, one has to accept an important multiplicity of sensory inputs and motor outputs. (For a review of the visual sensory systems, see Cowey, 1985; for an analysis of the morphology and physiological characteristics of the auditory sensory cortices, see Fitzpatrick & Imig, 1982; Imig *et al*, 1982; Brugge & Reale, 1985; Seldon, 1985). Thus, greater constancy seems to be observed the closer the lesion is located in the vicinity of the primary acoustic receiving cortex. (For an extensive review, see Zatorre, 1984.) In the para-acoustic areas, and particularly in cases of isolated and bilateral damage, the clinical picture of auditory agnosia emerges, and in those cases there is a constant accompaniment of an amusia of the perceptual type. Thus, nearly every case of auditory object agnosia is also a case of receptive amusia.

This should not be surprising since the closer the lesion is to the primary acoustic sensory areas, the easier it is to show that, if not all, at least some of the deficits are psychoacoustic in nature (i.e. deficits in pitch and rhythm discrimination, abnormalities in temporal distribution of acoustical events). Anomalies in timbre are rarely described as pure disorders in man.

Bilateral para-acoustic lesions in man may give rise to auditory agnosias. One of our patients was able to detect normally even subtle onsets of auditory events, (onset, duration, offset). However, qualitative judgments were prominent, describing human voices as "noises" or typewriter rattling and music as "door squeakings". In this case, the elementary nature of auditory stimulation was preserved while the complex structure of the sounds was easily misjudged. This case was obviously much more than a pure abnormality of timbre perception.

In summary, disorders of music perception do not seem to result from well defined localized foci. To the contrary, they often tend to fuse and mix with the complex abnormalities of language or deficits of auditory object perception (auditory agnosias). (For a review, see Whitfield, 1985.)

Amusias do not seem to correspond to those rather elementary deficits that, in the past, I have designated as "neuronal dependent processes" (Marin, 1987), which are processes of information, usually within well-defined single sensory modalities, that can be conceived as processed by discrete clusters of well-differentiated neurons, well-circumscribed and well-localized within the cortical mantle. (For a definition of biological preconditions for localized cortical functions, see Marin & Gordon, 1979; i.e., color discrimination, motor cortical deficits, cortical sensory abnormalities). The problem is then whether it is an acceptable hypothesis that music is sufficiently defined as an assortment of acoustical events that, just for its perception, needs to be processed in psychoacoustical terms. Such a definition of music seems to be quite insufficient. Since it is true that music is made of acoustical events distributed in time, what really seems to constitute a sine qua non part of the definition is that these acoustical events, as they are distributed in time, must show that they have an internal organization which the hearer must be able to capture or, at least, to reconstruct and display in his or her mind. The essential internal orgnaization of music may be rhythmic, temporal, or timbral combinations, or pitch interrelations. At other times such organizational aspects can be quite complex, as in the case of stylistic characteristics, musical formal displays, harmonic or contrapuntal aspects. If these organizational aspects of music are so basic and fundamental, even for the definition of music itself, perception of music can hardly be restricted to a series of psychoacoustical neuropsychological events. Music, by definition, involves perception of complex, and sometimes abstract, relations. The brain processing of such organizations cannot be considered elementary or simple and therefore is impossible to be conceived of as neuronal dependent processes. Music processing, and hence amusias, are complex phenomena which must depend on a complex neuronal substratum and can hardly be dependent on the functioning of a circumscribed neurological cortical localization. Thus, for this writer, the main explanation for the elusiveness of amusias in spite of predictable fixed and restricted lesions is in the nature of music itself.

It is interesting to note that in the recent past musicians and composers have been willing to reexamine basic aspects of their musical language, i.e. tonality (atonal, polytonal music), traditional aspects of tonal harmony (polytonal music, new harmonies), intervallic aspects (microtonal scales), rhythmic aspects (polyrhythmic music), and timbral aspects (new sounds in music, novel musical clusters). However, musicians have resisted accepting a definition of music as merely sounds devoid of an internal organization of some kind. Contemporary composers may accept radical changes in the medium of expression and their acoustic exteriorization, but have resisted making music devoid of structure. In their mind, internal hierarchies, equilibrium and contrasts of forms, identification of units, have remained the basis of their work and the justification of it as art. At the very bottom, music must be defined as acoustic events within an organized system of relations. This system must be captured and reconstructed in the mind of the hearer. This defines music in the past and present not only as words but as an organization. Such internal complex relations also define poetry and, for that matter, other expressions of art.

Thus, amusias, by the very nature of musical events, seem to correspond to a much greater complex structure, unlikely processed directly by solely specialized clusters of sound sensitive neurons. It must therefore depend on greater functional neuronal substrata, more widely located within general sensory areas of some specialization ("network dependent processes" such as phonological speech decoding of verbal deafness, letter reading). Are we not dealing then with levels of organization that are complex enough to be comparable to those that characterize lexicosemantic aspects of language, where similar attempts to reduce them to constant fixed localizations has thus far failed? If human music cannot be reduced to sounds alone, its neural substrata can hardly be reduced to the activity of fixed sound sensitive auditory neurons.

Cognitive processing models and music perception

A neuropsychological study of a function should include: 1) a thorough understanding of the psychological or cognitive structure of the function, and an understanding of the organization of that function itself, 2) should provide hypotheses or models concerning the information processing of that function by the human nervous system. Such a study should also include: 3) knowledge regarding the biological nervous system substratum that sustains the function and should provide ideas regarding the structures involved, their localization and their brain morphological and physiological characteristics. In summary, a neuropsychological study of a function comprises both the knowledge of "software" of the function and of the biological "hardware" apparatus that sustains it.

In some instances the advancement of our knowledge has been unequal and we comprehend better some aspects than others. For instance, there has been substantial advancement in our knowledge of the cognitive structure of reading and good hypotheses have been advanced regarding possible information processing in cases of normal and abnormal reading. In such cases our knowledge seems to be predominantly of the "software" structure and organization of the function of reading. This contrasts however with the very scanty information regarding the neurobiological substratum of normal and dyslexic behavior. (For an extensive review of the neuropsychological cognitive aspects, see Coltheart, 1985).

In other instances, our knowledge seems to be greater in relation to aspects of the "hardware" while, in contrast, our understanding of the functional organization is relatively weak. Such is the case in vision, where research in the last decades has greatly advanced our knowledge of the morphology and functional organization of the primary sensory retinotopic cortical representations. (For a review see Cowey, 1985; for a more recent review see Livingstone & Hubel, 1988). In these cases we have a fairly good knowledge of the morphology of the primary receiving cortical areas and their connectivity towards the more pluri-modal associative cortex. Thus we have a fairly good understanding of the "hardware" organization of such connectivity and increasing complexity of the function of the various stages from area 17 towards the infero-temporal associative cortex. This fairly good knowledge of the "hardware" of visual function does not correlate with an equally detailed understanding of the psychological information processing aspects of vision in object perception, visual gnosis, reading, etc. In this case our hardware knowledge seems to be greater than our detailed understanding of the informational flow processing.

The value of cognitive processing models for music can hardly be overestimated. Such a model in music would have great heuristic value, by providing direction and generating empirical objective questions for future investigation. If such a model could be agreed upon, we could focus much more easily on its empirical aspects, that would allow an objective progress in the knowledge of musical cognitive information processing. If organizational aspects of the acoustic events seem to be central to the structure of music (and this immediately generates consequences for the localization and characteristics of the biologial substratum related to the perception of music and amusias), it seems to be obvious that cognitive processing models of music will provide equally valuable guidelines for the study of music structure and music cognition. In the text that follows we hope to provide such a model which we contrast with that of another human manifestation, namely language and speech. Since music and language and speech are to be used as representatives of such contrasting models, it follows that, at least for this author, the relations between music and language are of a more superficial and not very significant nature.

Whenever individuals engage in verbal exchange, read a text, contemplate a sculpture, listen to poetry or a piece of music, their brains become immediately active and begin to participate actively in the processing of the verbal, motor or incoming perceptual information. Their first aim is perhaps to "tune in" and to activate those mechanisms that will appropriately decode and further process the information (i.e. arousal of attention, orienting response, dishabituation). The ultimate goal is not only to "tune in" but to carry the cognitive process to allow it to "make sense" of the information and decode its meaning. The individual's brain does not wait for the initiation of this process until all information is collected but initiates it almost simultaneously. For this reason it is better to designate such activities as "concomitant cognitive processes". They work in parallel, concomitantly to the incoming stimuli.

Among the types of concomitant cognitive processes there are two modalities that one may like to distinguish and differentiate. One deals with the cognitive processes that are activated in our brains by verbal exchanges, the other includes the cognitive processes operating in non-verbal situations such as music hearing, some motor skills, observing a sculpture, hearing poetry or playing some games, such as chess.

The radical difference between verbal and non-verbal cognitive processes is that in the former case, the verbal exchange, to achieve its ultimate semantic goals, presupposes that our brain has previous experience with the kind of information that will be exchanged. It knows the English sound that will be the constituent of the message; it recognizes the word to be used; it knows about the word or the syntactic phonological markers that will be inserted in the messages; and finally, it will be familiar with the mechanics of the words and sentences to be used. Finally, the individual should be capable of transferring the verbal meaning into the descriptions or actions occurring in the real world. What seems to be essential in this case is that during the decoding and cognitive processing of this verbal information the recipient already has an extensive previous experience, knowledge of the codes, knowledge and familiarity with the rules and procedures, and will be needing to refer much of the incoming information to already pre-existing vocabularies and internalized representations. Because of this required previous experience and previous cognitive representation of most of the substance of this information, I think that this concomitant cognitive processing may also be called "representational" (Table 1). This is in open contrast with the case of music hearing, poetry hearing, or some examples of motor skill performances in which the cognitive processing does not presuppose previous experience, detailed knowledge of the cognitive units or codes, familiarity with the rules and procedures or previous semantic representation. The stimuli may be novel in various degrees from familiar to entirely new. In some cases the hearer has some knowledge of the sound characteristics of the music he or she will hear. This anticipated knowledge allows one to predict the possible ending of such and such melodic line, anticipate changes of intensity or harmonic structures. In some other cases, often in contemporary music pieces, one is grossly unprepared as to the way the various musical structures are going to be treated and, as a consequence, one finds oneself unable to anticipate any possible future resolution or outcome. In the former case one can say that one has a previous internal mental representation while, in the latter situation, such a mental representation is largely absent (Chase & Simon, 1973; Charness, 1976; Ericsson, 1985; Psychology of Skills, 1985; Cranberg & Albert, 1988).

Table 1 Two modalities of cognitive processing

I	Representational (i.e. language)
	Cognitive processes that presuppose previous experience and internalized representations and stores. Presupposes agreed upon codes, rules and procedures.
II	Organizational perceptual processing (i.e. music)
	Does not presuppose previous experience. Develops greater details and complexity with repeated experience.

In contrast to what happens in the case of language, in perceptual organizational processes the individual may have no previous experience and information – its unitary components, its possible organization, its ultimate emotional impact, or its "meaning" – may be entirely novel. In various degrees individuals can say with certainty that they do not have previous familiarity or knowledge with information previously represented and internalized in their minds. These are obviously non-representational cognitive processes and because in so many instances the information is so predominantly a perceptual one, it is possible to designate them as concomitant "perceptual organizational" cognitive processes.

In music for instance, the individual may have no previous experience, no internal representation is available. The task will consist in hearing this new assembly of acoustic events and, whether purposely or not, "tune in" and "make sense" of it. In confronting this novel experience, one will be facing a similar situation as hearing poetry, looking at a new painting or sculpture, playing a game of chess or learning a new skill.

By "making sense" one soon recognizes that there is no meaning in the message, no direct referent to elements or properties of the external world and no precise semantic referent. One begins by a noncomitant analytical segmentation of the information, identifications of pitch, intensity, and timbre will be the first attempt to identify constituent units. This perceptual fragmentation will be guided to a large extent by many of the principles already described by the Gestalt psychologists. The likelihood in most cases is that in hearing music, or the activities already mentioned, no clear and perceptual homogeneous set of units will emerge, although as in the case of music, for instance, all bits of information are part of the same sensory modality. Eventually, as has been masterfully described by Chase & Simon (1973), with repeated exposure the individual will initiate perceptual organization by creating higher complexity units (perceptual chunking), by creating perceptual patterns, and eventually by creating a network of chunk and pattern coordination. This information will be coordinated and inter-related, but will not constitute a homogeneous set derived from a unitary code, or the codes will tend to be grouped into" files", "catalogues" and "libraries".

Table 2 Perceptual organizational processing development of perceptual skills (expertise)

– does not require previous experience
– develops concomitantly with repeated exposures
– rules and procedures are not well-defined
– rules and procedures are not universally defined
– they are predominantly perceptual

Naive:	– initial attempt at analysis
	– initial segmentation and search for low level units
	– perceptual relations (closely related to Gestalt principles)
	– perceptual grouping, perceptual chunking
	– creation of perceptual patterns (complex units)
Skilled:	– development of pattern relations and coordinations
	– creation of perceptual pattern "files", "libraries", "indices", and "catalogues": "lexicalization of the information"
Expert:	– at this level perceptual organizational processing begins to relate to representational cognitive processing

The expert interacts with the incoming information in an active set of arousal, activation, creation and resolution of tension and expectation. This creates a strong emotional reaction and relates this theory with the currently accepted theory of activational effects of emotions.

Thus, expert musicians, poets, expert chess players, will have accumulated over time extensive "libraries" and "catalogues" of these complex perceptual fragments. They will commit them to memory and although the categories vary greatly, these "libraries" are somewhat equivalent to our verbal lexicon. Experienced musicians, with increase of exposure and experience, will commit to memory an increasingly large collection of chunks, units and patterns, that will constitute the equivalent of building of a kind of special lexicon. For this reason I have spoken, perhaps not very appropriately, of the "lexicalization of the information". The expert has accumulated in time not only a large "catalogue" and "file" but has gained through experience.

In summary, we propose that a) perception of music is a complex set of phenomena that needs to capture and extract from acoustical events a series of relations, comparisons, contrasts, that constitute an abstract musical organization which provides music with an abstract structure; b) the hearer may or may not have previous knowledge of the musical structure about to be heard. One may or may not be familiar with the kind of sounds, their timbre characteristics, loudness, or temporal distribution. In other words, one may or may not have an previous internal representation. The task, however, is to "make sense" of it. This is accomplished by a perceptual organization of the acoustic events; c) previous and/or repeated experience plays an important role, and the ability to create a perceptual organization is very similar in nature to the development of other expertises and skills. The literature on skills and and expertise development is therefore quite pertinent and appropriate for music cognitive processing.

References

Brugge, J.F. & Reale, R.A. (1985) Auditory cortex. In *Cerebral Cortex Vol.4: Association and Auditory Cortex*, 229–272. A. Peters & E.G. Jones (eds.) Plenum Press.

Charness, N. (1976) Memory for chess positions: Resistance to interface. *Journal of Experimental Psychology: Human Learning and Memory*, **2**.

Chase, G.W. & Simon, A. (1973) The mind's eye in chess. *Visual Information Processing*, W.G. Chase (ed.), New York: Academic Press.

Coltheart, M. (1985) Cognitive neuropsychology and the study of reading. In *Attention and Performance XI*, M. Posner & O.S.M. Marin (eds), Hillsdale, N.J.: Lawrence Erlbaum Associates.

Cowey, A. (1985) Aspects of cortical organization related to selective attention and selective impairments of visual perception: A tutorial review. In *Attention and Performance XI*, M. Posner & O.S.M. Marin (eds), Hillsdale, N.J.: Lawrence Erlbaum Asociates.

Cranberg, L.D. & Albert, M.L. (1988) The Chess Mind in the exceptional brain, (L. Obler and D. Fein, eds) Guildford Press.

Ericcson, A.K. (1985) Memory skill, *Canadian Journal of Psychology*, **39**.

Fitzpatrick, K.A. & Imig, T.J. (1982) Organization of auditory connections: The primate auditory cortex. In *Cortical Sensory Organization. Vol. 3. Multiple Auditory Areas*, C.N. Woolsey (ed.), Clifton N.J.: Humana Press.

Imig T.J., Reale, R.A. & Bruge, J.F. (1982) Patterns of corticocortical projections related to psysiological maps in the cat. In *Cortical Sensory Organization, Vol. 3, Multiple Auditory Areas*, C.N. Woolsey (ed.), Clifton, N.J.: Humana Press.

Livingstone, M. & Hubel, D. (1988) Segregation of form, color, movement, and depth: Anatomy, physiology, and perception. Science, **240**: 740–750.

Marin, O.S.M. & Gordon, B. (1979) Neuropsychological aspects of aphasia. In *Current Neurology*. Vol.II. 305–343. D. Dawson, R. Tyler (eds) Boston. Mass.: Houghton Mifflin Professional Publishers.

Marin, O.S.M., Schwartz, M.F. & Saffran, E.M. (1979) The origins and distribution of language. In *Handbook of Neurobiology: Neuropsychology*. M. Gazzaniga (ed.), New York: Plenum Press.

Marin, O.S.M. (1982) Neurological aspects of music perception and performance. In *The Psychology of Music*, D. Deutsch (ed.), New York: Academic Press Inc.

Marin, O.S.M. (1987) Dementia and visual agnosia. In *Visual Object Processing. A Cognitive Neuropsychological Approach*, G.W. Humphreys & M.J. Riddoch (eds.) London: Lawrence Erlbaum.

Psychology of Skills (1985) Special Issue on Skill. *Canadian Journal of Psychology*, 39.

Seldon, J.L. (1985) The anatomy of speech perception. Human auditory cortex. In *Cerebral Cortex, Vol. 4. Association and Auditory Cortex*. 273–327. A. Peters & E.G. Jones (eds), New York: Plenum Press.

Whitfield, I.C. (1985) The role of auditory cortex in behavior. In *Cerebral Cortex. vol. 4 Association and Auditory Cortices*. 329–347. A. Peters & E.G. Jones (eds), New York: Plenum Press.

Zatorre, R.J. (1984) Musical perception and cerebral function: A critical review. *Music Perception,* **2**: 196–221.

Contemporary Music Review,
1989, Vol. 4, pp. 265–277
Photocopying permitted by license only

Effects of temporal neocortical excisions on musical processing

Robert J. Zatorre

Montreal Neurological Institute and Hospital, McGill University, 3801 University St., Montreal, Quebec H3A 2B4, Canada

Subjects who had undergone unilateral temporal-lobe excisions for the relief of epilepsy were tested in order to study the relation between musical processing and cerebral function. In one study it was found that only right temporal-lobe lesions including Heschl's gyri (the primary auditory cortex) resulted in a significant deficit in judging pitch changes when the fundamental of a complex tone was missing. In melodic discrimination tasks right-temporal lobectomy had a deleterious effect, but the excisions of Heschl's gyri from either side resulted in a more marked deficit. Other experiments involving identification of familiar distorted tunes and recognition of lyrics of songs primarily show effects of left temporal-lobe lesions. However, a case of absolute pitch ability showed no disturbance from a left temporal-lobe lesion. The results are discussed in terms of the possible contribution of different cortical regions to specific aspects of musical processing.

KEY WORDS: Temporal lobe, Heschl's gyri, pitch, melody, discrimination.

Introduction

The extraction of meaningful information from the environment may be considered a fundamental aspect of cognition. In the auditory domain, speech and music are two important classes of highly patterned information-bearing stimuli. It appears that our auditory nervous system is endowed with specialized mechanisms that permit complex processing of such signals to be carried out. Over the past several decades, experimental psychologists have achieved considerable progress in understanding the processing of complex auditory signals, including music, but there has not been as much progress in the neuropsychology of music processing. The concepts and paradigms derived from experimental and cognitive research provide a rich source of valuable heuristics, which I have endeavored to apply to the study of cerebral function and musical perception. This paper will summarize many of the studies I have carried out at the Montreal Neurological Institute over the past several years; it is not meant to be a review of prior research on this topic, however, for which the reader is referred to other sources (e.g., for studies with brain-damaged populations: Benton, 1977; Marin, 1982; Zatorre, 1984; for studies with neurologically intact subjects: Peretz & Morais, 1988).

In the research to be described below, the general approach has been to study the effects of unilateral, discrete cortical lesions in groups of patients in whom the site and extent of cerebral damage is well-documented. This approach has several advantages: (1) it permits testing under controlled conditions, (2) it avoids the

selection biases inherent in choosing subjects according to the behavioral manifestations of certain lesions, and (3) it allows comparison of the effect of similar
lesions in the right and left cerebral hemispheres. For the most part, I have concentrated on subjects with no formal musical training, choosing to study those
musical abilities that are most widely represented in the general population.

Patients studied had all undergone unilateral cerebral excision at the Montreal
Neurological Hospital for the relief of medically intractable epileptic seizures. The
nature of the lesions was generally static. Subjects who had rapidly growing tumors
were excluded because of potentially confounding mass effects; also, no subject
with a known degenerative disease was studied. Other criteria for exclusion
included any evidence of a bilateral lesion, or neurological evidence (such as
hemiparesis or hemianopia) of damage extending beyond the area of the surgical
removal. Lesions usually dated from birth or early life. In this report I shall concentrate on the effects of anterior left or right temporal lobectomy, which is the most
commonly performed surgical procedure. The excisions in these cases usually
involve between 4–6 cm of cortical tissue along the lateral surface of the temporal
lobe, and always include the amygdala, uncus, and varying amounts of the hippo-
campus and parahippocampal gyrus. Of greatest interest for the study of auditory
function is that the primary auditory cortex, corresponding in humans to the transverse gyri of Heschl (Celesia, 1976; Galaburda & Sanides, 1980), is sometimes
included in part or in whole in the removal (see Figure 1). This permits the contribution of this region to various tasks to be examined in detail. The patients are
classified according to the neurosurgeon's report at the time of surgery. Subjects
with left temporal (LT) or right temporal (RT) lesions are further classified according
to the integrity or excision of the primary auditory cortex, forming four groups,
those with complete sparing of this region (represented by the symbols LTa and
RTa), and those with partial or complete excision of Heschl's gyri (LTA and RTA).

The cognitive deficits displayed by patients who have undergone temporal
lobectomy are often rather subtle. These patients do not suffer from aphasia,
amnesia, or other gross intellectual deficits that would impair their ability to comprehend or attend to complex task demands. All patients studied obtained IQ
scores within the normal range on standardized intelligence tests. Moreover, all
subjects were either known to possess left-hemisphere speech representation
based on the intracarotid sodium Amytal test (Rasmussen & Milner, 1977), or this
was presumed based on right-handedness and neuropsychological test data. In
addition to the patient groups, normal control (NC) subjects, matched for age and
educational background to the patients, were tested in all the studies carried out
for purposes of comparison.

A point of departure for my studies was Milner's (1962) report that patients with
RT lesions were impaired in several of the subtests of the Seashore test of musical
ability. In particular, she reported that pitch discrimination was not disturbed by
temporal lobectomy; however, temporal-lobe lesions on the right, but not the left
produced significant deficits in the tonal memory test, which involves comparison of two short melodies.

Pitch perception

It has long been known that listeners typically perceive the pitch corresponding
to the fundamental period of vibration of a complex tone, even when no energy

Central Sulcus

O

A
A

F

Sylvian
fissure

T

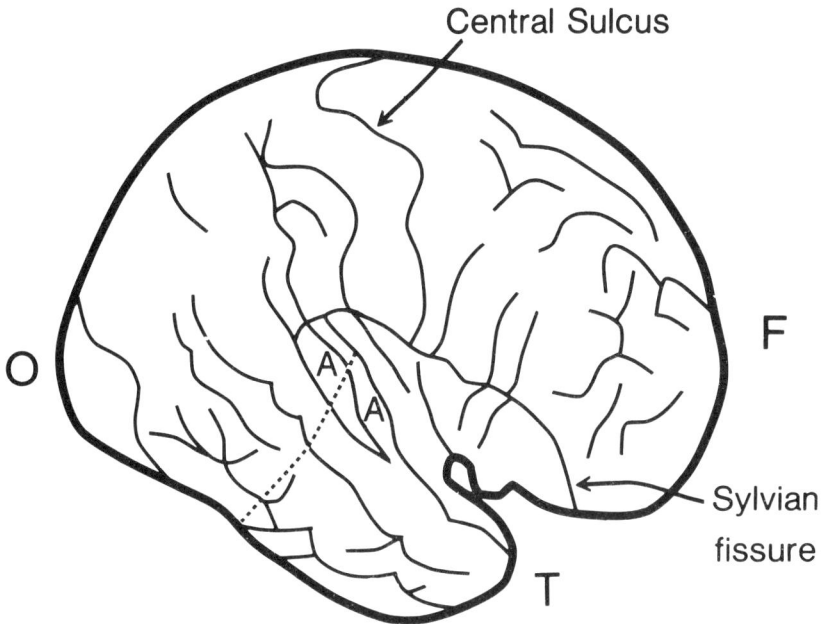

Figure 1 Lateral view of the right cerebral hemisphere with Sylvian Fissure opened to expose upper bank of temporal lobe. Dotted line indicates posterior extent of temporal-lobe excision in a case in which the transverse gyri of Heschl (labelled A in figure) were partially resected. In cases where this region was spared the line of resection would lie anterior to the dotted line. Abbreviations: O, occipital pole; T, temporal pole; F, frontal pole.

is present at the fundamental (see Green, 1976 chap. 7, for a review). There is evidence that central auditory mechanisms, particularly the auditory cortex, may play an important role in perception of the pitch of the missing fundamental. Psychophysical results suggest a central locus for this phenomenon because listeners perceive the missing fundamental even when two different harmonics are presented, one to each ear (Houtsma & Goldstein,1972). There is also electrophysiological evidence (DeRibaupierre, Goldstein & Yeni-Komshian, 1972) that some neurons in the primary auditory cortex respond in a way that would allow coding of the pitch of the fundamental in complex tones. Finally, there have been some behavioral studies with animals (Symmes, 1966; Whitfield, 1980) in which it was found that bilateral lesions of the primary auditory cortex and surrounding regions impair the ability to respond to the fundamental pitch. Little is known, however, about the neural substrate underlying this aspect of pitch perception in humans.

In the first study I will describe (Zatorre, 1988), I investigated more fully the effect of temporal cortical lesions on pitch perception. In this study the subjects heard a pair of tones on each trial and simply were to indicate if the pitch rose or fell. I prepared two sets of complex tones: for the control task they contained a prominent fundamental frequency component. In the missing fundamental task, only three or four upper harmonics were present such that the mean and range of spectral energy was identical within a pair, but the periodicity, or (missing) fundamental frequency, differed; thus, the only way to solve the task is to extract the pitch corresponding to the fundamental. All subjects retained for study were able to perform well on the control task, indicating adequate comprehension of the task. This result is also in agreement with numerous studies indicating that simple frequency discrimination (i.e., with pure tones, or with complex tones when the fundamental is present) is not permanently disrupted even by large bilateral ablations of auditory cortex in animals (Butler, Diamond & Neff, 1957; Meyer & Woolsey, 1957; Kelly & Whitfield, 1971; Whitfield, 1980),nor by unilateral temporal-lobe lesions in humans (Milner, 1962).

In contrast, on the missing fundamental task, patients in the RTA group were significantly impaired in making pitch judgments as compared to normal. Patients with left temporal-lobe lesions or with anterior right temporal-lobe excisions were unimpaired. This result suggests that the right primary auditory cortex plays a crucial role in extracting the pitch corresponding to the fundamental frequency from a complex stimulus. This is consistent not only with the animal studies cited above, but also with a number of findings that implicate structures in the human right cerebral hemisphere (especially the right temporal cortex), in the discrimination of timbre (Milner,1962), or in matching the pitch of complex tones (Sidtis & Volpe, 1981; Sidtis, 1984; Robin, Eslinger, Tyler & Damasio, 1987), tasks that probably depend in some way on the ability to analyze the spectral pattern. These results are also compatible with the idea that there exists a central "pitch processor" (Whitfield, 1970; Wilson,1974) whose function is cortically mediated. According to this account, damage to Heschl's gyri and adjacent cortex in the right temporal lobe disrupts the pattern-matching process that must take place for successful pitch extraction to occur. However, when the fundamental is present the task can be accomplished, presumably due to information processing at lower levels.

It would appear that the loss of the ability to extract the fundamental pitch from a complex sound would constitute a serious obstacle for many musically relevant tasks, and it may account for many aspects of the musical processing deficits observed following lesions of the right cerebral hemisphere. Nevertheless, many of these deficits are probably not directly related to fundamental frequency extraction, but rather involve other pattern-matching processes, insofar as they appear even with sequences composed of sinusoidal waveforms (Zatorre, 1985a), a topic to which we turn next.

Melodic discrimination

Milner's (1962) principal finding was that discrimination of tonal patterns was disrupted by RT lesions. In a study carried out several years ago (Zatorre, 1985a), I attempted to examine the nature of this deficit further by constructing a tonal discrimination task that involved the use of either scale or contour cues, or both (Dowling, 1978). Briefly, a task was prepared in which two six-note tonal melodies were presented on each trial. The comparison melody differed by one note on half the trials, and this note could alter either the scale or the contour or both of the original melody. As expected based on Dowling's findings, the results indicated that scale and contour may serve as cues to distinguish one melody from another, so that when both cues are present the two melodies are easily distinguished, whereas when neither cue is present performance is poor. Patients with right temporal-lobe lesions performed below normal on this task. However, their pattern of responses was similar to that of normal subjects; i.e., discrimination was easiest when both scale and contour cues were present, intermediate when only one cue was available, and worst when neither cue could be used. This result suggests, therefore, that the deficit in melodic processing observed following right temporal lobectomy cannot be attributed to a failure to utilize particular types of cues present in melodies. Rather it seems to be some more general type of deficit whose characteristics have yet to be specified precisely.

The most interesting finding to emerge from this study was not expected, and is shown in Figure 2. It was observed that when the excision encroached upon Heschl's gyri on either side, this resulted in a melodic discrimination deficit which appears to be independent from, but additive with the impairment resulting from right-temporal lobectomy. This result raises the question of a possible contribution of structures in the left temporal lobe to discrimination tasks such as this. In order to test the generality and replicability of this result, a new series of subjects was tested with a simpler three-note melodic discrimination task (Samson & Zatorre, 1988). The results of this experiment were largely in agreement with the previous one (Zatorre, 1985a) in that deficits were obtained both in the case of RT lesions as well as with LT lesions when the excision extended into Heschl's gyri (i.e., group LTA was impaired, whereas group LTa was not).

The question remains: why do lesions including Heschl's gyri from either the left or the right side affect melodic discrimination tasks? One hypothesis that was initially entertained was that, possibly, Heschl's gyri were implicated in short-term auditory memory. In order to test this notion a version of Deutsch's (1970) pitch memory task was constructed (Zatorre & Samson, unpublished). The task required the subject to indicate if two complex tones were identical in pitch or not; in the control condition only a silent interval separated the two tones, but in the experimental condition the two comparison tones were separated by a series of interference notes. Deutsch has shown that under these circumstances there is a significant decrement in performance, which is specific to tonal short-term memory. We posited that if such a memory system is linked to the function of the auditory cortex, then deficits should be apparent in this task only after lesions encroaching onto Heschl's gyri. The results were not at all consistent with this prediction, however. Instead, we found that in the experimental condition both groups RTa and RTA were impaired, while groups LTa and LTA both performed normally. All subjects were able to perform well in the control condition, in further agreement with the results of simple pitch discrimination presented above (Zatorre, 1988). Thus we must conclude that lesions of the anterior right temporal lobe are sufficient to disrupt short-term tonal memory, but the contribution of left-temporal lobe structures to musical processing uncovered in the other experiments (Zatorre, 1985a; Samson & Zatorre, 1988) remains to be explained.

Contribution of verbal mediation to melodic processing

The next topic to be examined concerns perceptual processing of musical materials in which there is a significant verbal component, either explicit or implicit. Several investigators have documented deficits in processing familiar melodies in patients suffering from left-hemisphere lesions (e.g., Shankweiler, 1966, Gardner, Silverman, Denes, Semenza & Rosenstiel, 1977; Grossman,

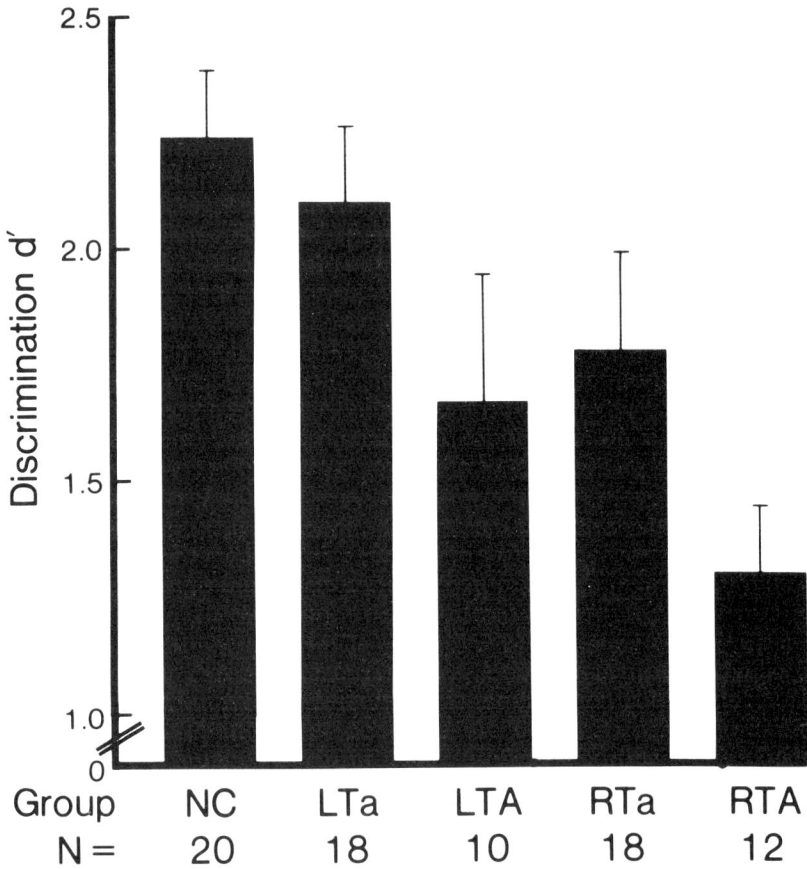

Figure 2 Discrimination of unfamiliar tonal melodies: d' score (discriminability index) for each group of subjects. Abbreviations: NC, normal control group; LTa, LTA, groups with left temporal lobectomy, sparing or including the primary auditory cortex in the resection, respectively; RTa, RTA, groups with right temporal lobectomy, sparing or including the primary auditory cortex in the resection, respectively. Bars indicate one standard error of the mean. (from Zatorre, 1985a)

Shapiro & Gardner, 1981; Shapiro, Grossman & Gardner, 1981). Although the tasks used in these studies were heterogenous, the possible mediating role played by the verbal lyrics to these melodies cannot be overlooked. A similar effect was observed in an experiment I carried out (Zatorre, 1985b) which was designed to study the role of the temporal lobes in extracting invariant information from a stimulus. Rather than ask, as in the previous studies, whether a slight alteration could be detected, the question here was turned around insofar as the task required the subject to identify a familiar melody despite significant distortion. Studies in cognitive psychology have indicated that familiar tunes can be altered in various ways and still be accurately identified so long as the tone chroma and the contour are preserved (Deutsch, 1972; Idson & Masaro, 1978). Thus a secondary aim was to examine the ability to use these cues after temporal lobectomy.

For this task five well-known melodies (without lyrics) were used without rhythmic cues that could differentiate them. In addition to the original (O) tune, there were three types of transformations: in the linear transformation (LIN) each interval in the original tune was multiplied by two, in the octave preserving-contour transformation (OPC) each tone was transposed one or more octaves from its original position, preserving the original intervallic direction, and in the contracted contour condition (CC) the change was similar to the OPC condition, but each tone was transposed 10 or 11 semitones. Note that whereas all three transformations preserve the contour, only OPC also retains chroma, while LIN preserves relative interval magnitude. The subjects' task was simply to listen to each excerpt and to find the correct title of the tune from a list before them. The results, shown in Figure 3, indicated that the LT group was significantly impaired as compared to the NC group. In this task no further deficits were evident as a function of the excision of Heschl's gyri. Transformation CC was the most difficult for all subjects, while both transformations LIN and OPC yielded more errors than condition O.

These results were surprising in that no significant deficit could be documented for the RT group. However, there was considerable variability in this group, and further work will have to be done to confirm whether such a task is indeed unaffected by RT lesions. Patients with LT lesions have well-documented verbal memory deficits (Milner, 1978), and also show mild naming deficits under some circumstances; their deficit on this melodic identification task suggests that a certain degree of verbal processing is necessary in order to match the stimulus melody with a long-term memory trace, because the lyrics are closely associated to the tune.

As for the use of chroma information, it appears that all groups are able to make use of this cue to assist in identification since performance on condition CC was significantly worse for all subjects as compared to the untransformed melodies. This finding accords well with the previously described result (Zatorre, 1985a) that temporal lobectomy does not impair the use of contour or scale information in melodic processing.

More direct evidence for the importance of LT mechanisms in memory for explicitly verbal aspects of musical stimuli has recently been obtained: in a study currently in progress (Samson & Zatorre, in preparation) we have administered Serafine, Crowder & Repp's (1984) song memory task to our groups of patients. Briefly, in this task a subject first hears a set of songs (sung with lyrics but no accompaniment), and subsequently must judge if test items contain either lyrics or tunes heard previously. Preliminary findings indicate a clear deficit for recognizing the lyrics after LT lobectomy, whereas patients with RT lesions perform as well as NC subjects. These results offer further evidence that when verbal memory plays a role in a musical tak, then lesions of the LT lobe are likely to produce significant impairments.

Absolute pitch

The final research area to be discussed, absolute pitch (AP), may be defined as the ability to name and/or produce specific musical tones without making use of a standard. It differs from the abilities examined in the studies discussed above in that it is not a skill that is very widely represented in the population. Thus,

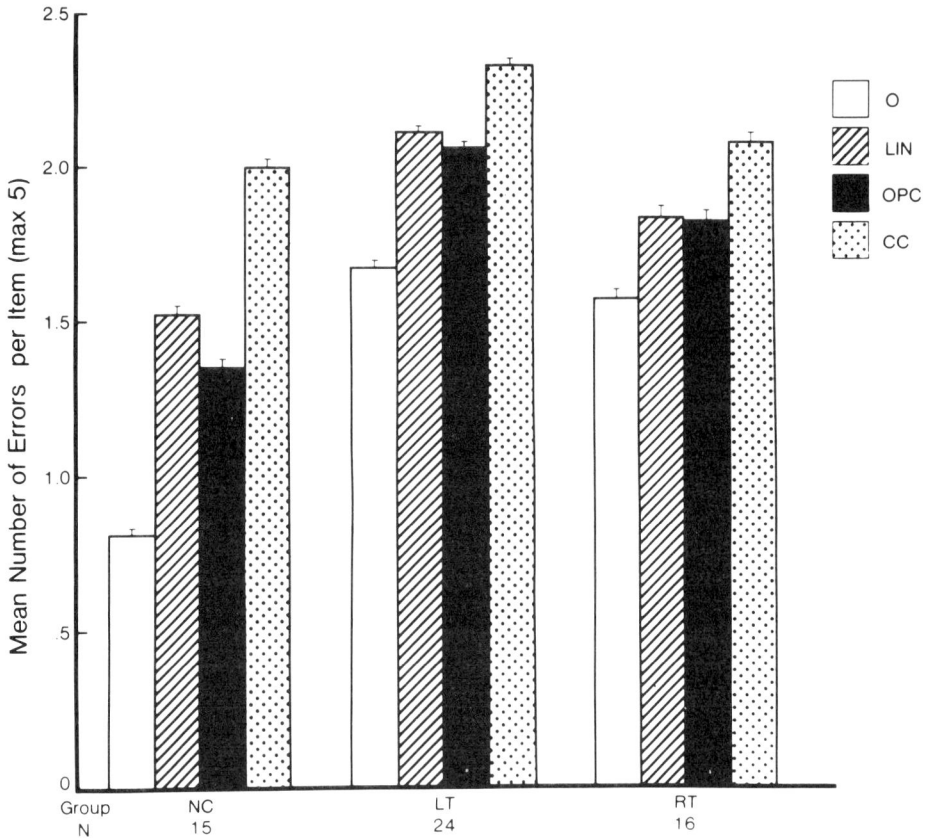

Figure 3 Average number of errors on distorted familiar melody identification task for each group of subjects. O: original; LIN: linear transformation; OPC: octave preserving contour transformation; CC: contracted contour transformation. Bars indicate one standard error of the mean. (From Zatorre, 1985b)

studying groups of subjects is not possible; rather, I have been able to investigate in depth the performance of an individual AP possessor who underwent a left temporal lobectomy, sparing Heschl's gyri, for seizure control (Zatorre, in press). This patient was studied before and after surgery with a variety of musical tasks, thereby permitting assessment of the specific effects of the temporal-lobe resection.

On a pitch naming task, in which the patient was simply required to identify randomly chosen piano tones, certain consistent errors were noted before surgery: he tended to underestimate the pitch on one day, and overestimate on another day. After surgery, however, he was much more accurate, and a follow-up study one year later showed nearly flawless performance. The preoperative fluctuations may have been due to changes in medication, or possibly to subclinical seizure activity. The improvement following left temporal lobectomy suggests that this region does not play a major role in absolute pitch. Possibly, with the removal of the epileptogenic focus, there was less interference with overall cerebral function, thereby permitting closer to optimal performance.

A further interesting dissociation was observed in the patient's verbal short-term memory, as compared to his tonal memory. It has been established (Milner, 1978) that left temporal lobectomy impairs short-term retention of verbal materials. This patient was no exception: recall of three spoken letters after 18 sec of verbal interpolated activity (counting backwards) was significantly impaired. In contrast, in a pitch memory task three tones were played which the subject identified; after 18 sec of verbal interpolated activity recall of the note names was nearly perfect. This implies that the tones could be encoded nonverbally, making them more resistant to interference from verbal distraction. This hypothesis was tested and supported in a study with normal subjects who possessed absolute pitch (Zatorre & Beckett, in press), in which we found that these subjects could retain the names of notes nearly perfectly while performing a verbal distracting task, something they could not do as well with strictly verbal memoranda.

The only other case report of AP ability following cerebral insult is that of Wertheim & Botez (1961). They found that AP was disturbed by a left-hemisphere lesion that resulted in a mixed but predominantly receptive aphasia in a violinist who had AP before his stroke. Although the locus and extent of lesion were not documented, one may assume that it involved the posterior part of the left hemisphere. There is a certain contradiction between these results and those I obtained in the case described above. The probably very different sites of lesion in the two cases may well explain the discrepancy. Apart from this, however, it is not clear from their report whether Wertheim & Botez's patient suffered a true loss of AP or rather a "rescaling" of his internal standard, insofar as many of his errors were reported to be a perfect fourth above the target. Thus, even that subject may not have lost all AP ability.

The results of these case studies do not, of course, exclude the possibility that idiosyncratic patterns of cerebral organization may exist for special skills such as AP, and that therefore each case may be somewhat different. As for other specialized musical skills, there exist several detailed case reports of musicians (without AP) who suffered extensive left-hemisphere damage but who were nonetheless able to continue performing and composing, and who showed no significant deficits in most musical tasks despite marked aphasic deficits (e.g., Luria, Tsvetkova & Futer, 1965; Basso & Capitani, 1985; Signoret, Van Eeckhout, Poncet & Castaigne, 1987). Thus, many questions remain regarding specialized musical skills and the underlying neural structures that are important. Nevertheless, we may tentatively conclude that there exists a considerable degree of independence between the function of the left temporal lobe and the region or regions that subserve many (though not all) specialized musical functions, including AP.

Conclusions

What have we learned from the foregoing experimental investigations? We may attempt an answer by summarizing the results (Table 1); the tasks are arranged in such a way as to permit a pattern to emerge. It is apparent that the breakdown of musical abilities following focal cortical lesions is quite systematic: whereas some abilities, such as simple frequency discrimination, are not affected at all by cortical lesions, others are disturbed only by lesions that include the auditory cortex. Moreover, certain tasks are affected by lesions in either temporal lobe, while other tasks are sensitive only to lesions on one side.

Table 1 Summary of results: performance of patient groups on various musical tasks

Stimulus	Task	Lesion groups showing impairments			
		LTa	LTA	RTa	RTA
Complex Tones Fundamental Present	Direction of Pitch Change	–	–	–	–
Complex Tones Missing Fundamental	Direction of Pitch Change	–	–	–	+
Complex Tones	Pitch Change w/Interference	–	–	+	+
3-note Sequences	Same–Different Discrimination	–	+	+	+
Unfamiliar Tonal Melodies	Same–Different Discrimination	–	+	+	+
Familiar Distorted Melodies	Identification of Title	+	+	– (?)	– (?)
Unfamiliar Songs	Recognition of Lyrics	+	+	–	–

Note: Normal performance is indicated by – sign, impaired performance is indicated by + sign. Abbreviations as in Figure 2.

At this point in our understanding of these phenomena, it is clearly too early to articulate an all-encompassing theoretical framework to explain these results or to make predictions. Nevertheless, several points are clear from these studies. First, it should be concluded that both the task demands and the type of stimulus to be processed will jointly determine which cerebral structures will come into play in any given situation. Thus, going from a full complex tone to a complex without a fundamental component is sufficient to bring out a deficit in group RTA, even though the task requirement is identical. By the same token, there are clearly situations in which the same stimulus may be processed differently depending on task demands. For example, although simple pitch discrimination is not affected by temporal-lobe removals, when there is an important memory component, as in the interference task, deficits appear after right temporal lobectomy. Before we achieve a more coherent understanding of the mechanisms underlying musical processing it will also be necessary to specify how these factors interact in more realistic situations.

The second point to emerge is that certain musical tasks encompass an important verbal component, whether it be implicit or explicit. Presumably, this accounts for the deficits in groups LTa and LTA in the last two experiments of Table 1. This factor is likely orthogonal to other processing requirements, insofar as the verbal aspect of a tune may be to some extent independent of other, more strictly musical aspects.

A third point that should be stressed is that, in agreement with many previous investigations of musical function and hemispheric specialization, the right cerebral hemisphere does play an important, and perhaps predominant role in many aspects of musical processing. The most consistent and severe deficits are generally obtained after damage to right temporal-lobe structures. Also, it was found that specialized musical skills such as AP were not affected by LT lobectomy. This asymmetry, however, is by no means absolute, as in certain cases the importance of left-hemisphere structures is also apparent. Nevertheless, there would seem to be a definite specialization of function, which may be considered in some respects complimentary to the well-established verbal predominance of the left hemisphere.

Finally, let us consider the possibility that the pattern of results shown in Table 1 reflects in some way the different levels of processing that are tapped by each task. This notion, though possibly somewhat difficult to define adequately, may provide a valuable heuristic to explain the results. With the exception of the last two tasks, Table 1 shows a ranking from tasks that require only a certain discriminative capacity to those that demand more in the way of pattern-recognition ability. Presumably, certain types of processing (e.g., pitch extraction) would have to occur before other processes can take place (e.g., melodic discrimination). There is a relationship between this ordering of tasks and the contribution made by various cortical regions. For tasks that are presumed to be relatively early in the processing stream, deficits are evident only after lesions to restricted areas. For tasks that may require input from one or several prior stages, deficits appear after several different types of lesions.

It may be hypothesized that subcortical auditory structures are responsible for the initial spectro-temporal analysis of incoming auditory signals, with extraction of the fundamental being carried out by mechanisms in the right primary auditory cortex. As tasks require more elaborate processing, calling upon various perceptual and mnemonic abilities, there is more participation from secondary, or so-called association areas; this is reflected by the significant deficits obtained following excisions limited to the anterior regions of the right temporal lobe. For certain tasks, there is a further contribution from the left primary auditory cortex, as well.

This scheme is not meant to be unidimensional: information processing certainly is not a single continuum, with information flowing in just one direction. As cognitive psychology uncovers more details of how music is processed, we will be in a better position to understand the contribution of different cerebral structures to each aspect of a given task. This will also be of importance in describing the function of regions not studied here, including the frontal and parietal lobes, which are bound to be important in many aspects of musical perception and production.

Acknowledgments

The preparation of this paper and much of the research reported herein were supported by an operating grant from the Medical Research Council of Canada (MA9598) to the author. I thank I. Peretz for helpful suggestions on an earlier version of the manuscript.

References

Basso, A. & Capitani, E. (1985) Spared musical abilities in a conductor with global aphasia and ideomotor apraxia. *Journal of Neurology, Neurosurgery and Psychiatry*, **48**, 407–412.
Benton, A.L. (1979) The amusias. In *Music and the Brain*, M. Critcheley & R.Henson (eds), Thomas: Springfield, Ill.
Butler, R.A., Diamond, I.T. & Neff, W.D. (1957) Role of auditory cortex in discrimination of changes of frequency. *Journal of Neurophysiology*, **20**, 108–120.
Celesia, G. (1976) Organization of auditory cortical areas in man. *Brain*, **99**, 403–414.
De Ribaupierre, F., Goldstein, M.H. & Yeni-Komshian, G. (1972) Cortical coding of repetitive acoustic pulses. *Brain Research*, **48**, 205–225.

Deutsch, D. (1970) Tones and numbers: specificity of interference in short-term memory. *Science*, **168**, 1604–1605.

Deutsch, D. (1972) Octave generalization and tune recognition. *Perception and Psychophysics*, **11**, 411–412.

Dowling, W.J. (1978) Scale and contour: two components of a theory of memory for melodies. *Psychological Review*, **85**, 341–354.

Galaburda, A. & Sanides, F. (1980) Cytoarchitectonic organization of the human auditory cortex. *Journal of Comparative Neurology*, **190**, 597–610.

Gardner, H., Silverman, J., Denes, G., Semenza, C. & Rosenstiel, A.K. (1977) Sensitivity to musical denotation and connotation in organic patients. *Cortex*, **13**, 242–256.

Green, D.M. (1976) *An Introduction to Hearing*. Hillsdale, N.J.: Erlbaum.

Grossman, M., Shapiro, B.E. & Gardner, H. (1981) Dissociable musical processing strategies after localized brain damage. *Neuropsychologia*, **19**, 425–425–433.

Houtsma, A.J.M. & Goldstein, J.L. (1972) The central origin of the pitch of complex tones: Evidence from musical interval recognition. *Journal of the Acoustical Society of America*, **51**, 520–529.

Idson, W.L. & Massaro, D.W. (1978) A bidimensional model of pitch in the recognition of melodies. *Perception and Psychophysics*, **24**, 551–565.

Kelly, J.B. & Whitfield, I.C. (1971) Effect of auditory cortical lesions on discriminations of rising and falling frequency-modulated tones. *Journal of Neurophysiology*, **34**, 802–816.

Luria, A.R., Tsvetkova, L.S. & Futer, J.C. (1965) Aphasia in a composer. *Journal of Neurological Science*, **2**, 288–292.

Marin, O.S.M. (1982) Neurological aspects of musical perception and performance. In *The Psychology of Music*, D. Deutsch (ed.), Academic Press: New York.

Meyer, D.R. & Woolsey, C.N. (1957) Effects of localized cortical destruction on auditory discriminative conditioning in the cat. *Journal of Neurophysiology*, **15**, 149–162.

Milner, B. (1962) Laterality effects in audition. In *Interhemispheric Relations and Cerebral Dominance*, V.B. Mountcastle (ed.), John Hopkins University Press: Baltimore.

Milner, B. (1978) Clues to the cerebral organization of memory. In *Cerebral Correlates of Conscious Experience*, P. Buser & A. Rougeul-Buser (eds.), INSERM Symposium No. 6, Amsterdam: Elsevier/North Holland.

Peretz, I.& Morais, J. (1988) Determinants of laterality for music: towards an information-processing account. In *Handbook of Dichotic Listening: Theory, Methods and Research*, K. Hugdahl (ed.), New York. Wiley.

Rasmussen, T. & Milner, B. (1977) The role of early left-brain injury in determining lateralization of cerebral speech functions. *Annals of the New York Academy of Sciences*, **299**, 355–369.

Robin, D.A., Eslinger, P., Tyler, R. & Damasio, H. (1987) Impaired pitch perception following focal right hemisphere damage. *Neurology*, 37 (Suppl. 1), 128.

Samson, S. & Zatorre, R.J. (1988) Discrimination of melodic and harmonic stimuli after unilateral cerebral excisions. *Brain and Cognition*, 7, 348–360.

Serafine, M.L., Crowder, R.G. & Repp, B.H. (1984) Integration of melody and text in memory for songs. *Cognition*, **16**, 285–303.

Shapiro, B.E., Grossman, M. & Gardner, H. (1981) Selective processing deficits in brain damaged populations. *Neuropsychologia*, **19**, 161–169.

Shankweiler, D. (1966) Defects in recognition and reproduction of familiar tunes after unilateral temporal lobectomy. Paper presented at the meeting of the Eastern Psychological Association, New York.

Sidtis, J.J. (1984) Music, pitch perception and the mechanisms of cortical hearing. In *Handbook of Cognitive Neuroscience*, M.S. Gazzaniga (ed.), 91–114, Plenum Press: New York.

Sidtis, J.J. & Volpe, V.T. (1981) Right hemisphere lateralization of complex pitch perception: A possible basis for amusia. *Neurology*, **31**, 101.

Signoret, J.L., Van Eeckhout, P., Poncet, M. & Castaigne,P. (1987) Aphasie sans amusie chez un organiste aveugle. *Revue Neurologique*, **143**, 172–181.

Symmes, D. (1966) Discrimination of intermittent noise by macaques following lesions of the temporal lobe. *Experimental Neurology*, **16**, 201–214.

Wertheim N. & Botez, M.I. (1961) Receptive amusia: a clincial analysis. *Brain*, **84**, 19–30.

Whitfield, I.C. (1970) Neural integration and pitch perception. In *Excitatory Synaptic Mechanisms*, P. Anderson J.K. Jenson (eds), Univ. Forlaget, Oslo), pp. 277–285.

Whitfield, I.C. (1980) Auditory cortex and the pitch of complex tones. *Journal of the Acoustical Society of America*, **67**, 644–647.

Wilson, J.P. (1974) Psychoacoustical and neurophysiological aspects of auditory pattern recognition. In *The Neurosciences: Third Study Program*, F.O. Schmitt & F.G. Warden (eds.), 147–153, Cambridge, Mass: M.I.T. Press.

Zatorre, R.J. (1984) Musical perception and cerebral function. *Music Perception*, **2**, 196–221.

Zattore, R.J. (1985a) Discrimination and recognition of tonal melodies after unilateral cerebral excisions. *Neuropsychologia*, **23**, 31–41.

Zattore, R.J. (1985b) Identification of distorted melodies after unilateral temporal lobectomy. Paper presented at the 13th Annual Meeting of the International Neuropsychological Society, San Diego, California.

Zatorre, R.J. (1988) Pitch perception of complex tones and human temporal-lobe function. *Journal of the Acoustical Society of America*. **84**, 566–572.

Zatorre, R.J. (in press) Intact absolute pitch ability after left temporal lobectomy. *Cortex*.

Zatorre, R.J. & Beckett, C. (in press) Multiple coding strategies in the retention of musical tones by possessors of absolute pitch. *Memory and Cognition*

Contemporary Music Review,
1989, Vol. 4, pp. 279–293
Photocopying permitted by license only

Music and modularity

Isabelle Peretz[a] and José Morais[b]

[a]*Département de Psychologie, Université de Montréal, C.P. 6128 Succ. A, Montréal, PQ, H3C 3J7, Canada*
[b]*Laboratoire de Psychologie Expérimentale, Université Libre de Bruxelles, 117 av. Adolphe Buyl, B-1050 Brussels, Belgium*

It is argued that the current modular conception of the human mind has important implications for the status of music processing in the architecture of the cognitive system. This conceptualization led us to treat several issues that have been neglected in the cognitive study of music. The major issue concerns the importance of specifying both models and experimental tasks in terms of stages in information processing. This approach is advocated as a preliminary step for identifying separable components in the processing of music and for assessing whether these comonents possess modular properties. In this perspective, and on the grounds of the available empirical facts, encoding of pitch information in terms of tonal scales is suggested to be a serious candidate for modularity. These computations appear to be made in an automatic way and seem to be acquired precociously and without explicit tutoring. This would support the proposal that music processing cannot be wholly attributed to general-purpose mechanisms.

KEY WORDS: Musical modules, neuropsychology of music, encoding of pitch, stages of musical information processing.

For the last ten years or so, music has become a distinct object of study in the field of cognitive psychology. There has been an explosion in research activity, as attested to by the regular appearance of articles in widely acclaimed journals, such as *Cognitive Psychology, Cognition, Journal of Experimental Psychology, Perception & Psychophysics* (a whole issue in 1987), and by the recent publication of a variety of textbooks (Howell, Cross & West, 1985; Sloboda, 1985; Dowling & Harwood, 1986). This productivity has been stimulated by the idea that music offers a unique opportunity to understand the human mind. Indeed, like speech, music is complex and uniquely human. Since music data are systematic, relatively clear and accessible, it is theoretically and methodologically advantageous to study music as a way to study the mind. In other words, music may serve as a model of the human mind. Such a perspective has often led to the characterization of music as the product of a general-purpose cognitive architecture. This general-purpose characterization of musical abilities may obscure the possibility that music "is wholly unlike anything else" (McAdams, 1987, p. 13). In the present paper, we will seriously contemplate the issue of specificity for music. More specifically, we will address this question following the contemporary notion of the modularity of the mind.

According to the modularity thesis, the human cognitive system is composed of physically separate subsystems, each endowed with a specific corpus of procedural and declarative knowledge. Three main research fields have contributed to the popularity of this approach. First, research in artificial intelligence and computer science has demonstrated that modular computerized systems, which have the property of being able to undergo computational changes without causing a large number of compensatory changes in other parts, are more efficient than non-modular ones (Marr, 1976). Second, research in neuropsychology has revealed that brain injury can cause a large number of highly selective deficits, which suggests that computational specificity in the human brain depends on physical separability (Shallice, 1981). Third, the investigations on perceptual processes, especially of those related to language, have described various phenomena that seem to suggest that the specific nature of the perceptual input coupled with the apparent necessity to preserve the veridicality of perception require interpretive mechanisms that are both specific and unaffected by general knowledge-based processes (Fodor, 1983). The existence of such modular systems for music perception has been put forth by Fodor (1983), by Gardner (1983), and more recently by Jackendoff (1987). The object of the present paper is to weigh the validity of the modularity thesis for music percpetion, along Fodor's lines, by examining the available empirical facts.

Fodor (1983) has provided us with the most thorough and explicit account of the essential properties that may characterize a modular processing system. For now, only a brief review of these properties is needed. To begin, two properties concern specificity. Modules are "domain specific" (property 1 in Fodor's list) and are associated with specific, identifiable neural systems, thus having the potential to exhibit "specific breakdown patterns" (property 8). Other properties are related to autonomy of processing. A module has its own processing capacity and its own memory resources. It is unaffected by processing by other modules or by general processors: it is "informationally encapsulated" (property 5). There is generally no central access to the internal representations of the module; the central processors can only have access to a module's output (property 3). Still other properties are related to the notion that modules are specialized devices built in the course of biological evolution in order to accomplish particularly important functions. The operation of a module is like a cognitive reflex. Its operation is mandatory, i.e. it is mediated by automatic processes which are obligatorily applied to particular properties of the input (property 2), and it is very fast (property 4). The module is directly associated with a fixed neural architecture (property 7), and its ontogeny exhibits a characteristic pace and sequencing (property 9). Nevertheless, there is room left for the imposition of interpretative mechanisms by more central processors, which allow belief fixation and the integration of pragmatic knowledge, since a module delivers "shallow" or superficial outputs (property 6).

Thus, in his essay, Fodor gives special prominence to neuropsychological evidence. When Fodor states that modular systems are modular not only functionally, but also physically in their neural implementation, he is undoubtedly refering to the modules that are most familiar, i.e. the modules for speech. These are, for the most part, lateralized in the left hemisphere of the brain. Moreover, predispositions for processing speech on a left hemispheric basis are found to be present at birth. Furthermore, pathologies of these neural areas exhibit highly specific breakdown patterns of language functioning. The resulting deficits, identified under the generic term "aphasia", cannot be explained by mere quantitative decrements in memory and attentional capacities.

Very similar claims can be made for music perception. First, many researchers posit that music has a special site in the right hemisphere. For example, Galaburda, Lemay, Kemper & Geshwind (1978) have suggested that a *planum temporale* (i.e. a particular neural area of the temporal lobe) that is larger on the left side of the brain might indicate important aspects of verbal activity while a *planum temporale* that is larger on the right side might "mean a high degree of musical potential" (p. 85). Similar to the findings that the left hemisphere is involved in speech perception as early as a few hours after birth, there are indications that the right hemisphere is more active in listening to music (see Mehler, 1984, for a review). Finally, "pure amusias", characterized by selective breakdown of music processing following brain damage without any concommittant disturbance in other spheres of cognitive functioning, have been reported (see Dorgeuille, 1966, and Marin, 1982, for reviews). Conversely, spectacular cases of spared musical abilities in the presence of profound disturbances in other cognitive domains are not uncommon (Luria, Tsvetkova & Futer, 1965; Basso & Capitani, 1985; Signoret, Van Eeckhout, Poncet & Castaigne, 1987). Taken together, these facts provide the basis for postulating specific neural circuitries for music.

Most researchers in the field of neuropsychology of music have, however, been reluctant to adopt such a modularistic view. Their scepticism is backed up by suggested empirical and theoretical evidence. For instance, many have pointed out that findings related to cerebral asymmetries have been far more variable than, say, the ones related to speech and language (see Zatorre, 1984, and Peretz, 1985, for reviews of the literature on a pathological population; and Peretz & Morais, 1988, for a review of the literature on a normal population). More specifically, it has been suggested that musicians and nonmusicians process melodies in opposite hemispheres (Bever & Chiarello, 1974). Thus, the research, which is based mainly on normals, has been guided by the implicit idea that music perception (see Sergent, 1982, for a similar idea with respect to vision) involves the execution of general-purpose mechanisms (Peretz & Morais, 1988). While this notion may be valid for some components of music processing, there are some aspects of music perception that may be specific and could eventually be identified with a fixed substrate in the brain. Support for such aspects will be outlined in the remainder of this paper.

Screening the candidates for a musical module

When Fodor (1983) asserts that input systems are domain specific, he cautions against equating those input systems with actual "visual" or "language" processing. Instead he is referring to highly specialized computational mechanisms for domains "in which perceptual analysis requires a body of information whose character and content is specific to that domain" (p. 49). For the domain of audition, he suggests that there are separate modular mechanisms subserving pitch organization, or melody, and temporal organization, or rhythm. Nonetheless, this simple hypothesis is not straightforward. It is a frequent practice among researchers to describe pitch organization independently of temporal organization, and many consider these two components to be distinct structures in their theoretical descriptions (for example, Deutsch & Feroe, 1981, and Krumhansl & Kessler, 1982, for pitch organization; Povel, 1981, and Longuet-Higgins & Lee, 1982, for temporal organization). The problem, however, is whether this structural automony is translatable into processing autonomy.

That melody and rhythm of sequential patterns are integrated at some level in the process of music perception is unquestionable. This is attested to by various observations. Listeners are more accurate at discriminating embedded pitches that coincide with important temporal events (Jones, Boltz & Kidd, 1982) and at transcribing melodies compatible at the level of pitch and temporal structure (Deutsch, 1980; Boltz & Jones, 1986). These effects could reflect the fact that allocating attention to both musical components is advantageous. Nevertheless, when decisional independence is promoted, that is, when the listeners are explicitly instructed to concentrate on one particular dimension at a time, they still exhibit response patterns that are affected by the irrelevant dimension (Jones, 1987; Pitt & Monahan, 1987). Thus, pitch and temporal organization appear to be intimately related. But to what extent are they related? Under some circumstances the two types of organization do not appear to interact. Such independence for rhythm and melody has been reported for judgments such as musical phrase completion (Palmer & Krumhansl, 1987a,b), familiar tune recognition (White, 1960) and for similarity judgments (Halpern, 1984; Monahan & Carterette, 1985). This suggests that before integration they have functional autonomy.

The problem is that perceptual independence is conceptually easy to formulate but difficult to verify experimentally. Experiments on perception usually require subjects to make decisional evaluations, which can fundamentally alter the percept, thus making perceptual independence difficult to test (Ashby & Townsend, 1986). In all the studies mentioned above, the tasks either involved some kind of post-perceptual judgment (judging similarity, sameness, and goodness) or had an important memory component (written recall and recognition). Given that melody and rhythm are intertwined in most music, integration of the two components is highly desirable, and in some sense, even inevitable. But this does not eliminate the possibility that listeners separate the two components in early stages of processing. What is certain is that the information is integrated somewhere in later stages, perhaps at the decision-making level.

In order to demonstrate that pitch and temporal organization are autonomously processed at the early stages of perceptual analysis, one would have to implement tasks that do not explicitly require subjects to attend to one of the two components. An alternative is to infer what the subjects perceive by examining the extent to which they confuse the components. An excellent example of such a paradigm is provided by the illusory-conjunction phenomenon observed in visual perception: when asked to detect the occcurrence of a red X, the observer detects it incorrectly in a display containing a red O and a green X that are presented under conditions which do not permit allocation of selective attention (Treisman, 1986; see also Studdert-Kennedy & Shankweiler, 1970, for a similar phenomenon in speech perception). This sort of finding strongly argues that separate systems for dealing with color and form exist in vision, and that the outputs of these two systems are later integrated in the decision making process. However, the above example shows that these are sometimes integrated erroneously, thus giving the experimenter a chance to observe the effects of early processes. Unfortunately, as far as we know, no paradigms have been used in the study of music perception that correspond to the one just cited.

The necessity to interpret experimental findings in terms of stages of processing may be illustrated by the following example, that deals with the segmentation of musical sequences. We have studied the role of various determinants of segmentation in three different experimental situations, each expected to tap a different processing stage (Peretz, in press). In one of these situations, already used with music (Deliège, 1987), the listeners were required to divide sequences into their "natural" parts. This is an introspectionist task, since the evidence relies on the listeners' conscious inspection of what they hear. The outcome of this situation is valuable to the extent that it is the subjects' ability to consciously and explicitly segment the musical input that we wish to examine (see also Morais, Alegria & Content, 1987, for a discussion of similar enquiries with respect to speech). Under this condition, we observed that, for instance, the temporal pause inserted between two groups of tones served as a segmentation marker for both musicians and nonmusicians, although more systematically in the former group (98% versus 75% of the responses, respectively). That this sort of intentional segmentation does not reflect perceptual processing is illustrated in other situations, which were inspired from current experimental paradigms in cognitive psychology. One, already applied to music (Dowling, 1973; Tan, Aiello & Bever, 1981), is known as the probe recognition technique. In this task, listeners are presented with a musical sequence followed by an excerpt; their task is to decide whether or not the excerpt is part of the sequence. Positive probes either fall within a cluster, or cross two adjacent clusters (delimited here by a temporal pause). Two different versions of this task were used. In the standard version, the probe followed the sequence. This is an "off-line" task; the listeners have to search their memory representation of the sequence. In the second version, the probe preceded the sequence, thus serving as a to-be monitored target. Such a condition allows one to make "on-line" measurements; i.e. measurements made *during* the processing of the sequence. The results in the two conditions are quite different. In the "on-line" task, the influence of the temporal pause is quite large, whereas in the "off-line" task it is in the opposite direction, albeit negligible (see Figure 1). Thus, subjects appear to process musical sequences by segmenting them according to temporal proximity. As we saw, this principle loses its impact when subjects are required to consult their memory representation of the same musical events. Another important result is that musical training had no effect on the pattern of responses. This latter result stands in sharp contrast to those obtained in the introspectionist task. Therefore, we can assume that the three different paradigms (intentional segmentation and probe verification with probe being presented before and after the test sequence) tap different stages of musical processing. This claim is further substantiated by the fact that all paradigms used the same musical objects and focused on the subjects' segmentation abilities.

It is in the context of the stage-of-processing approach that we can best understand the apparently contradictory sets of data on processing pitch and temporal organization. Those studies which find that these musical components are extracted separately can be explained in terms of autonomous mechanisms that function early in the processing of the musical object. At later stages, features emerging from the relations between the two types of organization are probably implicated in most recognition tasks. Pitt & Monahan (1987) appear to endorse such a view, since they state that subjects integrated "rhythm and pitch into a final percept" (p. 545) which determines similarity judgments. Indeed both pitch

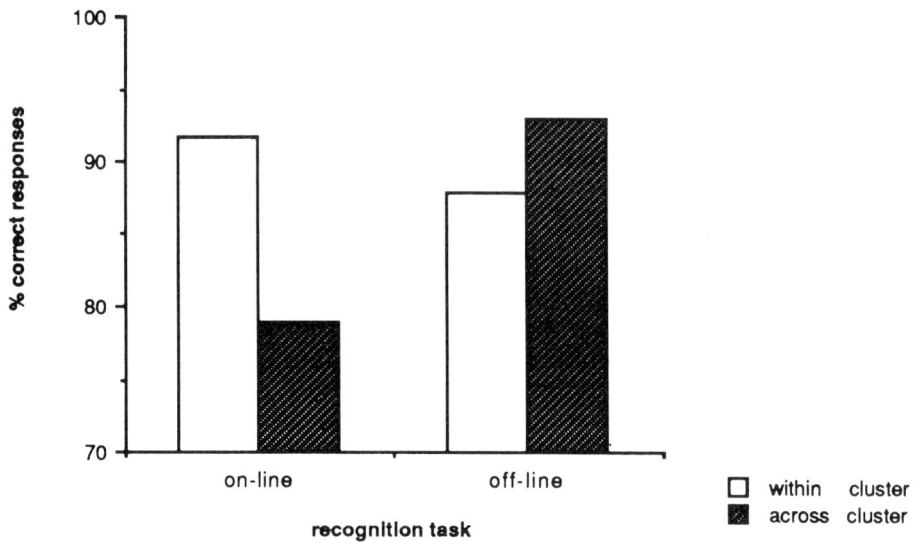

Figure 1 Plot of percent correct responses for probes falling within a cluster or crossing two clusters delimited by a temporal pause as a function of task, i.e. probe being presented before test sequence (on-line) or after test sequence (off-line).

proximity and tonal relatedness have uniform effects across all rhythm combinations. Thus, rather than arguing against modularity, these results support the idea of early separate extraction of pitch and temporal structure.

The proposal that melody and rhythm are autonomously processed prior to integration is suported by the behavioral dissociations that naturally occur as a consequence of brain insult. The most convincing evidence is undoubtedly provided by the phenomenon of double dissociation (Teuber, 1955). For those unfamiliar with neuropsychology, this phenomenon occurs in cases where it can be shown that one patient is still able to process adequately, for example, the rhythmic component of musical patterns but not the melodic one (namely providing evidence for dissociation in one direction) while another patient exhibits the opposite pattern (thus, providing evidence of dissociation in the opposite direction). Such powerful demonstrations of functional autonomy of the two underlying component mechanisms have been repeatedly observed for music. In singing, rhythm can be preserved while melody is impaired (Dorgeuille, 1966). Conversely, melody can be spared while rhythm is defective (Mavlov,1980; Brust, 1980). In reading, the same picture emerges with selective impairment of rhythm (Dorgeuille, 1966; Brust, 1980) or of melody (Dorgeuille, 1966, Assal, 1973). The same holds true for auditory perception (Dorgeuille, 1966). Our own investigations (Peretz, in preparation) have uncovered such striking dissociations. The corresponding data are presented below.

The one patient who sustained a lesion in the left hemisphere could no longer discriminate sound patterns differing in temporal structure, though he could still discriminate sequences on the basis of pitch structure at a normal level. The reverse pattern of performance was found in a patient with right brain damage. These outcomes can hardly be attributed to intervening task parameters, that is,

Table 1 Percentage of correct responses for the discrimination of sequential patterns differing solely in
terms of either pitch organization (melody) or
temporal organization (rhythm)

	Melody	Rhythm
1 Left brain-damaged	87.5	41.7
1 Right brain-damaged	41.7	91.7
2 Matched normals	91.7	100.0

to decision-making processes, since they were both obtained from same-different classification tests. Thus, the neuropsychological data provide a strong support for the notion that melody and rhythm are subserved by independent systems.

Given the indications of some functional autonomy between pitch and temporal organization in normal processing, which is further supported by neural independence, the possibility of a musical module that comprises both components seems unlikely. Rather, pitch organization and temporal organization will be considered as two separate candidates for modularity. If this is correct, the next question that must be addressed is whether, and perhaps to what extent, the mechanisms that compute pitch and temporal organization are specific to the perception of music.

With respect to computing temporal organization, it is difficult to argue that it is not inherent to many human activities. Most notably, it contributes to speech perception. If this is so, then doubt can be shed on the idea that the processing of temporal information in music is performed by a system uniquely, and originally, designed for music. Jackendoff (1987) acknowledges these shared aspects between language and music, but argues that the differences (i.e. at the level of the metrical structure) are substantiated enough that musical rhythmic structure cannot be simply attributed to a general-purpose temporal patterning device. However, delineation from those aspects that are truly specific to music is still fuzzy and there is not as yet any empirical work devoted to this issue. So, despite the possibility that the mechanisms that are involved in the temporal organization of music may be distinct from those that are involved in other cognitive domains, there is not enough evidence to forcefully demonstrate that they are specific to music.

In contrast, some aspects of pitch organization are clearly domain-specific and can be considered as the "germ around which a musical faculty could have evolved" (Jackendoff, 1987, p. 257). Central to pitch organization is the perception of pitch along musical scales. Pitch variations generate in music a determinate scale, whereas in normal human speech the intonation contours do not elicit such effects (Balzano, 1982). As Sloboda (1985) writes "that people represent music in a tonal space such that notes are assigned harmonic functions, is certainly different from any suggestion psychologists have made about cognitive representation in other spheres" (pp. 58–59). Moreover, it is speculated that perception of tonal pitch requires universal processing mechanisms. Even though the commonly used scales differ somewhat from culture to culture, most have common properties. Most musical scales make use of pitches an octave apart and are organized around 5 to 7 focal pitches (Dowling, 1978, 1982). These structural properties are interpreted as inherent to the constraints of the human cognitive apparatus (cf. the number of identifiable categories on a continuous dimension 7 +/– 2 as enunciated originally by Miller, 1956) and to the requirement that scales, by having an asymmetric interval structure, afford reference points and thus dynamic motion or tonal function (Balzano, 1980; Shepard, 1982).

Perception of pitch by reference to tonality as a modular system

Although the sensory encoding of frequency, apparently computed on a logarithmic continuum, is a necessary stage for perceiving pitch height, there is now substantial evidence that *musical* pitch perception is recoded in forms that are quite different from the early sensory codes. Such transformations, presumably mediated by various cognitive operations, make contact with a system of knowledge about pitch collections that are typically used within the musical traditions, and more specifically in the tonal tradition, about diatonic scales. In this system of knowledge, the tones assume not only a fixed pattern of asymmetric intervals (scale steps) that repeats in every octave, but also an internal organization around a reference tone (the tonic). This organization allows the establishment of a particular key that is more or less distantly related to other keys. This structure is presumably applicable to tones presented simultaneously, namely chords. While tonal structure most certainly pre-supposes a more elaborate description than the one just outlined, this brief summary of the knowledge that appears to determine the perception of pitch in a musical context is already quite elaborate and sufficiently well documented to be considered as part of the knowledge stored in a module.

Models of how these abstract properties may be represented in a multi-dimensional space have already been proposed (Shepard, 1982; Longuet-Higgins, 1978). However, most researchers have tended to focus their attention on the representational aspects of frequency rather than on specifying what stages in the system are concerned with specific frequency transformations and what computable procedures are involved in transforming codes between those stages. Some suggestions have been put forth but they have been limited to local aspects. For instance, Shepard & Jordan (1984; Jordan & Shepard, 1987) have proposed a sort of pitch template which is tuned to the pattern of intervals of the major diatonic scale with an interpretation of the first tone as the tonic by default. For chord relatedness, and possibly tones, Bharucha and his collaborators (Bharucha & Stoeckig, 1986, 1987; Bharucha & Olney, this volume) have proposed a connectionist model that links related chords by mechanisms of spreading activation. These two types of mechanisms may account for the successive transformations of pitch height that Dowling (1978, 1984a) has identified as the tuning stage and the modal stage, respectively. The tuning level corresponds to a level of analysis whereby pitches are mapped onto the diatonic scale, which is distinguished from a higher modal level, where these diatonic tones are hierarchically organized around the tonic. While such a distinction may correspond to the successive stages of processing of pitch information, thereby imposing future refinement about the specific content of a module for musical pitch computation, there is not yet any empirical evidence for endorsing such a view.

In any case, it is now well established that tonal regularities influence pitch processing. On the one hand, the distinction between scale (diatonic) tones and nonscale (nondiatonic) tones has been found to influence the recognition of single tones (Krumhansl, 1979) as well as the detection of pitch changes either in melodic sequences (Francès, 1972; Dewar, Cuddy & Mewhort, 1977; Cuddy, Cohen & Miller, 1979) or in chord sequences (Bharucha & Krumhansl, 1983). These latter effects have been shown to be valid to the extent that nonscale tones cannot be assimilated (or anchored) to the scale of the sequence (Bharucha, 1984). Recognition of diatonic sequences is advantageous because the embedded tones or intervals can be more accurately encoded than a collection of nonscale tones that fail to activate the musical scale structure. On the other hand, sensitivity to specific aspects of this structure is reflected in the subjects' ability to identify particular elements within the scale as being most central, like the tonic and the perfect fifth via the judgments of good completion of a scale (Krumhansl & Shepard, 1979; Krumhansl & Kessler, 1982) and the easiness of excerpt recognition (Tan, Aiello & Bever, 1981). Furthermore, proximity between musical keys has been shown to affect recognition of transposed melodic sequences (Cuddy, Cohen & Miller, 1979; Bartlett & Dowling, 1980) and judgments of good completion of tone and chord sequences (Krumhansl & Kessler, 1982; Bharucha & Krumhansl, 1983). It also facilitates speeded intonation decisions for chords (i.e. it generates "priming" effects, Bharucha & Stoeckig, 1986, 1987). All these results confirm the supposition that the abstract properties of musical scales determine pitch processing.

Serafine (1983) argues that encoding of pitch in terms of musical scales cannot be part of the perceptual system, and *a fortiori* of a module, since nonmusicians exhibit little sensitivity to scale structure (for example, Krumhansl & Shepard, 1979; Dowling, 1984b; Tan *et al*, 1981). Accordingly, scales would be an artifact of music reflection and their use in perception tasks would be the product of central processes acquired through explicit tutoring. However, several very recent studies have succeeded in obtaining effects of tonal organization that are insensitive to musical expertise (for example, Cuddy & Badertscher, 1987; Bharucha, 1984; Bharucha & Stoeckig, 1986, 1987). What is critical about these studies is that they did not merely show subjects' sensitivity to scale versus nonscale tones (as Dewar *et al*, 1977, and Cross, Howell & West, 1983, have observed previously in nonmusicians as well) but also a comparable sensitivity to tonal hierarchy. Thus, the conclusion to be drawn is that the main argument for the post-perceptual nature of scale interpretation no longer seems valid.

The fact that under certain conditions nonmusicians are as successful as musicians in displaying effects of tonal organization clearly indicates that they do possess this knowledge, albeit implicitly. Previous negative findings were probably related to experimental tasks. The methods may have allowed the intervention of formal knowledge, that is only available to musicians. This point seems illustrated in a study performed by Cuddy & Badertscher (1987). In this experiment, they used a derivative of the tone-profile technique developed by Krumhansl & Shepard (1979). The original task consisted of presenting subjects with a major scale and asking them to rate the suitability of tones drawn from the octave as completions of the sequence. Results obtained from this task indicate that nonmusicians made judgments based on proximity of pitch height while musicians took into account the suitability of members of the tonic triad. Cuddy

& Badertscher (1987) transformed this technique in several ways. One of these changes was to add musical significance to the task by asking subjects to help the experimenter make up good song endings (an instruction that was, in fact, used by Krumhansl & Keil, 1982, with children, but not with adult nonmusicians). Another important adaptation was to obviate the supplementary difficulty of transposing the tone-probe to the octave that is appropriate to the context by using tones in which pitch height dimension is reduced (following Shepard, 1964). These adaptations were found to be successful. Nonmusicians (as well as children) exhibited recovery of the tonal hierarchy. In addition, it was shown that so long as musicians were willing to conform to the instructions, they displayed the same profiles as the untrained. However, when required to rate completion of the songs according to their *formal knowledge* (not how good the completion was, but how correct it was), their profiles became different. This latter finding illustrates the extent to which musicians can anticipate and modulate their answers with respect to the experimenter's expectations. By the same token, it suggests that judgments observed with the tone-profile technique may be somewhat distant from perceptual experience. The tonal hierarchy that is observed when this method is used may well be produced by the intervention of central processors during the decision-making phase.

There are paradigms, like those showing priming effects, that elicit comparable sensitivity to tonal organization in the trained and the untrained. These effects probably occur because the required judgments are relatively free of strategy effects. This situation was used by Bharucha & Stoeckig (1986, Experiment 2 & 3; 1987) in which subjects were presented with a prime chord followed by a target chord for which they had to make a rapid intonation decision (in/out of tune). The prime chord was found to facilitate their decisions as long as it was related harmonically to the target. Since the decisions were orthogonal to the effect of tonal organization, which occurred nonetheless, it can be maintained that tonal hierarchy is not the sole effect of decisional processes but may be governed by a modular system.

Having reviewed the relevant data that support the perceptual reality of the tonal encoding of musical pitch, attention should be paid to other potentially modularistic properties. It will be argued that tonal encoding of pitch exhibits several of the modular properties enunciated by Fodor. First, the tonal system seems to mediate perception of musical pitch in an automatic way and without conscious awareness. Second, it seems to operate very early in ontogenetic development. Both of these are briefly developed hereafter.

First, Shepard (1982) has noted that the application of the knowledge that we have about musical scales appears mandatory and cognitively impenetrable. Phenomenologically, when listening to the eight successive tones of the major scale *(do, re, mi, . . . ,do)*, we tend to hear the successive steps as equivalent, even though we know that two of these intervals *(mi–fa* and *si–do)* are only half as large as the others (on a log frequency continuum). Shepard and Jordan (1984; Jordan & Shepard, 1987) have provided empirical support of this phenomenon. They have shown that listeners attribute tones to the diatonic scale even when the tones are equally spaced on a log frequency continuum (a series that does not correspond to any standard musical scale). They do so even when judgments are to be made with respect to physical relationship and not to any musical relationship. Related evidence demonstrating the lack of flexibility of listeners for interpreting the tones in scales different from the diatonic scale has also been reported by Watkins & Dyson (1985). Apparently, just as in vision where we cannot voluntarily avoid the mechanism of size constancy in Ponzo's illusion despite our knowledge of the illusion, we can hardly override the musical tendency to interpret tones in terms of the diatonic scale (i.e. that the intervals in a scale are physically equivalent)[1]. Thus, assignment of pitches to musical scales appears to be triggered automatically and "encapsulated" from general knowledge or beliefs. Second, with respect to development, children seem to have a natural ability to learn the regularities of tonal music through exposure to examples (like language). Improvisatory songs and memorization of nursery rhymes exhibit progressive mastery of tonal structure that is achieved around the age of five (for detailed reviews see Sloboda,1985; Dowling & Harwood, 1986; Hargreaves, 1986). Although children by this age may appear to be able to use the underlying tonal structure to guide their song performance, most studies have shown, paradoxically, that they do not exhibit this knowledge for discrimination tasks. Sensitivity to the tonal context in the discrimination of a pitch change in short sequences is not manifested before the age of 7 (Zenatti, 1969). It is around the age of 8 that children exhibit sensitity to key distance (Bartlett & Dowling, 1980) and by the end of elementary school that they can detect key changes in tunes (Imberty, 1969).

That acquisition of tonal organization proceeds in such orderly manner and mostly during the period of elementary school has been illustrated in a more precise fashion by both Imberty (1981) and Krumhansl & Keil (1982). Imberty (1981) has shown that around the age of 6 or 7, children are able to distinguish between the presence and absence of a cadence. By the age of 8, the child begins to differentiate cadences ending on the tonic from other types of endings. At the end of elementary school, a cadence on the tonic is fully differentiated from the one that modulates to the dominant. This progressive differentiation of tonal functions closely parallels the one observed by Krumhansl & Keil (1982). However, recovery of the tonal hierarchy may be found as early as the age of 6, if task parameters are suitably tailored (Speer & Meeks, 1985; Cuddy & Badertscher, 1987).

Here again, the influence of task factors appears crucial. Although, according to Zenatti (1969), sensitivity to tonal context does not manifest itself before the age of 7, Cohen, Thorpe & Trehub (1987; and see Trehub,1987, for a review of related data) have shown that it already present in infants that are 8 to 11 months old. The discrepancy between these two studies can be related to their methods. In Zenatti's study, children had not only to differentiate between pitch sequences but they also had to localize the discrepant tone that was embedded in the sequence. In Cohen *et al's* study, children simply turned their head upon presentation of the differing pattern in order to receive visual reinforcement. While these recent findings are more consistent with the view that children have precocious predispositions for organizing pitch in terms of tonal scales that will manifest themselves in both song and perceptual performance in the preschool child, they obscure somewhat the indications previously obtained about the order in which the various aspects of this knowledge is acquired. For the present, since the findings are so task bound, it appears that the issue of whether there exists a fixed sequencing in the acquisition of tonal organization, as suggested for example by the results obtained by Imberty and Krumhansl & Keil, remains inconclusive.

In summary, there are serious indications that translation of pitch onto tonal scales is subserved by a modular system. This system is specific to music (Fodor's property 1), seems to operate mandatorily (property 2), appears to be informationally encapsulated (property 5) and exhibits early ontogenetic development (property 9). Other properties are not yet empirically verified, most notably the property that describes the system as having a fixed neural architecture (properties 7 and 8). And there is one property of the system that may not be modular, namely the criterion that there is limited access to the internal representations that the system computes (property 3). Assuming that the output of such a system is a representation of pitches coded in terms of scale steps, music listeners, unlike speech listeners, must still have access to the "uncategorized" frequency information, that is, to early encodings in terms of pitch height. Otherwise, a chord, for instance, could not be heard as out of tune by less than the smallest musical unit. In fact, Bharucha & Stoeckig (1986, 1987) demonstrated this ability in requiring the listeners to make intonation decisions on tones that were out of tune by an eight-tone. This ability cannot be easily dismissed by the claim that the task does not involve the musical module since effects of tonal organization were obtained directly from the intonation decisions (cf. the priming effects described earlier). Thus, scale representation does not appear to preclude access to earlier codes. Indeed, a modular system may exhibit most but not all properties., or it may exhibit them only to some degree.

Conclusions

In the present paper, we have attempted to identify separate processors in music organization that can be viewed as modular. Modular systems are supposed to be involved early in the hierarchy of processing. Since there are both theoretical and empirical reasons to consider that early transformations of pitch information are computed independently of temporal organization, the possibility that they constitute separate candidates for modularity is envisaged. It appears that tonal encoding of pitch exhibits many properties of a modular system.

Another attempt at evaluating the modularity hypothesis for music is provided by Jackendoff (1987, of which we became acquainted while writing the final version of this chapter). He proposes a modular organization for music for rather late stages of processing, i.e. beyond the computations involved in the musical surface (and which corresponds perhaps to the level of representation on which we focused our attention). The levels of representations that he has focused upon (formally developed in Lerdahl & Jackendoff, 1983) consist of the grouping structure, the metrical structure, the time-span reduction and the prolongational reduction. While these subsequent levels of representation might correspond to a hierarchy of modular systems, there is presently scant empirical support for distinguishing them and *a fortiori* for assessing the nature and the locus of the interactions[2] that Jackendoff incorporates into his model. The latter issue is fundamental because it may violate the essential benefit of a modular system vis-à-vis an interactive one (Tannenhaus & Lucas, 1987).

In any case, both his and our approach attribute central importance to tonality[3]. Thus, although the essence of our approach bears some resemblance to his, we are more restrictive in the range of abilities to which the modularity thesis might be applied. Since the potential of the modular conception of music processing has only begun to be explored, the future of its exploitation is wide open.

Acknowledgments

The present paper was written while the first author was supported by a research fellowship and a grant from the National Sciences and Engineering Research Council of Canada, and the second author by the Belgian Fonds de la Recherche Fondamentale Collective under convention 2.4562.86.

Notes

1. It should be mentioned that these illusions were in part obtained with an adaptation of the tone-profile technique. As argued previously, this technique can hardly be regarded as an ideal task for uniquely tapping the perceptual system. This task is sensitive to cognitive bias. However, to demonstrate that, even under such circumstances, judgments are not modulated by scientific knowledge constitutes striking evidence that tonal encoding is mandatory and inflexible.
2. Jackendoff assumes that processing between a pair of levels is bidirectional and that this characteristic accounts for the fact that "in perception top-down evidence refines and fills in lower-level representations . . ." (p. 258).
3. It is noteworthy that, according to Jackendoff, the tonal system is so central to music processing that "it might be possible to think of metrical structure and time-span reduction as having evolved to provide a way to use a tonal system . . ." (p. 258–259).

References

Ashby, F. & Townsend, J. (1986) Varieties of perceptual independence. *Psychological Review*, **93**, 154–179.

Assal, G. (1973) Aphasie de Wernicke chez un pianiste. *Revue Neurologique*, **29**, 251–255.

Balzano, G.(1980) The group-theoretic description of twelvefold and microtonal pitch system. *Computer Music Journal*, **4**, 66–84.

Balzano, G. (1982) The pitch set as a level of description for studying musical pitch perception. In *Music, Mind and Brain*, M. Clynes (ed.) pp. 321–351. New York: Plenum Press.

Bartlett, J. & Dowling, W. (1980) Recognition of transposed melodies: a key-distance effect in developmental perspective. *Journal of Experimental Psychology: Human Perception and Performance*, **6**, 501–515.

Basso, A. & Capitani, E. (1985) Spared musical abilities in a conductor with global aphasia and ideomotor apraxia. *Journal of Neurology, Neurosurgery and Psychiatry*, **48**, 407–412.

Bever, T. & Chiarello, R. (1974) Cerebral dominance in musicians and nonmusicians. *Science*, **185**, 537–539.

Bharucha, J. (1984) Anchoring effects in music: the resolution of dissonance. *Cognitive Psychology*, **16**, 485–518.

Bharucha, J. & Stoeckig, K. (1986) Reaction time and musical expectancy: priming of chords. *Journal of Experimental Psychology: Human Perception and Performance*, **12**, 403–410.

Bharucha, J. & Stoeckig, K. (1987) Priming of chords: spreading activation or overlapping frequency spectra. *Perception & Psychophysics*, **41**, 519–524.

Bharucha, J. & Krumhansl, C. (1983) The representation of harmonic structure in music: Hierarchies of stability as a function of context. *Cognition*, **13**, 63–102.

Boltz, M. & Jones, M.R. (1986) Does rule recursion make melodies easier to reproduce? If not, what does? *Cognitive Psychology*, **18**, 389–431.

Brust, J. (1980) Music and language: musical alexia and agraphia. *Brain*, **103**, 367–392.

Cohen, A., Thorpe, L. & Trehub, S. (1987) Infants' perception of musical relations in short transposed tone sequences. *Canadian Journal of Psychology*, **41**, 33–47.

Cross, I., Howell, P. & West, R. (1983) Preferences for scale structure in melodic sequences. *Journal of Experimental Psychology: Human Perception and Performance*, **9**, 444–460.

Cuddy, L. & Badertscher, B. (1987) Recovery of the tonal hierarchy: some comparisons across age and levels of musical experience. *Perception & Psychophysics*, **41**, 609–620.

Cuddy, L., Cohen, A. & Miller, J. (1979) Melody recognition: the experimental application of musical rules. *Canadian Journal of Psychology*, **33**, 149–157.

Deliège, I. (1987) Grouping conditions in listening to music: an approach to Lerdahl & Jackendoff's grouping preference rules. *Music Perception*, **4**, 325–360.

Deutsch, D. (1980) The processing of structured and unstructured tonal sequences. *Perception and Psychophysics*, **28**, 325–36

Deutsch, D. & Feroe, J. (1981) The internal representation of pitch sequences in tonal music. *Psychological Review*, **88**, 503–522.

Dewar, K., Cuddy, L. & Mewhort, J. (1977) Recognition memory for single tones with and without context. *Journal of Experimental Psychology: Human Learning and Memory*, **3**, 60–67.

Dorgeuille, C. (1966) *Introduction à l'étude des amusies.* Unpublished doctoral dissertations, Paris.

Dowling, W. (1973) Rhythmic groups and subjective chunks in memory for melodies. *Perception and Psychophysics*, **14**, 37–40.

Dowling, W. (1978) Scale and contour: two components of a theory of memory for melodies. *Psychological Review*, **85**, 341–354.

Dowling, W. (1982) Musical scales and psychological scales: their psychological reality. In *Cross-cultural Perspectives on Music*, R. Falk & T. Rice (eds) pp. 20–28. Toronto: University of Toronto Press.

Dowling, W. (1984a) Assimilation and tonal structure: comment on Castellano, Bharucha, and Krumhansl. *Journal of Experimental Psychology: General.* **113**, 417–420.

Dowling, W. (1984b) Context effects on melody recognition: scale-step versus interval representations. *Music Perception*, **3**, 281–296.

Dowling, W. & Harwood, D. (1986) *Music Cognition.* Series in cognition and perception. New York: Academic Press.

Fodor, J. (1983) *The Modularity of Mind*, Cambridge, Mass: MIT Press.

Francès, R. (1972) *La perception de la musique*, Paris: Vrin. (Originally published, 1958).

Galaburda, A., Lemay, M., Kemper, T., & Geshwind, N. (1978) Right-left asymmetries in the brain. *Science*, **199**, 852–856.

Gardner, H. (1983) *Frames of Mind, The Theory of Multiple Intelligences.* New York: Basic Books.

Halpern, A. (1984) Perception of structure in novel music. *Memory and Cognition*, **12**, 163–170.

Hargreaves, D. (1986) *The Developmental Psychology of Music.* Cambridge: Cambridge University Press.

Howell, P., Cross, I. & West, R. (1985) (eds) *Musical Structure and Cognition.* London: Academic Press.

Imberty, M. (1969) *L'acquisition des structures tonales chez l'enfant.* Paris: Klincksieck.

Imberty, M. (1981) L'acculturation tonale chez l'enfant. Basic Musical Function and Musical Ability. Royal Swedish Academy of Music, **32**, 81–105.

Jackendoff, R. (1987) *Consciousness and the Computational Mind.* Cambridge: MIT Press, a Bradsfort book.

Jones, M. (1987) Dynamic pattern structure in music: recent theory and research. *Perception & Psychophysics*, **41**, 621–634.

Jones, M., Boltz, M. & Kidd, G. (1982) Controlled attending as a function of melodic and temporal context. *Perception & Psychophysics*, **32**, 221–218.

Jordan, D. & Shepard, R.(1987) Tonal schemas: evidence obtained by probing distorted musical scales. *Perception & Psychophysics*, **41**, 489–504.

Krumhansl, C.(1979) The psychological representation of musical pitch in a tonal context. *Cognitive Psychology*, **11**, 346–374.

Krumhansl, C. & Keil, F. (1982) Acquisition of the hierarchy of tonal functions in music. *Memory and Cognition*, **10**, 243–251.

Krumhansl, C. & Kessler, (1982) Tracing the dynamic changes in perceived tonal organization in a spatial representation of musical keys. *Psychological Review*, **89**, 334–368.

Krumhansl, C. & Shepard, R. (1979) Quantification of the hierarchy of tonal functions within a diatonic context. *Journal of Experimental Psychology: Human Perception and Performance.* **5**, 579–594.

Lerdahl, F. & Jackendoff, R. (1983) *A Generative Theory of Tonal Music*, Cambridge: MIT Press.

Longuet-Higgins, H. (1978) The perception of music. *Interdisciplinary Science Review*, **3**, 148–156.

Longuet-Higgins, H. & Lee, C. (1982) The perception of musical rhythms, *Perception*, **11**, 115–128.

Luria, A., Tsvetkova, L. & Futer, J. (1965) Aphasia in a composer. *Journal of Neurological Science*, **2**, 288–292.

Marin, O. (1982) Neurological aspects of music perception and performance. In *The Psychology of Music* D. Deutsch (ed.) pp. 453–473. New York: Academic Press.

Marr, D. (1976) Early processing of visual informations. *Philosophical Transactions of the Royal Society of London*, **275**, 483–534.

Mavlov, L. (1980) Amusia due to rhythm agnosia in a musician with left hemisphere damage: a non auditory supramodal defect. *Cortex*, **16**, 321–338.

McAdams, S. (1987) Music: A science of the mind? In "Music and Psychology: A Mutual Regard" S. McAdams (ed.) *Contemporary Music Review*, **2**, 1–61. London: Harwood Academic Publishers.

Mehler, J. (1984) Language related dispositions in early infancy. In *Neoneate Cognition: Beyond the Buzzing, Blooming Confusion*, J. Mehler & R. Fox (eds). New Jersey: Lawrence Erlbaum Associates.

Miller, G. (1956) The magic number seven, plus or minus two. *Psychological Review*, **63**, 81–97.

Monahan, C. & Caterette, E. (1985) Pitch and duration as determinants of musical space. *Music Perception*, **3**, 1–32.

Morais, J., Alegria, J. & Content, A. (1987) Segmental awareness: respectable, useful, and almost always necesary. *Cahiers de Psychologie Cognitive*, **7**, 530–556.

Palmer, C. & Krumhansl, C. (1987a) Independent temporal and pitch structures in determination of musical phrases. *Journal of Experimental Psychology: Human Perception and Performance.* **13**, 116–126.

Palmer, C. & Krumhansl, C. (1987b) Pitch and temporal contribution to musical phrase perception: effects of harmony, performance timing, and familiarity. *Perception and Psychophysics*, **41**, 505–518.

Peretz, I. (1985) Asymétrie hémisphérique dans les amusies, *Revue Neurologique*, **141**, 169–183.

Peretz, I. (in press) Determinants of clustering music: an appraisal of task factors. *International Journal of Psychology*.

Peretz, I. (submitted) Processing of local and global musical information by unilateral brain-damaged patients.

Peretz, I. & Morais, J. (1988) Determinants of laterality for music: towards an information processing account.In *Handbook of dichotic listening: Theory, Methods and Research* K. Hughdahl (ed.) New York: Wiley.

Pitt, M. & Monahan, C.(1987) The perceived similarity of auditory polyrhythms. *Perception & Psychophysics*, **41**, 534–546.

Povel, D.(1981) Interval representation of simple temporal pattern. *Journal of Experimental Psychology: Human Perception and Performance*, **7**, 3–18.

Serafine, M.(1983) Cognition in music. *Cognition.* **14**, 119–183.

Sergent, J. (1982) The cerebral balance of power: confrontation or cooperation? *Journal of Experimental Psychology: Human Perception and Performance.* **8**, 253–272.

Shallice, T. (1981) Neurological impairment of cognitive processes. *British Medical Bulletin*, **37**, 187–192.

Shepard, R. (1964) Circularity of judgments of relative pitch. *Journal of the Acoustical Society of America*, **36**, 2346–2353.

Shepard, R. (1982) Geometrical aproximations to the structure of musical pitch. *Psychological Review*, **89**, 305–333.

Shepard, R. & Jordan, E. (1984) Auditory illusions demonstrating that tones are assimilated to an internalized musical scale. *Science*, **226**, 1333–1334.

Signoret, J., Van Eeckhout, P., Poncet, M. & Cataigne, P. (1987) Aphasie sans amusie chez un organiste aveugle. *Revue Neurologique*, **143**, 172–181.

Sloboda, J. (1985) *The Musical Mind: The Cognitive Psychology of Music.* London: Oxford University Press.

Speer, J. & Meeks, P. (1985) School children's perception of pitch in music. *Psychomusicology*, **5**, 49–56.

Studdert-Kennedy, M. & Shankweiler, D. (1970) Hemispheric specialization for speech. *Journal of the Acoustical Society of America*, **48**, 579–584.

Tan, N., Aiello, R. & Bever, T. (1981) Harmonic structure as a determinant of melodic organization. *Memory and Cognition*, **9**, 533–539.

Tanenhaus, M. & Lucas, M.(1987) Context effects in lexical processing. In *Spoken Word Recognition* U. Frauenfelder and L. Komisarjevsky Tyler (eds). pp.213–234. Cambridge: MIT Press, Bradford Books.

Teuber, H. (1955) Physiological psychology. *Annual Review of Psychology*, **9**, 267–296.

Trehub, S. (1987) Infants' perception of musical patterns. *Perception & Psychophysics*, **41**, 635–641.

Treisman, A. (1986) Features and objects in visual processing. *Scientific American*, **255**, 114–125.

Watkins, A. & Dyson, M. (1985) On the perceptual organization of tone sequences and melodies. In *Musical Structure and Cognition*, P. Howell, I. Cross and R. West (eds). pp. 71–120. London: Academic Press.

White, B. (1960) Recognition of distorted melodies. *American Journal of Psychology*, **73**, 100–107.

Zatorre, R. (1984) Musical perception and cerebral function: a critical review. *Music Perception*, **2**, 196–221.

Zenatti, A. (1969) Le développement génétique de la perception musicale. *Monographies Françaises de Psychologie*, **17**, 1–110.

Contèmporary Music Review,
1989, Vol. 4, pp. 295–310
Photocopying permitted by license only

Modeling music listening: General considerations

Richard D. Ashley

*School of Music, 711 Elgin Road, Northwestern University, Evanston,
Illinois 60208, USA*

A number of important issues in the construction of cognitive models of music listening are explored. These include the essential starting-point of the model, the kinds of abstractions a model will make, and the features of the musical experience which a model preserves and those which it obscures. A number of approaches to modeling music listening are surveyed; these include linguistically-oriented models, those based on schemata, and simulation models, including those embodied in computer programs. Three main issues concerning the development and use of a model of music listening are considered: choice of a model's formalism, choosing which elements of cognition to include in a model, and ways in which a model may be evaluated. Special attention is given to the questions raised in modeling musical processes as computer programs. A computer model of melodic learning is described and evaluated as an example of how these considerations may be addressed.

KEY WORDS: Music psychology, music listening, cognitive modeling, schema, production systems.

Introduction

Listening to music is the most basic and important of music cognitive process. Nevertheless, it remains steeped in mystery, due in large part to the difficulties one faces when studying a cognitive activity which, most typically, yields little or no external behavior which may be recorded and used as data. Two main approaches have been taken to the study of music listening: experimentation, in the traditions of psychophysics and experimental cognitive psychology, and modeling, in the traditions of artificial intelligence and linguistics. This paper outlines some approaches which have been taken to modeling music listening and proposes some criteria for constructing and evaluating models of listening.

Models in the study of music: An overview

Models are, in the most general sense of the term, representations for or analogs of some object or process. They are used in many disciplines and may take different forms. Modeling is valuable for its ability to capture what an investigator believes to be the most interesting or salient characteristics of the object of study, while dealing less with others. It may also allow an investigator to study the behavior of complex systems with interacting parts through the use of a simulation model.

Numerous models have been used in studying music cognition. Not all of these models have to do with music listening *per se*; for example, Johnson-Laird (1988, pp. 260–265) describes a model of improvisation for jazz bass lines, Clarke (1987) has produced a model for the internal representation of hierarchic rhythmic structures, and Todd (1985) has developed a model of expressive timing in performance based on parabolic functions. Within models dealing with listening in some fashion, there is a wide diversity of approach and direction. Some are concerned with matters such as the structure of the basic musical materials or the music as represented in the score, or the knowledge which a listener might use to understand the music: others are more process-oriented and focus on other areas, such as allocation of attention or learning through listening. Some of the more important kinds of models are:

- linguistically-oriented models, using grammars or other elements derived from language;
- mathematical models, including those which are statistical, geometric, set-theoretic, and group-theoretic in scope;
- models based on schemata, or structured sets of relationships among attributes of a phenomenon;
- simulation models, whether embodied in computer programs or in some other fashion.

Let us now briefly survey a number of musical models in each of these categories.

Examples of musical models

Linguistically-oriented Models

The relationship between language and music has interested scholars for a long time, and has served as the impetus for a number of models of music based in some manner on linguistic principles or metaphors. Foremost among these are models based on grammars. Other interesting approaches, such as the semiological ones (Nattiez, 1976), have also been developed; unfortunately, limitations of space do not allow consideration of these here.

One well-known approach to linguistic models for music is that of generative grammars, as for example Sundberg & Lindblom (1976), where the structure and style of a class of folk-tunes has been modelled, or Steedman (1984), which provides a grammar for harmonic progressions in the twelve-bar blues. Another recent musical theory which is embodied in a grammar is found in the work of Lerdahl & Jackendoff (see esp. their 1983, or Lerdahl's chapter in this volume for a short review). Their theory is of particular interest for its multiply-hierarchical basis (musical structures are understood as being hierarchical in a number of ways: through grouping, rhythm and meter, and tonal prolongation) and for its use of "preference rules" which help a listener to decide between legal, or well formed, structures which may be assigned to the music.

Mathematical Models

Psychologists and musicians have made use of mathematical models for years as part of their work. In studies of music cognition, these techniques have been applied to pitch-materials in atonal music, internal representation of pitch sequences in tonal music, tonal and harmonic factors, aspects of musical scales and psychological relationships between timbres. These models have emphasized the nature of structural relationships in these musical materials, thus providing a foundation from which other considerations of the process of listening may proceed (see reviews in Deutsch, 1982; Risset & Wessel, 1982; and Shepard, 1982).

In general, the music set-theorists (e.g. Forte, 1974) have been isolated from empirical currents which surface in music theory. An exception is found in the work of Hasty (1981, 1986), who has worked to embed a theory of segmentation in post-tonal music into what may broadly be considered an information-processing framework. His interest here seems to be one of developing a general but useful set of plausible psychological constraints on the ways in which the pitches of a piece may be grouped together. Hasty is thus one of a group of younger American music theorists revising existing theories to fit into the new "cognitive" *zeitgeist*. In another domain, Deutsch & Feroe (1981) have proposed a model of the organization of pitch structures for tonal music which has been widely discussed (cf. West, Howell, & Cross, 1985). The model uses a highly-developed notion of hierarchy for pitch structures, based on a number of primitives of "alphabets", such as triads, diatonic scales, and chromatic scales. Such a notion is appealing, and has a strong relation to the idea of "chunking" as a means of overcoming stimulus complexity in interaction with limited resources in short-term memory (Miller, 1956).

A different kind of approach to the use of mathematically-oriented models of music listening is seen in a group of studies on the structure of scales, and tonal and timbral relationships (Krumhansl, 1979; Wessel, 1979; Balzano, 1980, Shepard, 1982; Bharucha & Krumhansl, 1983). These models use several main techniques (multidimensional scaling being foremost among them), but all involve mathematical or geometric representations of structural aspects of these musical elements. These techniques have also been used to study thematic relationships in Liszt's b minor piano sonata (Pollard-Gott, 1983), showing their versatility.

Schema Models

Among other important lines of research involving modeling are various schema theories. "Schema" is a notoriously vague term with many different definitions; at the risk of overgeneralizing, it may be understood as a relatively high-level or large-scale representation of a concept, object, or event in which care is taken to show relationships between the whole and its attributes in a structured manner (Rumelhart, 1980). The idea of a schema is widespread; it has been used, for instance, in studies of memory (Bartlett, 1932), machine vision (Minsky, 1975), and categorization (Rosch & Mervis, 1975). In studies related to music cognition, it may be seen in music theory in the work of Meyer (1973), Narmour (1977, this volume) and Gjerdingen (1986, 1988), and in the experimental literature in Krumhansl & Castellano (1983).

Much of the modern work on music cognition stems, directly or indirectly, from the work of Leonard Meyer (1956, 1973). He has developed the "implication–

realization" theory of melodic process – in effect, a schema theory for melody. Meyer is looking for a simple and powerful way to discuss and understand the behavior of tonal melodies, and uses the notion of "implications" in melodic phenomena, as understood by the listener, with the listener's task to make judgements concerning the types of "realizations" which these implications do and do not use. Meyer's work has been extended by his colleague Eugene Narmour (1977, this volume) and his student Robert Gjerdingen (1986, 1988). Their efforts have gone far to deal more formally with the question of what constitutes a musical style, and to raise significant questions about the nature of cognition for melodies.

The dynamic nature of schema theories, where the selection, use, and refinement of a schema takes place over time, is exploited in Krumhansl & Castellano (1983) to explain how a listener might make use of tonal information while listening to a musical work. This same dynamic element of schema theories has led to work implementing them in computer programs simulating schematic comprehension of music; these efforts are discussed in the next section.

Simulation Models

Many aspects of music listening can be modelled as states of knowledge or of affairs; however, listening itself is a process and some models have been constructed which are oriented toward this explicitly dynamic element of listening. Due to a confluence of theoretical ideas and the ready availability of computer systems which allow for the precise modeling of processes as computer programs, there is now a burgeoning interest in artificial intelligence-style modeling of music cognition, either as an alternative or an adjunct to experimentation. The models constructed are of many types, and use many different methods for their implementation. Musicians' attempts to build more comprehensive models of some kinds of music listening processes are still quite young, in part due to the special kinds of expertise needed to design and implement the computer programs which form the underlying mechanism they use. Even so, a number of studies exist which it is well to mention.

Although not expressed in a running computer program, the model of music listening developed by Jos Kunst (1978) is one of the most sophisticated and provocative works in the literature, and has spawned other efforts in this area. Kunst has taken a unique approach to modeling, based on logics that use quantifiers to show temporal relationships and "modal" relationships – in this case, those dealing with possibility and necessity. His interest is in music listening as a kind of puzzle-solving, in which the task of the listener is to maintain cognitive and conceptual "mastery" over the music. This "mastery" involves a listener in building, maintaining, and updating internal "worlds" which are models of the behavior of the music consisting of a set of proposed musical "laws". When these "laws" fail, the listener is no longer in control of his listening process. His task is then to create new laws, yielding a constant pattern of unlearning old laws and learning new ones.

Otto Laske's work (1977, 1980) has provided one of the best- known sources of ideas for constructing computational models of music listening. He bases his proposals on an eclectic group of sources: systems for speech understanding, modal logic, production systems, and generative grammars all find their way into his ideas. Overall, Laske has been most interested in flexible architectures which yield highly responsive models for music listening; unfortunately, none of them seem to have been fully implemented in a running program to date.

Rule-based systems have been used widely as models of cognition (Newell & Simon, 1972; Newell, 1973; Anderson, 1983). In these models, knowledge is encapsulated in small program units called "rules" which carry out some action when a certain state of affairs comes to pass. Rule-based models have been proposed for musical activities by a number of researchers. Sloboda (1985, pp. 215–233) introduces the production system formalism into his discussion of musical skill acquisition, and a number of studies (Ashley, 1985, 1986, 1987, 1989; Marsden, this volume) have proposed the use of some kind of rule-based program as a basis for modeling music cognition. The penultimate section of this paper gives an example of one such model.

A number of efforts have been made to produce computer programs which utilize schema frameworks for modeling some aspects of music listening (Holland, 1987; Baker, this volume). The desire to have schema models be very flexible is one of the reasons work in neural network or parallel distributed processing (PDP) models has arisen as a way of representing schemata (Rumelhart, Smolensky, McClelland, & Hinton, 1986). In these systems, a large number of independent feature detectors are arranged in a network and create larger patterns through their combinations. A valuable and interesting aspect of these models is that they can learn by experience. These are attractive features and have stimulated a number of essays in musical PDP systems (Bharucha, 1987; Lischka, 1987; Bharucha & Olney, this volume; Leman, this volume). This represents the most "modern" line of research into computer modeling of music listening, and combines some of the best features of schema and geometric approaches with the explicitly dynamic behavior of a simulation system. In addition, the PDP models' emphasis on learning through experience is a most salutary addition to the concerns addressed by students of music cognition.

Not all efforts in computer modeling of music listening fall as easily into these formalisms. Among other interesting approaches are those of Longuet-Higgins and his associates (Longuet-Higgins, 1976; Longuet-Higgins & Lisle, 1988) and of Povel (Povel & Essens, 1985). Longuet-Higgins' work represents the truly pioneering efforts in this area and continues to be very interesting. The basic activity he models is a kind of dictation or transcription task, where the listener/program is to produce a written representation of a melody which is performed on a keyboard. The internal workings of the model are based on a kind of stochastic procedure for interpreting pitch and duration patterns in a tonal-melodic framework. In Povel's case, the question deals with the nature of rhythmic understanding, especially with regard to meter. Povel postulates the existence of an "internal clock" which most typically will be triggered during the course of music listening, providing, through the interaction of durations and accents, a metric interpretation of the music. This conception of the clock was developed using both experimentation and a computer model.

Methodological issues in modeling music cognition

Now that a number of different models of aspects of music listening have been reviewed, it will be useful to attempt to establish some criteria by which such models may be evaluated. Of a large number of issues facing the cognitive modeller (see Polson, Miller & Kintsch, 1984 for a useful discussion), three questions might usefully addressed here:

- What kinds of criteria might be used for selecting a formalism for a model?
- What elements of music cognition should a model include?
- How should the model be evaluated?

Each of these is fraught with difficulties and is the subject of much heated debate; we can only hope to make a few suggestions here.

Choice of Formalism

First, how should one go about choosing how to model the phenomenon of interest? The primary criterion is that of the suitability of some representational framework. Any model will concentrate on some elements of a phenomenon and deemphasize others. Therefore, specific formalisms may be helpful in dealing with the elements in listening which are of special interest. For example, grammatical models have been used successfully for modeling a listener's competence in or knowledge of a certain body of music. Mathematical or geometric models are useful for showing relationships in pitch structures or between timbres; such considerations may also be embedded in a simulation model through a PDP or other connectionist system. If, on the other hand, a modeler wishes to focus on some other aspect of listening such as selective attention, a production system may be a good solution.

A second consideration is that of the level of detail needed for the model to describe its domain adequately. It has been proposed that PDP systems are well-suited for modeling perceptual tasks which happen relatively quickly, (Rumelhart, Smolensky, McClelland & Hinton, 1986), and that symbolic representations such as production systems may be more useful for tasks occupying longer times-spans. In addition, PDP systems may work best for very detailed or "low-level" phenomena, with many features, and more symbolic models for more generalized or "high-level" aspects of cognition. However, these points are open to dispute; some (Newell, 1973; Anderson, 1983) would contend that a unified representation such as the production system is appropriate at all levels of cognition. In addition, the relative transparency or opaqueness of different representations may be an issue. If the model will be used to implement an intelligent tutor, for example, some relatively explicit and high-level representation such as schemata or rules may be of considerable advantage.

Element of Cognition in Models

There are a large number of aspects of music cognition which a modeler might choose to address. These include: the structural nature of the musical materials involved; the listener's internal representation of these materials; the knowledge the listener brings to the music; the way in which listeners learn through listening; and features of the human cognitive architecture, such as memory and attention-allocation methods. These together produce a framework for a relatively comprehensive picture of music listening.

To include all of these elements in a single model is difficult, and most models do not attempt to deal with them all. However, this creates situations where many questions are left open. For example, a model of musical structure which is hierarchical in nature or uses chunking methods can easily yield superhuman levels of performance in terms of memory capability. This indicates that such a model would be made more complete by taking such things as memory structures, control processes (such as allocation of attention) and the time-demands of musical processing into account. Likewise, models which use symbolic representations of the musical input (i.e., a score of some kind) should not presume too highly that these representations are isomorphic to the listener's internal representation of the music. A grammatical model of a listener's knowledge in a style would be enhanced by some suggestions as to how the knowledge is used. Finally, all modeling efforts in music listening should consider that knowledge of music and internal representations of pieces of music are learned, and that learning on a regular, routine, and unavoidable basis is most characteristic of music listening – where much is learned without apparent intent or effort, in many cases.

Evaluating models

The evaluation of a model of music listening is, at one level, reasonably straightforward: one provides the model with some kind of input, and sees if its output is like that which a listener would produce. However, this only raises two difficult issues: what is the nature of the "input" the system should be given, and how does one know what kind of "output" is "like that a listener would produce?" The means by which these are done vary widely from study to study. Let us examine these by looking at three points: the level of description in a model, the desirability of a computable model, and the relationship of modeling to experimentation.

What level of description should a model seek to have? Models may have any of a number of levels of description. At one level, a modeler might consider it sufficient to give his model some input and have its output be similar to that a human would produce – a kind of "Turing test" for music cognition. This kind of modeling has often been done by workers with an artificial intelligence orientation, where getting a system that will operate in a reasonable fashion is often quite sufficient. While this makes sense in a field where general principles of intelligence are at issue, it makes for less satisfactory cognitive psychology, where the point is not so much how an abstract symbol-processing system behaves as how people do.

It would be preferable if models, especially those of a computational or simulation variety, could be shown to have components which behave as do the corresponding mechanisms in human beings. In this way, one might cast the results of experimental studies into a component of more integrated models. Such an approach would have the effect of helping to draw the computational and experimental approaches closer to each other, and should yield more fruitful discussions between AI-oriented and experimentally-oriented researchers. Models in other domains (Kosslyn, 1980; Anderson, 1983) have served this unifying and integrating purpose; however, at the early stage in which most musical model-building exists now, a rough simulation of input and output may be a more realistic expectation.

Should models be expressed as computer programs? At this time, a good deal of discussion in the cognitive sciences revolves around the issue of the place of computability in theories of cognition. Some see it as a powerful tool for aiding clear thinking, but others find it an isolated pursuit unto itself and having little to do with the empirical facts of cognition – those investigated through experiment. At the least, producing a computer program as a model from some theoretical framework indicates that the model is precise and coherent. This can help to further refine intuitive theories which have heretofore been incompletely formalized and to sharpen fuzzy thinking. In this way, the different factors which contribute to some intuitive judgment may be ferreted out (and others which were thought important may prove to have relatively little impact).

Let us consider an example from Lerdahl & Jackendoff's (1983) theory. It provides a competence theory for the knowledge needed by a "native speaker" of tonality in order for him to make use of musical structures in this idiom. It is not a performance theory, in that the processes which would make use of this knowledge base are not specified; it also lacks consideration of the kinds of cognitive architecture (for example, memory structures) which these musical competences would use.

However, there is an interesting kind of semi-computational component in the theory. Lerdahl & Jackendoff have provided two kinds of rules in their grammar for structures in tonal music: one set which assigns legal structures to the score (the well-formedness rules), and another which helps the listener to choose between alternate legal structures (the preference rules). The preference rules form an incipient control structure which would help the listener make decisions about what he is or she is hearing and allocate his or her cognitive resources accordingly. This control source is "incipient" because it is neither sufficiently detailed nor complete enough to permit its casting into a computable form, either mechanically or by hand. Rather, it must be interpreted by the analyst, possibly yielding more than one predicted structural interpretation of the same passsage. This kind of informal element can be greatly refined by trying to implement it as part of a computable system, in that the various factors which go into our intuitions may be uncovered (Baker, this volume). This heuristic value of computer modeling is not unknown to workers in some other areas of music-sound synthesis, for example – and should serve students of music cognition as well.

Another advantage which some hope to gain from computational modeling is that of being able to deal with more complete or complex systems rather than with the mechanisms and structures studied in individual experiments. This would allow a modeler to embed a number of different elements in a system and to study their interplay. In this way, it would help to indicate the ways in which individual elements of a system – for example, a pitch processing mechanism and one handling rhythm or meter – interact with one another, a kind of insight of which one sees relatively little. Unfortunately, this approach has its problems; among them is the difficulty of specifying mechanisms which combine to uniquely provide an explanation of the behavior of the system. There are suggestions as to how this problem may be attacked (Van Lehn, Brown & Greeno, 1984), but no fully adequate solution is seen at present.

What should be the relationship between modeling and experimentation? Models vary widely with regard to their development cycle. Some tend to be more "bottom-up" in nature, where individual experiments are completed and the results combined to produce the model. This has the advantage of giving a strong empirical anchor to the whole enterprise, but contains the seeds of other difficulties; for example, that of inducing general mechanisms from experimental evidence, or specifying the ways in which the mechanisms proposed would be integrated into the cognitive system. In other, more "top-down" studies, the model is worked on first, possibly (but not always) leading to experimentation in order to test the model's behavior or predictions. Such seems to be the case with, for example, Longuet-Higgins' work. Thus, two kinds of research paradigms are seen here, both found in cognitive science.

Although a model developed from intuition in a top-down fashion can be an excellent means of advancing a theory's development, it is somewhat troubling to see models developed which make no use of experimentation, or which use experimentation only *post hoc* – a situation which certainly exists outside of research in music as well. In computational and grammatical models, for example, successively closer approximations to the desired behavior are often reached informally, through the modeler's intuitive judgements, rather than making use of the methods experimental psychology could provide. This can limit the eventual growth of the system. One begins to see hopeful signs that the relationship between model-building and experimentation is growing closer, however. There are now music-theoretic models which are suitable for hypothesis formation and testing through experiment; Rosner & Meyer (1982) and I. Deliège (1987) are examples of this kind of experimental work, based respectively on the work of Meyer and Lerdahl & Jackendoff. A similar trend may be seen in the use of computational models as well (Povel & Essens, 1985; Bharucha, 1987, this volume; Ashley, 1989; Longuet-Higgins & Lisle, 1988), as more modelers begin to take experimental verification into account as a necessary and useful part of their efforts.

Having said this, subjecting the results of modeling to our musical judgments of their successes and failures is not without merit. A musical ear and mind joined together as the intuitive judge of the worth of our systems are quite valuable. Nevertheless, many modeling ventures in music are still in their infancy. Our ears need to guide us in improving our thinking, not to convince us at this early stage of the game that no progress is possible.

What guiding principles might be stated for modeling music listening? From this discussion, a few summarizing points may be drawn:

- Model of music listening should use formalisms appropriate to their goals and subject matter.
- Models of music listening should consider how they fit into a broader framework, including musical structure, internal representation, knowledge a listener brings to the music, learning through listening; and features of the human cognitive architecture.
- Models of music listening should be stated in a precise and coherent fashion; computer models provide a means of assuring precision and coherence.
- Models of music listening should make use of experimentation in both their development and testing phrases, to ensure that essential elements of the model have a sufficient empirical basis.

An example in melodic learning

Can all of these points be addressed in a single model? I have attempted to do so in a computer program which simulates a listener learning a melody by rote. The system, called LM, attempts to capture a range of typical phenomena one sees in people learning melodies, and to use general constraints – relatedness of musical materials, real-time concerns, memory limitations – which will allow for further study of the way in which detailed specifications of the cognitive architecture have implications for music-cognitive processes. Details of implementation are omitted here (see Ashley, 1989); the paper will instead concentrate on the more general design and operation of LM.

Melodic Learning: Human Behavior

Little is found in the literature on music cognition concerning the means by which listeners build their internal representaions of musical compositions. Studies of text comprehension over the last half-century have shown (cf. Bartlett, 1932) that people do not represent stories internally as literal copies of the prose. Rather, they store a higher-level version of the story, and reconstruct the details within this more global representation. In the more recent and music-specific literature, this has been paralleled in Sloboda & Parker (1985), in which listeners were asked to sing back what they could remember of a melody after each of a number of hearings. Thus, a schema framework may be appropriate for modeling how listeners represent melodies internally.

Except for the very best of listeners and the very simplest of melodies, repeated hearings of a melody are often necessary for it to be learned well. An examination of the errors made in learning a melody can, in conjunction with an analysis of the melody's structure, gives clues as to the processes by which the melody is being learned. These errors in may occur for several reasons, such as structure substitution, memory failures, and time-sharing difficulties. Structure substitutions are found when the representation possessed by the learner is related to, but different from, that found in the original music. Memory failures are common in learning melodies. For example, one commonly seen pattern of errors in melodic dictation is that in which the student transcribes the first 7–8 notes accurately, then has little or nothing correct until the very end. These indicate the limitations of short-term memory, as well as primacy and recency effects (where the beginning and ending of a series are better remembered than the rest). Time-sharing difficulties take place when two simultaneous processes are being carried out in such a manner as to interfere with one another. This effect can be seen, for example, when a performance or a transcription interferes with the process of rehearsal which allow the internal representation of the music to be maintained, possibly through competition for short-term memory.

A Melodic Example: Human Protocol

Let us begin by looking at part of a musician's process of learning a melody by rote. The melody, a folk-tune, is shown below in Figure 1. This melody is long enough not to be learned completely in a single hearing, but does not need to be broken up into phrases one at a time to be encoded. There is a noticable degree of parallelism and a clear hierarchic phrase structure of 2+ 2 + 2 + 2, yielding a quickly comprehensible structure. The clarity of the phrase structure in the example would lead one to suppose that it would be readily remembered, at least in general terms of there being two large movements each divided into half, with each fourth of the melody occupying the same time-span, In addition, there are clear harmonic "anchors" in the melody, corresponding to the end of the phrases.

Figure 1 Folk-melody for rote learning.

Figure 2 shows a transcription of a musician's sung reproduction of this melody after hearing it one time and four times respectively. A single comma indicates a breath, and a double comma a longer pause, breaking the rhythm of the performance. In the first reproduction, some of the errors are more easily understood than others. One factor in the substitution of the ending into the first phrase would be the similar harmonic underpinnings (tonic harmony) of Phrases 4 and 1 – a kind of structure substitution. There seems to be a primacy effect stimulating helping to emphasize Phrase 4; taken together, these two could account for placing Phrase 4 into Phrase 1's place. In the later reproduction, the beginning has been corrected but the second phrase's accuracy suffers; this may be due to a kind of deficit of attention caused by focusing overmuch on the first phrase. These kinds of incremental improvements, often accompanied by the introduction of some new errors, are typical of patterns of melodic learning. A model of melodic learning would need to exhibit behaviors like this in order to produce plausible patterns of performance.

Figure 2 Partial human protocol for melodic rote learning.

Melodic Learning: Computer Simulation

LM is implemented in Common Lisp and in KSM, a production system language (Ashley, 1985). LM uses a set of three independent production systems to carry out its actions. One serves to parse an input stream into musical segments; a second serves to focus attention on problem areas; a third is resonsible for reproductions (LM's version of singing the melody). All of the production systems share a common "goalstack", or list of the goals the system is trying to attain, and also a common working memory. Working memory acts as a kind of "blackboard" or central database on which the production systems operate and through which they communicate with one another.

A melody represented in LM's working memory is constructed from schemata stored in long-term memory. These schemata are arranged in memory in a heterarchy, and are indexed by contour, triadic or scalar content, and metric positioning. Together these features are used to determine "similar" or "related" judgements between two schemata. Schemata in this system are not at the level of generality found in most studies. Much of our listening to music – certainly our learning of music and our memory for it – must operate at a level of *concreteness* not seen in the pitch structures discussed in these studies. The schemata seen here are more like what a jazz musician would call "licks" (Perlman & Greenblatt, 1981); they have distinct harmonic, rhythmic, and melodic content which is essential to their nature. LM is biased toward the recalling, usage, and preservation of concrete schemata because it is only at a relatively high level of concreteness that a musical activity such as singbacks can be carried out. If a very specific schema cannot be found, LM moves to whatever level allows a good match to the percept in working memory.

LM is not designed to mimic some specific individual's learning experiences. Although it is possible to get LM to do this through a careful tuning of the system's contents and biases (production systems have the computing power of Turing machines), this is somewhat arbitrary modeling. Rather, LM learns in a manner *outwardly similar* to that seen in people, in that it produces the appropriate classes of errors and learning sequences.

LM proceeds in the following way. On the first hearing of a melody, it parses the incoming perceptual stream (represented as an event-list) into time-spans, or "trajectories", by a production system using rules based on Lerdahl & Jackendoff's Grouping Preference Rules. An attempt is made to either activate an existing schema which matches the material well, or to construct a new one. The time-span is stored as a "chunk" if it is followed by more music, or as an internalized even-list if it is not. The trajectories operate as a network of mutual reinforcement and inhibition; similar materials reinforce each other, whereas differnet materials interfere with each, causing partial forgetting to occur.

Once these trajectories have been constructed and chunked, LM's task is to discover places where the internal representation of the melody is not accurate, and to make such changes as are necessary to improve its accuracy. The following exmaple (Figure 3) gives some indication of how this works. After the first "hearing", LM is able to reproduce the final phrase well. This is for two main reasons: a recency effect, where the fiinal material is not "covered" by other music, and by the reinforcement which it shares with Phrase 2 due to their parallelism. According to the "structural rehearsal" which takes place between phrases as LM learns them, Phrase 4 should be the most easily remembered, followed in order by Phrase 1, Phrase 2, and Phrase 3. In the second hearing, LM has focused on the first phrase as being wrong and needing correction. A reasonable approximation of this phrase is produced, but the attention allocated to it causes other errors to be introduced. This exlains the faulty cadence point still found in measure 4 and the lacking details which differentiate the beginning of Phrase 3 from Phrase 1. In its third hearing, LM gets as close as it will to the original melody. Attention has once again been allocated to Phrase 1, this time due to the desire to check its correctness; the erroneous beginning pitch of the phrase has been corrected as has the cadence, and the third phrase can now be set on its proper ending as well.

Playback 1

Playback 2

Playback 3

Figure 3 LM protocol for melodic rote learning.

This brief example shows LM's basic level of performance. Although the system's performance is not the same as that of the actual human learner, the errors follow a similar pattern and arise from a relatively few considerations, such as strength connections between phrases in short-term memory and limitations of attention. LM is able to learn melodies in a fashion yielding behaviors like that seen in musicians learning melodies by rote and singing them back during the process. I have found the exercise of making the system behave decently very illuminating as to the interacting nature of musical processes and constraints. I have seen very few studies which insist on the level of concreteness in internal representation of music which I find necessary for LM (two notable exceptions being Perlman & Greenblatt, 1981 and Gjerdingen, 1988). I have tried to balance this by embedding these concrete schemata in a more flexible structure, that of the trajectory.

How does LM fare in terms of the principles given before for evaluating models of music listening? It uses a mixture of two formalisms to model melodic learning: schemata for representing melodies, and production systems for representing processing and control elements in the system. Each of these is suitable for its intended purpose, although a PDP model might work as well or better in some regards. LM was explicitly designed to explore the relationships among structural aspects of melodies, allocation of attention, and chunking in working memory, and to see if these elements could be combined to yield human-like behavior in learning melodies. In this regard, it attempts to be true to a number of aspects of cognition simultaneously. Since it is a computer model there is no lack of specificity about it. The development of LM has made use of experimental data from the beginning, but has not included as much evidence from others' studies as it might (or ought). The primary concern was to create a model which would behave reasonably and then refine it incrementally. There are thus *ad hoc* elements in the system which need to be replaced by more empirically founded ones; in particular, the low-level processing elements need to be refined, for example by taking into account the results of studies into rhythmic perception such as in Clarke (1987).

Summary

Many workers in music cognition have a desire to see their work tied more closely to "real-life" situations, dealing with more substantive musical materials and more substantive musical tasks. As we approach these goals, the use of models of cognitive behaviors are of great use, not least in the construction of better theories and hypotheses. There are sufficiently well-understood formalisms for producing such models, and when modeling is combined with experimentation both can benefit. Embodying these models in computer programs has become much simpler with the advent of more affordable systems, and holds out the promise of helping the results of individual studies be integrated with one another in ways not previously possible.

References

Anderson, J.R. (1983) *The Architecture of Cogniton.* Cambridge, Massachusetts: Harvard University Press.

Ashley, R. (1985) KSM: An essay in knowledge representation in music. In *Proceedings of the International Computer Music Conference 1985,* B.Truax (ed.), 383–390, San Francisco: Computer Music Association.

Ashley, R. (1986) A knowledge-based approach to assistance in timbral design. In *Proceedings of the International Computer Music Conference 1986,* P. Berg (ed.), 11–16, San Francisco: Computer Music Association.

Ashley, R. (1987) Listen and learn: On the use of formal models of music cognition. Presented to the Society for Music Theory Annual Meeting, Eastman School of Music, Rochester, New York.

Ashley, R. (1989) A model of melodic learning. Technical Report, Northwestern Computer Music, Northwestern University, Evanston, Illinois.

Balzano, G.J. (1980) The group-theoretic description of twelvefold and microtonal pitch systems. *Computer Music Journal,* **4,** 66–84.

Bartlett, F.C. (1932) *Remembering: A study in experimental and social psychology.* Cambridge: Cambridge University Press.

Bharucha, J.J. (1987) Music cognition and perceptual facilitation: A connectionist framework. *Music Perception,* **5** (1),1–30.

Bharucha, J.J. & Krumhansl, C.L. (1983) The representation of harmonic structure in music: Hierarchies of stability as a function of context. *Cognition* **13,** 63–102.

Clarke, E. (1987) Levels of structure in the organization of musical time. In S. McAdams (ed.) "Music and Psychology: A Mutual Regard", *Contemporary Music Review,* **2** (1), 211–238.

Deliège, I.(1987) Grouping conditions in listening to music: An approach to Lerdahl & Jackendoff's grouping preference rules. *Music Perception,* **4,** 325–359.

Deutsch, D. & Feroe, J.(1981) The internal representation of pitch sequences in tonal music. *Psychological Review,* **88,** 503–522.

Forte, A. (1974) *The Structure of Atonal Music.* New Haven: Yale University Press.

Gjerdingen, R.O. (1986) the formation and deformation of Classic/Romantic phrase schemata. *Music Theory Spectrum,* **8,** 25–43.

Gjerdingen, R.O. (1988) *A Classic Turn of Phrase: Music and the Psychology of Convention.* Philadelphia: University of Pennsylvania Press.

Hasty, C.F. (1981) Segmentation and process in post-tonal music. *Music Theory Spectrum,* **3,** 54–73.

Hasty, C.F. (1986) On the problem of succession and continuity in twentieth-century music. *Music Theory Spectrum,* **8,** 58–74.

Holland, S. (1987) New cognitive theories of harmony applied to direct manipulation tools for novices. In *Proceedings of the International Computer Conference 1987,* J. Beauchamp (ed.), 182–189, San Francisco: Computer Music Association.

Johnson-Laird, P.N. (1988) *The Computer and the Mind: An Introduction to Cognitive Science.* Cambridge, Massachusetts: Harvard University Press.

Kosslyn, S.M. (1980) *Image and Mind.* Cambridge, Massachusetts: Harvard University Press.

Krumhansl, C.L. Castellano, M.A. (1983) Dynamic processing in music perception. *Memory and Cognition*, **11**, 325–333.

Krumhansl, C.L. (1979) The representation of musical pitch in a tonal context. *Cognitive Psychology*, **11**, 346–374.

Kunst, J.(1978) *Making Sense in Music: An Enquiry into the Formal Pragmatics of Art*. Ghent: Communication and Cognition.

Laske, O. (1977) *Music, Memory and Thought*. Ann Arbor: UMI Press.

Laske, O. (1980) Toward an explicit cognitive theory of music listening. *Computer Music Journal*, **4** (2), 73–83.

Leman, M. (1985) Dynamic-Hierarchical networks as perceptual memory representations of music. *Interface*, **15**, 125–164.

Lerdahl, F. & Jackendoff, R. (1983) *A Generative Theory of Tonal Music*. Cambridge, Massachusetts: MIT Press.

Lischka, C. (1987) Connectionist models of musical thinking. In *Proceedings of the International Computer Musical Conference 1987*, J. Beacuchamp (ed.), 190–196, San Francisco: Computer Music Association.

Longuet-Higgins, H.C. (1976) Perception of melodies. *Nature*, **263**, 646–53.

Longuet-Higgins, H.C. & Lisle, E.R. (1988) Modeling musical cognition. Unpublished paper.

McAdams, S., Gladkoff, S., and Keller, J.P. (1984) AISE: A prototype laboratory for musical research and the development of conceptual tools. *Proceedings of the International Computer Music Conference 1984, Paris*, D. Wessel (ed.), 143–162, San Francisco: Computer Music Association.

Meyer, L.B. (1956) *Emotion and Meaning in Music*. Chicago: University of Chicago Press.

Meyer, L.B. (1973) *Explaining Music: Essays and Explorations*. Berkeley: University of California Press.

Miller, G. (1956) The magical number seven, plus or minus two. *Psychological Review*, **63**, 81–97.

Minsky, M. (1975) A framework for representing knowledge. In *The Psychology of Computer Vision*, P.H. Winston (ed.), 211–277, New York: McGraw-Hill.

Narmour, E. (1977) *Beyond Schenkerism*. Chicago: University of Chicago Press.

Nattiez, J.J. (1976) *Fondements d'une semiologie de la musique*. Paris: Union générale d'editions.

Newell, A. (1973) Production systems: Models of control structure. In *Visual Information Processing*, W. Chase (ed.), 463–526, New York: Academic Press.

Newell, A. & Simon, H., (1972) *Human Problem Solving*. Englewood Cliffs: Prentice-Hall.

Perlman, A.M. & Greenblatt, D. (1981) Miles Davis meets Noam Chomsky: Some observations on jazz improvisation and language structure. In *The Sign in Music and Literature*, W. Steiner (ed.), 169–183, Austin, Texas: University of Texas Press.

Pollard-Gott, L. (1983) Emergence of thematic concepts in repeated listenings to music. *Cognitive Psychology*, **15**, 69–94.

Polson, P.G., Miller, J.R., & Kintsch, W.(1984) Methods and tactics reconsidered. In *Method and Tactics in Cognitive Science*, W. Kintsch, J.R. Miller and P.G. Polson (eds), 277–296, Hillsdale: Lawrence Erlbaum.

Povel, D.J. & Essens, P. (1985) Perception of temporal patterns. *Music Perception* 3(1),411–440.

Risset, J.C., & Wessel, D.L. (1982) Exploration of timbre by analysis and synthesis.In *The Psychology of Music*, D. Deutsch (ed.), 25–58, New York: Academic Press.

Rosch, E., & Mervis, C.B. (1975) Family resemblances: Studies inthe internal structure of categories. *Cognitive Psychology*, **7**, 573–605.

Rosner, B.S., & Meyer, L.B. (1982) Melodic processes and the perception of music.In *The Psychology of Music*, D. Deutsch (ed.), 317–314, New York: Academic Press.

Rumelhart, D.E. (1980) Schemata: The building blocks of cognition. In *Theoretical Issues in Reading Comprehension*. R. Spiro, B. Bruce, & W. Brewer (eds), 33–58, Hillsdale: Lawrence Erlbaum.

Rumelhart, D.E., Smolensky, P., McClelland, J.L. & Hinton, G.E. (1986). Schemata and sequential thought processes in PDP models. In *Parallel Distributed Processing: Explorations in the Microstructure of Cognition, vol. 2*. J.L. McClelland & D.E. Rumelhart (eds), 7–57, Cambridge, Massachusetts: MIT Press.

Shepard, R. (1982) Structural representations of musical pitch. In D. Deutsch (ed.), *The Psychology of Music*, 343–390, New York: Academic Press.

Sloboda, J. (1985) *The Musical Mind: The Cognitive Psychology of Music*. Oxford: Oxford University Press.

Sloboda, J. & Parker, D. (1985) Immediate recall of melodies. In *Musical Structure and Cognition*, P. Howell, I. Cross, & R. West (eds), 143–167, London: Academic Press.

Steedman, M. (1984) A generative grammar for jazz chord sequences. *Music Perception*, **2** (1).

Sundberg, J. & Lindblom, B. (1976) Generative theories in language and music descriptions. *Cognition*, **4**, 99–122.

Todd, N.P. (1985) A model of expressing timing in tonal music. *Music Perception,* **3** (1), 33–58.

VanLehn, K., Brown, J.S., & Greeno, J. (1984) Competitive argumentation in computational theories of cognitiion. In *Method and Tactics in Cognitive Science,* W. Kintsch, J.R. Miller, and P.G. Olson (eds), 235–262, Hillsdale: Lawrence Erlbaum.

Wessel, D.L. (1979) Timbre space as a musical control structure. *Computer Music Journal,* **3** (2), 45–52.

West, R., Howell, P., & Cross, I. (1985) Modelling perceived musical structure. In *Musical Structure and Cognition,* P. Howell, I. Cross, & R. West (eds), 21–52, London: Academic Press.

Contemporary Music Review,
1989, Vol. 4, pp. 311–325
Photocopying permitted by license only

A computational approach to modeling musical grouping structure

Michael Baker

*Institute of Educational Technology, Centre for Information Technology in Education,
The Open University, Milton Keynes MK7 6AA, Great Britain.*

A prototype cognitive model for the processing of musical grouping structures from discrete pitches is described, focusing on the level of the *phrase* for *tonal melodies.* The AGA system ("Automated Grouping Analysis") based on this model, has been implemented as a rapid prototype in Common Lisp on an Apollo Domain AI workstation. AGA exploits two ways in which the grouping and time-span reduction components of Lerdahl & Jackendoff's (1983) theory interrelate, in terms of the *normal forms* of time-span reduction and the *parallelism* exhibited at deep reductional levels. Normal forms are implemented as the highest level rules of a grammar of chord function, to identify phrase level boundaries, which are evaluated in terms of parallelism displayed by reductions based on well formed parse-trees according to the grammar. We conclude that processing of grouping at this level is an activity which requires a great deal of knowledge of the specific genre concerned in the form of *processing heuristics,* and that the listener's prior expectations could be understood within the framework of *schema theory.*

KEY WORDS: Artificial intelligence, cognitive modeling, harmonic grammars, music cognition, musical grouping structure, musical reductions.

Introduction

This research aims to produce a cognitive model of how listeners segment the "musical surface" of tonal melodies into grouping structures. The model is based on a reformation of the Grouping Structure and Time-span Reduction components of Lerdahl & Jackendoff's *A Generative Theory of Tonal Music* (1983), and the resulting prototype formal model is embodied in a set of computer programs written in Common Lisp (Steele,1984) running on an Apollo Domain AI workstation. We shall describe a *rapid prototype* of the Automated Grouping Analysis system (AGA) which analyzes grouping structures for tonal melodies at the level of the phrase.

Before summarizing the theoretical basis of the model, it is important to be clear about its nature and purpose, and the kinds of claims which could be made concerning the cognitive validity of computational models. Cohen (1983) makes a distinction between artificial intelligence (AI) programs and computer simulations. The primary aim of AI systems is to get a computer to perform some task commonly done by humans – such as text translation – where the criterion of success is the extent to which the program actually *works,* without necessarily making any claims that it does so in a manner which simulates how humans do that task. An initial definition of computer simulation might be that it aims to instantiate and test a theory of human cognition. However, this is an inadequate description of actual research methodology in cognitive science, since, as Cohen (1983) points out

> . . . the main barrier to successful computer simulation is our ignorance of many aspects of human performance. We cannot simulate processes which we cannot describe.   (p. 220)

Since we presently have little knowledge of precise psychological mechanisms involved in musical grouping perception, one appropriate methodology for producing new theories is to develop a series of *rapid prototype* computer simulations, based on existing theory, and attempt to successively refine these to incorporate known psychological constraints and evidence, where these become available. The first prototype simulation is therefore based on the existing body of theory which has been developed by Lerdahl & Jackendoff (1983). In practice, the AI/cognitive simulation distinction is often (fruitfully) blurred:

> . . . an AI system may reflect psychological theories when these happen to suggest a feasible way to do the job. AI may also yield psychological insights in the course of developing and refining a system.
> (Cohen, 1983, p. 194).

There are other advantages to using computer simulation as a means of developing theories. Theorists are often unaware of the extent to which they have not completely formalized musical intuition, so adopting a methodological criterion of "implementability" could enable us to develop fully formal theories of music cognition. In summary, therefore, the prototype implementation which we describe here should be understood in terms of the methodology of AI computational models and cognitive simulations. *We are not claiming that this first prototype is psychologically valid*, but rather that it represents a stage in the development of such a theory, in terms of a methodology of successive iterations of simulation, empirical testing, and refinement. Accordingly, after describing each component of the model, we shall attempt to suggest ways in which the prototype could be modified to more effectively model human cognition. We shall not describe such modifications in detail here (see Baker, 1989).

The system starts from a sequence of discrete pitches represented symbolically in Lisp, and so is probably best understood as modeling processes at the level of what McAdams (1987) terms "the extraction of the musical lexicon", at a level of abstraction above Lerdahl & Jackendoff's (1983) view of the "musical surface" as "the physical signal of a piece when it is played." Our approach exploits two relationships between the time span reduction component and the grouping structure component of Lerdahl & Jackendoff's (1983) theory. The first relationship concerns the *normal forms* of time-span reduction and grouping structure at the level of the phrase. The second concerns the parallelism exhibited at deep levels in time-span reduction. Time-span reductions are implemented using a context-free general rewrite grammar of harmonic function, which provides both a means of generating well-formed parse trees according to the grammar, and a method for actually performing reductions. Once a set of reductional levels has been generated for each parse tree, the degree to which successive levels exhibit similarity of parallelism between phrase groups is used as a criterion for preferring one well-formed parse tree (with attendant phrase-level boundaries) over another.

An approach to analyzing grouping structures

Criticisms of the work by Lerdahl & Jackendoff from the perspectives of psychology and music theory are now well documented in the literature (Peel & Slawson, 1984; Clarke, 1986). Possibly the most serious problem facing the grouping component of their theory concerns the notion of "parallelism" (Lerdahl & Jackendoff, 1983, p. 52 ff). As Lerdahl & Jackendoff themselves state, the problem is not only to formalize what parallelism *is* (how similar must two passages be before they are construed as parallel?), but of how to compare parallelism with anything else. The problem is an instance of a more general problem with the theory, of formalizing how global features interact with local surface detail. Although we recognize Lerdahl & Jackendoff's important theoretical advance in identifying grouping structure as an analytically separable component, we maintain that *any approach to grouping analysis must concentrate on the problem of how grouping interacts with other musical factors.*

AGA exploits *one* of these interrelationships, being the relationship between *grouping structure, parallelism* and *time-span reductions.* The relationship obtains in two main ways: (1) between grouping at the phrase level and the "normal forms" of time-span reduction: (2) between grouping at the phrase level and the deep linear parallelism between antecedent and consequent phrases at successive levels in time-span reductions. Relationship (1) is depicted in Figure 1, showing the normal form for the so-called interrupted forms, which identifies a kind of template or schema to which time-span reductions must conform (Lerdahl & Jackendoff refer to it as a "background" structure, or "skeleton"; 1983 p.139ff).

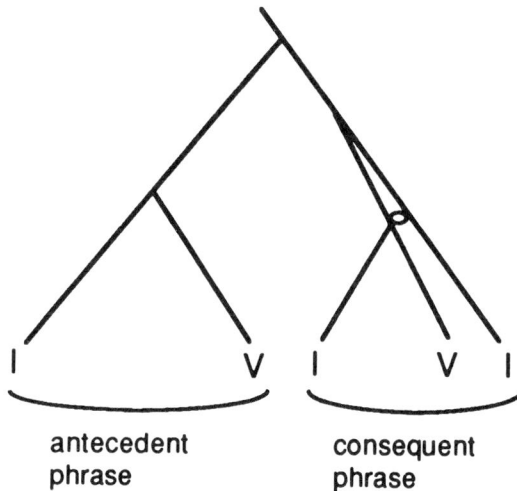

antecedent   consequent
phrase   phrase

Figure 1 The "normal form" for the interrupted form.

Since time-span reductions for a piece must conform to a normal form for that piece, an acceptable time-span reduction will depend on the normal form being based on a correct identification of phrase boundaries. Once a set of grammatically well-formed time-span reduction trees has been generated, each of which embodies hypothesized phrase boundaries, we can use relationship (2) to constrain the space of possible parse trees to those which accord with musical intuition. Figure 2 shows an example of deep reductional parallelism exhibited by the J.S. Bach chorale "O Haupt voll Blut und Wunden" (St. Matthew Passion), according to the Lerdahl & Jackendoff time-span reduction (1983, p. 144).

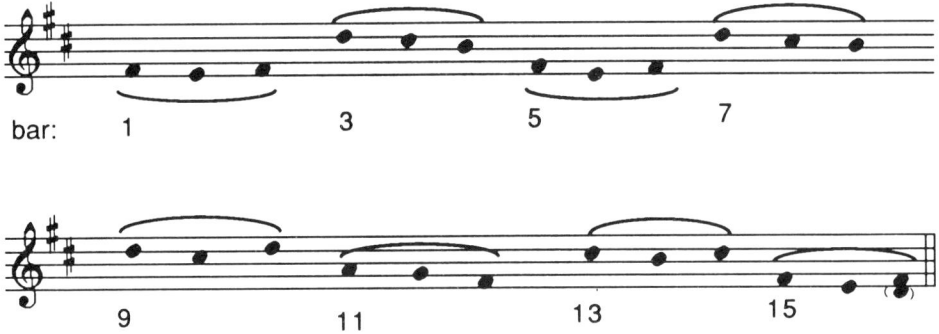

Figure 2 A section of the time-span reduction from the chorale "O Haupt voll Blut und Wunden" (J.S. Bach, St. Matthew Passion).

Our underlying hypothesis is that

for certain well defined musical subcultures, phrase level groups identified by parsing according to the most appropriate normal form, will exhibit a greater degree of parallelism at some reductional level than any other phrase level groups which are grammatically well formed.

"Greater degree" of parallelism is defined in the next section, and the term "musical subculture" is used in the sense understood by Steedman (1984), to be a subset of tonal pieces which can be characterized by a formal context-free grammar.

The normal form of Figure 1 is notationally equivalent to the rewrite rules

$$s \rightarrow L\ R$$
$$L \rightarrow I\ V$$
$$R \rightarrow I\ V\ I$$

where **s** is the melody, **L** is what we term an "antecedent phrase", **R** is a "consequent phrase" and **I** and **V** are chord function symbols with their usual theoretical meaning. It is possible to abstract from Lerdahl & Jackendoff's time-span reduction theory (in combination with conventional music theory) a more extended grammar which encapsulates chord function: **ii** → **vi ii**, **vi** → **iii vi**, **V** → **ii V**, are examples of rules which in effect extend a left-branching cadence backwards. **I** → **I V**, **I** → **I IV**, are examples where a "structural beginning"

(Lerdahl & Jackendoff) is extended forwards. Any number of "trivial" substitution rules are possible, according to the subculture being modeled, for example I → vi, V → V7, V → vii7, and so on. Finally, the modeling of different musical forms requires different normal forms, or different combinations of normal forms as the highest level rule of the grammar.

The remainder of this paper describes the prototype implementation of AGA.

The Automated Grouping Analysis system

AGA can be divided into four main phrases: lexical analysis (harmonization), parsing, reductions and pattern matching under limited transformations. The melody, its meter and a chord lexicon are input to the "lexical analyser", which returns a set of chord functions assigned to each metric unit, from the bar level down to each beat. This is taken as input to a *chart parser*, together with the harmonic grammar appropriate to that melody, which returns a set of possible parse trees for the melody. Each parse tree (together with the chord lexicon) provides the basis for time-span reductions, each of which are evaluated for maximal parallelism displayed at each level. Finally, a simple algorithm is used to assess the degree of parallelism displayed, to sort the small number of possible boundary-sets into order of preference. The final outcome is a small ordered list of possible phrase-level boundary-sets for the given melody.

From the Musical Surface to the Musical Lexicon

The "lexical analysis" program generates a set of lexical items (chord functions) for metric units in the input melody. Melodies can be input via MIDI ("Musical Instrument Digital Interface"), "captured" within the Common Lisp environment,
and converted to a simple list representation where a pitch event is a list of the form.

(<pitch-number n1><start-time n1><velocity n1><duration n1>)

Duration is measured in units of the shortest note duration, and start-times are expressed as the sum of durations. Pitches are represented as numbers of semitones above or below a defined tonic (= 0) for the melody. A melody is simply a list of these pitch-event lists, being a representation which facilitates the use of elegant and efficient recursive list processing algorithms. Since harmonic units are defined by metric rather than grouping division, the program needs information as to how the list of notes should be divided into bars and beats, including the position of the first bar. In addition, it needs a "chord lexicon", being simply a list which pairs chord functions with the notes which can match that function. For example, the first element of the list

(I.(0 4 7) ii.(2 5 9) ii7.(0 2 5 9) . . . .)

states that where 0 is defined as the tonic, chord I matches with any group of pitches which are identical to, or the octave equivalents of, that tonic, and the tones, four and seven semitone above if, respectively. All of these kinds of information are stored in a special data structure (an "object") which is created for that melody.

Lexical analysis can be divided into two main phases: (1) isolating metric units in the melody and (2) returning the possible harmonizations for metric units, according to the chord lexicon. At the most general level, the program attempts to return a harmonization for each bar of the melody, and within each bar for the half-bars and each beat (depending upon the meter of the melody). In this respect the harmonization process differs from existing work in this field, since we cannot make assumptions that the piece will display a particular harmonic rhythm (Taft-Thomas, 1985), nor do we possess an existing harmonization, to which we need to assign a harmonic analysis (Winograd,1968). Since metric and grouping boundaries are distinct, we cannot assume that the phrase boundary will coincide with the bar or half-bar lines.

For each metric unit, the "harmonize" is called from a series of *melodic viewpoints*. Melodic viewpoints correspond to the possible kinds of melodic figuration for that melody, and are implemented as functions which aim to isolate the pitches in a metric group which should be treated as harmonic tones, i.e., those deriving from the chord of the current key. Once isolated, the harmonic tones (when compressed to equivalents within a single octave) are simply matched with the chord lexicon. The harmonization for a metric unit is the combination of matched chord functions, under each applicable melodic viewpoint. At present, melodic viewpoints implemented are "onbeat notes", "onbeat-passing tones", "arpeggio", "upper-auxiliary", "lower-auxiliary" and "changing-notes". In effect, they correspond to possible harmonic reductions for that section of the melody. For example, the "onbeat-notes" function considers the possible melodic figuration that the harmony notes are those on the beat, and so simply returns these notes to be matched with the chord lexicon. The "arpeggio" viewpoint attempts to treat all of the notes as belonging to the same chord: if it succeeds, then no further viewpoints are considered for that unit, nor for the metric units into which it could be divided. (The melodic section is already "reduced" to tones which can all be viewed as part of the same chord, this being the goal of alternative melodic viewpoints.)

It is clear that music is so potentially "lexically ambiguous" in comparison with natural languages, that a great deal of constraining knowledge, or heuristic guidance, is required to limit this ambiguity. In formal terms, our model shows that the problem of inferring harmony implicit in a group of pitches, in a purely "bottom-up" manner, is a *combinatorially unconstrained* problem. Our notion of melodic viewpoints is designed to capture the set of possible melodic figurations for groups of melodies, from which we can attempt to infer harmonic tones, but for any set of pitches considered devoid of musical context it is clear that any number of – or even all – viewpoints could be assigned, which gives us very little theoretical leverage. Take, for example, the first three notes of the second bar of Figure 3, and consider possible harmonizations using a single chord, where (at least) the following melodic viewpoints apply:

> *onbeat tones*: select tones on the beat as harmonic tones
> *passing notes*: for any three consecutive three tones move in an ascending or descending diatonic scale, select the first and third as harmonic tones.

With the first viewpoint, the single B natural as the harmonic tone would return possible harmonizations **iii,V** and **vii**, given a suitable chord vocabulary. For the second viewpoint we have a B natural and a D natural to harmonize, which is harmonized as chord **V** or **vii**, so the total possible harmonizations are **iii, V** and **vii**. Add to this the fact that many genres would require a much richer harmonic vocabulary, and that harmonic rhythm could vary from piece to piece, and we see that considered "bottom up", tonal music possesses a very high degree of indeterminacy at the level of individual harmonies (in comparison to lexical categories which could be assigned to isolated words, for example). The fact that listeners simply could not – in information processing terms – unconsciously infer harmony with this degree of indeterminacy reveals the extent to which listeners must be guided by *top-down* expectations concerning likely "grammatical" continuations from one chord to the next, and by knowledge of harmonic rhythm and vocabulary. A simple method of adjusting the model to incorporate the listener's use of top-down knowledge would be to integrate the harmonization and parsing processes, to make top-down predictions for chords to continue a sequence (Baker, 1989), and to incorporate genre-specific knowledge in the form of *heuristics*. Using such heuristic knowledge simply means that search is constrained by knowledge of the genre concerned, which a listener might be expected to have acquired. Specifically, the program needs knowledge of the following kinds: (a) of which chords should be allowed in the lexicon; (b) of harmonic rhythm (it is only at the drive to a final cadence, for example, that the harmonic rhythm usually extends down to the beat level); (c) of which kinds of melodic figuration occur in that subculture. Finding such a set of heuristics which adequately constrain a particular "musical subculture" is itself a non-trivial problem, especially since heuristic knowledge of harmonic rhythm may vary from piece to piece, and within particular pieces.

The Parsing Process

A *chart parser* is used to build possible parse trees from the lexical items according to the grammar. We briefly describe the parsing process not because such parsers are not well known (Winograd, 1983, p. 116), but in order to describe our specific approach to using this method.

Prior to parsing, the output of the lexical analyzer (chords assigned to metric units) is initialized into a "chart" data-structure. The chart consists of *edges*, spanning *vertices*, which for our purposes can be thought of as the time-spans which chord functions apply to, and the points between the edges, respectively. For example, in Figure 3 an "edge" would be stored for each of chord **i**, chord **IV** and chord **vi**, assigned to the first beat. These edges would be recorded as "outgoing" edges to the first vertex (v0) and incoming edges to the second vertex (v1).

During the course of the parse, new edges are built by continuing existing edges according to the rules in the grammar, and are stored in the chart as incoming or outgoing edges to a vertex. For example, in Figure 3, if we have an edge from v0 to v1 with label **I**, and an edge from v1 to v2, with label **IV**, then from a rule **I → I IV**, matching with the right-hand-side enables us to build a new edge from v0 to v2, with its label as the left-hand-side of the rule, i.e. **I**, which would be placed on the chart (providing such an edge was not already present, which it is in this example). The parser terminates, for our purposes, when there are no further edges which could be continued, and returns all the edges which span the whole chart.

In order to use information residing in the chart for the reductional process,

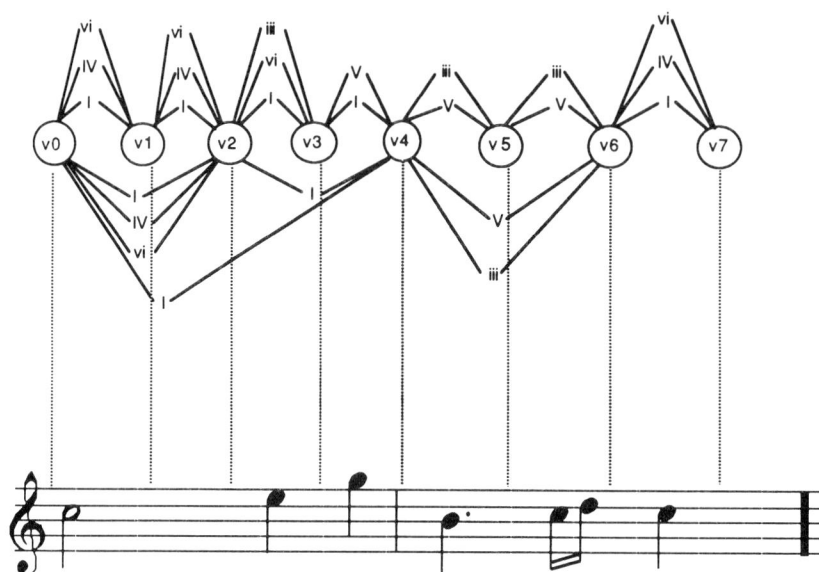

Figure 3 Chord functions derived from the first two bars of Mozart piano sonata in C, K545, in the chart data-structure.

each new edge needs to record its "children" i.e. the edges from which it is built. In order to retrieve the full parse tree you simply have to recursively look for the children of an edge in the chart, terminating with edges which have no children.

The main reason for using a chart parser here is that it provides a completely flexible data-structure with which to conduct the parsing process in a manner which best models human processing. The main possibilities are to parse bottom-up, or top-down, and either left-to-right or some complex combination of these methods (see Elsom-Cook & du Boulay, 1986). At present, AGA uses a combination of bottom-up and top-down methods (a "left corner parse"), which is arguably the most psychologically plausible mechanism for natural language processing (Johnson-Laird, 1983, p.355). Formal properties of the grammar (as it stands) which we use would preclude a purely top-down approach in any case. For any top-down parser, a grammar which is left-recursive will loop indefinitely, since the first element of the right-hand-side will be continually proposed for extension at the same vertex. Left-recursive rules have the form $x \rightarrow x\ y$ (for example, our rule $I \rightarrow I\ V$). Parsing backwards will not avoid this in our grammar, since we also have right-recursive rules, such as $V \rightarrow ii\ V$. Top-down parsers *can* be used with such a grammar, but only if it is rewritten to a *weakly equivalent* form prior to parsing (Winograd, 1983, p.112), where for example, the rules $A \rightarrow I\ V$, and $I \rightarrow V$ would be replaced in the grammar by $A \rightarrow I\ x\ V$ and $x \rightarrow V$. The two grammars are weakly equivalent in that they will recognize the same set of strings in the language, but will assign different parse trees. We have not adopted this approach since the insertion of such symbols is clearly psychologically arbitrary, and would greatly complicate the reductional procedure based upon such parse trees.

The parsing process makes extremely high information processing and storage demands, since many edges will be created, stored and used to continue other edges, which do not ultimately lead to a parse for the full melody. It seems unlikely that human information processing would be so inefficient and still be able to parse serially input pitches in real-time, given limitations on working memory. The parsing process can be viewed as a *search* through the space of well-formed substrings in the chart with a set of *heuristics* to guide that search. One source of heuristic rules – there may well be others – can be found in the Lerdahl & Jackendoff grouping preference rules. We have implemented four of these rules (GPR2a, GPR2b, GPR3d) as functions which return a set of positions in the melody where each rule is instantiated. It seems to be generally true that although there are many redundant boundaries, nevertheless, the musically acceptable phrase boundaries are contained within the total set predicted. Accordingly, we can apply these rules as a rather weak set of heuristics, by *not* building a new edge where its starting and end vertices predict a possible phrase boundary which is not a member of the set predicted by the grouping preference rules. Heuristic search methods for solving problems are characterized by the fact that they are not *guaranteed* to find a correct solution. However, Ebcioglu (1986) has shown convincingly, that the specification of a detailed set of appropriate heuristics can be an effective method for modeling a specific musical style. Our use of grouping preference rules as a set of *informal heuristics* significantly differs from their role in Lerdahl & Jackendoff's (1983) theoretical system. In our model the theoretical role of grouping preference rules is as a set of "clues" or "indices" (I. Deliege, 1987, this volume) present on the musical surface, which guide harmonic parsing. Finally, it must again be stressed that our model is strictly an idealisation which assumes complete and exhaustive perception of possible harmonizations. Clearly, our perception of harmony is much more fragmentary, and there will be many interpersonal differences in the extent to which harmonies and their relationships are perceived.

The Reductional Process

The reductional procedure is based on the parse trees which can be extracted from the chart data structure, and on a number of the Lerdahl & Jackendoff principles for performing time-span reductions. We assume that our grammar has correctly encapsulated the way in which the notes within the time-span of one harmony relate to an adjacent time-span, since the grammar specifies how the chords *function*. For example, if the adjacent harmonies I and V have the chord I as a parent, then according to the rule I → I V, the notes which originally fell under the compass of chord I will be retained in the reduction in favor of those covered by chord V, since the rule expresses the fact that I "dominates" V in this context. Where both siblings in a tree match the parent chord – such as in the rule I → I I – then the context of the subtree in either an antecedent or consequent group is used to ascertain the "dominance" relation in antecedent groups, the left-hand sibling dominates, and the converse is true with consequent groups. The resulting reductions are primarily harmonic in nature – they reveal a kind of "harmonic skeleton" for the melody. Most reductional procedures seem to be a combination of the top-down approach of looking for larger-scale recurring linear patterns with a bottom-up reducing away of "inessential" notes. Our reductional algorithm takes this into account by exploiting the fact that the parsing process has already identified the larger-scale top-down divisions in the melody. The reductional algorithm therefore combines the exploitation of hierarchical harmonic relationships expressed by the parse trees with a bottom-up reduction of non-harmonic tones, and tones which are less "harmonically stable", using a number of simple criteria specified by Lerdahl & Jackendoff (1983, p. 161 ff). Figure 4 summarizes the reductional process.

```
function:     reduce
·nputs:       melody      - the melody
              tree        - the parse tree for the melody, derived from the chart
              lexicon     - an association list of chord functions with lists of notes
              normal-form      - the highest level rule for the grammar

ilgorithm :
    level-0  ← list of pairs: (<group of notes><terminal chord symbol>)
    level-1  ← remove-non-harmonic-tones   level-0
    level-2  ← collapse-repeated-tones   level-1
    level-3  ← remove-unstable-tones   level-2

    successive-levels  ←
        do
            for each sibling pair in level-3,
            retain the single tone whose chord symbol matches its parent

            create a new level; set its value to the new 'generation' of ρarent symbols
        terminate
            when the remaining chord symbols match the right-hand-side
            of normal-form
    return   (level-0 level-1 level-2 level-3 successive-levels)
    end.
```

Figure 4 A simplified algorithm for performing reductions.

   Levels 1 to 3 aim to reduce the melody to a single tone within the scope of each chord function. A simple criterion of "stability" is used to reduce harmony notes with respect to each other – after non-harmonic and repeated tones have been removed – where less stable tones are those further up in the stack of thirds above a root, and so on. For successive levels, the parse tree not only specifies which tones should be reduced, but more importantly, it specifies which tones are to be compared with each other. Working bottom-up, the "reduce" function generates a new level from the parent nodes to the previous level, until only the symbols of the normal form remain. Figure 5 gives a simple example of how such an algorithm performs a reduction. We deliberately choose an example which has been much analyzed by other theorists (Schenker, 1935/1979, Figure g. 72/3; Meyer, 1973, p. 26 ff; Lerdahl & Jackendoff, 1983, pp. 172–173) for purposes of comparison. Note that there are other well-formed parse trees for this set of symbols, which would generate different analyses. It is our hypothesis that the

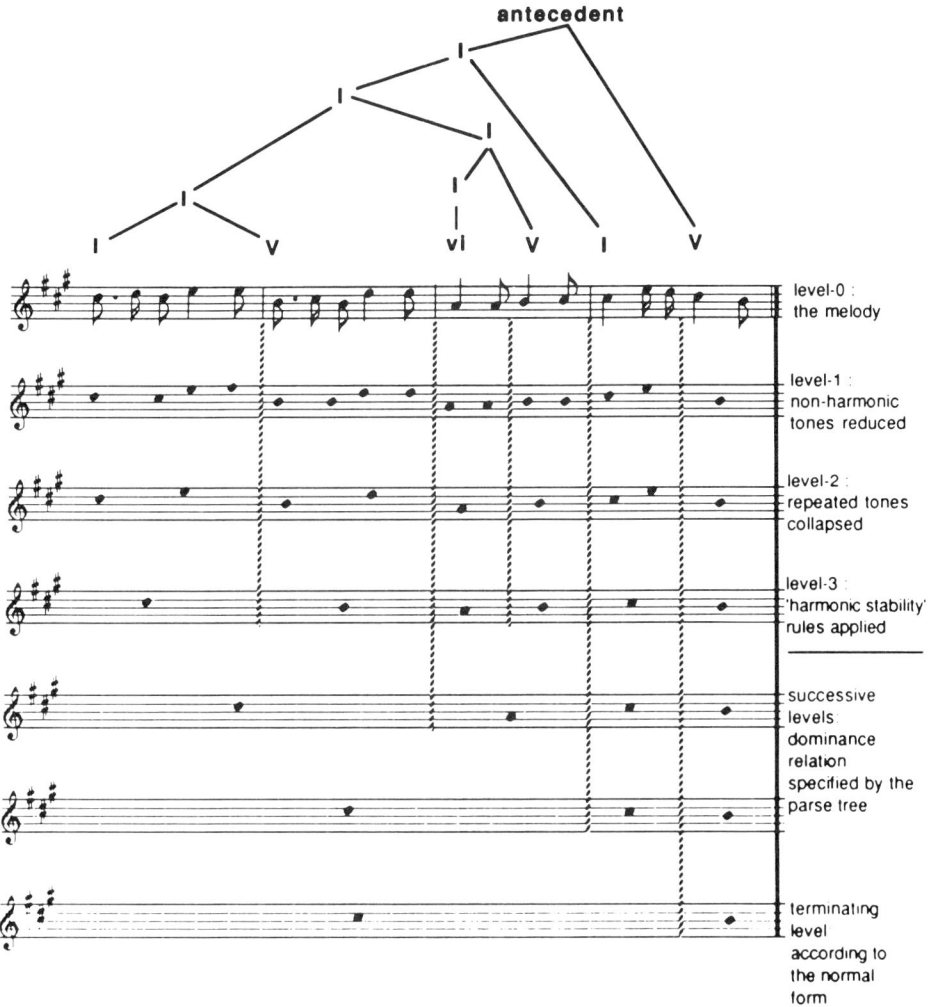

Figure 5 An example reduction of the first phrase of Mozart piano sonata in A, K331.

parse tree which displays the greatest "stability" in terms of deep reductional parallelism will be the musically preferred analysis, and that this indeterminacy between possible analyses can do justice to cases where grouping perception is genuinely ambiguous.

The reductional process just described is viewed as the early stages in the description of a formal theory of how reductions can be performed. As such it makes many simplifications, in comparison with the richness of Lerdahl & Jackendoff's theory of time-span reductions. These simplifications were made for methodological reasons, assuming that the best way to do justice to the full complexity of musical reductions is to specify initially clear and simple algorithms, which can then be successively refined. To our knowledge, no other methods exist which can form the basis of a computational algorithm for reductions. As Ebcioglu puts it, ". . . a formal hierarchical theory of harmony along the lines of Schenker . . . is to present knowledge an as yet unachieved research goal" (Ebcioglu, 1986, p. 192).

At present the model is relatively crude in a number of respects which we state but do not discuss: (a) it uses a simplistic criterion of stability of one note with respect to another; (b) it needs to use a degree of "lookahead", for linear parallelism in selecting the single tone to represent a time-span;(c) (related to a and b), the reductions are primarily harmonic, and take little acount of melodic and rhythmic factors. We believe that a *research program* which addressed these and other shortcomings could form the basis of a formal approach to musical reductions. We would not claim that listeners are able to perceive all such levels of reduction in a melody, but simply that our very perception of harmony implies perception of reductions in some sense.

Deep Reductional Parallelism

Once a set of reductional levels has been generated for each of the well-formed parses, pattern-matching techniques are used to search for recurring patterns in harmony and pitch contour at each level. Earlier attempts at using pattern matching techniques (Simon & Sumner, 1968) had failed to pick out musically relevant patterns from the combinatorial debris of patterns which occur in any melody. Our method has the advantages that the parsing process constrains the search for patterns to those which occur between possible well-formed phrase-level groups, and that at reductional levels, "inessential" notes have been removed to make the patterns which occur much simpler. At present we use a simple set of criteria for preferring one of the well-formed phrase-level boundaries over another: the parse tree is preferred which displays the greatest extent of matching at the highest reductional level, since this corresponds to a match which is in a sense more "obvious". If no such match is found for any of the sets of levels, the system repeats the matching process under successive "limited transformations" until such a decision is reached. A "limited transformation" is an operation on the pitch-set such as simple transposition or inversion. This forms the weakest part of the model, and an area which requires much further work. Questions which remain to be answered include (a) how can we achieve an ordering of the relative "distance" of transformations – is a motif which is inverted thereby perceptibly altered greater than if the motif is transposed? (b) which transformations would apply to any given piece, in order to avoid exhaustive search for the most appropriate?, and (c) how can we avoid a combinatorial explosion in cases where one section relates to another via the application of multiple transformations? The attempts to answer such questions would constitute a research program which attempted to fully formalize Lerdahl & Jackendoff's notion that for a certain class of tonal pieces, analytically separable components (grouping, meter, time-span and prolongational reductions) coexist in a relationship of *mutual stability* (Lerdahl & Jackendoff, 1983, p. 52). Our attempt to use deep reductional parallelism to constrain the space of "grammatical" phrase level grouping structures therefore rests on the presumption that this elusive notion of stability can be so defined.

Despite the relative simplicity of the methods used here at present, they are nevertheless sufficient to model musical parallelism in a reasonably large number of tonal melodies, and we believe that the precise specification of the kinds of transformations required may be a matter which is specific to the "musical subculture" being modeled. A number of analyses have shown that where a melody *is* of the kind which exhibits parallelism between well-formed phrase groups, then the parse tree which exhibits quite clear deep reductional parallelism is the one which would be preferred by musical intuition.

Grouping at the Sub-phrase Level

This research in modeling grouping at the phrase level suggests that the global factors of "tonal motion" and parallelism take precedence over grouping preference rules which operate on the musical surface. We would argue that once phrase level boundaries have been determined using the method embodied in AGA, it is feasible to process grouping structures at smaller levels. Although we have not extended our model so far to cope with these sub-phrase grouping structures, we believe that AGA could be extended using a combination of Lerdahl & Jackendoff's well-formedness and grouping preference rules, with sophisticated pattern matching techniques which search for perceptually significant "clues" on the musical surface (I. Deliege, 1987).

Conclusions and further work

AI cognitive modeling techniques typically proceed through several iterations of a cycle which involves constructing prototype models which simulate some cognitive activity, then refining the model in the light of empirical evidence. AGA has yet to pass through a complete cycle, so we shall try to state what the model suggests about human information processing in musical grouping perception and suggest ways in which future versions could be refined.

The overall model of human information processing which is suggested is one where bottom-up unconscious inference of well-formed harmonic progressions leading to segmentation at the phrase-level is guided by a *great deal* of top-down knowledge of the specific musical style concerned. In the previous section we discussed the way in which heuristic knowledge is required on a number of levels of processing. At the level of building the "harmonic lexicon", knowledge is required of the allowable chord vocabulary, harmonic rhythm, and melodic figuration. As lexical items are combined into well-formed progressions, clues on the musical surface give heuristic guidance to constrain a combinatorial explosion of possibilities: and, finally, the search for musically significant parallelisms proceeds at a level of abstraction from the musical surface, guided by possible well-formed grouping structures. At sub-phrase levels, these clues on the musical surface become more important in determining grouping structures. We suggest that the formalization of the kinds of processing heuristics which we have described, is consistent with the top-down knowledge postulated by several recent versions of *schema theory* (Stoffer, 1985; McAdams, 1987) applied to music cognition. In its present form AGA suffers from a major deficiency in explanatory power: since it uses only one "normal form" (implemented as a high-level grammar rule) it could only tell us the position of phrase boundaries in a melody, given that we already know that the melody *does* have the kind of grouping structure encapsulated in that normal form. We argue (Baker, 1989) that the model could achieve greater generality, and psychological plausibility, by recasting the abstraction of grouping structure embodied in high-level grammar rules into the form of a system of related *group schemata*.

A number of limitations of the model have been mentioned in describing individual components, in terms of the amount and direction of processing. There is a further major respect in which the prototype is implausible as a model of human cognition, in terms of the relationship between different processing modules. In its present form, AGA performs several phases of processing across the entire melody, passing new sets of symbols to subsequent processes. It assigns possible harmonic functions to the entire melody and builds up several parse trees and sets of reductional levels. Clearly, no listener has access to the entire course of a melody in working memory, nor could successive processing components access new sets of symbols in working memory. A possible solution is to integrate the component processes to make the parser the central control mechanism, which called integrated harmonization and reduction functions in a largely left-to-right sweep through the melody. Given that we are attempting to use some kind of selection criterion between well-formed parse trees, it would be more plausible and efficient to attempt to apply such criteria as constraints during the parsing process itself. Given such a psychologically plausible parser, it could be integrated within a system of grouping schemata, which invoked the parser when driven by top-down expectations. We leave detailed discussion of such refinements for further work (Baker, 1989).

Acknowledgments

Thanks to my supervisor, Mark Elsom-Cook, for unfailing encouragement and inspiration, and to Simon Holland for pointing me in the right direction. This research is supported by an award from the Science and Engineering Research Council of Great Britain.

References

Baker, M.J. (1989) An artificial intelligence approach to musical grouping analysis. In "Music, Mind and Structure", E.F. Clarke & S. Emmerson (eds.), *Contemporary Music Review*, 3 (1), 43–68, London: Harwood Academic Publishers.

Clarke, E. (1986) Theory, analysis and the psychology of music: A critical evaluation of Lerdahl, F. and Jackendoff, R. *A Generative Theory of Tonal Music. Psychology of Music*, **14**, 3–16.

Cohen, G. (1983) *The Psychology of Cognition*.

Deliege, I.(1987) Grouping conditions in listening to music: An approach to Lerdahl & Jackendoff's grouping preference rules. *Music Perception*, **4**, 325–360.

Ebcioglu, K. (1986) *An Expert System for Harmonization of Chorales in the Style of J.S. Bach*. PhD thesis, Department of Computer Science, University of New York at Buffalo, USA.

Elsom-Cook, M. & du Boulay, B. (1986) A Pascal program checker. *Proceedings of the European Conference on Artificial Intelligence 1986*, vol.II, pp. 90–95.

Johnson-Laird, P. (1983) *Mental Models*. Cambridge University Press.

Lerdahl F.& Jackendoff, R. (1983) *A Generative Theory of Tonal Music*. Cambridge, Mass.: MIT Press.

McAdams, S. (1987) Music: A science of the mind? In "Music and Psychology: A Mutual Regard", S. McAdams, (ed.), *Contemporary Music Review*, **2**, 1–61, London: Harwood Academic Publishers.

Meyer, L.B. (1973) *Explaining Music*. University of California Press.

Peel, J.& Slawson, W. (1984) Review of *A Generative Theory of Tonal Music*, by F. Lerdahl & R. Jackendoff. *Journal of Music Theory*, **28**, 271–294.

Schenker, H. (1935/1979) *Free Composition*, trans. Ernst Oster. Longman.

Simon, H. & Sumner, R.(1968) Pattern in music. In *Formal Representation of Human Judgement*. Kleinmuntz,B., (ed.) New York: Wiley & Sons.

Steedman, M.(1984) A generative grammar for jazz chord sequences. *Music Perception*, **2,** 53–77.

Steele, Guy L, Jr (1984) *COMMON LISP The Language.* Digital Press.

Stoffer, T.H. (1985) Representation of phrase structure in the perception of music. *Music Perception*, **3,** 191– 220.

Taft-Thomas, M. (1985) VIVACE: A rule-based AI system for composition. *Proceedings of the International Computer Music Conference, 1985, Vancouver,* pp. 267–274. San Francisco: Computer Music Association.

Winograd, T.(1968) Linguistics and the computer analysis of tonal harmony. *Journal of Music Theory*, **12,** 2– 49.

Winograd, T.(1983) *Language as a Cognitive Process, Volume 1: Syntax* Addison-Wesley.

Contemporary Music Review,
1989, Vol. 4, pp. 327-340
Photocopying permitted by license only

Listening as discovery learning[1]

Alan A. Marsden

Department of Music, The Queen's University of Belfast, Belfast BT7 1NN, U.K.
(Formerly of Department of Music, University of Lancaster)

Much current work in musical cognition is based on the notion of *grammar,* but there are problems in using this as a basis for modeling the process of listening as one of parsing. Not only are there unresolved issues in modeling listeners' abilities to accommodate a multiplicity of musical styles, including novel styles, but also problems occur in modeling the recognition of recurrent patterns in a suitably flexible way. *Discovery* and *learning* are found to have a crucial role in the listening process, and so should be at the heart of a listening model. Learning models from other domains of cognitive science offer a potential basis for such models. This is illustrated through a model, based on Thagard and Holyoak's PI ("Processes of Induction") system to learn the concept of beat by exposure to a metrical sequence of taps. Possibilities for the development of more sophisticated musical models along similar lines are explored.

KEY WORDS: Listening processes, musical models, musical grammars, learning systems.

Listening as parsing or learning

Within the branch of musical scholarship which aims for rigorous theories of music, the notion of "grammar" has had recent, and largely well-deserved, popularity, even attracting a whole conference to itself (Baroni & Callegari, 1984; see also Roads, 1979; and Baroni, 1983). The notion originates in linguistics, of course, but it has taken on an existence of its own, so that those advocating the use of grammars in musical research do not necessarily imply a strong parallel between music and language. A grammar, in the formal sense used here, is a definition of the set of symbolic sequences ("utterances") which make up a language or, in musical applications, a musical style or corpus. The importance of the grammar is that, by employing formalisms such as generative rewrite rules, it can be quite compact while the set of utterances may be very large or even infinite. The normal test for a grammar is that it be capable of generating *all* the utterances in the given corpus, and *only* utterances which either are members of the corpus or meet some acceptability criterion. It is common, furthermore, to regard a grammar as revealing in an utterance the structures which are in some sense *pertinent* (Baroni, 1983, pp.183–4; Baroni, Brunetti, Callegari & Jacoboni, 1984, pp. 201–205).

The summarizing power of a grammar in the study of a corpus of music is not in doubt, and it is reasonable to assume that the structures of a grammar will in some way reflect the structures of musical knowledge. However, when it comes to making models, there are serious shortcomings in thinking of the process of listening as one of parsing according to the appropriate grammar. The role of a model is not that it be an exact copy of a process but that its behavior mimic the system under investigation in significant ways, without being obscured by

insignificant details. Its appropriateness thus depends on the criterion of significance, and so models of listening based on parsing will have their place. It will be
argued, though, that such models cannot easily reflect some aspects of listening
which seem significant with regard to the value listeners find in music. The
intention is not to discount the notion of grammar, but to discuss its limitations in
this area. Arguments have already been advanced for flexible modeling
frameworks on the grounds of the fluidity of musical style (Marsden & Pople,
1989) and the conceptual fragmentation and re-integration evident in music
theory and analysis (Marsden & Pople, in press). Here a particular basis for such
flexible models in the idea of discovery learning will be advanced.

The role of learning in listening has already been stressed in the work of other
authors. Narmour (1977) similarly concerned with a lack of flexibility in music
theory, stresses the role of implication in listening, and discusses the process of
style development as the expansion of a repertoire of implicative "style forms"
(pp. 127–134). Kunst (1978) expounding a theory more formal in nature, concen-
trates on a particular type of unlearning-plus-learning process (the "bivalence
function"), involving the listener's discarding of one proposition about the music
heard and the derivation of a new proposition. Minsky explores the idea of
"sonata as teaching machine" (1981, pp.29–34), and suggests that "perhaps what
we learn is not the music itself but *a way to hear it*" (1981, p. 29, my emphasis).

The principal difficulty with the use of grammars in models of musical listening
is that grammars are fixed and rigid while structuring in actual music appears very
fluid. If a grammar is to be at all detailed, it must refer to a limited corpus of music,
in some cases extremely limited (e.g."twelve bar blues", Steedman, 1984; or the
openings of Schubert Lieder, Camilleri, 1984). A more wide-ranging approach
requires a multiplicity of grammars, possibly hierarchically organized, reflecting
a multiplicity of styles (Baroni *et al*, 1984, pp. 201–202). Here some of the
shortcomings of the approach become more apparent. It is implied that a model
of listening, if it is to be applicable to more than one musical style, must have
available a number of alternative grammars. It must therefore also have some
mechanism for selecting the appropriate grammar, and indeed a mechanism to
derive a new grammar from an existing one to model listeners' behavior on
encountering an unfamiliar style (e.g. Schumann *Lieder* having become familiar
with Schubert *Lieder*), but the features of these components cannot be derived
from the general principles of a parsing-based approach. The two aspects of
behavior missing from a simple parsing model are *discovery* – listeners find out
things in and about a piece of music without external guidance – and *learning* –
listeners are able to use what they discover in subsequent listening.

Even when a parsing model is intended to apply to music in a single style, it
faces difficulties of fluidity. This will be illustrated by discussion of the opening of
the Allegro of the first movement of Mozart's *String Quartet in C, K.465, the "Dissonance"* (1785). (The discussion below is based on a fuller analysis in Marsden,
1987, pp. 149–182.).

Even naive listeners have a notion of the "theme" of a piece of music as its
recurrent or main melodic pattern, which evidently reflects an important facet of
listening, *viz.* the recognition of recurrent patterns. How would a model based on
parsing reflect such behavior? Obviously it is not in the role of a parser to find
recurrent patterns – for that a model requires a pattern matching component – but
some sort of interpretation and structuring such as a parser performs is necessary

for patterns to become recognizable. This implies a two-stage model, with a parser structuring raw input and then passing its output (e.g. a parse tree) to a pattern matcher. Here an immediate problem occurs: what level of interpretation should be passed to the matcher? Significant patterns occur in the first violin of the Mozart example (Figure 1) in terms of pitches (bars 29 and 38), pitch classes (bars 23–26 and 31–34), absolute intervals (the minor 6ths in bars 28 and 29) and tonal intervals (i.e. the number of steps in a diatonic scale; see for example bars 23 and 25 where whole tones are matched by semitones).

Even if consideration is restricted to the most general of these categories, tonal intervals, there are problems in modeling the recognition of patterns by a two stage parsing-then-matching approach. Figure 2 gives a rudimentary grammar sufficient to reveal the patterns in the six extracts in the Figure. (Extracts 4 and 5 come from bars 90 and 96 respectively.) Some previous stage of processing is assumed to have extracted sequences of tonal intervals from the sequences of pitches in each extract. Each numeral represents an interval by the number of steps in the diatonic scale of C (for extracts 1–3 and 6) or G (for extracts 4 and 5). For simplicity the direction of intervals is ignored. The grammar consists of only two rewrite rules: rule (a) embodies the notion of a neighbor-note; rule (b) represents a type of passing-note figure. The right hand column of the Figure gives the parse tree for each extract. The role of the grammar and parser is clearly illustrated

Figure 1 Extract from Mozart *String Quartet in C, K.465, the "Dissonance"*.

Rewrite rules: 1. X -> (X+1) 1
                 2. X -> (X−3) 1 1 1

Figure 2 Parsing of extracts from Mozart K.465 to reveal matches. Numerals refer to tonal intervals, e.g. 1 = whole tone or semitone. The rewrite rules state that the interval on the left of the arrow can be replaced by the sequence of intervals on the right. X can match any interval. The parse trees show the derivation, from top to bottom, of the sequence of intervals in each extract from a single "root" interval by application of the rewrite rules indicated to the right.

in enabling a match between the parse tree for extract 3 and the first level of the parse trees for extracts 1 and 2. Similarly, a match between extract 5 and extracts 1 and 2 is revealed through their equivalent trees, though the roots are different (interval 4 in extract 5, interval 3 in extracts 1 and 2). On the other hand, a match between extracts 4 and 5 is not so simple. Certainly their roots are the same, but it seems clear that a listener would recognize in these extracts not only the common overall interval 4, but also the common neighbor-note figure. In the parse trees this involves a more complex match of both the roots and the bottom levels. Furthermore, if intervals 3 and 4 (perfect 4th and 5th respectively) are considered matchable (as implied by the matching of extracts 1, 2 and 5), enabling a match of extracts 1 and 2 with extract 4, the same match occurs in terms of parse trees with extract 6, but this is probably not reflected in a listener's recognition. The recognition of the match with extract 4 depends crucially on similarities of pitch and rhythm between extracts 4 and 5 not enjoyed by extract 6. Matching to model listeners' behaviors must therefore be performed by a complex process and must depend on a multiplicity of information.

There are two possible approaches based on the notion of grammar and parsing to reflect this sort of behavior. Firstly the model could be, as implied, a two stage parse-then-match process. In this case the parser must pass on to the matcher a great number of alternative interpretations, to ensure that the matcher is provided with all the information that it required. This is obviously very inefficient, and, given known cognitive processing constraints, unsatisfactory as a cognitive model. The alternative is to involve the matcher somehow in the process of parsing so that useless alternatives are weeded out at an early stage. In other words parsing would be *guided* by some control component designed to lead to successful matches. The parsing process would then be not simply an implementation of the concepts embodied in the grammar.

Fluidity seems to be required, however, not only in how a grammar is applied, as in the "guided parser" notion above, but also in the rules of the grammar itself. This is clear from earlier discussion with respect to the multiplicity of musical styles, but is also true within the more restricted scope of an individual style. It seems that sometimes the *general* features of a style, such as might be embodied in the rules of a grammar, are weakened or even overridden by *idiosyncratic* features of an individual piece. One such case occurs in Beethoven's *"Eroica" Symphony* (1804) in the statement of the theme by the second horn just before the start of the recapitulation in the first movement (Figure 3). The usual rules governing harmony and the resolution of dissonances are not kept in this extract, yet listeners do not generally react to it as a mistake, as a rigid grammatical approach would imply. It seems that local characteristics of the piece (e.g. the ubiquity of the theme and the established pattern of long areas of one harmonic function encompassing sometimes intense local dissonances) have combined to neutralize those rules. This is but an extreme example of a type of problem which continually causes music teachers embarrassment when they have to claim to their students that some rule of harmony does not apply in some specific case in a piece by an acknowledged master.

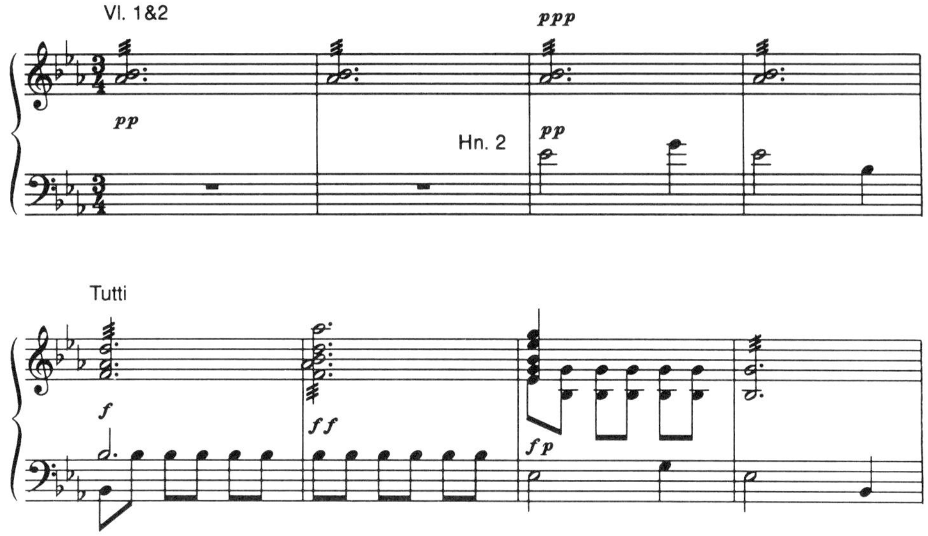

Figure 3 Extract from Beethoven *Symphony no. 3, "Eroica"*.

Modeling listening as discovery learning

A picture is emerging of a model in which rules will continue to play a part, but discovery and learning will have a crucial role in governing the application of rules and in the adaptation of the rule base. This suggests that perhaps the idea of learning rather than the idea of grammar should form the basis of the model.

A researcher taking this course will find guidance from work in other domains of cognitive modeling, where learning systems are very much a current concern, most conspicuously in the "parallel (distributed processing" (PDP) or "connectionist" movement (see Rumelhart & McClelland, 1986; Bharucha & Olney, this volume). The framework considered below is at a higher level of abstraction than PDP models, but shares many of their adaptive characteristics. It is based on the PI ("processes of induction") model of Thagard & Holyoak (Holland, Holyoak, Nisbett & Thagard, 1986).

At the heart of PI is a set of production rules but, unlike most production systems, these all act in parallel without any controlling interpreter to decide which rule to apply and every rule has associated with it a measure of strength. Rules' conditions are matched against the current state represented by a "message list", and their actions are to write messages to a new message list, which replaces the previous message list on the next processing cycle (see Figure 4). The message list is of restricted size (reflecting memory and processing constraints in human cognition), and conflicts between rules are resolved by competition for place in this message list on the basis of rule strength (a measure of a rule's past usefulness), support (the strength of messages matching conditions) and activation (a measure of a rule's association with other active rules). Rules are thus analogous to knowledge in long-term memory, and the message list to short-term memory.

PI (which in 1986 was still under development) has two learning mechanisms. One (similar to the learning mechanism in PDP systems) is through the revision

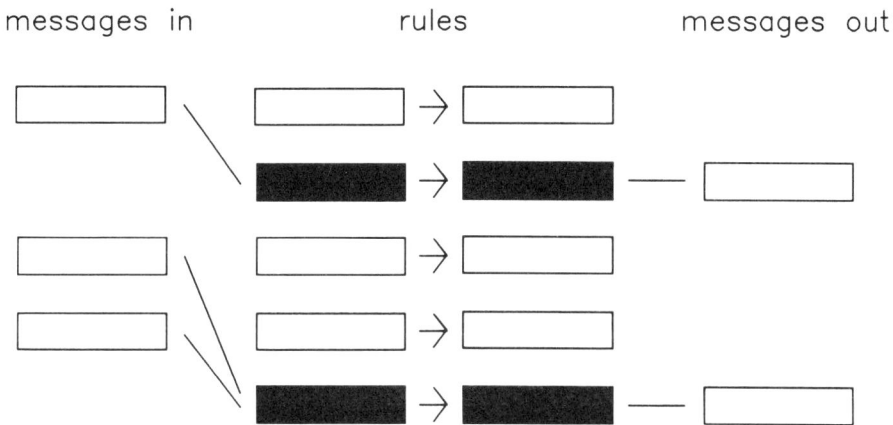

Figure 4 PI processing cycle. Messages are matched with the left-hand sides (conditions) of rules, which are thereby activated to produce new messages from their right-hand sides to be used on the next processing cycle.

of rule strengths. A rule which proves to be useful (i.e. whose action achieves the system's objective) has its strength increased, and this increase is passed back through the system to those rules which have contributed to that rule's success. Conversely, rules which turn out to be harmful or not useful have their strengths reduced. This is illustrated in Figure 5. The strength revision algorithm used here is to add to a rule half of the difference between its strength and the strength of the rule using its message. This is similar in effect to the "bucket brigade" algorithm of Holyoak & Thagard in which, as the posting rule passes its message to the receiving rule, it receives in return a "payment" of a portion of the receiving rule's strength. This revision of strengths means that rules which have proven useful in the past are more likely to win in the competition to post their messages, and so the overall performance of the system is likely to improve.

Old strengths

50		75		100
rule1	— message1 —	rule2	— message2 —	payoff
62.5		87.5		100

New strengths

Old strengths

50		25		(0)
rule1	— message1 —	rule2	— message2 —	(unused)
37.5		12.5		(0)

New strengths

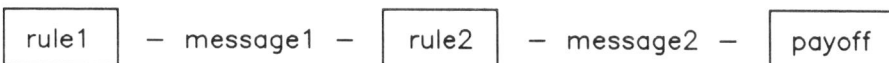
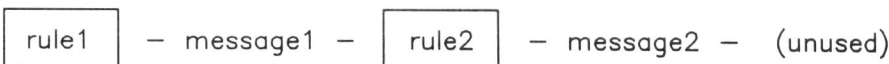

Figure 5 Rule strength revision.

The second learning mechanism is the derivation of new rules. This aspect of PI is less well defined. Certain "operating principles" (essentially rule-forming heuristics) will govern when new rules will be formed and what those rules will be. (See Lenat, 1983, for a discussion of the importance of heuristics in learning systems.) Usually new rules are formed on the basis of existing rules by generalization, specialization, or similar processes. The important point is that new rules, once added to the system, are *tested* in the normal operation of PI. Good rules will have their strengths increased and come to replace similar rules which do not perform so well; bad rules will have their strengths decreased and eventually be effectively forgotten.

The designers of PI argue convincingly for its framework in the modeling of human cognition. In particular, its basis on pragmatic factors – learning is driven by the system's goals, achievements and failures – enables the model to overcome some of the problems in other learning theories such as conditioning (Holland *et al*, 1986, pp. 173–178), and to provide some explanation for otherwise puzzling aspects of human behavior such as the failure to apply logical rules (pp. 265–284) or the retention of beliefs which in scientific terms are erroneous but which are useful in everyday life (pp. 205–211). The potential of the framework for modeling in the musical domain therefore deserves exploration.

Infants acquire procedural musical knowledge, such as the ability to follow the beat of a piece of music, simply through exposure, much as they acquire language. This is a clear case of discovery learning, and provides a suitable initial modeling exercise. A model should start with some very basic rules, such as might be reasonably believed innate, and *learn*, by exposure to musical input, the concept of beat. This learning, as stressed above, must be directed towards some goal, but it is not clear at this stage what goal should be considered to govern the process of listening to music. The choice among the various possibilities (e.g. recall or recognition of the music heard, maximum escape from everyday concerns etc.) must be a subject of research, and may well turn out to be quite complex. For the present, it is assumed that listeners aim to be able to predict what they will hear. This is credible from the point of view of survival value – it is important in everyday domains to be able to foresee the course of events, and this may carry over into the domain of music – and it is also congruent with the music theories of Meyer and Narmour.

The model presented here, based on PI, has three operating principles to govern rule generation (Figure 6). The first, specialization of conditions, applies when a rule has been unexpectedly successful, i.e. when it receives a large increase in strength. The assumption is that if the rule has proved successful in the present circumstances, it will also probably be successful when the circumstances recur, so a more specialized version of the rule which adds to its conditions other messages present on the message list is generated. This new rule will compete with the original and may in time prove more successful. The second operating principle, generalization of conditions, applies when the message matching a rule's action should have been present but was not or was only weakly supported. The assumption is that the rule or rules producing that action are too specialized and so conditions not present in the message list at the time are dropped. A special case of this principle applies where there are no existing rules which might produce the required action. A new rule is then generated whose conditions consist of all the current messages. The final principle, specialization of rule coupling, applies when a rule proves useful in those circumstances when the message matching (one of) its conditions comes from one previous rule but not when it comes from another. Here two new rules are formed with new matching messages in their action and condition parts respectively, so that the second rule will fire only when it is preceded by a firing of the first rule. In generating a new message, should it prove useful in time, the system effectively learns a new concept.

1. Specialisation of conditions (condition2 present):

$$\text{condition1} \;\rightarrow\; \text{action}$$
$$\Rightarrow \quad \text{condition1} + \text{condition2} \;\rightarrow\; \text{action}$$

2. Generalisation of conditions (condition2 absent):

$$\text{condition1} + \text{condition2} \;\rightarrow\; \text{action}$$
$$\Rightarrow \qquad\qquad \text{condition1} \;\rightarrow\; \text{action}$$

3. Specialisation of rule coupling (concept formation):

$$\text{condition} \rightarrow \text{message} \qquad \dots \qquad \text{message} \rightarrow \text{action}$$
$$\Rightarrow \quad \text{condition} \rightarrow \text{new message} \; \dots \; \text{new message} \rightarrow \text{action}$$

Figure 6 Principles governing rule generation.

The model starts with two rules which simply keep a record of past messages, effectively implementing a memory. The first takes any (non-"historical") message as its condition and posts the message that this occurred one cycle ago. The second rule matches these "historical" messages and increments their cycle count. The strength of these rules is set at such a level as to cause the support for "historical" messages to decline with age, and so events long past are eventually forgotten because they fail in the competition for places on the message list. The model deals at this stage with an extremely impoverished musical input, corresponding to a metrical sequence of taps: the message "tap" is added to the message list on the appropriate processing cycle to indicate that a tap has occurred at that time. As stated above, the goal of the model is to predict events, so it aims to produce the message "predict tap" to coincide with input of the message "tap".

When presented with a metrical input, the model does learn to predict taps at the right time, and in so doing it learns the concept of beat. The precise steps by which this takes place will of course depend on the precise input, but the broad outlines of the process are as illustrated in Figure 7. At the first tap there are no previous messages, and so no new rule can be formed – there is no basis on which to predict when the next tap will occur. At the second tap the special case of the second operating principle can be applied: the message "predict tap" should have been produced but there are as yet no rules to produce it, so rule 1 is formed. Now when the circumstances recur, a tap is predicted, and this prediction often proves correct, but incorrect predictions occur when taps occur between beats. (The first of these taps off the beat will be unpredicted and will lead to the formation of new rules, but these can be ignored at present. They will be weak rules because, in the type of sequence used here, taps between beats are essentially not predictable and so any rules attempting to predict them will often fail and lose strength.) Rule 1 will, for example, predict a tap at point B in the sequence of taps in Figure 7 on the basis of the tap at point A, which leads to a decrease of the rule's strength. At point C, however, the tap is correctly predicted, and the success triggers the first operating principle, the specialization of conditions. The intitial rules will have kept records not only of when taps occur but also of when taps have been predicted, and so one specialization which will be added to the set of rules, to be tested along with others, is to add the condition that not only must a tap have occurred n cycles ago, but that tap must also have been predicted, producing rule 2. This rule tends to work better than rule 1 by avoiding making false predictions at points like B. Rule 1 will remain, however, and at points such as E will happen to correctly predict a tap on the basis of the tap at point D. Now rule 2 will also predict a tap at point F, which is false. Because this failure is based on a message supplied by rule 1, while success at points such as G is based also on a message supplied by an earlier occurrence of rule 2, the third operating principle is activated, and the coupling between rule 2 and itself is specialized, producing rule 3. This operates in a similar way to rule 2, but because of the addition of the new message "new-concept" it is only activated by previous predictions made by itself and not by those made by rule 1. The final step is to cope with points like H where no tap occurs on the beat. The failure for the tap at I to be predicted leads, through the second operating principle, to a generalization of rule 3 to rule 4. This rule states that some notional event "new-concept" will occur every $n+1$ cycles, and that a tap is predicted at the same time. This is precisely the common concept of a "beat".

Clearly a model to deal with more realistic musical input would be considerably more complex, but the same framework is likely to prove useful. The model could continue to have the same goal of prediction: instead of aiming to simply predict the occurrence of events, the system would aim also to predict their qualities (e.g. pitch). This would introduce problematic issues concerning apropriate rewards (e.g. is it better to predict the wrong pitch at the right time or the right pitch at the wrong time?), and would complicate issues of concept formation, but once these are overcome, it would be feasible to use real pieces of music as input.

A model of this type need not, of course, begin with an empty set of rules, but rather might initially contain rules representing knowledge about music in a particular style. The record of the learning steps taken by the model in response to input representing a particular piece would form a sort of "map" of the process of listening to that piece (this is similar to Kunst's 1978, idea of networks of "bivalence functions" reflecting real and potential listening; see also Kunst & van den Bergh, 1984). Given the extract from the Mozart quartet as input, for example, a model like the one discussed above would quite naturally infer rules recognizing the recurrent patterns, because it is in these that notes are most successfully

Initial rules

             (X) -> (ago 1 X)

             (ago N X) -> (ago N+1 X)

    1.   (ago n tap) -> (predict tap)

Specialise conditions

    2.   (ago n tap) (ago n predict tap) -> (predict tap)

Specialise coupling 2-2

    3.   (ago n tap) (ago n predict tap) (ago n new-concept)
                            -> (predict tap) (new-concept)

Generalise conditions

    4.   (ago n predict tap) (ago n new-concept)
                            -> (predict tap) (new-concept)

Figure 7 Learning the concept of beat. Rule 1 is activated by a message which, through the initial rules, indicates that a tap occurred n cycles ago (corresponding to the duration of a crotchet, or quarter-note). Rule 2, a specialization of rule 1, is activated only when there are messages to record both the occurrence of a tap n cycles ago, and a prediction of that tap. Rule 3 specializes this still further by the addition of a new type of message with the effect that the rule can only be activated n cycles after a previous activation of itself. Rule 4 drops the requirement for there to have been a tap n cycles ago, thereby keeping time through an abstract concept corresponding to a "beat".

predicted. This is illustrated in Figure 8. The events in bars 23–24 will produce, among others, rule 1, which predicts intervals of a third followed by a second given the pattern repeated note, second, second. (As in Figure 2, numerals here represent steps in a diatonic scale.) This prediction is confirmed at bar 26, and so the rule is strengthened. At bar 28, however, the prediction from this rule proves to be false, and so a revision of the rule is implied.

(It is assumed that in a more complex model to deal with real musical input, the operating principles governing rule formation will be more sophisticated than those presented above. Indeed they should properly be subject to revision and testing in the same manner as the rules, so that the system not only learns rules, but also learns principles on which to revise rules. [Lenat, 1983, similarly suggested, from experience with AM, that the guiding heuristics of that system should be subject to adaptation.] The system would therefore make a guess at the rule revision most appropriate in the light of the current circumstances and the other rules it possesses embodying knowledge about the style.)

The model is assumed to already possess rules like A and B, which state that if a notional interval of a second is expected (here the word "notional" adumbrates the Schenkerian concept of "higher level"), predict both a second and the interval of a third followed by a second, thus embodying the concept of a neighbor-note. The presence of these rules will cause the system to generate rule 2, which will coexist with rule 1, but will not supplant it because its predictions, though more often correct than those of rule 1, are not as accurate. The reward it receives is mediated by rules A and B, which of course do not always make correct predictions and so are not of maximum strength. Thus rule 2 is strengthened to a lesser degree on correct predictions than is rule 1 whose reward is not mediated through any other rule. So the system comes to contain two alternative notions of the theme, embodied in the two rules, whose relative importances are represented by their relative strengths.

A.   predict notional 1 -> predict 1

B.   predict notional 1 -> predict 2 1

1.   0 1 1 -> predict 2 1

2.   0 1 1 -> predict notional 1

3.   ago ♩ note-sounding 4/5 -> predict 1

Figure 8 Learning responses to Mozart K.465. As in Figure 2, numerals refer to tonal intervals. Rules A and B correspond to the idea of an appoggiatura. Rule 1 predicts the interval sequence 2 1 following the sequence 0 1 1. Rule 2 is activated in the same circumstances but predicts a "notional" interval 1, which by rules A and B can be realized as either interval 1 or the sequence 2 1. Rule 3 predicts interval 1 whenever the note sounding a minim (half note) ago is at an intervallic distance of 4 or 5 from the present note.

Such multiple representations can extend also to the problematic parallel between bar 90 (extract 4 in Figure 2) and the theme. Rule 3 in Figure 8, states that when the note sounding a minim (half note) ago was a fifth or sixth away from the present note, predict the next interval to be a second. This makes correct predictions throughout the extract in Figure 1, and at bar 90, and despite its curious formulation, it can successfully coexist with the other rules above. Any interpretation of a sequence as passing-notes or neighbor-notes by one rule need not prejudice the operation of another rule because all act in parallel and multiple representations can be simultaneously entertained. Furthermore, representations are retained in the system only when there are rules such as the initial rules in Figure 7 to pass the relevant messages from the old message list to the new, and the pragmatic basis for the generation and testing of rules will lead to more selective "remembering" rules, ensuring that only potentially useful representations are retained.

Obviously a considerable amount of work remains to be done before these conjectures can be tested in a working model. Problems of assigning appropriate credit to rules and determining a basis for that credit, i.e. the goal of the learning system, have already been alluded to. In addition, as with any dynamic system, the behavior of such a model can be very complex and make considerable demands on computing resources. It may transpire that the particular approach adopted here, based on PI, is not the best framework for a model of listening processes, but a strong case remains for modeling on the basis of the idea of listening as a process of discovery and learning. Narmour (1977) sees points of crucial musical significance where the realizations of implied continuations are disrupted. Kunst (1978) similarly believes that the crucial activity in listening occurs when some conception of the music is found to be mistaken and the listener is forced to make a new one. Minsky (1981) charts the continual reworkings of the theme of Beethoven's *Fifth Symphony*, and similar reworkings occur to the theme of the Mozart piece discussed above. Notwithstanding the dangers of this line of argument, it seems that it is Mozart's intention to always present the listener with something slightly changed and unexpected; the listener's desire to predict the course of the music is being played with. There are, of course, regularities in music and in listeners' conceptions of music, and these are appropriately revealed in musical grammars, which from the perspective of this paper might be viewed as essentially static abstractions from a listening process which is essentially dynamic. It seems, though, that these regularities only serve to allow for irregularities, which are the points at which discovery and learning occur. Any model which aims to reflect what listeners find of value must take account of this.

Note

1. The author gratefully acknowledges the financial support of the Leverhulme Trust in this research.

References

Baroni, M. (1983) The concept of musical grammar. *Music Analysis*, 2 (2), 175–208.
Baroni, M., Brunetti, R., Callegari, L. & Jacoboni, C. (1984) A grammar for melody: Relationships between melody and harmony. In *Musical Grammars and Computer Analysis*, M. Baroni & L. Callegari (eds), 201–218, Florence: Olschki.
Baroni, M. & Callegari, L. (1984) (eds) *Musical Grammars and Computer Analysis*. Florence: Olschki.
Beethoven, L. (1804) *Symphony No. 3 in E flat major*, Op.55. London: Eulenberg, n.d.
Camilleri, L. (1984) A grammar of the melodies of Schubert's Lieder. In *Musical Grammars and Computer Analysis*, M. Baroni & L. Callegari (eds), 229–236, Florence: Olschki.
Holland, J.H., Holyoak, K.J., Nisbett, R.E. & Thaggard, P.R. (1986) *Induction*. Cambridge Mass.: M.I.T. Press.
Kunst, J. (1978) *Making Sense in Music, an Enquiry into the Formal Pragmatics of Art*. Ghent: Communication and Cognition, Ghent University.

Kunst, J. & van den Bergh, H. (1984) The analysis of musical meaning: a theory and an experiment. *Interface*, **13**, 75–106.

Lenat, D.B. (1983) The role of heuristics in learning by discovery: Three case studies. In *Machine Learning: An Artificial Intelligence Approach*, R.S. Michalski, J.G. Carbonell & T.M. Mitchell (eds), Los Altos, Cal.: Tioga.

Marsden, A.(1987) Analysing Music as Listeners' Cognitive Activity; A Study with Reference to Mozart. Ph.D. dissertation, University of Cambridge.

Marsden, A. & Pople, A. (1989) Modelling musical cognition as a community of experts. In "Music, Mind and Structure", E.F. Clarke & S. Emmerson (eds.), *Contemporary Music Review*, **3** (1), 29–43, London: Harwood Academic Publishers.

Marsden, A. & Pople, A. (in press) Towards a connected distributed model of musical listening. *Interface*.

Minsky, M. (1981) Music, mind and meaning. *Computer Music Journal*, **5** (3), 28–44. Also in *Music Mind and Brain*, M. Clynes (ed.), 1–19, New York: Plenum Press (1982), and A.I. memo no. 616, M.I.T. Press, Cambridge, Mass. (1981).

Mozart, W.A. (1785) *String Quartet in C major*, K.465. London: Eulenberg, 1968.

Narmour, E. (1977) *Beyond Schenkerism: The Need for Alternatives in Music Analysis*. Chicago and London: University of Chicago Press.

Roads, C. (1979) Grammars as representations for music. *Computer Music Journal*, **3** (1), 48–55.

Rumelhart, D.E., McClelland, J.R. & the PDP Research Group (1986) *Parallel Distribute Processing: Explorations in the Microstructure of Cognition* (two vols.). Cambridge Mass.: MIT Press.

Steedman, M.J. (1984) A generative grammar for jazz chord sequences. *Music Perception*, **2** (1), 52–77.

Contemporary Music Review,
1989, Vol. 4, pp. 341–356
Photocopying permitted by license only

Tonal cognition, artificial intelligence and neural nets

Jamshed J. Bharucha and Katherine L. Olney

Department of Psychology, Dartmouth College, Hanover, New Hampshire 03755, U.S.A.

We discuss a class of computational models that provide promising explanations of the processes underlying music cognition. These models, called neural net, connectionist, or parallel distributed models, are suited to music cognition because they can learn from passive exposure to the structural regularities of a musical culture. They have the potential to account for (1) the development, in the mind of the average listener, of cognitive schemas for music and (2) the subsequent generation of musical expectations based on these schemas. Using Western harmony and Indian *rāgs* as examples, we illustrate how one can simulate the expectancies of a native of one culture listening to the music of another. We show how a network can be constructed according to known music-theoretic constraints in order to study how some properties emerge from others. Finally, we review the results of experiments that test predictions about expectancies generated by these models.

KEY WORDS: Artificial intelligence, cognition, harmony, Indian music, neural nets, psychology.

Introduction

Cultural influences on the perceptual interpretation of music are mediated by cognitive structures that are often called perceptual schemas. Perceptual schemas for music encode the regularities of a musical genre through extended passive exposure. They serve to generate expectations following a musical context, facilitate the recognition of expected patterns, and render expected tones more consonant than others (Bharucha, 1987b). This schematic knowledge does not depend on explicit musical training, and is said to be tacit or implicit, reflecting the average listener's impoverished ability to articulate it. But what, precisely, is a schema? How, precisely, is tacit knowledge encoded? And how, precisely, is it learned?

The empirical knowledge and the theoretical and technical tools now exist to elucidate the concept of a schema with greater specificity. In this paper, we explore the extent to which recent breakthroughs in psychology and computer science can point to answers to the above questions. We explicate a class of computational models called neural net models, parallel distributed models, or connectionist models. These models have recently received considerable attention in psychology and computer science because of their neurophysiological plausibility, their ability to recognize patterns under conditions of variability, and their ability to learn (see Feldman & Ballard, 1982; McClelland & Rumelhart, 1986; Rumelhart & McClelland, 1986). Although early forms of these models have existed for some time (see Rosenblatt, 1962), even for music (see Deutsch, 1969), the development of more powerful learning algorithms and recent evidence from neurophysiology have resurrected them as strong candidates for theories of perception and cognition.[1]

A neural net is a network of interconnected neuron-like units (See Figure 1, left). Units transmit activation to other units much as neurons excite or inhibit other neurons across synapses. The connections between units can vary in strength, and a unit excites or inhibits another in proportion to the strength (weight) of the connection between them. Even though each unit alone is capable only of receiving and transmitting activation, a network as a whole can exhibit intelligent behavior on the basis of many units, with numerous interconnections, acting in concert. The behavior of the network is thus determined by the way in which units are connected and the strengths of these connections. A neural net learns by incrementally altering the strengths of these connections until some target behavior is achieved.

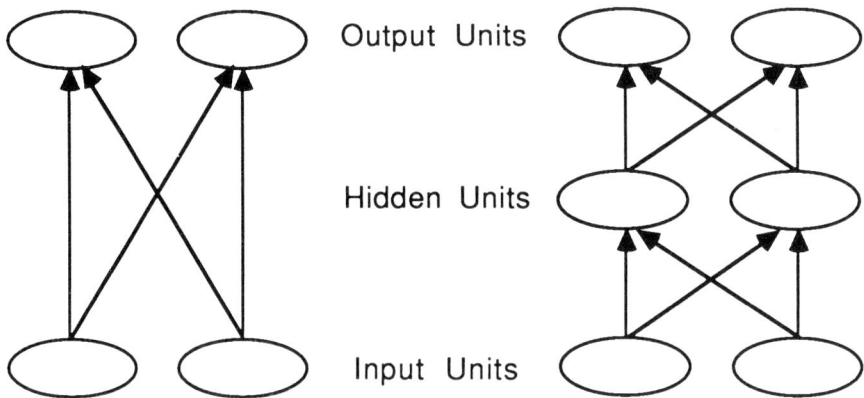

Figure 1 *(Left)*A neural net with a set of input units feeding into a set of output units. Input units are sensitive to particular features of the music (e.g., pitches within a certain range, pitch-classes, chords). The degree to which an input unit is activated represents the degree to which a feature is either present or remembered to be present in the music. An output unit receives activation from the input units in proportion to the strengths (weights) of the connections between them. The degree to which an output unit is activated represents the degree to which a feature is suggested, expected or implied. The network learns by incrementally altering the strengths of the connections so that, over the course of hearing repeated patterns, the expectations or implications represented by the activation levels of the output units more closely match the structure of the music. *(Right)* Sometimes extra units are necessary to mediate between input and output units, representing intermediate abstractions or feature combinations. These are called hidden units.

Neural Nets and the Relationships between Psychology and Artificial Intelligence (AI)

The term "neural net" has come to refer not only to networks of neurons in the brain but also to computational networks of simple processing units. Neural nets that are constrained by psychological data and that generate testable predictions are psychological models of cognition awaiting neurophysiological validation. Although units in these networks are unlikely to correspond to individual neurons in the brain, they may correspond to assemblies of neurons at a functional level. Neural nets that are not constrained by psychological data may be used to build artificial intelligence systems, since the mathematical properties of certain classes of neural nets are well understood. Neural nets may therefore be loosely divided into those that serve as psychological models of human cognition and those that serve to build intelligent machines. The former are attempts to answer *psychological* questions ("How does the brain accomplish x?"), whereas the latter are attempts to answer *AI* questions ("How can a machine be built to accomplish x?").

Our research is motivated by psychological questions. However, we find that asking AI questions is a fruitful way to come up with prospective networks that can then be evaluated as answers to the psychological questions.[2] This methodology underlies the close relationship between cognitive psychology and artificial intelligence. The networks we describe in this paper constitute an exploration of the promise of neural nets for understanding music perception and cognition. As such, they represent the process of answering AI questions with the eventual goal of answering psychological questions.

Rules

At the heart of the neural net approach is a departure from a reliance on the explicit mental representation of rules as advocated by Chomsky (1980) and Fodor (1975). Although the behavior of a neural net can be formally described by the rules of a grammar, these rules are not explicitly represented in the network. Rule-based theories that are offered as formal descriptions are vital contributions to an understanding of cognition because they specify constraints that any theory of the underlying processes must meet. However, rule-based theories that go beyond formal description to claim that rules are explicitly represented, as in a computer program, and that cognitive processes are symbolic operations performed on these representations (see Fodor, 1975), are fundamentally different from neural nets in their conception of cognition.[3]

Given music theory's traditional focus on the formulation of rules, a few words about the relationship between traditional music theory and the neural net approach are in order. The rules proposed by a theory of music (of a given style) can be construed as falling into one or more of the following categories: (1) analytic tools for understanding the structure of compositions independently of how they are perceived, (2) guidelines for composing in that style, or (3) hypotheses about how we perceive music in that style. There are a number of possible construals of rules within category 3, among them: (3a) hypotheses about the formal structure of the organized musical percept,[4] or (3b) hypotheses about the psychological processes that bring about the organized musical percept. Our approach is at odds with 3b. We claim that, for the average listener, with no formal musical training but substantial passive exposure, perceptual intuitions about music are a result not of the application of explicitly represented rules but rather of pattern completion.

Pattern completion is a process by which the mind anticipates, suggests, implies, or seems to "fill in" features that are typically present in familiar patterns. In a rule-based system, this "filling-in" would take the form of an inference. In a neural net, it is a consequence of the activation of associated features and organizational units, resulting in the perception of wholes or gestalts. Pattern completion is central to perception, for example, in reading handwriting, understanding natural speech, and perceiving the continuity of object edges that are partially occluded.

Learning and Innateness

Perhaps the most attractive feature of neural nets is their ability to learn. In the brain, neurons are connected by synapses, and recent evidence of synaptic changes following learning (Lynch, 1986) suggests that altering the connectivity between neurons is one way in which the brain learns. Computational algorithms have recently been developed that specify how a neural net can learn by altering the strengths of its connections until it converges on an optimal set of weights (Rumelhart, Hinton & Williams, 1986).

Although there are compelling arguments that some aspects of music cognition derive from structures that have evolved for other purposes, such as language, it is difficult to argue that specific evolutionary pressures existed for the level of musical sophistication of even the average listener. Some fundamental constraints on the representation of pitch must have been imposed through evolution, delimiting the kinds of structural regularities that can be learned (Shepard, in press). These constraints would include the basic auditory dimensions (such as pitch) that can be registered by the senses and relational properties such as invariance under transposition. Within these constraints, however, specific musical regularities (some of which may distinguish the music of different cultures and some of which may be universal) could be acquired through exposure. A powerful algorithm for passive perceptual learning (such as the generalized delta rule of Rumelhart, *et al*, 1986, which we employ in the simulations discussed below) thus enables us to address age-old debates about nature versus nurture with a new sophistication. Cognitive influences on music perception can be thought of as the consequence of constrained networks that employ general principles of perceptual learning to encode musical regularities through extended passive exposure.

We propose a three-part guideline for positing innate perceptual patterns for music. A pattern is unlikely to be innately encoded if: (1) the pattern is highly prevalent in the environment and (2) the brain can learn it through passive exposure, with the qualification that (3) knowledge of the pattern is not needed soon after birth and does not seem to have been needed at any time during evolution prior to the development of the learning capability in 2 above. Note that a pattern will be universal if it satisfies conditions 1 and 2, but is unlikely to be innate if it satisfies condition 3. Thus universality doesn't entail innateness. One must consider the pattern's prevalence in the environment and its learnability.

Consider the perceived similarity of pitches separated by octaves (referred to as octave equivalence). Whether octave equivalence is innate or learned has been the topic of considerable debate. Only in the context of a well-specified theory of perceptual learning are any new insights likely to be forthcoming. Neural net learning algorithms permit us to model the learning of auditory patterns through passive exposure, thereby suggesting the hypothesis that any auditory pattern that is ubiquitous and learnable will be learned. Octaves are ubiquitous, given that they occur in the energy spectrum of the speech signal. We are exposed to octaves for many hours each day from birth, across a continuous pitch range. A very simple neural net exposed to such an environment will learn to associate any pitch within the speech range with its octaves. We are compelled by parsimony to conclude, at least in the absence of evidence to the contrary, that octave equivalence is almost certain to be universal yet unlikely to be innate.[5]

Pattern association

Introduction to Pattern Associators

Most neural nets associate one pattern with another. If we present a network with some stimulus pattern P, the input units (i.e., the units that can be activated directly from outside the network) are given some pattern of activation. Activation then spreads through the network, constrained by the network's connectivity. The resulting pattern of activation suggests a pattern Q. By "suggest" we will mean either a simultaneous association or a sequential expectation. The units whose activation represents the suggested pattern are called output units.

For the purpose of this paper, each input or output unit can be thought of as registering the presence or absence of a feature. The degree to which an input unit is activated represents the degree to which a feature is either present or remembered to be present. The degree to which an output unit is activated represents the degree to which a feature is suggested, i.e., the confidence or expectancy that the feature was, is, or will be, present. The knowledge represented by a network is embodied in its connectivity, and the perceptual interpretation of some stimulus – in the present case, a musical event or a sequence of events – is the pattern of activation distributed across the output units.

The entire set of input units thus represents the feature space that defines the input pattern, and the entire set of output units represents the feature space that defines the output pattern. Input and output patterns may be in either the same perceptual domain (e.g. vision, audition, etc.) or in different domains. Even if the input and output domains are the same, the feature spaces may be different. Four examples illustrate the range of possibilities. First, both input and output patterns could be defined over the chromatic set, causing one pattern of tones to suggest another. Second, the input could be a fine-grained pitch set and the output could be the chromatic set, resulting in the assimilation of the pitch continuum to a chromatic schema. Third, the input could be the chromatic set and the output the set of major and minor chords, resulting in the assimilation of chromatic tones to a harmonic schema. Finally, the input could be a visual pattern from the written score and the output could be either an auditory or motoric pattern, as in the case of an experienced sight-reader.

Other units (besides input and output) may be involved that serve only to mediate between input and output units, and are often called hidden units or internal units (see Figure 1, right). Hidden units do not typically code for individual features of the input or output domains, but may come to represent intermediary abstractions. The use of hidden units overcomes some of the severe limitations of simple input-output associative networks. These limitations were once considered definitive grounds for rejecting neural nets as accounts of perception and cognition (see Minsky & Papert, 1988), because the early learning algorithms (e.g., Rosenblatt, 1962) were limited to a single layer of links between input and output. The use of hidden units in networks that can learn thus distinguishes contemporary neural net research from traditional associationism.

Suppose stimulus patterns P and Q frequently occur together or in succession. On each such occurrence, the output generated by the presence of P is compared with Q, and the weights are adjusted incrementally so as to reduce the disparity. Over the course of repeated exposure, the network finds a set of weights that enables P to suggest Q. Several learning algorithms exist for determining the adjustment of weights on each presentation so as to converge to an optimal set of weights. The learning algorithms we have used in this paper are the delta rule and the generalized delta rule (also called the error back-propogation learning rule) developed by Rumelhart, *et al*, (1986). (Further details are given in the Appendix.)

Learning Octave Equivalence through Autoassociation

Consider as our first example a neural net for auditory perception that predicts that octaves will be heard as similar, given exposure only to speech. A simple network that exhibits this property is one that learns to associate a pattern with itself. Such a network consists of an array of input units and an array of output units, such that each input unit feeds into each output unit. Initially (at "birth") the strengths of the connections from input to output units are either zero or random, representing the state prior to any exposure. Any given sound signal, such as a speech signal, will activate input units whose receptive fields correspond to partials present in the signal. The output units receive their activation from the input units via the connections between them, in proportion to the weights. Since the weights are initially zero or random, the output units will respond to the sound with either zero or random activation. However, the output units have independent access to the sound, and can therefore register the mismatch between the sound spectrum and the random pattern of activation received through the connections. The learning algorithm specifies how the weights are altered so that the next time the sound is heard, the output activation received through the connections will more closely match the sound.

Through repeated exposure, the network finds an optimal or near-optimal set of weights that reproduce the input pattern in the output. A network with this property is called an autoassociative network because it associates a pattern with itself. Autoassociative networks seem almost ludicrously simple at first, but have remarkable properties. They can complete, in the mind, patterns that are present in incomplete form. Thus, having learned to output a certain sound spectrum given that spectrum as input, a presentation of that spectrum with some elements missing will result in a "filling in" of these missing elements at the output level. Since many of the prominent spectral components in the speech signal form octaves, the network will have a tendency to suggest octaves more than other intervals.

The formation of feature hierarchies: From sensory to cognitive units

Must we limit our efforts to the sensory level of elementary frequency detectors as in the above network? How can we start to model higher – more cognitive – levels of musical structure?

There is mounting evidence that the brain represents patterns in a hierarchy of feature-specific units, with elementary feature detectors feeding into units that code for larger organizations. Extensive exposure to any combination of elementary features will result in the formation of a unit (representation) that stands for that combination. The network described at the end of the paper and shown in Figure 2 is an example of this. Pitch-class (tone) units are connected to chord units, which are connected to key units. How do these chord and key units get there? For that matter, how do the pitch-class units get there?

A number of algorithms exist that permit units with no innate specialization to become specialized to respond to the presence of some frequently occurring pattern. Once they have specialized, these units are essentially abstract feature detectors. Thus units might develop that are specialized for particular musical intervals or chords. Neural nets that have these properties are said to be self-organizing. Some of the most successful algorithms for self-organization involve competitive learning (Kohonen, 1984; Rumelhart & McClelland, 1986).

In a competitive learning network, some units are present from the outset with the sole purpose of awaiting some future specialization. Input units that respond to elementary features in the environment are linked to these generic units with randomly weighted connections. These generic units are linked to each other by inhibitory connections in a "winner-takes-all" network such that only the one that receives the most activation is able to remain activated. When a pattern consisting of some set of these elementary features occurs, the corresponding input units fire, and in turn activate the generic units to which they are connected. Some arbitrary generic unit will emerge as the winner, and will gradually become specialized to respond to that pattern by strengthening the connections that fed it activation from that pattern and weakening the connections that did not. With repeated presentations of the pattern, this unit becomes more and more likely to respond to that pattern (or patterns similar to it) and less and less likely to respond to different patterns. Other generic units will, in similar fashion, become specialized for other patterns. In this way, a hierarchical network develops with units representing elementary features at the lowest level and units representing abstract features or entire patterns at the highest level.

This mechanism can account for the formation of pitch-class units that are octave invariant, for units specializing in frequently heard chords, and possibly for units specializing in even more abstract features such as keys. In what follows, we shall assume the prior formation of pitch-class units and chord units and key units as a result of competitive learning.

Learning tonal schemas

Learning Tonal Schemas through Autoassociative Networks

The activation of a tonal schema based on partial sets of scale tones can be viewed as a pattern completion problem. In the context of a piece of music that typifies the constraints of a musical culture, some familiar subset of the 12 chromatic tones (e.g. the major diatonic set or the notes in an Indian *rāg*) plays a more important role than the other tones (Krumhansl, 1979; Bharucha,1984; Castellano, Bharucha, & Krumhansl,1984). Scale tones can be facilitated or suggested even with just a partial context, i.e., even when only a subset of the scale tones have been played (Bharucha, 1987b).

Consider a simple autoassociative network that implements major scale schemas. There are twelve input and twelve output units tuned to the twelve chromatic tones C to B. The network is exposed repeatedly to all twelve diatonic major sets, and learns to generate a diatonic major set as output given the same set as input.

Once it has learned, the network serves as a pattern recognition device, and "fills in" missing notes given an incomplete pattern. Thus, the set {D,E,F,G,A,B} fills in C. The set {C,D,E,F,G,A} fills in B and B♭, because it is a subset of the frequently heard patterns {C,D,E,F,G,A,B} and {C,D,E,F,G,A,B♭}, representing the keys of C and F, respectively. In fact, an even smaller set, {C,E,G}, representing a C major chord, fills in all the diatonic tones in the keys of C and F. Of the remaining tones, F# is the most highly activated, reflecting the C major chord's subdominant function in the key of G. It is important to remember when considering the results of these analyses that no knowledge of chords and their relationships was presented to this network. The network's behavior thus illustrates the extent to which complex structural relationships in music fall out of simpler ones, in this case as a result of simply associating diatonic major sets with themselves.

During learning, this network discovers, without explicit rules to guide its behavior, some of the abstract properties of diatonic scale systems that have been captured in the formal work of music theorists. The network exhibits a tacit knowledge of the circle of fifths. Weights are positive between tones separated by less than 90° around the circle, resulting in excitation. Weights are zero between tones separated by 90°, resulting in no activation. Weights are negative between tones separated by more than 90°, resulting in inhibition. These emergent properties of the network are consistent with Krumhansl's (Krumhansl & Schmuckler, 1987) view that cognitive structures for music have internalized the correlational structure of tonal music.

We can expand the scope this exercise to include other modes. Consider, for example, an autoassociative network exposed to the 24 major and harmonic minor diatonic sets. Here one sees the expected ambiguities between major and minor modes given partial diatonic sets. Thus, {C,D,E,F,A,B} fills in both G and G#, representing the related keys of C major and A minor.

Learning Indian Rāg Schemas through Autoassociative Networks

Consider a network exposed to ten common *rāgs* in North Indian music. The *rāgs* chosen for this simulation were those used in the study by Castellano, Bharucha & Krumhansl (1984) and are listed in Table 1. After learning, {Sa,Ga,Ma,Pa,Dha–, Ni} fills in Re– to suggest *rāg* Bhairav. In fact, a much smaller subset is sufficient: {Ga,Ma,Dha–,Ni} fills in Sa, Re–, and Pa. This is in accord with reaction time measurements of tones presented to Indian subjects following a partial presentation of *rāg* Bhairav: Tones that are typically present in this context but absent in the present rendition are facilitated, as measured by faster processing and greater intonational sensitivity (Bharucha, 1987b).

Table 1 Notes used in ten North Indian *Rāgs*[a]

Rāg	Notes used in rāg
Bhairav	Sa,Re–,Ga,Ma,Pa,Dha–,Ni
Yaman	Sa,Re,Ga,Ma+,Pa,Dha,Ni
Bilaval	Sa,Re,Ga,Ma,Pa,Dha
Khamaj	Sa,Re,Ga,Ma,Pa,Dha,Ni–,Ni
Kafi	Sa,Re,Ga–,Ma,Pa,Dha,Ni–
Asavri	Sa,Re–,Ga–,Ma,Pa,Dha–,Ni–
Bhairvi	Sa,Re–,Re,Ga–,Ma,Ma+,Pa,Dha–,Ni–
Todi	Sa,Re–,Ga–,Ma,+,Pa,Dha–,Ni
Purvi	Sa,Re–,Ga,Ma,Ma+,Pa,Dha,Ni
Marva	Sa,Re–,Ga,Ma+,Dha,Ni

[a]The Indian *swara* (note) names (Sa,Re,Ga,Ma,Pa,Dha,Ni) are equivalent to the Solfege (Do,Re,Me,Fa,So,La,Ti) in that order. In this paper, we use + to indicate sharp, – to indicate flat. Note that the number of *swaras* is not constant (see Bilaval and Khamaj, for example) across these *rāgs*, even though the *thats* (scales) that theoretically underlie them are septatonic. In this exercise, we have used the *rāg* notes, not the *that* notes.

A Westerner Listening to Indian Music

Neural nets can generate explicit hypotheses about how people of one culture hear the music of another. Consider, for example, the network exposed only to the major and harmonic minor diatonic sets. After learning, if the network is presented with all the notes of *rāg* Bhairav, it faithfully reproduces the input pattern in its output. However, if it is presented with a partial set of the tones in Bhairav, say with Re– missing, it fails to fill in Re–.

Some informal queries about the intuitions of Western musicians listening to Bhairav suggest that Sa is heard more as a dominant than as a tonic, and that Ma is the preferred tonic. (The lower ratings given to Ma in the Castellano, *et al* (1984) study could be due to Sa's presence in the drone). It may be of some interest to see which which keys, if any, are most activated by Indian *rāgs* when heard by a Western listener. We therefore taught a network to recognize keys so that it would activate one of 24 major and minor key units in response to a major or harmonic minor diatonic set. After learning, the network was presented with the tone sets for 10 *rāgs*. Only Bhairav, Yaman, Bilaval, Kafi and Asavri activated any keys, and all of these except Bhairav activated a major mode. Consistent with the intuitions of our Western informants, Bhairav activated a minor mode with Ma as the tonic. Bilaval was ambiguous as to a major mode with Sa as the tonic or with Ma as the tonic, because neither Ni nor Ni– are present. Kafi activated a major mode with Ni– as tonic, since it consists precisely of the major diatonic set.

These results should be construed only in the limited context in which these preliminary simulations were conducted, since other cues (including metrical cues, phrasing, and the presence of the drone) would no doubt strongly influence the perception of mode and of a tonic in a realistic rendition of a *rāg*. However, the neural net approach is highly conducive to the inclusion of these other factors, since they can all be represented as patterns defined over feature spaces with a continuum of activation available for each feature.

Learning Chord Expectancies

Consider a network that registers the current chord as its input pattern and generates expectancies for chords to follow as its output pattern. We can present a neonatal network (i.e., one that hasn't yet been exposed to any music) with chord pairs that are representative of a certain musical genre. For example, we can expose the network to harmony of the common practice period by presenting it with chord pairs that reflect the transition probabilities of chords as they occur in that genre.

We estimated transition probabilities from Piston's (1962) table of usual root progressions in major keys. Since the chord transitions given by Piston are stated in terms of harmonic functions, and the network obviously can't know about functionality before it has been exposed to any chords, chord transitions for individual chords were estimated from the functional transitions by enumerating the possible functions of each chord in each key (i.e. any major chord can be I, IV, or V, and any minor chord can be ii, iii, or vi).[6]

Initially, the network generates a random pattern of activation when presented with a chord. This pattern is then compared with the pattern corresponding to the succeeding chord and the weights are incrementally altered, as dictated by the delta rule, to reduce the disparity. In this way, the network eventually comes to generate a pattern of activation that mirrors the transition probabilities for chords to follow.

Although the network learns pairwise chord transitions, activation is allowed to accumulate at the output units over the course of a sequence, decaying over time. This model enables us to explore the extent to which pairwise learning can predict patterns of activation that result from an entire sequence of chords. Its behavior in this respect is virtually identical to the behavior of the constraint-satisfaction model described below. It predicts the build up of a tonal center over the course of a tonal sequence, and it predicts key ambiguities.

Our success in modeling learning of harmonic expectancies by learning pairwise transitions should not be assumed to generalize to other aspects of music learning. We would not expect this to be true for the learning of patterns of melodic contour, patterns of voice leading, motivic patterns, and patterns that come under the rubric of phrasing. The networks for these aspects of music would undoubtedly have to support more interaction among elements of the context.

A Constraint-Satisfaction Network for Harmony

Even though the real power of contemporary neural nets lies in their ability to learn and self-organize through passive exposure, it is often useful to construct networks whose connections conform to some known music-theoretic constraints and then observe the network's behavior. Such networks – called constraint-satisfaction networks – can test for redundancies in a theory of music (Which constraints are absolutely necessary? Which constraints will emerge unsolicited from the behavior of the network?) and enable one to observe multiple constraints operating simultaneously, sometimes in concert and sometimes in conflict.

In this section we summarize a constraint-satisfaction network for harmony, described in greater detail elsewhere (Bharucha, 1987a,b). The goal in the development of this model was to determine to what extent simple constraints of Western harmony can account for more subtle and complex ones. We built a network that embodies only two elementary constraints: (1) which tones are components of which chords and (2) which chords are members of which keys. Tone–chord relationships and chord-key relationships are wired in by bidirectional connections between tone, chord and key units (see Figure 2).

In this model, a unit responds to the change in activation of units to which it is connected. The onset of a chord causes a change in the activation of its component tones. These changes, weighted by the connection strengths, cause changes in the activations of their parent chords. Then, those changes cause changes in both the member tones and parent keys, and the tones and keys re-activate chords, and so on. This spread of activation continues (we call this reverberation) until the network settle into a state of equilibrium, reflecting the simultaneous satisfaction of all the constraints embodied in it.

Activation is allowed to accumulate in the network over the course of a sequence of chords, subject to decay. So, if another chord is heard before activation has decayed completely, the activation due to the new chord is added to the residual activation from the previous chords. Absolute activations thus reflect the effect of the entire sequence, weighted according to recency.

The activation of this network makes explicit the acoustically driven influence of shared tones and the learned, cognitively driven influence of having heard chords in standard groupings. When the chord units are first activated by the tone units, before activation has had a chance to reverberate back from the key units,

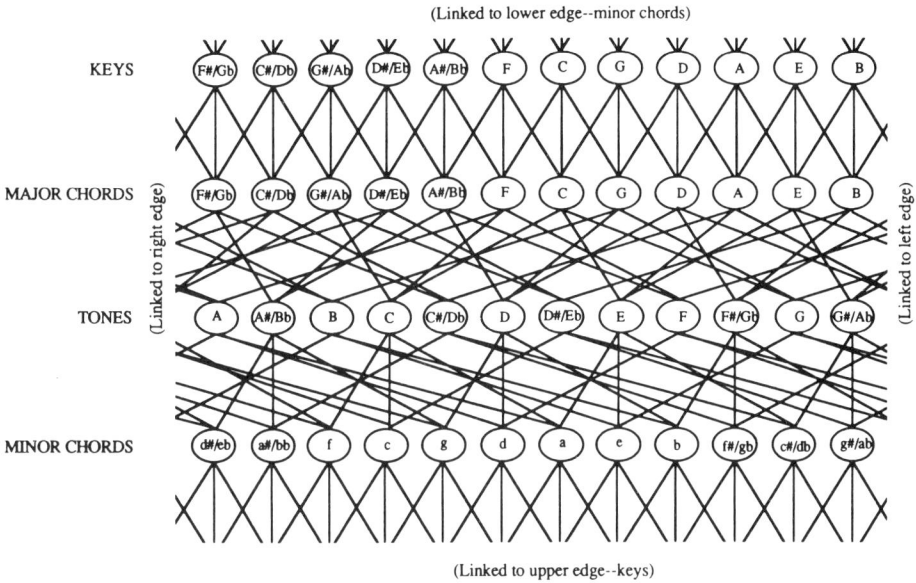

Figure 2 A constraint-satisfaction network representing relationships between tones, chords and keys. A musical context activates tone units, and activation spreads through the network, reverberating until it settles into a state of equilibrium. The pattern of activation at equilibrium represents chordal expectations and key implications, and influences the consonance and recognition of events that follow. (From Bharucha, 1987a, Copyright by the Cognitive Science Society).

the pattern of activation of the chord units represents the pattern of shared tones between chords. This is the "bottom-up" processing component of harmonic expectancy, since it is based on purely acoustic relationships between chords. For example, a C major chord will, via bottom-up processing, activate all and only chords that share tones with it. For example, the A major chord unit will receive some activation (since the A major chord shares a tone with the C major chord, namely E), but the D major chord unit will receive no activation at all.

Once activation has had a chance to percolate through the upper echelons of the network and filter down, the pattern of activation of the chord units represents the pattern of shared tones as well as the pattern of learned relationships. This is the "top-down" component of harmonic expectancy, since it embodies the learned cultural influences over and above acoustic relationships. By this time, the C major chord will have activated some chord units that do not share tones with it, for example, D major. In fact, the D major chord unit ends up with more activation than the A major chord unit.

Each chord exerts an independent influence on the accumulating effect of the sequence. This provides the basis for pivoting from one key to another, since an individual chord's ambiguity is not completely overriden by the context. There is an analog of this process in language. An ambiguous word activates its entire array of meanings, regardless of the constraints placed by the prior context (Swinney, 1979). The context biases the interpretation in one direction or another.

This model closely mimics the responses of subjects in earlier experiments (Krumhansl, Bharucha & Castellano, 1982; Bharucha & Krumhansl, 1983) on relatedness judgments of chords following a context and memory judgments of chord sequences (Olney, 1985). It also makes specific empirical predictions in addition to exhibiting a knowledge of musical structures not explicitly wired into it (see Bharucha, 1987b for details). One example of this is the high level of expectancy for the C major chord and the C major key after presenting the network with an F major chord followed by a G major chord. Furthermore, the expected hierarchy of stability of chord functions emerges with the presentation of a tonal context, even though a chord is linked equally to each of its parent keys. In other words, tonic chords turn out to be more highly activated than dominants and subdominants in a tonal context, even though the weights of tonic links (i.e., the links between major chord units and the key units of the same name) are no different from the weights of dominant or subdominant links. This means that some functional differentiation emerges as a result of the overall pattern of connectivity, representing the simultaneous application of multiple constraints.

Evidence for cognitively mediated activation in music

The fundamental differences between neural net theories and rule-based theories of the processes underlying music cognition lead to empirical predictions that can be tested experimentally, with the qualification that we are referring here only to rule-based accounts that claim that rules constitute the underlying cognitive process.

Network models as we have characterized them predict that expectancies are mediated by the activation of units representing the expected features. In a musical sequence, expected events should therefore be processed more quickly than unexpected events, because the appropriate units in the former case will have been processed in advance. This prediction was tested experimentally for chords (Bharucha & Stoeckig, 1986).[7] A context chord (called the prime) was followed by a chord (called the target) about which a decision was to be made. The target was either internally in tune or slightly mistuned. The subject's task was to decide, as quickly as possible, whether or not the target chord was in tune, by pressing one of two designated keys on a computer keyboard. The target chord was either highly expected or unexpected given the prime. If, for example, the prime was C major, the expected target was G major and the unexpected target was F# major. Subjects were significantly faster to make a correct decision for expected than for unexpected target chords. This was true regardless of the level of musical training.

The faster recognition of the related targets was due in part to a bias to hear the related targets as in tune and the unrelated targets as mistuned (see Bharucha & Stoeckig, 1986). We therefore believe that expectations and the context's influence on consonance go hand in hand. Chords that are expected are processed more quickly and are heard as more consonant than chords that are unexpected.

The expected target chord in the above experiment shared a component tone with the prime chord, whereas the unexpected chord did not. One might argue that a lingering perceptual effect of this common tone was responsible for the faster decision for the expected target. We therefore replicated this effect for expected chords that do not share component tones with the prime (Bharucha & Stoeckig, 1987). For example, if the prime was C major, then the expected target was B♭ major. Since C and B♭ major do not share component tones, the experiment wasn't biased in favor of the expected chord.

However, since our chords were rich with overtones, the expected chord shared some overtones with the prime while the unexpected chord did not. One might argue that a lingering perceptual effect of these common overtones was responsible for the faster decision for the expected target. We therefore replicated the experiment with chords stripped of any shared overtones. Although the overall decision times were slower, subjects were still significantly faster for the expected chords than for the unexpected chords. This last manipulation establishes definitively that expectancies in harmony cannot be accounted for solely by the lingering effects of shared overtones. They must be mediated by the indirect activation of units at a cognitive level.

An analogous experiment was conducted in India on the expectation of tones while hearing an Indian *rāg* (Bharucha, 1987b). *Rāg* Bhairav (see Table 1) was chosen because it is common in both North and South Indian music, so a wider selection of subjects in India are likely to have heard it. A rendition of Bhairav was presented to Indian subjects with an important note missing. It was predicted that units coding for this missing note would receive activation via learned connections that encode the regularities of this *rāg*. Following the rendition, subjects heard either the missing note or a control note (which does not belong in the *rāg*) and made a speeded true/false decision about this note (see Bharucha, 1987b for details). The missing note was processed more quickly than the control, suggesting that a perceptual unit that codes for that note was activated by the context.

Future directions in the modeling of musical sequences

Our current research is directed toward modeling more precisely the expectancies that result from a particular sequence as it unfolds. In particular, we are interested in the development of a sequential schema as a result of exposure to specific sequences, since this more accurately represents schema learning in the natural setting, i.e., we hear specific pieces of music, and in doing so acquire a schema. This is a particularly challenging problem, because there are many possible (and often very complex) mappings between a sequential context at any given point in a sequence and the expectancies for tones to follow.

These complex mappings cannot be learned by networks consisting of only input and output units and links from input to output. Consider, as an exercise, a hypothetical musical genre played with two bells, Bell 1 and Bell 2, with the following constraints: Bell 1 is followed by Bell 2, Bell 2 is followed by Bell 1 and Bell 2 together, and Bell 1 and Bell 2 together are followed by Bell 1. How does a neural net learn what to expect? One might begin by considering a network with two input units representing the bells that are played, two output units representing the bells that are expected to follow, and links from input to output units (as in Figure 1,left). Even after tens of thousands of presentations of these pairs, the network fails to find a set of weights that will generate (to a sufficient approximation) the expectancies that correspond to its experience.

The problem can be represented as a truth table (see Table 2). If Bell 1 is played alone, the input pattern can be expressed as [1 0] and the expected pattern is [0 1]; if Bell 2 is played alone, the input pattern is [0 1] and the expected pattern is [1 1], and so on. The last row represents the expectation of silence given silence. If we were only interested in how the network learns when to expect Bell 1, the problem is trivial, since the Bell 1 output is identical to the Bell 2 input in all four rows. The most obvious solution is a positive weight on the link from the Bell 2 input to the Bell 1 output and zero weights on all the other links.

Table 2 A musical genre that cannot be learned without hidden units

Input pattern		Expected pattern	
Bell 1	Bell 2	Bell 1	Bell 2
1	0	0	1
0	1	1	1
1	1	1	0
0	0	0	0

Learning when to expect Bell 2 is, however, an insurmountable problem for this network, because no solution exists. The logical function relating the input pattern to the Bell 2 output is nothing but XOR (exclusive OR): Bell 2 is expected after either Bell 1 or Bell 2 is heard, but not after both are heard together. A network with only one layer of links between input and output units cannot learn XOR (Minsky & Papert, 1969). If, however, the network is given hidden units that mediate between input and output units (as in Figure 1, right), it easily converges to a solution using the generalized delta rule. Thus the use of hidden units is essential for any attempt to venture into learning more complex sequential patterns.

Conclusion

We have explored some ways in which neural nets can be employed to model the acquisition of pitch schemas for music. In doing so, we have attempted to spell out, in precise terms, a hypothesis of what a schema is and how it is learned. In doing so, we have attempted to sharpen the language in which issues of innateness and learning in music are debated. We have also attempted to demonstrate a mode of theorizing that emphasizes the postulation of general cognitive principles (rather than music-specific cognitive principles) that, when coupled with a highly structured acoustic and musical environment, give rise automatically to music-specific cognitive phenomena.

Although it is widely recognized that neural net or connectionist models represent a breakthrough in our understanding of perception, their potential ability to account for complex syntactic phenomena, particularly in language, is highly controversial (Fodor & Pylyshyn, 1988; Pinker & Prince, 1988). Fodor & Pylyshyn (1988) argue vehemently against the possibility that neural nets could play a role other than to implement rule-based computational systems. We claim, at least for music, that the incremental learning of which neural nets are capable far outstrips any known mechanism for acquiring rules by passive exposure.

We maintain that although some aspects of music perception that seem to have a syntactic flavor (most notably, the recognition of motivic patterns under transformation) may prove to be a challenge for these models, their explanatory power and parsimony for a wide range of fundamental musical phenomena compel us to fully explore their potential as psychological theories.

Appendix

The activation of a unit
If $w_{i,j}$ is the weight of a link from unit i to unit j, then the activation of unit is given by:

$$a_i = f\,(net_i),\ where\ net_i = \sum_j w_{i,j}a_j.$$

f must be a differentiable and nondecreasing function for the generalized delta rule below, if the hidden units are to make a difference.

The delta rule
Let $a_{i,P}$ be the activation of input unit i given by pattern $P, a_{j,P}$ be the activation of output unit j received from pattern P, Q_j be the activation of output unit j that would suggest pattern Q, and v be a constant representing a learning rate. The change in the weight of a link from unit i to unit j is given by

$$\Delta w_{i,j} = v\,a_{i,P}\,(Q_j - a_{j,P}).$$

The generalized delta rule
(see Rumelhart, *et al*, 1986, for more details).

$\Delta w_{i,j} = v\,a_{i,P}\partial_j$, where ∂_j is an error signal at unit j. When j is an output unit,

$$\partial_j = f'(net_j)\,(Q_j - a_{j,P}),\ where\ f'\ is\ the\ derivative\ of\ f.$$

When j is a hidden unit linked to output units k,

$$\partial_j = f'\,(net_j)\,\sum\,w_{j,k}\partial_k.$$

The accumulation of activation over the course of a sequence of chords
(See Bharucha, 1987 a,b, for more details). Let $\Sigma a_{i,e}$ be the phasic activation received by unit i following chord e after the network has reached equilibrium. Let d be the decay of activation in one time unit following the offset of e. The total activation accumulated at unit i is thus:

$$a_{i,e} = \sum_c \Delta a_{i,c}(1-d)^t e^{-t}c.$$

Acknowledgments

The development of the ideas in this paper has benefited from comments or probing questions from a number of people, among them the following: David Jones, Carol Krumhansl, Fred Lerdahl, Stephen McAdams, Jay McClelland, Eugene Narmour, David Rumelhart, Kristine Taylor and Peter Todd.

Notes

1. See Feldman & Ballard (1982) for more discussion of the general properties of these models. See Bharucha (1987b) for more discussion of the musical properties of these models.
2. The reverse question sequence is also common. The concept of a neural net arose as an answer to psychological questions and now is providing answers to AI questions.
3. Rule-based systems *can* be implemented in neural nets and vice versa. However, a neural net that learns through passive exposure does not typically establish the same set of connections that it would if it were explicitly implementing a rule-based system.
4. The theory of Lerdahl and Jackendoff (1983) would seem to fall into category 3a. They write, at the very outset of their book: "We take the goal of a theory of music to be a formal description of the musical intuitions of a listener who is experienced in a musical idiom." (p. 1)

5. The universality of octave equivalence does not require that octaves be found in the music of all cultures, actual or possible. A culture may choose to assiduously avoid octaves for this very reason.
6. We limited this simulation to major keys.
7. Similar evidence for the facilitation of chords has been obtained by Marin & Barnes (1987).

References

Bharucha, J.J. (1984) Anchoring effects in music: The resolution of dissonance. *Cognitive Psychology,* **16,** 485–518.

Bharucha, J.J. (1987a) MUSACT: A connectionist model of musical harmony. In *Proceedings of the Cognitive Science Society.* Hillsdale, NJ: Erlbaum.

Bharucha, J.J. (1987b) Music cognition and perceptual facilitation: A connectionist framework. *Music Perception.*

Bharucha, J.J. & Krumhansl, C.L. (1983) The representation of harmonic structure in music: Hierarchies of stability as a function of context. *Cognition,* **13,** 63–102.

Bharucha, J.J. & Stoeckig, K. (1986) Reaction time and musical expectancy: Priming of chords. *Journal of Experimental Psychology: Human Perception & Performance,* **12,** 1–8.

Bharucha, J.J. & Stoeckig, K. (1987). Priming of chords: Spreading activation or overlapping frequency spectra? *Perception & Psychophysics,* **41,** 519–524.

Castellano, M.A., Bharucha, J.J. & Krumhansl, C.L. (1984) Tonal hierarchies in the music of North India. *Journal of Experimental Psychology: General,* **113,** 394–412.

Chomsky, N. (1980) *Rules and Representations.* New York: Columbia University Press.

Deutsch, D. (1969) Music recognition. *Psychological Review,* **76,** 300–307.

Feldman, J.A. & Ballard, D.H. (1982) Connectionist models and their properties, *Cognitive Science,* **6,** 205–254.

Fodor, J.A. (1975) *The Language of Thought.* New York: Crowell.

Fodor, J.A.& Pylyshyn, Z.W. (1988) Connectionism and cognitive architecture: A critical analysis. *Cognition,* **28,** 3–72.

Kohonen, T. (1984) *Self Organization and Associative Memory.* Berlin: Springer-Verlag.

Krumhansl, C.L. (1979) The representation of musical pitch in a tonal context. *Cognitive Psychology.* **11,** 346– 374.

Krumhansl, C.L., Bharucha, J. & Castellano, M.A. (1982) Key distance effects on perceived harmonic structure in music. *Perception & Psychophysics,* **32,** 96–108.

Krumhansl, C.L. & Schmuckler, M.A. (1987) Key-finding in music: An algorithm based on pattern matching to tonal hierarchies. Paper presented at the Mathematical Psychology Meeting, 1986.

Lerdahl, F. & Jackendoff, R. (1983) *A Generative Theory of Tonal Music.* Cambridge: MIT Press.

Lynch, G. (1986) *Synapses, Circuits, and the Beginnings of Memory.* Cambridge: MIT Press.

Marin, O.S.M. & Barnes, S. (1987) Acceptability of chord sequences as functions of their tonal relations. Unpublished manuscript.

McClelland, J.L. & Rumelhart, D.E. (1986) *Parallel Distributed Processing: Explorations in the Microstructure of Cognition.* **Vol 2.** Cambridge: MIT Press.

Meyer, L. (1956) *Emotion and Meaning in Music.* Chicago: University of Chicago Press.

Minsky, M. & Papert, S. (1988) *Perceptrons* (Expanded ed.). Cambridge: MIT Press.

Olney, K.L. (1985) *Computer Simulation of Harmonic Processing.* Honors Thesis, Dartmouth College, 1985.

Pinker, S. & Prince, A. (1988) On language and connectionism: Analysis of a parallel distributed processing model of language acquisition. *Cognition,* **28,** 73–194.

Piston, W. (1962) *Harmony* (3rd ed.). New York: Norton.

Rosenblatt, F. (1962) *Principles of Neurodynamics.* New York: Spartan.

Rumelhart, D.E., Hinton, G. & Williams, R. (1986) Learning internal representations by error propogation. In D.E. Rumelhart & J.L. McClelland (eds), *Parallel Distributed Processing: Explorations in the Microstructure of Cognition.* **Vol. 1.** Cambridge: M.I.T. Press.

Rumelhart, D.E. & McClelland, J.L. (1986) *Parallel Distributed Processing: Explorations in the Microstructure of Cognition.* **Vol.1.** Cambridge: M.I.T. Press.

Shepard, R.N. (in press). Internal representation of universal regularities: A challenge for connectionism. In L. Nadel, L.A. Cooper, P. Cullicover, & R.M. Harnish (eds), *Neural Connections and Mental Computation.* Cambridge: M.I.T. Press.

Swinney, D.A. (1979) Lexical access during sentence comprehension: (re)consideration of context effects. *Journal of Verbal Learning and Verbal Behavior.* **18,** 645–659.

Terhardt, E. (1984) The concept of musical consonance: A link between music and psychoacoustics. *Music Perception,* **1,** 276–295.

Contemporary Music Review,
1989, Vol. 4, pp. 347–362
Photocopying permitted by license only

Adaptive dynamics of musical listening

Marc Leman

University of Ghent, Seminar of Musicology, Institute for Psychoacoustics and Electronic Music, Blandijnberg 2, B-9000 Ghent, Belgium.

The paper addressess issues related to the self-organization of the *musical* mind during perceptual learning: in particular, adaptation and changes of mental musical represenations. The change of representation in response to perceptual information is called *adaptive dynamics:* a key concept in our understanding of all musical information processing mechanisms. An analysis of adaptive dynamics in the musical listening context is given in terms of *symbolic* and *subsymbolic* processing.

KEY WORDS: music cognition, listening, knowledge representation, adaptive dynamics, neural networks.

Introduction

Cognitive scientists, among them Piaget, have long maintained that our perceptive and cognitive system tends to equilibrate towards more stable states with respect to the environment. We assimilate the information which we encounter in our environment and accommodate to it by changing our conceptual representation of it.

In cases of repeated listening, perceptual learning involves the adjustment of expectancies to correctly anticipate perception which then results in a better performance of some activity under consideration. Pollard-Gott (1983) reports an experiment in which the listener's ability to construct higher level concepts was investigated. The gain in performance was measured in terms of similarity ratings. Research of this type is important, not only for the methodology used in the study of higher-level musical information processing in natural settings, but also for its relevance to a theory of perceptual learning in music. The results of the study confirm what we all knew long before, i.e. that during repeated listening our perceptual knowledge about music steadily grows and changes. However, a number of new questions are raised about the mechanisms which underlie this so-called "growth" and "change" of representations.

The present paper deals with these questions and focuses on issues related to the self-organizational of the *musical* mind during perceptual learning: in particular, adaptation and changes of representation. The change of representation in response to perceptual information is called *adaptive dynamics:* a key concept in our understanding of musical information processing mechanisms. We give an analysis of adaptive dynamics and uncover some of the basic techniques and problems encountered in modeling this notion in the musical listening context.

Account of dynamics

The role of dynamics and conceptual change in musical listening has often been discussed in the literature on *aesthetics* and the *phenomenology of music*. Musical dynamics is considered to be highly relevant for the causation of emotion and affect (Meyer, 1956) and is at the core of semantic and pragmatic theories of musical interpretation (Broeckx, 1981; Smith, 1979). Until recently, however, no systematic research has been undertaken to investigate the basic information processing mechanisms that underlie this dynamic behavior.

The outstanding exception is a formal theory of musical dynamics developed by Kunst (1976, 1978) in which listening is considered as a walk through a labyrinth of possible perceptual paths. The formalism used allows a description of this walk in terms of a temporal, interpreted, modal logic extended with some dynamic function called a *bi-valence function*. The approach has been integrated into a Production System design by Laske (1977, 1980). An attempt at empirical evaluation was carried out by Kunst & Vanden Bergh (1984).

The theory is very appealing from a phenomenological point of view since many listeners tend to describe their listening experience in terms of some kind of conscious concentration on musical sounds. One of the subjects which we asked to describe her musical listening experiences use the expression "changing fixations on sounds", which we think captures very well the spirit in which Kunst developed his so-called *formal pragmatics*.

From a cognitive point of view, however, listening is more than just a change of semiotic units and "fixation on sounds". What we are interested in is a basic understanding of the mental processes that underlie this change of meaning and conscious concentration. To speak metaphorically: we are not merely interested in the walk through the labyrinth but also in the decision processes which govern that walk.

Listening is a very complex mental activity in which a number of fundamental dynamic dimensions can be distinguished, such as:

(a) the dynamics of forming hierarchical relationships and associations between musical concepts,
(b) the dynamics of hypothesis formation and rejection,
(c) the dynamics of short term memory (STM) performance and attention in its relation to adaptation,
(d) the dynamics of perceptual learning.

In the following sections we develop an analysis of these dimensions in terms of information processing activities. We start the presentation of the model from a *symbol* processing point of view and argue that making the model more psychologically apt necessitates the introduction of a deeper level of description. *Subsymbolic* processing offers a number of alternative implementation techniques which account for some perceptual and cognitive phenomena that are otherwise very difficult to implement at the symbolic level. The central idea is that the concepts emerging at the symbolic level appear as patterns of activated microfeatures at the lower level. Finally some remarks are made with respect to the methodology used and some suggestions are offered for guiding new research.

Adaptive dynamics from a symbol processing point of view

The symbol processing paradigm holds that the human mind is a symbol manipulating system. This approach has been very popular in cognitive science for almost two decades. The core assumption is very straightforward: the basic unit of information in the system is called a *symbol* and symbols are processed ("manipulated") by *rules* of the form "if symbol A and symbol B and symbol C and . . . are the case, then symbol D is the case".

From this perspective a listener is conceived of as a symbol-manipulating system which captures the musical information stream and processes this stream so that emotion and meaning arise. The model developed here involves a number of particular hypotheses about the specific way this information stream is processed as well as the type of meaningful and emotional activity that is involved.[1]

The central idea is that the stream of information is first categorized and then associated in one way or another to the listener's knowledge. During listening, then, musical knowledge is used to process the perceived information in an efficient way. This process involves expectancies and anticipation of new perceptual information. The effect of using this strategy is that known information can be very rapidly processed so that processing effort can be used to elaborate the network at other, possibly higher, levels. This is a basic strategy in our understanding of perceptual learning. But as we all know, the perceived information may also falsify the anticipation so that the associative structure which caused that anticipation needs some refinement and change. This is part of the game that has some importance for the theory: the net result of the mutual interaction between listener and musical environment is a *learning process*, but this is not the most important consequence. Actually, we believe that it is the *pragmatic involvement* in adjusting and elaborating our perceptual associations, i.e., the *adaptive dynamics*, that is the effective cause of musical enjoyment.[2]

Dynamic Hierarchical Networks

We now turn to a more detailed description of the intuitive ideas put forward in the preceding section. The bulk of the model is a theory of mental musical representation called *Dynamic Hierarchical Network (DHN) theory*.

A DHN is a formalism to represent musical knowledge from a symbol processing point of view (Leman, 1985). The formalism resembles the structure of a linguistic semantic network (Findler, 1979) in that musical knowledge is represented by concepts and relationships between concepts. The associative structure is *hierarchical* in the sense that some concepts are more abstract than other concepts.

DHN's have a number of properties which distinguish them from the classical semantic networks in computational linguistics: (1) DHNs represent perceptual knowledge rather than linguistic or lexical knowledge; (2) the associative structure is *dynamic* in the sense that (a) it is built up during listening and is thus time dependent, and that (b) the structure can be used during perception and changed in response to perception.

The concepts and relationships together form an associative structure or network that is processed by means of rules. A distinction can be made between three levels of processing at work in the model: (1) Concept Acquisition, (2) Organization, and (3) Adaptation. During listening these three levels run simultaneously.

Concept Acquisition
A low-level signal processing system or musical data acquisition still doesn't exist to our knowledge, so we are compelled to stay within the constraints of a score representation. This is an unrealistic simplification with consequences that go beyond the current level of description of the model, but it has the advantage that a straightforward account is possible which should give the reader an idea of the core assumptions of the model. Attempts toward a finer-grained analysis are undertaken in the subsequent parts of this paper.

The first layer is concerned with the acquisition of musical concepts. We base our account on a model described in Heeffer & Leman (1986). Musical information, here represented by the score, enters the concept acquisition module which, in turn, produces chunks of information called *musical concepts*. This is achieved in three steps:

(a) there is a segmentation part, based on the Gestalt segmentation rules put forward by Lerdahl & Jackendoff (1983),
(b) a conflict resolution part, in which conflicts between segmentation (e.g. "one note between two segmentation marks is not allowed") are resolved based on a hierarchy discovered by I. Deliège (1987), and
(c) a chunking part, in which all data between two segmentations are collected. This collection is called a *basic structural unit* or a *basic musical concept*.

Basic concepts typically consist of from two to a maximum of six notes. Figure 1 displays the outcome of the concept acquisition module for the first few bars of *Density 21.5*, for flute by Varèse. The weights for the segmentation rules (see Heeffer & Leman, 1986) were set as follows: a segmentation rule for interval-difference (= 0.2), for attack-difference (= 0.3), for articulation-change (= 0.4), for slur-rest (= 0.2) and for loudness-difference (= 0.3).

Organization
Network organization is that stage of processing in which the basic musical concepts, which form the outcome of the concept acquisition layer, are associated with each other by means of explicit, labeled relationships. A distinction is made between two types of relationships: *semantic* and *episodic*. The first category specifies relations of *similarity, tonality, generality*, as well as *part-of* relationships, to mention but a few. The second category specifies time organization in terms of *immediate success, overlapping, is long after* and so on.

The processing at this level is directed towards detecting relationships between the concepts, as well as detecting new concepts. For example, when two concepts are almost similar, the system will generate a new concept which captures the features of both.

The resulting network can be displayed as a graph with boxes (concepts) and linked circles (relationships between concepts). An example is given in Figure 2. The whole network, as well as the processing steps, can be described in terms of Predicate Logics (Leman, 1986a).

Adaptation
This layer of processing accounts for so-called "knowledge-driven" perception.

Figure 1 Output of the segmentation program for *Density 21.5* by Varèse. Reproduced with the kind permission of G. Ricordi, E.C.p.S.A., copyright owner.

By this it is understood that some knowledge is used in order to process incoming information.

To give an example that copes with the experiment of Pollard-Gott (1983): assume that a listener has built up some knowledge of the piece of music just listened to. This knowledge is incomplete and only partial, may be wrong, but when listening for the second time, the listener may use that knowledge to very quickly process the incoming information. Unknown and new

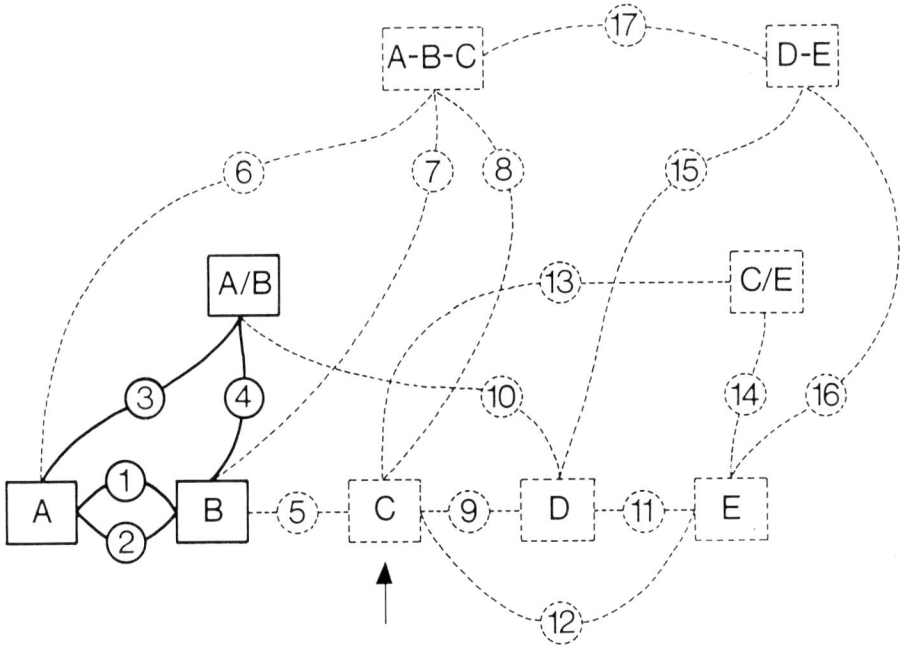

Figure 2 (a) DHN before C enters. (See text for explanation.)

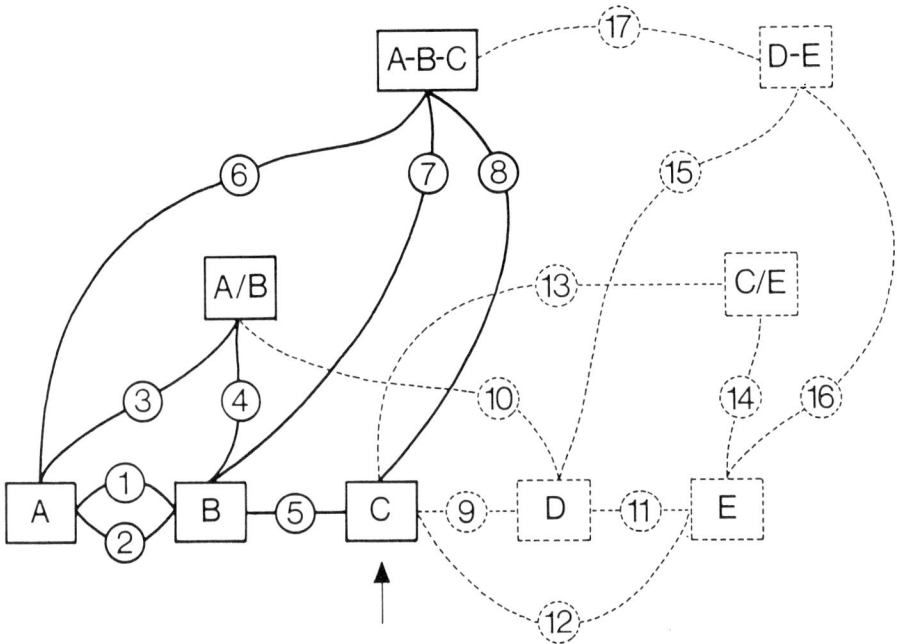

Figure 2 (b) DHN adaptation after C was confirmed.

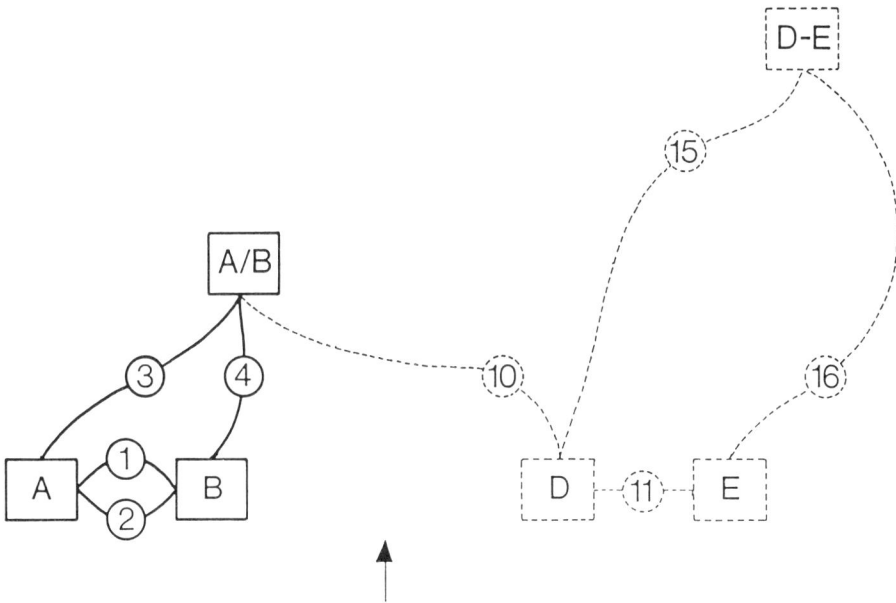

Figure 2 (c) DHN adaptation after *C* was rejected.

information will be processed from scratch and wrongly anticipated musical events result in a partial change of the associated structure. What we need is some means of control that handles perception in the context of what is expected.

Expectation and change of representation in response to new perceptual information can be described in terms of *default logics*. Default logics are characterized by the fact that the consistency of the knowledge is assumed in the absence of any evidence to the contrary. When a contradiction appears, some rules of reasoning are changed and/or part of the deduction may become invalid.

Default reasoning is invoked when knowledge about future events is primed. Then the rules which govern the network adaptation suppose the consistency of this knowledge with the information that is expected. Given that the incoming data are consistent with what was expected (i.e. there is a match between the knowledge and the information coming in), then that part of the network which assumed consistency for that information is *confirmed*. The consistency is no longer a supposition but a *fact*. *Confirmation* implies also that the incoming information is recognized as part of a context, which is determined by other concepts and relationships. The final result of this process is a very fast integration of the recognized concept within the existing knowledge structure. The effect of this is that processing effort is liberated to further elaborate the associative structure (= learning).

If, on the other hand, the information that comes in does not correspond with what is expected, then some procedure is invoked which adapts the existing knowledge structure to the new perceptual situation. This is achieved by changing that part of the network which wrongly supported the consistency of this concept. As a result, the system has to integrate the new encountered information chunk from scratch. We call this an *unlearning plus learning process:* first, part of the knowledge structure is destroyed (= unlearning), then the new concept is integrated into the remaining knowledge structure by seeking new relationships (= learning).[3]

The basic principles for the adaptation of a DHN representation are illustrated in Figure 2. The basic concepts are labeled A, B, C, D, and E. The concepts labeled A/B and C/E represent generalized concepts based on A and B, and on C and E. The boxes labeled A–B–C and D–E represent clusters of basic concepts. The relations have a number but their actual meaning is not relevant in this *Gedanken* experiment. The network expands as a function of the new basic concepts that come in: first A, then B, then C, and so on. Given the time constraints and processing capabilities, as many relationships and new concepts as possible are derived. If we ignore the difference between completed lines and dashed lines, then this graph represents a DHN going from A to E.

Since this knowledge is retained in memory (assume that it is built up during a first listening), it may be used during subsequent listening.[4] A DHN or part of it may be primed and used for processing new information. Assume that the whole network was primed just before the concept A comes in. Then the DHN may be conceived of as an anticipatory knowledge structure: all concepts of this network are expected to occur so that the structure will be confirmed in the absence of any evidence to the contrary.

Now consider Figure 2a. We are at the point where concepts A and then B have been encountered. As a result A/B was automatically confirmed because it depends on both A and B. (Completed lines stand for stable knowledge, while dashed lines represent expectations). At this moment, the very next concept expected is C.

Figure 2b displays the result after it would have appeared that C did indeed correspond with the incoming information. The part of the network which depends on the confirmed basic concepts is then automatically confirmed (some of the dashed lines are now complete). Learning is possible because processing effort, due to automatic integration, is liberated.

Figure 2c shows what would have happened if there was no correspondence between C and the incoming information. (1) All concepts and relationships which depend on C are eliminated from the representation (= unlearning). (2) The new concept must be integrated into the network from the very beginning (= learning). A formal account in terms of non-monotonic logics is given in Leman (1986b).

Spreading of activation

The model developed thus far gives an account of dynamics in terms of hierarchical concepts, associations, and issues related to confirmation and rejection of anticipated knowledge. Despite the rigorous method of description used it is possible to simulate aspects of the dynamics related to perceptual learning in human listening activities.

However, from a psychological point of view, the model still has a number of important short-comings of which the most important are the lack of *short-term memory* and *attention*.

This section introduces these concepts by elaborating the network in terms of a spreading activation model (McClelland & Rumelhart, 1986; Rumelhart & McClelland, 1986; Grossberg, 1987). The basic idea is that if a concept is activated it spreads activation along its connections to other concepts. However, spreading of activation introduces a type of computation which is rather different from symbol manipulation because what is spread through the network are not *symbols* but *activations*. This has important consequences from a modeling point of view (more about this in the following section).

A DHN can be implemented with spreading of activation. What we need is:

   (i) some value (e.g. between 0 and 1) associated with the level of activation of each musical concept,
  (ii) a weight associated with each relation,
 (iii) a way of computing the spreading of activation.

Spreading of activation accounts for a number of interesting phenomena such as the *priming effect, short-term memory processing,* and *attention.*

Semantic and Episodic Priming

Semantic priming has been studied experimentally for chord progressions in tonal contexts (Bharucha & Stoeckig, 1986; Bharucha, 1987): chords that are harmonically closeley related to a preceding context are processed more quickly than chords that are harmonically distant from the context. We believe that priming also occurs in a melodic or structural context (motives, figures). For example, when a listener has some well-defined knowledge about some piece of music, the recognition of a particular musical concept may activate a number of concepts that together belong to the *episodic* and *semantic* context of that concept. The priming effect can be simulated in a DHN as follows: the unit recognized spreads activation through the network and the concepts that are tightly connected get high activation in turn which accounts for the increase in reaction times for judgments involving related concepts. As a result, the activated part of the knowledge structure may contain information about expected musical events.

Short-term Memory (STM)

STM is defined as a functional temporary state containing the currently most highly activated concepts. STM can also be conceived of as an interactive schedule for the system to build up its associations: concepts with the highest level of activation are the most probable candidates for subsequent processing (e.g. for detecting new relationships and concepts out of them).

From a symbolic point of view STM functions as a kind of "blackboard" on which highly activated concepts are visible for the rules. The system then detects relationships between the concepts activated. Since the content of STM changes rapidly, depending on the amount of information perceived, the rules that build up the knowledge structure can only fire within some limited time constraints. Given the limited amount of processing effort, this would explain the fact that the representation would be very poor after a first listening. It also explains why confirmation of anticipated knowledge is so important: the listener need not traverse the processing steps all over again and can liberate processing effort for new "discoveries".

Attention

The activation value of a concept depends on the attention directives of the system. For example, when a listener is asked to listen to the violin part of a quartet, some attention directives are set such that the concepts associated with the violin get stronger activation than the other voices coming in. Though salient features of the music itself may call for attention of the listening system, attention may also be directed via knowledge other than purely musical knowledge (but this is beyond the topic of this paper.)

We set up a limited computer experiment to illustrate the basic ideas put forward here. Each concept of a hypothetical DHN is represented by a unit and relations are given a weight value such that activation is spread in proportion to the strength of connection between the concepts. A decay mechanism reduces the activation levels as a function of time and STM is conceived of as the functional temporary state containing the seven most highly activated concepts. All basic concepts which enter the system get maximal activation.[5]

Figure 3 displays the different stages of STM as the (hypothetical) music goes on. The vertical axis stands for the different stages, while the horizontal axis contains different concepts. Small boxes represent low activation, big boxes represent high activation values. Black boxes represent the basic musical units arriving, the white boxes represent the associated concepts. Each row shows a snapshot of the STM-store, each column shows the history of a particular concept in terms of activation. Interestingly, all boxes which are at the right side of the diagonal formed by the black boxes are the expected events. The concepts at the left represent the immediate remembrance of past concepts. It can be shown that the STM performance for expectations and past events is better when the knowledge structure is more elaborated.

Microfeature and subsymbolic processing

The technique of spreading activation is a powerful method for implementing cognitive models. This section explores the possibilities to further develop the models in terms of the parallel distributed processing paradigm (Rumelhart & McLelland, 1986). There are a number of reasons for doing this. One of the most compelling arguments, apart from the one that spreading activation models have some close analogy with the way our brain works, is that symbolic processing is not flexible enough to account for essential characteristics of human (musical) intelligence.

Making symbol systems more intelligent involves the use of techniques that go beyond the limits of the logics on which the basic reasoning capabilities of artificial intelligence systems are built. The language Prolog, as it currently exists (Clocksin & Mellish, 1981), is an excellent example of this. The DHN-theory described above was implemented in Prolog. Prolog functions as a store-house for facts and rules, and provides ways for making references from one fact (symbol) to another. Prolog's inference engine is based on the principle of resolution which tells how one symbol configuration can follow from others. The tool for carrying out this logical inference is *unification,* or matching of terms (i.e. symbol configurations). The problem is that unification is an all-or-non procedure: *either there is an exact match, or there is no exact match of terms.* Hence, probabilistic reasoning, fuzzy reasoning

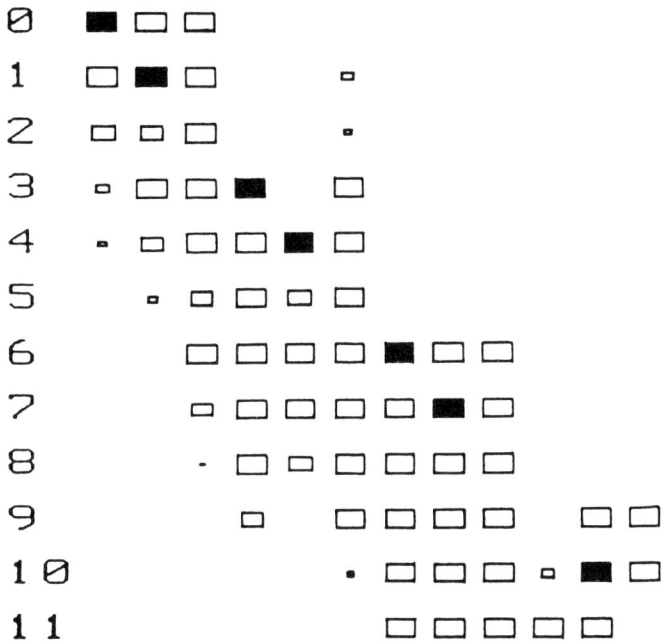

Figure 3 Example of a hypothetical STM-store dynamics. (See text for explanation.)

and default reasoning have to be introduced to cope with problems of flexibility and creativity. However, we all know that introducing flexibility at one point does not guarantee flexibility at other points. This way of modeling is purely *ad hoc* (Leman, 1988a).

These and a number of other arguments have led many authors to the viewpoint that symbols are *not* the basic units of information in the system, rather they should be conceived as having an *internal structure* expressed in terms of a set of *activated microfeatures* (Hinton & Anderson, 1981). Accordingly, the interactions between the symbols are determined by this internal structure in terms of large networks of simple processing units that use some form of message passing through spreading activation on a massively parallel basis rather than governed by stored explicit rules.

The question of how neural nets can be linked to the current theory and how far the symbolic description of DHN behavior can be implemented on a massively parallel basis is still an open problem, but an example may give an idea of the appealing processing capabilities if we should succeed.

We performed a microfeature analysis of the musical concepts from *Density 21.5* (Figure 1). The microfeatures were categorized in four feature sets (Table 1): a set of *pitch* units, a set of *interval* units, a set of *contour* units and a set of *duration* units. A "1" indicates which microfeatures apply for each of the 19 concepts (U1–U19).

Table 1 The units in each feature set are indicated by labels: p1, p2, . . . , i1, . . . and so on. Whenever one or more particular feature units are present in a concept, they are given a value of 1 in the Table. Labels have the following meaning:

Pitch units

unit label	p1	p2	p3	p4	p5	p6	p7	p8	p9	p10	p11
pitches	C	C#	D	D#	E	F	F#	G	G#	A	A#

Interval units

unit label	i1	i2	i3	i4	i5	i6	i7	i8	i9	i10	i11	i12	i13
intervals	0	+1	+2	+3	+4	+5	+6	-1	-2	-3	-4	-5	-6

Contour units the following convention is used:

•   indicates that the beginning or the end of an interval is closed: this occurs at the beginning or the end of a concept.

⊃   indicates that the beginning or the end of an interval is open: an up or down interval has occurred before or after.

  indicates upward direction.

  indicates downward direction.

unit label	c1	c2	c3	c4	c5	c6	c7	c8
contour								

Duration units the following convention is used:

•   indicates that the beginning or the end of a duration is closed: this occurs at the beginning or the end of a concept.

⊃   indicates that the beginning or the end of a duration is open: another duration has occurred before or after.

—   indicates short duration (maximum a quarter note, or crotchet).

--   indicates medium duration (maximum a half note, or minim).

---   indicates long duration (more than a half note, or minim).

unit label	d1	d2	d3	d4	d5	d6	d7	d8	d9
duration									

C.M.R. — N

We then designed a network where each set represents a pool of units. The concepts are also represented in a pool, called the *instance* pool. Each unit from this pool sends and receives excitatory activation to and from the feature units which constitute the concept. Within each pool, including the *instance* pool, each unit sends inhibitory activation to all the other units of that pool. The network was then presented to the *iac* (interactive activation and competition) program of McClelland & Rumelhart, 1988).[6]

We briefly report some of the characteristics of this network. For example, when two instantiation units are clamped (i.e. input is sent to them), activation is spread toward feature units until the system settles down in a stable configuration that makes up a *generalized* concept. For example, when U1 and U2 are clamped, generalization is poor: we get a strong activation of *p7, c2, d1, d2* and *d9*. On the other hand, activation of *U1* and *U9* results in the activation of the microfeatures *i8, c2, c6, d1, d2,* and *d9*, which constitute a more coherent abstract concept. A *resonance* effect may be obtained by setting the parameters of the network appropriately. Resonance in the above example produces activation of *U3, U12,* and *U18*, which in turn produce a strong effect on the activation of *p5, p6,* and *i3*. The so-called resonance effect is actually an effect caused by interactive connections between the units so that mutually excitatory connections enhance each other. It allows retrieval of the correct concept given incomplete input information and is a basic mechanism for priming contextual information.

Of course, this is actually an example of a flexible and creative content-addressable musical database instead of a memory-trace of a hypothetical listener. More could be said about this network and its application to musical information processing but the example demonstrates fairly well how musical concepts can be processed on a subsymbolic level in terms of spreading of activation. Where a symbolic approach would come up with a sophisticated program in order to cope with features such as generalization and resonance, this program has these "human-like" features as a natural effect.

Similar experiments with competitive and self-adaptive networks, along with work done in the field of speech recognition, have convinced us that it should be possible to build a musical data acquisition module based on sub-symbolic processing. Basically, this would consist of a feature detection module and a competitive self-adaptive network which would categorize these features into chunks of information. This would allow a far more realistic approach to cognitive modeling.

Acknowledgments

I wish to thank Stephen McAdams and Herman Sabbe for their comments on this paper.

Notes

1. Intuitive accounts of these hypotheses have been described earlier by Meyer (1956, 1973), Broeckx (1981), and Apostel, Sabbe & Vandamme (1986). A number of stimulating ideas concerning symbolic processing can be found in the pioneering work of Laske (1977, 1985).
2. A more thorough discussion is beyond the scope of this paper, but there are some very strong arguments to believe that emotional behavior is causally connected to the aspects of dynamics distiguished here. One class of emotional experiences (mentioned earlier by Meyer, 1956) is related to the falsification of anticipatory structures. Psychological foundations are found in Mandler (1980).

The basic idea is that the interruption of a process of thought evokes arousal. Emotional experience then arises out of a Gestalt-like concatenation of the visceral arousal and a cognitive evaluation.

3. According to Kunst (1976, 1978), the "learning" process is a process by which a past is attached to a percept. The "unlearning" process comes down to a change of an already formed concept as the result of an action of new concepts. These percepts are incompatible with the conceptual usage, they decompose these habits and lead to the formation of new concepts. Our account differs in that a theory is provided for the inference mechanisms and decision processes that carry out this change. Also, a DHN network is a totally different representation schema than the description schema Kunst used.

4. We restrict our account to DHN knowledge only. Other possible sources of knowledge, such as knowledge of style, composers' love affairs, literary program, and so on are not taken into account. This is a restriction, but we do believe that the principles of adaptive dynamics for these types of knowledge are similar.

5. The activation of a unit i (representing a concept) at time t is computed by a simple threshold function:

$$a_i(t + 1) = 1 \text{ if } [a_i(t) + net_i(t)] > 1$$
$$a_i(t + 1) = 0 \text{ if } [a_i(t) + net_i(t)] < 0$$

else

$$a_i(t + 1) = [a_i(t) + net_i(t)] \tag{1}$$

$$\text{where } net_i(t) = \sum_j w_{ij}a_j(t) \tag{2}$$

6. In gb 1 mode (based on an analysis by Grossberg of the *iac* program, the change of activation of a unit i is computed by:

$$\Delta a_i = (1 - a_i)exi_i - (a_i - 1)ini_i - \delta a_i \tag{3}$$

where a_i stands for the activation of unit i, exi_i is the exitatory input and ini_i is the inhibitory input computed as follows:

$$exi_i = \alpha \sum_j w_{ij}a_j \quad \text{for } a_j > 0 \tag{4}$$

$$ini_i = \beta \sum_j w_{ij}a_j \quad \text{for } a_j < 0 \tag{5}$$

The external input on i is added to exi_i if > 0 and to ini_i if < 0. α, β are parameters that constrain the summation. δ is the decay value. For more details we refer the reader to McClelland & Rumelhart (1988).

References

Apostel, L., Sabbe, H. & Vandamme, F. (eds) (1986) *Reason, Emotion and Music*. Gent: Communication and cognition.

Bharucha, J.J. (1987) Music cognition and perceptual facilitation: A connectionist framework. *Music Perception,* **5,** 1–30.

Bharucha, J.J. & Stoeckig, K. (1986) Reaction time and musical expectancy: Priming of chords. *Journal of Experimental Psychology: Human Perception & Performance,* **12,** 1–8.

Broeckx, J.L. (1981) *Muziek, Ratio en Affect*. Antwerpen: Metropolis.

Clocksin, W.F. & Mellish, C.S. (1981) *Programming in Prolog*. Berlin: Springer Verlag.

Deliège, I. (1987) Grouping conditions in listening to music: An approach to Lerdahl & Jackendoff's preference rules. *Music Perception,* **4,** 325–359.

Findler, N.V. (ed.) (1979) *Associative Networks: The Representation and Use of Knowledge by Computers*. New York: Academic Press.

Grossberg, S. (ed.) (1987) *The Adaptive Brain*. Amsterdam: North-Holland.

Heeffer, A. & Leman, M. (1986) Chunking as a method for concept acquisition. *Proceedings of the ECAI–86,* **vol.II,** 79–83.

Hinton, G.E. & Anderson, J.A. (eds) (1981) *Parallel Models of Associative Memory*. NJ: Lawrens Erlbaum Ass.

Kunst, J. (1976) Making sense in music, I: The use of mathematical logic. *Interface, Journal of New Music Research*, **5**, 3–68.

Kunst, J. (1978) *Making Sense in Music*. Gent: Communication & Cognition.

Kunst, J. & Vanden Bergh, H. (1984) The analysis of musical meaning: A theory and an experiment. *Interface, Journal of New Music Research*, **13**, 75–106.

Laske, O.E. (1977) *Music, Memory and Thought*. University of Microfilms International.

Laske, O.E. (1980) Toward an explicit cognitive theory of musical listening. *Computer Music Journal*, **4**, (2) 73–83.

Laske, O.E. (1985) Can we formalize and program musical knowledge? An inquiry into the scope of cognitive musicology. *Musikometrica*, 1.

Leman, M. (1985) Dynamical-hierarchical networks as perceptual memory representations of music. *Interface, Journal of New Music Research*, **14** (3–4), 125–164.

Leman, M. (1986a) A process model for musical listening based on DH-Net-works. *CC–AI, Journal for the Integrated Study of Artificial Intelligence, Cognitive Science and Applied Epistemology*, **3**, 225–239.

Leman, M. (1986b) Using dynamical dialectical logics for an account of de-fault reasoning in musical listening. *CC–AI, Journal for the Integrated Study of Artificial Intelligence, Cognitive Science and Applied Epistemology*, **3**, 121–131.

Leman, M. (1988a) *Symbolic and Subsymbolic Processing in Models of Musical Communication and Cognition*. Reports from the Seminar of Musicology – Institute for Psychoacoustics and Electronic Music, 7, University of Ghent.

Leman, M. (1988b) Massive parallel computer methods in music research. In *Gentse Bijdragen tot de Kunstgeschiedenis en Oudheidkunde*, 27,Leuven: Peeters, (in press).

Lerdahl, F. & Jackendoff, R. (1983) *A Generative Theory of Tonal Music*. The MIT Press.

Mandler, G. (1980) The generation of emotion: A psychological theory. In Plutchik R. and Kellerman H. (eds.) (1980), *Emotion: Theory, Research and Experience, vol 1*, London: Academic Press.

McClelland, J.L. & Rumelhart, D.E. (eds) (1986) *Parallel Distributed Processing: Explorations in the Microstructure of Cognition*, Vol. 2 Cambridge, Mass.: The MIT Press.

McClelland, J.L. & Rumelhart, D.E. (1988) *Explorations in Parallel Distributed Processing*. Cambridge, Mass: The MIT Press.

Meyer, L.B. (1956) *Emotion and Meaning in Music*. Chicago: University of Chicago Press.

Meyer, L.B. (1973) *Explaining Music: Essays and Explorations*. Berkeley: University of California Press.

Pollard-Gott, L. (1983) "Emergence of thematic concepts in repeated listening to music. *Cognitive Psychology*, **15**, 66–94.

Rumelhart, D.E. & McClelland, J.L. (eds) (1985) *Parallel Distributed Processing: Explorations in the Microstructure of Cognition*, vol.1. Cambridge, Mass: The MIT Press.

Smith, F.J. (1970) *The Experience of Musical Sound; Prelude to a Phenomenology of Music*. New York: Gordon and Breach Science Publ.

Contemporary Music Review,
1989, Vol. 4, pp. 373–380
Photocopying permitted by license only

Models and metaphors: Formalizations of music

André Riotte

Université de Paris VIII, 28 rue Danton, F-93310 Le Pré Saint-Gervais, France

From theoretical formalizations to computer models, a "modeling" approach is becoming more wide-spread among researchers working along the chain extending from the conception of music to its perception. Based on various approaches described in this volume, this article seeks to clarify the levels on which models now being developed actually function, by comparing them to the metaphorical approach often cited by composers as stimulating their creative processes. These two attitudes seem to have points in common, and both scientists and artists resort to each in turn.

KEY WORDS: Formalization, models, formal system, metaphors, simulation.

It could be observed during the symposium that while approaches involving modeling were limited to the scientific study of music listening, certain aspects of other approaches related to form and musical language could also be considered as pertaining to a type of modeling. Yet when composers spoke of form during the symposium, it was striking to note that most of them either invoked (as did Kaija Saariaho) or even fully relied on (François Bayle, Marco Stroppa) metaphors rather than models as "catalysts for forms". That is why I have decided to make several basic observations concerning the use of these two notions, with the goal of clarifying the concepts of model and metaphor, not so much to differentiate between them as to discover potential points in common. In so doing, it would be worthwhile to briefly reconsider the definition of terms increasingly used in the field of music, such as models, formalizations, and simulation, in order that the concepts they are supposed to cover become clear in our minds.

Formal models and simulation

Scientists isolate the phenomenon to be observed; they select a discrete number of measurable dimensions, the reading of which constitutes a description of the phenomenon.[1] They seek to establish the conditions under which the phenomenon can be reproduced, and to systematize the results of these observations by establishing hierarchies between measured dimensions, their relationships and constraints. In favorable circumstances, this can lead to the definition of a model of the phenomenon studied.

This type of mathematical model or system is an assembly of symbols sharing well-defined functional relations whose mathematical properties are known. The abstract description of the model may derive from various branches of mathematics – a set of analytical formulas, a system of differential equations, or a formal grammar.

The model may be determinist, if it employs only causal relations, or stochastic if it uses relations described in terms of probabilities.

Scientists seek to generalize their observations whenever possible by inferring slight but distinct changes in a given phenomenon.

Finally, they may develop a speculative model, that is to say one describing a family of as yet unverified phenomena of general scope. Strictly speaking, this constitutes the elaboration of a theory concerning these phenomena, and subsequent observation will thus confirm or refute the model's validity.

Formal systems belong primarily to this approach, their ambition being not to describe a specific aspect of reality, but rather to establish a web of relations logically deducible from coherent definitions, which thus assume an axiomatic nature.

To sum up this overview of models, the following types can be singled out:

- Models stemming from *observation* of phenomena. Their goal is to describe a set of relations linking the characteristic dimensions of these phenomena (a physics formula – the manipulation of symbols – already meets this definition since it can predict the value of a measurable physical variable).
- Models resulting from the *extrapolation* of observations. These often result from the above, their goal being to predict the behavior of a known phenomenon (system) in as yet untested circumstances (for example, a non-linear differential equation describing the movement of a pendulum whose fixed pointed is periodically perturbed).
- Models born of *speculation,* on a higher plane than the first two types of model, corresponding to a set of relationships which are supposed to explain the behavior of a class of phenomena, thus constituting a theory (see, for example, the system of "unified" equations that have appeared in theoretical physics with the goal of revealing a common formulation for phenomena covering electromagnetism, electrostatics, and gravity).

Finally, the entire evolving set of models constitutes and enhances our representation of the world.

These approaches all share the condition of *validity,* of "refutability"[2] linked to the correlation of their solutions with observation of the corresponding phenomena (granting certain approximations), whenever this is (or becomes) possible. Sooner or later, this validation determines the model's acceptability, through confrontation with a strictly defined aspect of physical reality.

Lastly, the specific case of "computer" models should be added to the foregoing notion of "mathematical" or "formal" models. Transposing an abstract model into a computer model lends a new dimension to the whole approach, particularly for those which use time as a parameter or independent variable and thus have a "dynamic" behavior. Through "simulation", changes in a model can be observed in those frequent cases where purely mathematical solutions for the system aren't possible. This gives birth to a new, intermediate concept, which Claude Cadoz (1988) calls the "materialized model". It is no longer reality which is being observed, but a simulation of reality.

Musical strategies corresponding to the different forms of models cited above depend on their place in the chain of events that represents the phenomenon of music. As a reminder of the major elements in this chain, from gestation of music up to its entry into memory, I propose the following simplified breakdown:

Conception → Production → Transmission → Perception → Assimilation

Formal or computer models have been developed at almost every stage in the chain.

Models and music composition

If, in composing a score, a composer establishes a formal coding of the musical phenomenon being conceived, this coding does not represent a model since it is limited to the description of a succession of events, without establishing logical links between them. In order to constitute a model, it is essential that:

- the representation be more economical than a simple listing of events, and
- the system of symbols constitute a formal syntax describing the logical (algorithmic) functioning of the model. If I construct a computer model from a musical score, the validity of my work will be determined by the reconstruction of the score from elements of the model supplied to the computer (cf. Riotte & Mesnage, 1988).

Intermediate stages exist, the ancestors of which are now well known, such as Mozart's tossing dice to compose waltzes. Computerized in 1959 by D. A. Chaplin (Hiller, 1970), this provided the outline of an automaton producing varied realizations of a single tonal trajectory. Even the rebuses in Bach's *Musical Offering* (1747) suppose a certain pre-existing functioning, to the extent that they are not completely "realized".

An open – though thoroughly composed – work, where possibilities for divergence and choice are finite and specified (such as Boulez' *Troisième sonate pour piano*, 1961), can be largely considered as an automaton. Its overall form can be described using an oriented graph which would constitute an initial "macroscopic" approach, that is to say articulating non-formalized fragments of discourse. Stockhausen's *Klavierstück No. 11* (1975), despite the vast (though finite) number of solutions, represents the same type of intermediate stage.

If, on the other hand, the work is constituted of repertories of symbols from which the performer draws at will, supplying missing data where needed (as in, for example, Boucourechliev's *Archipels I* (1968), potential realizations can be only partly represented by set-theoretic relations. This constitutes neither model nor automaton.

In terms of predictability, all possible attitudes now coexist, from that of the conventional composer who exerts prior control over the unequivocal course of the work to that of Cage who invents only modalities for producing symbols, the product itself having no interest apart from its unpredictability.

Models and the physics of sound

The various levels of modeling must still be identified. Pure analytic research into the production of sound, notably that of Cadoz (1988a,b), has established models of physical systems (vibrating fluids and substances) which produce sounds. This is a purely scientific approach, which is necessary if one seeks, like Cadoz (1987), to create gesture-model transducers permitting the "manual" real-time control of parameters for synthesis models. Such an approach can lead to extrapolations like, for instance, a computer model able to synthesize particular classes of inharmonic sounds (Riotte, 1984), the goal being once again to control sound synthesis phenomena even when they depart from simple periodicity. A global vision of formal processes related to timbral processing, on the other hand, is described in Jean-Baptiste Barrière's article in this volume. We have thus arrived at the next level in the chain described above, that of sound production.

However, even the intermediate stage of transmission now employs modeling. Without so much as touching on remote transmission systems in this rapid overview, it should at least be mentioned that the projection of sound in concert halls in now the object of sophisticated modeling done by acousticians, laying the foundations for architectural acoustics (Jullien, Warusfel, Malcurt & Lavandier, 1986).

Models of music listening

Cognitive models of perception are among the most ambitious in terms of principles involved, for they imply the simulation of a mental representation of materials common to both conception and assimilation of a musical work, materials that undergo constant evolution.

While the models mentioned above in the context of composition can be broken down into score models and synthesis models, cognitive models should in theory cover the entire chain, though it should be admitted that composers don't hear their works in the same way as even sophisticated listeners do (unless, as in Cage's case, the work is – by its very necessity – unpredictable).

Richard D. Ashley's presentation (this volume) offered a documented review of the various levels of music listening models and formalizations employed.

Among the models the closest to the use of a score is Ashley's, just mentioned, which simulates the learning of melodies through repeated listening, as well as that of Michael J. Baker (this volume). Both resort in varying degree to methods and algorithms of phrase reduction using the grouping preference rules from Lerdahl & Jackendoff's (1983) research.

Alan A. Marsden's listening model (this volume) is based on the hypothesis that a musical work establishes its own formal grammar. Learning is consequently expressed in the model by a control element able to create new rules by extrapolating from existing rules, and by a mechanism for weighting these rules, creating dynamic feedback to the original syntax.

Marc Leman's model (this volume) has up to now only been validated by a partial simulation on the level of short-term memory. Based on the notion of dynamic hierarchical networks (DHN), it remains therefore partly at a theoretical stage. The adaptive dynamics of this type of model mean that is self-structuring, in stages. But the underlying concepts and relations between them still have to be experimentally put into practice.

Finally, the model proposed by Jamshed J. Bharucha and Katherine L. Olney (this volume) seems particularly promising. It belongs to the family of connectionist artificial intelligence models which simulate a neural type of functioning, each information unit representing a piece of data linked to others by a more or less strong connection depending on the evolving state of the global structure. The network for "learning musical scales" actually tested by Bharucha is based on the cycle of fifths in the equal-tempered system and is therefore represented by an autoassociative network. The tonal structure is symbolized by preferential links associating major and minor triads. It is thus able to activate the missing notes of the tonal scales supplied, and to react to scales of *rāgs* by taking the tonal structures involved into account. It would be interesting to develop other network "sensitivities", notably towards subgroups on the chromatic scale.

The complexity of the work implied by such models, though they deal only with basic relationships of tonal harmony or grouping preference, gives an idea of the distance yet to be traveled in linking up with elaborate models of score description (though all the problems of harmonic approximation related to equal temperament, as well as their assimilation by the ear, are presumed to have been resolved).

Composers and metaphors

> Your eyes are doves behind your veil,
> Your hair is like a flock of goats, moving down the slopes of Gilead.
> Your teeth are like a flock of shorn ewes that have come up from the washing . . .
> Your lips are like a scarlet thread, and your mouth is lovely.
> Your cheeks are like halves of a pomegranate behind your veil . . ."
>
> *– The Song of Solomon*

Analogy was originally the poet's instrument, and a string of specific analogies – like those in this biblical passage – implicitly provide the outline for a potential network of representations applicable to another, interior, space. Metaphor, of itself, is almost indefinable. "A metaphor is the artifice which allows you to speak metaphorically," quipped Umberto Eco (1980), all the while evoking similar terms such as symbol, model, creativity, paradigm, representation, not to mention language, sign, and . . . meaning. And he added: "Considering metaphor to be cognitive does not however mean analyzing it in terms of conditions of truthfulness". The two language-related options Eco proposed contain, just below the surface, the two poles suggested in this article.

a) "language, by nature and by origin, is metaphorical . . . rules arise in order to discipline (and impoverish) this metaphorical wealth . . ."
b) "language . . . is a mechanism . . . governed by rules . . . which dictates . . . among the general sentences, those which are 'endowed with meaning'; metaphor is the breakdown of this machine . . ."

Without necessarily opting for one or the other of these hypotheses, at least two complementary attitudes can be discerned. One affirms the primacy of invention, the search for meaning in disorganized proliferation, and the other seeks to institute language(s) as formal systems(s).

It is well known that, in music, meaning itself is the problem; no unambiguous relationship can be established between a melisma and an idea, between a harmonic field and a semantic field.

The slavish imitation of reality (the recording of a nightingale's song added to the score of Respighi's *The Pines of Rome*, 1924) can be clearly differentiated from the imitative metaphor exemplified by the transcoded bird songs used by Oliver Messiaen in many of his works (for instance, *Réveil des Oiseaux*, 1953). In the former case, it is a question of an "icon" in a semiotic sense, while the latter, endowed with its own system of representation and syntax (the potential rigor of which could only be revealed by a formalization procedure) has an operative value.

Musical transposition of a poetic text is already in itself a metaphorical undertaking yet often covers more deeply hidden formal correspondences, such as in Boulez' *Improvisations sur Mallarmé* (1975), or my own *Anamorphoses* (Riotte, 1983).

For composers, metaphor seems above all to serve as efficient reinforcement to imagination at work, through "relational" borrowing from a completely different sector of nature or human activity. Taking for example, the metaphor explicitly employed by Marco Stroppa in his "Musical Information Organisms" (this volume), it is noteworthy that he declares it fruitful because it engenders a network of "functional" relationships. In so far as this network constitutes a metaphor in action, it represents a clear parallel with models, apart from the fact that these latter must sooner or later be verified by reality. But if consideration is limited to the development of a formal computer model designed to "simulate" a music composition process, that is to say a formal grammar (deriving from the corresponding recent branch of mathematics), it then appears that the validity of the relationships generated by this grammar is independent of the meaning attributed to the symbols involved.

From there it can be seen that for composers at least, the two paths converge sharply. Whether metaphors or formal systems are used, the mechanisms brought into play work on the level of coherence and not on the level of meaning. It is no longer a question of confrontation with an extrinsic reality, but of a more or less acute consciousness of this coherence, leading to an individual venture toward which only one collective response is appropriate: each individual is *sensitive* to certain forms of coherence.

Scientists and metaphors

> "Lean firmly on your principles . . .
> and they always wind up giving way."   (*Anonymous*)

Scientists also use metaphors in elaborating their theories. René Thom's catastrophe theory (1980) completely transformed the very sense of the qualifying term (in the highly abstract field in which it operates) since the oh-so-evocative dramatization which initially characterized it was transformed into the promise of survival for the system subjected to it.

Physicists seeking to model highly complex phenomena of fluid turbulence have succeeded by pushing the determinism of their models (notably represented by systems of non-linear differential equations) to the point of chaos (Bergé, Pomeau & Vidal, 1985). And they baptized the key parameters of this paradoxal situation, notably due to the extreme dependence of these models on variations in initial conditions, with the highly metaphorical expression of "strange attractors".

Finally, Henri Atlan's (1979) theory of noise complexification should be mentioned, which tends to show the process by which a living organism (represented by a multiple-feedback higher-level dynamic system) can transform the meaningless into the meaningful, echoing Isabelle Stenger's (1984) comment that, "In the world of the living, everything makes sense".

In conclusion

Over twenty years ago, I concluded a lecture on the new relationship between Art and Science, between musical composition and mathematics, with a metaphor which has since become commonplace: that of composers awaiting the availability of the spaceship which would free them from the constraints of (historical) gravity, enabling them to fix the trajectory of works to come (even if their destination appeared inaccessible or even unknowable). It would seem that through the increasingly precise definition of formal instruments now becoming accessible, the metaphor of yesterday is transforming itself into a range of computer models which by their very existence should launch, in turn, new metaphors operating on new levels.

Translated from the French by Deke Dusinberre

Notes

1. This opening synopsis of scientific procedures is drawn from Riotte & Mesnage (1988).
2. In the sense in which Popper uses the term.

References

Atlan, H. (1979) Désordres et organisation: complexité par le bruit. *Entre le cristal et la fumée*, 13–130. Paris: Seuil.
Bergé, P., Pomeau, Y. & Vidal, C. (1985) Attracteurs étranges. *L'ordre dans le chaos*, 117–164. Paris: Hermann.
Boucourechliev, A. (1968), *Archipel I* for two pianos and two percussion instruments. London: Universal Editions.
Boulez, P. (1961) *Troisième Sonate* for piano. London: Universal Editions.
Boulez, P. (1975) Nouvelles convergences avec la poésie. *Par volonté et par hasard*, C. Deliège (ed.), 121–128. Paris: Seuil.
Cadoz, C. & Luciani, A. (1987), Environnement de transducteurs gestuels. *Rapport de recherche ACROE*, Grenoble.
Cadoz, C. & Luciani, A. (1988a) Geste instrumental et composition musicale. *Rapport de recherche ACROE*, Grenoble.
Cadoz, C. & Luciani, A. (1988b) Processus de création et outil de création. Presentation at the *Music and the Cognitive Sciences Symposium*, March 1988, Paris.
Eco, U. (1988) Métaphore et sémiosis. *Sémantique et philosophie du langage*, 139–187, Paris: Presses Universitaires de France.
Hiller, L. (1970) Music composed by computer – A historical survey. *In the Computer and Music*, Harry B. Lincoln (ed), 47–49. Ithaca & London: Cornell University Press.
Jullien, J.P., Warusfel, O., Malcurt, C. & Lavandier, C. (1986). Virtual concert hall, *IRCAM Annual Report 1986*, 44–50, Paris: IRCAM.
Lerdahl, F. & Jackendoff, R. (1983) Grouping Structure. *A Generative Theory of Tonal Music*, 37–67. Cambridge, Mass: MIT Press.
Messiaen, O. (1953) *Le Réveil des Oiseux*, for piano and orchestra. Paris: Durand.
Riotte, A. (1984) Un modèle informatique pour la transformation continue de sons inharmoniques. *Proceedings of the ICMC 1984*, 43–52, San Francisco: Computer Music Association.

Riotte, A. & Mesnage, M. (1988) Analyse musicale et systèmes formels: Un modèle informatique de la première quatuor à cordes de Stravinsky. *Analyse Musicale,* **10,** 51–67, Paris: Société Francaise d'Analyse Musicale.

Rombaut, M. & Riotte, A. (1983) Anamorphoses, transcodage musical. *Matière d'oubli,* 57–78, Paris: Belfond.

Stengers, I. (1984) Multiplicité, raison et sens. *Approches du réel,* M.O. Monchicourt (ed), Paris: Le Mail.

Stockhausen, K. (1975) *Klavierstück XI.* London: Universal Edition.

Thom, R. (1980) La théorie des catastrophes. *Paraboles et Catastrophes,* 59–113, Paris: Flammarion.

Part IV
Musical Performance

Contemporary Music Review,
1989, Vol. 4, pp. 381–389
Photocopying permitted by license only

Cognition and affect in musical performance

L. Henry Shaffer

Department of Psychology, University of Exeter, Exeter EX4 4QG, England

The cognitive basis of musical performance is discussed in the context of the problem of how to construct a humanoid robot that could play a Chopin waltz. This allows the discussion to focus critically on issues ranging from the mechanics of movement to the cognitive representation in planning a performance. In doing so it makes explicit the varieties of knowledge buried in the nervous system, most of which are inaccessible to introspection. Finally it raises the possibility that knowledge may not be enough and that we have to give the robot feelings about itself as a performer and about the social context and tradition of music making.

KEY WORDS: Cognition, affect, music performance, motor skill, tacit knowledge, musical expression.

In recent years I have set as an essay for our Psychology students the question: "Could a robot play a Chopin waltz?". They happily write about the mechanical fingers of the robot clattering on the piano keys, missing the point that what is required of them is an inquiry into how people are able to perform highly skilled actions. The body after all is an elaborately articulated automaton, a skeleton equipped with muscle actuators, waiting for instruction to do something. Reflexes acting through the spinal cord can arrange the muscle tonus needed to maintain bodily posture and the coordination of such basic actions as stepping and walking given an appropriate stimulus. The automaton is however incapable of initiating action and needs continuous and detailed instructions from the brain of what to do and how to do it.

I shall pursue the robotics problem to several ends which I think are related. It is a constructive way of considering brain function in musical performance: it allows us to explore the limits of what may be achieved in robotics; and it offers a perhaps different view of music as performance.

A musical performance can be described at a number of levels, each of which can provide insights into the nature of performance. It exists as an abstract representation of intention, which is a mental plan improvised or derived from a score; as a sequence of commands for movement derived from the plan from which messages to the muscles are constructed; as a pattern of muscle contractions acting on the skeleton; as a motor geometry performed in space and time by the body; and as a pattern of sounds produced by the movements acting on an instrument, which may be the human voice.

By the time a musician has reached concert standard of performance, the intermediate levels between score and sound have for the most part become experientially transparent. They have ceased to engage attention leaving the mind free to consider matters of interpretation. They intrude on attention only at moments

By the time a musician has reached concert standard of performance, the intermediate levels between score and sound have for the most part become experimentally transparent. They have ceased to engage attention leaving the mind free to consider matters of interpretation. They intrude on attention only at moments of actual or potential breakdown, which can arise from losing place in the score, from playing wrong notes, from a disturbance of concentration, or if tension or fatigue draws attention to the movements themselves. Even then, what enters awareness has to do with ways of coping with the breakdown rather than with the processes of production. It is only when we pose the robotics problem that the complexity of these hidden processes become apparent.

The automaton

The human skeleton has evolved as a hierarchy of articulated segments. Nature has thus provided an excellent solution for a system that has to combine large movements of transportation with precise manipulation. Combined with this, the flexibility of rotation at many of the joints confers on the system an enormous freedom in composing kinematic solutions to motor problems. We shall take for granted that it is within the scope of modern technology to build such a structure. The major difficulties for the engineer begin in designing actuators that can match the properties of human muscle.

A muscle acts as a spring and has a capability almost unmatched among physical materials: it can exert force by varying its stiffness and can achieve this over a wide range. It can assume a high stiffness to produce large accelerations of movement or it can be highly compliant for the purpose of grasping a butterfly. Furthermore it can change from one extreme to the other in a very short space of time, and this is illustrated when say, a pianist goes quickly from a *sforzando* to a *pianissimo* on the keyboard.

Muscles typically act collectively in groups to produce torque about a joint, where the property of variable elasticity allows a simple principle of motor control: rotation about a joint to a target position can be achieved merely by setting the relative stiffness of muscles opposed about that joint. This solution is the envy of the robotics engineer, who has to deal with much less tractable materials.

Movements create geometries in space and time, and usually they involve kinematic chains containing two or more joints. Sometimes, as in dance and gymnastics, the performer attempts to control the overall geometry of movement over the chain, which can include the whole body: while at other times, as in typing and writing, only the geometries described by the end effectors, the fingertips or the pen tip, are relevant. A simple illustration reveals a profound engineering property of human movement. Asked to draw a line between two fixed points or to move the hand to a given target, the person typically moves the hand in a straight line. Yet this requires quite complex rotations at the elbow and shoulder. We learn two things from this: that the brain represents movement in terms of the geometry it wishes to control rather than directly in terms of muscle contractions, and that it has to solve a complex problem in joint rotations to achieve this. The joints are capable of an infinity of combinations of rotation and a motor solution involves a choice among these (Morasso & Tagliasco, 1986, Ch. 1).

Such apparently simple acts as plucking a violin string or striking a particular piano key present major problems in kinematics and dynamics to the robotics engineer, who has to take account of the masses of the limb segments and the pull of gravity in computing muscle forces. Yet the musician is willing to undertake more stringent requirements of the action, that it should have a certain timing determined by the musical rhythm, impart a certain accenting and perhaps timbre (when these can be independent) to the sound produced, and achieve a certain articulation between successive sounds. Furthermore, musicians seldom maintain a rigid spatial relationship with the instrument, and this flexibility adds to the length of the effective kinematic chain and hence to the degrees of freedom in the movement, which heavily increases the complexity of computation.

Skilled musicians will not be grateful for having their attention drawn to the complexity of their motor control. However, it may become more comprehensible to them why it requires so much practice for the beginner to achieve mastery and why laying off practice for a while can lead to loss of precision. The motor problems the engineer attempts to solve analytically have been solved by the brain by means of successive approximation over myriad repetitions of movements. These progressively refined solutions are more or less general algorithms stored in the brain as motor knowledge. It is tacit knowledge, in the sense that it is not accessible to introspection but is available for use when it is needed. Alas, the knowledge deteriorates over time unless it is continually tuned with practice.

Motor geometry

Getting the fingers to the right locations on an instrument is important but only part of the motor task in playing. The performer can learn to shape the trajectories of movement so as to achieve timing of rhythm and variation of dynamic and tone quality with an economy of motor effort. Above all, the motor geometry can be used to shape the musical phrase. Since the geometry can serve multiple ends, it is not always clear what are the optimal solutions, and it is all too easy for the performer to adopt more or less benign mannerisms that contribute little to the efficiency of movement or quality of performance.

Fingering techniques have changed in different periods of the history of many instruments, and these can have consequences for the style of performance required by the music. The player concerned with authenticity of style may thus need to learn different motor geometries for the music of different periods and even of different composers. Also, a keyboard player switching between the harpsichord and the modern piano has to accommodate the differences in touch between the keyboards and even to differences in spacing between the keys. The harpsichord spacing is typically slightly less than the piano and can differ between one harpsichord and another. The ability of skilled players to negotiate these changes suggests that their motor knowledge is hierarchically organized, so that parameter changes can apply to sets of motor algorithms. This applies similarly to actors having to produce speech in different dialects of the language.

The roles of motor geometry are not confined to the production of musical sound. Playing music is a social act involving other players or an audience. Placed in this context the trajectories of playing movements can take on gestural qualities that serve a mimetic role to help the audience follow the musical argument, or to cue other players and help coordinate their timing, or even to add a touch of theatre to the occasion.

Motor programming

Every skilled action proceeds from a mental plan that contains a goal together with a description of how to achieve it. From the viewpoint of motor kinematics and muscle contractions it is a quite abstract description. The translation from plan to performance thus requires the addition of further levels of detailed information, and because the amount of detail is typically very large and therefore not portable in memory, it has to be constructed during performance by a process of motor programming.

Let us consider a fragment of music about the size of a melodic phrase played on a piano. It is a sequence of sounds created by a pattern of movement, which is realized by a complex pattern of muscle contractions. This can involve muscles throughout the body: fingers, hands, arms, trunk, and legs can all participate in the motor pattern, so that at any moment there is not just one movement but a distributed pattern of concurrent movements, many of which have to be precisely coordinated in time. Even breathing can become locked into the temporal coordination. The number of motor parameters that have to be specified is quite large, and it is likely they are computed not together but in a structure of component representations that coordinate at different levels. This offers an economical way of combining the musical intention with motor requirements arising from the physical context of performance, such as the need to suppress a sneeze, to change bodily position, or to turn the page of the score.

The fundamental constraints on motor programming are of timing. They can arise from the real world, as in ball games, or from rhythmic requirements of the action, as in speaking, dancing or playing music, and they arise also from the need to conserve energy in movement.

Skilled performance looks easy. It appears to flow without effort, because movement tends to be continuous and avoid abrupt changes in direction as much as possible. In general, it aims at the minimum acceleration that is compatible with the task. Yet if we examine the biomechanics of movement we see that the moving parts of the body have masses that may require large forces to move them to distant destinations, and that a finite time is required to mobilize these forces in muscles. In addition, the nervous system requires a finite time to construct messages to the muscles. The nontrivial time scale of these events becomes apparent if we have to react without warning, say, to catch a glass falling off the edge of a table.

The brain deals with these timing factors, when possible, by preparing much of the information well in advance of movement and initiating movements as early as possible to reach their targets at appointed times. It is not, then, mere curiosity that leads musicians to read ahead of the fingers when playing from a score. The eye-hand span, typically of the order of one or two phrases (Sloboda, 1985, ch. 3), allows the brain time to prepare the material read from the score for motor output. It serves, of course, a further purpose of allowing the player to determine a structural grouping for the material, which can be conveyed in an expressive form over the sequence.

It is a major breakthrough in acquiring performance technique when the player can freely prepare ahead the continuation of the music being played at the moment. As long as performance is under conscious control the mind clings to the conservative habit of doing things serially. It has to be coaxed from this mode of control into allowing different manipulations of information to proceed autonomously and concurrently, to engage in effect in mental juggling. Once distributed control is achieved the eyes can read music independently of what the hands are playing, and different fingers can move concurrently to their respective targets. This is important for shaping a phrase and for playing the simultaneous voices in polyphonic music (Shaffer, 1981).

There are too few invariants between a mental plan and movement to make the translation from one to the other feasible in a single step. The movement required to play a particular note can vary enormously depending on the notes that precede and follow it, and on the manner in which the note should sound. This could lead to an infinitude of specifications in trying to allow for all possible contingencies. A more compact way of representing motor knowledge is to make use of two steps of translation. One of these constructs a representation of movement, in effect a motor image, in terms of such variables as finger assignment, the coordinates of location relative to the topography of the instrument, timing, dynamic and manner of touch. The other step adds to this representation by assigning a movement geometry together with kinetic details, and computes a patterning of muscle stiffness that will achieve the overall specification of the finger dance.

On examination, the fine structure of timing in musical performance appears to involve two levels of timing control. As we might expect, one level is concerned with the timing of the abstract pulse of the music, and the other with the timing of note production in relation to this pulse. This fits in well with the conception of two-step motor programming: the pulse can impose a timescale on the motor image, and the specifications of note timing relative to this can be used in computing the trajectories of movement (Shaffer, Clarke & Todd, 1985).

Cognitive planning

The cognitive requirements in playing music differ depending on whether it is an improvisation or a performance on a given text, or score, but they depend on similar kinds of musical knowledge. As with motor knowledge, it is part of the tacit knowledge acquired with experience. The player can verbally describe some of it, but in performance the knowledge is brought into use as it is needed, without mental rehearsal. Such rehearsal would limit the speed or fluency of performance by adding an intermediary step to its use, with the attendant risk of distorting it.

In an improvisation, such as in jazz, the player starts with a melodic idea, which may or may not be explicitly stated, and creates from it a sequence of phrases that transform or elaborate it, usually in terms of its chordal structure. The improvisation succeeds to the extent that it makes interesting use of its material and remains within the conventions of its genre, or at least makes a musically convincing case for departing from them. This requires extensive knowledge, including a knowledge of harmony, a knowledge of the genre and, perhaps, a theory of genre that allows controlled departure from current conventions. The speed at which jazz music is often played places severe real-time constraints on improvisation, making it likely that much of the knowledge is coded in the form of algorithms for making choices among the rules of generative grammars (Johnson-Laird, 1987).

In composed music, on the other hand, much or all of the structural choice has been made by the composer. The exceptions are mainly in the use of ornament or the instantiation of a figured bass in Baroque music, and in the occasional freedom to improvise offered by modern aleatoric music. Apart from these the freedom left to the player is in interpreting the musical structure and the use of expression, which includes modulation of timing and dynamic and variation of timbral quality. An interpretation is formed within a theory of musical structure, and there are many theories to choose from, emphasizing different aspects of structure; expression is formed within the conventions of a tradition, relating to the period of the music and the style of the composer, and by the interpreted structure. One of the functions of expression is to make the structural interpretation clear to the listener.

The parallels with improvised jazz become apparent if composed music is played at sight. There is a similar reliance on a knowledge of musical structure both general and specific to a genre, though in playing from a score it is used to parse the given music. Improvisation is transferred from constructing music to interpreting the structure of a text and providing an expressive commentary on that structure. Again, given the playing speeds attained in sight-read performances it is likely that the player has efficient algorithms for parsing the music and for assigning expressive forms to the parsed structures.

Of course, both classical and jazz musicians can leave as much or as little to chance in performance as they wish by preparing their materials in advance. This can take some of the burden off performance algorithms, but it does not reduce the required musical knowledge. Rather it adds an ancillary role to that knowledge, since a concert performer may play without the score, using the structural parse as a mnemonic aid in committing the music to memory. A useful side effect of remembering the surface detail of the music within a structural description is that if there is a momentary forgetting of detail during performance it can be plausibly reconstructed.

Robot performance

We now have a humanoid robot articulated with all the subtlety of the human being and equipped with a computer brain that can store and act upon a wide variety of knowledge. I have indicated some of the kinds of knowledge it would need in order to play music with a semblance of musicality and with a fluidity of movement resembling that of a human performer. This includes knowledge about its own capabilities as a mobile and manipulating system, about the effects of motor geometries on the production of sound, about the structures of music and of musical genre, and about conventions of expression. Though they are implicit in the description, I have not discussed the perceptual capabilities of the robot, its ability to interpret symbols in a score, to recognize the sounds it produces, and to make use of tactile feedback from its playing movements.

If our theories of these kinds of knowledge were sufficiently advanced it would be feasible to arrange for the robot to play a Chopin waltz. We might, however, soon tire of the performance. The original question was ambiguous about whether the robot had to play a particular waltz or any of the Chopin waltzes, and it did not specify a quality of performance. I have tried in the discussion to anticipate the requirements of a general ability to play more than one piece, but it remains for me to discuss the issue of quality and of the gap that may still exist between the robot and the human performer.

The focus of the issue is on the question of whether it is sufficient to give the robot knowledge, of music and of musical technique, to turn it into a performing musician. The robot I have discussed so far is essentially a symbol manipulating device together with a set of actuators, which will on demand give a performance observing every detail and nuance that is within the scope of its instructions. Beyond this it is indifferent to the performance and its possible effect on an audience, it knows nothing about music as experience, and it has no sense of itself as a performer. We have not given the robot feelings and consequently all these are irrelevant considerations. The issue is, of course, a familiar one to any music teacher who has had to deal with pupils auditioning as robots.

I do not feel confident discussing the matter of emotion in music, yet the direction of the argument so far leads inexorably to this step. So here goes.

The emotional factor in music has several dimensions. Music making is typically a social event, involving an audience or other players, and the player needs to have a sense of social occasion. The player also needs to have the feeling of playing within a musical tradition rather than playing a piece as an isolated exercise. Again, there is an element of sensuousness in the physical movements of playing music and a player who does not experience this is missing some of the point of playing. Finally, however much weight one attaches to its abstract structure music has inescapable connotations of mood and a player has to be sensitive to these.

It is a chicken and egg question whether the patterning of mood is a consequence of the musical structure or whether the structure was chosen to convey this pattern. Even the composer may not be clear on this point, since the wellsprings of invention are not freely open to introspection. All we can say with confidence is that in a well-knit piece, mood and structure are closely associated. A player developing an interpretation of the piece needs to find a patterning of expression that works at both levels, but whereas a structure for the music can be determined by analysis, the patterning of mood must be felt. This is not to say that the player has to experience the mood at the time of playing. It is sufficient to be able to simulate the motor concomitants of mood so that it is conveyed in sound through the gestures of playing, just as an actor is able to adopt different persona. The repertoire of expressive devices the player acquires may be shaped to deal with structure but may receive its fine tuning from the needs to express mood.

Thus the parameters of expression may be only approximately evaluated within the motor program leaving fine adjustment to a simulation of mood. There seems to be a catch, however, in that a mood may not be reliably simulated. The player may have to be in a suitable frame of mind to sucessfully adopt the simulation and this cannot be planned. Hence a player with complete mastery of a piece of music may give an inspired performance on one occasion and a merely competent one on another. It is difficult to account for this if one supposes that expression is determined only by cognitive factors.

There are different ways in which frame of mind might affect a simulation of mood. One is that the mood of the player may be incompatible with the mood to be simulated, making the simulation inaccessible. Another, less psychodynamic, possibility is that the player's mood may affect the refinement of motor control needed to convey the subtleties of expression associated with the patterning of mood. We do not yet know a great deal about the relationship between mood and motor control. It seems clear that states of fear or anger can lead to a loss of control, and so it is possible to consider the converse, that states of excitement can lead to a heightening of control, perhaps making the muscles themselves more responsive to nuances of instruction.

The mood of the player can be influenced by a host of factors only some of which have to do with the musical context. Within that context, it can arise from a sense of occasion induced by the acoustics of the hall, the responsiveness of the audience, rapport with the other players or an affinity with the music. Such factors can raise the level of sensitivity of the player, inducing a feeling of being intimately connected to the music. Apart from these it may arise from the bodily sensations of movement in producing the musical sound, and this itself can be a complex factor. It can include a feeling of pleasure in being in precise control of the production of movement-sound. Related to but different from this is the kinesthetic pleasure that can arise in executing difficult motor patterns that the composer has designed for the virtuoso performer. I have in mind here such pieces as the Chopin *Etudes* with their ostinato patterns played at speed, each involving a slightly different configuration of the hands. Finally and not least is the feeling of embodying the musical rhythm. This last can be experienced by anyone playing within their level of competence. It can be experienced by an autistic child banging out an accompaniment to a rhythm as much as by a concert musician.

A great deal has been claimed for dancing and playing music, or at least beating time to music, as forms of therapy. If these claims are valid, this suggests that the connection between music and its mimetic movement is quite primitive. Playing music is perhaps the supreme instance in which the rhythms of movement both shape and mimic the end product. If we look for this intimacy of relationship elsewhere, perhaps the nearest approximation is in such crafts as wood carving and sculpting, in which the rhythms of chiselling create the textures of the surface.

It is not difficult to find a physiological mechanism for the subjective feeling of embodying a musical rhythm. If muscles singly and collectively act as springs then they can enter oscillatory modes of behavior, and sensory feedback from the muscles to the brain can provide a very direct sense of rhythmicity. It is overly simple to suppose this is restricted to periodic oscillation. Perhaps marching in step is the nearest one gets to pure periodicity in movement, and it was just this activity that led the Russian physiologist Bernstein (1967) to his now classical studies of rhythmic movement. More generally, the periodicity of muscle varies with its stiffness and this can be continuously modulated in time. Also, at any moment periodicity can be distributed in complex patterns over the body. Hence the experience of rhythmic involvement can be quite rich, though it may only achieve this richness in the highly skilled performer.

I close with two observations:

Cognitive scientists who have followed the argument so far may become impatient and point out that any transformation over a set of expressive parameters, affecting timing, dynamic, touch, and so on, yields a similar set of such parameters, and these could have been planned in the first place, and even given to a robot. Thus there is no fundamental difference between good and inspired playing, except in the choice of parameters, and no need to complicate a theory of performance with emotional factors. Yet the fact remains that players cannot determine through practice the occasion of an inspired performance, and cannot fake their own mood by going through the motions. Listeners can detect the difference even in recordings of a performance. The difference seems to be not in the choice of parameters but in a quality of articulation that runs through the performance. The structural interpretation of the piece remains the same but only sometimes the players' own mood allows them to fully catch the mood of the music, and this is felt by both the players and the listeners.

Composers are at liberty to define music in any way they like, and to choose to work within or alter any of its conventions. However, if music is an important part of human experience, and composers aim at shared experience rather than private satisfaction, then it is reasonable to raise the question whether the departures from a tradition replace it with something of comparable value. I have discussed the possibility that the richness of musical experience derives not just from sounds but from the physical and social aspects of producing them. If, as has sometimes happened in recent years, music is divorced from a rhythmic pulse or from direct human means of production, then one is entitled to ask what it has to offer in compensation. It may be fun programming robots or synthesizers to produce music and the output may be fun to listen to, but the therapeutic balm of participation may be lost in the processs.

Acknowledgments

This research is supported by a grant, C00232213, from the Economic and Social Research Council.

References

Bernstein, N. (1967) *The Coordination and Regulation of Movements*. Oxford: Pergamon.
Johnson-Laird, P.N. (1987) Reasoning, imagining and creating. *Bulletin of the British Psychological Society*, **40**, 121–129.
Morasso, P. & Tagliasco, V. (1986) *Human Movement Understanding*, Ch. 1. Amsterdam: North-Holland.
Shaffer, L.H. (1981) Performances of Chopin, Bach and Bartok: Studies in motor programming. *Cognitive Psychology*, **13**, 327–376.
Shaffer, L:H., Clarke, E. & Todd, N. (1985) Meter and rhythm in piano playing. *Cognition*, **20**, 61–77.
Sloboda, J.A. (1985) *The Musical Mind*, Ch. 3. Oxford: Clarendon Press.

Contemporary Music Review,
1989, Vol. 4, pp. 391–404
Photocopying permitted by license only

Speech and music performance: Parallels and contrasts

Rolf Carlson, Anders Friberg, Lars Frydén, Björn Granström
& Johan Sundberg[1]

Department of Speech Communication and Music Acoustics,
Royal Institute of Technology (KTH), Box 70014, S-10044 Stockholm, Sweden

Speech and music performance are two important systems for interhuman communication by means of acoustic signals. These signals must be adapted to the human perceptual and cognitive systems. Hence a comparitive analysis of speech and music performances is likely to shed light on these systems, particularly regarding basic requirements for acoustic communication. Two computer programs are compared, one for text-to-speech conversion and one for note-to-tone conversion. Similarities are found in the need for placing emphasis on unexpected elements, for increasing the dis-similarities between different categories, and for flagging structural constituents. Similarities are also found in the code chosen for conveying this information, e.g. emphasis by lengthening and constituent marking by final lengthening.

KEY WORDS: Communication, duration, intonation, music performance, music synthesis, phrasing, prosody, speech synthesis.

Introduction

Much has been written and said about parallels between language and music regarding their structural aspects (Winograd, 1968; Bernstein, 1976; Sundberg & Lindblom, 1976; Lerdahl & Jackendoff, 1983). Striking similarities are generally found, such as a hierarchic structure with several levels. This hierarchical structure reflects the relations between different parts of the messsage. These relations have basic simple forms. With the help of variations and violations of this form, a speaker can focus on various important aspects of the message. The communicative success of these transformations is dependent on the listener's knowledge of the basic form and the speaker's presupposition about the listener's knowledge. In speech and music research, the relation between the speaker/ performer and the listener at all structural levels is, or should be, of prime interest. In the present article we will concentrate on some interesting similarities and contrasts between language and music that seem to exist at the surface level.

Both language and music are realized in acoustic signals. Linguistics has introduced the term *speech* for the acoustic realization of language. In music science, no corresponding terminological distinction has been established. In this article we will use the term *music performance* for the acoustic realization of music. Thus, while the term language is equivalent to music, the term speech is equivalent to music performance.

One major problem both in speech and music performance research is that many different prosodic factors are mixed together as one single acoustic parameter. For instance, segmental inherent pitch, word tone, sentence type, lexical stress, emphasis etc. can all be signaled by one single parameter, such as the voice fundamental frequency. In the same way, the duration of speech sounds is affected by a variety of conditions including stress, position in the utterance, and local phonetic context. An extensive review of the factors that have been found to influence the duration of speech sounds are reported in a paper by Klatt (1976) and in special issues of *Phonetica* (1981, 1986). All of this is taken into account by the listener in the perceptual decoding process.

The same applies to music. There are many different reasons to lengthen or shorten a note beyond its nominal duration as specified in the score. Apparently, such perturbations of the nominal duration serve different purposes, e.g. emphasis, marking of phrase endings, and sharpening the contrast between categories. This results in rather complicated interactions making it hard to use conventional analytic methods. As a consequence, analysis-by-synthesis is a powerful tool in both speech and music performance research.

In recent years, the use of computers has led to great advances in both speech and music sciences. With the help of fast analysis tools, new knowledge has been gained and new models simulated. It is now possible to study the acoustic behavior of articulatory models or to compare duration models to natural recorded speech in data banks.

Speech recognition systems have attracted a lot of research money and some of it has been fruitfully invested in basic speech research. Text-to-speech programs have been productive in increasing the understanding of the speech communication process. With the help of models formulated as transformation rules, we have been able to test our current knowledge and to reject or accept ideas.

Similarly, our work with developing computer-generated music performances, by means of note-to-tone programs, has been revealing as to basic aspects of music communication. In this article, we will analyze some similarities that we have observed in our parallel working with text-to-speech and note-to-tone programs.

Text-to-speech and note-to-tone programs

We have previously reported on the long-term effort to develop high quality text-to-speech systems for several languages (Carlson & Granström 1975a; Carlson, Granström & Hunnicutt, 1982). The approach taken has been to formulate the process in a coherent framework. One criterion was that linguistics involved in creating, refining, and maintaining the text-to-speech software should be able to work with constructs and conventions familiar to them without necessarily mastering conventional computer programming. Consequently, *distinctive features* and *phonemes* are primes in our system. Also, the rule notation borrows heavily on that used in generative phonology, although it is expanded to easily handle continuous variables such as synthesizer parameters. This makes it possible to formulate pronunciation rules for coarticulation and utterance final lengthening in the same framework as the rules used for translating spelled text into phonetic transcription. Another important goal was to streamline the transfer to a real-time system, which has the dual advantage of speeding up the testing of rules and of facilitating practical use in different applications.

Our current text-to-speech system consists of a structure of rule components and various lexica. The lexica have two important functions. The most important is to separate function words from content words. The function words, e.g., articles, prepositions, and pronouns, are mainly used to build up the grammatical structure of a language. Each language has a limited number of such words. These words are normally unstressed and often violate the pronunciation rules in a language. Content words follow pronunciation rules to a greater extent. The rules are written in the same formalism throughout the system and, in order to refer to different-level units, we attach appropriate features to our single stock of symbols. In this way everything from syntactic analysis to detailed sub-phonemic manipulations is handled in a coherent way.

The note-to-tone program is basically the same as the phonetic part of the text-to-speech program and was reformulated for musical purposes by coauthors Carlson and Granström (Sundberg, 1978; Sundberg, Askenfelt & Frydén, 1983). The modification regards the input format, being a transformation of the musical score, which can be executed automatically. Each note is defined as a sound possessing a pitch name (e.g. F sharp), an octave number and a duration, and each voice of a score is stored, represented in this way, as a separate input file.

Apart from this, information is also added regarding chords and phrase and sub-phrase boundaries. It would have been possible to write computer programs also performing chord and phrase analysis. However, this project aims at a description of music performance rather than music analysis. Therefore, it appeared preferable to do these analyses in the conventional way, i.e. using one's musical judgement.

The musical equivalents of the pronunciation rules in the text-to-speech program are the *performance rules*. These have been gradually developed over a long period of time. In this process, a professional music teacher and musician, Lars Frydén, has played a decisive role. He has "instructed" the computer on what to change in the performance in order to improve it musically. These instructions have been organized into a set of ordered, context-dependent rules, most of which have been tested in experiments with panels of expert listeners (Thompson, Friberg, Frydén & Sundberg, 1986).

In summary, parallel experiences have accumulated from working with speech synthesis (coauthors Carlson and Granström) and music performance synthesis (coauthors Friberg, Frydén and Sundberg) using similar tools. This allowed a more detailed comparison than is usually possible. Therefore, it seemed an interesting task to compare these experiences and to discuss the implications of similarities and dissimilarities.

An important difference in focus should be mentioned at this point. In the case of speech, the instrument producing the acoustic signal consists of the human voice organ. This is an exceedingly flexible instrument producing a highly variable acoustic signal. Consequently, synthesizing the output is a complicated task, and intelligibility rather than beauty has been the primary concern in this synthesis work.

Another difference between a normal text and music is also of general interest. It is relatively easy to generate the phonetic transcription from the spelled text.

In this transcription, only the segmental quality is marked. On the other hand, it is a major task to make some kind of syntactic and semantic interpretation of the text. Such information is in most cases needed in order to generate really convincing speech performance. In present text-to-speech systems, this problem is normally approached simply by identifying function words and perhaps accessing parts of speech (word class) information in a lexicon.

Normally, spelled text or phonetic transcription lack markings of phrases, emphasis, and most other indicators of higher-level relations. This has led current text-to-speech systems to concentrate on lower levels and primitive syntax analysis. Much less has been studied to formulate the acoustic correlates of larger syntactic structures. Even discourse structure, however, is known to affect, for example the acoustically realized duration and intonation (Lehiste, 1975).

The problems presenting themselves in attempts to synthesize music performance are, in part, different. By contrast to the vocal tract, most music instruments are built of rigid parts of wood or metal. This leads to an acoustically much more stable, less flexible signal, so that synthesizing the sheer instrument signals per se is by no means as complicated a task as in the case of the human voice. Therefore, in music performance synthesis, the main concern has been the expressive deviations by means of which the performer shows his musical interpretation of the piece. Fortunately for the musician, the music also contains more information about the composers' intentions at a higher level. This difference between speech and music performance synthesis work limits the possibilities of making exhaustive comparisons.

The human voice is undoubtedly a musical instrument when used for singing. Parallels between speech and singing are too obvious to be interesting and will mostly be disregarded in this paper.

Basic contrasts

Representation Levels

Both speech and music can be represented by means of graphical signs, viz., the orthography and the music score. However, in the case of speech, the phonetic transcription exists as an intermediate level of representation between orthography and speech. The relation between the orthography and the phonetic representation varies between languages; in some languages such as Finnish or Spanish, the relation is very straightforward making the intermediate level almost unnecessary. In other languages, like English, the relation is quite complicated and not entirely according to a set of conventions/rules. In this case, the speaker or synthesis program needs to rely on a phonetic transcription.

In a sense, an equivalent intermediate level of description exists also in music, viz., when the player or the composer complements the score by a great number of additional signs, such as dots, dashes, wedges, slurs, etc. This type of score has not formally been distinguished from the orthographic representation as clearly as in the case of speech. Also, this intermediate level seems more needed in speech. This can be concluded from the fact that the speech produced by the concatenation of sounds directly corresponding to the letters not only sounds extremely unnatural, but is also even practically impossible to understand; music produced from a nominal realization of the note signs, on the other hand, is still recognizable, even though very boring to listen to.

Quantization

Although both music and language can be represented by graphical signs that in some way can be regarded as symbols for the corresponding acoustic signals, the relationship between this graphical representation and the sound signals differs in one important respect.

In the music score, pitch and duration are represented by symbols according to a system of *quantized categories*. For instance, a quarter note (crotchet), is nominally twice as long as an eighth note (quaver), and a C is almost 6% lower in fundamental frequency than a C sharp.

In orthography, on the other hand, neither pitch, nor duration are specified in quantitative terms. In most languages it is rather the time derivative of pitch that is predictable from the orthography, such as in cases of question, quotation, accents, etc. or from the linguistic content, such as in cases of so-called focus. (Focus is a term used in linguistics to mark the part of the sentence which carries the most important information). In so-called tone languages, pitch is predictable within non-quantized categories, such as high, middle, low, rising, and falling. Duration can sometimes be predicted qualitatively from orthography, such as "long" and "short" vowels and consonants. However, prediction of phonetic transcription sometimes fails so that a lexicon is needed in order to arrive at correct word pronunciation.

Parallels

Role of the Author/Composer

The fact that we can formulate rule systems that generate intelligible speech and music performance of a decent musical quality apparently means that the acoustic realization is implied in the orthography and the music score. This suggests that the author limits the number of possible acoustic realizations of his text in a similar way as the composer limits the possible acoustic realizations of his score. This is probably an essential requirement on a useful symbol system, such as the orthography and the music score. This similarity indicates that, in this regard, similar processes underlie speech and music performances. However, the final acoustic realization is not of the same prime concern for authors as for composers. This is also why writing systems can have a more vague relation to the acoustic realization.

Stress and Emphasis

An important premise of the comparisons carried out in the present article is the difference between *emphasis* and *stress* in speech. While emphasis is content-dependent, the distinction between stressed and unstressed is a word-level phenomenon. This means that emphasis and stress exist at different levels in speech, stress being at a lower level. It seems that an equivalent distinction can be made in music, in that stress is a property that is dependent on the position in the bar, while emphasis is rather dependent on higher-level aspects of the musical structure.

Communicative Purposes

Predictability and emphasis

In both speech and music, a listener can predict most acoustic events due to his linguistic or musical experience and competence. For instance, we are very skilled in filling gaps in the acoustic information occurring because of interference with noise. Even if a door is banging in the middle of somebody's speech, we can mostly hear what the person is saying. It is often even hard to tell which speech sound was masked by the noise. Some classical perceptual studies have shown that the perceived location in time of a disturbing sound is judged to be a place in the conversation where it causes as little harm as possible, i.e., close to a syntactic break.

However, the meaning of an utterance does not always survive a door bang. In some places, the sentence is vulnerable and if information is lost in such places, the meaning of the sentence could not be restored. From this, we can conclude that predictability varies along a spoken utterance.

A similar reasoning seems applicable to music. Mostly we can complement a melodic line correctly, even if one note is missing. For instance, deleting a passing-note would be completely harmless. According to Sloboda (1977) the eyes of musicians tend to jump to beginnings and endings of phrases, thus apparently inferring the intermediate notes. On the other hand, there are also more important notes in a melody. In the second theme from the first movement of Schubert's *B minor symphony, D759*, there is a modulation from D major to B major, see Figure 1. The modulation is announced by a D sharp. If this note is cut out, the harmonic interpretation of the following notes will be affected. Thus, this D sharp seems to be a crucial note for the melody. It seems obvious that such important notes have a low predictability, and it can be assumed that predicability is dependent on the inverse of the information rate.

Figure 1 Second theme from first movement of Schubert's *Symphony in B minor, D 759*. The top line of numbers symbolizes the harmonies in terms of the distance, in semitones, between the root of the chord and the root of the tonic.

The parallel ocurrence of a time-varying predictability in both speech and music is by no means trivial. Its existence in both suggests that possibly it represents a way of meeting an essential limitation of the perceptual system. For instance, this system may be incapable of processing signals having an invariably high information rate.

Predictability of words has been studied by several authors. In a now classical study by Lieberman (1963), the relationship between context redundancy and keyword intelligibility was studied. It was shown that predictability had a strong effect on how clearly a word was pronounced. This experiment was later repeated by Hunnicutt (1985, 1987a). In a text-to-speech system, Coker, Umeda & Browman (1973) included factors such as word frequency and repetition of earlier mentioned words. These parameters added to the naturalness of the speech quality. Similar ideas about predictability are included in modern communication aids for the handicapped. It can be shown that a prediction program working only on the surface structure can predict at least 50% of the typed letters in a running text (Hunnicutt, 1987b).

Predictability in speech is present at many different levels such as phoneme sequence, choice of word endings, and even syntatic constructs. At a structural level, we know that certain phrase or word combinations are very probable. It is even likely that certain word sequences are lexicalized just like certain single words, and that we perceive these phrases as single units.

The varying predictability in a sentence is significant to its acoustical realization, i.e., to speech. In order to make speech easy to understand and natural sounding, it is necesary to emphasize important, or less predictable words, and to deemphasize unimportant, predictable elements.

The varying predictability is significant also to the quality of music performance. In our rule system for music performance we have introduced a notion which we have called *melodic charge* in order to take into account the need for emphasizing certain notes and deemphasizing others. Melodic charge is defined with the aid of the circle of fifths, where the root of the prevailing chord has zero melodic charge, as illustrated in Figure 2. It is correlated with listeners' concepts of what is a good continuation of a scale, according to probe tone rating experiments carried out by Krumhansl & Kessler (1982). Also, according to Knopoff & Hutchinson (1983), it is positively correlated with the occurrence of the various scale tones in Schubert songs, so that, in some sense, it would reflect the negation of predictability, or *remarkableness* of the notes in a melody.

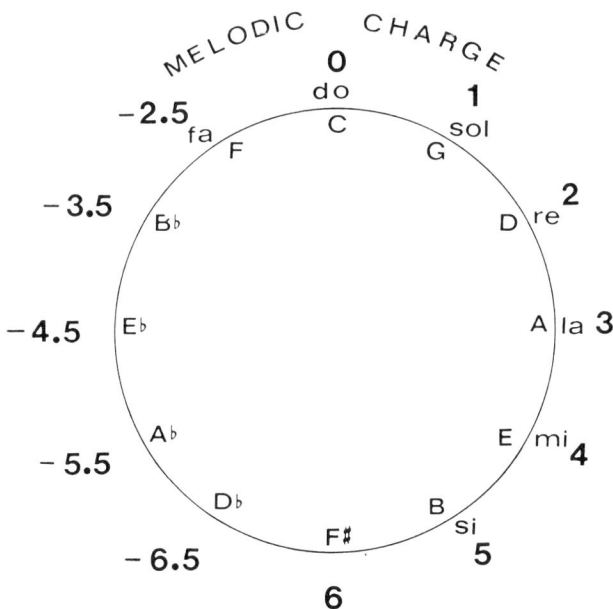

Figure 2 Definition of melodic charge by means of the circle of fifths.

The fact that the negation of predictability is marked by emphasis in both speech and music performance seems to suggest that adjusting the performance to the predictability is an important property of communication by acoustic signals.

Category separation
Some rules in the music performance program seem to serve the purpose of increasing the contrast between different categories. For example, minor seconds are played narrower than their nominal value, and major seconds are played wider. Also, short notes are shortened and long notes are lengthened. Another example is the *inégalles,* a playing manner from the Baroque era which is applied to long series of notes of the same nominal duration; in such series, duration is transferred from the unstressed to the stressed notes, the quantity transferred being slightly less than in the case of a punctuation. The result is that emphasis is laid on the differences between stressed and unstressed positions in the bar.

In speech, pitch and duration are specified in non-quantized categories as previously mentioned. Therefore, contrast sharpening is more difiicult to discern in speech than in music performance. Still, it is evident that categories exist also in speech. For example, there are long and short vowels, and the contrast between these categories is increased by formant frequency differences. Thus, a short Swedish /a/ has higher first and second formants than a long /a/. Word emphasis constitutes another example. In a study by Erikson & Rapp (described in Carlson, Erikson, Granström, Lindblom & Rapp, 1975), where emphasis was placed on different words in the same sentence, it could be seen that the syllables neighboring the emphasized word were pronounced with shorter durations and lesser fundamental frequency movements, while the duration of the emphasized word was increased and its fundamental frequency was quickly changing (see Figures 3 and 4). Finally, a classic observation from English is the marked difference between the length of a vowel before voiced and voiceless consonants. Phonetic contrasts are also exaggerated when there is a contextual need to distinguish two similar words, like Emigrant/Immigrant.

Constituent marking
Both speech and music have a hierarchical structure, as mentioned, and one of the obvious parallels is that phrases and other constituents in the hierarchical structure are marked in both. Moreover, the structure is evident from the graphic representation in both, at least for a human observer who is familiar with the language or the type of music.

In orthography, various signs such as periods, commas, semicolons, and spaces are used to mark the structure; but less explicit structural indicators are also used, such as word order and special words like conjunctions. In speech, these constituents are marked in many different ways, primarily by durational and modifications, voice source changes, and pausing. According to Klatt (1976) constituent marking as evidenced from segmental duration can be observed at different levels, e.g., even at the word level.

In music, phrase endings are marked in a number of different ways; in nursery tunes, phrase and sub-phrase endings were marked by long notes, and certain harmonic and melodic stereotypes (Lindblom & Sundberg, 1970).In the music performance program, phrase and sub-phrase endings are marked in the input notation. Then, the final notes of these two constituents are marked in the

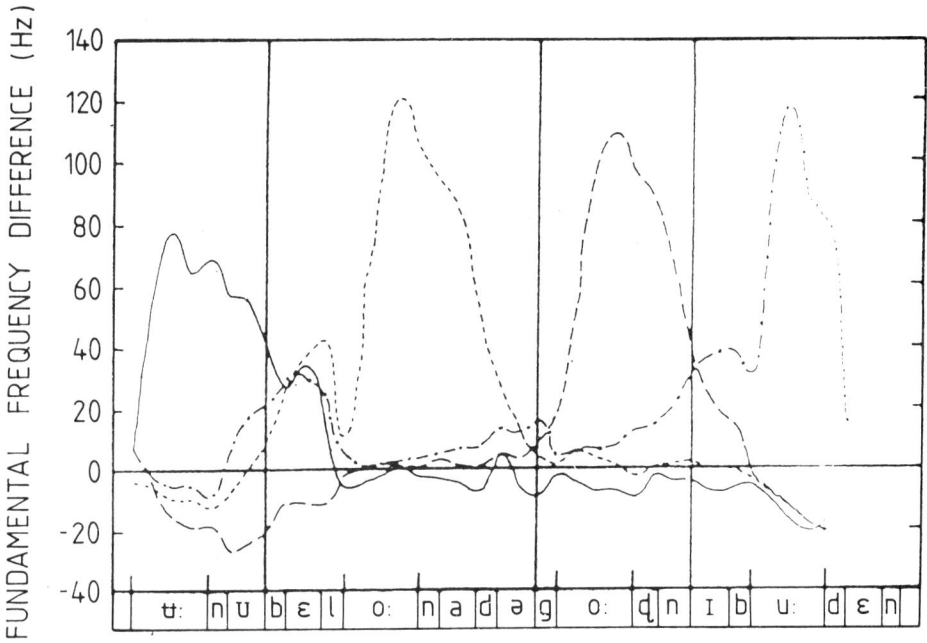

Figure 3 Fundamental frequency differences between emphatic productions and the averaged neutral production of the Swedish sentence "Uno belanåde gården i Boden", (Uno mortgaged the farm in Boden). The different curves pertain to emphasis on the four main words.

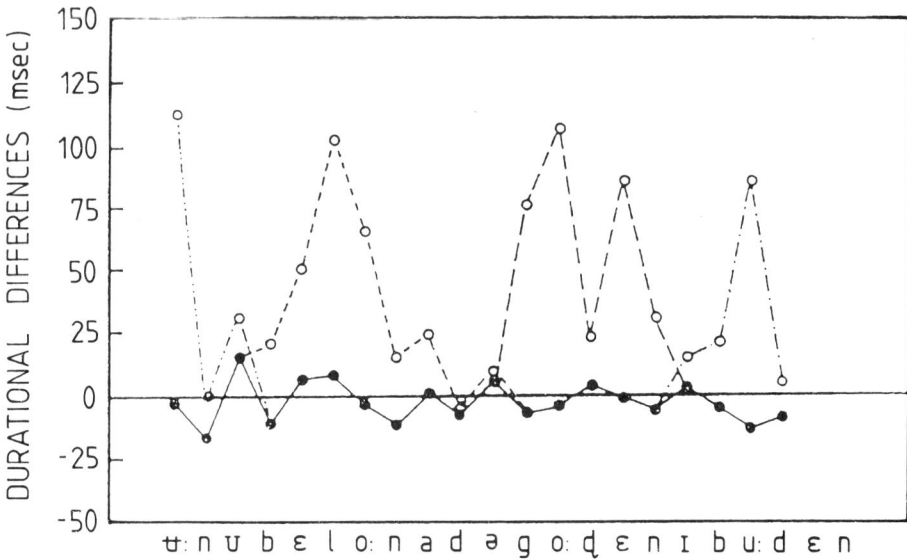

Figure 4 Durational differences between segments in emphatic and neutral utterances. The solid curve indicates the difference between segments in nonemphasized words of emphatic utterances and neutral production. The other curves pertain to the increase in duration of the words when pronounced emphatically.

performance (Friberg, Sundberg & Frydén, 1987). This marking seems to be an essential requirement in a music performance (Thompson *et al*, 1986). Measurements on music performance support the same assumption and also indicate that constituent marking takes place at different levels in the hierarchy (Todd, 1985).

Phrase marking is an instance of the general principle of marking constituents in a structure. This principle is often referred to as *grouping* which seems esssential in any type of communication. It seems that constituents at many different levels are marked. For instance, word boundaries are marked not only in speech, as mentioned above, but also in orthography with a space. Also in understanding the speech of a foreign language, a major step is to be able to detect the boundaries between words.

The fact that constituent marking appears not only in speech and music performance, but also in the orthography and the music score suggests that the marking of constituents is a paramount demand in many kinds of inter-human communication.

Choice of Acoustic Code

As both speech and music performance use acoustic signals for communication, it is interesting to compare the codes used. If speech and music performance use similar codes, the understanding of music requires a competence which is partly the same as that required for understanding speech. Thus, comparing the codes will shed some light on the basic requirements for understanding music.

Emphasis
As mentioned earlier, the main correlates for emphasis in speech are relatively greater pitch changes, increased durations, and, to some extent, greater vocal effort, as was illustrated in Figures 3 and 4. By and large, as pitch and duration in music are decided upon by the composer, much less leeway is left to the performer than to a speaker. However, while our sensitivity to differences in the duration of notes presented in isolation is modest, the sensitivity to minute perturbations of the duration appearing in a regular sequence of notes of similar duration is quite high. Under these conditions, perturbations as small as 10 msec can be detected (van Noorden, 1975). Thus, by arranging sequences of notes of similar duration, the composer seems to offer the player the possibility to communicate emphasis in terms of lengthening and shortening of notes.

Similar observations have been made with regard to speech. The lower boundary for perceiving durational differences has been found to be on the order of 10 msec (Huggins, 1972; Klatt & Cooper, 1975). The just noticeable difference has been shown to vary with the type of sound and its phonetic context (Carlson & Granström 1975b, Fujisaki, Nakamura & Imoto, 1975).

Musicians seem to take advantage of this high sensitivity to durational perturbation. As was mentioned above, melodic charge is a property of a note that reflects the remarkableness of the note. Similarly, the *harmonic charge* seems to reflect the remarkableness of a chord. Remarkableness seems to call for emphasis in the performance.

According to the performance rules, a high melodic charge is marked by increases in sound level, vibrato extent, and duration. The method is straightforward; the increment of sound level, vibrato extent, and duration is calculated as a constant multiplied by the melodic charge of the individual note. The result is that notes with a high melodic charge sound emphasized. Similarly, increases in harmonic charge generate crescendos, and the associated increments in sound level are used for calculating the increases in duration and vibrato extent. According to formal listening experiments with musically trained subjects, the musical quality of a performance is raised if melodic charge is marked in this way (Thompson *et al*, 1986).

These examples seem to indicate that emphasis is signaled by adding duration, resulting in a slowing of the tempo. The same means are also used in speech. This slowing down of the tempo seems perceptually adequate; the listener is given more time to process the unexpected information.

Melodic charge and increases in harmonic charge are also reflected in the vibrato extent, as mentioned. Here, the parallel with speech is less obvious, but the following speculation is tempting. The perceptual system seems very sensitive to changes, e.g. in pitch, and one emphasis marker in speech is pitch change. Vibrato actually increases the rate of change of fundamental frequency, though without changing the mean perceived pitch. From this perspective, vibrato could be seen as an elegant way of exploiting pitch change for expressive purposes without changing the melodic patterns.

Constituent marking

In speech as in music performance, it is necessary to mark structural constituents at different levels. In speech, the most apparent example is the phrase and clause ending which is signaled by a lengthening of the last syllable or syllables. This way of announcing the ending of a constituent is common to most languages (Lindblom, 1979). Actually, final lengthening is so important for both Swedish and English that speech synthesized without such a rule is perceived as accelerating at the end of each clause.

In speech, constituents of many sizes, from paragraphs to words, are marked, not only with duration but also with other parameters like intonation, and vocal source settings. Also, micro-pauses are introduced at major syntatic breaks even if there is no need for breathing, e.g. after words followed by a period, a comma, or a semicolon. Durational data on these effects have been reported for several languages and are also formulated into coherent rule systems.

Prosodic models have an obvious importance in the general description of languages and find application in text-to-speech systems. Several of these models have been tested by Carlson, Granström & Klatt (1979), and the more elaborate models give advantages both in naturalness and intelligibility.

One durational description of Swedish is historically based on a tree structure of a sentence with phrase boundaries and syllables on separate branches. Support for this model was found in reiterant speech (Carlson & Granström, 1973; Lindblom & Rapp, 1973). The model had a cyclic rule that increased the final lengthening to an extent reflecting the hierarchical position of the boundary. A similar model has been found extremely productive in describing timing data from piano music performance (Todd, 1985).

Another type of prosodic model for speech is based on a general structure proposed by Klatt (1979). The rules have as input the inherent duration, which is the typical duration of the phoneme in a word-initial position before a stressed vowel. The second parameter is the minimal duration, which is a measure of the phoneme's compressibility. Finally, a correction factor is used to calculate the duration. This factor is set depending on local and global parameters. This model has proven to be good at describing duration effects in running speech. The experiences from the music performance program reveal that a similar model, including restrictions on compressibility, would also be productive in music performance.

There seems to be a contradiction between these two models for describing duration phenomena. The first model is probably suited for a well-prepared reading of text with a high amount of speech pre-planning, while the other is typical of less planned speech with rules of a more local nature.

According to Todd (1985), the ending of a phrase is often played with a small retard while the beginning is played with a small accelerando. It is well known that the last notes of a piece are often played with a final retard (Sundberg & Verrillo, 1980). In the music performance program, the last note of a phrase is lengthened by 40 msec and terminated by a micro-pause. A sub-phrase termination is marked by a micro-pause only. In addition, there are a number of other rules that shorten and lengthen notes depending on the context, and these rules sometimes seem to serve the purpose of constituent marking. For instance, in combination with the marker of phrase endings, they actually sometimes generate small retards at phrase endings.

Why is the code for marking structural constituents similar in speech and music performance? A tempting hypothesis is that the code in music is imported from speech in this regard; as all music listeners have acquired a competence in decoding speech, it would be safe to use the same code in music performance. However, some languages, e.g. Danish, do not use final lengthening, and yet, musicians from these countries are obviously quite as competent musicians as their colleagues from other countries. This shows that the code used in music performance may not be borrowed from speech, but might lean on other kinds of common experience.

As far as the final retard is concerned, there is a striking similarity with the decreasing rate of footsteps in a stopping runner who keeps the step length and the braking force constant throughout the stopping process (Kronman & Sundberg, 1987). Under these conditions, the slowing down of the footsteps follows the same curve as the average retard in motor music from the baroque era. Thus, the final lengthening seems to allude to a well-known experience, namely that of stopping locomotion. We may speculate that the final lengthening in phrase endings are also faint allusions to locomotion. If so, the code would be very robust in the sense that anybody acquainted with locomotion is likely to know the code.

Outlook

We can discern three apparently very basic principles used in speech and music performance. The first one is increasing the difference between categories, which would facilitate communication by helping the listener to make correct identifications. A second principle is the *emphasis* which is called for by varying *predictability*. In speech, predictability would serve the purpose of making the message robust. In music performance, on the other hand, this may or may not be the purpose; while speech is often required to function in a noisy environment, Western music is likely to be performed in less disturbed situations. In any event, it seems likely that it is the cognitive system that asks for varying degrees of emphasis. Perhaps, this system cannot digest long series of equally unexpected elements in communication. Emphasis is signaled acoustically in similar ways in speech and music.

Another common basic principle in speech and music performance is *constituent marking*. The parts that constitute blocks in the structure are marked in the acoustic realization, e.g. phrases and clauses in speech, and phrases and sub-phrases in music. This appears to reflect a requirement of the cognitive system, and is often referred to as the principle of *grouping*. Also, the acoustic code by means of which constituent marking is communicated is simpler in speech and music.

Why all these numerous parallels? What do they imply? The parallels are not astonishing. Both speech and music are examples of formalized inter-human communication by means of acoustic signals. Both must be devised for the same perceptual and cognitive systems. The limitations and capabilities of these systems must contribute importantly to the development of both speech and music.

Acknowledgments

The speech part of the work reported in this paper was supported by The Swedish Board for Technical Development (STU) Contract No. 84–3667 and the music performance part by the Bank of Sweden Ter-centenary Foundation, Contract 84/171.

Notes

1. The authors' names are arranged in alphabetical order.

References

Bernstein, L. (1976) *The Unanswered Question*. Cambridge, Mass.: MIT Press.

Carlson, R., Erikson, Y., Granström, B., Lindblom, B & Rapp, K. (1975) Neutral and emphatic stress patterns in Swedish. In *Speech Communication*, Vol 2, G. Fant (ed.), 209–218, Stockholm: Almqvist Wiksell.

Carlson, R. & Granström, B. (1973) Word accent, emphatic stress, and syntax in a synthesis by rule scheme for Swedish. *STL–QPSR*, **2–3/1973**, 31–36.

Carlson, R. & Granström, B. (1975a) A phonetically-oriented programming language for rule description of speech. In *Speech Communication*, Vol 2, G. Fant (ed.), 245–253, Stockholm: Almqvist & Wiksell.

Carlson, R. & Granström, B. (1975b) Perception of segment duration. In *Structure and Process in Speech Perception*, A. Cohen & S. Nooteboom (eds.), 90–196, Heidelberg: Springer Verlag.

Carlson, R. & Granström, B. (1986) Linguistic processing in the KTH multi-lingual text-to-speech system. *Conference Record, IEEE–ICASSP, Tokyo*, 2403–2406.

Carlson, R. Granström, B. & Hunnicutt, S. (1982) A multi-language text-to-speech module. *Conference Record, IEEE–ICASSP, Paris*, 1604–1607.

Carlson, R., Granström, B. & Klatt, D. (1979) Some notes on the perception of temporal patterns in speech. In *Frontiers in Speech Communication Research*, B. Lindblom & S. Öhman (eds.), 233–244, New York: Academic Press.

Coker, C.H., Umeda, N. & Browman, C.P. (1973) Automatic synthesis from text. *IEEE Transactions in Audio Electroacoustics*, *AU–21*, 293–297.

Friberg, A., Sundberg, J. & Frydén, L. (1987) How to terminate a phrase: An analysis-by-synthesis experiment on a perceptual aspect of music performance. In *Action and Perception of Rhythm and Music*, A. Gabrielsson (ed.) 49–55, Publ. no. 55, Stockholm: Royal Swedish Academy of Music.

Fujisaki, H., Nakamura, K. & Imoto, T. (1975) Auditory perception of duration of speech and non-speech stimuli. In *Auditory Analysis and Perception of Speech*, G. Fant & M. Tatham (eds.) 197–200, New York: Academic Press.

Huggins, A.W.F. (1972) Just noticeable differences for segment duration in natural speech. *Journal of the Acoustical Society of America*, **51**, 1270–1278.

Hunnicutt, S. (1985) Intelligibility versus redundancy – conditions of dependency. *Language and Speech*, **28**, 47–56.

Hunnicutt, S. (1987a) Acoustic correlates of redundancy and intelligibility. *STL–QPSR*, **2–3**, 7–14.

Hunnicutt, S. (1987b) Input and output alternatives in word production, STL–QPSR 2–3, 15–29.

Klatt, D.K. (1976) Linguistic uses of segmental duration in English: Acoustic and perceptual evidence, *Journal of the Acoustical Society of America*, **59**, 1208–1221.

Klatt, D.K. (1979) Synthesis by rule of segmental durations in English sentences. In *Frontiers in Speech Communication Research*, B. Lindblom & S. Öhman (eds), 287–299, New York: Academic Press.

Klatt, D.K. & Cooper, W.E. (1975) Perception of segment duration in sentence contexts. In *Structure and Process in Speech Perception*, A. Cohen & S. Nooteboom (eds), 69–86, Heidelberg: Springer Verlag.

Knopoff, L. & Hutchinson, W. (1983) Entropy as a measure of style: The influence of sample length, *Journal of Music Theory*, **27**, 75–97.

Kohler, K.J. (1981) (ed.) "Temporal Aspects of Speech Production and Perception", *Phonetica*, **38**, 1–3.

Kohler, K.J. (1986) (ed.) "Prosodic Cues for Segments", *Phonetica*, **43**, 1–3.

Kronman, U. & Sundberg, J. (1987) Is the musical retard an allusion to physical motion? In *Action and Perception of Rhythm and Music*, A. Gabrielsson (ed.), 57–68, Publ. no. 55, Stockholm: Royal Swedish Academy of Music.

Krumhansl, C.L. & Kessler, E.J. (1982) Tracing the dynamic changes in perceived tonal organization in spatial representation of musical keys. *Psychological Review*, **89**, 334–368.

Lehiste, I. (1975) The phonetic structure of paragraphs. In *Structure and Process in Speech Perception*, A. Cohen & S. Nooteboom (eds), 195–203, Heidelberg: Springer Ferlag.

Lerdahl, F. & Jackendoff, R. (1983) *A Generative Theory of Tonal Music*. Cambridge, Mass: MIT Press.

Lieberman, P. (1963) Some effects of semantic and grammatical context on the production and perception of speech. *Language and Speech*, **6**, 172–187.

Lindblom, B. (1979) Final lengthening in speech and music. In *Nordic Prosody*, E. Gårding, G. Bruce & R. Bannert (eds), 85–101, Lund: Travaux de l'Institut de Linguistique de Lund XIII.

Lindblom, B. & Rapp, K. (1973) Some temporal regularities of spoken Swedish. University of Stockholm, Dept. of Linguistics, Publ. No. 21.

Lindblom, B. & Sundberg, J. (1970) Towards a generative theory of melody. *Svensk Tidskrift för Musikforskning* (Swedish Journal of Musicology), **52**, 171–181.

van Noorden, L.P.A.S. (1975) *Temporal Coherence in the Perception of Tone Sequences*. Dissertation, Technical University, Eindhoven.

Sloboda, J.A. (1977) Phrase units as determinants of visual processing in music reading. *British Journal of Psychology*, **68**, 117–124.

Sundberg, J. (1978) Synthesis of singing. *Svensk Tidskrift för Musikforskning*, (Swedish Journal of Musicology), **60**, 107–112.

Sundberg, J. (in press), Synthesis of singing using a computer-controlled formant synthesizer, manuscript to be published by the Music Department, Stanford University

Sundberg, J. & Lindblom, B. (1976) Generative theories in language and music descriptions. *Cognition*, **4**, 99–122.

Sundberg, J. & Verrillo, V. (1980) On the anatomy of the retard: A study of timing in music. *Journal of the Acoustical Society of America*, **68**, 772–779.

Sundberg, J., Askenfelt, A. & Fryden, L. (1983) Musical performance: A synthesis-by-rule approach. *Computer Music Journal*, **7**, 37–43.

Thompson, W.F., Friberg, A., Frydén, L. & Sundberg, J. (1986) Evaluating rules for the synthetic performance of melodies. *STL–QPSR*, **2–3**, 27–44.

Todd, N. (1985) A model of expressive timing in tonal music, *Music Perception*, **3**, 33–57.

Winograd, T. (1968) Linguistics and the computer analysis of tonal harmony. *Journal of Music Theory*, **12**, 2–49.

Contemporary Music Review,
1989, Vol. 4, pp. 405–416
Photocopying permitted by license only

Towards a cognitive theory of expression:
The performance and perception of rubato

Neil Todd

Department of Psychology, University of Exeter, Exeter EX4 4QG, England

Expression is examined from the viewpoint of communication theory and it is argued that a proper understanding of expression involves an integrated description of both performance and perception. A framework is developed in which to couch a general theory of expression. As an example, a number of algorithms, implemented in Lisp are described which model the performance and perception of rubato. The model is based on two factors: 1) the use of "phrase final lengthening" to signal a group boundary and 2) the ability of the listener to track a variable tempo. The study shows that rubato is a rich source of information for the listener and that any realistic music parser must take this into account. On the other hand any performance model must take into account the constraints of perception.

KEY WORDS: Cognition, computational modeling, musical expression, music performance, music perception, rubato.

Introduction

It can be agreed that expression is a form of communication. So formally, a theory of expression must describe the process of communication – the message to be communicated, the signal encoding the message, and also the recovery of the message from the signal. On the other hand a performer playing "with expression" will invariably employ the use of various devices, depending on the instrument and style, which include variations in tempo (rubato), loudness (dynamics), timbre (tone quality) and note offset time (articulation). We may regard these variations as *signals* between performer and listener and the variables themselves as *channels* (Shannon & Weaver, 1949).

An important corollary of this is that to understand properly the nature of expression in music, we must consider both performance and perception. Of course, the processes of performance and perception are separate but a performance is only functional if it can be comprehended, at least in principle. Therefore, in a functional performance the processes of performance are constrained by the competence of the listener, even if we accept a degree of redundancy in the performance. And vice-versa, the processes of perception are constrained by the structure of the performance. More importantly though, the perception of expression is an essential testing ground for any performance theory.

This viewpoint raises a number of questions. What message or information is the performer conveying in these variations of tempo, etc? How is that message encoded or mapped into the variations? How is the information recovered from the variations by the listener? What is the function of the message? The goal of this paper is to go some way towards answering these questions.

Methodology

The essential methodological problem in the study of expression is that we have no direct access to the encoding or decoding processes or to the internal representation of the message to be communicated. We can only directly observe the performance or signal. Fortunately, we are helped in this matter by the fact that Western notation for music reveals much of the musical structure (Longuet-Higgin & Steedman, 1971). So some of the techniques of analysis which have been developed by music theorists may be of use.

The approach adopted here is computational; that is, human cognition is viewed as a form of information processing. The goal of the approach is taken to be the representation of knowledge in terms of data structures and the representation of processes in terms of "effective procedures" (Johnson-Laird, 1983). A suitable high-level language for the implementation of such structures and procedures is Lisp. The utility of this methodology is that it forces the formulation of theories which are logically consistent and allows us to make precise predictions which can be tested. Of course this is no guarantee that a model constructed on this basis is the actual process used in a human performance.

One of the greatest insights of David Marr (1982) was that an information-processing system has three levels of explanation. At one level is the computational theory of the system in which its performance is characterized as the mapping of one kind of information into another. At a second level is the choice of representation of an algorithm, its input and output. And at a third level is the physical realization of the system. In this paper, expression will be discussed at the first two levels, each having its own form of notation, the particular physical realization not being of importance here. At the level of computational theory Greek symbols are used for unobservables, such as an internal representation or process, whereas Latin symbols are used to denote observables, such as loudness or duration. At the algorithmic level the various objects are just referred to by their *filename.*

A General Framework – The Computational Theory

Let us formulate the problem in symbolic terms. If we let Ψ represent the internal representation and P represent the performance – a series of events in time which have certain properties such as duration and loudness – we can think of the process of performance as a mapping $\Psi \rightarrow P$ and the process of perception as the inverse mapping $P \rightarrow \Psi$. So, making the idealization that the internal representation is fully recovered, we can represent the process of expression thus:

$$\Psi \rightarrow P \rightarrow \Psi \tag{1}$$

The performance mapping can be represented by a *performance procedure* Π which takes Ψ as its input and in which is embedded an *encoding function* γ such that:

$$\Pi\,(\Psi,\gamma) \rightarrow P \tag{2}$$

The encoding function γ defines a time series Y_t such that:

$$Y_t = \gamma(t;\theta_1,\theta_2,\ldots,\theta_p) + \epsilon_t, \qquad t = 1,2,\ldots,T \tag{3}$$

where $\theta_i = (\theta_1,\theta_2,\ldots,\theta_p)'$ is a *vector of parameters*, which may be discrete or continuous; Y_t is a dependent variable such as duration or loudness; and ϵ_t is a random noise component, which is assumed to have zero mean, $E(\epsilon) = 0$, and variance $V(\epsilon) = \sigma^2$. Another way of thinking of Π is that its job is to determine a path in the parameter space as the performance unfolds.

The process of perception can be represented by a *listening procedure* Λ in which is embedded a *set of decoding functions* $\delta_i = (\delta_1, \delta_2, ..., \delta_p)'$ such that:

$$\Lambda\ (P, \delta_i) \rightarrow \Psi \tag{4}$$

The decoding functions δ_i are such that:

$$\theta_i = \delta_i(Y_t) \tag{5}$$

enabling the reconstruction of the path in parameter space and the prediction of future values of Y.

We can now redefine our problem in symbolic terms – given the data from P, a theory of expression must determine for each channel the following:

a) a representation for Ψ
b) an encoding function γ
c) a performance procedure Π
d) a vector of parameters θ_i
e) a set of decoding functions δ_i
f) a listening procedure Λ

The theory sketched out above is sufficiently general to cover any variable of expression. At the same time it is agnostic as to what is being communicated, be it structure, emotion, or extra-musical reference.

Rubato

So far our discussion has been at the abstract computational level. In this section, I will attempt to apply the above computational theory to the variation of tempo or rubato at the algorithmic level.

A fundamental distinction is made here between time variation at and above the level of the beat, and variation within the beat (Shaffer, 1981; Clarke, 1985). This distinction accords with the idea that there is a most salient metrical level or tactus at which primary timing control takes place. The principles governing these two components, which we may refer to as beat timing and note timing, are different. We shall focus our attention here on the first component whose encoding function will be referred to by ρ_B such that:

$$D_t = \rho_B(t; \theta_i) + \epsilon_t, \qquad t = 1, 2, ..., T \tag{6}$$

where D_t is beat duration.

Internal Representation Ψ

One of the features which characterizes the duration structure of a performance is that it is made up of a series of segments or gestures (Shaffer, Clarke & Todd, 1985; Todd, 1985; Shaffer & Todd, 1987). We may assume then that the segments in the duration structure correspond to the grouping structure of the music the music (Lerdahl and Jackendoff, 1983). In other words the performer is communicating information about the way in which phrases are organized.

A suitable representation for grouping is Lerdahl & Jackendoff's time-span reduction which can easily be adapted to Lisp (see Fig. 1) (Todd, 1989). This representation is called *tsr*.

```
(setq tsr '((G1) (G2)) )
(setq G1 '((g1) (g2)) )
(setq G2 '((g3) (g4)) )
(setq g1 '(1 1 1 1) )
(setq g2 '(1 1 1 1) )
(setq g3 '(1 1 1 1) )
(setq g4 '(1 1 1 1) )
```

Figure 1 A Lisp representation of Lerdahl & Jackendoff's time-span reduction *tsr*. The Lisp brackets correspond to Lerdahl & Jackendoff's bracket notation and the integers in the surface groups represent a beat. The example has two levels, an intermediate level and a surface level. On the intermediate level there are two groups *G1* and *G2* where *G1* contains the two surface groups *g1* and *g2*, and *G2* contains *g3* and *g4*.

In a more complex representation the integers would be replaced by atoms which have a property list. However, this skeletal description of the rhythmic structure is sufficient to model beat timing. Note that it makes no reference to any tonal information and therefore could apply to atonal music.

Performance Π, ρ_B

Having established a suitable representation *tsr*, we need to find a procedure and encoding function. In Todd (1985) a model was established which generated a duration structure from a structural description of the music. The basic idea of the model was that the performer uses "phrase final lengthening" to signal a boundary – the degree of slowing being determined by the importance of the boundary. In the model, a parabolic encoding function with 6 parameters ($p=6$) was used to model the segments in the duration structure. This function had the following form:

$$\rho_B(t, \theta_i) = \theta_1 + \frac{\theta_2}{(1-\theta_6)^2} \left\{ \frac{t}{\theta_3} - \frac{(\theta_4 - 1)}{\theta_5} - \theta_6 \right\}^2, \qquad t = 1,2,...,T \qquad (7)$$

where

θ_1 = *tempo*,
θ_2 = *amplitude*,
θ_3 = *length of phrase*,
θ_4 = *boundary strength*,
θ_5 = *upper limit of boundary strength*,
θ_6 = *offset of parabola minimum*.

$(1 - \theta_6)^{-2}$ is a normalization factor such that if the boundary strength $\theta_4 = 1$ and $t = \theta_3$ then θ_2 represents the true amplitude (Todd, 1985). As for the values of the parameters, θ_1 and θ_2 are input at the start of the algorithm *play*; θ_3 and θ_4 are computed for each group as the program runs; and θ_5 and θ_6 are set within the program with $\theta_6 = 0.52$ and $\theta_5 = 11$ in Todd (1985).

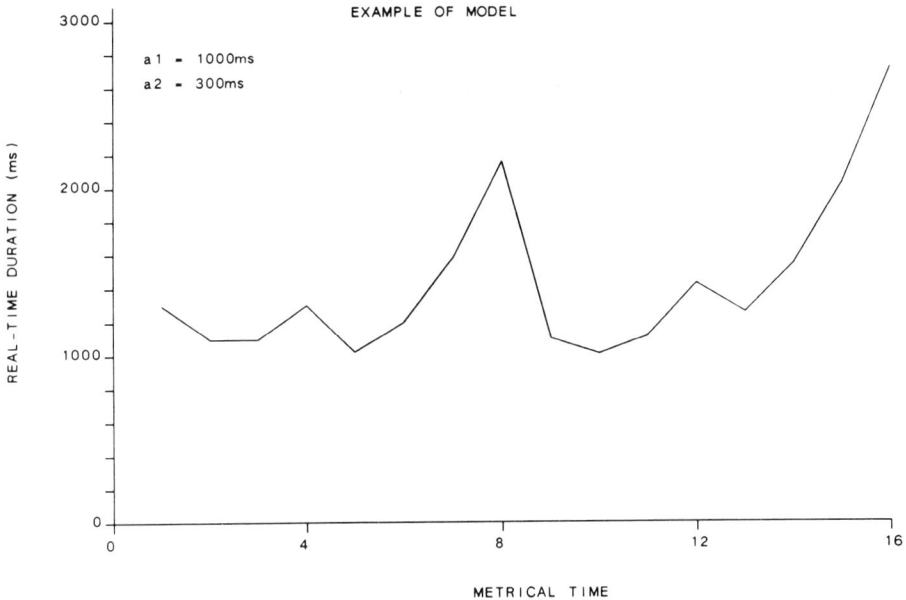

Figure 2 The output of the algorith *play* as in Todd (in press). This example takes as its input the *tsr* as in Figure 1, and therefore has two timing components corresponding to the two structural levels. $\theta_1 = 1000$ms and $\theta_2 = 300$ms, (a_1 and a_2 in figure).

In a later model (Todd, in press), the same function was used but was applied recursively at a number of levels and $\theta_5 = 3$ because the number of possible boundary strengths is reduced. The performance procedure in the model, which is called *play*, involved looking ahead and planning the shape of the phrasing at each level. When a surface group was reached the planned phrasings were superposed beat by beat. When a surface group was completed the program backtracked to the next level and so on until all the surface groups were played. The output of the program is a list of durations, which is called *data* (See Figure 2).

Perception Λ,g

We now need to answer the question how does the listener recover grouping from a varying tempo? From Equations (1), (2), and (4), a procedure for the recovery of the internal representation must satisfy the requirement that $\Lambda(\Pi(\Psi)) \to \Psi$.

In terms of constructing an algorithm, which we will call *listen*, this requirement means that if the performance procedure *play* generates performance *data* from *tsr* then the listening procedure *listen* must reconstruct *tsr* from *data*.

Presented in Appendix 1 is an algorithm which is based on the detection of the pattern of durations short-long-short to signal the start of a new group (see function *phrase-final*, Appendix 1). The algorithm allows an input buffer which holds the current duration D_t plus the previous two durations D_{t-1} and D_{t-2} so that a boundary is detected when the following conditions are met:

$$D_t < D_{t-1} \quad \text{and} \quad D_{t-2} < D_{t-1} \tag{8}$$

A boundary showing ratio r is defined (see function *boundary-ratio*, Appendix 1) such that:

$$r = \frac{D_{t-1}}{2} \left\{ \frac{1}{D^t} + \frac{1}{D_{t-2}} \right\} \tag{9}$$

The boundary strength θ_4, the number of right brackets, is recovered by the decoding function δ_4 which is a step function of the boundary slowing ratio such that:

$$\delta_4 = \begin{cases} 0 & \text{for } 1 \leq r < r_1 \\ 1 & \text{for } r_1 \leq r < r_2 \\ 2 & \text{for } r_2 \leq r < r_3 \end{cases}$$

where r_1 is a noise threshold so that if $r_1 = 1$ then the algorithm assumes there is no noise, that is, $V(\epsilon) = 0$. The output of the algorithm *listen* is again a Lisp representation of grouping (see Figure 3), but the groups are defined in order of occurence – which is the reverse of that in Figure 1.

```
(setq sg1 '(1 1 1 1))
(setq sg2 '(1 1 1 1))
(setq ig1 '((sg1) (sg2)))
(setq sg3 '(1 1 1 1))
(setq sg4 '(1 1 1 1))
(setq ig2 '((sg3) (sg4)))
(setq tsr '((ig1) (ig2)))
```

Figure 3 The output of the algorithm *listen* as in Appendix 1 which used as an input the data generated by *play*, as in Figure 2. This algorithm is fixed at two levels but could easily be adapted to more. *sgn* refers to the *n*th surface group. *ign* refers to the *n*th intermediate group.

Whilst the algorithm *listen* can reconstruct the *tsr* remarkably well, it ignores tempo variation before the final slowing. This leaves unresolved two questions.

First, the pre-final variation obviously contains a lot of information. Is it possible then to find values for the parameters θ_i by regression, given a suitable function such as ρ_B? Second, the listener must be able to predict the tempo at least one beat in advance in order to parse the rhythmic structure (Longuet-Higgins, 1976). so, can we find an auto-regression function for beat duration?

At first sight the idea of using regression on Eq. 7 looks very attractive holding out the prospect that we can find a value for θ_3 before reaching the end of the phrase. There are however a number of problems with this. First, Eq. 7 is non-linear in three of the parameters and thus requires the use of a numerical approximation such as the Gauss-Newton method (Draper & Smith, 1981). The calculations for this are unwieldy (it is beyond the scope of this paper to show them here) and involve the use of iteration to find an optimal solution. So, even if we were prepared to tolerate such calculations they would require an unacceptable amount of time to perform on line, particularly for a language such as Lisp. Second, the six unknown parameters require at least 6 data points to find a unique solution, which implies that each phrase would have to be at least six beats in length ($T=6$) before the listener could make any predictions – which is obviously nonsense.

One way out of the problem is to assume that the listener uses a simpler regression equation such as:

$$\rho_B(t, \theta_i) = \theta_1 + \theta_2(t - \theta_3)^2, \qquad t=1,2...,T \qquad (11)$$

which can be solved using a non-statistical algebraic method by taking ·alues at t, $t-1$ and $t-2$. Even more simple is a linear function which yields the auto-regression equation:

$$D_t = 2D_{t-1} - D_{t-2} \qquad (12)$$

Michon (1967) found that Eq. 12 gave a reasonable approximation to a sinusoidal input in a simple temporal tracking task. So, it seems reasonable that this approximation might also apply to a parabolic input as in the case of rubato.

Another possible solution is that the listener passes the more stable parameters, such as θ_5 and θ_6 of Eq. 7, from one phrase to the next. This solution would leave an initial period of ambiguity at the start but reduce the amount of calculation as the performance progresses. Once the stable parameters had been established they would only be abandoned if there was very strong counter-evidence such as an abrupt change of tempo. This accords with the idea that the perception of music involves the establishing of a conceptual framework from which to interpret an input (Longuet-Higgins, 1976).

However, the problem itself has arisen because the durations used in the calculations are from only one metrical level. Much information about tempo is given at metrical levels below the tactus and in the durations of actual notes. So, the representation needs to be extended downwards to include note timing, which would mean that a rubato handler would have to work in cooperation with a metrical parser, one feeding the other. Clearly, a lot more work is needed in this area.

Discussion

Let us recapitulate. A general framework was described which enabled us to discuss expression in a formal manner. The essential idea was that performance involves the mapping of some internal representation into a series of events in time and that perception involves the recovery of the internal representation from the time series. The expressive variation of tempo was looked at and it was shown that it is possible to find algorithms to model the mapping and recovery processes. Finally, solutions to the twin problems of parameter estimation and auto-regression were discussed.

I think it is clear, certainly in the domain of expression, that the processes of performance and perception must be looked at together. Rubato contains a great deal of information which the listener uses in the comprehension of music. A number of points can be made on this.

Any theories of music perception must take rubato into account in at least two ways. First, most metrical or grouping parsers (Longuet-Higgins & Steedman, 1971; Longuet-Higgins & Lee, 1984; Baker, 1987) are incapable of dealing with tempo variation or at best treat it as "noise". Even parsers which have been designed to handle a fluctuating tempo, such as that of Chafe, Mont-Reynaud & Rush (1982), however ingenious, still treat rubato as "noise" rather than as *a structured source of information*. (The Chafe *et al* parser also suffers from the problem of being a multiple-pass system – a luxury which the human listener doesn't share). So they must use an auto-regression equation of the kind discussed above in order to be able to predict the next beat. Second, one of the problems in parsing is reducing multiple readings to find the "correct" path. Clearly, the inclusion of a rubato handler would enable the parser to eliminate many readings early on.

Further, the algorithms make no reference to any tonal information. In other words they are agnostic as to whether the music is atonal or not. Therefore, a rubato handler could be a vital component of any theory of grouping in the perception of atonal music. A complete theory must of course, include dynamics, articulation and timbre. It must also describe a number of performance modes. Thus for example, a "Romantic" mode might have a deep rubato, whilst a "Baroque" mode would have little rubato but with emphasis on dynamics and articulation. However, the basic theory sketched at the beginning of this paper, the mapping into and recovery from a time series of some internal representation, must be the basis on which a complete theory of expression is constructed.

Acknowledgments

Many thanks to Exeter University Computer Science Department for the use of facilities and advice on Lisp programming; to Exeter University Computer Unit for help in the production of this paper; and to Exeter University Psychology Department whose generous support made possible the presentation of this paper at IRCAM.

Appendix: Two-level algorithm "listen" (Franz Lisp, Opus 38.91)

The executive function start: a) opens Port for input of datafile; b) opens oport for output to tsrfile; c) calls the function set-up-vars; d) calls the main function listen; e) closes port and oport.

```
(defun start()
    (prog()
        loop
        (patom "listen to what data?")
        (setq datafile (concat "data/" (read)))
        (setq port (fileopen datafile ' "r"))
        (patom "name of tsrfile?")
        (setq tsrfile (concat "tsr/" (read)))
        (setq oport (fileopen tsrfile ' "w"))
        (set-up-vars)
        (listen port)
        (close port)
        (close oport)
        (patom "listen more?")
        (setq answer (read))
        (cond ((eq answer 'no) (return 'finished)))
        (go loop)))
```

The function set-up-vars initializes: a) the input buffer input, a three element list; b) the time-span reduction tsr, a list of intermediate-groups; c) the current surface-group current-sgroup, a list of "beats"; d) the current intermediate-group current-igroup, a list of surface-groups; e) a count of surface-groups sindex; f) a count of intermediate groups iindex. set-up-vars also sets: a) the ratio sratio (r_1 in Eq. 10); b) the ratio iratio (r_2 in Eq. 10).

```
(defun set-up-vars()
    (setq input '(nil nil nil))
    (setq tsr '())
    (setq current-sgroup '())
    (setq current-igroup '())
    (setq sindex 1)
    (setq iindex 1)
    (setq sratio 1)
    (setq iratio 1.15))
```

The main function listen is recursive. It takes Port as its input and returns a value for the time span reduction tsr. On each new call it updates input with the function update-input which reads the next beat duration from datafile. Listen upates current-sgroup until it reaches a group boundary, which is detected by end-of-group. If it is a surface-group it defines a new surface-group with the function def-sgroup and updates current-igroup. If it is an intermediate-group it defines new surface and intermediate groups and updates current-igroup and tsr. The program finishes when the end of datafile is detected.

```
(defun listen(Port)
   (prog()
      (update-input Port)
      (cond
         ((end-of-piece)
            (prog()
               (def-sgroup current-sgroup)
               (update-igroup)
               (def-igroup current-igroup)
               (update-tsr)
               (def-tsr tsr)))
         ((end-of-group)
            (cond
               ((intermediate group)
                  (prog()
                     (def-sgroup current-sgroup)
                     (update-igroup)
                     (def-igroup current-igroup)
                     (update-tsr)
                     (listen Port)))
               ((surface-group)
                  (prog()
                     (def-sgroup current-sgroup)
                     (update-igroup)
                     (listen Port)))))
         (t (prog()
            (update-sgroup)
            (listen Port)))))))

(defun update-input(Port)
   (Setq input (list (read Port) (cr input) (cadr input))))

(defun end-of-piece()
   (cond  ((null (car input)) t)
          (t nil)))

(defun end-of-group()
   (cond  ((start-of-piece) nil)
          ((phrase-final) t)
          (tnil)))

(defun start-of-piece()
   (cond  ((or (null (cadr input))
               (null (caddr input))) t)
          (t nil)))

(defun phrase-final ()
   (cond ((and (lessp (car input) (cadr input))
               (lessp (caddr input) (cadr input))) t)
          (t nil)))

(defun surface-group()
   (cond ((greaterp (boundary-ratio) sratio) t)
          (t nil)))

(defun intermediate-group()
   (cond ((greaterp (boundary-ratio) iratio) t)
          (t nil)))

(defun boundary-ratio()
   (times (quotient (float (cadr input)) 2)
          (plus (quotient 1 (float (car input)))
                (quotient 1 (float (caddr input))))))
```

```
(defun update-sgroup()
   (setq current-sgroup (append current-sgroup '(1))))

(defun update-igroup()
   (prog()
      (setq current-igroup (append current-igroup (list (list sg))))
      (setq current-sgroup '(1))))

(defun update-tsr()
   (prog()
      (setq tsr (append tsr (list (list ig))))
      (setq current-igroup '())))

(defun def-sgroup(Group)
   (prog()
      (setq sg (concat 'sg sindex))
      (print (list 'setq sg (list 'quote Group))) (terpr)
      (print (list 'setq sg (list 'quote Group)) oport) terpr oport)
      (set sg Group)
      (setq sindex (add1 sindex))))
(defun def-igroup(Group)
   (prog()
      (setq ig (concat 'ig iindex))
      (print (list 'setq ig (list 'quote Group))) (terpr)
      (print (list 'setq ig (list 'quote Group)) oport) (terpr )port(
      (set ig Group)
      (setq iindex (addi iindex))))

(defun def-tsr(tsr)
   (prog()
      (setq tsrfile (concat (substring tsrfile 5)))
      (print (list 'setq 'tsr (list 'quote tsr))) (terpr)
      (print (list 'setq tsrfile (list 'quote tsr)) oport)
      (terpr oport)))
```

References

Baker, M.J. (1987) *Automated Analysis of Musical Grouping Structures*, CITE Report No. 23, Institute of Educational Technology. The Open University.

Clarke, E. (1984) *Structure and Expression in the Rhythm of Piano Performance*. Ph.D. Thesis, University of Exeter.

Chafe, C., Mont-Reynaud, B. & Rush, L. (1982) Towards an intelligent editor of digital audio: Recognition of musical constructs. *Computer Music Journal* **6**, (1) 30–41.

Draper, N.R. & Smith, H. (1981) *Applied Regression Analysis*, (Second Edition). New York: Wiley.

Johnson-Laird, P.N. (1983) *Mental Models: Towards a Cognitive Science of Language, Inference and Consciousness*. Cambridge: Cambridge University Press.

Lerdahl, F. & Jackendoff, R. (1983) *A Generative Theory of Tonal Music*. Cambridge, Mass: MIT Press.

Longuet-Higgins, H.C. (1976) The perception of melodies, *Nature* **263**, 646–653.

Longuet-Higgins, H.C. & Lee, C.S. (1984) The rhythmic interpretation of monophonic music. *Music Perception*, **1** (4), 424–441.

Longuet-Higgins, H.C. & Steedman, M.J. (1971) On interpreting Bach, *Machine Intelligence* **6**: Edinburgh University Press.

Marr, D. (1982) *Vision: A Computational Investigation into the Human Representation and Processing of Visual Information*. San Francisco: W.H. Freeman and Company.

Michon, J.A. (1967) *Timing in Temporal Tracking*. Institute for Perception RVO–TNO, Soesterberg.

Shaffer, L.H. (1981) Performances of Chopin, Bach and Bartok: Studies in motor programming. *Cognitive Psychology*, **13**, 326–376.

Shaffer, L.H., Clarke, E. & Todd, N.P. (1985) Meter and rhythm in piano playing. *Cognition*, **20**, 61–77.

Shaffer, L.H., Clarke, E. & Todd, N.P. (1987) The interpretive component in musical performance in A. Gabrielson (ed.) *Action and Perception in Rhythm and Meter*. Royal Swedish Academy of Music No. 55.

Shannon, C.E. & Weaver, W. (1949) *The Mathematical Theory of Communication.* Urbana: University of Illinois Press.

Todd, N.P. (1985) A model of expressive timing in tonal music. *Music Perception* **3**, 33–58.

Todd, N.P. (1989) A computational model of rubato. In "Music, Mind and Structure", E.F. Clarke & S. Emmerson (eds.), *Contemporary Music Review,* **3** (1), 69–88.

Contemporary Music Review,
1989, Vol. 4, pp. 417–435
Photocopying permitted by license only

Score, vision, action

Kari Kurkela

Sibelius Academy, Music Research Institute, PL 86, SF-00251 Helsinki, Finland

The aim of the paper is to conceptualize some aspects in the understanding of a note text. The process of performing a note text is divided into two parts, referred to as *interpretive* and *executive* levels; the main features of the phases are dealt with in the beginning of the paper. The interpretive level is then examined more closely from two points of view. First, the question of *notional competence* is clarified within the framework of a *model-theoretic semantics of notation,* developed by the author during recent years. Notational competence is approached by explicating the logical connection between notation and the sound universe as a clarification of a competent user's intuition of notation. Then *information processing* during the understanding of the meaning of a note expression is preliminarily modeled on the basis of a *production theory* (ACT*) provided by John R. Anderson (1983). Even if being notationally competent and understanding note expressions have the same "surface" manifestations, the "deep" structures connected to the two phenomena are assumed to differ considerably from each other.

KEY WORDS: Performance, interpretation, notation, meaning, semantics, cognition, mental symbolic computation.

In this paper I shall try to conceptualize some aspects in the understanding of a note text. My purpose is to make the interpretive process, carried out by a musician, more comprehensible and to crystallize some phenomena for empirical studies in the performance of music. The article has three main parts. First, I shall deal with some *general questions* concerning the process of interpreting and executing note texts. Then the phenomenon that I call *notational competence* – or as it also could be put – the *logical* or *semantic* nature of understanding a note text, will be briefly studied. And finally, the question of understanding a note text will be approached by using the concepts of *cognitive psychology.*

Interpretation and execution

In a general action-theoretic framework, a goal-directed act can be categorized as including (i) an agent's intention ("I will do q"), (ii) the agent's belief concerning what one has to do in order to achieve the intended goal ("if I do p, then q"), (iii) the agent's causal influence upon the environment (p) and (iv) a change in the environment as a result of the agent's action (q). The act of performing a score is apparently a goal-directed act, and therefore we can ask: how could the process of performing a score be applied to the above framework?

Suppose that a pianist is at the point of performing a certain fragment of a note text. For this purpose, the performer must know what the note text means. Therefore, the process of performing the fragment is assumed to include a *semantic interpretation* that results in understanding the *basic meaning* of the passage. Usually, the understanding of the basic meaning is not enough; an artistic fine adjustment is needed. This part of interpretation, based on some aesthetic principles, could be called an *artistic interpretation* – or more generally a *communicative interpretation*. In principle, then, an *executive* act is preceded by a twofold *interpretive* process yielding the actual goal for an execution. This is, of course, only the *logical* order of the steps of the procedure. In practice, an output of an interpretive process may be a result of a long process in time where the two phases are tightly entwined.

After the pianist has acquired – as a result of the twofold interpretive process – a conception of what should be realized, he or she has yet to outline an execution strategy, that is, acquire a cognitive state of readiness to produce performances exemplifying the refined artistic vision of the note text. One can hypothesize that in many cases the outlining of an execution strategy is not so much a conceptualized process as a proceduralized or automatized application of acquired skills to the actual situation. In any case, the performer has to be aware of his or her physical and psychic state, as well as of the properties of the instrument, the acoustic environment and other factors affecting the executive process at the moment.[1]

When an execution strategy has been calculated and the situation is otherwise appropriate, an act of playing can be carried out, resulting in a *performance* of the passage.

In principle, the process of performing a fragment of a note text can be considered a sequence of goals and their fulfillments. The goal of performing the fragment is achieved by first setting a subgoal to calculate a basic meaning for the note text. This is followed by a subgoal to refine the rough vision for artistic purposes. Then a subgoal to caluclate an execution strategy is established, followed by the final subgoal to play (Figure 1).

Attempts to improve a performance are based on motor-kinesthetic and auditory feedback.[2] This means that one or more of the factors affecting the process of performing may be modified. A gradual deepening of insight into the musical work[3] is described as modifications on the interpretive level. Executive power is strengthened by "tuning" the execution strategy and by reinforcing technical resources to correspond to the demands of the execution strategy. Changes on the interpretive level are reflected on the executive level. But even though the vision of the score was not changed, the execution strategy may be altered.

Figure 1 manifests the supposition that different skills are required for carrying out the different goal-directed subacts. So, for instance, *understanding* notation does not necessarily imply that one knows how to proceed in order to *play* a note text. On the other hand, knowing what one should do in order to create a performance does not, unfortunately, imply that one can do it.

Notational Competence

After these general remarks on the process of performing a note text, let us consider the interpretive level somewhat more closely. It seems that so far it has been studied less than the executive level. The question of understanding a note text will be illuminated briefly from two points of view: what is notational competence (as a philosophical question), and how could the cognitive process of

AN ACT OF PERFORMING

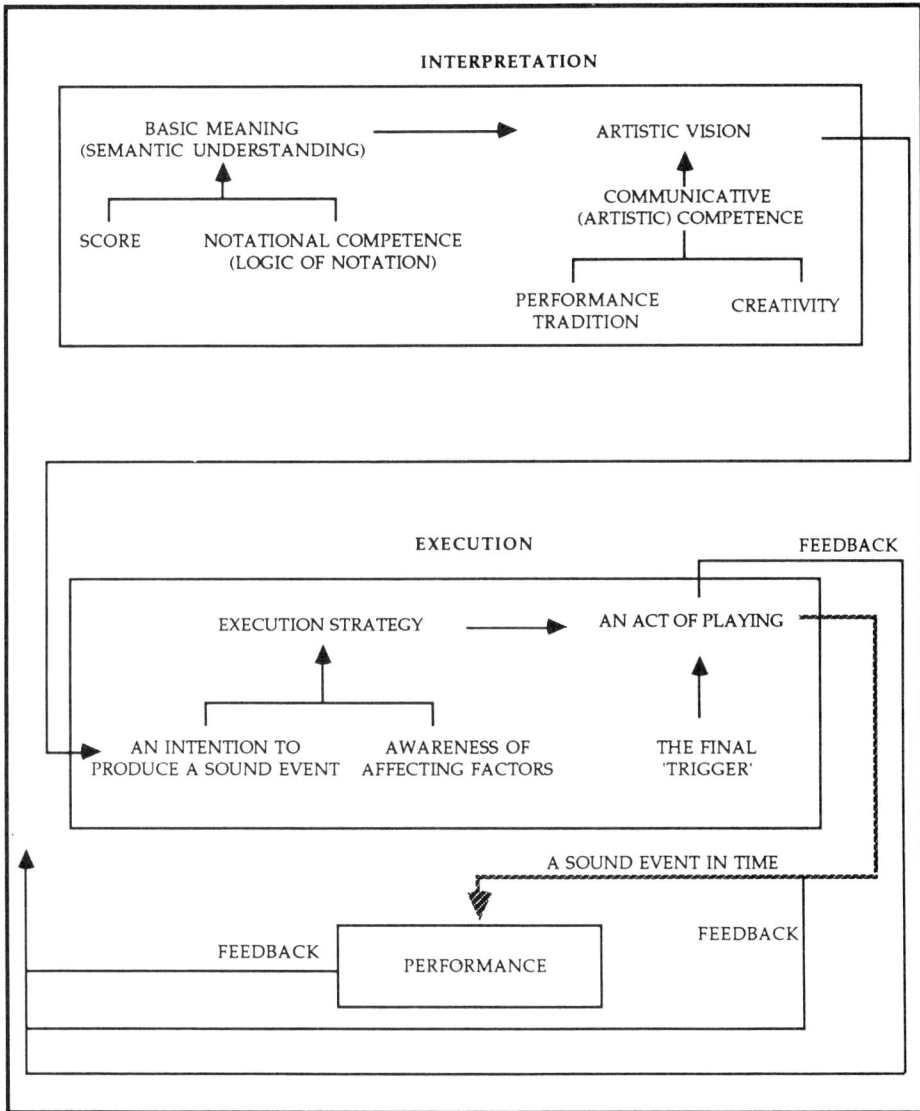

Figure 1 An act of performing a score.

understanding a note text be preliminarily modeled (for psychological inquiry)?
We have to limit our considerations primarily to the understanding of the basic
meaning of the note text.

As Marvin Minsky (1986) has stated, "In science, one can learn the most by
studying what seems the least". So let us restrict our concentration to a modest
but important note symbol of conventional staff notation, such as the following:

Note symbols of this type will be referred to as *formulae* in the rest of the paper. Even if we concentrate on formulae, our semantic conclusions can in principle be applied to note texts consisting of horizontal and vertical combinations of formulae. There are of course, specific problems in the process of understanding a larger chunk of notational material. However, the understanding of a chunk usually presupposes that its constituents are understood. And we try to clarify this part of the question.[4]

Mastering notation

What is the ability to understand a note text? To answer this question is to deal with another question: what is notational competence? Let us loosely define notational competence as *an ability to understand and produce an indefinite number of note expressions such that the ability is based on the mastering of a system of rules.* Now a further question arises: what do these rules deal with? Mastering of notation is knowledge of how note expressions and their combinations are connected to sounds. Thus, *to explicate notational competence is to explicate the rules that govern the relationship between notation and the sound universe in a given (temporal, cultural, etc.) context.*

In a general framework, an explanation of the connections between notation and sounds is a *logical* treatment. A composer must proceed logically when describing his or her sounding ideas, just as a performer has to know this logic in order to be able to understand the composer's notational signs. Consequently, knowledge of how sound events should be reported on a staff and how the written note symbols should be understood can be considered an ability to proceed according to certain logical principles. Therefore, *to explicate notational competence is to explicate a logical connection between notation and the sound universe.*

One question further: what is the explication of a logic of notation? As I have suggested elsewhere (Kurkela, 1986), conventional staff notation can be regarded as a written language such that a formula (as in Example 1), corresponds to a declarative sentence of a natural language. Therefore, *an explication of notational logic can be seen as a specification of a syntax and semantics for notation.*

It has to be emphasized that the relationship between notation and its meaning is *not* compared to that between written and spoken forms of a natural language, but in fact, to the relationship between a declarative sentence and its semantic content. On the other hand, we are not dealing with musical meanings but, in fact, with the meaning of the note text.

Abstractness of notational semantics

How could we test a person's ability to understand a note expression (as in Example 1)? Probably the simplest way is to inform the person of the tempo, pitch, and volume level at the moment and then to present a series of sounds and to query after each example whether the given sound matches the formula or not. If the person knows the meaning of the formula, he or she can make the right selections.

Why can the person make the right selections? The formula specifies some of the relational properties the sound must have in order to correspond to the formula. The ability to infer these restrictions from the note text is to know the basic meaning of the formula. We may state this as follows: *understanding the basic meaning of a formula is to have conceptual knowledge about the properties that a sound must have under given indexical constraints in order to correspond semantically to the formula.*

Even if the consequences of understanding a formula are concrete, our way of understanding the meaning of a formula turns out to be rather abstract. At least the following four aspects have to be taken into acount in a satisfactory description of our notational competence:

1. *Quantification and possibility.* A formula does not have a single referent (in contrast to a proper noun, for instance). Rather, it is a *quantified* expression (cf. next section). By specifying some restrictions, each formula outlines a certain range of possibilities. Understanding a formula is to be aware of the possibilities that the formula allows.
2. *Indexicality.* Usually the constituents of a formula are indexical expressions. That is, their absolute meaning (such as tempo, pitch, or dynamic value) and the meaning of the formula, consequently, are dependent on fixed reference values at a given moment.
3. *Principle of Compositionality and intensionality.* According to our intuition of notation, if two formulae comprise parts with different meanings, then the formulae have different meanings. Therefore, the logic of notation must be based on the Principle of Compositionality.[5] This requirement leads to a need for intensional logic. To clarify this notion, let us postulate two different formulae such that neither one has (or can have) a single sound correlate in our world. Therefore the two formulae have an empty set as their reference set in our world. If a semantics of notation were extensional and not intensional, then the two formulae would have the same meaning, that is, an empty set. This can, however, go against our intuition because we suppose that differences between two formulae may result in two different meanings.[6]
4. *Conceptuality.* To understand a formula is *not* to hear a sound event. One can, of course, imagine a sound event corresponding to a formula under certain indexical constraints; however, to be able to do this one must already know the meaning of the formula. Correspondingly, a composer usually knows what he or she means by a formula without having imagined a single sounding correlate to the formula. That is, understanding a basic meaning of a formula is a conceptual process that may lead to an auditory imagination and/or to an executive process.

Model-theoretic treatment of notational competence

In a *model-theoretic* framework, an explication of linguistic competence can be carried out with mathematical accuracy. There is no space for a detailed account of the matter in this context.[7] However, let us outline briefly some principles of a model-theoretic treatment of notational competence that takes the above four remarks into account.

We define a *possible sound situation* as a pair comprising a possible sound event and a possible package of convenient indexical constraints:
a sound situation = <a sound event, indexical constraints>.

A possible sound event is a sound event that may or may not exist in our actual world. Indexical constraints determine an absolute content for indexical note symbols. Metronome marks, for instance, indicate typical indexical constraints.

Now a model-theoretic semantic value for a formula can be defined. *The basic meaning of a formula is associated with a function (operation) from a set of possible sound situations such that the function picks out all the possible sound situations corresponding to the formula* (Figure 2).

When the meaning of a formula is associated with a function from the set of possible sound situations, the above four requirements are fulfilled. Thus as to the quantification and possibility aspect, the meaning of formula is not attached to a single sound, but to a function. This function picks out a subset of possible sound

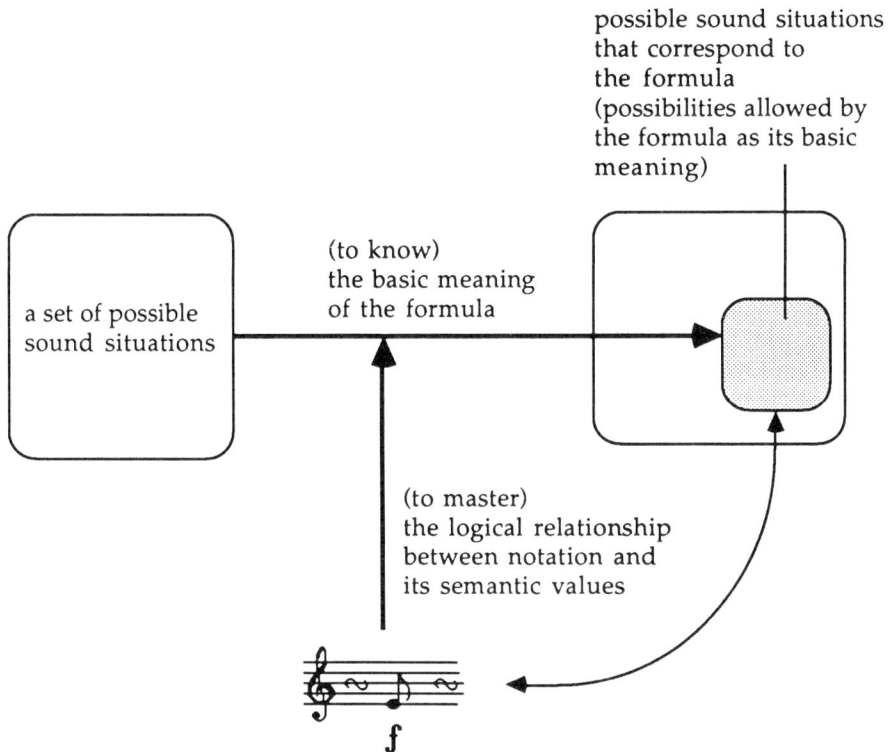

Figure 2 (Understanding) the meaning of a note text.

situations such that in each of the situations the relation of certain properties of sound events to the corresponding indexical constraints remain constant. Due to the relational constancy between sound properties and indexical constraints, the selected sound situations have a semantic correspondence to the formula. By picking out a subset of possible sound situations, the function, in other words, illustrates the sounding possibilities allowed by the formula as its basic meaning.[8]

As to the second and third requirement above, the indexical nature of note symbols has been taken into account clearly in the discussed interpretation. And the Principle of Compositionality holds in the discussed intensional model-theoretic interpretation even with the formulae that never have explicit correlates in our "real" world.

Also satisfied is the requirement of conceptuality: the meaning function of a formula is, in fact, a compact conceptual principle for selecting sound situations (cf. next section). From a practical point of view, to know the meaning of a formula is to know what relational properties a sound event must have in order to be considered a sounding correlate of the formula. This preparedness to make right selections has, then, a model-theoretical counterpart in the form of a characteristic function from the set of possible sound situations. Thus, the above model-theoretic treatment illustrates linguistic competence of notation as an ability to infer conceptual knowledge of the conditions that a sound situation must fulfill in order to corresond to the give note expression (see Figure 2).

Composition of the meaning of a formula

How is the meaning function of a formula as a compact conceptual principle based on the meaning of the parts following the Principle of Compositionality? That is, what is the *logic* when the criteria for sound objects matching the note expression are inferred?[9] In this section, this question will be briefly clarified. The formula in Example 1 consists of three semantically independent parts (see Figure 3). The note is assumed to stand for an unspecified sound event having the property of lasting for *n* time units. And the following specifications represent the property of having the pitch E4 and the property of having strong intensity.[10]

There are several simple alternatives for deriving the formula syntactically from its parts. However, too much simplicity on the syntactic level must be paid back as ambiguity on the semantic level. Because it is convenient to deal with a syntax that is in a one-to-one correspondence to the semantics of notation, we must abandon some syntactically simple alternatives. We can avoid the quantification problems by forming a somewhat more complex analysis tree. The analysis tree in Figure 4 is my suggestion based on Montague's (1973) treatment of corresponding problems with quantified sentences in English.[11]

A note variable has been introduced in the analysis tree that, however, occurs only in the deep structure of the formula. The note variable is used to form a complex qualifier that occurs in the middle level of the analysis tree. This complex qualifier stands for the complex property of having the pitch E4 and strong intensity; it is the result of an operation referred to as a *lambda operation, abstraction operation* or *binder operation* by logicians and computer scientists.[12] Thanks to the binder operation, we can combine a quantified note with this complex qualifier

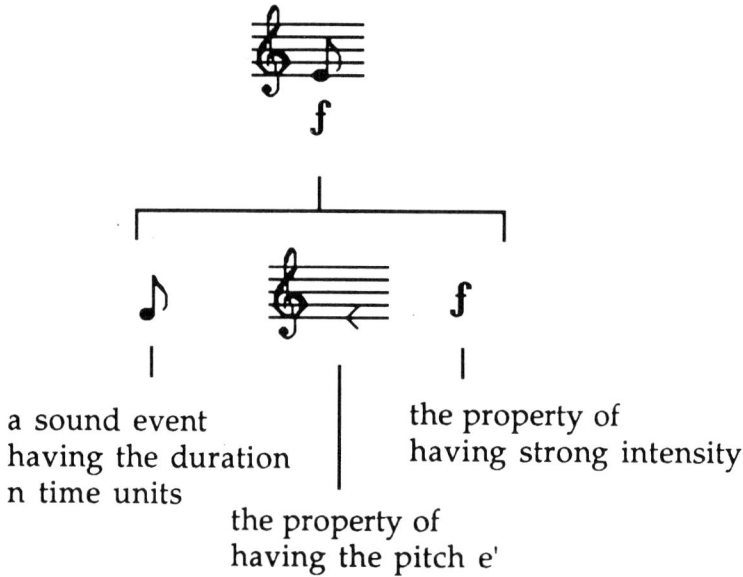

Figure 3 Parts of a formula.

without undesirable semantic complications. The resulting expression asserts that a sound event lasting for n time units has the complex property of having pitch E4 and strong intensity.

The model-theoretic meaning of the top-node expression has been defined as a function picking out a subset of sound situations. The analysis tree outlines how this satisfaction condition is derived logically from the parts of the formula. As such, it illustrates explicitly the linguistic intuition inherently shared by competent users of notation.

Artistic competence

We have outlined model-theoretically how a note symbol as such, without extra-notional additions, is connected to the sound universe. Understanding the basic meaning of a note text is, however, only the first part of notational competence. As we know, an *acceptable* performance of a score is usually not in a rigid one-to-one correspondence to the note text; expressive variation is needed. Even a performance with mistakes may be accepted rather than a basically correct but hopelessly mechanical realization. Communicative (artistic) competence,[13] thus, includes an ability to pay attention to contextuality essential features and to ignore the inessential ones. And as we know, some of the essential factors are not necessarily noted on the staff at all, whereas some noted features may be found inessential.

We have pointed out that notational competence includes an ability to understand note expressions such that the ability is based on the mastering of a system of rules. It can be seen by now that if we are dealing with communicative (artistic)

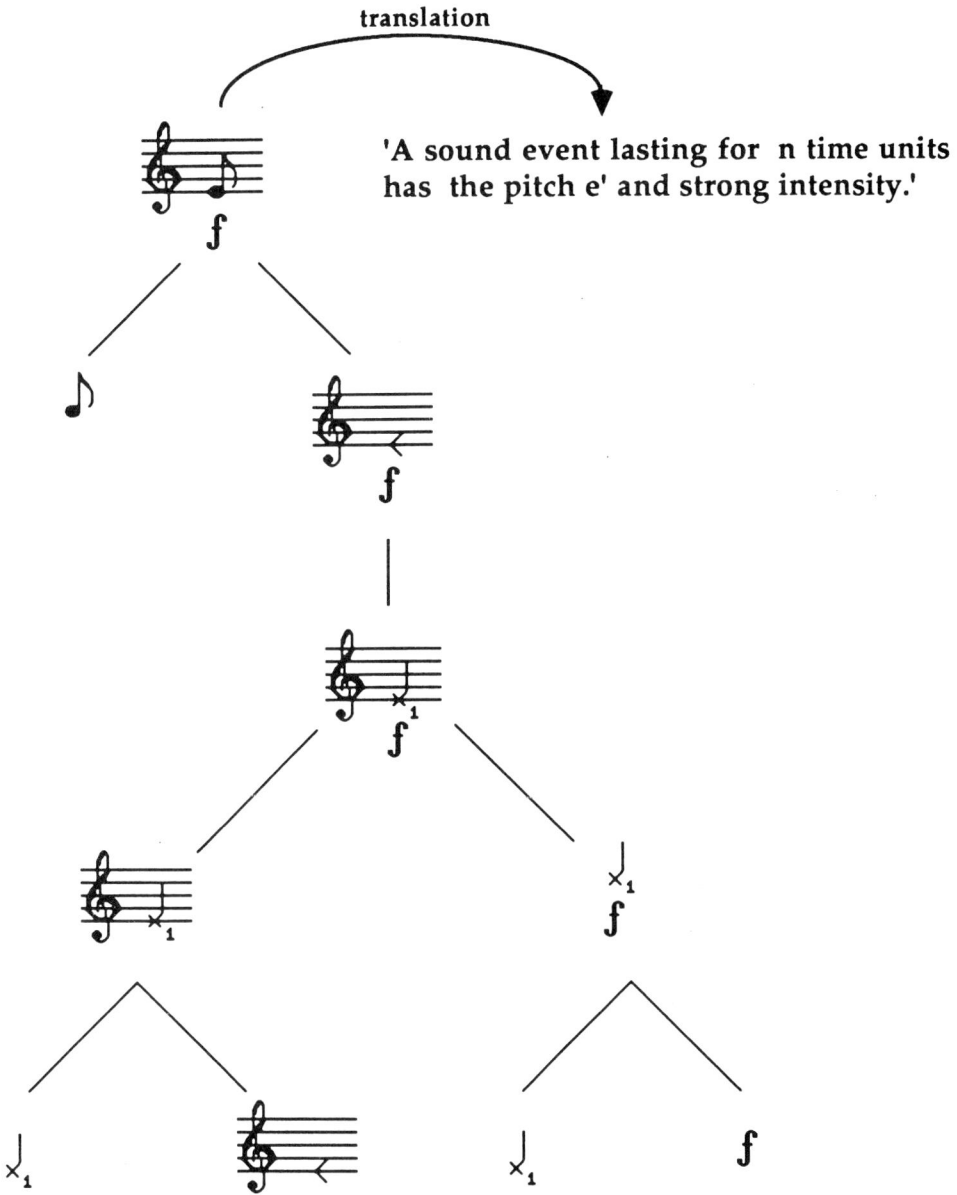

Figure 4 Logical derivation of a formula. A semantically unambiguous analysis tree.

competence, the rules in question may even be in discordance with those connected purely to notational basic competence (linguistic competence). That is, as far as artistic competence can be systematized, the explication has to determine the logical role of extra-notational factors that can overrule the factors affecting the formation of basic meaning.[14]

Without even trying to outline in this context what a rational connection of a given note text and its artistic meaning might be,[15] let us consider briefly the two extra-notational factors that have been pointed out in Figure 1: performance tradition and creativity. We can suppose that performance traditions develop under the pressure of general, perhaps universal laws that govern our ways of patterning acoustic events. Creativity in this context might be defined shortly as an idiosyncratic, basically spontaneous deviation from an accepted performance tradition. Although a reference group may object to a product of a creative act because of its deviation from actual conventions in performing the piece, the new idea may become established in use little by little and thus result in a modification of the performance tradition.

Artistic or communicative competence of notation includes an ability to understand note expressions "properly" – that is, in an acceptable way. This ability can be considered the skill to apply certain extra-notational rules in connection with the rules specifying the basic meaning of a note expression. However, what is considered acceptable or proper is dependent on the given reference group. On the other hand, we have supposed that creativity may be considered a part of artistic competence. And a creative act can cause objections in the given context because of its deviation from the established rules and conventions. Thus, if creativity is considered a part of artistic competence, a structural discordance is found in it: both acceptability and rejection are presumed.

Understanding a formula

Characteristic to a semantic treatment like the one above is its pursuit of parsimony, generality and intuitive acceptance. It may be true that the treatment could be carried out in a simpler way than suggested above but not, I suppose, without loss of intuitive acceptability and generality. Parsimony and generality are good principles in models of cognitive processes, as well. However, one may not be allowed to assume that human information processing matches one-to-one with the simplest possible description (cf. Anderson, 1983, pp. 40–44). On the other hand, a well-founded description of a cognitive process may not be intuitively satisfying in one respect: to be conscious of the result of a cognitive process does not imply that one is conscious of the factors participating in the cognitive process (cf. Minsky, 1982 & 1986).

Production theory

Now let's compare the above semantic treatment of understanding note texts to a cognitive approach and see what similarities and differences the two points of view may have. As pointed out, conventional staff notation is a kind of written language. Therefore, the process of understanding a note text may have as much in common with the understanding of a written language as with purely musical problems; on the other hand, the process of understanding and performing a score apparently has characteristics shared by goal-directed acts in general.[16] And the understanding of a note text as an act of problem solving is typically a matter of higher level cognition that includes phenomena such as memory and learning.

These processes have been studied extensively in cognitive psychology, and some studies might also provide a relevant basis for clarification of the process of understanding and executing a note text. For this purpose, I have selected a well-known production system framework presented by John R. Anderson and his colleagues. Called Adaptive Control of Thought, abbreviated ACT*, it is presented thoroughly in Anderson's book *The Architecture of Cognition* (1983). A pictorial presentation of some of the main functions of the ACT* system is presented in Figure 5.[17]

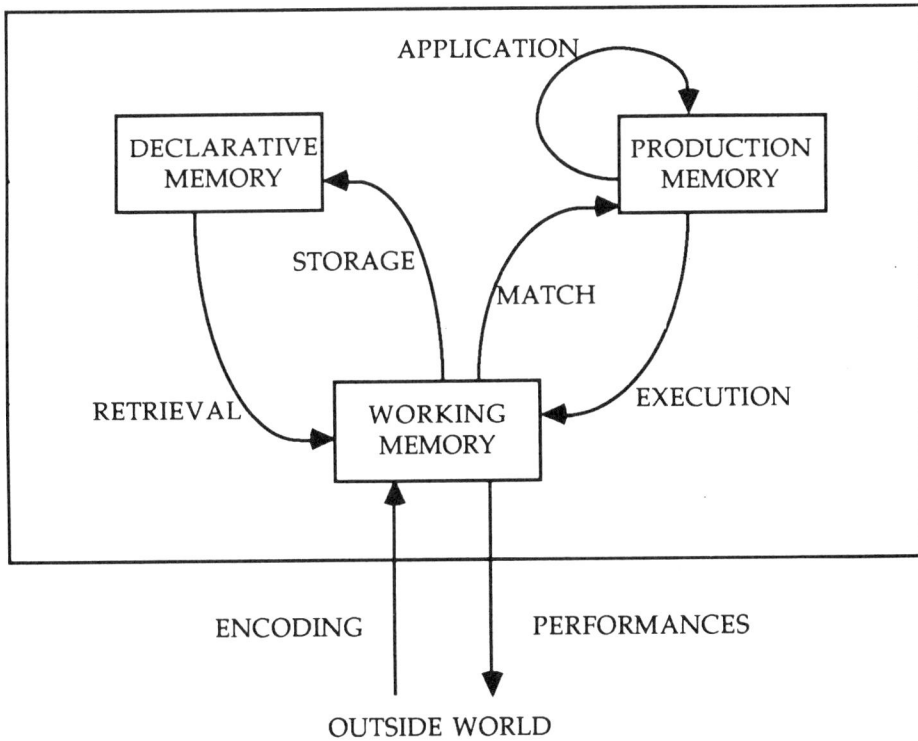

Figure 5 Main functions of the ACT* production system (Anderson, 1983).

The ACT* system illustrates the basic principles of operation present in the human cognitive system. It consists of three memories: *working, long-term declarative* and *production*. The content of the working memory is retrieved from the long-term declarative memory as well as deposited by encoding processes from the outside world and by the action of productions. In principle, knowledge representation is supposed to by propositional or in the form of temporal string codes or spatial image codes. Productions are condition-action pairs. The condition specifies some data patterns, and if elements matching these patterns are in the working memory, then the production can apply and result in new data elements specifying, for instance, how to proceed in the given situation (Anderson, 1983, pp. 7–84).

Goals have an important role in the conditions of productions: if the current goal matches a data pattern specified by a condition of a production, then the goal becomes a powerful source of activation for that production. A plan of action can be reflected as a hierarchical goal structure that controls the application of productions (Anderson, 1983, p.33). Thus we might assume that the sequence of goals involved in the act of performing a score (as illustrated in Figure 1) controls the application of the productions needed in understanding and executing a score (see also Figure 7).

Productions in understanding a formula

In this paper we are interested in a description of processes involved in understanding the basic meaning of a formula. The rather long lists of productions needed in the ACT* framework for an explication of how a novice may understand a formula – as well as the corresponding computational implementations – are beyond the scope of this paper[18]. However, let us consider briefly some of the principles of this matter.

The system needs production for perceptual recognition of note symbols and their combinations. In this case, the condition part of a production has descriptions of patterns and the action part involves labeling of the perceived object (Anderson 1983, p.30). Informally stated, the general form of productions might be somewhat as follows:

P1   IF a position contains a stem of type $|$
            and of a closed oval of type ●
            THEN the position is a note symbol of type ♩
            and it is called a quarter note.

Productions of this kind are assumed to specify a type for each note expression under consideration and to name the type.[19] So recognition of a given note expression is supposed to be based on certain crucial properties of the stimulus that match the condition of a production. A pattern-matching process is complete if the structural and attributive properties of a note expression match all the clauses of a condition. But a production can apply even if all of its condition clauses are not matched. For instance, a person accustomed to typed note text may recognize both of the following examples as tokens of the same formula type, despite the apparent differences between the expressions:

It can be understood easily that difficulties in performing a blurred note text, such as a manuscript, begin with recognizing problems, namely with the fact that the data structure does not perfectly match any condition of existing productions. This situation is supposed to lead to attempts to find a production condition that is matched best to the given situation. As a consequence, a partially matching production may apply and result in a conception of the type of the blurred note expression and its parts. However, there are inhibitory factors, such as the influence of competing productions, that in this case force the playing process to be slower and more exhausting than normal.

In Figure 6, a hypothesized knowledge representation of the expression in Example 2 has been outlined.[20]

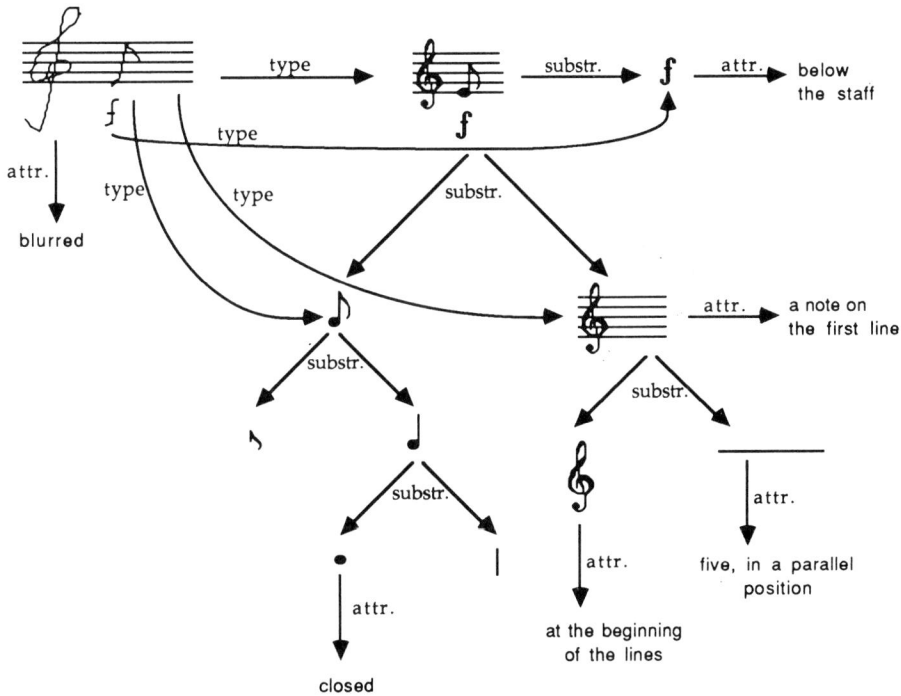

Figure 6 A hypothesized knowledge representation of the structure of a formula. (Attr. stands for attributive information and substr. for substructure information.)

When the syntactic type of the note expression has been determined, the process of interpreting the basic meaning can be carried out. (The understanding of note symbols as representatives of certain syntactic types is then an interpretative act as such.) Actually, the object of the interpretative process is a knowledge representation – such as the hierarchic structure in Figure 6.

A presentation of a process of how a novice with a specific learning history could be assumed to understand a formula is given in Figure 7.[21]

The process consists of five main sections. In the first section, the system acknowledges the goal of studying an uninterpreted note expression of a certain type, in this case a formula; further, it includes the setting of the subgoal to interpret an unstudied part of the formula. The second section (flow 2 from the node 'study an unstudied part of F') refers to the enterprise of finding out the

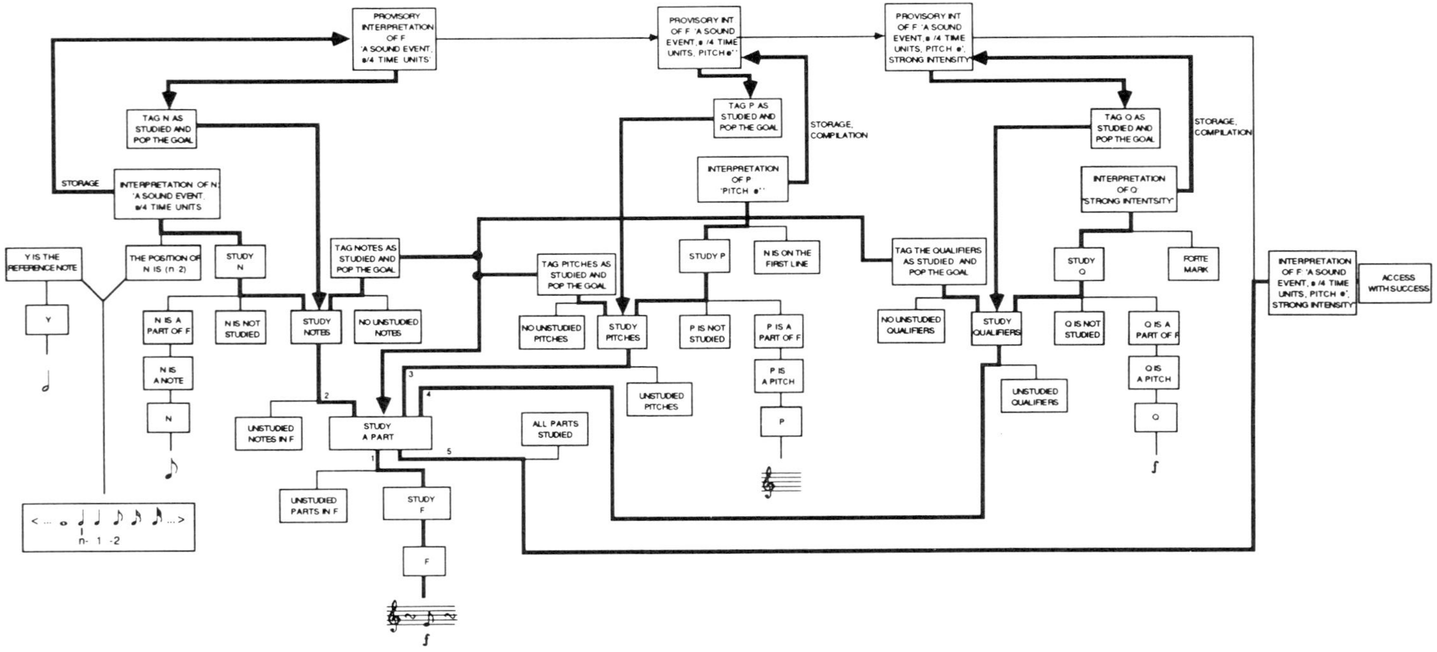

Figure 7 A hypothesized flow of productions in understanding a note expression.

basic meaning of the note that is a part of the formula. It has been assumed in our example that the formula is not the first one in the given context. Therefore, the time value of the note has to be related to a reference value, say, to a half note having a certain temporal value of s time units as the metrical basic unit in the given musical context. The interpretation of the note – as of each part in the formula – ends with a storage operation.

The third and fourth flows illustrate the processes of interpreting the pitch and the rest of the formula. The fifth flow refers to the accomplishment of the interpretation.

The order of the steps of the procedure has been fixed in our figure; and it has been implicitly presumed that, given a note expression, the system calculates the meaning of all the parts of the same type – notes, e.g. – before moving to the next type. However, it is presumable that this is not the only possibility. One can hypothesize several factors, such as learning history, which may influence the order of the steps.

It is evident that it takes time for a system to carry out a complex procedure like the above. And if the system is open to external and internal interference, as is the case with the human cognitive system, complexity is a source of mistakes. In fact, each experienced music teacher knows that a novice needs considerable time while calculating a meaning for a complex expression. On the other hand, it has been presupposed in the above model that the system can retrieve information (of the order of notes, for intance) from long-term memory without considerable effort. However, the retrieving of information from long-term memory may cause problems in the stocking of knowledge in the working memory. The situation where a novice's working memory runs out before the interpretation of a complex note expression has been completed is also familiar to music teachers.

It is apparent that Figure 7 is not an illustration of an expert's way of interpreting the basic meaning of a formula. However, it is possible to illustrate procedural learning in the ACT* framework[22]. Productions which apply in sequence can be combined into a single production. This process is called *composition*. Each production needs time to apply and a composition of productions needs less time than a sequence of single productions combined in it. Thus, composition reflects the fact that the time needed for understanding of note expressions decreases with increasing experience. For example, let us take the following four productions:

P2   IF the goal is to interpret a note expression x,
          and there are parts in the note expression x that are not studied,
          THEN the subgoal is to study the unstudied parts of the note expression x.

P3   IF the subgoal is to study the unstudied parts of a note expression x
          and there are notes in the expression x that are not studied
          THEN the subgoal is to study the unstudied notes.

P4   IF the subgoal is to study the unstudied notes
          and the note y is a part of the note expression x
          and the note y is not studied,
          THEN the subgoal is to study the note y

P5   IF the subgoal is to study the note y.
          and M is a $(n+1)$-tuple of notes as follows: $M = <\ldots \, \flat,\flat,\flat,\flat,\flat \ldots>$
          and the reference note is the nth member of M
          and the note y is the $(n \pm i)$th member of M
          and the relative time value of the reference note is s,
          THEN the relative time value of the $(n+i)$th member of M is $s/2^i$
          and the relative time value of the $(n - i)$th member of M is $2^i s$.

Several successful and specific applications of the above productions in sequence might finally result in the following specific composition:

P6   IF the goal is to interpret a note expression x,
         and an eighth note y is an unstudied part of the note expressing x
         and the relative time value of a half note as the reference note is s,
         THEN the relative time value of the eighth note y is $s/4$.

It would be interesting to question how communicative (artistic) understanding could be described in the given framework. There is not space for a detailed treatment of the question here. However, I suppose that certain rules determine the criteria for a musical performance in general and others specify how just a note text – by Chopin, e.g. – should be performed. So as a general type of a production for a situation like the one in question, something as follows could be represented:

P7   IF the basic meaning of a note expression x is p
         and the structural context is w
         and the composer is u,
         THEN the artistic meaning of the note expression x is q.

Let us assume that q contains parts $a, b, c, \ldots, n$. Now, the acquistion of q means that the person can evaluate sound situations. For example:

P8   IF a sound situation z matches the clauses $a, b, c, \ldots, n$,
         THEN the sound situation z is an artistically acceptable
         performance of the note text x.

As a principle, we could assume that if the matching is not complete in the cases such as P8, then the artistic value of a sound situation is not regarded as the highest possible and the diminution in communicative value corresponds to the rate of mismatch and saliency of features that are missing.

Knowledge representation

As a result of interpretative processes such as those described above, the system acquires declarative knowledge of a note expression's basic and artistic content. As already pointed out, cognitive units in the ACT* framework are supposed to be propositional or in the form of temporal string codes or spatial image codes. As candidate for an additional code, a kinesthetic and/or motor code has been suggested. It is worth questioning what the type or types of knowledge representation could be as a person understands the basic and artistic meaning of a note text (such as p and q in P7). According to Anderson, music possibly has its own code or is an instance of a motor-kinesthetic code. However, as Anderson points out, there must be empirical data that cannot be explained by existing types and there must have been time in our evolutionary history to create a representation before it is reasonable to introduce additional types of knowledge representation into the ACT* framework (Anderson, 1983, pp. 45–46, 308).

A representation in the ACT* framework can be a tangled hierarchy comprising cognitive units of different types[23]. Consequently, an artistic vision of a note text or of its fragment might be a temporal list possibly having a substructure and attributive specifications assigned to its elements; the specifications might be propositional, spatial[24] and kinesthetic by nature. It has to be emphasized that a vision based on understanding a note text is not an imagined sound situation but rather a kind of a slot such that to imagine (or otherwise produce) a sound situation is, so to say, to fill the slot (i.e. the sound situation matches the condition part of a production, as in P8).

In any case, we may presume that to calculate an execution strategy, that is, to "translate" an artistic vision into a motor programming mode, is to create a knowledge structure which presumably is a string of motor-kinesthetic units and can have a substructure and attributive elements.

Conclusion

We have illuminated the process of understanding a note text from two points of view. Based on these general remarks, some similarities and differences can be seen. Both approaches are based on the assumption that conventional staff notation is a language. Notational competence means to be intuitively aware of the logical connection between note symbols and a sound universe. An explication of this connection involves first a clarification of a syntax and semantics of notation and then requires an explanation of what in the given context is considered communicatively (artistically) satisfying. On the other hand, we have modeled the practical process of understanding a note text hypothetically as a sequence of cognitive operations or an application of cognitive skills called productions. Acquisition of productions makes a person notationally competent. So the two phenomena are connected to each other and have certain fundamental similarities. However, considerable structural differences can be seen between the logical deep structure of a note expression and the sequence of productions in understanding the meaning of the expression, the nature of which has to be specified in further empirical studies.

Notes

1. For more about the process of translating an intention into performance (response output) and about "programming the motor output" from a cognitive point of view, see Shaffer (1976, 1981). About performance plans in general, see Sloboda (1982).
2. About feedback in performance, see Sloboda (1982), which includes discussion of the matter.
3. "Artistic vision" and insight into a musical work are treated as synonyms in this context. For more about the concept "musical work", see Kurkela (1986, 1987, 1988a) and Kurkela & Grund (1987). See also note 13 below.
4. On the other hand, understanding a separate formula may differ from understanding it as a constituent of a larger unit in some situations. However, a novice usually interprets separate formulae. Advanced strategies – for example, the very sophisticated ones applied by a skilled sight reader (cf. Sloboda 1985) – are, in turn, supposed to be based on more elementary faculties, basically on understanding separate formulae. And the full understanding of the advanced strategies presupposes that we know how they are developed from more elementary ones. So, the clarification of elementary strategies is also motivated from this point of view.
5. This is known also as the Principle of Frege and can be stated as follows: the meaning of a complex expression is based on the meaning of the parts and their mode of combination.
6. Correspondingly, it is intuitively satisfying to state that if John seeks a unicorn, he seeks something else than when he seeks a mermaid even if in both cases John seeks something that is an empty set in our actual world.
7. A detailed model-theoretic interpretation of conventional notation is given in my book *Note and Tone*. I have also dealt with the main points of a treatment of this kind in some other papers (published in English as well as in French). Cf. References.

8. For a more detailed discussion on the matter, see Kurkela (1986, 1987, 1988a) and Kurkela & Grund (1987).
9. It has to be emphasized that we are dealing with a logical connection between two systems (notation and sound universe). The cognitive processes involved in this question are discussed in the section on "Understanding a Formula" below.
10 For more about sound properties and about how a note stands for sound events, see Kurkela (1986, 1987, 1988a).
11. Montague (1973). For a more detailed treatment of the matter, see Kurkela (1986).
12. For more about lambda operators in this context, see Kurkela (1986).
13. When talking of acceptability or communicative competence, we are actually dealing with a pragmatic matter of which "artistry" is only one, though very salient, aspect in the context of concert music.
14. The performer has, in other words, to presume affecting factors that are not stated on the staves. To be communicatively competent is to master the "right" assumptions. For a more detailed treatment of the matter, see also Kurkela & Grund (1987, §5–§7) and Kurkela (1986, 1987, 1988a,b).
15. See, for example, Sundberg, Frydén & Askenfelt (1983) and McAdams (1987, p. 15).
16. About notation and language reading, see also Sloboda (1976). About similarities between music performance, speech and typing, see Shaffer (1976).
17. See also Neves & Anderson (1981) and Anderson, Greeno, Kline & Neves (1981). This presentation is based on Anderson (1983). Cognitive models tend to be more or less theoretical by nature because we do not have direct access to our cognitive system. The aspects to be presented in the following sections are not an exception to this rule. As stated in the beginning of the paper, it will be used as a basis for empirical studies and therefore the sections also contain hypotheses. The general principles presented by Anderson (1983) that I have adopted here are, however, at least partly empirically supported. An important source for the musical observations has been my activity as a concert pianist and experience as a piano teacher with children and young people ranging in their skills from novices to post graduate students.
18. I shall follow the practice adopted in Anderson (1983) and present the (types of) productions in an English-like syntax for readability and intuitive understanding of the matter. The actual Prolog implementation of the algorithm presented in Figure 7 can be obtained by writing to me. We will concentrate on the question of how a novice might understand notation, because it is assumed that the strategies applied by an expert are based on the productions used as a novice. Cf. note 4 and the discussion about compositions in this paper.
19. Types or patterns – at least as far as knowledge representation is in the form of spatial images – are not fixed to an absolute size; cf. Anderson (1983, p. 56). P1, as a general type of a production, contains undefined concepts such as "position" and "contain". I think we can disregard them here because defining them is not a specifically musical problem (for more about the matter, see for example Anderson, 1983, pp. 31, 81–84, and 144). It is apparent that if we define the understanding and execution of a note text thoroughly, exact knowledge about many non-musical phenomena is needed.
20. There are different notations for visual images and one "chooses a notation to make salient the information being used by the processes operating on the representation" (Anderson, 1983, p. 57). In our example, it is essential to know whether the note has a flag or not, whether there are the usual number of lines or not, what is the exact location of the note on the staff, and so on. Figure 6 is one way to make explicit the visual material used in the semantic understanding of the note expression.
21. One may see the correspondence between the network and production rules in Figure 8, opposite. The application of a production – and thus the actual flow of productions – depends naturally on how the condition part of each production is fulfilled.
22. Anderson (1983), Neves & Anderson (1981) and Anderson *et al* (1981).
23. On the other hand, it is not unreasonable to assume that in many cases a representation of a certain type could be "translated" into some others at least to some degree.
24. Concepts such as "length", "pitch" and "volume" have, indeed, spatial associations. In this context, "spatiality" might be understood in a general way, i.e. not only as a phenomenon of pure visuality, but as a concept of some other cognitive modes of experiencing as well.

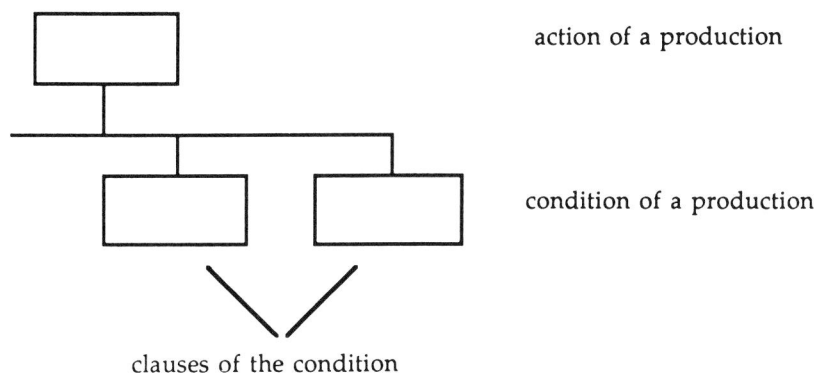

action of a production

condition of a production

clauses of the condition

Figure 8

References

Anderson, J.R. (1983) *The Architecture of Cognition*. Cambridge and London: Harvard University Press.

Anderson, J.R., Greeno, J.G., Kline, P.J. & Neves, D.M. (1981) Acquisition of problem-solving skill. In *Cognitive Skills and Their Acquisition*, John R. Anderson (ed.) 191–230. Hillsdale,N.J.: Erlbaum Associates.

Kurkela, K. (1986) *Note and Tone. A Semantic Analysis of Conventional Music Notation*. Helsinki: The Musicological Society of Finland.

Kurkela, K. (1987) Entre la note et le ton. Fondements de la sémantique de la notation musicale, *Degrés. Revue de synthese a orientation semiologique*, **52**, hiver 1987, 25–30, Bruxelles.

Kurkela, K. (1988a) How a note denotes. In "Essays on Philosophy of Music", *Acta Philosophica Fennica* Vol. 43, V. Rantala, L. Rowell & E. Tarasti (eds.) 70–96, Helsinki: University of Helsinki.

Kurkela, K. (1988b) Music in performance and its study. *Finnish Music Quarterly*, **2/1988**, 36–43.

Kurkela, K.& Grund, C. (1987) Notation and its interpretation: some music theoretical concepts, especially for studies in the performance of music. In *The Semiotic Web '86. An International Yearbook*, T.A. Sebeok & J.Umiker Sebeok (eds.) 484–490, Berlin: Mouton de Gruyter

McAdams, S. (1987) Music: A science of the mind? In "Music and Psychology: A Mutual Regard". S. McAdams, (ed.),*Contemprary Music Review*, **2**,(1) 1–61, London: Harwood Academic Publishers.

Minsky, M. (1982) Music, mind and meaning. In *Music, Mind and Brain; The Neuropsychology of Music*, M. Clynes (ed.) chap. 1, New York: Plenum Press.

Minsky, M. (1986) *The Society of Mind*. New York: Simon and Schuster.

Montague, R. (1973) The proper treatment of quantification in ordinary English. In *Formal Philosophy. Selected Papers of Richard Montague* (1974), R. Thomason (ed.) 247–270, New Haven: Yale University Press.

Neves, D.M. & Anderson, J.R. (1981) Knowlege compilation: mechanisms for automatization of cognitive skills. In *Cognitive Skills and their Acquisition*, John R. Anderson (ed.), 57–84, Hillsdale, N.J.: Erlbaum Associates.

Shaffer, L.H. (1976) Intention and performance. *Psychological Review*, **83**, 375–393.

Shaffer, L.H. (1981) Performance of Chopin, Bach and Bartok: Studies in motor programming. *Cognitive Psychology*, **13**, 326–376.

Sloboda, J.A. (1976) Visual perception of musical notation: Registering pitch symbols in memory. *Quarterly Journal of Experimental Psychology*, **28**, 1–16.

Sloboda, J.A. (1982) Music performance. In *The Psychology of Music*, D. Deutsch (ed.) 479–496, New York, London: Academic Press.

Sloboda, J.A. (1985) *The Musical Mind: The Cognitive Psychology of Music*. Oxford: Clarendon Press.

Sundberg, J., Frydén, L. & Askenfelt, A. (1983) What tells you the player is musical? An analysis-by-synthesis study of music performance. In *Studies of Music Performance*, J. Sundberg (ed.) 61–75, Stockholm: Royal Swedish Academy of Music.

Contemporary Music Review,
1989, Vol. 4, pp. 437–446
Photocopying permitted by license only

Command performances, performance commands

Gerald J. Balzano

Department of Music, B-026, University of California at San Diego, La Jolla, California 92093, USA

This chapter reviews some major concerns in the study of music cognition, focusing on musical performance and composition. An attempt is made to discern the nature of the hybrid term "performance". The different chapters dedicated to performance in this volume (by Shaffer; Carlson, Friberg, Frydén, Granström & Sundberg; Todd; and Kurkela) are discussed. Possible directions for the future of performance, composition, and music education are proposed in light of developments both in personal-computer/music-synthesis environments and in our understanding of the acquisition of musical skills. A strong need is expressed for cognitive studies to devote more attention to composition, which necessarily implies the participation of willing composers. A critique of the subject-object split that plagues the science of performance is developed. Finally, some thoughts on the future of music and the cognitive sciences are advanced with a critique of some of the basic assumptions of Cognitive Science and an examination of some alternatives in the realms of neural nets and ecological psychology.

KEY WORDS: Music performance, music composition, computer learning environments, musical universals, perceptual learning, subjective-objective, neural nets, ecological psychology.

On performance

"Performance" is a hybrid term, a term with several meanings. When a psychologist tells someone, particularly a musician, "I am interested in performance," he is apt to be misunderstood. There is a journal in the *Journal of Experimental Psychology* series entitled *Human Perception and Performance*, and it is not, except very occasionally, a journal of music articles. To be sure, the title emphasizes a reciprocity that is important, between receptive and expressive capacities, but if one looks for examples of "Human Performance" as shown in this journal, we see firstly that they are much harder to come by than articles about "Human Perception", but also that what passes for performance are often very brief snippets of behavior, not very much in the way of connected, meaningful, expressive behavior at all. To the extent that we *do* see connected, meaningful, expressive behavior studied in the "Perception & Performance" journal, there is generally a very limited analysis of what is going on. Perception and performance are in one sense inverses of one another, reciprocally related processes. But one is so much harder to study scientifically than the other!

This situation is mirrored within the cognitive-scientific study of music. We have many studies of our receptive, listening abilities, and comparatively few of our expressive capabilities as manifested in performance. As risky as it is to look at listening when the objects of our study are brief, decontextualized hunks, it is even riskier to look at performance in this fashion. Actually, psychoacoustics is well-known for doing just this, namely looking at listening out of context almost as a methodological credo. In this sense psychoacoustics is to behaviorism as perception is to performance. But we have seen in this conference neither psychoacoustic studies of listening nor behavioristic studies of performance, and I for one feel that is appropriate, as neither approach shows a proper appreciation of *context*.

However, it is one thing to show a proper appreciation of context and quite another to do something more productive about it. When we are looking at listening, we extend our vista outward into more connected meaningful contexts with some difficulty, but at least the stimulus for listening is nominally under the scientist's control. When, on the other hand, we study more connected, meaningful *performances*, the object of our study is very clearly not under our control, else it would not be somebody else's expressive performance. So the methodological problems of examining more connected extended contexts are compounded in the study of performance over what they are in perception. It is not so much that it is hard to control somebody's performance as that to do so would defeat the purpose of studying it.

And once we have admitted a potentially wild and woolly performance of a musical work into our laboratory, what shall we do with it? What kinds of observations do we wish to make about it? Do we wish to arrive at "reductions" of a performance like we might arrive at "reductions" of a score? Obviously the performance in and of itself is much too complex to look at in its full splendor, and yet at the same time it is clear that the methods used to reduce scores on which some – but by no means all – performances are based, are just not appropriate to understanding and appreciating performance.

Overview of the performance chapters in this volume

All this is by way of celebrating the bravery of those who presented original work on the topic of performance, to my mind the most difficult topic of all those engaged at this symposium. I'd like to look briefly at the tactics they took in doing this, and make a few comments.

One way of getting a handle on the complexity of performance is given in Shaffer's (this volume) thought-experiment strategy of designing a musical robot. This is an example of forming an idealization of some complicated thing, where the idealized form is perhaps understandable in ways that the real thing is not. Shaffer's robot is an idealization that forces us to think through some of the complexities of music performance in a novel way.

Kurkela's (this volume) work approaches but does not quite reach actual performance, being a very fine-grained look at what it takes to get from a "note" to a "tone". Again the complexities and subtleties involved here in even the apparently most straightforward act of music reading give us pause. What is most interesting about Kurkela's analysis is the reminder that examining the process from the standpoint of its logical requirements and looking at it from the standpoint of the psychological processes that generate it are by no means identical.

Todd's (this volume) work most clearly reflects an appreciation of the reciprocity between performance and perception alluded to above. Like Shaffer and Kurkela, he is trying to *generate* some aspect of a performance, but in this case the basis for generation is more explicitly based on information gleaned from a prior analysis of a performance. And while Shaffer is concerned with the overall organization of the performance and Kurkela is concerned with its most elementary score-based constituent, Todd is specifically concerned with an important ingredient of its expressive aspect, *rubato,* perhaps the most pervasive means by which the performance goes beyond the notated indications in the score.

For Carlson *et al* (this volume), the preferred methodology harks back to a number of early discussions in the symposium. Whenever we attempt to understand something by comparing it to something else, actually both objects of the comparison are illuminated by the critical act of holding them side by side. This happens in all metaphor making, and we have found it to be particularly true when the objects of the comparison are language and music. The Carlson *et al* work fits into the session on Performance rather than the one on Music and Language because of their specific concern with *production* of music and speech. They have also used the tactic employed by Shaffer and Todd of using simplified descriptions of how performances are shaped – performance "rules" – and observing how the idealized performance-by-prescription compares with a real one. And one of the most significant instruments for assessing that comparison, appropriately enough, is the ear of the musical listener. I shall return in particular to this point.

Any further attempt to compare these exceedingly diverse approaches is no doubt doomed to vacuity. Besides, the authors speak quite well for themselves. Read their chapters.

Thoughts on the future of performance, composition and education

Music continues to evolve, and for a long time the primary focus of that evolution has been in the realm of composition. Contemporary performance practice has changed that to some extent, but now the advent of the computer as both a perceptual and productional aid to performance has really changed it with a vengeance. To date, work in cognitive science on human-machine interactions and interfaces has centered around mundane activities like sending and receiving electronic mail, but there is a potential for much livelier possibilities here. So while scientists work on performance, the nature of performance itself does not sit still but changes even as we speak. This is as it should be.

I want to make two further comments related to this. The first stems from the fact that my own work has increasingly been in this area. I have been interested in designing computer-based environments for music learning. These environments have the property that all of them present a particular model or representation with which the user works; they are all interactive and they all make quite a bit of noise while they are being used. They are "models with handles", if you will. Years ago we might have only used such models to *analyze* ready-made musical structures (and I did). But lately I have come to believe that if something is a good model then it is also a good tool, and can be used equally well to *generate* new structures as to analyze existing ones.

So, for example, the group-theoretic representations of pitch spaces that I have been so fond of in recent years (Balzano, 1980, 1986a,b) have found a new home as one of these so-called learning environments. But it and the others are really not just "learning" environments in the sense that their usefulness is limited to novices and music students. I would argue, on the contrary, that they are also each a new kind of *musical instrument* on which one can do this ever-changing thing called performance. What is unusual about these new kinds of musical instruments is their simultaneous status as representations. They are instruments that are self-describing; their appearance is that of the model that generates them. I'd like to think that we shall be seeing more of their kind in the near future, and that they will cause us to rethink music education as well as performance and composition. I would also like to say that I think the design of these "instruments" is a worthwhile activity for cognitive scientists who are frustrated with the limitations of the laboratory. And I note that were quite a few of us who, for one reason or another, did not present any new "data" from our experimental laboratories at this symposium. (See Balzano, 1987a, for further discussion of interdisciplinary musical "microworlds".)

The second further comment I wish to make concerns the issue of universals. With music evolving all the time our list of universals must of course stand susceptible to constant revision. I am amused when I think of music graduate students at the University of California at San Diego frothing at the mouth when the time comes in my course to talk of universals. Indeed, what would you do if you were a graduate student interested in exploring the frontiers of musical possibility, and somebody tells you "No music has property X"? I don't know about you, but I would take this as a mandate to run off and try to compose a piece of music that *does* have property X. And this too, I think, is as it should be. Better we should shift our talk to focus on properties of musics that are more or less widespread, in the world and through history, properties that recur frequently versus ones that do not, rather than debating universality. Actually, I think that what is *unique* about a particular music is every bit as interesting as that which it shares with all other musics.

A word about human flexibility follows right along here. I would very much like to believe, with H. de la Motte, that there is little or no limit to our flexibility as listeners, performers, composers. I have designed the just-discussed music learning environments precisely to broaden these limits. So it should be clear where my sympathies, and even my energies, lie. But I think it is important for us to keep our eyes open for contrary evidence here. For example, I have to believe that if we were more flexible, there would already be a more thriving production and consumption of microtonal music. I attribute the relative lack in this direction both to limitations on our flexibility as listeners to *perceive* what goes on in a microtonal piece and limitations on our flexibility as composers to *conceive* of what should go on in such a piece. Certainly, we all need to push ourselves a lot harder to realize the true potential of the flexibility I believe we possess. The lesson of Bharucha's (1987; this volume) neural nets "brought up" on Western tonality is very much worth bearing in mind. Categorical perception of old categories need not describe the end-state of our musical potential, but some hard work is needed to escape this easy fate.

I would be remiss if I didn't say something specifically about composition. If studies of music performance are hard to find, studies of musical composition are virtually nonexistent. Many composers doubtless feel that the process by which they create is at once rather personal and rather boring. Composing is not meant to be publicly observed like performances presumably are, nor does composing honor any real-time constraints like a performance presumably does.

Yet I feel we need to open up the cognitive science of music to composition for a number of reasons. One is that, to be sure, there is no defensible reason to leave it out, once we have let performance in the door. And there is reason to believe that as personal microcomputer/MIDI-based systems become increasingly widespread, the activity of composing will come earlier and earlier into the musical lives of amateurs. Again, the "learning environments" on which I have worked recently (Balzano, 1987a) are an explicit attempt in this direction. Right now, virtually everybody sings, a much smaller number of people have some experience playing a musical instrument, and a much smaller number than that do some composing in their lifetimes. What I am saying is that I believe we can look forward to significant changes in these numbers in the future. Giving our children powerful tools for musical composition-and-performance should, if nothing else, help to demystify the musical offerings of the gods of MTV[1].

My second reason for wishing those inclined toward cognitive studies to devote more attention to composition is situated at virtually the opposite end of the spectrum, at the professional rather than the novice end. We have heard frequently from composers – both over the years and during this symposium – that the scientists who look at music have on the whole very limited models of what music and musical structure is. One antidote to this would be for present-day composers to speak to cognitive scientists – from what would essentially be an autobiographical perspective – about the alternative models of musical structure with which they themselves work. This is not a call for discussions and revelations of idiosyncratic compositional methods, although I am not ruling them out either. It is rather a way to try and open up our view of musical structure by asking those who have thought the most about it in the most open-ended-way – composers – to share their thoughts and ideas on the subject. At least, to criticize scientists for taking a limited view of structure but to be unwilling to work through and articulate one's own more expanded view borders on the disingenuous. With such expanded views on the table, all of us, whether we are interested in listening, performance, composition, modeling, form-bearing elements, or music-as-language . . . all of us stand to benefit. We might even get some new computer-based learning environments out of the process, wherein the rest of us could come to see and hear music in a new way.

On "subjectivity" and a science of performance

It is a good sign for music performers and music theorists to begin talking to one another in a productive fashion. Indeed, it's a good sign that they're talking to one another at all. The two groups don't have a history of very good relations. In part this is because so much music theorizing has had the ring of prescriptiveness to it. As a classic case, I'd like to consider theories of musical intervals. Traditionally, these are defined as whole-number frequency ratios; the octave is 2:1, the perfect fifth is 3:2, and so forth.

This looks like pure *description*, but it quickly turns to *prescription* when the tuning theorist declares that intervals not conforming to the specification are "out of tune". This characterization has been repeatedly applied to tuning schemes like equal temperament, and it is noncontroversially, even conversationally, applied to the sound of pianos. Interestingly – if not surprisingly – the same (non-piano) performer who might disparage pianos' out-of-tuneness due to their failure to conform to frequency ratio prescriptions will very likely be affronted when his or her own playing is accorded a similar description on these grounds.

Despite such lapses into inconsistency, it is the performer's view, and not the theorist's, that has my support. It is not just that no performer likes to hear someone say his or her performance is out of tune – and, to be sure, no one has said this about my piano playing lately. It is rather that no *a priori* scheme could ever decide something like in-tuneness. At the least, what makes something in tune is a highly contextual thing, not a static absolute like a 3:2 ratio.

But there is more than that, and this is what makes the story of tuning and ratios such a textbook case for scientific approaches to musical performance. It has almost always been part of becoming "scientifically respectable" to put one's trust in machines and other mechanized measuring instruments. The deliverances of such devices have the critical virtue of "objectivity", while human judgments are "subjective", or so we are told. Though we may be eager, even hasty, to embrace the trappings of science to study music in general and musical performance in particular, I would urge that we leave this particular chestnut behind. I know that the objective-subjective distinction has a most honorable tradition in the history of ideas, and that it is considered to be near the very core of psychoacoustics. As Fechner (1860/1966), the grandfather of psychophysics, has taught us, tone frequency is objective but pitch is subjective; tone intensity is objective but loudness is subjective; and so on. But the distinction is insidious, and in the case of music it discredits the very capacities it should celebrate. Instead, the canons of objectivity would have us celebrate the capacities of mechanical devices, even though the set of measuring instruments that exists at any point in history hardly picks out a principled set of real-world properties.

Some of this came home to me recently when I was reading a book on constructing so-called "objective" tests of musical ability and achievement. This book, which could have been any one of several and shall therefore remain nameless, took no small pains to establish the objective-subjective distinction. (Nor can any self-respecting book in the tests-and-measurements tradition afford to be lax about it). Objective information, we are told, is that which can be verified by any observer. This seems to be an innocuous definition, but let's take a closer look.

To fix ideas, consider the case of trying to determine the skillfulness of a musical performance or a set of musical performances. The definition says that no property of a musical performance that cannot be heard or detected by all observers may be called objective. An objective test of a performer's ability, to phrase it alternately, may "measure" only qualities of a performance that can be heard by musician and nonmusician alike. At this point I feel it is important to ask, what is the purpose of a music education? What, if it is successful, does an education in music do to the learner? Performer, composer, and theorist alike all presumably develop (among other things) their *perceptual* abilities while in the business of learning to be musicians. This perceptual learning leads to their ability to hear properties of the music that cannot be heard by the novice. It is curious, then, to take the very dimensions of sensitivity along which someone has developed in the process of becoming musical, and rule just these dimensions out as (scientifically) illegitimate indicators of musicality. But this is precisely what occurs under the banner of objectivity; the informed perceptual judgments of skilled music perceivers are subtly – or not so subtly – discredited, because there is no instrument that measures them, and because they refer to properties of the music that, by definition of "music perceptual learning", are not equally heard by all listeners.

I think it is critically important to recognize that there is another view, one that is equally scientific but that rejects the objective-subjective distinction. The alternative view, simply put, is that *there are perfectly objective properties of the world for which the only measuring instrument we have is a properly attuned human perceiver.* (See Balzano, 1987b, for a related discussion). It seems to me that if we accept this proposition, we must either deny the subjective-objective distinction outright, or recognize it as so inscrutable that it is useless for doing science.

And so we must come to reevaluate the business of in-tuneness. We see that musicians who endorse the (again, seemingly innocuous) idea that "in tune" intervals are constituted by small integral frequency ratios are actually supporting the objective-subjective distinction. They are tacitly certifying a science of music that will, logically and inexorably preceding from these granted premises, undermine musicians' hard-won abilities to hear by relegating the fruits of such abilities forever to the realm of the subjective.

In fact, one does not even have to be a great musician to bear witness to one of the great mysteries of musical performance: that the bent notes of a master jazz singer are somehow exquisitely expressive while the (in some sense) equally bent notes of a TV-show amateur are painfully discordant. This is a mystery because we scientists have not yet provided any principled account of it. We cannot get at questions like these by even the most cleverly created synthetic performances (e.g. Clynes, 1983); we can only do it by analysis of performances that have exemplars of all the varieties of "bent" notes . . . as measured by human listeners.

Part of what makes this such a difficult project is that we may take no fixed, externally defined acoustical framework as the ground from which to measure "bentness". We cannot use small-integer ratios, and we cannot use equal temperament, as standards. Jenkins, Wald & Pittenger (1986) have said that psychologists need to let perceivable events themselves define the features by which they (events) may be apprehended (as opposed to invoking pre-wired "feature detectors"). A similar directive in the tuning arena would be to let some conjunction of the performer's actions (over a whole tune) and the listener's perceptions set the standard. Anything less will surely send us on the road to pseudo-explanations, if not pseudo-science.

So what is a musical interval, if not a frequency ratio? I have suggested that it is an element in a structure, one which is mathematical but which is not tied to acoustics (Balzano, 1980; Balzano, 1982). It is not equal temperament plus categorical perception. Nor is it, obviously, wholly independent of sound. It is, if you like, a mutual "construction" of performer and perceiver, but this is not at all the same as "subjective".

If I am a performer and I have played major 3rds and minor 3rds and I am trying to establish a new place somewhere between the two – a "blue" 3rd, perhaps – there are certain constraints which my performance must meet. The distributional history of my major- and minor- 3rd intonation choices in the tune I am playing have to have been sufficiently separated to leave a "hole" for the new category to "fill".

My new, blue 3rd has to fill that hole in a way that not only has its own distributional integrity, but does not violate the distributional integrity of the major and minor 3rds that flank it.

This is no easy task. But it is in many ways no different from the case of the novice (a) singing a song in C major, with many F's and G's but no chromatic tones, and then (b) trying to find and establish a "place" for F#. Not all who try, succeed. But then, not all would-be jazz-singers succeed in establishing that blue 3rd either. The main difference between the two enterprises is that the C major scale implicitly generates the "place" for F# by virtue of the scale's structure, while the jazz singer is more on his or her own to find that blue 3rd. In neither case will an appeal to readymade tuning systems tell us whether the note was found or not. It depends, rather on the structure of the performer's intonations-in-context, and it will also depend on the apprehension of that structure by a human listener.

Musicians have frequently insisted that "in tune is what the performer says is in tune", but it has been thought that this bit of folk wisdom had to be left on the cutting-room floor when scripting a scientific approach to musical performance. On the contrary, I am saying that the spirit, if not the letter, of this idea is in fact the only hope for real answers in our attempts to study that most challenging area of musicality, performance.

Closing thoughts on the future of "Music and the Cognitive Sciences"

Cognitive Science is currently in somewhat of a tumultuous state. Now (1988) is an exciting time, but it is also riddled with controversy. Cognitive Science's root metaphors, its leading models, and its core methodologies hang in the balance. Up until a few years ago, the root metaphor of cognition as computation seemed comfortably entrenched. Explaining behavior meant giving a listing of the internal "program" controlling the computation. Performance commands were the stuff from which performances were built. One can find a prototypical example of this style of theorizing in J. Sloboda's (1985) wonderfully lucid introductory text.

But only a few years in the wake of that book, Cognitive Science is being taken by storm by models of the "neural-net", "(neo-)connectionist", or "parallel distributed processing (PDP)" variety. (See Bharucha, this volume; see also Rumelhart & McClelland, 1986). Here the root metaphor is more biological, of interacting "neurons" or units propagating patterns of excitation and inhibition among themselves. The language of computation, though it can be appropriated to the goings-on in such networks, seems only to be a crude, high-level "gloss" of the real mechanisms at work, and is usually quite dispensible for the purpose of understanding them.

Another alternative is that of the "ecological approach" to cognition. This approach is also gaining popularity, albeit much more slowly than the connectionist approach. It is an ecological approach that informs the ideas in the present chapter. One of the hallmarks of this approach is the rejection of organism-environment dualisms. These include both the classic mind-body dualism and the subjective-objective dualism discussed in the previous section. According to the ecological approach to cognition, one should not use different language for talking about organisms and environments; one should consider them sub-systems of a larger system. Properties of organisms should be described relative to their environments and properties of environments should be described relative to organisms. (See Gibson, 1979, for foundations of the ecological approach; Balzano, 1982, 1986a,b, for some applications to music perception; and Still & Costall, in press, and Gaver, 1988, for related discussions to which the present one is indebted.)

One important consequence of the ecological approach is that Cognitive Science really does need to be just as concerned with properties of environments as with properties of organisms. It is decidedly *not* acceptable for the Cognitive Scientist to treat description of environments as the purview of physics, nor to take descriptions proffered by physics as a starting point for understanding cognition, perception, or action (Runeson, 1977). We saw the mischief this could cause in our discussion of tuning. Only accounts of environments and organisms that "point both ways" can have the proper emphasis on the mutuality of the perceiver and perceived, of the knower and the known.

Mainstream Cognitive Science and all its intellectual cousins still court the dualisms, and mystify the process of knowing the world. When we sever an internal state of an organism from the environmental conditions that naturally coexist and coordinate with it and make our object of study this decontextualized internal state, it is easy to fall into the trap of thinking that "only" the internal state is important for understanding behavior. This is one step too far down the slippery slope of solipsism, which is the belief that "I exist" is the only sure truth and all else might just as easily be illusion, or even orchestrated for my benefit. This makes great science fiction on occasion (e.g. Dick, 1969, 1973), but never great science. Cognitive Science sells itself down the river as a mere grabbag of curiosities if it sells itself as the study of illusions.

From this ecological perspective, one of the most important things about the study of musical performance is the way it highlights the extensiveness of a person's potential coordination with a part of his or her environment. When a master instrumentalist puts on a command performance, the coordination between the musician and the instrument becomes so sublimely complete, we may even say that the boundary between organism and environment has actually shifted, that the instrument has become "part of", an extension of, the musician.

It is this coordination we should be looking at, not musical illusions or performance "errors". The implication for network modeling is that *the environment is part of the network too,* and that we need to be looking at the ways organism-subnetworks and environment-subnetworks couple and uncouple in their patterns of activity. So far the new Cognitive Scientific theories, like their computational ancestors, have only been doing half the job. But this need not be the case; it is not a necessary feature of such models. I hope we will begin to see network models with explicit representation of environments from the Cognitive Scientific community; musical performance may actually be quite a fertile ground for such an endeavor. The next several years could be quite interesting.

Notes

1. An American musical video-clip television station [*Editors' note*].

References

Balzano, G.J. (1980) The group-theoretic description of 12-fold and microtonal pitch systems. *Computer Music Journal,* **4** (4), 66–84.

Balzano, G.J. (1982) The pitch set as a level of description for studying musical pitch perception. In *Music, Mind and Brain: The Neuropsychology of Music,* M. Clynes (ed.), 321–351, New York: Plenum Press.

Balzano, G.J. (1986a) Music perception as detection of pitch-time constraints. In *Event Cognition: An Ecological Perspective,* V. McCabe & G.J. Balzano (eds.) 217–233, Hillsdale, N.J.: L. Erlbaum Associates.

Balzano, G.J. (1986b) What are musical pitch and timbre? *Music Perception,* **3,** 297–314.

Balzano, G.J. (1987a) Reconstructing the curriculum for design. *Machine-Mediated Learning,* **2,** 83–109.

Balzano, G.J. (1987b) Measuring music. In *Action and Perception in Rhythm and Music,* A. Gabrielsson (ed.) 177–199, Stockholm: Royal Swedish Academy of Music, Publication No. 55.

Bharucha, J.(1987) Music cognition and perceptual facilitation: A connectionist framework. *Music Perception,* **5,** 1–30.

Clynes, M. (1983) Expressive microstructure in music, linked to living qualities. In *Studies of Music Performance,* J. Sundberg (ed.) 76–181, Stockholm: Royal Swedish Academy of Music, Publication No. 39.

Dick, P.K. (1969) *Ubik.* New York: Doubleday.

Dick, P.K. (1974) *Flow my Tears, the Policeman Said.* New York: Doubleday.

Fechner, G. (1966) *Elements of Psychophysics.* (H. Adler, Trans.) New York: Holt, Rinehart, & Winston. (Original work published 1860).

Gaver, W.W. (1988) *Everyday Listening and Auditory Icons.* Ph.D. Dissertation, Department of Cognitive Science, U.C. San Diego.

Gibson, J.J. (1979) *The Ecological Approach to Visual Perception.* Boston: Houghton-Mifflin.

Jenkins, J.J., Wald, J. & Pittenger, J.B. (1986) Apprehending pictorial events. In *Event Cognition: An Ecological Perspective,* V. McCabe & G.J. Balzano (eds) 117–133, Hillsdale, N.J.: L. Erlbaum Associates.

Rumelhart, D.E. & McClelland, J.L. (1986) *Parallel Distributed Processing: Explorations in the Microstructure of Cognition,* vol. 1. Cambridge, Mass.: MIT Press.

Runeson, S. (1977) On the possibility of "smart" perceptual mechanisms. *Scandinavian Journal of Psychology,* **18,** 172–179.

Sloboda, J. (1985) *The Musical Mind: The Cognitive Psychology of Music.* Oxford: Clarendon Press.

Still, A. & Costall, A. (in press) Mutual elimination of dualism in Vygotsky and Gibson. *Newsletter of the Laboratory of Comparative Human Cognition.*

Name index

Page numbers in *bold italic* type denote references

Subject index

Contemporary Music Studies Volume 1

CHARLES KOECHLIN

(1867-1950)

HIS LIFE AND WORKS

By Robert Orledge

In 1942 Wilfred Mellers classed Koechlin "among the select number of contemporary composers who really matter", yet it is only in the 1980s that Koechlin has begun to achieve the recognition he deserves as a composer of breadth, vision and powerful originality: a pioneer of polytonality and a master orchestrator who was greatly admired by contemporaries such as Fauré, Debussy, Satie and Milhaud.

Lavishly illustrated with photographic and musical examples, this book provides the first comprehensive evaluation of Koechlin's life and works. As well as concentrating on major symphonic works like Koechlin's *Jungle Book* cycle, it also discusses his attraction to the early sound film and the music inspired by such stars as Lilian Harvey, Marlene Dietrich and Charlie Chaplin in the 1930s.

Koechlin's career provides a fascinating study of the triumph of integrity and independence over almost overwhelming odds, and his rich and varied output offers a veritable treasure-trove for performers, scholars and enthusiasts alike.

About the author

Robert Orledge was born in Bath, England in 1948 and was educated at Clare College, Cambridge where he gained a BA Honours Degree in Music in 1968, an MA in 1972 and a PhD in 1975 for his dissertation on Charles Koechlin. He is an Associate of the Royal College of Organists, and a member of the Royal Musical Association, the Association des Amis de Charles Koechlin, the Centre de Documentation Claude Debussy, and the Fondation Erik Satie.

His special area of research interest is French music between 1860 and 1950. He has published books on Fauré and Debussy and is currently writing a book on Satie. Dr Orledge is Reader in Music at the University of Liverpool, UK.

Contents

Koechlin's life . Koechlin's reputation . Early works to 1910 . 1911-24: the 'perilous domain of chamber music' . 1924-33: the interrelationship of didactic works, contrapuntal exercises and original compositions . 1933-8: music for the early sound film and for the people . 1938-50: orchestral music and the 'art monodique' . Koechlin the composer . Koechlin's musical techniques . Epilogue . A translation of Koechlin's autobiographical study . Catalogue of Koechlin's works . Bibliography of texts by and about Koechlin.

November 1989   512pp.
Hardcover 3-7186-4898-9 $78.00
Harwood Academic Publishers

NOTES FOR CONTRIBUTORS

Typescripts

Papers should be typed with double spacing on good quality paper and submitted in duplicate to the Editor, **Contemporary Music Review**, c/o Harwood Academic Publishers, at

P.O. Box 197	or	P.O. Box 786	or	14–9 Okubo 3-chome
London WC2E 9PX		Cooper Station		Shinjuku-ku
England		New York, NY 10276		Tokyo 160
		USA		Japan

or directly to the issue editor. Submission of a paper to this journal will be taken to imply that it represents original work not previously published, that it is not being considered elsewhere for publication, and that if accepted for publication it will not be published elsewhere in the same form, in any language, without the consent of the editors and publishers. It is a condition of the acceptance by the editor of a typescript for publication that the publisher acquires automatically the copyright of the typescript throughout the world.

Languages

Papers are accepted only in English.

Abstract

Each paper requires an abstract of 100–150 words summarizing contents.

Key words

Up to six key words (index words) should be provided by the author. These will be published at the front of the paper.

Illustrations

All illustrations should be designated as "Figure 1" etc., and be numbered with consecutive arabic numerals. Each illustration should have a descriptive caption and be mentioned in the text. Indicate an approximate position for each illustration in the margin, and note the paper title, the name of the author and the figure number on the back of the illustration (please use a soft pencil for this, not a felt tip pen).

Preparation: All illustrations submitted must be of a high enough standard for direct reproduction. Line drawing should be prepared in black (india) ink on quality white card or paper or on tracing paper, with all the necessary lettering included. Alternatively, good sharp photographs ("glossies") are acceptable. Photographs intended for halftone reproduction must be good, glossy original prints of maximum contrast. Unusable illustrations and examples will not be redrawn or retouched by the printer, so it is essential that figures are well prepared.

Musical examples

These, like the illustrations, must be of a high enough standard for direct reproduction. Musical examples should be prepared in black (india) ink on quality white card or white music manuscript paper, or on tracing paper, with any necessary lettering included. If staves are hand drawn, ensure that the lines are of uniform thickness. Unusable musical examples will not be redrawn or retouched by the printer, so it is essential that figures are well prepared.

References and notes

References and notes are indicated in the text by consecutive superior arabic numerals (without parentheses). The full list should be collected and typed at the end of the paper in numerical order. Listed references should be complete in all details, including article titles and journal titles in full. In multiauthor references, the first six authors' names should be listed in full, then "*et al.*" may be used. Examples:

1. Smith, F.J. (1976) Editor. *In Search of Musical Method*, pp. 70–81. New York and London: Gordon and Breach.
2. Cockrell, D. (1982) A study in French Romanticism. *Journal of Musicological Research*, **4** (1/2), 85–115.

NB Authors must check that reference details are correct and complete; otherwise the references are useless. As a final check, please make sure that references tally with citings in the text.

Proofs

Contributors will receive page proofs (including illustrations) by air mail for correction, which must be returned to the printer within 48 hours of receipt. Please ensure that a full postal address is given on the first page of the typescript, so that proofs arrive without delay. Authors' alterations in excess of 10% of the original composition cost will be charged to authors.

Page charges

There are no page charges to individuals or institutions.

Forthcoming Issues

Live Electronics, New Music and Dance, New Uses of Tonality,
Music and Text, Opera, Development of the Orchestra,
New Electronic Instruments, British Composers: The New
Generation, The Microcomputer Music Revolution,
Contemporary Choral Techniques, Pop versus Serious
Contemporary Music, Harmony, Tradition and Innovation in
Russian Music, Tonality, Percussion in Performance,
New Developments in German Contemporary Music

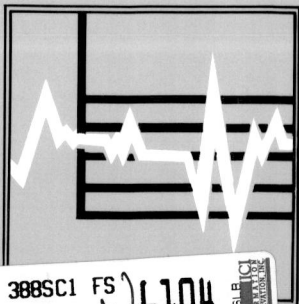